1985

CLASSICS OF MODERN FICTION

Ten Short Novels

Third Edition

CLASSICS OF MODERN FICTION

Ten Short Novels

Third Edition

Edited by **Irving Howe**

*Hunter College and the Graduate Center
of The City University of New York*

HARCOURT BRACE JOVANOVICH, INC.

*New York / San Diego / Chicago / San Francisco / Atlanta
London / Sydney / Toronto*

ISBN: 0-15-507647-7

Library of Congress Catalog Card Number: 79-91647

Printed in the United States of America

COPYRIGHTS AND ACKNOWLEDGMENTS

For permission to use the selections reprinted in this book, the author is grateful to the following publishers and copyright holders:

Notes from Underground (1864) by Fyodor Dostoevsky. Reprinted from *White Nights and Other Stories* by Fyodor Dostoevsky, translated by Constance Garnett. Reprinted by permission of the publisher, William Heinemann Ltd., London.

The Death of Ivan Ilych (1886) by Leo Tolstoy, translated by Aylmer Maude (World's classics 432). Reprinted by permission of the publisher, Oxford University Press, London.

The Machine Stops (1909) by E. M. Forster. Reprinted from *The Eternal Moment and Other Stories* by E. M. Forster. Copyright, 1928 by Harcourt Brace Jovanovich, Inc.; copyright, 1956, by E. M. Forster. Reprinted by permission of the publisher.

The Secret Sharer (1912) by Joseph Conrad. Reprinted from *'Twixt Land and Sea: Three Tales* (1912) by Joseph Conrad. Reprinted by permission of the publisher, J. M. Dent & Sons, Ltd., London, and the Trustees of the Joseph Conrad Estate.

Death in Venice (1912) by Thomas Mann. Copyright, 1930, 1936 by Alfred A. Knopf, Inc. Reprinted from *Stories of Three Decades* by Thomas Mann, translated by H. T. Lowe-Porter, by permission of the publisher.

iv

The Metamorphosis (1916) by Franz Kafka. Reprinted by permission of Schocken Books Inc. from *The Penal Colony: Stories and Short Pieces* by Franz Kafka, copyright © 1948 by Schocken Books Inc., New York, translated by Willa and Edwin Muir.

The Displaced Person (1955) by Flannery O'Connor. Copyright, 1977, by Flannery O'Connor. Reprinted from her volume *A Good Man Is Hard to Find and Other Stories* by permission of Harcourt Brace Jovanovich, Inc.

Seize the Day (1956) by Saul Bellow. Copyright © 1956 by Saul Bellow. Reprinted by permission of The Viking Press, Inc.

No One Writes to the Colonel (1961) by Gabriel García Marquéz. Reprinted from *No One Writes to the Colonel* by Gabriel García Marquéz. Copyright © 1961 by Aguirre Editor, Colombia, South America. Copyright © 1968 in the English translation by Harper & Row, Publishers, Inc. Reprinted by permission of the publisher.

The Temptation of Jack Orkney (1963) by Doris Lessing. Reprinted from *Stories* by Doris Lessing. Copyright 1972, 1978 by Doris Lessing. Reprinted by permission of Alfred A. Knopf, Inc., and Curtis Brown Ltd.

The quotation on pages 6–7 is from *Politics and the Novel* by Irving Howe. Copyright © 1957 by Irving Howe. Reprinted by permission of the publisher, Horizon Press, Inc.

The quotations on pages 273 and 277–78 are from *The Ironic German: A Study of Thomas Mann* by Erich Heller, by permission of Erich Heller. Copyright © 1958 by Erich Heller.

The quotations on pages 348, 350, and 352 are from "Kafka's 'Metamorphosis' and Modern Spirituality" by Martin Greenberg, published in *Tri-Quarterly*, No. 6, Spring 1966. Reprinted by permission of *Tri-Quarterly* and the author.

CREDITS FOR PHOTOGRAPHS ON BACK COVER
(Dostoevsky) Brown Brothers
(Tolstoy) Bettmann Archive
(Forster) Serena Wadham / Photo Trends
(Conrad) Brown Brothers
(Mann) German Information Center
(Kafka) Culver Pictures
(O'Connor) Wide World Photos
(Bellow) United Press International
(García Márquez) Fina Torres, Gamma / Liaison
(Lessing) Peter Lessing

Contents

THOMAS MANN
Death in Venice

FRANZ KAFKA
The Metamorphosis

FLANNERY O'CONNOR
The Displaced Person

SAUL BELLOW
Seize the Day

GABRIEL GARCÍA MÁRQUEZ
No One Writes to the Colonel

DORIS LESSING
The Temptation of Jack Orkney

To the Student

This is a textbook, and it is meant for classroom study. There is no way to disguise that fact nor any reason to try. But it is an unusual textbook in this respect: it ought to give a great deal of pleasure.

These ten short novels—or, as we shall also call them, novellas—range in character from universally acknowledged masterpieces by Tolstoy and Dostoevsky to major works by great "modernist" writers of the twentieth century, Franz Kafka and Thomas Mann. There are also distinguished works by more recent writers, such as Saul Bellow and Flannery O'Connor, both from the United States, Gabriel García Márquez, a highly gifted South American, and Doris Lessing, raised in South Africa but now living in England. The experience of reading such literature should enrich your sense of life and your sense of language and thereby achieve the purpose of literature: to give pleasure.

Why, then, should literature be studied at all? Some people believe that it should not; they believe that great works of literature ought not to be chewed over in class or ground into the dust of analysis by critics. They say that anyone who is literate and not hostile to the human imagination ought to be able to read *Death in Venice* or *The Secret Sharer* entirely by himself, without the aid of teachers, critics, and editors.

Perhaps so. But there is a counterargument worth considering. Few pleasures in life are spontaneous. Most pleasures in life are produced, or at least heightened, by a process of learning and cultivation. The pleasure of responding to a subtle story by Tolstoy;

the pleasure of grasping the intellectual tangles of a story by Dostoevsky and seeing how you can simultaneously admire it and disagree with the author's premises; the pleasure of involving yourself in a story by Thomas Mann even if you would not care to know real people who are like his characters—these are all *learned responses*. No one is simply born with them. Some students will take more easily to the fiction in this book than others will, but no one should foreclose on his potentialities.

The process of cultivation need never come to an end. Every human being is capable of steady development, even though in practice we all have our limitations. Ideally—if a happy three-sided relation develops between student, teacher, and text—you should experience, by reading and studying this book, both the pleasure of growth and the growth of pleasure.

As you undergo this experience, you will soon realize that the editor's introductions to each novella are very far from being the last word. In regard to literature, there is no last word. You may find yourself in partial disagreement with an introduction. Your instructor may use it as an opinion to argue against. Fair enough. There can be value in matching judgments and comparing interpretations. All I am doing is providing critical opinion that will help you, through suggestion and contrast, to make your own judgments.

Toward that end, I urge that you read the introductions not before but after you have read the novellas themselves. In that way you will be able to form your own impressions and then see where you agree and disagree with what I have written. To be sure, an introduction may be read first. But my guess is that you will get more out of it by reading a novella and then turning to its introduction.

There remain to be said a few words about the form of fiction in this book. In the simplest terms, a short novel is a prose narrative considerably longer than a short story but considerably shorter than a full-length novel, and for the study of fiction it offers many of the advantages of both. The genre also has a rich and distinctive life of its own, which we can perhaps best explore by making some points of comparison with the short story and the novel.

The short story characteristically focuses on a single incident, a bit of action that is usually dramatic and ends in some sort of revelation—a flash of irony, comprehension, or insight. What visibly *happens*—quickly, abruptly—is crucial. If a story is to make a strong impression on us, it will do so not merely through the intensity of its concentrated action but also through the implications that event suggests.

The novel, by contrast, concerns itself with an extended series of actions, often with subsidiary groups of events (called subplots) and generally shows a considerable number of characters in the course of change or development. The novel tends to be loose in form, since to the novelist full and vivid representation of reality matters more than the neatness or rigor of his composition. The novel presents a full span of experience: it suggests the completeness, the roundedness, of a life or group of lives. And the novel tends to mix the author's summarizing narrative with climactic and dramatic scenes in which the characters speak out directly. We think of the novel as the fictional genre in which human character is most fully displayed and investigated and in which, as a rule, complex plots are required in order to show character in a wide range of circumstances, under a variety of pressures, and from a multiplicity of perspectives.

The short novel does not rely on incident alone, like the short story, yet neither can it contain a complex and many-stranded plot, like the novel. As a rule, it moves a single line of action into rapid fulfillment or completion—for example, the course of Ivan Ilych's death or the adventure of initiation in *The Secret Sharer*. From this genre we gain a sense of character in depth, character as it reveals itself through a central test or crisis. But necessarily there can be only a few characters in the novella—indeed, most of the novellas in this book intensely scrutinize a single character as he approaches a turning point in his experience, often a point where he must discover what he really is as a human being. That is why the events in these short novels are strictly confined to a brief span of time.

Because it moves along a single line of action—sometimes focusing on the climactic point in that action—the short novel is not merely a cut-down novel. The rhythm of its narration differs from that of the full-scale novel: it is tight and exclusive rather than expansive and inclusive. It would be hard to imagine Charles Dickens, for example—with his fondness for eccentric minor characters and amusing side-shows—turning to the short novel as a genre. In the short novel, we are almost always aware of the strong executive hand of the writer, molding and shaping, cutting and tightening: he must adhere to a strict standard of relevance when deciding what can be included. As compensation, however, he often achieves a clearer narrative design than the novelist does. Professor Ronald Paulson has remarked, "Artistry, style, a fine polish—these are characteristics of the novelette that set it off from the novel and, to a lesser degree, from the short story. The novel, it has been said, requires careless, sloppy writing to suggest a close, sweaty hold on reality." Sustained over the full length of a novel, the highly polished prose common to many short novels could become wearisome. Furthermore, such prose tends to draw attention to itself and thereby may sacrifice verisimilitude (the surface appearance of commonplace reality). But reading a short novel is like watching a virtuoso violinist perform a sonata. The sense of *performance* becomes central. (This, however, applies more to such writers as Mann and Conrad than to Dostoevsky and Tolstoy.)

Whereas the short-story writer tries to strike off a flash of insight and the novelist hopes to create the illusion of a self-sufficient world, the author of the short novel is frequently concerned with showing an arc of human conduct that has a certain symbolic significance. The short novel is a form that encourages the writer to struggle with profound philosophic or moral problems through a compact yet extended narrative.

The material in a short novel is full enough to allow its symbolic significance to emerge with greater complexity than could be expected from a short story; it is also brief enough to ensure the work's being self-contained, compressed, and disciplined. Perhaps the best illustration of this point is Conrad's *The Secret Sharer*, in which the young captain undergoes his initiation into the dangers and values of human experience. *The Secret Sharer* is long enough to provide sufficient detail for us to be convinced of its reality and to be enticed into sharing the complicated responses of the main character; but, once the captain's ordeal has been completed, the narrative abruptly closes and we are not invited to pursue the remainder of his career as we might be in a full-scale novel. We pick up his story and then drop it just at the point required to fulfill Conrad's intention.

Had Conrad tried to fit his action into a short story, it would have been too cramped and might have read like an outline for a longer piece of writing. We would not have had sufficient space and time to live through the young captain's experience. Had Conrad tried to stretch out his action, it would have become thin or padded, with a resultant loss of suspense. In this short novel, as in other masterpieces of the genre, the action forms a harmonious equivalent to the motivating idea. The short novel always needs a good fit.

And the fully achieved short novel occupies a position elegantly described by Vladimir Nabokov: "There is . . . in the dimensional scale of the world a kind of delicate meeting-place between the imagination and knowledge, a point, arrived at by diminishing large things and enlarging small ones, that is intrinsically artistic."

Irving Howe

FYODOR DOSTOEVSKY

Notes from Underground

A NOVEL

Translated by Constance Garnett

Introduction

What first strikes the reader of *Notes from Underground* is that ideas play a role on every page, a far more crucial role, or at least a far more direct one, than in any other piece of fiction in this book. If the student is troubled by the relationship between Dostoevsky's ideas and characters, then let him be assured that this is a difficulty shared by critics. In fact, almost every problem an inexperienced reader confronts in literature is also—if on a more complex level—a problem for the experienced reader.

In responding to a piece of fiction where ideas seem central, or where they "stick out," there are at least two dangers to watch for.

First: the danger of taking the ideas used by the writer completely at face value, as if he were composing a tract, with the result that we praise or dispraise his work according to whether we agree or disagree with his views. We thereby lose sight of the fact that he is trying to create a work of art—in which, it must be remembered, the views expressed by the characters, even by the main character, can be sharply different from the author's.

Second: the danger of assuming that the writer didn't really care very strongly about his ideas and used them simply as "raw material" for a story, with the result that we may miss much of the intellectual urgency of the work and take the writer with insufficient seriousness.

A mature reading of *Notes from Underground* requires that we recognize simultaneously that Dostoevsky did want his ideas to be taken seriously in their own right but also wanted us to respond to his novella as a work of art. And one of the problems, a very complicated problem, that follows is to decide whether or in what way the narrator of *Notes from Underground* speaks for Dostoevsky. It is difficult to hold in balance the perspective of ideas and the perspective of art, but that is just where the challenge and the pleasure lie in reading this kind of fiction.

Let me phrase the matter in another, more complicated way. All of us live in a world of commonplace reality—the world of classrooms, bombs, kitchens, checkbooks, and parents. When we read a work of fiction, we enter "another" world, one that has been imagined by the writer. For this "other world" to excite our minds and grip our hearts, it must bear some deep and credible relationship to our experience. It must reflect or illuminate or transform our sense of commonplace reality. Yet in order for this to happen, the writer's "other world" must be given a shape and structure of its own, just as a building or a piece of sculpture must have a shape and structure. And because the literary structure is created, it has to be different from the world of commonplace reality.

As long as these two worlds—the one we are born into and the one a writer imagines—are kept both distinct and connected in our minds, all is well. But in a novel or story in which ideas figure prominently, these two worlds are brought into a relationship so tense and so close that the result can become confusing. Dostoevsky presents imaginary characters and an imaginary situation—that much is clear. But the issues he raises (such as individualism, socialism, rationalism, and free will) are so important and arouse in us such strong feelings of approval or distaste that we find it hard to remember that *Notes from Underground* is a work of fiction. We tend to react as if we were in a heated political debate. We tend to lose what literary critics have called our "esthetic distance." It becomes a temptation to applaud or dismiss Dostoevsky's writing by saying that we agree with or dislike the ideas *we think* are in his story. And yet the whole point of reading fiction is that, even while responding to a writer's ideas as such, we must also respond to the whole composition as a piece of literature.

Let us look at the ideas that cluster in and around *Notes from Underground*. It is often described as a revolutionary work that helped introduce a distinctively *modern* feeling or style into European culture. The term "modern" is here both elusive and essential. With different writers it takes on different shades of meaning. But when we speak of *Notes from Underground* as a forerunner of a distinctively "modern" sensibility, one that has dominated Western culture for about the last century, we have in mind at least the following:

+ *the replacement of religious certainty and moral absolutes by skepticism, doubt, agnosticism, and intellectual relativism (the view that there are no unalterable moral commandments binding upon all men in all circumstances but that judgments of conduct and ideas must be made relative to changing circumstances)*

+ *a strong stress upon estrangement—or, as it is often called, alienation—from the prevalent standards of society, which are seen as corrupted (materialistic) or mediocre (bourgeois) or hypocritical (falsely pious)*

+ *a fascination with human subjectivity—that is, the view that what matters most in our time is not so much the nature of either the external physical world or the social world but, rather, the way in which our impressions of these worlds are registered in human consciousness*

+ *a feeling that in a universe deprived of God and the comforts of religion, man has been left "homeless," a stranger in the universe, and must therefore consume himself with introspective anxiety and self-mortification*

+ *an increasing doubt as to the value or relevance of rational thought, now seen not as a path to knowledge and wisdom but as a way of classifying and thereby squeezing the life out of intuitions and perceptions*

+ *a feeling that, with the collapse of moral certainties, there remains nothing for men but to engage in the boldest experiments, to forge a new order of values in personal relationships and in the creation of art and the destruction and reconstitution of society*

✦ *and, finally, a gnawing doubt as to the purpose or even value of human life. This doubt can lead to the tacit conclusion that our existence on this earth is pointless, a transitory encounter with pleasure and a prolonged exposure to pain, all of which may end with the doctrine or mood of nihilism (the denial of meaning in life and thereby, if pushed hard enough, a denial of life itself).*

Modernism, then, is a cultural outlook that insists that human existence is profoundly and inherently problematic. It insists that human beings are caught up in a constant struggle to recreate freshly the terms of their lives, rather than having simply to abide by commandments that have been handed down to us. And it insists that the classical precepts which are supposed to contain the wisdom of the past no longer help men very much.

Modernism has been the dominant strain in Western culture for at least a century: a strain at once brilliant, unsettling, and corrosive. And in Dostoevsky it found an often reluctant spokesman, one of the few great writers who really have changed the way people think and feel. Let me quote a few paragraphs from an essay of mine concerning Dostoevsky's ideas, because I think they may help prepare the reader for *Notes from Underground.*

Dostoevsky dreaded the autonomous intellect, the faithless drifting he had himself experienced and was later to portray in Ivan Karamazov [in his novel *The Brothers Karamazov*]; he feared that the intellectual, loosed from the controls of Christianity and alienated from the heart-warmth of the Russian people, would feel free to commit the most monstrous acts to quench his vanity. Once man is free from responsibility to God, what limit can there be to his presumption?—an argument that might be more convincing if there were evidence that believers as a group have been less arrogant than skeptics. Together, it should be noticed, with the messianic strain in his religion, there is an element of coarse "pragmatism": God as celestial overseer.

Though a tendentious moralist, Dostoevsky was an entirely honest novelist, and in his novels he could not but show that while the will to faith is strong in some modern intellectuals, it seldom leads them to the peace of faith. His God-seekers, like Shatov in *The Possessed* [another novel by Dostoevsky], are men peculiarly driven by anguish: the more serious their desire for God, the more must they acknowledge the distance separating them from Him . . . . Since the quest of such characters is partly motivated by an intense dislike for commercial civilization, they often find themselves in unexpected conflict with society. Their ideas, it is true, have little in common with socialist doctrine, but their values lead them to an uneasy kinship with socialism as a critical activity.

[Note: Dostoevsky wrote *Notes from Underground* a good many years before *The Possessed*, but the narrator of the earlier story can be seen as an anticipation of several characters in the later novel.]

Yet they cannot accept socialism. Dostoevsky despised it as "scientific" . . . the twin of rationalist atheism; he rejected it, also, because he feared that man might barter freedom for bread. No political system which located salvation in the secular world could have been acceptable to him, and in a sense R. P. Blackmur is right when he says that Dostoevsky's politics were those of a man "whose way of dealing with life rested on a fundamental belief that a true rebirth, a great conversion, can come only after a great sin." It is even profitable to think of Dostoevsky's novels as rituals of rebirth, with a series of plebeian heroes . . . reenacting the drama of the Resurrection. . . .

Dostoevsky's politics were indeed, as Blackmur says, "non-social" and hence apocalyptic, but they were also colored by an intense fascination for the social politics of his time. Though he despised the ideas of the revolutionary intellectuals, he had been soaked in the atmospheres that nourished them, and as a result, his intellectual divergence signified less than his temperamental affinities. He "translated" the political radicalism of the 1840s, the radicalism of fraternity and utopia, into Christian terms—highly unorthodox and closer in spirit to primitive Christianity than to any church of his or our day.

The relationship of Dostoevsky to cultural modernism is thus extremely complex. He releases, more dramatically than any other nineteenth-century writer, a good many of the feelings and impulses we associate with modernism, but he also resists and mocks these at the very same time. It is this doubleness of perspective that lies at the heart of *Notes from Underground*.

Let's now turn to the story itself. It was originally intended as a polemic against the socialists and radicals who, in the Czarist Russia of the 1860s, had begun to speak out with considerable forcefulness. More particularly, it was meant as an attack upon and a parody of the Utopian novel *What Is To Be Done?* (1863) by Nicolai Chernyshevsky, one of the leading Russian radicals. Chernyshevsky wrote in behalf of reason. He expressed faith in the inherent goodness of man. He advocated the application of science to social problems in order to build a perfect society. But Dostoevsky, even while drawn to the radicals temperamentally and sharing many of their complaints and resentments, was their most scathing intellectual opponent. In contrast to the radicals, Dostoevsky believed that men were inherently evil, irrational, and destructive, that reason could not finally solve their problems, and that only faith in Christ could help control the turmoil of their impulses. And to demonstrate all this through narrative and drama, Dostoevsky created the "underground man," as the narrator of *Notes from Underground* has come to be known—the "underground man" who embodies, both in psychological condition and as an extreme parody, the dilemmas of the mind that is content neither with faith nor rationality, religion nor skepticism.

The entire first part of *Notes from Underground* consists, apparently, of direct argument or what we call dialectic: that is, an interplay of statement and counterstatement. In a little while I shall try to give a sketch of the narrator's argument, but first it ought to be absolutely clear that Dostoevsky was not writing a polemic pure-and-simple, even if at some point it does seem to be that (in fact, the closer it comes to a polemic pure-and-simple, the less interesting it is). What we hear throughout this first section is the voice of a human being. It is a voice urgent, slightly hysterical, jeering at his imaginary listeners and himself. One of Dostoevsky's critics, Ralph Matlaw, says some illuminating things about this technique of narration:

> The narrator, by his own admission, is writing a confession, and he maintains that the oratorical flourishes simply exist so that he may express himself more easily and clearly. But this in turn gives the work the *illusion of dialogue* and makes it seem like a sustained polemic against an opponent, as if the narrator were anticipating objections. Like all confessions, the narrator's confession postulates the existence of an auditor, but psychologically, the auditor here is never passive and cannot be passive, for this is *a confession to one's self*— the author and the confessor are one. The "Notes" may even be considered as a parody of confession which, in religious terms, is ostensibly preceded by contrition, but here is replaced by proud (though ambivalent) self-defense. [Italics added—I. H.]

Dostoevsky manages to do something here that is extremely difficult in fiction. He presents not a finished or static thought but *the mind in process of thought.* This mind is shown sometimes arguing against itself and sometimes mocking itself. It is a mind that twists and turns and, with an almost malicious glee, anticipates and destroys counterarguments before they can be made. And because Dostoevsky did not wish to spare anyone, least of all his narrator, the voice we hear turns inward, upon itself, to undercut its own arguments. The process involved might be described as intellectual corrosion.

We get here, in an extreme version, the portrait of a mind that is both brilliant and diseased, a sensibility that is both delicate and coarse. For Dostoevsky was a master at portraying mixed states of feeling and perception, the mind at war with itself and the same mind burlesquing or parodying its war with itself. None of us can easily identify with the speaker, for few of us are either so agile in argument or so neurotic in character as this man from the spiritual underground. But which of us can claim that he is entirely free from the narrator's complaints or his malaise? It is part of Dostoevsky's greatness that, no matter how spiritually feverish or intellectually intoxicated his characters may be, they all manage to involve us in their destinies. And they do this because they are, above all, suffering men.

Notes from Underground is divided into two parts. What is their relation? If we can answer this question plausibly, we may reach an understanding of Dostoevsky's narrative strategy. So let us see if we can, by a ruthless simplification, reduce the brilliant first part to a group of statements or propositions:

✦ *Intelligence is a disease from which man cannot escape: it dooms him to self-pride and narcissism.*

✦ *Man is hopelessly split between the side of himself that wishes to act and the side that wishes to observe.*

✦ *It is often impossible to make a clear distinction between man's pride and his humility: one masks the other.*

✦ *Consciousness is the distinctive mark of humanity, yet consciousness drives man into self-division, cutting his mind off from his inner resources and impulses, so that he runs the danger of becoming "divorced from life" as he thinks about life.*

✦ *Man is trapped in a struggle between will—that which drives him to desire things he may even know to be evil or reprehensible—and reason, the faculty of mind that at least occasionally controls his will but that cannot really command the chaos of existence.*

✦ *We are all subject to a constant inner division between our need for freedom and our need to submit ourselves to authority. The need for freedom can be arbitrary, irrational, even to the point of insisting that two plus two equals five.*

✦ *The one freedom possible to man that matters most is the freedom of choice, and insofar as rationality and social organizations threaten this freedom, even in its destructive aspects, they can be enemies of life.*

✦ *Those who try to reform human existence on rational principles, be they liberals or socialists, are the enemies of freedom, for they would transform life into a death-like automatism, an ant-heap, a well-regulated slave camp.*

✦ *What redeems life and gives it meaning is human suffering, an experience which, in its fullness of consciousness, is possible only to mankind.*

Other such propositions could be developed, and those above could be stated with greater exactness or more detail. But I think it is correct to say that statements of this general order can be inferred from the first part of *Notes from Underground*. They come from the narrator in two ways: either as his direct expressions of opinion or as conclusions we are driven to draw when the narrator parodies an extreme version of rationalism. But as I so baldly summarize these opinions, I do not at all do justice to what is most important in this first section: its portrait of a mind tormenting itself with doubts, reflections, and polemics. No critical summary can convey a full sense of *that*; there is no substitute for a direct reading of the work itself. And what emerges from such a reading is a dramatic encounter with the mind and emotions of "the undergound man," a major new figure in Western culture.

What is he really like, this "underground man"? He refuses clear definition, fixity, coherence. Meek and arrogant at the same time, both resourceful in argument and derisive of intellect, starved for love and scornful of those who offer it, he lives in a chaos of subterranean passions. Beneath each layer of his being there quivers another, in radical conflict with the first. He can move in quick succession from satanic pride to abject humility and then, with a mocking self-approval, recognize that the humility is no more than a curtain for his pride. Nor need the sequence of exposure end there. In principle, the narrator of *Notes from Underground* could go on talking forever, each time peeling off another layer of his vanity. From a conviction of his inferiority he abases himself toward everyone—toward everyone but the men of ordinary decent sentiments who seem to have escaped from his abyss of suffering and are therefore regarded by him as objects of contempt. Yet to say this is also to notice that he holds strong convictions of superiority, for at heart he is gratified by the signs of his plight and regards his pain as evidence of his distinction. Gratified, he indulges in a vast self-pity; but this psychic quick-change artist can also be mercilessly ironic about that self-pity. Above all else, he is a master of parody.

By the end of the first part, then, the narrator is at an absolute impasse. He has talked himself into a dead-end. He has reasoned himself into impotence. And now, I think, comes Dostoevsky's most brilliant stroke. For what would most of us say to "the underground man" after having listened to his outpouring? Would we not say to him: "You just can't go on this way, you are trapped in your own cycle of argument; there is only one recourse open to you and that is to plunge directly into life itself, to open yourself to experience and find your meaning in work or love or the day-to-day affairs of commonplace existence."

It is as if Dostoevsky had already heard us saying this; as if, with his sardonic mind, he therefore tells himself: "Very well, we will plunge our 'hero' into life, we will show what happens to him—this chattering wretch with his big ideas—when he encounters love and friends." What the second part of the story shows is that the recommendation that Christians, psychoanalysts, and ordinary persons might all make to "the underground man"—the recommendation of action as therapy—proves to be hopeless. To be sure, the "life" into which the narrator enters in Part II might strike some of us as pretty feeble, as not really giving "life" much of a chance. But it is as much as the narrator can manage; it is as much as he can get hold of—and it undoes him; it defeats him. As the chain of incidents in

Part II shows, there is no way for him to escape from his contaminated self, neither when he is alone nor when he is in society, neither through thought nor through action. It is a burden he must always bear.

And we too?

Notes from Underground

A NOVEL

PART I · UNDERGROUND

I

I am a sick man. . . . I am a spiteful man. I am an unattractive man. I believe my liver is diseased. However, I know nothing at all about my disease, and do not know for certain what ails me. I don't consult a doctor for it, and never have, though I have a respect for medicine and doctors. Besides, I am extremely superstitious, sufficiently so to respect medicine, anyway (I am well-educated enough not to be superstitious, but I am superstitious). No, I refuse to consult a doctor from spite. That you probably will not understand. Well, I understand it, though. Of course, I can't explain who it is precisely that I am mortifying in this case by my spite: I am per-

The author of the diary and the diary itself are, of course, imaginary. Nevertheless it is clear that such persons as the writer of these notes not only may, but positively must, exist in our society, when we consider the circumstances in the midst of which our society is formed. I have tried to expose to the view of the public more distinctly than is commonly done, one of the characters of the recent past. He is one of the representatives of a generation still living. In this fragment, entitled "Underground," this person introduces himself and his views, and, as it were, tries to explain the causes owing to which he has made his appearance and was bound to make his appearance in our midst. In the second fragment there are added the actual notes of this person concerning certain events in his life. [AUTHOR'S NOTE.]

fectly well aware that I cannot "pay out" the doctors by not consulting them; I know better than any one that by all this I am only injuring myself and no one else. But still, if I don't consult a doctor it is from spite. My liver is bad, well—let it get worse!

I have been going on like that for a long time—twenty years. Now I am forty. I used to be in the government service, but am no longer. I was a spiteful official. I was rude and took pleasure in being so. I did not take bribes, you see, so I was bound to find a recompense in that, at least. (A poor jest, but I will not scratch it out. I wrote it thinking it would sound very witty; but now that I have seen myself that I only wanted to show off in a despicable way, I will not scratch it out on purpose!)

When petitioners used to come for information to the table at which I sat, I used to grind my teeth at them, and felt intense enjoyment when I succeeded in making anybody unhappy. I almost always did succeed. For the most part they were all timid people—of course, they were petitioners. But of the uppish ones there was one officer in particular I could not endure. He simply would not be humble, and clanked his sword in a disgusting way. I carried on a feud with him for eighteen months over that sword. At last I got the better of him. He left off clanking it. That happened in my youth, though.

But do you know, gentlemen, what was the chief point about my spite? Why, the whole point, the real sting of it lay in the fact that continually, even in the moment of the acutest spleen, I was inwardly conscious with shame that I was not only not a spiteful but not even an embittered man, that I was simply scaring sparrows at random and amusing myself by it. I might foam at the mouth, but bring me a doll to play with, give me a cup of tea with sugar in it, and maybe I should be appeased. I might even be genuinely touched, though probably I should grind my teeth at myself afterwards and lie awake at night with shame for months after. That was my way.

I was lying when I said just now that I was a spiteful official. I was lying from spite. I was simply amusing myself with the petitioners and with the officer, and in reality I never could become spiteful. I was conscious every moment in myself of many, very many elements absolutely opposite to that. I felt them positively swarming in me, these opposite elements. I knew that they had been swarming in me all my life and craving some outlet from me, but I would not let them, would not let them, purposely would not let them come out.

They tormented me till I was ashamed: they drove me to convulsions and—sickened me, at last, how they sickened me! Now, are not you fancying, gentlemen, that I am expressing remorse for something now, that I am asking your forgiveness for something? I am sure you are fancying that. . . . However, I assure you I do not care if you are. . . .

It was not only that I could not become spiteful, I did not know how to become anything: neither spiteful nor kind, neither a rascal nor an honest man, neither a hero nor an insect. Now, I am living out my life in my corner, taunting myself with the spiteful and useless consolation that an intelligent man cannot become anything seriously, and it is only the fool who becomes anything. Yes, a man in the nineteenth century must and morally ought to be pre-eminently a characterless creature; a man of character, an active man is pre-eminently a limited creature. That is my conviction of forty years. I am forty years old now, and you know forty years is a whole lifetime; you know it is extreme old age. To live longer than forty years is bad manners, is vulgar, immoral. Who does live beyond forty? Answer that, sincerely and honestly. I will tell you who do: fools and worthless fellows. I tell all old men that to their face, all these venerable old men, all these silver-haired and reverend seniors! I tell the whole world that to its face! I have a right to say so, for I shall go on living to sixty myself. To seventy! To eighty! . . . Stay, let me take breath. . . .

You imagine no doubt, gentlemen, that I want to amuse you. You are mistaken in that, too. I am by no means such a mirthful person as you imagine, or as you may imagine; however, irritated by all this babble (and I feel that you are irritated) you think fit to ask me who am I—then my answer is, I am a collegiate assessor.[2] I was in the service that I might have something to eat (and solely for that reason), and when last year a distant relation left me six thousand roubles in his will I immediately retired from the service and settled down in my corner. I used to live in this corner before, but now I have settled down in it. My room is a wretched, horrid one in the outskirts of the town. My servant is an old country-woman, ill-natured from stupidity, and, moreover, there is always a nasty smell about her. I am told that the Petersburg climate is bad for me, and that with my small means it is very expensive to live in Petersburg. I know all that better than all these sage and experienced counsellors and monitors. . . . But I am remaining in Petersburg; I am not

[2] A minor bureaucratic post.

going away from Petersburg! I am not going away because . . . ech!
Why, it is absolutely no matter whether I am going away or not
going away.

But what can a decent man speak of with most pleasure?

Answer: Of himself.

Well, so I will talk about myself.

II

I want now to tell you, gentlemen, whether you care to hear it or
not, why I could not even become an insect. I tell you solemnly,
that I have many times tried to become an insect. But I was not
equal even to that. I swear, gentlemen, that to be too conscious is an
illness—a real thoroughgoing illness. For man's everyday needs, it
would have been quite enough to have the ordinary human consciousness, that is, half or a quarter of the amount which falls to the
lot of a cultivated man of our unhappy nineteenth century, especially one who has the fatal ill-luck to inhabit Petersburg, the most
theoretical and intentional town on the whole terrestrial globe.
(There are intentional and unintentional towns.) It would have
been quite enough, for instance, to have the consciousness by which
all so-called direct persons and men of action live. I bet you think I
am writing all this from affectation, to be witty at the expense of
men of action; and what is more, that from ill-bred affectation, I am
clanking a sword like my officer. But, gentlemen, whoever can pride
himself on his diseases and even swagger over them?

Though, after all, every one does do that; people do pride themselves on their diseases, and I do, may be, more than any one. We
will not dispute it; my contention was absurd. But yet I am firmly
persuaded that a great deal of consciousness, every sort of consciousness, in fact, is a disease. I stick to that. Let us leave that, too, for a
minute. Tell me this: why does it happen that at the very, yes, at
the very moments when I am most capable of feeling every refinement of all that is "good and beautiful," as they used to say at one
time, it would, as though of design, happen to me not only to feel
but to do such ugly things, such that . . . Well, in short, actions
that all, perhaps, commit; but which, as though purposely, occurred
to me at the very time when I was most conscious that they ought
not to be committed. The more conscious I was of goodness and of
all that was "good and beautiful," the more deeply I sank into my

mire and the more ready I was to sink in it altogether. But the chief point was that all this was, as it were, not accidental in me, but as though it were bound to be so. It was as though it were my most normal condition, and not in the least disease or depravity, so that at last all desire in me to struggle against this depravity passed. It ended by my almost believing (perhaps actually believing) that this was perhaps my normal condition. But at first, in the beginning, what agonies I endured in that struggle! I did not believe it was the same with other people, and all my life I hid this fact about myself as a secret. I was ashamed (even now, perhaps, I am ashamed): I got to the point of feeling a sort of secret abnormal, despicable enjoyment in returning home to my corner on some disgusting Petersburg night, acutely conscious that that day I had committed a loathsome action again, that what was done could never be undone, and secretly, inwardly gnawing, gnawing at myself for it, tearing and consuming myself till at last the bitterness turned into a sort of shameful accursed sweetness, and at last—into positive real enjoyment! Yes, into enjoyment, into enjoyment! I insist upon that. I have spoken of this because I keep wanting to know for a fact whether other people feel such enjoyment. I will explain: the enjoyment was just from the too intense consciousness of one's own degradation; it was from feeling oneself that one had reached the last barrier, that it was horrible, but that it could not be otherwise; that there was no escape for you; that you never could become a different man; that even if time and faith were still left you to change into something different you would most likely not wish to change; or if you did wish to, even then you would do nothing; because perhaps in reality there was nothing for you to change into.

And the worst of it was, and the root of it all, that it was all in accord with the normal fundamental laws of over-acute consciousness, and with the inertia that was the direct result of those laws, and that consequently one was not only unable to change but could do absolutely nothing. Thus it would follow, as the result of acute consciousness, that one is not to blame in being a scoundrel; as though that were any consolation to the scoundrel once he has come to realize that he actually is a scoundrel. But enough. . . . Ech, I have talked a lot of nonsense, but what have I explained? How is enjoyment in this to be explained? But I will explain it. I will get to the bottom of it! That is why I have taken up my pen. . . .

I, for instance, have a great deal of *amour propre*. I am as suspicious and prone to take offence as a humpback or a dwarf. But upon my word I sometimes have had moments when if I had happened to be slapped in the face I should, perhaps, have been positively glad of it. I say, in earnest, that I should probably have been able to discover even in that a peculiar sort of enjoyment—the enjoyment, of course, of despair; but in despair there are the most intense enjoyments, especially when one is very acutely conscious of the hopelessness of one's position. And when one is slapped in the face—why then the consciousness of being rubbed into a pulp would positively overwhelm one. The worst of it is, look at it which way one will, it still turns out that I was always the most to blame in everything. And what is most humiliating of all, to blame for no fault of my own but, so to say, through the laws of nature. In the first place, to blame because I am cleverer than any of the people surrounding me. (I have always considered myself cleverer than any of the people surrounding me, and sometimes, would you believe it, have been positively ashamed of it. At any rate, I have all my life, as it were, turned my eyes away and never could look people straight in the face.) To blame, finally, because even if I had had magnanimity, I should only have had more suffering from the sense of its uselessness. I should certainly have never been able to do anything from being magnanimous—neither to forgive, for my assailant would perhaps have slapped me from the laws of nature, and one cannot forgive the laws of nature; nor to forget, for even if it were owing to the laws of nature, it is insulting all the same. Finally, even if I had wanted to be anything but magnanimous, had desired on the contrary to revenge myself on my assailant, I could not have revenged myself on any one for anything because I should certainly never have made up my mind to do anything, even if I had been able to. Why should I not have made up my mind? About that in particular I want to say a few words.

III

With people who know how to revenge themselves and to stand up for themselves in general, how is it done? Why, when they are possessed, let us suppose, by the feeling of revenge, then for the time there is nothing else but that feeling left in their whole being. Such a gentleman simply dashes straight for his object like an infuriated bull with its horns down, and nothing but a wall will stop him. (By the way: facing the wall, such gentlemen—that is, the "direct" persons and men of action—are genuinely nonplussed. For them a wall is not an evasion, as for us people who think and consequently do nothing; it is not an excuse for turning aside, an excuse for which we are always very glad, though we scarcely believe in it ourselves, as a rule. No, they are nonplussed in all sincerity. The wall has for them something tranquillizing, morally soothing, final— maybe even something mysterious . . . but of the wall later.)

Well, such a direct person I regard as the real normal man, as his tender mother nature wished to see him when she graciously brought him into being on the earth. I envy such a man till I am green in the face. He is stupid. I am not disputing that, but perhaps the normal man should be stupid, how do you know? Perhaps it is very beautiful, in fact. And I am the more persuaded of that suspicion, if one can call it so, by the fact that if you take, for instance, the antithesis of the normal man, that is, the man of acute consciousness, who has come, of course, not out of the lap of nature but out of a retort (this is almost mysticism, gentlemen, but I suspect this, too), this retort-made man is sometimes so nonplussed in the presence of his antithesis that with all his exaggerated consciousness he genuinely thinks of himself as a mouse and not a man. It may be an acutely conscious mouse, yet it is a mouse, while the other is a man, and therefore, et cætera, et cætera. And the worst of it is, he himself, his very own self, looks on himself as a mouse; no one asks him to do so; and that is an important point. Now let us look at this mouse in action. Let us suppose, for instance, that it feels insulted, too (and it almost always does feel insulted), and wants to revenge itself, too. There may even be a greater accumulation of spite in it than in *l'homme de la nature et de la vérité*.[3] The base and nasty desire to vent that spite on its assailant rankles perhaps even more nastily in it than in *l'homme de la nature et de la vérité*. For through his innate stupidity the latter looks upon his revenge as justice pure and simple; while in consequence of his acute consciousness the mouse does not believe in the justice of it. To come at last to the deed itself, to the very act of revenge. Apart from the one fundamental nastiness the luckless mouse succeeds in creating around it so many other nastinesses in the form of doubts and questions, adds to the one question so many unsettled questions that there inevitably works up around it a sort of fatal brew, a stinking mess, made up of its doubts, emotions, and of the contempt spat

---

[3] The man of nature and truth.

upon it by the direct men of action who stand solemnly about it as judges and arbitrators, laughing at it till their healthy sides ache. Of course the only thing left for it is to dismiss all that with a wave of its paw, and, with a smile of assumed contempt in which it does not even itself believe, creep ignominiously into its mouse-hole. There in its nasty, stinking, underground home our insulted, crushed and ridiculed mouse promptly becomes absorbed in cold, malignant and, above all, everlasting spite. For forty years together it will remember its injury down to the smallest, most ignominious details, and every time will add, of itself, details still more ignominious, spitefully teasing and tormenting itself with its own imagination. It will itself be ashamed of its imaginings, but yet it will recall it all, it will go over and over every detail, it will invent unheard of things against itself, pretending that those things might happen, and will forgive nothing. Maybe it will begin to revenge itself, too, but, as it were, piecemeal, in trivial ways, from behind the stove, incognito, without believing either in its own right to vengeance, or in the success of its revenge, knowing that from all its efforts at revenge it will suffer a hundred times more than he on whom it revenges itself, while he, I daresay, will not even scratch himself. On its deathbed it will recall it all over again, with interest accumulated over all the years and. . . .

But it is just in that cold, abominable half despair, half belief, in that conscious burying oneself alive for grief in the underworld for forty years, in that acutely recognized and yet partly doubtful hopelessness of one's position, in that hell of unsatisfied desires turned inward, in that fever of oscillations, of resolutions determined for ever and repented of again a minute later—that the savour of that strange enjoyment of which I have spoken lies. It is so subtle, so difficult of analysis, that persons who are a little limited, or even simply persons of strong nerves, will not understand a single atom of it. "Possibly," you will add on your own account with a grin, "people will not understand it either who have never received a slap in the face," and in that way you will politely hint to me that I, too, perhaps, have had the experience of a slap in the face in my life, and so I speak as one who knows. I bet that you are thinking that. But set your minds at rest, gentlemen, I have not received a slap in the face, though it is absolutely a matter of indifference to me what you may think about it. Possibly, I even regret, myself, that I have given so few slaps in the face during my life. But enough . . . not another word on that subject of such extreme interest to you.

I will continue calmly concerning persons with strong nerves who do not understand a certain refinement of enjoyment. Though in certain circumstances these gentlemen bellow their loudest like bulls, though this, let us suppose, does them the greatest credit, yet, as I have said already, confronted with the impossible they subside at once. The impossible means the stone wall! What stone wall? Why, of course, the laws of nature, the deductions of natural science, mathematics. As soon as they prove to you, for instance, that you are descended from a monkey, then it is no use scowling, accept it for a fact. When they prove to you that in reality one drop of your own fat must be dearer to you than a hundred thousand of your fellow-creatures, and that this conclusion is the final solution of all so-called virtues and duties and all such prejudices and fancies, then you have just to accept it, there is no help for it, for twice two is a law of mathematics. Just try refuting it.

"Upon my word, they will shout at you, it is no use protesting: it is a case of twice two makes four! Nature does not ask your permission, she has nothing to do with your wishes, and whether you like her laws or dislike them, you are bound to accept her as she is, and consequently all her conclusions. A wall, you see, is a wall . . . and so on, and so on."

Merciful Heavens! but what do I care for the laws of nature and arithmetic, when, for some reason, I dislike those laws and the fact that twice two makes four? Of course I cannot break through the wall by battering my head against it if I really have not the strength to knock it down, but I am not going to be reconciled to it simply because it is a stone wall and I have not the strength.

As though such a stone wall really were a consolation, and really did contain some word of conciliation, simply because it is as true as twice two makes four. Oh, absurdity of absurdities! How much better it is to understand it all, to recognize it all, all the impossibilities and the stone wall; not to be reconciled to one of those impossibilities and stone walls if it disgusts you to be reconciled to it; by the way of the most inevitable, logical combinations to reach the most revolting conclusions on the everlasting theme, that even for the stone wall you are yourself somehow to blame, though again it is as clear as day you are not to blame in the least, and therefore grinding your teeth in silent impotence to sink into luxurious inertia, brooding on the fact that there is no one even for you to feel vindictive against, that you have not, and perhaps never will have, an object for your spite, that it is a sleight of hand, a bit of juggling, a card-sharper's trick, that it is simply a mess, no knowing what and no knowing who, but in spite of all these uncertainties and jugglings, still there is an ache in you, and the more you do not know, the worse the ache.

IV

"Ha, ha, ha! You will be finding enjoyment in toothache next," you cry, with a laugh.

"Well? Even in toothache there is enjoyment," I answer. I had toothache for a whole month and I know there is. In that case, of course, people are not spiteful in silence, but moan; but they are not candid moans, they are malignant moans, and the malignancy is the whole point. The enjoyment of the sufferer finds expression in those moans; if he did not feel enjoyment in them he would not moan. It is a good example, gentlemen, and I will develop it. Those moans express in the first place all the aimlessness of your pain, which is so humiliating to your consciousness; the whole legal system of nature on which you spit disdainfully, of course, but from which you suffer all the same while she does not. They express the consciousness that you have no enemy to punish, but that you have pain; the consciousness that in spite of all possible Vagenheims [4] you are in complete slavery to your teeth; that if some one wishes it, your teeth will leave off aching, and if he does not, they will go on aching another three months; and that finally if you are still contumacious and still protest, all that is left you for your own gratification is to thrash yourself or beat your wall with your fist as hard as you can, and absolutely nothing more. Well, these mortal insults, these jeers on the part of some one unknown, end at last in an enjoyment which sometimes reaches the highest degree of voluptuousness. I ask you, gentlemen, listen sometimes to the moans of an educated man of the nineteenth century suffering from toothache, on the second or third day of the attack, when he is beginning to moan, not as he moaned on the first day, that is, not simply because he has toothache, not just as any coarse peasant, but as a man affected by progress and European civilization, a man who is "divorced from the soil and the national elements," as they express it nowadays. His moans become nasty, disgustingly malignant, and go on for whole days and nights. And of course he knows himself that he is doing himself no

---

[4] Petersburg dentists.

sort of good with his moans; he knows better than any one that he is only lacerating and harassing himself and others for nothing; he knows that even the audience before whom he is making his efforts, and his whole family, listen to him with loathing, do not put a ha'porth of faith in him, and inwardly understand that he might moan differently, more simply, without trills and flourishes, and that he is only amusing himself like that from ill-humour, from malignancy. Well, in all these recognitions and disgraces it is that there lies a voluptuous pleasure. As though he would say: "I am worrying you, I am lacerating your hearts, I am keeping every one in the house awake. Well, stay awake then, you, too, feel every minute that I have toothache. I am not a hero to you now, as I tried to seem before, but simply a nasty person, an impostor. Well, so be it, then! I am very glad that you see through me. It is nasty for you to hear my despicable moans: well, let it be nasty; here I will let you have a nastier flourish in a minute. . . ." You do not understand even now, gentlemen? No, it seems our development and our consciousness must go further to understand all the intricacies of this pleasure. You laugh? Delighted. My jests, gentlemen, are of course in bad taste, jerky, involved, lacking self-confidence. But of course that is because I do not respect myself. Can a man of perception respect himself at all?

V

Come, can a man who attempts to find enjoyment in the very feeling of his own degradation possibly have a spark of respect for himself? I am not saying this now from any mawkish kind of remorse. And, indeed, I could never endure saying, "Forgive me, Papa, I won't do it again," not because I am incapable of saying that—on the contrary, perhaps just because I have been too capable of it, and in what a way, too! As though of design I used to get into trouble in cases when I was not to blame in any way. That was the nastiest part of it. At the same time I was genuinely touched and penitent, I used to shed tears and, of course, deceived myself, though I was not acting in the least and there was a sick feeling in my heart at the time. . . . For that one could not blame even the laws of nature, though the laws of nature have continually all my life offended me more than anything. It is loathsome to remember it all, but it was loathsome even then. Of course, a minute or so later I would realize wrathfully that it was all a lie, a revolting lie, an affected lie, that is, all this penitence, this emotion, these vows of reform. You will ask why did I worry myself with such antics: answer, because it was very dull to sit with one's hands folded, and so one began cutting capers. That is really it. Observe yourselves more carefully, gentlemen, then you will understand that it is so. I invented adventures for myself and made up a life, so as at least to live in some way. How many times it has happened to me—well, for instance, to take offence simply on purpose, for nothing; and one knows oneself, of course, that one is offended at nothing, that one is putting it on, but yet one brings oneself, at last, to the point of being really offended. All my life I have had an impulse to play such pranks, so that in the end I could not control it in myself. Another time, twice, in fact, I tried hard to be in love. I suffered, too, gentlemen, I assure you. In the depth of my heart there was no faith in my suffering, only a faint stir of mockery, but yet I did suffer, and in the real, orthodox way; I was jealous, beside myself . . . and it was all from *ennui*, gentlemen, all from *ennui*; inertia overcame me. You know the direct, legitimate fruit of consciousness is inertia, that is, conscious sitting-with-the-hands-folded. I have referred to this already. I repeat, I repeat with emphasis: all "direct" persons and men of action are active just because they are stupid and limited. How explain that? I will tell you: in consequence of their limitation they take immediate and secondary causes for primary ones, and in that way persuade themselves more quickly and easily than other people do that they have found an infallible foundation for their activity, and their minds are at ease and you know that is the chief thing. To begin to act, you know, you must first have your mind completely at ease and no trace of doubt left in it. Why, how am I, for example, to set my mind at rest? Where are the primary causes on which I am to build? Where are my foundations? Where am I to get them from? I exercise myself in reflection, and consequently with me every primary cause at once draws after itself another still more primary, and so on to infinity. That is just the essence of every sort of consciousness and reflection. It must be a case of the laws of nature again. What is the result of it in the end? Why, just the same. Remember I spoke just now of vengeance. (I am sure you did not take it in.) I said that a man revenges himself because he sees justice in it. Therefore he has found a primary cause, that is, justice. And so he is at rest on all sides, and consequently he carries out his revenge calmly and successfully, being persuaded that he is doing a just and honest thing.

But I see no justice in it, I find no sort of virtue in it either, and consequently if I attempt to revenge myself, it is only out of spite. Spite, of course, might overcome everything, all my doubts, and so might serve quite successfully in place of a primary cause, precisely because it is not a cause. But what is to be done if I have not even spite (I began with that just now, you know). In consequence again of those accursed laws of consciousness, anger in me is subject to chemical disintegration. You look into it, the object flies off into air, your reasons evaporate, the criminal is not to be found, the wrong becomes not a wrong but a phantom, something like the toothache, for which no one is to blame, and consequently there is only the same outlet left again—that is, to beat the wall as hard as you can. So you give it up with a wave of the hand because you have not found a fundamental cause. And try letting yourself be carried away by your feelings, blindly, without reflection, without a primary cause, repelling consciousness at least for a time; hate or love, if only not to sit with your hands folded. The day after to-morrow, at the latest, you will begin despising yourself for having knowingly deceived yourself. Result: a soap-bubble and inertia. Oh, gentlemen, do you know, perhaps I consider myself an intelligent man, only because all my life I have been able neither to begin nor to finish anything. Granted I am a babbler, a harmless vexatious babbler, like all of us. But what is to be done if the direct and sole vocation of every intelligent man is babble, that is, the intentional pouring of water through a sieve?

VI

Oh, if I had done nothing simply from laziness! Heavens, how I should have respected myself, then. I should have respected myself because I should at least have been capable of being lazy; there would at least have been one quality, as it were, positive in me, in which I could have believed myself. Question: What is he? Answer: A sluggard; how very pleasant it would have been to hear that of oneself! It would mean that I was positively defined, it would mean that there was something to say about me. "Sluggard"—why, it is a calling and vocation, it is a career. Do not jest, it is so. I should then be a member of the best club by right, and should find my occupation in continually respecting myself. I knew a gentleman who prided himself all his life on being a connoisseur of Lafitte. He considered this as his positive virtue, and never doubted himself. He died, not simply with a tranquil, but with a triumphant, conscience, and he was quite right, too. Then I should have chosen a career for myself, I should have been a sluggard and a glutton, not a simple one, but, for instance, one with sympathies for everything good and beautiful. How do you like that? I have long had visions of it. That "good and beautiful" weighs heavily on my mind at forty. But that is at forty; then—oh, then it would have been different! I should have found for myself a form of activity in keeping with it, to be precise, drinking to the health of everything "good and beautiful." I should have snatched at every opportunity to drop a tear into my glass and then to drain it to all that is "good and beautiful." I should then have turned everything into the good and the beautiful; in the nastiest, unquestionable trash, I should have sought out the good and the beautiful. I should have exuded tears like a wet sponge. An artist, for instance, paints a picture worthy of Gué. At once I drink to the health of the artist who painted the picture worthy of Gué, because I love all that is "good and beautiful." An author has written As you will: at once I drink to the health of "any one you will" because I love all that is "good and beautiful."

I should claim respect for doing so. I should persecute any one who would not show me respect. I should live at ease, I should die with dignity, why, it is charming, perfectly charming! And what a good round belly I should have grown, what a treble chin I should have established, what a ruby nose I should have coloured for myself, so that every one would have said, looking at me: "Here is an asset! Here is something real and solid!" And, say what you like, it is very agreeable to hear such remarks about oneself in this negative age.

VII

But these are all golden dreams. Oh, tell me, who was it first announced, who was it first proclaimed, that man only does nasty things because he does not know his own interests; and that if he were enlightened, if his eyes were opened to his real normal interests, man would at once cease to do nasty things, would at once become good and noble because, being enlightened and understanding his real advantage, he would see his own advantage in the good and nothing else, and we all know that not one man can, consciously, act against his own interests, consequently, so to say, through necessity, he would begin doing good? Oh, the babe! Oh, the pure, innocent child! Why, in the first place, when in all these thousands of years has there been a time when man has acted only from his own interest? What is to be done with the millions of facts that bear witness that men, *consciously*, that is, fully understanding their real interests, have left them in the background and have rushed headlong on another path, to meet peril and danger, compelled to this course by nobody and by nothing, but, as it were, simply disliking the beaten track, and have obstinately, wilfully, struck out another difficult, absurd way, seeking it almost in the darkness. So, I suppose, this obstinacy and perversity were pleasanter to them than any advantage. . . . Advantage! What is advantage? And will you take it upon yourself to define with perfect accuracy in what the advantage of man consists? And what if it so happens that a man's advantage, *sometimes*, not only may, but even must, consist in his desiring in certain cases what is harmful to himself and not advantageous? And if so, if there can be such a case, the whole principle falls into dust. What do you think—are there such cases? You laugh; laugh away, gentlemen, but only answer me: have man's advantages been reckoned up with perfect certainty? Are there not some which not only have not been included but cannot possibly be included under any classification? You see, you gentlemen have, to the best of my knowledge, taken your whole register of human advantages from the averages of statistical figures and politico-economical formulas. Your advantages are prosperity, wealth, freedom, peace—and so on, and so on. So that the man who should, for instance, go openly and knowingly in opposition to all that list would, to your thinking, and indeed mine, too, of course, be an obscurantist or an absolute madman: would not he? But, you know, this is what is surprising: why does it so happen that all these statisticians, sages and lovers of humanity, when they reckon up human advantages invariably leave out one? They don't even take it into their reckoning in the form in which it should be taken, and the whole reckoning depends upon that. It would be no great matter, they would simply have to take it, this advantage, and add it to the list. But the trouble is, that this strange advantage does not fall under any classification and is not in place in any list. I have a friend for instance . . . Ech! gentlemen, but of course he is your friend, too; and indeed there is no one, no one, to whom he is not a friend! When he prepares for any undertaking this gentleman immediately explains to you, elegantly and clearly, exactly how he must act in accordance with the laws of reason and truth. What is more, he will talk to you with excitement and passion of the true normal interests of man; with irony he will upbraid the shortsighted fools who do not understand their own interests, nor the true significance of virtue; and, within a quarter of an hour, without any sudden outside provocation, but simply through something inside him which is stronger than all his interests, he will go off on quite a different tack—that is, act in direct opposition to what he has just been saying about himself, in opposition to the laws of reason, in opposition to his own advantage, in fact in opposition to everything. . . . I warn you that my friend is a compound personality, and therefore it is difficult to blame him as an individual. The fact is, gentlemen, it seems there must really exist something that is dearer to almost every man than his greatest advantages, or (not to be illogical) there is a most advantageous advantage (the very one omitted of which we spoke just now) which is more important and more advantageous than all other advantages, for the sake of which a man if necessary is ready to act in opposition to all laws; that is, in opposition to reason, honour, peace, prosperity—in fact, in opposition to all those excellent and useful things if only he can attain that fundamental, most advantageous advantage which is dearer to him than all. "Yes, but it's advantage all the same" you will retort. But excuse me, I'll make the point clear, and it is not a case of playing upon words. What matters is, that this advantage is remarkable from the very fact that it breaks down all our classifications, and continually shatters every system constructed by lovers of mankind for the benefit of mankind. In fact, it upsets everything. But before I mention this advantage to you, I want to compromise myself personally, and therefore I boldly declare that all these fine systems, all these theories for explaining to mankind their real normal interests, in order that inevitably striving to pursue these interests they may at once become good and noble—are, in my opinion, so far, mere logical exercises! Yes, logical exercises. Why, to maintain this theory of the regeneration of mankind by means of the pursuit of his own advantage is to my mind almost the same thing as . . . as to affirm, for instance, following Buckle, that through civilization mankind becomes softer, and consequently less bloodthirsty and less fitted for warfare. Logically it does seem to follow from his arguments. But man has such a predilection for systems and abstract deductions that he is ready to distort the truth intentionally, he is ready to deny the evidence of his senses only to justify his logic. I take this example because it is the most glaring instance of it. Only look about you: blood is being spilt in streams, and in the merriest way, as though it were champagne. Take the whole of the nineteenth century in which Buckle lived. Take Napoleon—the Great and also the present one. Take North America—the eternal union. Take the farce of Schleswig-Holstein. . . . And what is it that civilization softens in us? The only gain of civilization for mankind is the greater capacity for variety of sensations—and absolutely nothing more. And through the development of this many-sidedness man may come to finding enjoyment in bloodshed. In fact, this has already happened to him. Have you noticed that it is the most civilized gentlemen who have been the subtlest slaughterers, to whom the Attilas and Stenka Razins could not hold a candle, and if they are not so conspicuous as the Attilas and Stenka Razins it is simply because they are so often met with, are so ordinary and have become so familiar to us. In any case civilization has made mankind if not more bloodthirsty, at least more vilely, more loathsomely bloodthirsty. In old days he saw justice in bloodshed and with his conscience at peace exterminated those he thought proper. Now we do think bloodshed abominable and yet we engage in this abomination, and with more energy than ever. Which is worse? Decide that for yourselves. They say that Cleopatra (excuse an instance from Roman history) was fond of sticking gold pins into her slave-girls' breasts and derived gratification from their screams and writhings. You will say that that was in the comparatively barbarous times; that these are barbarous times too, because also, comparatively speaking, pins are stuck in even now; that though man has now learned to see more clearly than in barbarous ages, he is still far from having learnt to act as reason and science would dictate. But yet you are fully convinced that he will be sure to learn when he gets rid of certain old bad habits, and when common sense and science have completely re-educated human nature and turned it in a normal direction. You are confident that then man will cease from *intentional* error and will, so to say, be compelled not to want to set his will against his normal interests. That is not all; then, you say, science itself will teach man (though to my mind it's a superfluous luxury) that he never has really had any caprice or will of his own, and that he himself is something of the nature of a piano-key or the stop of an organ, and that there are, besides, things called the laws of nature; so that everything he does is not done by his willing it, but is done of itself, by the laws of nature. Consequently we have only to discover these laws of nature, and man will no longer have to answer for his actions and life will become exceedingly easy for him. All human actions will then, of course, be tabulated according to these laws, mathematically, like tables of logarithms up to 108,000, and entered in an index; or, better still, there would be published certain edifying works of the nature of encyclopædic lexicons, in which everything will be so clearly calculated and explained that there will be no more incidents or adventures in the world.

Then—this is all what you say—new economic relations will be established, all ready-made and worked out with mathematical exactitude, so that every possible question will vanish in the twinkling of an eye, simply because every possible answer to it will be provided. Then the "Palace of Crystal" will be built.[5] Then . . . . In fact, those will be halcyon days. Of course there is no guaranteeing (this is my comment) that it will not be, for instance, frightfully dull then (for what will one have to do when everything will be calculated and tabulated), but on the other hand everything will be extraordinarily rational. Of course boredom may lead you to anything. It is boredom sets one sticking golden pins into people, but all that would not matter. What is bad (this is my comment again) is that I dare say people will be thankful for the gold pins then. Man is stupid, you know, phenomenally stupid; or rather he is not at all stupid, but he is so ungrateful that you could not find another like him in all creation. I, for instance, would not be in the least surprised if all of a sudden, à propos of nothing, in the midst of general prosperity a gentleman with an ignoble, or rather with a reactionary and ironical, countenance were to arise and, putting his arms akimbo, say to us all: "I say, gentlemen, hadn't we better kick over the whole show and scatter rationalism to the winds, simply to send these logarithms to the devil, and to enable us to live once more at our own sweet foolish will!" That again would not matter, but what is annoying is that he would be sure to find followers—such is the nature of man. And all that for the most foolish reason, which, one would think, was hardly worth mentioning: that is, that man everywhere and at all times, whoever he may be, has preferred to act as he chose and not in the least as his reason and advantage dictated. And one may choose what is contrary to one's own interests, and

---

[5] This refers to the Crystal Palace erected in London for the Great Industrial Exhibition of 1851. In European literary and intellectual circles, the Crystal Palace became a symbol for the rise of an urban and industrial civilization.

sometimes one *positively ought* (that is my idea). One's own free unfettered choice, one's own caprice, however wild it may be, one's own fancy worked up at times to frenzy—is that very "most advantageous advantage" which we have overlooked, which comes under no classification and against which all systems and theories are continually being shattered to atoms. And how do these wiseacres know that man wants a normal, a virtuous choice? What has made them conceive that man must want a rationally advantageous choice? What man wants is simply *independent* choice, whatever that independence may cost and wherever it may lead. And choice, of course, the devil only knows what choice.

VIII

"Ha! ha! ha! But you know there is no such thing as choice in reality, say what you like," you will interpose with a chuckle. "Science has succeeded in so far analysing man that we know already that choice and what is called freedom of will is nothing else than—"

Stay, gentlemen, I meant to begin with that myself. I confess, I was rather frightened. I was just going to say that the devil only knows what choice depends on, and that perhaps that was a very good thing, but I remembered the teaching of science . . . and pulled myself up. And here you have begun upon it. Indeed, if there really is some day discovered a formula for all our desires and caprices—that is, an explanation of what they depend upon, by what laws they arise, how they develop, what they are aiming at in one case and in another and so on, that is a real mathematical formula —then, most likely, man will at once cease to feel desire, indeed, he will be certain to. For who would want to choose by rule? Besides, he will at once be transformed from a human being into an organstop or something of the sort; for what is a man without desires, without free will and without choice, if not a stop in an organ? What do you think? Let us reckon the chances—can such a thing happen or not?

"H'm!" you decide. "Our choice is usually mistaken from a false view of our advantage. We sometimes choose absolute nonsense because in our foolishness we see in that nonsense the easiest means for attaining a supposed advantage. But when all that is explained and worked out on paper (which is perfectly possible, for it is contemptible and senseless to suppose that some laws of nature man will never understand), then certainly so-called desires will no longer exist. For if a desire should come into conflict with reason we shall then reason and not desire, because it will be impossible retaining our reason to be *senseless* in our desires, and in that way knowingly act against reason and desire to injure ourselves. And as all choice and reasoning can be really calculated—because there will some day be discovered the laws of our so-called free will—so, joking apart, there may one day be something like a table constructed of them, so that we really shall choose in accordance with it. If, for instance, some day they calculate and prove to me that I made a long nose at some one because I could not help making a long nose at him and that I had to do it in that particular way, what *freedom* is left me, especially if I am a learned man and have taken my degree somewhere? Then I should be able to calculate my whole life for thirty years beforehand. In short, if this could be arranged there would be nothing left for us to do; anyway, we should have to understand that. And, in fact, we ought unwearyingly to repeat to ourselves that at such and such a time and in such and such circumstances nature does not ask our leave; that we have got to take her as she is and not fashion her to suit our fancy, and if we really aspire to formulas and tables of rules, and well, even . . . to the chemical retort, there's no help for it, we must accept the retort too, or else it will be accepted without our consent. . . ."

Yes, but here I come to a stop! Gentlemen, you must excuse me for being over-philosophical: it's the result of forty years underground! Allow me to indulge my fancy. You see, gentlemen, reason is an excellent thing, there's no disputing that, but reason is nothing but reason and satisfies only the rational side of man's nature, while will is a manifestation of the whole life, that is, of the whole human life including reason and all the impulses. And although our life, in this manifestation of it, is often worthless, yet it is life and not simply extracting square roots. Here I, for instance, quite naturally want to live, in order to satisfy all my capacities for life, and not simply my capacity for reasoning, that is, not simply one twentieth of my capacity for life. What does reason know? Reason only knows what it has succeeded in learning (some things, perhaps, it will never learn; this is a poor comfort, but why not say so frankly?) and human nature acts as a whole, with everything that is in it, consciously or unconsciously, and, even if it goes wrong, it lives. I suspect, gentlemen, that you are looking at me with compassion; you tell me again that an enlightened and developed man, such, in short, as the future man will be, cannot consciously desire anything disadvantageous to himself, that that can be proved mathematically. I thoroughly agree, it can—by mathematics. But I repeat for the hundredth time, there is one case, one only, when man may consciously, purposely, desire what is injurious to himself, what is stupid, very stupid—simply in order to have the right to desire for himself even what is very stupid and not to be bound by an obligation to desire only what is sensible. Of course, this very stupid thing, this caprice of ours, may be in reality, gentlemen, more advantageous for us than anything else on earth, especially in certain cases. And in particular it may be more advantageous than any advantage even when it does us obvious harm, and contradicts the soundest conclusions of our reason concerning our advantage—for in any circumstances it preserves for us what is most precious and most important—that is, our personality, our individuality. Some, you see, maintain that this really is the most precious thing for mankind; choice can, of course, if it chooses, be in agreement with reason; and especially if this be not abused but kept within bounds. It is profitable and sometimes even praiseworthy. But very often, and even most often, choice is utterly and stubbornly opposed to reason . . . and . . . and . . . do you know that that, too, is profitable, sometimes even praiseworthy? Gentlemen, let us suppose that man is not stupid. (Indeed one cannot refuse to suppose that, if only from the one consideration, that, if man is stupid, then who is wise?) But if he is not stupid, he is monstrously ungrateful! Phenomenally ungrateful. In fact, I believe that the best definition of man is the ungrateful biped. But that is not all, that is not his worst defect; his worst defect is his perpetual moral obliquity, perpetual—from the days of the Flood to the Schleswig-Holstein period. Moral obliquity and consequently lack of good sense; for it has long been accepted that lack of good sense is due to no other cause than moral obliquity. Put it to the test and cast your eyes upon the history of mankind. What will you see? Is it a grand spectacle? Grand, if you like. Take the Colossus of Rhodes, for instance, that's worth something. With good reason Mr. Anaevsky [6] testifies of it that some say that it is the work of man's hands, while others maintain that it has been created by nature herself. Is it many-coloured? May be it is many-coloured, too: if one takes the dress uniforms, military and civilian, of all peoples in all ages—that

---

[6] A contemporary novelist who was the object of much critical derision.

alone is worth something, and if you take the undress uniforms you will never get to the end of it; no historian would be equal to the job. Is it monotonous? Maybe it's monotonous too: it's fighting and fighting; they are fighting now, they fought first and they fought last—you will admit, that it is almost too monotonous. In short, one may say anything about the history of the world—anything that might enter the most disordered imagination. The only thing one can't say is that it's rational. The very word sticks in one's throat. And, indeed, this is the odd thing that is continually happening: there are continually turning up in life moral and rational persons, sages and lovers of humanity who make it their object to live all their lives as morally and rationally as possible, to be, so to speak, a light to their neighbours simply in order to show them that it is possible to live morally and rationally in this world. And yet we all know that those very people sooner or later have been false to themselves, playing some queer trick, often a most unseemly one. Now I ask you: what can be expected of man since he is a being endowed with such strange qualities? Shower upon him every earthly blessing, drown him in a sea of happiness, so that nothing but bubbles of bliss can be seen on the surface; give him economic prosperity, such that he should have nothing else to do but sleep, eat cakes and busy himself with the continuation of his species, and even then out of sheer ingratitude, sheer spite, man would play you some nasty trick. He would even risk his cakes and would deliberately desire the most fatal rubbish, the most uneconomical absurdity, simply to introduce into all this positive good sense his fatal fantastic element. It is just his fantastic dreams, his vulgar folly that he will desire to retain, simply in order to prove to himself—as though that were so necessary—that men still are men and not the keys of a piano, which the laws of nature threaten to control so completely that soon one will be able to desire nothing but by the calendar. And that is not all: even if man really were nothing but a piano-key, even if this were proved to him by natural science and mathematics, even then he would not become reasonable, but would purposely do something perverse out of simple ingratitude, simply to gain his point. And if he does not find means he will contrive destruction and chaos, will contrive sufferings of all sorts, only to gain his point! He will launch a curse upon the world, and as only man can curse (it is his privilege, the primary distinction between him and other animals), may be by his curse alone he will attain his object—that is, convince himself that he is a man and not a piano-key! If you say that all this, too, can be calculated and tabulated—chaos and darkness and curses, so that the mere possibility of calculating it all beforehand would stop it all, and reason would reassert itself, then man would purposely go mad in order to be rid of reason and gain his point! I believe in it, I answer for it, for the whole work of man really seems to consist in nothing but proving to himself every minute that he is a man and not a piano-key! It may be at the cost of his skin, it may be by cannibalism! And this being so, can one help being tempted to rejoice that it has not yet come off, and that desire still depends on something we don't know?

You will scream at me (that is, if you condescend to do so) that no one is touching my free will, that all they are concerned with is that my will should of itself, of its own free will, coincide with my own normal interests, with the laws of nature and arithmetic.

Good Heavens, gentlemen, what sort of free will is left when we come to tabulation and arithmetic, when it will all be a case of twice two make four? Twice two makes four without my will. As if free will meant that!

IX

Gentlemen, I am joking, and I know myself that my jokes are not brilliant, but you know one can't take everything as a joke. I am, perhaps, jesting against the grain. Gentlemen, I am tormented by questions; answer them for me. You, for instance, want to cure men of their old habits and reform their will in accordance with science and good sense. But how do you know, not only that it is possible, but also that it is *desirable*, to reform man in that way? And what leads you to the conclusion that man's inclinations *need* reforming? In short, how do you know that such a reformation will be a benefit to man? And to go to the root of the matter, why are you so positively convinced that not to act against his real normal interests guaranteed by the conclusions of reason and arithmetic is certainly always advantageous for man and must always be a law for mankind? So far, you know, this is only your supposition. It may be the law of logic, but not the law of humanity. You think, gentlemen, perhaps that I am mad? Allow me to defend myself. I agree that man is pre-eminently a creative animal, predestined to strive consciously for an object and to engage in engineering—that is, incessantly and eternally to make new roads, *wherever they may lead*. But the reason why he wants sometimes to go off at a tangent may just be that he is *predestined* to make the road, and perhaps, too, that however stupid the "direct" practical man may be, the thought sometimes will occur to him that the road almost always does lead *somewhere*, and that the destination it leads to is less important than the process of making it, and that the chief thing is to save the well-conducted child from despising engineering, and so giving way to the fatal idleness, which, as we all know, is the mother of all the vices. Man likes to make roads and to create, that is a fact beyond dispute. But why has he such a passionate love for destruction and chaos also? Tell me that! But on that point I want to say a couple of words myself. May it not be that he loves chaos and destruction (there can be no disputing that he does sometimes love it) because he is instinctively afraid of attaining his object and completing the edifice he is constructing? Who knows, perhaps he only loves that edifice from a distance, and is by no means in love with it at close quarters; perhaps he only loves building it and does not want to live in it, but will leave it, when completed, for the use of *les animaux domestiques*—such as the ants, the sheep, and so on. Now the ants have quite a different taste. They have a marvellous edifice of that pattern which endures for ever—the ant-heap.

With the ant-heap the respectable race of ants began and with the ant-heap they will probably end, which does the greatest credit to their perseverance and good sense. But man is a frivolous and incongruous creature, and perhaps, like a chess player, loves the process of the game, not the end of it. And who knows (there is no saying with certainty), perhaps the only goal on earth to which mankind is striving lies in this incessant process of attaining, in other words, in life itself, and not in the thing to be attained, which must always be expressed as a formula, as positive as twice two makes four, and such positiveness is not life, gentlemen, but is the beginning of death. Anyway, man has always been afraid of this mathematical certainty, and I am afraid of it now. Granted that man does nothing but seek that mathematical certainty, he traverses oceans, sacrifices his life in the quest, but to succeed, really to find it, he dreads, I assure you. He feels that when he has found it there will be nothing for him to look for. When workmen have finished their work they do at least receive their pay, they go to the tavern, then they are taken to the police-station—and there is occupation for a week. But where can man go? Anyway, one can observe a certain awkwardness about him when he has attained such objects. He loves the process of attaining, but does not quite like to have attained, and that, of course, is very absurd. In fact, man is a comical creature; there seems to be a kind of jest in it all. But yet mathematical certainty is, after all, something insufferable. Twice two makes four seems to me simply a piece of insolence. Twice two makes four is a pert coxcomb who stands with arms akimbo barring your path and spitting. I admit that twice two makes four is an excellent thing, but if we are to give everything its due, twice two makes five is sometimes a very charming thing too.

And why are you so firmly, so triumphantly, convinced that only the normal and the positive—in other words, only what is conducive to welfare—is for the advantage of man? Is not reason in error as regards advantage? Does not man, perhaps, love something besides well-being? Perhaps he is just as fond of suffering? Perhaps suffering is just as great a benefit to him as well-being? Man is sometimes extraordinarily, passionately, in love with suffering, and that is a fact. There is no need to appeal to universal history to prove that; only ask yourself, if you are a man and have lived at all. As far as my personal opinion is concerned, to care only for well-being seems to me positively ill-bred. Whether it's good or bad, it is sometimes very pleasant, too, to smash things. I hold no brief for suffering nor for well-being either. I am standing for . . . my caprice, and for its being guaranteed to me when necessary. Suffering would be out of place in vaudevilles, for instance; I know that. In the "Palace of Crystal" it is unthinkable; suffering means doubt, negation, and what would be the good of a "palace of crystal" if there could be any doubt about it? And yet I think man will never renounce real suffering, that is, destruction and chaos. Why, suffering is the sole origin of consciousness. Though I did lay it down at the beginning that consciousness is the greatest misfortune for man, yet I know man prizes it and would not give it up for any satisfaction. Consciousness, for instance, is infinitely superior to twice two makes four. Once you have mathematical certainty there is nothing left to do or to understand. There will be nothing left but to bottle up your five senses and plunge into contemplation. While if you stick to consciousness, even though the same result is attained, you can at least flog yourself at times, and that will, at any rate, liven you up. Reactionary as it is, corporal punishment is better than nothing.

X

You believe in a palace of crystal that can never be destroyed—a palace at which one will not be able to put out one's tongue or make a long nose on the sly. And perhaps that is just why I am afraid of this edifice, that it is of crystal and can never be destroyed and that one cannot put one's tongue out at it even on the sly.

You see, if it were not a palace, but a hen-house, I might creep into it to avoid getting wet, and yet I would not call the hen-house a palace out of gratitude to it for keeping me dry. You laugh and say that in such circumstances a hen-house is as good as a mansion. Yes, I answer, if one had to live simply to keep out of the rain.

But what is to be done if I have taken it into my head that that is not the only object in life, and that if one must live one had better live in a mansion. That is my choice, my desire. You will only eradicate it when you have changed my preference. Well, do change it, allure me with something else, give me another ideal. But meanwhile I will not take a hen-house for a mansion. The palace of crystal may be an idle dream, it may be that it is inconsistent with the laws of nature and that I have invented it only through my own stupidity, through the old-fashioned irrational habits of my generation. But what does it matter to me that it is inconsistent? That makes no difference since it exists in my desires, or rather exists as long as my desires exist. Perhaps you are laughing again? Laugh away; I will put up with any mockery rather than pretend that I am satisfied when I am hungry. I know, anyway, that I will not be put off with a compromise, with a recurring zero, simply because it is consistent with the laws of nature and actually exists. I will not accept as the crown of my desires a block of buildings with tenements for the poor on a lease of a thousand years, and perhaps with a signboard of a dentist hanging out. Destroy my desires, eradicate my ideals, show me something better, and I will follow you. You will say, perhaps, that it is not worth your trouble; but in that case I can give you the same answer. We are discussing things seriously; but if you won't deign to give me your attention, I will drop your acquaintance. I can retreat into my underground hole.

But while I am alive and have desires I would rather my hand were withered off than bring one brick to such a building! Don't remind me that I have just rejected the palace of crystal for the sole reason that one cannot put out one's tongue at it. I did not say because I am so fond of putting my tongue out. Perhaps the thing I resented was, that of all your edifices there has not been one at which one could not put out one's tongue. On the contrary, I would let my tongue be cut off out of gratitude if things could be so arranged that I should lose all desire to put it out. It is not my fault that things cannot be so arranged, and that one must be satisfied with model flats. Then why am I made with such desires? Can I have been constructed simply in order to come to the conclusion that all my construction is a cheat? Can this be my whole purpose? I do not believe it.

But do you know what: I am convinced that we underground folk ought to be kept on a curb. Though we may sit forty years underground without speaking, when we do come out into the light of day and break out we talk and talk and talk. . . .

XI

The long and the short of it is, gentlemen, that it is better to do nothing! Better conscious inertia! And so hurrah for underground! Though I have said that I envy the normal man to the last drop of my bile, yet I should not care to be in his place such as he is now (though I shall not cease envying him). No, no; anyway the underground life is more advantageous. There, at any rate, one can . . . Oh, but even now I am lying! I am lying because I know myself that it is not underground that is better, but something different, quite different, for which I am thirsting, but which I cannot find! Damn underground!

I will tell you another thing that would be better, and that is, if I myself believed in anything of what I have just written. I swear to you, gentlemen, there is not one thing, not one word of what I have written that I really believe. That is, I believe it, perhaps, but at the same time I feel and suspect that I am lying like a cobbler.

"Then why have you written all this?" you will say to me. "I ought to put you underground for forty years without anything to do and then come to you in your cellar, to find out what stage you have reached! How can a man be left with nothing to do for forty years?"

"Isn't that shameful, isn't that humiliating?" you will say, perhaps, wagging your heads contemptuously. "You thirst for life and try to settle the problems of life by a logical tangle. And how persistent, how insolent are your sallies, and at the same time what a scare you are in! You talk nonsense and are pleased with it; you say impudent things and are in continual alarm and apologizing for them. You declare that you are afraid of nothing and at the same time try to ingratiate yourself in our good opinion. You declare that you are gnashing your teeth and at the same time you try to be witty so as to amuse us. You know that your witticisms are not witty, but you are evidently well satisfied with their literary value. You may, perhaps, have really suffered, but you have no respect for your own suffering. You may have sincerity, but you have no modesty; out of the pettiest vanity you expose your sincerity to publicity and ignominy. You doubtlessly mean to say something, but hide your last word through fear, because you have not the resolution to utter it, and only have a cowardly impudence. You boast of consciousness, but you are not sure of your ground, for though your mind works, yet your heart is darkened and corrupt, and you cannot have a full, genuine consciousness without a pure heart. And how intrusive you are, how you insist and grimace! Lies, lies, lies!"

Of course I have myself made up all the things you say. That, too, is from underground. I have been for forty years listening to you through a crack under the floor. I have invented them myself, there was nothing else I could invent. It is no wonder that I have learned it by heart and it has taken a literary form. . . .

But can you really be so credulous as to think that I will print all this and give it to you to read too? And another problem: why do I call you "gentlemen," why do I address you as though you really were my readers? Such confessions as I intend to make are never printed nor given to other people to read. Anyway, I am not strong-minded enough for that, and I don't see why I should be. But you see a fancy has occurred to me and I want to realize it at all costs. Let me explain.

Every man has reminiscences which he would not tell to every one, but only to his friends. He has other matters in his mind which he would not reveal even to his friends, but only to himself, and that in secret. But there are other things which a man is afraid to tell even to himself, and every decent man has a number of such things stored away in his mind. The more decent he is, the greater the number of such things in his mind. Anyway, I have only lately determined to remember some of my early adventures. Till now I have always avoided them, even with a certain uneasiness. Now, when I am not only recalling them, but have actually decided to write an account of them, I want to try the experiment whether one can, even with oneself, be perfectly open and not take fright at the whole truth. I will observe, in parenthesis, that Heine says that a true autobiography is almost an impossibility, and that man is bound to lie about himself. He considers that Rousseau certainly told lies about himself in his confessions, and even intentionally lied, out of vanity. I am convinced that Heine is right; I quite understand how sometimes one may, out of sheer vanity, attribute regular crimes to oneself, and indeed I can very well conceive that kind of vanity. But Heine judged of people who made their confessions to the public. I write only for myself, and I wish to declare once and for all that if I write as though I were addressing readers, that is simply because it is easier for me to write in that form. It is a form, an empty form—I shall never have readers. I have made this plain already. . . .

I don't wish to be hampered by any restrictions in the compilation of my notes. I shall not attempt any system or method. I will jot things down as I remember them.

But here, perhaps, some one will catch at the word and ask me: if you really don't reckon on readers, why do you make such compacts with yourself—and on paper too—that is, that you won't attempt any system or method, that you jot things down as you remember them, and so on, and so on? Why are you explaining? Why do you apologize?

Well, there it is, I answer.

There is a whole psychology in all this, though. Perhaps it is simply that I am a coward. And perhaps that I purposely imagine an audience before me in order that I may be more dignified while I write. There are perhaps thousands of reasons. Again, what is my object precisely in writing? If it is not for the benefit of the public why should I not simply recall these incidents in my own mind without putting them on paper?

Quite so; but yet it is more imposing on paper. There is something more impressive in it; I shall be better able to criticize myself and improve my style. Besides, I shall perhaps obtain actual relief from writing. To-day, for instance, I am particularly oppressed by one memory of a distant past. It came back vividly to my mind a few days ago, and has remained haunting me like an annoying tune that one cannot get rid of. And yet I must get rid of it somehow. I have hundreds of such reminiscences; but at times some one stands out from the hundred and oppresses me. For some reason I believe that if I write it down I should get rid of it. Why not try?

Besides, I am bored, and I never have anything to do. Writing will be a sort of work. They say work makes man kind-hearted and honest. Well, here is a chance for me, anyway.

Snow is falling to-day, yellow and dingy. It fell yesterday, too, and a few days ago. I fancy it is the wet snow that has reminded me of that incident which I cannot shake off now. And so let it be a story à propos of the falling snow.

PART II · À PROPOS OF THE WET SNOW

When from dark error's subjugation
My words of passionate exhortation
  Had wrenched thy fainting spirit free;
And writhing prone in thine affliction
Thou didst recall with malediction
  The vice that had encompassed thee:
And when thy slumbering conscience, fretting
  By recollection's torturing flame,
Thou didst reveal the hideous setting
  Of thy life's current ere I came:
When suddenly I saw thee sicken,
  And weeping, hide thine anguished face,
Revolted, maddened, horror-stricken,
  At memories of foul disgrace.
                                NEKRASOV (*translated by Juliet Soskice*)

I

At that time I was only twenty-four. My life was even then gloomy, ill-regulated, and as solitary as that of a savage. I made friends with no one and positively avoided talking, and buried myself more and more in my hole. At work in the office I never looked at any one, and I was perfectly well aware that my companions looked upon me, not only as a queer fellow, but even looked upon me—I always fancied this—with a sort of loathing. I sometimes wondered why it was that nobody except me fancied that he was looked upon with aversion? One of the clerks had a most repulsive, pock-marked face, which looked positively villainous. I believe I should not have dared to look at any one with such an unsightly countenance. Another had such a very dirty old uniform that there was an unpleasant odour in his proximity. Yet not one of these gentlemen showed the slightest self-consciousness—either about their clothes or their countenance or their character in any way. Neither of them ever imagined that they were looked at with repulsion; if they had imagined it they would not have minded—so long as their superiors did not look at them in that way. It is clear to me now that, owing to my unbounded vanity and to the high standard I set for myself, I often looked at myself with furious discontent, which verged on loathing, and so I inwardly attributed the same feeling to every one. I hated my face, for instance: I thought it disgusting, and even suspected that there was something base in my expression, and so every day when I turned up at the office I tried to behave as independently as possible, and to assume a lofty expression, so that I might not be suspected of being abject. "My face may be ugly," I thought, "but let it be lofty, expressive, and, above all, *extremely* intelligent." But I was positively and painfully certain that it was impossible for my countenance ever to express those qualities. And what was worst of all, I thought it actually stupid looking, and I would have been quite satisfied if I could have looked intelligent. In fact, I would even have put up with looking base if, at the same time, my face could have been thought strikingly intelligent.

Of course, I hated my fellow clerks one and all, and I despised them all, yet at the same time I was, as it were, afraid of them. In fact, it happened at times that I thought more highly of them than of myself. It somehow happened quite suddenly that I alternated between despising them and thinking them superior to myself. A cultivated and decent man cannot be vain without setting a fearfully high standard for himself, and without despising and almost hating himself at certain moments. But whether I despised them or thought them superior I dropped my eyes almost every time I met any one. I even made experiments whether I could face so and so's looking at me, and I was always the first to drop my eyes. This worried me to distraction. I had a sickly dread, too, of being ridiculous, and so had a slavish passion for the conventional in everything external. I loved to fall into the common rut, and had a whole-hearted terror of any kind of eccentricity in myself. But how could I live up to it? I was morbidly sensitive, as a man of our age should be. They were all stupid, and as like one another as so many sheep. Perhaps I was the only one in the office who fancied that I was a coward and a slave, and I fancied it just because I was more highly developed. But it was not only that I fancied it, it really was so. I was a coward and a slave. I say this without the slightest embarrassment. Every decent man of our age must be a coward and a slave. That is his normal condition. Of that I am firmly persuaded. He is made and constructed to that very end. And not only at the present time owing to some casual circumstances, but always, at all times, a decent man is bound to be a coward and a slave. It is the law of nature for all decent people all over the earth. If any one of them happens to be valiant about something, he need not be comforted nor carried away by that; he would show the white feather just the same before something else. That is how it invariably and inevitably ends. Only donkeys and mules are valiant, and they only till they are pushed up to the wall. It is not worth while to pay attention to them for they really are of no consequence.

Another circumstance, too, worried me in those days: that there was no one like me and I was unlike any one else. "I am alone and they are *every one*," I thought—and pondered.

From that it is evident that I was still a youngster.

The very opposite sometimes happened. It was loathsome sometimes to go to the office; things reached such a point that I often came home ill. But all at once, *à propos* of nothing, there would come a phase of scepticism and indifference (everything happened in phases to me), and I would laugh myself at my intolerance and fastidiousness, I would reproach myself with being *romantic*. At one time I was unwilling to speak to any one, while at other times I would not only talk, but go to the length of contemplating making friends with them. All my fastidiousness would suddenly, for no rhyme or reason, vanish. Who knows, perhaps I never had really had it, and it had simply been affected, and got out of books. I have not decided that question even now. Once I quite made friends with them, visited their homes, played preference, drank vodka, talked of promotions. . . . But here let me make a digression.

We Russians, speaking generally, have never had those foolish transcendental "romantics"—German, and still more French—on whom nothing produces any effect; if there were an earthquake, if all France perished at the barricades, they would still be the same, they would not even have the decency to affect a change, but would still go on singing their transcendental songs to the hour of their death, because they are fools. We, in Russia, have no fools; that is well known. That is what distinguishes us from foreign lands. Consequently these transcendental natures are not found amongst us in their pure form. The idea that they are is due to our "realistic" journalists and critics of that day, always on the look out for Kostanzhoglos and Uncle Pyotr Ivanitchs and foolishly accepting them as our ideal; they have slandered our romantics, taking them for the same transcendental sort as in Germany or France. On the contrary, the characteristics of our "romantics" are absolutely and directly opposed to the transcendental European type, and no European standard can be applied to them. (Allow me to make use of this word "romantic"—an old-fashioned and much respected word which has done good service and is familiar to all.) The characteristics of our romantic are to understand everything, *to see everything and to see it often incomparably more clearly than our most realistic minds see it*; to refuse to accept anyone or anything, but at the same time not to despise anything; to give way, to yield, from policy; never to lose sight of a useful practical object (such as rent-free quarters at the government expense, pensions, decorations), to keep their eye on that object through all the enthusiasms and volumes of lyrical poems, and at the same time to preserve "the good and the beautiful" inviolate within them to the hour of their death, and to preserve themselves also, incidentally, like some precious jewel wrapped in cotton wool if only for the benefit of "the good and the beautiful." Our "romantic" is a man of great breadth and the greatest rogue of all our rogues, I assure you. . . . I can assure you from experience, indeed. Of course, that is, if he is intelligent. But what am I saying! The romantic is always intelligent, and I only meant to observe that although we have had foolish romantics they don't count, and they were only so because in the flower of their youth they degenerated into Germans, and to preserve their precious jewel more comfortably, settled somewhere out there—by preference in Weimar or the Black Forest.

I, for instance, genuinely despised my official work and did not openly abuse it simply because I was in it myself and got a salary for it. Anyway, take note, I did not openly abuse it. Our romantic would rather go out of his mind—a thing, however, which very rarely happens—than take to open abuse, unless he had some other career in view; and he is never kicked out. At most, they would take him to the lunatic asylum as "the King of Spain" if he should go very mad. But it is only the thin, fair people who go out of their minds in Russia. Innumerable "romantics" attain later in life to considerable rank in the service. Their many-sidedness is remarkable! And what a faculty they have for the most contradictory sensations! I was comforted by this thought even in those days, and I am of the same opinion now. That is why there are so many "broad natures" among us who never lose their ideal even in the depths of degradation; and though they never stir a finger for their ideal, though they are arrant thieves and knaves, yet they tearfully cherish their first ideal and are extraordinarily honest at heart. Yes, it is only among us that the most incorrigible rogue can be absolutely and loftily honest at heart without in the least ceasing to be a rogue. I repeat, our romantics, frequently, become such accomplished rascals (I use the term "rascals" affectionately), suddenly display such a sense of reality and practical knowledge that their bewildered superiors and the public generally can only ejaculate in amazement.

Their many-sidedness is really amazing, and goodness knows what it may develop into later on, and what the future has in store for us. It is not a poor material! I do not say this from any foolish or boastful patriotism. But I feel sure that you are again imagining that I am joking. Or perhaps it's just the contrary, and you are convinced that I really think so. Anyway, gentlemen, I shall welcome both views as an honour and a special favour. And do forgive my digression.

I did not, of course, maintain friendly relations with my comrades and soon was at loggerheads with them, and in my youth and inexperience I even gave up bowing to them, as though I had cut off all relations. That, however, only happened to me once. As a rule, I was always alone.

In the first place I spent most of my time at home, reading. I tried to stifle all that was continually seething within me by means of external impressions. And the only external means I had was reading. Reading, of course, was a great help—exciting me, giving me pleasure and pain. But at times it bored me fearfully. One longed for movement in spite of everything, and I plunged all at once into dark, underground, loathsome vice of the pettiest kind. My wretched passions were acute, smarting, from my continual, sickly irritability. I had hysterical impulses, with tears and convulsions. I had no resource except reading, that is, there was nothing in my surroundings which I could respect and which attracted me. I was overwhelmed with depression, too; I had an hysterical craving for incongruity and for contrast, and so I took to vice. I have not said all this to justify myself. . . . But, no! I am lying. I did want to justify myself. I make that little observation for my own benefit, gentlemen. I don't want to lie. I vowed to myself I would not.

And so, furtively, timidly, in solitude, at night, I indulged in filthy vice, with a feeling of shame which never deserted me, even at the most loathsome moments, and which at such moments nearly made me curse. Already even then I had my underground world in my soul. I was fearfully afraid of being seen, of being met, of being recognized. I visited various obscure haunts.

One night as I was passing a tavern I saw through a lighted window some gentlemen fighting with billiard cues, and saw one of them thrown out of the window. At other times I should have felt very much disgusted, but I was in such a mood at the time, that I actually envied the gentleman thrown out of the window—and I envied him so much that I even went into the tavern and into the billiard-room. "Perhaps," I thought, "I'll have a fight, too, and they'll throw me out of the window."

I was not drunk—but what is one to do—depression will drive a man to such a pitch of hysteria? But nothing happened. It seemed that I was not even equal to being thrown out of the window and I went away without having my fight.

An officer put me in my place from the first moment.

I was standing by the billiard-table and in my ignorance blocking up the way, and he wanted to pass; he took me by the shoulders and without a word—without a warning or explanation—moved me from where I was standing to another spot and passed by as though he had not noticed me. I could have forgiven blows, but I could not forgive his having moved me without noticing me.

Devil knows what I would have given for a real regular quarrel —a more decent, a more *literary* one, so to speak. I had been treated like a fly. This officer was over six foot, while I was a spindly little fellow. But the quarrel was in my hands. I had only to protest and I certainly would have been thrown out of the window. But I changed my mind and preferred to beat a resentful retreat.

I went out of the tavern straight home, confused and troubled, and the next night I went out again with the same lewd intentions, still more furtively, abjectly and miserably than before, as it were, with tears in my eyes—but still I did go out again. Don't imagine, though, it was cowardice made me slink away from the officer: I never have been a coward at heart, though I have always been a coward in action. Don't be in a hurry to laugh—I assure you I can explain it all.

Oh, if only that officer had been one of the sort who would consent to fight a duel! But no, he was one of those gentlemen (alas, long extinct!) who preferred fighting with cues or, like Gogol's Lieutenant Pirogov, appealing to the police. They did not fight duels and would have thought a duel with a civilian like me an utterly unseemly procedure in any case—and they looked upon the duel altogether as something impossible, something free-thinking and French. But they were quite ready to bully, especially when they were over six foot.

I did not slink away through cowardice, but through an unbounded vanity. I was afraid not of his six foot, nor of getting a sound thrashing and being thrown out of the window; I should have had physical courage, enough, I assure you; but I had not the moral courage. What I was afraid of was that every one present, from the insolent marker down to the lowest little stinking, pimply clerk in a greasy collar, would jeer at me and fail to understand when I began to protest and to address them in literary language. For of the point of honour—not of honour, but of the point of honour (*point d'honneur*)—one cannot speak among us except in literary language. You can't allude to the "point of honour" in ordinary language. I was fully convinced (the sense of reality, in spite of all my romanticism!) that they would all simply split their sides with laughter, and that the officer would not simply beat me, that is, without insulting me, but would certainly prod me in the back with his knee, kick me round the billiard-table, and only then perhaps have pity and drop me out of the window.

Of course, this trivial incident could not with me end in that. I often met that officer afterwards in the street and noticed him very carefully. I am not quite sure whether he recognized me, I imagine not; I judge from certain signs. But I—I stared at him with spite and hatred and so it went on . . . for several years! My resentment grew even deeper with years. At first I began making stealthy inquiries about this officer. It was difficult for me to do so, for I knew no one. But one day I heard some one shout his surname in the street as I was following him at a distance, as though I were tied to him—and so I learnt his surname. Another time I followed him to his flat, and for ten kopecks learned from the porter where he lived, on which storey, whether he lived alone or with others, and so on

—in fact, everything one could learn from a porter. One morning, though I had never tried my hand with the pen, it suddenly occurred to me to write a satire on this officer in the form of a novel which would unmask his villainy. I wrote the novel with relish. I did unmask his villainy, I even exaggerated it; at first I so altered his surname that it could easily be recognized, but on second thoughts I changed it, and sent the story to the *Otetchestvenniya Zapiski*. But at that time such attacks were not the fashion and my story was not printed. That was a great vexation to me.

Sometimes I was positively choked with resentment. At last I determined to challenge my enemy to a duel. I composed a splendid, charming letter to him, imploring him to apologize to me, and hinting rather plainly at a duel in case of refusal. The letter was so composed that if the officer had had the least understanding of the good and the beautiful he would certainly have flung himself on my neck and have offered me his friendship. And how fine that would have been! How we should have got on together! "He could have shielded me with his higher rank, while I could have improved his mind with my culture, and, well . . . my ideas, and all sorts of things might have happened." Only fancy, this was two years after his insult to me, and my challenge would have been a ridiculous anachronism, in spite of all the ingenuity of my letter in disguising and explaining away the anachronism. But, thank God (to this day I thank the Almighty with tears in my eyes), I did not send the letter to him. Cold shivers run down my back when I think of what might have happened if I had sent it.

And all at once I revenged myself in the simplest way, by a stroke of genius! A brilliant thought suddenly dawned upon me. Sometimes on holidays I used to stroll along the sunny side of the Nevsky about four o'clock in the afternoon. Though it was hardly a stroll so much as a series of innumerable miseries, humiliations and resentments; but no doubt that was just what I wanted. I used to wriggle along in a most unseemly fashion, like an eel, continually moving aside to make way for generals, for officers of the guards and the hussars, or for ladies. At such minutes there used to be a convulsive twinge at my heart, and I used to feel hot all down my back at the mere thought of the wretchedness of my attire, of the wretchedness and abjectness of my little scurrying figure. This was a regular martyrdom, a continual, intolerable humiliation at the thought, which passed into an incessant and direct sensation, that I was a mere fly in the eyes of all this world, a nasty, disgusting fly—more intelligent, more highly developed, more refined in feeling than any of them, of course—but a fly that was continually making way for every one, insulted and injured by every one. Why I inflicted this torture upon myself, why I went to the Nevsky, I don't know. I felt simply drawn there at every possible opportunity.

Already then I began to experience a rush of the enjoyment of which I spoke in the first chapter. After my affair with the officer I felt even more drawn there than before: it was on the Nevsky that I met him most frequently, there I could admire him. He, too, went there chiefly on holidays. He, too, turned out of his path for generals and persons of high rank, and he, too, wriggled between them like an eel; but people like me, or even better dressed than me, he simply walked over; he made straight for them as though there was nothing but empty space before him, and never, under any circumstances, turned aside. I gloated over my resentment watching him and . . . always resentfully made way for him. It exasperated me that even in the street I could not be on an even footing with him.

"Why must you invariably be the first to move aside?" I kept asking myself in hysterical rage, waking up sometimes at three o'clock in the morning. "Why is it you and not he? There's no regulation about it; there's no written law. Let the making way be equal as it usually is when refined people meet: he moves half-way and you move half-way; you pass with mutual respect."

But that never happened, and I always moved aside, while he did not even notice my making way for him. And lo and behold a bright idea dawned upon me! "What," I thought, "if I meet him and don't move on one side? What if I don't move aside on purpose, even if I knock up against him? How would that be?" This audacious idea took such a hold on me that it gave me no peace. I was dreaming of it continually, horribly, and I purposely went more frequently to the Nevsky in order to picture more vividly how I should do it when I did do it. I was delighted. This intention seemed to me more and more practical and possible.

"Of course I shall not really push him," I thought, already more good-natured in my joy. "I will simply not turn aside, will run up against him, not very violently, but just shouldering each other—just as much as decency permits. I will push against him just as much as he pushes against me." At last I made up my mind completely. But my preparations took a great deal of time. To begin with, when I carried out my plan I should need to be looking rather more decent, and so I had to think of my get-up. "In case of emergency, if, for instance, there were any sort of public scandal (and the public there is of the most *recherché*: the Countess walks there; Prince D. walks there; all the literary world is there), I must be well dressed; that inspires respect and of itself puts us on an equal footing in the eyes of society."

With this object I asked for some of my salary in advance, and bought at Tchurkin's a pair of black gloves and a decent hat. Black gloves seemed to me both more dignified and *bon ton* than the lemon-coloured ones which I had contemplated at first. "The colour is too gaudy, it looks as though one were trying to be conspicuous," and I did not take the lemon-coloured ones. I had got ready long beforehand a good shirt, with white bone studs; my overcoat was the only thing that held me back. The coat in itself was a very good one, it kept me warm; but it was wadded and it had a raccoon collar which was the height of vulgarity. I had to change the collar at any sacrifice, and to have a beaver one like an officer's. For this purpose I began visiting the Gostiny Dvor and after several attempts I pitched upon a piece of cheap German beaver. Though these German beavers soon grow shabby and look wretched, yet at first they look exceedingly well, and I only needed it for one occasion. I asked the price; even so, it was too expensive. After thinking it over thoroughly I decided to sell my raccoon collar. The rest of the money—a considerable sum for me, I decided to borrow from Anton Antonitch Syetotchkin, my immediate superior, an unassuming person, though grave and judicious. He never lent money to any one, but I had, on entering the service, been specially recommended to him by an important personage who had got me my berth. I was horribly worried. To borrow from Anton Antonitch seemed to me monstrous and shameful. I did not sleep for two or three nights. Indeed, I did not sleep well at that time, I was in a fever; I had a vague sinking at my heart or else a sudden throbbing, throbbing, throbbing! Anton Antonitch was surprised at first, then he frowned, then he reflected, and did after all lend me the money, receiving from me a written authorization to take from my salary a fortnight later the sum that he had lent me.

In this way everything was at last ready. The handsome beaver replaced the mean-looking raccoon, and I began by degrees to get to work. It would never have done to act off-hand, at random; the plan had to be carried out skilfully, by degrees. But I must confess that after many efforts I began to despair: we simply could not run into each other. I made every preparation, I was quite determined—it seemed as though we should run into one another directly—and before I knew what I was doing I had stepped aside for him again and he had passed without noticing me. I even prayed as I approached him that God would grant me determination. One time I had made up my mind thoroughly, but it ended in my stumbling and falling at his feet because at the very last instant when I was six inches from him my courage failed me. He very calmly stepped over me, while I flew on one side like a ball. That night I was ill again, feverish and delirious.

And suddenly it ended most happily. The night before I had made up my mind not to carry out my fatal plan and to abandon it all, and with that object I went to the Nevsky for the last time, just to see how I would abandon it all. Suddenly, three paces from my enemy, I unexpectedly made up my mind—I closed my eyes, and we ran full tilt, shoulder to shoulder, against one another! I did not budge an inch and passed him on a perfectly equal footing! He did not even look round and pretended not to notice it; but he was only pretending, I am convinced of that. I am convinced of that to this day! Of course, I got the worst of it—he was stronger, but that was not the point. The point was that I had attained my object, I had kept up my dignity, I had not yielded a step, and had put myself publicly on an equal social footing with him. I returned home feeling that I was fully avenged for everything. I was delighted. I was triumphant and sang Italian arias. Of course, I will not describe to you what happened to me three days later; if you have read my first chapter you can guess that for yourself. The officer was afterwards transferred; I have not seen him now for fourteen years. What is the dear fellow doing now? Whom is he walking over?

II

But the period of my dissipation would end and I always felt very sick afterwards. It was followed by remorse—I tried to drive it away: I felt too sick. By degrees, however, I grew used to that too. I grew used to everything, or rather I voluntarily resigned myself to enduring it. But I had a means of escape that reconciled everything —that was to find refuge in "the good and the beautiful," in dreams, of course. I was a terrible dreamer, I would dream for three months on end, tucked away in my corner, and you may believe me that at those moments I had no resemblance to the gentleman who, in the perturbation of his chicken heart, put a collar of German beaver on his great coat. I suddenly became a hero. I would not have admitted my six-foot lieutenant even if he had called on me. I could not even picture him before me then. What my dreams were and how I could satisfy myself with them—it is hard to say now, but at the time I was satisfied with them. Though, indeed, even now, I am to some extent satisfied with them. Dreams were particularly sweet and vivid after a spell of dissipation; they came with remorse and with tears, with curses and transports. There were moments of such positive intoxication, of such happiness, that there was not the faintest trace of irony within me, on my honour. I had faith, hope, love. I believed blindly at such times that by some miracle, by some external circumstance, all this would suddenly open out, expand; that suddenly a vista of suitable activity—beneficent, good, and, above all, *ready made* (what sort of activity I had no idea, but the great thing was that it should be all ready for me)—would rise up before me—and I should come out into the light of day, almost riding a white horse and crowned with laurel. Anything but the foremost place I could not conceive for myself, and for that very reason I quite contentedly occupied the lowest in reality. Either to be a hero or to grovel in the mud—there was nothing between. That was my ruin, for when I was in the mud I comforted myself with the thought that at other times I was a hero, and the hero was a cloak for the mud: for an ordinary man it was shameful to defile himself, but a hero was too lofty to be utterly defiled, and so he might defile himself. It is worth noting that these attacks of the "good and the beautiful" visited me even during the period of dissipation and just at the times when I was touching the bottom. They came in separate spurts, as though reminding me of themselves, but did not banish the dissipation by their appearance. On the contrary, they seemed to add a zest to it by contrast, and were only sufficiently present to serve as an appetizing sauce. That sauce was made up of contradictions and sufferings, of agonizing inward analysis, and all these pangs and pin-pricks gave a certain piquancy, even a significance to my dissipation—in fact, completely answered the purpose of an appetizing sauce. There was a certain depth of meaning in it. And I could hardly have resigned myself to the simple, vulgar, direct debauchery of a clerk and have endured all the filthiness of it. What could have allured me about it then and have drawn me at night into the street? No, I had a lofty way of getting out of it all.

And what loving-kindness, oh Lord, what loving-kindness I felt at times in those dreams of mine! in those "flights into the good and the beautiful"; though it was fantastic love, though it was never applied to anything human in reality, yet there was so much of this love that one did not feel afterwards even the impulse to apply it in reality; that would have been superfluous. Everything, however, passed satisfactorily by a lazy and fascinating transition into the sphere of art, that is, into the beautiful forms of life, lying ready, largely stolen from the poets and novelists and adapted to all sorts of needs and uses. I, for instance, was triumphant over every one; every one, of course, was in dust and ashes, and was forced spontaneously to recognize my superiority, and I forgave them all. I was a poet and a grand gentleman, I fell in love; I came in for countless millions and immediately devoted them to humanity, and at the same time I confessed before all the people my shameful deeds, which, of course, were not merely shameful, but had in them much that was "good and beautiful!" something in the Manfred style. Every one would kiss me and weep (what idiots they would be if they did not), while I should go barefoot and hungry preaching new ideas and fighting a victorious Austerlitz against the obscurantists. Then the band would play a march, an amnesty would be declared, the Pope would agree to retire from Rome to Brazil; then there would be a ball for the whole of Italy at the Villa Borghese on the shores of the Lake of Como, the Lake of Como being for that purpose transferred to the neighbourhood of Rome; then would come a scene in the bushes, and so on, and so on—as though you did not know all about it! You will say that it is vulgar and contemptible to drag all this into public after all the tears and transports which I have myself confessed. But why is it contemptible? Can you imagine that I am ashamed of it all, and that it was stupider than anything in your life, gentlemen? And I can assure you that some of these fancies were by no means badly composed. . . . It did not all happen on the shores of Lake Como. And yet you are right—it really is vulgar and contemptible. And most contemptible of all it is that now I am attempting to justify myself to you. And even more contemptible than that is my making this remark now. But that's enough, or there will be no end to it: each step will be more contemptible than the last. . . .

I could never stand more than three months of dreaming at a

time without feeling an irresistible desire to plunge into society. To plunge into society meant to visit my superior at the office, Anton Antonitch Syetotchkin. He was the only permanent acquaintance I have had in my life, and wonder at the fact myself now. But I only went to see him when that phase came over me, and when my dreams had reached such a point of bliss that it became essential at once to embrace my fellows and all mankind; and for that purpose I needed, at least, one human being, actually existing. I had to call on Anton Antonitch, however, on Tuesday—his at-home day; so I had always to time my passionate desire to embrace humanity so that it might fall on a Tuesday.

This Anton Antonitch lived on the fourth storey in a house in Five Corners, in four low-pitched rooms, one smaller than the other, of a particularly frugal and sallow appearance. He had two daughters and their aunt, who used to pour out the tea. Of the daughters one was thirteen and another fourteen, they both had snub noses, and I was awfully shy of them because they were always whispering and giggling together. The master of the house usually sat in his study on a leather couch in front of the table with some grey-headed gentleman, usually a colleague from our office or some other department. I never saw more than two or three visitors there, always the same. They talked about the excise duty, about business in the senate, about salaries, about promotions, about His Excellency, and the best means of pleasing him, and so on. I had the patience to sit like a fool beside these people for four hours at a stretch, listening to them without knowing what to say to them or venturing to say a word. I became stupefied, several times I felt myself perspiring, I was overcome by a sort of paralysis; but this was pleasant and good for me. On returning home I deferred for a time my desire to embrace all mankind.

I had, however, one other acquaintance of a sort, Simonov, who was an old schoolfellow. I had a number of schoolfellows, indeed, in Petersburg, but I did not associate with them and had even given up nodding to them in the street. I believe I had transferred into the department I was in simply to avoid their company and to cut off all connection with my hateful childhood. Curses on that school and all those terrible years of penal servitude! In short, I parted from my schoolfellows as soon as I got out into the world. There were two or three left to whom I nodded in the street. One of them was Simonov, who had been in no way distinguished at school, was of a quiet and equable disposition; but I discovered in him a certain independence of character and even honesty. I don't even suppose that he was particularly stupid. I had at one time spent some rather soulful moments with him, but these had not lasted long and had somehow been suddenly clouded over. He was evidently uncomfortable at these reminiscences, and was, I fancy, always afraid that I might take up the same tone again. I suspected that he had an aversion for me, but still I went on going to see him, not being quite certain of it.

And so on one occasion, unable to endure my solitude and knowing that as it was Thursday Anton Antonitch's door would be closed, I thought of Simonov. Climbing up to his fourth storey I was thinking that the man disliked me and that it was a mistake to go and see him. But as it always happened that such reflections impelled me, as though purposely, to put myself into a false position, I went in. It was almost a year since I had last seen Simonov.

III

I found two of my old schoolfellows with him. They seemed to be discussing an important matter. All of them took scarcely any notice of my entrance, which was strange, for I had not met them for years. Evidently they looked upon me as something on the level of a common fly. I had not been treated like that even at school, though they all hated me. I knew, of course, that they must despise me now for my lack of success in the service, and for my having let myself sink so low, going about badly dressed and so on—which seemed to them a sign of my incapacity and insignificance. But I had not expected such contempt. Simonov was positively surprised at my turning up. Even in the old days he had always seemed surprised at my coming. All this disconcerted me: I sat down, feeling rather miserable, and began listening to what they were saying.

They were engaged in warm and earnest conversation about a farewell dinner which they wanted to arrange for the next day to a comrade of theirs called Zverkov, an officer in the army, who was going away to a distant province. This Zverkov had been all the time at school with me too. I had begun to hate him particularly in the upper forms. In the lower forms he had simply been a pretty, playful boy whom everybody liked. I had hated him, however, even in the lower forms, just because he was a pretty and playful boy. He was always bad at his lessons and got worse and worse as he went on;

however, he left with a good certificate, as he had powerful interest. During his last year at school he came in for an estate of two hundred serfs, and as almost all of us were poor he took up a swaggering tone among us. He was vulgar in the extreme, but at the same time he was a good-natured fellow, even in his swaggering. In spite of superficial, fantastic and sham notions of honour and dignity, all but very few of us positively grovelled before Zverkov, and the more so the more he swaggered. And it was not from any interested motive that they grovelled, but simply because he had been favoured by the gifts of nature. Moreover, it was, as it were, an accepted idea among us that Zverkov was a specialist in regard to tact and the social graces. This last fact particularly infuriated me. I hated the abrupt self-confident tone of his voice, his admiration of his own witticisms, which were often frightfully stupid, though he was bold in his language; I hated his handsome but stupid face (for which I would, however, have gladly exchanged my intelligent one), and the free-and-easy military manners in fashion in the " 'forties." I hated the way in which he used to talk of his future conquests of women (he did not venture to begin his attack upon women until he had the epaulettes of an officer, and was looking forward to them with impatience), and boasted of the duels he would constantly be fighting. I remember how I, invariably so taciturn, suddenly fastened upon Zverkov, when one day talking at a leisure moment with his school-fellows of his future relations with the fair sex, and growing as sportive as a puppy in the sun, he all at once declared that he would not leave a single village girl on his estate unnoticed, that that was his *droit de seigneur*, and that if the peasants dared to protest he would have them all flogged and double the tax on them, the bearded rascals. Our servile rabble applauded, but I attacked him, not from compassion for the girls and their fathers, but simply because they were applauding such an insect. I got the better of him on that occasion, but though Zverkov was stupid he was lively and impudent, and so laughed it off, and in such a way that my victory was not really complete: the laugh was on his side. He got the better of me on several occasions afterwards, but without malice, jestingly, casually. I remained angrily and contemptuously silent and would not answer him. When we left school he made advances to me; I did not rebuff them, for I was flattered, but we soon parted and quite naturally. Afterwards I heard of his barrack-room success as a lieutenant, and of the fast life he was leading. Then there came other rumours—of his successes in the service. By then he had taken to cutting me in the street, and I suspected that he was afraid of compromising himself by greeting a personage as insignificant as me. I saw him once in the theatre, in the third tier of boxes. By then he was wearing shoulder-straps. He was twisting and twirling about, ingratiating himself with the daughters of an ancient General. In three years he had gone off considerably, though he was still rather handsome and adroit. One could see that by the time he was thirty he would be corpulent. So it was to this Zverkov that my schoolfellows were going to give a dinner on his departure. They had kept up with him for those three years, though privately they did not consider themselves on an equal footing with him, I am convinced of that.

Of Simonov's two visitors, one was Ferfitchkin, a Russianized German—a little fellow with the face of a monkey, a blockhead who was always deriding every one, a very bitter enemy of mine from our days in the lower forms—a vulgar, impudent, swaggering fellow, who affected a most sensitive feeling of personal honour, though, of course, he was a wretched little coward at heart. He was one of those worshippers of Zverkov who made up to the latter from interested motives, and often borrowed money from him. Simonov's other visitor, Trudolyubov, was a person in no way remarkable—a tall young fellow, in the army, with a cold face, fairly honest, though he worshipped success of every sort, and was only capable of thinking of promotion. He was some sort of distant relation of Zverkov's, and this, foolish as it seems, gave him a certain importance among us. He always thought me of no consequence whatever; his behaviour to me, though not quite courteous, was tolerable.

"Well, with seven roubles each," said Trudolyubov, "twenty-one roubles between the three of us, we ought to be able to get a good dinner. Zverkov, of course, won't pay."

"Of course not, since we are inviting him," Simonov decided.

"Can you imagine," Ferfitchkin interrupted hotly and conceitedly, like some insolent flunkey boasting of his master the General's decorations, "can you imagine that Zverkov will let us pay alone? He will accept from delicacy, but he will order half a dozen bottles of champagne."

"Do we want half a dozen for the four of us?" observed Trudolyubov, taking notice only of the half dozen.

"So the three of us, with Zverkov for the fourth, twenty-one roubles, at the Hôtel de Paris at five o'clock to-morrow," Simonov, who had been asked to make the arrangements, concluded finally.

"How twenty-one roubles?" I asked in some agitation, with a show of being offended; "if you count me it will not be twenty-one, but twenty-eight roubles."

It seemed to me that to invite myself so suddenly and unexpectedly would be positively graceful, and that they would all be conquered at once and would look at me with respect.

"Do you want to join, too?" Simonov observed, with no appearance of pleasure, seeming to avoid looking at me. He knew me through and through.

It infuriated me that he knew me so thoroughly.

"Why not? I am an old schoolfellow of his, too, I believe, and I must own I feel hurt that you have left me out," I said, boiling over again.

"And where were we to find you?" Ferfitchkin put in roughly.

"You never were on good terms with Zverkov," Trudolyubov added, frowning.

But I had already clutched at the idea and would not give it up.

"It seems to me that no one has a right to form an opinion upon that," I retorted in a shaking voice, as though something tremendous had happened. "Perhaps that is just my reason for wishing it now, that I have not always been on good terms with him."

"Oh, there's no making you out . . . with these refinements," Trudolyubov jeered.

"We'll put your name down," Simonov decided, addressing me. "To-morrow at five o'clock at the Hôtel de Paris."

"What about the money?" Ferfitchkin began in an undertone, indicating me to Simonov, but he broke off, for even Simonov was embarrassed.

"That will do," said Trudolyubov, getting up. "If he wants to come so much, let him."

"But it's a private thing, between us friends," Ferfitchkin said crossly, as he, too, picked up his hat. "It's not an official gathering."

"We do not want at all, perhaps . . ."

They went away. Ferfitchkin did not greet me in any way as he went out, Trudolyubov barely nodded. Simonov, with whom I was left *tête-à-tête,* was in a state of vexation and perplexity, and looked at me queerly. He did not sit down and did not ask me to.

"H'm . . . yes . . . to-morrow, then. Will you pay your subscription now? I just ask so as to know," he muttered in embarrassment.

I flushed crimson, and as I did so I remembered that I had owed Simonov fifteen roubles for ages—which I had, indeed, never forgotten, though I had not paid it.

"You will understand, Simonov, that I could have no idea when I came here . . . I am very much vexed that I have forgotten. . . ."

"All right, all right, that doesn't matter. You can pay to-morrow after the dinner. I simply wanted to know. . . . Please don't . . . ."

He broke off and began pacing the room still more vexed. As he walked he began to stamp with his heels.

"Am I keeping you?" I asked, after two minutes of silence.

"Oh!" he said, starting, "that is—to be truthful—yes. I have to go and see some one . . . not far from here," he added in an apologetic voice, somewhat abashed.

"My goodness, why didn't you say so?" I cried, seizing my cap, with an astonishingly free-and-easy air, which was the last thing I should have expected of myself.

"It's close by . . . not two paces away," Simonov repeated, accompanying me to the front door with a fussy air which did not suit him at all. "So five o'clock, punctually, to-morrow," he called down the stairs after me. He was very glad to get rid of me. I was in a fury.

"What possessed me, what possessed me to force myself upon them?" I wondered, grinding my teeth as I strode along the street, "for a scoundrel, a pig like that Zverkov! Of course, I had better not go; of course, I must just snap my fingers at them. I am not bound in any way. I'll send Simonov a note by to-morrow's post. . . ."

But what made me furious was that I knew for certain that I should go, that I should make a point of going; and the more tactless, the more unseemly my going would be, the more certainly I would go.

And there was a positive obstacle to my going: I had no money. All I had was nine roubles, I had to give seven of that to my servant, Apollon, for his monthly wages. That was all I paid him—he had to keep himself.

Not to pay him was impossible, considering his character. But I will talk about that fellow, about that plague of mine, another time.

However, I knew I should go and should not pay him his wages.

That night I had the most hideous dreams. No wonder; all the evening I had been oppressed by memories of my miserable days at school, and I could not shake them off. I was sent to the school by distant relations, upon whom I was dependent and of whom I have heard nothing since—they sent me there a forlorn, silent boy, already crushed by their reproaches, already troubled by doubt, and looking with savage distrust at every one. My schoolfellows met me with spiteful and merciless jibes because I was not like any of them. But I could not endure their taunts; I could not give in to them with the ignoble readiness with which they gave in to one another. I hated them from the first, and shut myself away from every one in timid, wounded and disproportionate pride. Their coarseness revolted me. They laughed cynically at my face, at my clumsy figure; and yet what stupid faces they had themselves. In our school the boys' faces seemed in a special way to degenerate and grow stupider. How many fine-looking boys came to us! In a few years they became repulsive. Even at sixteen I wondered at them morosely; even then I was struck by the pettiness of their thoughts, the stupidity of their pursuits, their games, their conversations. They had no understanding of such essential things, they took no interest in such striking, impressive subjects, that I could not help considering them inferior to myself. It was not wounded vanity that drove me to it, and for God's sake do not thrust upon me your hackneyed remarks, repeated to nausea, that "I was only a dreamer," while they even then had an understanding of life. They understood nothing, they had no idea of real life, and I swear that that was what made me most indignant with them. On the contrary, the most obvious, striking reality they accepted with fantastic stupidity and even at that time were accustomed to respect success. Everything that was just, but oppressed and looked down upon, they laughed at heartlessly and shamefully. They took rank for intelligence; even at sixteen they were already talking about a snug berth. Of course, a great deal of it was due to their stupidity, to the bad examples with which they had always been surrounded in their childhood and boyhood. They were monstrously depraved. Of course a great deal of that, too, was superficial and an assumption of cynicism; of course there were glimpses of youth and freshness even in their depravity; but even that freshness was not attractive, and showed itself in a certain rakishness. I hated them horribly, though perhaps I was worse than any of them. They repaid me in the same way, and did not conceal their aversion for me. But by then I did not desire their affection: on the contrary I continually longed for their humiliation. To escape from their derision I purposely began to make all the progress I could with my studies and forced my way to the very top. This impressed them. Moreover, they all began by degrees to grasp that I had already read books none of them could read, and understood things (not forming part of our school curriculum) of which they had not even heard. They took a savage and sarcastic view of it, but were morally impressed, especially as the teachers began to notice me on those grounds. The mockery ceased, but the hostility remained, and cold and strained relations became permanent between us. In the end I could not put up with it: with years a craving for society, for friends, developed in me. I attempted to get on friendly terms with some of my schoolfellows; but somehow or other my intimacy with them was always strained and soon ended of itself. Once, indeed, I did have a friend. But I was already a tyrant at heart; I wanted to exercise unbounded sway over him; I tried to instil into him a contempt for his surroundings; I required of him a disdainful and complete break with those surroundings. I frightened him with my passionate affection; I reduced him to tears, to hysterics. He was a simple and devoted soul; but when he devoted himself to me entirely I began to hate him immediately and repulsed him—as though all I needed him for was to win a victory over him, to subjugate him and nothing else. But I could not subjugate all of them; my friend was not at all like them either, he was, in fact, a rare exception. The first thing I did on leaving school was to give up the special job for which I had been destined so as to break all ties, to curse my past and shake the dust from off my feet. . . . And goodness knows why, after all that, I should go trudging off to Simonov's!

Early next morning I roused myself and jumped out of bed with excitement, as though it were all about to happen at once. But I believed that some radical change in my life was coming, and would inevitably come that day. Owing to its rarity, perhaps, any external event, however trivial, always made me feel as though some radical change in my life were at hand. I went to the office, however, as usual, but sneaked away home two hours earlier to get ready. The great thing, I thought, is not to be the first to arrive, or they will think I am overjoyed at coming. But there were thousands of such great points to consider, and they all agitated and overwhelmed me. I polished my boots a second time with my own hands; nothing in the world would have induced Apollon to clean them twice a day, as he considered that it was more than his duties required of him. I stole the brushes to clean them from the passage, being careful he should not detect it, for fear of his contempt. Then I minutely examined my clothes and thought that everything looked old, worn and threadbare. I had let myself get too slovenly. My uniform, perhaps, was tidy, but I could not go out to dinner in my uniform. The worst of it was that on the knee of my trousers was a big yellow stain. I had a foreboding that that stain would deprive me of nine-tenths of my personal dignity. I knew, too, that it was very poor to think so. "But this is no time for thinking: now I am in for the real thing," I thought, and my heart sank. I knew, too, perfectly well even then, that I was monstrously exaggerating the facts. But how could I help it? I could not control myself and was already shaking with fever. With despair I pictured to myself how coldly and disdainfully that "scoundrel" Zverkov would meet me; with what dull-witted, invincible contempt the blockhead Trudolyubov would look at me; with what impudent rudeness the insect Ferfitchkin would snigger at me in order to curry favour with Zverkov; how completely Simonov would take it all in, and how he would despise me for the abjectness of my vanity and lack of spirit—and, worst of all, how paltry, *unliterary*, commonplace it would all be. Of course, the best thing would be not to go at all. But that was most impossible of all: if I feel impelled to do anything, I seem to be pitchforked into it. I should have jeered at myself ever afterwards: "So you funked it, you funked it, you funked the *real thing!*" On the contrary, I passionately longed to show all that "rabble" that I was by no means such a spiritless creature as I seemed to myself. What is more, even in the acutest paroxysm of this cowardly fever, I dreamed of getting the upper hand, of dominating them, carrying them away, making them like me—if only for my "elevation of thought and unmistakable wit." They would abandon Zverkov, he would sit on one side, silent and ashamed, while I should crush him. Then, perhaps, we would be reconciled and drink to our everlasting friendship; but what was most bitter and most humiliating for me was that I knew even then, knew fully and for certain, that I needed nothing of all this really, that I did not really want to crush, to subdue, to attract them, and that I did not care a straw really for the result, even if I did achieve it. Oh, how I prayed for the day to pass quickly! In unutterable anguish I went to the window, opened the movable pane and looked out into the troubled darkness of the thickly falling wet snow. At last my wretched little clock hissed out five. I seized my hat and, trying not to look at Apollon, who had been all day expecting his month's wages, but in his foolishness was unwilling to be the first to speak about it, I slipt between him and the door and jumping into a high-class sledge, on which I spent my last half rouble, I drove up in grand style to the Hôtel de Paris.

IV

I had been certain the day before that I should be the first to arrive. But it was not a question of being the first to arrive. Not only were they not there, but I had difficulty in finding our room. The table was not laid even. What did it mean? After a good many questions I elicited from the waiters that the dinner had been ordered not for five, but for six o'clock. This was confirmed at the buffet too. I felt really ashamed to go on questioning them. It was only twenty-five minutes past five. If they changed the dinner hour they ought at least to have let me know—that is what the post is for, and not to have put me in an absurd position in my own eyes and . . . and even before the waiters. I sat down; the servant began laying the table; I felt even more humiliated when he was present. Towards six o'clock they brought in candles, though there were lamps burning in the room. It had not occurred to the waiter, however, to bring them in at once when I arrived. In the next room two gloomy, angry-looking persons were eating their dinners in silence at two different tables. There was a great deal of noise, even shouting, in a room further away; one could hear the laughter of a crowd of people, and nasty little shrieks in French: there were ladies at the dinner. It was sickening, in fact. I rarely passed more unpleasant moments, so much so that when they did arrive all together punctually at six I was overjoyed to see them, as though they were my deliverers, and even forgot that it was incumbent upon me to show resentment.

Zverkov walked in at the head of them; evidently he was the leading spirit. He and all of them were laughing; but, seeing me, Zverkov drew himself up a little, walked up to me deliberately with a slight, rather jaunty bend from the waist. He shook hands with me in a friendly, but not over-friendly, fashion, with a sort of circumspect courtesy like that of a General, as though in giving me his hand he were warding off something. I had imagined, on the contrary, that on coming in he would at once break into his habitual thin, shrill laugh and fall to making his insipid jokes and witticisms. I had been preparing for them ever since the previous day, but I had not expected such condescension, such high-official courtesy. So, then, he felt himself ineffably superior to me in every respect! If he only meant to insult me by that high-official tone, it would not matter, I thought—I could pay him back for it one way or another. But what if, in reality, without the least desire to be offensive, that sheepshead had a notion in earnest that he was superior to me and could only look at me in a patronizing way? The very supposition made me gasp.

"I was surprised to hear of your desire to join us," he began, lisping and drawling, which was something new. "You and I seem to have seen nothing of one another. You fight shy of us. You shouldn't. We are not such terrible people as you think. Well, anyway, I am glad to renew our acquaintance."

And he turned carelessly to put down his hat on the window.

"Have you been waiting long?" Trudolyubov inquired.

"I arrived at five o'clock as you told me yesterday," I answered aloud, with an irritability that threatened an explosion.

"Didn't you let him know that we had changed the hour?" said Trudolyubov to Simonov.

"No, I didn't. I forgot," the latter replied, with no sign of regret, and without even apologizing to me he went off to order the *hors d'œuvres.*

"So you've been here a whole hour? Oh, poor fellow!" Zverkov cried ironically, for to his notions this was bound to be extremely funny. That rascal Ferfitchkin followed with his nasty little snigger like a puppy yapping. My position struck him, too, as exquisitely ludicrous and embarrassing.

"It isn't funny at all!" I cried to Ferfitchkin, more and more irritated. "It wasn't my fault, but other people's. They neglected to let me know. It was . . . it was . . . it was simply absurd."

"It's not only absurd, but something else as well," muttered Trudolyubov, naïvely taking my part. "You are not hard enough upon it. It was simply rudeness—unintentional, of course. And how could Simonov . . . h'm!"

"If a trick like that had been played on me," observed Ferfitchkin, "I should . . ."

"But you should have ordered something for yourself," Zverkov interrupted, "or simply asked for dinner without waiting for us."

"You will allow that I might have done that without your permission," I rapped out. "If I waited, it was . . ."

"Let us sit down, gentlemen," cried Simonov, coming in.

"Everything is ready; I can answer for the champagne; it is capitally frozen. . . . You see, I did not know your address, where was I to look for you?" He suddenly turned to me, but again he seemed to avoid looking at me. Evidently he had something against me. It must have been what happened yesterday.

All sat down; I did the same. It was a round table. Trudolyubov was on my left, Simonov on my right. Zverkov was sitting opposite, Ferfitchkin next to him, between him and Trudolyubov.

"Tell me, are you . . . in a government office?" Zverkov went on attending to me. Seeing that I was embarrassed he seriously thought that he ought to be friendly to me, and, so to speak, cheer me up.

"Does he want me to throw a bottle at his head?" I thought, in a fury. In my novel surroundings I was unnaturally ready to be irritated.

"In the N—— office," I answered jerkily, with my eyes on my plate.

"And ha-ave you a go-od berth? I say, what ma-a-de you leave your original job?"

"What ma-a-de me was that I wanted to leave my original job," I drawled more than he, hardly able to control myself. Ferfitchkin went off into a guffaw. Simonov looked at me ironically. Trudolyubov left off eating and began looking at me with curiosity.

Zverkov winced, but he tried not to notice it.

"And the remuneration?"

"What remuneration?"

"I mean, your sa-a-lary?"

"Why are you cross-examining me?" However, I told him at once what my salary was. I turned horribly red.

"It is not very handsome," Zverkov observed majestically.

"Yes, you can't afford to dine at cafés on that," Ferfitchkin added insolently.

"To my thinking it's very poor," Trudolyubov observed gravely.

"And how thin you have grown! How you have changed!" added Zverkov with a shade of venom in his voice, scanning me and my attire with a sort of insolent compassion.

"Oh, spare his blushes," cried Ferfitchkin, sniggering.

"My dear sir, allow me to tell you I am not blushing," I broke out at last; "do you hear? I am dining here, at this café, at my own expense, not at other people's—note that, Mr. Ferfitchkin."

"Wha-at? Isn't every one here dining at his own expense? You would seem to be . . ." Ferfitchkin flew out at me, turning as red as a lobster, and looking me in the face with fury.

"Tha-at," I answered, feeling I had gone too far, "and I imagine it would be better to talk of something more intelligent."

"You intend to show off your intelligence, I suppose?"

"Don't disturb yourself, that would be quite out of place here."

"Why are you clacking away like that, my good sir, eh? Have you gone out of your wits in your office?"

"Enough, gentlemen, enough!" Zverkov cried, authoritatively.

"How stupid it is!" muttered Simonov.

"It really is stupid. We have met here, a company of friends, for a farewell dinner to a comrade and you carry on an altercation," said Trudolyubov, rudely addressing himself to me alone. "You invited yourself to join us, so don't disturb the general harmony."

"Enough, enough!" cried Zverkov. "Give over, gentlemen, it's out of place. Better let me tell you how I nearly got married the day before yesterday. . . ."

And then followed a burlesque narrative of how this gentleman had almost been married two days before. There was not a word about the marriage, however, but the story was adorned with generals, colonels and kammer-junkers, while Zverkov almost took the lead among them. It was greeted with approving laughter; Ferfitchkin positively squealed.

No one paid any attention to me, and I sat crushed and humiliated.

"Good Heavens, these are not the people for me!" I thought. "And what a fool I have made of myself before them! I let Ferfitchkin go too far, though. The brutes imagine they are doing me an honour in letting me sit down with them. They don't understand that it's an honour to them and not to me! I've grown thinner! My clothes! Oh, damn my trousers! Zverkov noticed the yellow stain on the knee as soon as he came in. . . . But what's the use! I must get up at once, this very minute, take my hat and simply go without a word . . . with contempt! And to-morrow I can send a challenge. The scoundrels! As though I cared about the seven roubles. They may think . . . Damn it! I don't care about the seven roubles. I'll go this minute!"

Of course I remained. I drank sherry and Lafitte by the glassful in my discomfiture. Being unaccustomed to it, I was quickly affected. My annoyance increased as the wine went to my head. I longed all at once to insult them all in a most flagrant manner and then go away. To seize the moment and show what I could do, so that they would say, "He's clever, though he is absurd," and . . . and . . . in fact, damn them all!

I scanned them all insolently with my drowsy eyes. But they seemed to have forgotten me altogether. They were noisy, vociferous, cheerful. Zverkov was talking all the time. I began listening. Zverkov was talking of some exuberant lady whom he had at last led on to declaring her love (of course, he was lying like a horse), and how he had been helped in this affair by an intimate friend of his, a Prince Kolya, an officer in the hussars, who had three thousand serfs.

"And yet this Kolya, who has three thousand serfs, has not put in an appearance here to-night to see you off," I cut in suddenly.

For a minute every one was silent. "You are drunk already." Trudolyubov deigned to notice me at last, glancing contemptuously in my direction. Zverkov, without a word, examined me as though I were an insect. I dropped my eyes. Simonov made haste to fill up the glasses with champagne.

Trudolyubov raised his glass, as did every one else but me.

"Your health and good luck on the journey!" he cried to Zverkov. "To old times, to our future, hurrah!"

They all tossed off their glasses, and crowded round Zverkov to kiss him. I did not move; my full glass stood untouched before me.

"Why, aren't you going to drink it?" roared Trudolyubov, losing patience and turning menacingly to me.

"I want to make a speech separately, on my own account . . . and then I'll drink it, Mr. Trudolyubov."

"Spiteful brute!" muttered Simonov. I drew myself up in my chair and feverishly seized my glass, prepared for something extraordinary, though I did not know myself precisely what I was going to say.

"Silence!" cried Ferfitchkin. "Now for a display of wit!"

Zverkov waited very gravely, knowing what was coming.

"Mr. Lieutenant Zverkov," I began, "let me tell you that I hate phrases, phrasemongers and men in corsets . . . that's the first point, and there is a second one to follow it."

There was a general stir.

"The second point is: I hate ribaldry and ribald talkers. Especially ribald talkers! The third point: I love justice, truth and honesty." I went on almost mechanically, for I was beginning to shiver with horror myself and had no idea how I came to be talking like this. "I love thought, Monsieur Zverkov; I love true comradeship, on an equal footing and not . . . H'm . . . I love . . . But, however, why not? I will drink your health, too, Mr. Zverkov! Seduce the Circassian girls, shoot the enemies of the fatherland and . . . and . . . to your health, Monsieur Zverkov!"

Zverkov got up from his seat, bowed to me and said:

"I am very much obliged to you." He was frightfully offended and turned pale.

"Damn the fellow!" roared Trudolyubov, bringing his fist down on the table.

"Well, he wants a punch in the face for that," squealed Ferfitchkin.

"We ought to turn him out," muttered Simonov.

"Not a word, gentlemen, not a movement!" cried Zverkov solemnly, checking the general indignation. "I thank you all, but I can show him for myself how much value I attach to his words."

"Mr. Ferfitchkin, you will give me satisfaction to-morrow for your words just now!" I said aloud, turning with dignity to Ferfitchkin.

"A duel, you mean? Certainly," he answered. But probably I was so ridiculous as I challenged him and it was so out of keeping with my appearance that everyone, including Ferfitchkin, was prostrate with laughter.

"Yes, let him alone, of course! He is quite drunk," Trudolyubov said with disgust.

"I shall never forgive myself for letting him join us," Simonov muttered again.

"Now is the time to throw a bottle at their heads," I thought to myself. I picked up the bottle . . . and filled my glass. . . . "No, I'd better sit on to the end," I went on thinking; "you would be pleased, my friends, if I went away. Nothing will induce me to go. I'll go on sitting here and drinking to the end, on purpose, as a sign that I don't think you of the slightest consequence. I will go on sitting and drinking, because this is a public-house and I paid my entrance money. I'll sit here and drink, for I look upon you as so many pawns, as inanimate pawns. I'll sit here and drink . . . and sing if I want to, yes, sing, for I have the right to . . . to sing . . . h'm!"

But I did not sing. I simply tried not to look at any of them. I assumed most unconcerned attitudes and waited with impatience for them to speak *first*. But alas, they did not address me! And oh, how I wished, how I wished at that moment to be reconciled to them! It struck eight, at last nine. They moved from the table to the sofa. Zverkov stretched himself on a lounge and put one foot on a round table. Wine was brought there. He did, as a fact, order three bottles on his own account. I, of course, was not invited to join them. They all sat round him on the sofa. They listened to him, almost with reverence. It was evident that they were fond of him. "What for? What for?" I wondered. From time to time they were moved to drunken enthusiasm and kissed each other. They talked of the Caucasus, of the nature of true passion, of snug berths in the service, of the income of an hussar called Podharzhevsky, whom none of them knew personally, and rejoiced in the largeness of it, of the extraordinary grace and beauty of a Princess D., whom none of them had ever seen; then it came to Shakespeare's being immortal.

I smiled contemptuously and walked up and down the other side of the room, opposite the sofa, from the table to the stove and back again. I tried my very utmost to show them that I could do without them, and yet I purposely made a noise with my boots, thumping with my heels. But it was all in vain. They paid no attention. I had the patience to walk up and down in front of them from eight o'clock till eleven, in the same place, from the table to the stove and back again. "I walk up and down to please myself and no one can prevent me." The waiter who came into the room stopped, from time to time, to look at me. I was somewhat giddy from turning round so often; at moments it seemed to me that I was in delirium. During those three hours I was three times soaked with sweat and dry again. At times, with an intense, acute pang I was stabbed to the heart by the thought that ten years, twenty years, forty years would pass, and that even in forty years I would remember with loathing and humiliation those filthiest, most ludicrous, and most awful moments of my life. No one could have gone out of his way to degrade himself more shamelessly, and I fully realized it, fully, and yet I went on pacing up and down from the table to the stove. "Oh, if you only knew what thoughts and feelings I am capable of, how cultured I am!" I thought at moments, mentally addressing the sofa on which my enemies were sitting. But my enemies behaved as though I were not in the room. Once—only once—they turned towards me, just when Zverkov was talking about Shakespeare, and I suddenly gave a contemptuous laugh. I laughed in such an affected and disgusting way that they all at once broke off their conversation, and silently and gravely for two minutes watched me walking up and down from the table to the stove, *taking no notice of them.* But nothing came of it: they said nothing, and two minutes later they ceased to notice me again. It struck eleven.

"Friends," cried Zverkov getting up from the sofa, "let us all be off now, *there!*"

"Of course, of course," the others assented. I turned sharply to Zverkov. I was so harassed, so exhausted, that I would have cut my throat to put an end to it. I was in a fever; my hair, soaked with perspiration, stuck to my forehead and temples.

"Zverkov, I beg your pardon," I said abruptly and resolutely. "Ferfitchkin, yours too, and every one's, every one's: I have insulted you all!"

"Aha! A duel is not in your line, old man," Ferfitchkin hissed venomously.

It sent a sharp pang to my heart.

"No, it's not the duel I am afraid of, Ferfitchkin! I am ready to fight you to-morrow, after we are reconciled. I insist upon it, in fact, and you cannot refuse. I want to show you that I am not afraid of a duel. You shall fire first and I shall fire into the air."

"He is comforting himself," said Simonov.

"He's simply raving," said Trudolyubov.

"But let us pass. Why are you barring our way? What do you want?" Zverkov answered disdainfully.

They were all flushed: their eyes were bright: they had been drinking heavily.

"I ask for your friendship, Zverkov; I insulted you, but . . ."

"Insulted? *You* insulted *me?* Understand, sir, that you never, under any circumstances, could possibly insult *me.*"

"And that's enough for you. Out of the way!" concluded Trudolyubov.

"Olympia is mine, friends, that's agreed!" cried Zverkov.

"We won't dispute your right, we won't dispute your right," the others answered, laughing.

I stood as though spat upon. The party went noisily out of the room. Trudolyubov struck up some stupid song. Simonov remained behind for a moment to tip the waiters. I suddenly went up to him.

"Simonov! give me six roubles!" I said, with desperate resolution.

He looked at me in extreme amazement, with vacant eyes. He, too, was drunk.

"You don't mean you are coming with us?"

"Yes."

"I've no money," he snapped out, and with a scornful laugh he went out of the room.

I clutched at his overcoat. It was a nightmare.

"Simonov, I saw you had money. Why do you refuse me? Am I a scoundrel? Beware of refusing me: if you knew, if you knew why I am asking! My whole future, my whole plans depend upon it!"

Simonov pulled out the money and almost flung it at me.

"Take it, if you have no sense of shame!" he pronounced pitilessly, and ran to overtake them.

I was left for a moment alone. Disorder, the remains of dinner, a broken wine-glass on the floor, spilt wine, cigarette ends, fumes of drink and delirium in my brain, an agonizing misery in my heart and finally the waiter, who had seen and heard all and was looking inquisitively into my face.

"I am going there!" I cried. "Either they shall all go down on their knees to beg for my friendship, or I will give Zverkov a slap in the face!"

V

"So this is it, this is it at last—contact with real life," I muttered as I ran headlong downstairs. "This is very different from the Pope's leaving Rome and going to Brazil, very different from the ball on Lake Como!"

"You are a scoundrel," a thought flashed through my mind, "if you laugh at this now."

"No matter!" I cried, answering myself. "Now everything is lost!"

There was no trace to be seen of them, but that made no difference—I knew where they had gone.

At the steps was standing a solitary night sledge-driver in a rough peasant coat, powdered over with the still falling, wet, and as it were warm, snow. It was hot and steamy. The little shaggy piebald horse was also covered with snow and coughing, I remember that very well. I made a rush for the roughly made sledge; but as soon as I raised my foot to get into it, the recollection of how Simonov had just given me six roubles seemed to double me up and I tumbled into the sledge like a sack.

"No, I must do a great deal to make up for all that," I cried.

"But I will make up for it or perish on the spot this very night. Start!"

We set off. There was a perfect whirl in my head.

"They won't go down on their knees to beg for my friendship. That is a mirage, cheap mirage, revolting, romantic and fantastical —that's another ball on Lake Como. And so I am bound to slap Zverkov's face! It is my duty to. And so it is settled; I am flying to give him a slap in the face. Hurry up!"

The driver tugged at the reins.

"As soon as I go in I'll give it to him. Ought I before giving him the slap to say a few words by way of preface? No. I'll simply go in and give it to him. They will all be sitting in the drawing-room, and he with Olympia on the sofa. That damned Olympia! She laughed at my looks on one occasion and refused me. I'll pull Olympia's hair, pull Zverkov's ears! No, better one ear, and pull him by it round the room. Maybe they will all begin beating me and will kick me out. That's most likely, indeed. No matter! Anyway, I shall first slap him; the initiative will be mine; and by the laws of honour that is everything: he will be branded and cannot wipe off the slap by any blows, by nothing but a duel. He will be forced to fight. And let them beat me now. Let them, the ungrateful wretches! Trudolyubov will beat me hardest, he is so strong; Ferfitchkin will be sure to catch hold sideways and tug at my hair. But no matter, no matter! That's what I am going for. The blockheads will be forced at last to see the tragedy of it all! When they drag me to the door I shall call out to them that in reality they are not worth my little finger. Get on, driver, get on!" I cried to the driver. He started and flicked his whip, I shouted so savagely.

"We shall fight at daybreak, that's a settled thing. I've done with the office. Ferfitchkin made a joke about it just now. But where can I get pistols? Nonsense! I'll get my salary in advance and buy them. And powder, and bullets? That's the second's business. And how can it all be done by daybreak? And where am I to get a second? I have no friends. Nonsense!" I cried, lashing myself up more and more. "It's of no consequence! the first person I meet in the street is bound to be my second, just as he would be bound to pull a drowning man out of water. The most eccentric things may happen. Even if I were to ask the director himself to be my second to-morrow, he would be bound to consent, if only from a feeling of chivalry, and to keep the secret! Anton Antonitch. . . ."

The fact is, that at that very minute the disgusting absurdity of my plan and the other side of the question was clearer and more vivid to my imagination than it could be to any one on earth. But . . .

"Get on, driver, get on, you rascal, get on!"

"Ugh, sir!" said the son of toil.

Cold shivers suddenly ran down me. Wouldn't it be better . . . to go straight home? My God, my God! Why did I invite myself to this dinner yesterday? But no, it's impossible. And my walking up and down for three hours from the table to the stove? No, they, they and no one else must pay for my walking up and down! They must wipe out this dishonour! Drive on!

And what if they give me into custody? They won't dare! They'll be afraid of the scandal. And what if Zverkov is so contemptuous that he refuses to fight a duel? He is sure to; but in that case I'll show them . . . I will turn up at the posting station when he is setting off to-morrow, I'll catch him by the leg, I'll pull off his coat when he gets into the carriage. I'll get my teeth into his hand, I'll bite him. "See what lengths you can drive a desperate man to!" He may hit me on the head and they may belabour me from behind. I will shout to the assembled multitude: "Look at this young puppy who is driving off to captivate the Circassian girls after letting me spit in his face!"

Of course, after that everything will be over! The office will have vanished off the face of the earth. I shall be arrested, I shall be tried, I shall be dismissed from the service, thrown in prison, sent to Siberia. Never mind! In fifteen years when they let me out of prison I will trudge off to him, a beggar, in rags. I shall find him in some provincial town. He will be married and happy. He will have a grown-up daughter. . . . I shall say to him: "Look, monster, at my hollow cheeks and my rags! I've lost everything—my career, my happiness, art, science, *the woman I loved*, and all through you. Here are pistols. I have come to discharge my pistol and . . . and I . . . forgive you. Then I shall fire into the air and he will hear nothing more of me. . . ."

I was actually on the point of tears, though I knew perfectly well at that moment that all this was out of Pushkin's *Silvio* and Lermontov's *Masquerade*. And all at once I felt horribly ashamed, so ashamed that I stopped the horse, got out of the sledge, and stood still in the snow in the middle of the street. The driver gazed at me, sighing and astonished.

What was I to do? I could not go on there—it was evidently stupid, and I could not leave things as they were, because that would seem as though . . . Heavens, how could I leave things! And after such insults! "No!" I cried, throwing myself into the sledge again. "It is ordained! It is fate! Drive on, drive on!"

And in my impatience I punched the sledge-driver on the back of the neck.

"What are you up to? What are you hitting me for?" the peasant shouted, but he whipped up his nag so that it began kicking.

The wet snow was falling in big flakes; I unbuttoned myself, regardless of it. I forgot everything else, for I had finally decided on the slap, and felt with horror that it was going to happen *now, at once,* and that *no force could stop it.* The deserted street lamps gleamed sullenly in the snowy darkness like torches at a funeral. The snow drifted under my great-coat, under my coat, under my cravat, and melted there. I did not wrap myself up—all was lost, anyway.

At last we arrived. I jumped out, almost unconscious, ran up the steps and began knocking and kicking at the door. I felt fearfully weak, particularly in my legs and my knees. The door was opened quickly as though they knew I was coming. As a fact, Simonov had warned them that perhaps another gentleman would arrive, and this was a place in which one had to give notice and to observe certain precautions. It was one of those "millinery establishments" which were abolished by the police a good time ago. By day it really was a shop; but at night, if one had an introduction, one might visit it for other purposes.

I walked rapidly through the dark shop into the familiar drawing-room, where there was only one candle burning, and stood still in amazement: there was no one there. "Where are they?" I asked somebody. But by now, of course, they had separated. Before me was standing a person with a stupid smile, the "madam" herself, who had seen me before. A minute later a door opened and another person came in.

Taking no notice of anything I strode about the room, and, I believe, I talked to myself. I felt as though I had been saved from death and was conscious of this, joyfully, all over: I should have given that slap, I should certainly, certainly have given it! But now they were not here and . . . everything had vanished and changed! I looked round. I could not realize my condition yet. I looked mechanically at the girl who had come in: and had a glimpse of a fresh, young, rather pale face, with straight, dark eyebrows, and with grave, as it were wondering, eyes that attracted me at once; I should have hated her if she had been smiling. I began looking at her more intently and, as it were, with effort. I had not fully collected my thoughts. There was something simple and good-natured in her face, but something strangely grave. I am sure that this stood in her way here, and no one of those fools had noticed her. She could not, however, have been called a beauty, though she was tall, strong-looking, and well built. She was very simply dressed. Something loathsome stirred within me. I went straight up to her.

I chanced to look into the glass. My harassed face struck me as revolting in the extreme, pale, angry, abject, with dishevelled hair. "No matter, I am glad of it," I thought; "I am glad that I shall seem repulsive to her; I like that."

VI

. . . Somewhere behind a screen a clock began wheezing, as though oppressed by something, as though some one were strangling it. After an unnaturally prolonged wheezing there followed a shrill, nasty, and as it were unexpectedly rapid, chime—as though some one were suddenly jumping forward. It struck two. I woke up, though I had indeed not been asleep but lying half conscious.

It was almost completely dark in the narrow, cramped, low-pitched room, cumbered up with an enormous wardrobe and piles of cardboard boxes and all sorts of frippery and litter. The candle end that had been burning on the table was going out and gave a faint flicker from time to time. In a few minutes there would be complete darkness.

I was not long in coming to myself; everything came back to my mind at once, without an effort, as though it had been in ambush to pounce upon me again. And, indeed, even while I was unconscious a point seemed continually to remain in my memory unforgotten, and round it my dreams moved drearily. But strange to say, everything that had happened to me in that day seemed to me now, on waking, to be in the far, far away past, as though I had long, long ago lived all that down.

My head was full of fumes. Something seemed to be hovering over me, rousing me, exciting me, and making me restless. Misery and spite seemed surging up in me again and seeking an outlet. Suddenly I saw beside me two wide open eyes scrutinizing me curiously and persistently. The look in those eyes was coldly detached, sullen, as it were utterly remote; it weighed upon me.

A grim idea came into my brain and passed all over my body, as a horrible sensation, such as one feels when one goes into a damp and mouldy cellar. There was something unnatural in those two eyes, beginning to look at me only now. I recalled, too, that during those two hours I had not said a single word to this creature, and had, in fact, considered it utterly superfluous; in fact, the silence had for some reason gratified me. Now I suddenly realized vividly the hideous idea—revolting as a spider—of vice, which, without love, grossly and shamelessly begins with that in which true love finds its consummation. For a long time we gazed at each other like that, but she did not drop her eyes before mine and her expression did not change, so that at last I felt uncomfortable.

"What is your name?" I asked abruptly, to put an end to it.

"Liza," she answered almost in a whisper, but somehow far from graciously, and she turned her eyes away.

I was silent.

"What weather! The snow . . . it's disgusting!" I said, almost to myself, putting my arm under my head despondently, and gazing at the ceiling.

She made no answer. This was horrible.

"Have you always lived in Petersburg?" I asked a minute later, almost angrily, turning my head slightly towards her.

"No."

"Where do you come from?"

"From Riga," she answered reluctantly.

"Are you a German?"

"No, Russian."

"Have you been here long?"

"Where?"

"In this house?"

"A fortnight."

She spoke more and more jerkily. The candle went out; I could no longer distinguish her face.

"Have you a father and mother?"

"Yes . . . no . . . I have."

"Where are they?"

"There . . . in Riga."

"What are they?"

"Oh, nothing."

"Nothing? Why, what class are they?"

"Tradespeople."

"Have you always lived with them?"

"Yes."

"How old are you?"

"Twenty."

"Why did you leave them?"

"Oh, for no reason."

That answer meant "Let me alone; I feel sick, sad."

We were silent.

God knows why I did not go away. I felt myself more and more sick and dreary. The images of the previous day began of themselves, apart from my will, flitting through my memory in confusion. I suddenly recalled something I had seen that morning when, full of anxious thoughts, I was hurrying to the office.

"I saw them carrying a coffin out yesterday and they nearly dropped it," I suddenly said aloud, not that I desired to open the conversation, but as it were by accident.

"A coffin?"

"Yes, in the Haymarket; they were bringing it up out of a cellar."

"From a cellar?"

"Not from a cellar, but from a basement. Oh, you know . . . down below . . . from a house of ill-fame. It was filthy all round . . . Egg-shells, litter . . . a stench. It was loathsome."

Silence.

"A nasty day to be buried," I began, simply to avoid being silent.

"Nasty, in what way?"

"The snow, the wet." (I yawned.)

"It makes no difference," she said suddenly, after a brief silence.

"No, it's horrid." (I yawned again.) "The gravediggers must have sworn at getting drenched by the snow. And there must have been water in the grave."

"Why water in the grave?" she asked, with a sort of curiosity, but speaking even more harshly and abruptly than before.

I suddenly began to feel provoked.

"Why, there must have been water at the bottom a foot deep. You can't dig a dry grave in Volkovo Cemetery."

"Why?"

"Why? Why, the place is waterlogged. It's a regular marsh. So they bury them in water. I've seen it myself . . . many times."

(I had never seen it once, indeed, I had never been in Volkovo, and had only heard stories of it.)

"Do you mean to say, you don't mind how you die?"

"But why should I die?" she answered, as though defending herself.

"Why, some day you will die, and you will die just the same as that dead woman. She was . . . a girl like you. She died of consumption."

"A wench would have died in hospital. . . ." (She knows all about it already: she said "wench," not "girl.")

"She was in debt to her madam," I retorted, more and more provoked by the discussion; "and went on earning money for her up to the end, though she was in consumption. Some sledge-drivers standing by were talking about her to some soldiers and telling them so. No doubt they knew her. They were laughing. They were going to meet in a pot-house to drink to her memory."

A great deal of this was my invention. Silence followed, profound silence. She did not stir.

"And is it better to die in a hospital?"

"Isn't it just the same? Besides, why should I die?" she added irritably.

"If not now, a little later."

"Why a little later?"

"Why, indeed? Now you are young, pretty, fresh, you fetch a high price. But after another year of this life you will be very different—you will go off."

"In a year?"

"Anyway, in a year you will be worth less," I continued malignantly. "You will go from here to something lower, another house; a year later—to a third, lower and lower, and in seven years you will come to a basement in the Haymarket. That will be if you were lucky. But it would be much worse if you got some disease, consumption, say . . . and caught a chill, or something or other. It's not easy to get over an illness in your way of life. If you catch anything you may not get rid of it. And so you would die."

"Oh, well, then I shall die," she answered, quite vindictively, and she made a quick movement.

"But one is sorry."

"Sorry for whom?"

"Sorry for life."

Silence.

"Have you been engaged to be married? Eh?"

"What's that to you?"

"Oh, I am not cross-examining you. It's nothing to me. Why are you so cross? Of course you may have had your own troubles. What is it to me? It's simply that I felt sorry."

"Sorry for whom?"

"Sorry for you."

"No need," she whispered hardly audibly, and again made a faint movement.

That incensed me at once. What! I was so gentle with her, and she . . .

"Why, do you think that you are on the right path?"

"I don't think anything."

"That's what's wrong, that you don't think. Realize it while there is still time. There still is time. You are still young, good-looking; you might love, be married, be happy. . . ."

"Not all married women are happy," she snapped out in the rude abrupt tone she had used at first.

"Not all, of course, but anyway it is much better than the life here. Infinitely better. Besides, with love one can live even without happiness. Even in sorrow life is sweet; life is sweet, however one lives. But here what is there but . . . foulness? Phew!"

I turned away with disgust; I was no longer reasoning coldly. I began to feel myself what I was saying and warmed to the subject. I was already longing to expound the cherished ideas I had brooded over in my corner. Something suddenly flared up in me. An object had appeared before me.

"Never mind my being here, I am not an example for you. I am, perhaps, worse than you are. I was drunk when I came here, though," I hastened, however, to say in self-defence. "Besides, a man is no example for a woman. It's a different thing. I may degrade and defile myself, but I am not any one's slave. I come and go, and that's an end of it. I shake it off, and I am a different man. But you are a slave from the start. Yes, a slave! You give up everything, your whole freedom. If you want to break your chains afterwards, you won't be able to: you will be more and more fast in the snares. It is an accursed bondage. I know it. I won't speak of anything else, maybe you won't understand, but tell me: no doubt you are in debt to your madam? There, you see," I added, though she made no answer, but only listened in silence, entirely absorbed, "that's a bondage for you! You will never buy your freedom. They will see to that. It's like selling your soul to the devil. . . . And besides . . . perhaps I, too, am just as unlucky—how do you know—and wallow in the mud on purpose, out of misery? You know, men take to drink from grief; well, maybe I am here from grief. Come, tell me, what is there good here? Here you and I . . . came together . . . just now and did not say one word to one another all the time, and it was only afterwards you began staring at me like a wild creature, and I at you. Is that loving? Is that how one human being should meet another? It's hideous, that's what it is!"

"Yes!" she assented sharply and hurriedly.

I was positively astounded by the promptitude of this "Yes." So the same thought may have been straying through her mind when she was staring at me just before. So she, too, was capable of certain thoughts? "Damn it all, this was interesting, this was a point of likeness!" I thought, almost rubbing my hands. And indeed it's easy to turn a young soul like that!

It was the exercise of my power that attracted me most.

She turned her head nearer to me, and it seemed to me in the darkness that she propped herself on her arm. Perhaps she was scrutinizing me. How I regretted that I could not see her eyes. I heard her deep breathing.

"Why have you come here?" I asked her, with a note of authority already in my voice.

"Oh, I don't know."

"But how nice it would be to be living in your father's house! It's warm and free; you have a home of your own."

"But what if it's worse than this?"

"I must take the right tone," flashed through my mind. "I may not get far with sentimentality." But it was only a momentary thought. I swear she really did interest me. Besides, I was exhausted and moody. And cunning so easily goes hand-in-hand with feeling.

"Who denies it!" I hastened to answer. "Anything may happen. I am convinced that some one has wronged you, and that you are more sinned against than sinning. Of course, I know nothing of your story, but it's not likely a girl like you has come here of her own inclination. . . ."

"A girl like me?" she whispered, hardly audibly; but I heard it.

Damn it all, I was flattering her. That was horrid. But perhaps it was a good thing. . . . She was silent.

"See, Liza, I will tell you about myself. If I had had a home from childhood, I shouldn't be what I am now. I often think that. However bad it may be at home, anyway they are your father and mother, and not enemies, strangers. Once a year at least, they'll show their love of you. Anyway, you know you are at home. I grew up without a home; and perhaps that's why I've turned so . . . unfeeling."

I waited again. "Perhaps she doesn't understand," I thought, "and, indeed, it is absurd—it's moralizing."

"If I were a father and had a daughter, I believe I should love my daughter more than my sons, really," I began indirectly, as though talking of something else, to distract her attention. I must confess I blushed.

"Why so?" she asked.

Ah! so she was listening!

"I don't know, Liza. I knew a father who was a stern, austere man, but used to go down on his knees to his daughter, used to kiss her hands, her feet, he couldn't make enough of her, really. When she danced at parties he used to stand for five hours at a stretch, gazing at her. He was mad over her: I understand that! She would fall asleep tired at night, and he would wake to kiss her in her sleep and make the sign of the cross over her. He would go about in a dirty old coat, he was stingy to every one else, but would spend his last penny for her, giving her expensive presents, and it was his greatest delight when she was pleased with what he gave her. Fathers always love their daughters more than the mothers do. Some girls live happily at home! And I believe I should never let my daughters marry."

"What next?" she said, with a faint smile.

"I should be jealous, I really should. To think that she should kiss any one else! That she should love a stranger more than her father! It's painful to imagine it. Of course, that's all nonsense, of course every father would be reasonable at last. But I believe before I should let her marry, I should worry myself to death; I should find fault with her suitors. But I should end by letting her marry whom she herself loved. The one whom the daughter loves always seems the worst to the father, you know. That is always so. So many family troubles come from that."

"Some are glad to sell their daughters, rather than marrying them honourably."

Ah, so that was it!

"Such a thing, Liza, happens in those accursed families in which there is neither love nor God," I retorted warmly, "and where there is no love, there is no sense either. There are such families, it's true, but I am not speaking of them. You must have seen wickedness in your own family, if you talk like that. Truly, you must have been unlucky. H'm! . . . that sort of thing mostly comes about through poverty."

"And is it any better with the gentry? Even among the poor, honest people live happily."

"H'm . . . yes. Perhaps. Another thing, Liza, man is fond of reckoning up his troubles, but does not count his joys. If he counted them up as he ought, he would see that every lot has enough happiness provided for it. And what if all goes well with the family, if the blessing of God is upon it, if the husband is a good one, loves you, cherishes you, never leaves you! There is happiness in such a family! Even sometimes there is happiness in the midst of sorrow; and indeed sorrow is everywhere. If you marry *you will find out for yourself*. But think of the first years of married life with one you love: what happiness, what happiness there sometimes is in it! And indeed it's the ordinary thing. In those early days even quarrels with one's husband end happily. Some women get up quarrels with their husbands just because they love them. Indeed, I knew a woman like that: she seemed to say that because she loved him, she would torment him and make him feel it. You know that you may torment a man on purpose through love. Women are particularly given to that, thinking to themselves 'I will love him so, I will make so much of him afterwards, that it's no sin to torment him a little now.' And all in the house rejoice in the sight of you, and you are happy and gay and peaceful and honourable. . . . Then there are some women who are jealous. If he went off anywhere—I knew one such a woman, she couldn't restrain herself, but would jump up at night and run off on the sly to find out where he was, whether he was with some other woman. That's a pity. And the woman knows herself it's wrong, and her heart fails her and she suffers, but she loves—it's all through love. And how sweet it is to make it up after quarrels, to own herself in the wrong or to forgive him! And they are both so happy all at once—as though they had met anew, been married over again; as though their love had begun afresh. And no one, no one should know what passes between husband and wife if they love one another. And whatever quarrels there may be between them they ought not to call in their own mother to judge between them and tell tales of one another. They are their own judges. Love is a holy mystery and ought to be hidden from all other eyes, whatever happens. That makes it holier and better. They respect one another more, and much is built on respect. And if once there has been love, if they have been married for love, why should love pass away? Surely one can keep it! It is rare that one cannot keep it. And if the husband is kind and straightforward, why should not love last? The first phase of married love will pass, it is true, but then there will come a love that is better still. Then there will be the union of souls, they will have everything in common, there will be no secrets between them. And once they have children, the most difficult times will seem to them happy, so long as there is love and courage. Even toil will be a joy, you may deny yourself bread for your children and even that will be a joy. They will love you for it afterwards; so you are laying by for your future. As the children grow up you feel that you are an example, a support for them; that even after you die your children will always keep your thoughts and feelings, because they have received them from you, they will take on your semblance and likeness. So you see this is a great duty. How can it fail to draw the father and mother nearer? People say it's a trial to have children. Who says that? It is heavenly happiness! Are you fond of little children, Liza? I am awfully fond of them. You know—a little rosy baby boy at your bosom, and what husband's heart is not touched, seeing his wife nursing his child! A plump little rosy baby, sprawling and snuggling, chubby little hands and feet, clean tiny little nails, so tiny that it makes one laugh to look at them; eyes that look as if they understand everything. And while it sucks it clutches at your bosom with its little hand, plays. When its father comes up, the child tears itself away from the bosom, flings itself back, looks at its father, laughs, as though it were fearfully funny and falls to sucking again. Or it will bite its mother's breast when its little teeth are coming, while it looks sideways at her with its little eyes as though to say, 'Look, I am biting!' Is not all that happiness when they are the three together, husband, wife and child? One can forgive a great deal for the sake of such moments. Yes, Liza, one must first learn to live oneself before one blames others!"

"It's by pictures, pictures like that one must get at you," I thought to myself, though I did speak with real feeling, and all at once I flushed crimson. "What if she were suddenly to burst out laughing, what should I do then?" That idea drove me to fury. Towards the end of my speech I really was excited, and now my vanity was somehow wounded. The silence continued. I almost nudged her.

"Why are you—" she began and stopped. But I understood: there was a quiver of something different in her voice, not abrupt, harsh and unyielding as before, but something soft and shamefaced, so shamefaced that I suddenly felt ashamed and guilty.

"What?" I asked, with tender curiosity.

"Why, you . . ."

"What?"

"Why, you . . . speak somehow like a book," she said, and again there was a note of irony in her voice.

That remark sent a pang to my heart. It was not what I was expecting.

I did not understand that she was hiding her feelings under irony, that this is usually the last refuge of modest and chaste-souled people when the privacy of their soul is coarsely and intrusively invaded, and that their pride makes them refuse to surrender till the last moment and shrink from giving expression to their feelings before you. I ought to have guessed the truth from the timidity with which she had repeatedly approached her sarcasm, only bringing herself to utter it at last with an effort. But I did not guess, and an evil feeling took possession of me.

"Wait a bit!" I thought.

VII

"Oh, hush, Liza! How can you talk about being like a book, when it makes even me, an outsider, feel sick? Though I don't look at it as an outsider, for, indeed, it touches me to the heart. . . . Is it possible, is it possible that you do not feel sick at being here yourself? Evidently habit does wonders! God knows what habit can do with any one. Can you seriously think that you will never grow old, that you will always be good-looking, and that they will keep you here for ever and ever? I say nothing of the loathsomeness of the life here. . . . Though let me tell you this about it—about your present life, I mean; here though you are young now, attractive, nice, with soul and feeling, yet you know as soon as I came to myself just now

I felt at once sick at being here with you! One can only come here when one is drunk. But if you were anywhere else, living as good people live, I should perhaps be more than attracted by you, should fall in love with you, should be glad of a look from you, let alone a word; I should hang about your door, should go down on my knees to you, should look upon you as my betrothed and think it an honour to be allowed to. I should not dare to have an impure thought about you. But here, you see, I know that I have only to whistle and you have to come with me whether you like it or not. I don't consult your wishes, but you mine. The lowest labourer hires himself as a workman, but he doesn't make a slave of himself altogether; besides, he knows that he will be free again presently. But when are you free? Only think what you are giving up here. What is it you are making a slave of? It is your soul, together with your body; you are selling your soul which you have no right to dispose of! You give your love to be outraged by every drunkard! Love! But that's everything, you know, it's a priceless diamond, it's a maiden's treasure, love—why, a man would be ready to give his soul, to face death to gain that love. But how much is your love worth now? You are sold, all of you, body and soul, and there is no need to strive for love when you can have everything without love. And you know there is no greater insult to a girl than that, do you understand? To be sure, I have heard that they comfort you, poor fools, they let you have lovers of your own here. But you know that's simply a farce, that's simply a sham, it's just laughing at you, and you are taken in by it! Why, do you suppose he really loves you, that lover of yours? I don't believe it. How can he love you when he knows you may be called away from him any minute? He would be a low fellow if he did! Will he have a grain of respect for you? What have you in common with him? He laughs at you and robs you—that is all his love amounts to! You are lucky if he does not beat you. Very likely he does beat you, too. Ask him, if you have got one, whether he will marry you. He will laugh in your face, if he doesn't spit in it or give you a blow—though maybe he is not worth a bad halfpenny himself. And for what have you ruined your life, if you come to think of it? For the coffee they give you to drink and the plentiful meals? But with what object are they feeding you up? An honest girl couldn't swallow the food, for she would know what she was being fed for. You are in debt here, and, of course, you will always be in debt, and you will go on in debt to the end, till the visitors here begin to scorn you. And that will soon happen, don't rely upon your youth—all

that flies by express train here, you know. You will be kicked out.
And not simply kicked out; long before that she'll begin nagging at
you, scolding you, abusing you, as though you had not sacrificed
your health for her, had not thrown away your youth and your soul
for her benefit, but as though you had ruined her, beggared her,
robbed her. And don't expect any one to take your part: the others,
your companions, will attack you, too, to win her favour, for all are
in slavery here, and have lost all conscience and pity here long ago.
They have become utterly vile, and nothing on earth is viler, more
loathsome, and more insulting than their abuse. And you are laying
down everything here, unconditionally, youth and health and beauty
and hope, and at twenty-two you will look like a woman of five-and-
thirty, and you will be lucky if you are not diseased, pray to God for
that! No doubt you are thinking now that you have a gay time and
no work to do! Yet there is no work harder or more dreadful in the
world or ever has been. One would think that the heart alone would
be worn out with tears. And you won't dare to say a word, not half a
word when they drive you away from here; you will go away as
though you were to blame. You will change to another house, then
to a third, then somewhere else, till you come down at last to the
Haymarket. There you will be beaten at every turn; that is good
manners there, the visitors don't know how to be friendly without
beating you. You don't believe that it is so hateful there? Go and
look for yourself some time, you can see with your own eyes. Once,
one New Year's Day, I saw a woman at a door. They had turned her
out as a joke, to give her a taste of the frost because she had been
crying so much, and they shut the door behind her. At nine o'clock
in the morning she was already quite drunk, dishevelled, half-naked,
covered with bruises, her face was powdered, but she had a black
eye, blood was trickling from her nose and her teeth; some cabman
had just given her a drubbing. She was sitting on the stone steps, a
salt fish of some sort was in her hand; she was crying, wailing something about her luck and beating with the fish on the steps, and
cabmen and drunken soldiers were crowding in the doorway taunting her. You don't believe that you will ever be like that? I should
be sorry to believe it, too, but how do you know; maybe ten years,
eight years ago that very woman with the salt fish came here fresh as
a cherub, innocent, pure, knowing no evil, blushing at every word.
Perhaps she was like you, proud, ready to take offence, not like the
others; perhaps she looked like a queen, and knew what happiness
was in store for the man who should love her and whom she should

love. Do you see how it ended? And what if at that very minute
when she was beating on the filthy steps with that fish, drunken and
dishevelled—what if at that very minute she recalled the pure early
days in her father's house, when she used to go to school and the
neighbour's son watched for her on the way, declaring that he would
love her as long as he lived, that he would devote his life to her, and
when they vowed to love one another for ever and be married as
soon as they were grown up! No, Liza, it would be happy for you if
you were to die soon of consumption in some corner, in some cellar
like that woman just now. In the hospital, do you say? You will be
lucky if they take you, but what if you are still of use to the madam
here? Consumption is a queer disease, it is not like fever. The patient goes on hoping till the last minute and says he is all right. He
deludes himself. And that just suits your madam. Don't doubt it,
that's how it is; you have sold your soul, and what is more you owe
money, so you daren't say a word. But when you are dying, all will
abandon you, all will turn away from you, for then there will be
nothing to get from you. What's more, they will reproach you for
cumbering the place, for being so long over dying. However you beg
you won't get a drink of water without abuse: 'Whenever are you
going off, you nasty hussy, you won't let us sleep with your moaning,
you make the gentlemen sick.' That's true, I have heard such things
said myself. They will thrust you dying into the filthiest corner in
the cellar—in the damp and darkness; what will your thoughts be,
lying there alone? When you die, strange hands will lay you out,
with grumbling and impatience; no one will bless you, no one will
sigh for you, they only want to get rid of you as soon as may be;
they will buy a coffin, take you to the grave as they did that poor
woman to-day and celebrate your memory at the tavern. In the grave
sleet, filth, wet snow—no need to put themselves out for you—'Let
her down, Vanuha; it's just like her luck—even here, she is head-
foremost, the hussy. Shorten the cord, you rascal.' 'It's all right as it
is.' 'All right, is it? Why, she's on her side! She was a fellow-crea-
ture, after all! But, never mind, throw the earth on her.' And they
won't care to waste much time quarrelling over you. They will scatter the wet blue clay as quick as they can and go off to the tavern
. . . and there your memory on earth will end; other women have
children to go to their graves, fathers, husbands. While for you
neither tear, nor sigh, nor remembrance; no one in the whole world
will ever come to you, your name will vanish from the face of the
earth—as though you had never existed, never been born at all!

Nothing but filth and mud, however you knock at your coffin lid at night, when the dead arise, however you cry: 'Let me out, kind people, to live in the light of day! My life was no life at all; my life has been thrown away like a dish-clout; it was drunk away in the tavern at the Haymarket; let me out, kind people, to live in the world again.'"

And I worked myself up to such a pitch that I began to have a lump in my throat myself, and . . . and all at once I stopped, sat up in dismay, and bending over apprehensively, began to listen with a beating heart. I had reason to be troubled.

I had felt for some time that I was turning her soul upside down and rending her heart, and—and the more I was convinced of it, the more eagerly I desired to gain my object as quickly and as effectually as possible. It was the exercise of my skill that carried me away; yet it was not merely sport. . . .

I knew I was speaking stiffly, artificially, even bookishly, in fact, I could not speak except "like a book." But that did not trouble me: I knew, I felt that I should be understood and that this very bookishness might be an assistance. But now, having attained my effect, I was suddenly panic-stricken. Never before had I witnessed such despair! She was lying on her face, thrusting her face into the pillow and clutching it in both hands. Her heart was being torn. Her youthful body was shuddering all over as though in convulsions. Suppressed sobs rent her bosom and suddenly burst out in weeping and wailing, then she pressed closer into the pillow: she did not want any one here, not a living soul, to know of her anguish and her tears. She bit the pillow, bit her hand till it bled (I saw that afterwards), or thrusting her fingers into her dishevelled hair, seemed rigid with the effort of restraint, holding her breath and clenching her teeth. I began saying something, begging her to calm herself, but felt that I did not dare; and all at once, in a sort of cold shiver, almost in terror, began fumbling in the dark, trying hurriedly to get dressed to go. It was dark: though I tried my best I could not finish dressing quickly. Suddenly I felt a box of matches and a candlestick with a whole candle in it. As soon as the room was lighted up, Liza sprang up, sat up in bed, and with a contorted face, with a half insane smile, looked at me almost senselessly. I sat down beside her and took her hands; she came to herself, made an impulsive movement towards me, would have caught hold of me, but did not dare, and slowly bowed her head before me.

"Liza, my dear, I was wrong . . . forgive me, my dear," I began, but she squeezed my hand in her fingers so tightly that I felt I was saying the wrong thing and stopped.

"This is my address, Liza, come to me."

"I will come," she answered resolutely, her head still bowed.

"But now I am going, good-bye . . . till we meet again."

I got up; she, too, stood up and suddenly flushed all over, gave a shudder, snatched up a shawl that was lying on a chair and muffled herself in it to her chin. As she did this she gave another sickly smile, blushed and looked at me strangely. I felt wretched; I was in haste to get away—to disappear.

"Wait a minute," she said suddenly, in the passage just at the doorway, stopping me with her hand on my overcoat. She put down the candle in hot haste and ran off; evidently she had thought of something or wanted to show me something. As she ran away she flushed, her eyes shone, and there was a smile on her lips—what was the meaning of it? Against my will I waited: she came back a minute later with an expression that seemed to ask forgiveness for something. In fact, it was not the same face, not the same look as the evening before: sullen, mistrustful and obstinate. Her eyes now were imploring, soft, and at the same time trustful, caressing, timid. The expression with which children look at people they are very fond of, of whom they are asking a favour. Her eyes were a light hazel, they were lovely eyes, full of life, and capable of expressing love as well as sullen hatred.

Making no explanation, as though I, as a sort of higher being, must understand everything without explanations, she held out a piece of paper to me. Her whole face was positively beaming at that instant with naïve, almost childish, triumph. I unfolded it. It was a letter to her from a medical student or some one of that sort—a very high-flown and flowery, but extremely respectful, love-letter. I don't recall the words now, but I remember well that through the high-flown phrases there was apparent a genuine feeling, which cannot be feigned. When I had finished reading it I met her glowing, questioning, and childishly impatient eyes fixed upon me. She fastened her eyes upon my face and waited impatiently for what I should say. In a few words, hurriedly, but with a sort of joy and pride, she explained to me that she had been to a dance somewhere in a private house, a family of "very nice people, *who knew nothing*, absolutely nothing, for she had only come here so lately and it had all happened . . . and she hadn't made up her mind to stay and was certainly going away as soon as she had paid her debt . . ." and at that party there had been the student who had danced with her all the evening. He had talked to her, and it turned out that he had known her in old days at Riga when he was a child, they had played together, but a very long time ago—and he knew her parents, but *about this* he knew nothing, nothing whatever and had no suspicion! And the day after the dance (three days ago) he had sent her that letter through the friend with whom she had gone to the party . . . and . . . well, that was all.

She dropped her shining eyes with a sort of bashfulness as she finished.

The poor girl was keeping that student's letter as a precious treasure, and had run to fetch it, her only treasure, because she did not want me to go away without knowing that she, too, was honestly and genuinely loved; that she, too, was addressed respectfully. No doubt that letter was destined to lie in her box and lead to nothing. But none the less, I am certain that she would keep it all her life as a precious treasure, as her pride and justification, and now at such a minute she had thought of that letter and brought it with naïve pride to raise herself in my eyes that I might see, that I, too, might think well of her. I said nothing, pressed her hand and went out. I so longed to get away. . . . I walked all the way home, in spite of the fact that the melting snow was still falling in heavy flakes. I was exhausted, shattered, in bewilderment. But behind the bewilderment the truth was already gleaming. The loathsome truth.

VIII

It was some time, however, before I consented to recognize that truth. Waking up in the morning after some hours of heavy, leaden sleep, and immediately realizing all that had happened on the previous day, I was positively amazed at my last night's *sentimentality* with Liza, at all those "outcries of horror and pity." "To think of having such an attack of womanish hysteria, pah!" I concluded. And what did I thrust my address upon her for? What if she comes? Let her come, though; it doesn't matter. . . . But *obviously*, that was not now the chief and the most important matter: I had to make haste and at all costs save my reputation in the eyes of Zverkov and Simonov as quickly as possible; that was the chief business. And I was so taken up that morning that I actually forgot all about Liza.

First of all I had at once to repay what I had borrowed the day before from Simonov. I resolved on a desperate measure: to borrow fifteen roubles straight off from Anton Antonitch. As luck would have it he was in the best of humours that morning, and gave it to me at once, on the first asking. I was so delighted at this that, as I signed the I O U with a swaggering air, I told him casually that the night before "I had been keeping it up with some friends at the Hôtel de Paris; we were giving a farewell party to a comrade, in fact, I might say a friend of my childhood, and you know—a desperate rake, fearfully spoilt—of course, he belongs to a good family, and has considerable means, a brilliant career; he is witty, charming, a regular Lovelace, you understand; we drank an extra 'half-dozen' and . . ."

And it went off all right; all this was uttered very easily, unconstrainedly and complacently.

On reaching home I promptly wrote to Simonov.

To this hour I am lost in admiration when I recall the truly gentlemanly, good-humoured, candid tone of my letter. With tact and good breeding, and, above all, entirely without superfluous words, I blamed myself for all that had happened. I defended myself, "if I really may be allowed to defend myself," by alleging that being utterly unaccustomed to wine, I had been intoxicated with the first glass, which I said I had drunk before they arrived, while I was waiting for them at the Hôtel de Paris between five and six o'clock. I begged Simonov's pardon especially; I asked him to convey my explanations to all the others, especially to Zverkov, whom "I seemed to remember as though in a dream" I had insulted. I added that I would have called upon all of them myself, but my head ached, and besides I had not the face to. I was particularly pleased with a certain lightness, almost carelessness (strictly within the bounds of politeness, however), which was apparent in my style, and better than any possible arguments, gave them at once to understand that I took rather an independent view of "all that unpleasantness last night"; that I was by no means so utterly crushed as you, my friends, probably imagine; but on the contrary, looked upon it as a gentleman serenely respecting himself should look upon it. "On a young hero's past no censure is cast!"

"There is actually an aristocratic playfulness about it!" I thought admiringly, as I read over the letter. And it's all because I am an intellectual and cultivated man! Another man in my place would not have known how to extricate himself, but here I have got out of it and am as jolly as ever again, and all because I am "a cultivated and educated man of our day." And, indeed, perhaps, everything was due to the wine yesterday. H'm! . . . no, it was not the wine. I did not drink anything at all between five and six when I was waiting for them. I had lied to Simonov; I had lied shamelessly; and indeed I wasn't ashamed now. . . . Hang it all though, the great thing was that I was rid of it.

I put six roubles in the letter, sealed it up, and asked Apollon to take it to Simonov. When he learned that there was money in the letter, Apollon became more respectful and agreed to take it. Towards evening I went out for a walk. My head was still aching and giddy after yesterday. But as evening came on and the twilight grew denser, my impressions and, following them, my thoughts, grew more and more different and confused. Something was not dead within me, in the depths of my heart and conscience it would not die, and it showed itself in acute depression. For the most part I jostled my way through the most crowded business streets, along Myeshtchansky Street, along Sadovy Street and in Yusupov Garden. I always liked particularly sauntering along these streets in the dusk, just when there were crowds of working people of all sorts going home from their daily work, with faces looking cross with anxiety. What I liked was just that cheap bustle, that bare prose. On this occasion the jostling of the streets irritated me more than ever. I could not make out what was wrong with me, I could not find the clue, something seemed rising up continually in my soul, painfully, and refusing to be appeased. I returned home completely upset, it was just as though some crime were lying on my conscience.

The thought that Liza was coming worried me continually. It seemed queer to me that of all my recollections of yesterday this tormented me, as it were, especially, as it were, quite separately. Everything else I had quite succeeded in forgetting by the evening; I dismissed it all and was still perfectly satisfied with my letter to Simonov. But on this point I was not satisfied at all. It was as though I were worried only by Liza. "What if she comes," I thought incessantly, "well, it doesn't matter, let her come! H'm! it's horrid that she should see, for instance, how I live. Yesterday I seemed such a hero to her, while now, h'm! It's horrid, though, that I have let myself go so, the room looks like a beggar's. And I brought myself to go out to dinner in such a suit! And my American leather sofa with the stuffing sticking out. And my dressing-gown, which will not cover me, such tatters, and she will see all this and she will see Apollon. That beast is certain to insult her. He will fasten upon her in order to be rude to me. And I, of course, shall be panic-stricken as usual, I shall begin bowing and scraping before her and pulling my dressing-gown round me, I shall begin smiling, telling lies. Oh, the beastliness! And it isn't the beastliness of it that matters most! There is something more important, more loathsome, viler! Yes, viler! And to put on that dishonest lying mask again!" . . .

When I reached that thought I fired up all at once.

"Why dishonest? How dishonest? I was speaking sincerely last night. I remember there was real feeling in me, too. What I wanted was to excite an honourable feeling in her. . . . Her crying was a good thing, it will have a good effect."

Yet I could not feel at ease. All that evening, even when I had come back home, even after nine o'clock, when I calculated that Liza could not possibly come, she still haunted me, and what was worse, she came back to my mind always in the same position. One moment out of all that had happened last night stood vividly before my imagination; the moment when I struck a match and saw her pale, distorted face, with its look of torture. And what a pitiful, what an unnatural, what a distorted smile she had at that moment! But I did not know then, that fifteen years later I should still in my imagination see Liza, always with the pitiful, distorted, inappropriate smile which was on her face at that minute.

Next day I was ready again to look upon it all as nonsense, due to over-excited nerves, and, above all, as *exaggerated*. I was always conscious of that weak point of mine, and sometimes very much afraid of it. "I exaggerate everything, that is where I go wrong," I repeated to myself every hour. But, however, "Liza will very likely come all the same," was the refrain with which all my reflections ended. I was so uneasy that I sometimes flew into a fury: "She'll come, she is certain to come!" I cried, running about the room, "if not to-day, she will come to-morrow; she'll find me out! The damnable romanticism of these pure hearts! Oh, the vileness—oh, the silliness—oh, the stupidity of these 'wretched sentimental souls'! Why, how fail to understand? How could one fail to understand? . . ."

But at this point I stopped short, and in great confusion, indeed.

And how few, how few words, I thought, in passing, were needed; how little of the idyllic (and affectedly, bookishly, artificially idyllic too) had sufficed to turn a whole human life at once according to my will. That's virginity, to be sure! Freshness of soil!

At times a thought occurred to me, to go to her, "to tell her all," and beg her not to come to me. But this thought stirred such wrath in me that I believed I should have crushed that "damned" Liza if she had chanced to be near me at the time. I should have insulted her, have spat at her, have turned her out, have struck her!

One day passed, however, another and another; she did not come and I began to grow calmer. I felt particularly bold and cheerful after nine o'clock, I even sometimes began dreaming, and rather sweetly: I, for instance, became the salvation of Liza, simply through her coming to me and my talking to her. . . . I develop her, educate her. Finally, I notice that she loves me, loves me passionately. I pretend not to understand (I don't know, however, why I pretend, just for effect, perhaps). At last all confusion, transfigured, trembling and sobbing, she flings herself at my feet and says that I am her saviour, and that she loves me better than anything in the world. I am amazed, but . . . "Liza," I say, "can you imagine that I have not noticed your love, I saw it all, I divined it, but I did not dare to approach you first, because I had an influence over you and was afraid that you would force yourself, from gratitude, to respond to my love, would try to rouse in your heart a feeling which was perhaps absent, and I did not wish that . . . because it would be tyranny . . . it would be indelicate (in short, I launch off at that point into European, inexplicably lofty subtleties à la George Sand), but now, now you are mine, you are my creation, you are pure, you are good, you are my noble wife.

> Into my house come bold and free,
> Its rightful mistress there to be."

Then we begin living together, go abroad and so on, and so on. In fact, in the end it seemed vulgar to me myself, and I began putting out my tongue at myself.

Besides, they won't let her out, "the hussy!" I thought. They don't let them go out very readily, especially in the evening (for some reason I fancied she would come in the evening, and at seven o'clock precisely). Though she did say she was not altogether a slave there yet, and had certain rights; so, h'm! Damn it all, she will come, she is sure to come!

It was a good thing, in fact, that Apollon distracted my attention at that time by his rudeness. He drove me beyond all patience! He was the bane of my life, the curse laid upon me by Providence. We had been squabbling continually for years, and I hated him. My God, how I hated him! I believe I had never hated any one in my life as I hated him, especially at some moments. He was an elderly, dignified man, who worked part of his time as a tailor. But for some unknown reason he despised me beyond all measure, and looked down upon me insufferably. Though, indeed, he looked down upon every one. Simply to glance at that flaxen, smoothly brushed head, at the tuft of hair he combed up on his forehead and oiled with sunflower oil, at that dignified mouth, compressed into the shape of the letter V, made one feel one was confronting a man who never doubted of himself. He was a pedant, to the most extreme point, the greatest pedant I had met on earth, and with that had a vanity only befitting Alexander of Macedon. He was in love with every button on his coat, every nail on his fingers—absolutely in love with them, and he looked it! In his behaviour to me he was a perfect tyrant, he spoke very little to me, and if he chanced to glance at me he gave me a firm, majestically self-confident and invariably ironical look that drove me sometimes to fury. He did his work with the air of doing me the greatest favour. Though he did scarcely anything for me, and did not, indeed, consider himself bound to do anything. There could be no doubt that he looked upon me as the greatest fool on earth, and that "he did not get rid of me" was simply that he could get wages from me every month. He consented to do nothing for me for seven roubles a month. Many sins should be forgiven me for what I suffered from him. My hatred reached such a point that sometimes his very step almost threw me into convulsions. What I loathed particularly was his lisp. His tongue must have been a little too long or something of that sort, for he continually lisped, and seemed to be very proud of it, imagining that it greatly added to his dignity. He spoke in a slow, measured tone, with his hands behind his back and his eyes fixed on the ground. He maddened me particularly when he read aloud the psalms to himself behind his partition. Many a battle I waged over that reading! But he was awfully fond of reading aloud in the evenings, in a slow, even sing-song voice, as though over the dead. It is interesting that that is how he has ended: he hires himself out to read the psalms over the dead, and at the same time he kills rats and makes blacking. But at that time I could not get rid of him, it was as though he were chemically combined with my existence. Besides, nothing would have induced him to consent to leave me. I could not live in furnished lodgings: my lodging was my private solitude, my shell, my cave, in which I concealed myself from all mankind, and Apollon seemed to me, for some reason, an integral part of that flat, and for seven years I could not turn him away.

To be two or three days behind with his wages, for instance, was impossible. He would have made such a fuss, I should not have known where to hide my head. But I was so exasperated with every one during those days, that I made up my mind for some reason and with some object to *punish* Apollon and not to pay him for a fortnight the wages that were owing him. I had for a long time—for the last two years—been intending to do this, simply in order to teach him not to give himself airs with me, and to show him that if I liked I could withhold his wages. I purposed to say nothing to him about it, and was purposely silent indeed, in order to score off his pride and force himself to be the first to speak of his wages. Then I would take the seven roubles out of a drawer, show him I have the money put aside on purpose, but that I won't, I won't, I simply won't pay him his wages, I won't just because that is "what I wish," because "I am master, and it is for me to decide," because he has been disrespectful, because he has been rude; but if he were to ask respectfully I might be softened and give it to him, otherwise he might wait another fortnight, another three weeks, a whole month.

But angry as I was, yet he got the better of me. I could not hold out for four days. He began as he always did begin in such cases, for there had been such cases already, there had been attempts (and it may be observed I knew all this beforehand, I knew his nasty tactics by heart). He would begin by fixing upon me an exceedingly severe stare, keeping it up for several minutes at a time, particularly on meeting me or seeing me out of the house. If I held out and pretended not to notice these stares, he would, still in silence, proceed to further tortures. All at once, *à propos* of nothing, he would walk softly and smoothly into my room, when I was pacing up and down or reading, stand at the door, one hand behind his back and one foot behind the other, and fix upon me a stare more than severe, utterly contemptuous. If I suddenly asked him what he wanted, he would make me no answer, but continue staring at me persistently for some seconds, then, with a peculiar compression of his lips and a most significant air, deliberately turn round and deliberately go back to his room. Two hours later he would come out again and again present himself before me in the same way. It had happened that in my fury I did not even ask him what he wanted, but simply raised my head sharply and imperiously and began staring back at him. So we stared at one another for two minutes; at last he turned with deliberation and dignity and went back again for two hours.

If I were still not brought to reason by all this, but persisted in my revolt, he would suddenly begin sighing while he looked at me, long, deep sighs as though measuring by them the depths of my moral degradation, and, of course, it ended at last by his triumphing completely: I raged and shouted, but still was forced to do what he wanted.

This time the usual staring manœuvres had scarcely begun when I lost my temper and flew at him in a fury. I was irritated beyond endurance apart from him.

"Stay," I cried, in a frenzy, as he was slowly and silently turning, with one hand behind his back, to go to his room, "stay! Come back, come back, I tell you!" and I must have bawled so unnaturally, that he turned round and even looked at me with some wonder. However, he persisted in saying nothing, and that infuriated me.

"How dare you come and look at me like that without being sent for? Answer!"

After looking at me calmly for half a minute, he began turning round again.

"Stay!" I roared, running up to him, "don't stir! There. Answer, now: what did you come in to look at?"

"If you have any order to give me it's my duty to carry it out," he answered, after another silent pause, with a slow, measured lisp, raising his eyebrows and calmly twisting his head from one side to another, all this with exasperating composure.

"That's not what I am asking you about, you torturer!" I shouted, turning crimson with anger. "I'll tell you why you came here myself: you see, I don't give you your wages, you are so proud you don't want to bow down and ask for it, and so you come to punish me with your stupid stares, to worry me and you have no sus . . . pic . . . ion how stupid it is—stupid, stupid, stupid, stupid!" . . .

He would have turned round again without a word, but I seized him.

"Listen," I shouted to him. "Here's the money, do you see, here it is" (I took it out of the table drawer); "here's the seven roubles complete, but you are not going to have it, you . . . are . . . not . . . going . . . to . . . have it until you come respectfully with bowed head to beg my pardon. Do you hear?"

"That cannot be," he answered, with the most unnatural self-confidence.

"It shall be so," I said, "I give you my word of honour, it shall be!"

"And there's nothing for me to beg your pardon for," he went on, as though he had not noticed my exclamations at all. "Why, besides, you called me a 'torturer,' for which I can summon you at the police-station at any time for insulting behaviour."

"Go, summon me," I roared, "go at once, this very minute, this very second! You are a torturer all the same! a torturer!"

But he merely looked at me, then turned, and regardless of my loud calls to him, he walked to his room with an even step and without looking round.

"If it had not been for Liza nothing of this would have happened," I decided inwardly. Then, after waiting a minute, I went myself behind his screen with a dignified and solemn air, though my heart was beating slowly and violently.

"Apollon," I said quietly and emphatically, though I was breathless, "go at once without a minute's delay and fetch the police-officer."

He had meanwhile settled himself at his table, put on his spectacles and taken up some sewing. But, hearing my order, he burst into a guffaw.

"At once, go this minute! Go on, or else you can't imagine what will happen."

"You are certainly out of your mind," he observed, without even raising his head, lisping as deliberately as ever and threading his needle. "Whoever heard of a man sending for the police against himself? And as for being frightened—you are upsetting yourself about nothing, for nothing will come of it."

"Go!" I shrieked, clutching him by the shoulder. I felt I should strike him in a minute.

But I did not notice the door from the passage softly and slowly open at that instant and a figure come in, stop short, and begin staring at us in perplexity. I glanced, nearly swooned with shame, and rushed back to my room. There, clutching at my hair with both hands, I leaned my head against the wall and stood motionless in that position.

Two minutes later I heard Apollon's deliberate footsteps. "There is some woman asking for you," he said, looking at me with peculiar severity. Then he stood aside and let in Liza. He would not go away, but stared at us sarcastically.

"Go away, go away," I commanded in desperation. At that moment my clock began whirring and wheezing and struck seven.

IX

> Into my house come bold and free,
> Its rightful mistress there to be.

I stood before her crushed, crestfallen, revoltingly confused, and I believe I smiled as I did my utmost to wrap myself in the skirts of my ragged wadded dressing-gown—exactly as I had imagined the scene not long before in a fit of depression. After standing over us for a couple of minutes Apollon went away, but that did not make me more at ease. What made it worse was that she, too, was overwhelmed with confusion, more so, in fact, than I should have expected. At the sight of me, of course.

"Sit down," I said mechanically, moving a chair up to the table, and I sat down on the sofa. She obediently sat down at once and gazed at me open-eyed, evidently expecting something from me at once. This naïveté of expectation drove me to fury, but I restrained myself.

She ought to have tried not to notice, as though everything had been as usual, while instead of that, she . . . and I dimly felt that I should make her pay dearly for *all this*.

"You have found me in a strange position, Liza," I began, stammering and knowing that this was the wrong way to begin. "No, no, don't imagine anything," I cried, seeing that she had suddenly flushed. "I am not ashamed of my poverty. . . . On the contrary I look with pride on my poverty. I am poor but honourable. . . . One can be poor and honourable," I muttered. "However . . . would you like tea?" . . .

"No," she was beginning.

"Wait a minute."

I leapt up and ran to Apollon. I had to get out of the room somehow.

"Apollon," I whispered in feverish haste, flinging down before him the seven roubles which had remained all the time in my clenched fist, "here are your wages, you see I give them to you; but for that you must come to my rescue: bring me tea and a dozen rusks from the restaurant. If you won't go, you'll make me a miserable man! You don't know what this woman is. . . . This is—everything! You may be imagining something. . . . But you don't know what that woman is!" . . .

Apollon, who had already sat down to his work and put on his spectacles again, at first glanced askance at the money without speaking or putting down his needle; then, without paying the slightest attention to me or making any answer he went on busying himself with his needle, which he had not yet threaded. I waited before him for three minutes with my arms crossed *à la Napoléon*. My temples were moist with sweat. I was pale, I felt it. But, thank God, he must have been moved to pity, looking at me. Having threaded his needle he deliberately got up from his seat, deliberately moved back his chair, deliberately took off his spectacles, deliberately counted the money, and finally asking me over his shoulder: "Shall I get a whole portion?" deliberately walked out of the room. As I was going back to Liza, the thought occurred to me on the way: shouldn't I run away just as I was in my dressing-gown, no matter where, and then let happen what would?

I sat down again. She looked at me uneasily. For some minutes we were silent.

"I will kill him," I shouted suddenly, striking the table with my fist so that the ink spurted out of the inkstand.

"What are you saying!" she cried, starting.

"I will kill him! kill him!" I shrieked, suddenly striking the table in absolute frenzy, and at the same time fully understanding how stupid it was to be in such a frenzy. "You don't know, Liza, what that torturer is to me. He is my torturer. . . . He has gone now to fetch some rusks; he . . ."

And suddenly I burst into tears. It was an hysterical attack. How ashamed I felt in the midst of my sobs; but still I could not restrain them.

She was frightened.

"What is the matter? What is wrong?" she cried, fussing about me.

"Water, give me water, over there!" I muttered in a faint voice, though I was inwardly conscious that I could have got on very well without water and without muttering in a faint voice. But I was, what is called, *putting it on*, to save appearances, though the attack was a genuine one.

She gave me water, looking at me in bewilderment. At that moment Apollon brought in the tea. It suddenly seemed to me that this commonplace, prosaic tea was horribly undignified and paltry after all that had happened, and I blushed crimson. Liza looked at Apollon with positive alarm. He went out without a glance at either of us.

"Liza, do you despise me?" I asked, looking at her fixedly, trembling with impatience to know what she was thinking.

She was confused, and did not know what to answer.

"Drink your tea," I said to her angrily. I was angry with myself, but, of course, it was she who would have to pay for it. A horrible spite against her suddenly surged up in my heart; I believe I could have killed her. To revenge myself on her I swore inwardly not to say a word to her all the time. "She is the cause of it all," I thought.

Our silence lasted for five minutes. The tea stood on the table; we did not touch it. I had got to the point of purposely refraining from beginning in order to embarrass her further; it was awkward for her to begin alone. Several times she glanced at me with mournful perplexity. I was obstinately silent. I was, of course, myself the chief sufferer, because I was fully conscious of the disgusting meanness of my spiteful stupidity, and yet at the same time I could not restrain myself.

"I want to . . . get away . . . from there altogether," she began, to break the silence in some way, but, poor girl, that was just what she ought not to have spoken about at such a stupid moment to a man so stupid as I was. My heart positively ached with pity for her tactless and unnecessary straightforwardness. But something hideous at once stifled all compassion in me; it even provoked me to greater venom. I did not care what happened. Another five minutes passed.

"Perhaps I am in your way," she began timidly, hardly audibly, and was getting up.

But as soon as I saw this first impulse of wounded dignity I positively trembled with spite, and at once burst out.

"Why have you come to me, tell me that, please?" I began, gasping for breath and regardless of logical connection in my words. I longed to have it all out at once, at one burst; I did not even trouble how to begin. "Why have you come? Answer, answer," I cried, hardly knowing what I was doing. "I'll tell you, my good girl, why you have come. You've come because I talked sentimental stuff to you then. So now you are soft as butter and longing for fine sentiments again. So you may as well know that I was laughing at you then. And I am laughing at you now. Why are you shuddering? Yes, I was laughing at you! I had been insulted just before, at dinner, by the fellows who came that evening before me. I came to you, meaning to thrash one of them, an officer; but I didn't succeed, I didn't find him; I had to avenge the insult on some one to get back my own again; you turned up, I vented my spleen on you and laughed at you. I had been humiliated, so I wanted to humiliate; I had been treated like a rag, so I wanted to show my power. . . . That's what it was, and you imagined I had come there on purpose to save you. Yes? You imagined that? You imagined that?"

I knew that she would perhaps be muddled and not take it all in exactly, but I knew, too, that she would grasp the gist of it, very well indeed. And so, indeed, she did. She turned white as a handkerchief, tried to say something, and her lips worked painfully; but she sank on a chair as though she had been felled by an axe. And all the time afterwards she listened to me with her lips parted and her eyes wide open, shuddering with awful terror. The cynicism, the cynicism of my words overwhelmed her. . . .

"Save you!" I went on, jumping up from my chair and running up and down the room before her. "Save you from what? But perhaps I am worse than you myself. Why didn't you throw it in my teeth when I was giving you that sermon: 'But what did you come here yourself for? was it to read us a sermon?' Power, power was what I wanted then, sport was what I wanted, I wanted to wring out your tears, your humiliation, your hysteria—that was what I wanted then! Of course, I couldn't keep it up then, because I am a wretched creature, I was frightened, and, the devil knows why, gave you my address in my folly. Afterwards, before I got home, I was cursing and swearing at you because of that address, I hated you already because of the lies I had told you. Because I only like playing with words, only dreaming, but, do you know, what I really want is that you should all go to hell. That is what I want. I want peace; yes, I'd sell the whole world for a farthing, straight off, so long as I was left in peace. Is the world to go to pot, or am I to go without my tea? I say that the world may go to pot for me so long as I always get my tea. Did you know that, or not? Well, anyway, I know that I am a blackguard, a scoundrel, an egoist, a sluggard. Here I have been shuddering for the last three days at the thought of your coming. And so you know what has worried me particularly for these three days? That I posed as such a hero to you, and now you would see me in a wretched torn dressing-gown, beggarly, loathsome. I told you just now that I was not ashamed of my poverty; so you may as well know that I am ashamed of it; I am more ashamed of it than of anything, more afraid of it than of being found out if I were a thief, because I am as vain as though I had been skinned and the very air blowing on me hurt. Surely by now you must realize that I shall never forgive you for having found me in this wretched dressing-gown, just as I was flying at Apollon like a spiteful cur. The saviour, the former hero, was flying like a mangy, unkempt sheep-dog at his lackey, and the lackey was jeering at him! And I shall never forgive you for the tears I could not help shedding before you just now, like some silly woman put to shame! And for what I am confessing to you now, I shall never forgive *you* either! Yes—you must answer for it all because you turned up like this, because I am a blackguard, because I am the nastiest, stupidest, absurdest and most envious of all the worms on earth, who are not a bit better than I am, but, the devil knows why, are never put to confusion; while I shall always be insulted by every louse, that is my doom! And what is it to me that you don't understand a word of this! And what do I care, what do I care about you, and whether you go to ruin there or not? Do you understand? How I shall hate you now after saying this, for having been here and listening. Why, it's not once in a lifetime a man speaks out like this, and then it is in hysterics! . . . What more do you want? Why do you still stand confronting me, after all this? Why are you worrying me? Why don't you go?"

But at this point a strange thing happened. I was so accustomed to think and imagine everything from books, and to picture everything in the world to myself just as I had made it up in my dreams beforehand, that I could not all at once take in this strange circumstance. What happened was this: Liza, insulted and crushed by me, understood a great deal more than I imagined. She understood from all this what a woman understands first of all, if she feels genuine love, that is, that I was myself unhappy.

The frightened and wounded expression on her face was followed first by a look of sorrowful perplexity. When I began calling myself a scoundrel and a blackguard and my tears flowed (the tirade was accompanied throughout by tears) her whole face worked convulsively. She was on the point of getting up and stopping me; when I finished she took no notice of my shouting: "Why are you here, why don't you go away?" but realized only that it must have been very bitter to me to say all this. Besides, she was so crushed, poor girl; she considered herself infinitely beneath me; how could she feel anger or resentment? She suddenly leapt up from her chair with an irresistible impulse and held out her hands, yearning towards me, though still timid and not daring to stir. . . . At this point there was a revulsion in my heart, too. Then she suddenly rushed to me, threw her arms round me and burst into tears. I, too, could not restrain myself, and sobbed as I never had before.

"They won't let me . . . I can't be good!" I managed to articulate; then I went to the sofa, fell on it face downwards, and sobbed on it for a quarter of an hour in genuine hysterics. She came close to me, put her arms round me and stayed motionless in that position. But the trouble was that the hysterics could not go on for ever, and (I am writing the loathsome truth) lying face downwards on the sofa with my face thrust into my nasty leather pillow, I began by degrees to be aware of a far-away, involuntary but irresistible feeling that it would be awkward now for me to raise my head and look Liza straight in the face. Why was I ashamed? I don't know, but I was ashamed. The thought, too, came into my overwrought brain that our parts now were completely changed, that she was now the heroine, while I was just such a crushed and humiliated creature as she had been before me that night—four days before. . . . And all this came into my mind during the minutes I was lying on my face on the sofa.

My God! surely I was not envious of her then.

I don't know, to this day I cannot decide, and at the time, of course, I was still less able to understand what I was feeling than now. I cannot get on without domineering and tyrannizing over some one, but . . . there is no explaining anything by reasoning and so it is useless to reason.

I conquered myself, however, and raised my head; I had to do so sooner or later . . . and I am convinced to this day that it was just because I was ashamed to look at her that another feeling was suddenly kindled and flamed up in my heart . . . a feeling of mastery and possession. My eyes gleamed with passion, and I gripped her hands tightly. How I hated her and how I was drawn to her at that minute! The one feeling intensified the other. It was almost like an act of vengeance. At first there was a look of amazement, even of terror on her face, but only for one instant. She warmly and rapturously embraced me.

X

A quarter of an hour later I was rushing up and down the room in frenzied impatience, from minute to minute I went up to the screen and peeped through the crack at Liza. She was sitting on the ground with her head leaning against the bed, and must have been crying. But she did not go away, and that irritated me. This time she understood it all. I had insulted her finally, but . . . there's no need to describe it. She realized that my outburst of passion had been simply revenge, a fresh humiliation, and that to my earlier, almost causeless hatred was added now a *personal hatred*, born of envy. . . . Though I do not maintain positively that she understood all this distinctly; but she certainly did fully understand that I was a despicable man, and what was worse, incapable of loving her.

I know I shall be told that this is incredible—but it is incredible to be as spiteful and stupid as I was; it may be added that it was strange I should not love her, or at any rate, appreciate her love. Why is it strange? In the first place, by then I was incapable of love, for I repeat, with me loving meant tyrannizing and showing my moral superiority. I have never in my life been able to imagine any other sort of love, and have nowadays come to the point of sometimes thinking that love really consists in the right—freely given by the beloved object—to tyrannize over her.

Even in my underground dreams I did not imagine love except as a struggle. I began it always with hatred and ended it with moral subjugation, and afterwards I never knew what to do with the subjugated object. And what is there to wonder at in that, since I had succeeded in so corrupting myself, since I was so out of touch with "real life" as to have actually thought of reproaching her, and putting her to shame for having come to me to hear "fine sentiments"; and did not even guess that she had come not to hear fine sentiments, but to love me, because to a woman all reformation, all salvation from any sort of ruin, and all moral renewal is included in love and can only show itself in that form.

I did not hate her so much, however, when I was running about the room and peeping through the crack in the screen. I was only insufferably oppressed by her being here. I wanted her to disappear. I wanted "peace," to be left alone in my underground world. Real life oppressed me with its novelty so much that I could hardly breathe.

But several minutes passed and she still remained, without stirring, as though she were unconscious. I had the shamelessness to tap softly at the screen as though to remind her. . . . She started, sprang up, and flew to seek her kerchief, her hat, her coat, as though making her escape from me. . . . Two minutes later she came from behind the screen and looked with heavy eyes at me. I gave a spiteful grin, which was forced, however, to *keep up appearances*, and I turned away from her eyes.

"Good-bye," she said, going towards the door.

I ran up to her, seized her hand, opened it, thrust something in it and closed it again. Then I turned at once and dashed away in haste to the other corner of the room to avoid seeing, anyway. . . .

I did mean a moment since to tell a lie—to write that I did this accidentally, not knowing what I was doing through foolishness, through losing my head. But I don't want to lie, and so I will say straight out that I opened her hand and put the money in it . . . from spite. It came into my head to do this while I was running up and down the room and she was sitting behind the screen. But this I can say for certain: though I did that cruel thing purposely, it was not an impulse from the heart, but came from my evil brain. This cruelty was so affected, so purposely made up, so completely a product of the brain, of books, that I could not even keep it up a minute—first I dashed away to avoid seeing her, and then in shame and despair rushed after Liza. I opened the door in the passage and began listening.

"Liza! Liza!" I cried on the stairs, but in a low voice, not boldly.

There was no answer, but I fancied I heard her footsteps, lower down on the stairs.

"Liza!" I cried, more loudly.

No answer. But at that minute I heard the stiff outer glass door open heavily with a creak and slam violently, the sound echoed up the stairs.

She had gone. I went back to my room in hesitation. I felt horribly oppressed.

I stood still at the table, beside the chair on which she had sat and looked aimlessly before me. A minute passed, suddenly I started; straight before me on the table I saw . . . In short, I saw a crumpled blue five-rouble note, the one I had thrust into her hand a minute before. It was the same note; it could be no other, there was no other in the flat. So she had managed to fling it from her hand on the table at the moment when I had dashed into the further corner.

Well! I might have expected that she would do that. Might I have expected it? No, I was such an egoist, I was so lacking in respect for my fellow-creatures that I could not even imagine she would do so. I could not endure it. A minute later I flew like a madman to dress, flinging on what I could at random and ran headlong after her. She could not have got two hundred paces away when I ran out into the street.

It was a still night and the snow was coming down in masses and falling almost perpendicularly, covering the pavement and the empty street as though with a pillow. There was no one in the street, no sound was to be heard. The street lamps gave a disconsolate and useless glimmer. I ran two hundred paces to the cross-roads and stopped short.

Where had she gone? And why was I running after her?

Why? To fall down before her, to sob with remorse, to kiss her feet, to entreat her forgiveness! I longed for that, my whole breast was being rent to pieces, and never, never shall I recall that minute with indifference. But—what for? I thought. Should I not begin to hate her, perhaps, even to-morrow, just because I had kissed her feet to-day? Should I give her happiness? Had I not recognized that day, for the hundredth time, what I was worth? Should I not torture her?

I stood in the snow, gazing into the troubled darkness and pondered this.

"And will it not be better?" I mused fantastically, afterwards at home, stifling the living pang of my heart with fantastic dreams. "Will it not be better that she should keep the resentment of the insult for ever? Resentment—why, it is purification; it is a most stinging and painful consciousness! To-morrow I should have defiled her soul and have exhausted her heart, while now the feeling of insult will never die in her heart, and however loathsome the filth awaiting her—the feeling of insult will elevate and purify her . . . by hatred . . . h'm! . . . perhaps, too, by forgiveness . . . Will all that make things easier for her though? . . ."

And, indeed, I will ask on my own account here, an idle question: which is better—cheap happiness or exalted sufferings? Well, which is better?

So I dreamed as I sat at home that evening, almost dead with the pain in my soul. Never had I endured such suffering and remorse, yet could there have been the faintest doubt when I ran out from my lodging that I should turn back half-way? I never met Liza again and I have heard nothing of her. I will add, too, that I remained for a long time afterwards pleased with the phrase about the benefit from resentment and hatred in spite of the fact that I almost fell ill from misery.

Even now, so many years later, all this is somehow a very evil memory. I have many evil memories now, but . . . hadn't I better end my "Notes" here? I believe I made a mistake in beginning to write them, anyway I have felt ashamed all the time I've been writing this story; so it's hardly literature so much as a corrective punishment. Why, to tell long stories, showing how I have spoiled my life through morally rotting in my corner, through lack of fitting environment, through divorce from real life, and rankling spite in my underground world, would certainly not be interesting; a novel needs a hero, and all the traits for an anti-hero are *expressly* gathered together here, and what matters most, it all produces an unpleasant impression, for we are all divorced from life, we are all cripples, every one of us, more or less. We are so divorced from it that we feel at once a sort of loathing for real life, and so cannot bear to be reminded of it. Why, we have come almost to looking upon real life as an effort, almost as hard work, and we are all privately agreed that it is better in books. And why do we fuss and fume sometimes? Why are we perverse and ask for something else? We don't know what ourselves. It would be the worse for us if our petulant prayers were answered. Come, try, give any one of us, for instance, a little more independence, untie our hands, widen the spheres of our activity, relax the control and we . . . yes, I assure you . . . we should be begging to be under control again at once. I know that you will very likely be angry with me for that, and will begin shouting and stamping. Speak for yourself, you will say, and for your miseries in your underground holes, and don't dare to say all of us—excuse me, gentlemen, I am not justifying myself with that "all of us." As for what concerns me in particular I have only in my life carried to an extreme what you have not dared to carry half-way, and what's more, you have taken your cowardice for good sense, and have found comfort in deceiving yourselves. So that perhaps, after all, there is more life in me than in you. Look into it more carefully! Why, we don't even know what living means now, what it is, and what it is called! Leave us alone without books and we shall be lost and in confusion at once. We shall not know what to join on to, what to cling to, what to love and what to hate, what to respect and what to despise. We are oppressed at being men—men with a real individual body and blood, we are ashamed of it, we think it a disgrace and try to contrive to be some sort of impossible generalized man. We are stillborn, and for generations past have been begotten, not by living fathers, and that suits us better and better. We are developing a taste for it. Soon we shall contrive to be born somehow from an idea. But enough; I don't want to write more from "Underground."

[*The notes of this paradoxalist do not end here, however. He could not refrain from going on with them, but it seems to us that we may stop here.*]

LEO TOLSTOY

The Death of Ivan Ilych

Translated by Aylmer Maude

Introduction

The *Death of Ivan Ilych* is one of the most ambitious pieces of fiction ever written. Tolstoy set out not merely to describe a single segment of society or to present a single example of humanity but *to encompass within one story the fundamental patterns of human existence.* Tolstoy wished to write a story about which a fool might say, "True enough, but, after all, this does not concern me, for I am not like Ivan Ilych." More accurately, he wished to write a story to which all of us would first respond like the fool but about which we would finally be forced to harbor a second thought: "Ivan Ilych *is* me, not insofar as I am young or old, pretty or ugly, rich or poor, silly or wise, but insofar as I share with other men one overriding condition: I am mortal, I must die." And this realization of our common fate stabs our hearts.

The fact that all men must die is hardly news; and as an abstract statement it dulls our fears at least as much as it arouses them. In fact, the repetition of this kind of statement—"all men are mortal" —can itself become a way of avoiding the reality to which it points. Tolstoy wished to shake us out of our routine response and to assault our private little self-deception (*you and you may die, but not me*). To do this he had to find a way of making his abstract intention come to pulsing life. For he was not concerned merely with showing the death of some particular character, a circumstance from which the reader could soon find a way of squirming loose emotionally. Instead, Tolstoy wanted to render a universal experience but not as a mere abstraction, since abstraction has a tendency to become a psychological anesthetic.

EXAMPLE:
If I say, "All men must die," you nod in agreement and maybe even yawn. But if I were able to show you a picture of yourself as a corpse, you might take notice.

The strategy Tolstoy hit upon was to create a figure who, in his absolutely commonplace life and character, would indeed seem universal—he would be a man stripped of all those traits that distinguish one person from another, and there would be almost nothing left to him but the fact that he is a man. Almost anyone can feel superior to Ivan Ilych, that good gray nonentity; yet all of us share at least some of those trivialities and vanities that make up the bulk of Ivan Ilych's existence. By thus embodying his abstract idea in the life of an utterly ordinary man, Tolstoy hoped to make each detail of his story take on a universal significance. The concrete would become a way of conveying the abstract, and the life of Ivan Ilych would become—or seem to become—the life of all of us.

To achieve effects of this kind Tolstoy begins with a very clever stroke: he puts us, the readers, into the story. The narrative starts shortly after Ivan Ilych has died. The people around him, family and friends, are confronted with one of the most commonplace and, Tolstoy suggests, one of the most tiresome of duties. Because their former colleague has died, they have to put on long faces, even as they are thinking about "the changes and promotions it might occasion among themselves or their acquaintances." They have to pay their respects to the widow, who mildly tyrannizes over them by making them pretend to be more grieved than they really are but who is herself already considering the financial problems she will now have to face. And while quite ready to acknowledge that poor Ivan Ilych was quite a decent man (*though toward the end, you know, one couldn't recognize him!*), they are irritated that this mess may cause them to lose a good night's game of cards.

Meanwhile, each of the gentlemen in the opening section cannot suppress the thought that comes to everyone on such occasions: "Well, he's dead but I'm alive!" That life does go on can seem a shameful injustice at the moment of death.

Yet here we ought to be on guard against self-righteousness. The people around Ivan Ilych are certainly no more sinful than most of us. Nor are they evil. Their reactions form the common denominator of human existence, that which makes us all a little ashamed of being men but which we cannot escape precisely because we are men. And in truth, they do feel something, a vague sense of sympathy and loss, as they shuffle through the house over which Ivan Ilych was once master. In this respect there is a brilliant little passage that seems especially worth noting. A gentleman named Peter Ivanovich comes to pay his respects to the widow:

> Peter Ivanovich knew that, just as it had been the right thing to cross himself in that room, so what he had to do here was to press her hand, sigh, and say, "Believe me. . . ." So he did all this and as he did it felt that the desired result had been achieved: that both he and she were touched.

"Both he and she were touched." The two people go through the routine of condolence knowing it is a routine, and they are equally uncomfortable at the thought of a mutual insincerity; yet just because they do have to go through this routine of civilized life they are stirred, unexpectedly, to some genuine feeling. Tolstoy understood that the forms and conventions of civilization—manners, ceremonies, rituals—can deaden our finer and spontaneous feelings but that they can also enable those feelings to emerge and take shape. So Peter Ivanovich and the widow do reach a moment of genuine emotion: they are hypocrites but not merely hypocrites. And while Tolstoy may have slyly led us to suppose ourselves superior to these mediocre people whose response to death reveals the extent of their mediocrity, we soon recognize that in most circumstances we would behave in much the same way. Thereby we are less inclined to judge the gentlemen who go through the motions of condolence and then, with a sigh of nervous relief, settle down to a hand of cards. "What else," they might well ask, "is there to do?"

So much for the prelude, composed by Tolstoy with the idea of implicating all of us in the ordinary responses to the ordinary fact of an ordinary man's death. Tolstoy now turns back in time, to the life of Ivan Ilych. In a sentence that comes with the force of a blow, he writes: "Ivan Ilych's life had been most simple and most ordinary and therefore most terrible." Not until we have absorbed the entire story can we understand why a simple and ordinary life is "therefore most terrible." What Tolstoy means, I *think*, is that a commonplace life never prompts a man to confront himself and ask whether his experience has meaning or value. Such a man can go straight to the grave without once questioning himself, without once wondering whether he has done anything to justify the days he spent on earth. And to die as a clod after having lived all one's years as a clod—that is indeed terrible. It is to have missed everything, both the joy and the pain of awareness.

Would it be hard to picture Ivan Ilych as an American? He would be called John Smith, and he would probably be working for a corporation, living in a nice house in the suburbs, providing decently for his wife and children, and repeating quite sincerely all the standard opinions of our day. John Smith equals Ivan Ilych, a man neither remarkably good nor remarkably bad: a zero. But do not hasten to judge him; Ivan Ilych is an honorable man, and there you may go twenty-five or thirty years from now.

Ivan Ilych follows the path of his elders. He is an organization man. "He considered his duty to be what was so considered by those in authority." Yet Tolstoy does not sneer or mock. He writes as if he were a distant god recording the fate of a species. "All the enthusiasms of childhood and youth passed without leaving much trace on him; he succumbed to sensuality, to vanity, and latterly among the highest classes to liberalism, but always within limits which his instinct unfailingly indicated to him as correct." This sentence is acute: Ivan Ilych goes through the usual phases of experience, as these are shaped by our physical needs and our social condition, and since he lives at a moment when it is fashionable to flirt with liberalism, he does that, too, but always within limits, adds Tolstoy, "which his instinct unfailingly . . . ." What is that instinct? Obviously it is not a biological drive; in fact, it is not an instinct at all. Here Tolstoy is permitting himself one of his touches of visible irony: Ivan Ilych has only one "instinct," that for knowing how far he can go within the world while still being thoroughly accepted by it, the "instinct" for opportunism. What Tolstoy is really pointing to is Ivan Ilych's social conformism.

With time Ivan Ilych rises in the world, taking a few steps up the bureaucratic ladder, and thereby comes to taste a little power. And power can taste sweet. As Tolstoy writes in one of his marvelously concentrated and subtle sentences:

> Ivan Ilych never abused his power; he tried on the contrary to soften its expression, but the consciousness of it *and of the possibility of softening its effect*, supplied the chief interest and attraction of his office.

I have italicized the key phrase, for, as Tolstoy suggests, it is often through our sense of being kindly and even indulgent to other people that we are confirmed in our sense of holding power over them.

So the narrative moves along, in gray sentences which stake out a gray life. Ivan Ilych need never question himself; why should a citizen so useful to society ever think of questioning himself? Nor does Tolstoy pass judgment on Ivan Ilych. That would undermine his own story; it would call into question the use of Ivan Ilych as a representative man. Take, for example, Tolstoy's description of how Ivan Ilych gets married:

> To say that Ivan Ilych married because he fell in love with Praskovya Fëdorovna and found that she sympathized with his views of life would be as incorrect as to say that he married because his social circle approved of the match. He was swayed by both these considerations: the marriage gave him personal satisfaction, and at the same time it was considered the right thing by the most highly placed of his associates.

The tone here is solemn, or perhaps mock-solemn, quite as if Tolstoy were a lawyer balancing the fine points of a case or a judge trying in his charge to the jury to be fair to both sides. *On the one hand, but then on the other* . . . . You have to shake yourself to remember that these deadly sentences are being written about what is supposed to be one of the great emotional climaxes of human existence. And it isn't as if Tolstoy were unable to write in any other way. In many of his novels and stories he writes with enormous zest and bravura, with emotional freedom, with great streaks of verbal color. But here the prose has to fit, in tone and tint, the nature of the material. And so there follows the next paragraph, a solitary sentence, terrible in its isolation:

> So Ivan Ilych got married.

And not such a bad marriage either. It brings him the conveniences that a sensible man wants: dinner at home, bed, children, the proprieties. In time the marriage settles into a condition of commonplace boredom, interrupted by occasional flares of passion, as if passion were becoming more and more a memory, less and less an experience:

> There remained only those rare periods of amorousness which still came to them at times but did not last long. These were islets at

which they anchored for a while and then again set out upon that ocean of veiled hostility which showed itself in their aloofness from one another. This aloofness might have grieved Ivan Ilych had he considered that it ought not to exist, *but he now regarded the position as normal* . . . . [Emphasis added—I. H.]

And so, in this limbo which is neither vivid life nor utter death, Ivan Ilych must learn to fill up his time. He does work that he regards as useful; at least, society regards it as useful, and that, to him, is a sufficient validation. His great triumph comes when he receives a promotion "two stages above his former colleagues." And then—but keep watching Tolstoy very carefully to see how shrewd he is—the marriage between Ivan Ilych and his wife improves a little too. They are now in the third stage of marriage. The first flare of excitement ended quickly; then came the stage of bewildered hostility, in which each asks, "Was it for this that we . . . ?" But now, in the third and surely the longest stage of most marriages, "he and his wife were at one in their aims and moreover saw so little of one another, they got on together better than they had done since the first years of marriage." Besides, an interest in emotions is gradually replaced by an interest in objects. Husband and wife become enamored of a house: when people reach the age at which they ought to reflect upon their own mortality, they decide to erect a structure of wood and stone that will be immortal. No longer tormented by sensual desires, with his vanity as a public man somewhat slackened, Ivan Ilych turns to interior decoration.

And then he becomes sick. A human being reaches his moment of supreme trial—for is not all of life a steady progression toward the day of our death?—and he cannot even get a hearing in his own family. The paragraph Tolstoy writes here, so free of decoration or pretense, is beyond praise:

He reached home and began to tell his wife about it. She listened, but in the middle of his account his daughter came in with her hat on, ready to go out with her mother. She sat down reluctantly to listen to this tedious story, but could not stand it long, and her mother too did not hear him to the end.

It is only now, with the appearance of his fatal sickness, that Ivan Ilych really begins to live, for only now does he begin to reflect upon the nature of his life. Slowly, against his own great resistance, Ivan Ilych comes to see—or at least to sense—how empty his life has been, how utterly he has been enslaved to habit, convention, and vanity. He experiences one of the most terrifying revelations possible to a human being: the feeling that there is not enough time left, that everything is now too late, that all has been wasted. And meanwhile he struggles against the knowledge of his forthcoming death. Like most men, he acquiesces in the petty deceptions by which doctors and relatives try to veil the truth, for even—perhaps especially—at the deathbed, life must somehow continue. But because he has been forced to abandon his usual routines, because he must now lie on his back encountering the pain his body causes him, Ivan Ilych does begin to discover the possibilities of the human condition.

The German novelist Thomas Mann expresses in one of his essays the kinship Tolstoy is tracing between the decay of the body and the growth of the spirit:

> Disease has two faces and a double relation to man and his human dignity. On the one hand it is hostile; by overstressing the physical, by throwing man back upon his own body, it has a dehumanizing effect. On the other hand, it is possible to feel about illness [that it is] a highly dignified human phenomenon.

Disease, that is, shocks us into awareness: we can no longer live as if we have an indefinite number of days before us. (This is why certain existentialist writers say that a constant sense of death is a necessary condition for a full life.) Disease shatters the non-life of our customary existence and thereby restores us to a condition of freedom: for we must now struggle to assert our humanity over the torment of physical pain. But at the same time disease destroys our freedom, no man can finally stop the decay of his own body.

How, concretely, does Ivan Ilych begin to discover the truth about his humanity? In the simplest but most fundamental ways. First, through a quickened perception of everything about him. He sees through the smallness of the people with whom he lives, but he sees, also, his own smallness: there is no ground for any feeling of superiority or any inclination to judgment. He confronts the truth about his own life:

> His marriage, a mere accident, then the disenchantment that followed it, his wife's bad breath and the sensuality and hypocrisy: then that deadly official life and those preoccupations about money, a year of it, and two, and ten, and twenty, and always the same thing. And the longer it lasted the more deadly it became.

"What," he asks himself, "if my whole life has really been wrong?" An unbearable thought. But what matters is not so much which conclusion he can come to—for in truth no single conclusion about a human life can possibly tell the whole truth. What matters is that he is now struggling for the truth.

It is a truth which he cannot grasp conceptually, or at least not merely in conceptual terms. In the unassuming, kindly warmth of the peasant boy Gerasim, who relieves Ivan Ilych's pain and keeps him company without complaint, he discovers the sustaining possibilities of human relationships:

> He felt comforted when Gerasim supported his legs (sometimes all night long) and refused to go to bed, saying: "Don't you worry, Ivan Ilych. I'll get sleep enough later on," or when he suddenly became familiar and exclaimed: "If you weren't sick it would be another matter, but as it is, why should I grudge a little trouble?" Gerasim alone did not lie; everything showed that he alone understood the facts of the case and did not consider it necessary to disguise them, but simply felt sorry for his emaciated and enfeebled master. Once when Ivan Ilych was sending him away he even said straight out: "We shall all of us die, so why should I grudge a little trouble?" —expressing the fact that he did not think his work burdensome, because he was doing it for a dying man and hoped someone would do the same for him when his time came.

Here again we must stress that the end of Ivan Ilych is pretty much the end of all men: torment, confusion, panic, regret, and finally a span of unbroken pain. One of Tolstoy's critics, Philip Rahv, has forcefully underscored this observation:

> it would be utterly pointless if we were to see Ivan Ilych as a special type and what happened to him as anything out of the ordinary. Ivan Ilych is Everyman, and the state of absolute solitude into which he falls as his life ebbs away is the existential norm, the inescapable realization of mortality.

But let us not exaggerate and thereby provide Ivan Ilych's end with an "uplifting" moral. The last three days of his life he struggles "in that black sack into which he was being thrust by an invisible, resistless force." He can neither escape back into life nor "get right into" the sack. The pretense that his life has been good keeps him from finally yielding to the relief of death, and only after he abandons his illusions—but still more: only after he realizes, thereby in a sense forgiving himself, that it does not really matter any more whether his life has been good—can Ivan Ilych surrender himself.

In looking back on this remarkable story, we can hardly suppose that it is through a particular device or technique that Tolstoy establishes his mastery over our imaginations. At the end, I think we must fall back upon an idea which in the criticism of literature ought to be advanced with great caution and only in a few instances: the idea that we have submitted ourselves to the voice of a man who has reached the innermost depths of experience, who has purchased his wisdom at a heavy price in suffering, and who has thereby burned out of his writing all vanity and pretension. For if we must conclude that each of us is Ivan Ilych, we must not forget that Tolstoy was but another version of Ivan Ilych. And from the pain of that recognition, the story has been written.

The Death of Ivan Ilych

I

During an interval in the Melvinski trial in the large building of the Law Courts, the members and public prosecutor met in Ivan Egorovich Shebek's private room, where the conversation turned on the celebrated Krasovski case. Fëdor Vasilievich warmly maintained that it was not subject to their jurisdiction, Ivan Egorovich maintained the contrary, while Peter Ivanovich, not having entered into the discussion as the start, took no part in it but looked through the *Gazette* which had just been handed in.

"Gentlemen," he said, "Ivan Ilych has died!"

"You don't say so!"

"Here, read it yourself," replied Peter Ivanovich, handing Fëdor Vasilievich the paper still damp from the press. Surrounded by a black border were the words: "Praskovya Fëdorovna Goloviná, with profound sorrow, informs relatives and friends of the demise of her beloved husband Ivan Ilych Golovin, Member of the Court of Justice, which occurred on February the 4th of this year 1882. The funeral will take place on Friday at one o'clock in the afternoon."

Ivan Ilych had been a colleague of the gentlemen present and was liked by them all. He had been ill for some weeks with an illness said to be incurable. His post had been kept open for him, but there had been conjectures that in case of his death Alexeev might receive his appointment, and that either Vinnikov or Shtabel would succeed Alexeev. So on receiving the news of Ivan Ilych's death the first thought of each of the gentlemen in that private room was of the changes and promotions it might occasion among themselves or their acquaintances.

"I shall be sure to get Shtabel's place or Vinnikov's," thought Fedor Vasilievich. "I was promised that long ago, and the promotion means an extra eight hundred rubles a year for me besides the allowance."

"Now I must apply for my brother-in-law's transfer from Kaluga," thought Peter Ivanovich. "My wife will be very glad, and then she won't be able to say that I never do anything for her relations."

"I thought he would never leave his bed again," said Peter Ivanovich aloud. "It's very sad."

"But what really was the matter with him?"

"The doctors couldn't say—at least they could, but each of them said something different. When last I saw him I thought he was getting better."

"And I haven't been to see him since the holidays. I always meant to go."

"Had he any property?"

"I think his wife had a little—but something quite trifling."

"We shall have to go to see her, but they live so terribly far away."

"Far away from you, you mean. Everything's far away from your place."

"You see, he never can forgive my living on the other side of the river," said Peter Ivanovich, smiling at Shebek. Then, still talking of the distances between different parts of the city, they returned to the Court.

Besides considerations as to the possible transfers and promotions likely to result from Ivan Ilych's death, the mere fact of the death of a near acquaintance aroused, as usual, in all who heard of it the complacent feeling that, "it is he who is dead and not I."

Each one thought or felt, "Well, he's dead but I'm alive!" But the more intimate of Ivan Ilych's acquaintances, his so-called friends, could not help thinking also that they would now have to fulfil the very tiresome demands of propriety by attending the funeral service and paying a visit of condolence to the widow.

Fëdor Vasilievich and Peter Ivanovich had been his nearest acquaintances. Peter Ivanovich had studied law with Ivan Ilych and had considered himself to be under obligations to him.

Having told his wife at dinner-time of Ivan Ilych's death and of his conjecture that it might be possible to get her brother transferred to their circuit, Peter Ivanovich sacrificed his usual nap, put on his evening clothes, and drove to Ivan Ilych's house.

At the entrance stood a carriage and two cabs. Leaning against the wall in the hall downstairs near the cloak-stand was a coffin-lid covered with cloth of gold, ornamented with gold cord and tassels, that had been polished up with metal powder. Two ladies in black were taking off their fur cloaks. Peter Ivanovich recognized one of them as Ivan Ilych's sister, but the other was a stranger to him. His colleague Schwartz was just coming downstairs, but on seeing Peter Ivanovich enter he stopped and winked at him, as if to say: "Ivan Ilych has made a mess of things—not like you and me."

Schwartz's face with his Piccadilly whiskers and his slim figure in evening dress had as usual an air of elegant solemnity which contrasted with the playfulness of his character and had a special piquancy here, or so it seemed to Peter Ivanovich.

Peter Ivanovich allowed the ladies to precede him and slowly followed them upstairs. Schwartz did not come down but remained where he was, and Peter Ivanovich understood that he wanted to arrange where they should play bridge that evening. The ladies went upstairs to the widow's room, and Schwartz with seriously compressed lips but a playful look in his eyes, indicated by a twist of his eyebrows the room to the right where the body lay.

Peter Ivanovich, like everyone else on such occasions, entered feeling uncertain what he would have to do. All he knew was that at such times it is always safe to cross oneself. But he was not quite sure whether one should make obeisances while doing so. He therefore adopted a middle course. On entering the room he began crossing himself and made a slight movement resembling a bow. At the same time, as far as the motion of his head and arm allowed, he surveyed the room. Two young men—apparently nephews, one of whom was a high-school pupil—were leaving the room, crossing themselves as they did so. An old woman was standing motionless, and a lady with strangely arched eyebrows was saying something to her in a whisper. A vigorous, resolute Church Reader, in a frock-coat, was reading something in a loud voice with an expression that precluded any contradiction. The butler's assistant, Gerasim, stepping lightly in front of Peter Ivanovich, was strewing something on the floor. Noticing this, Peter Ivanovich was immediately aware of a faint odour of a decomposing body.

The last time he had called on Ivan Ilych, Peter Ivanovich had seen Gerasim in the study. Ivan Ilych had been particularly fond of him and he was performing the duty of a sick nurse.

Peter Ivanovich continued to make the sign of the cross, slightly inclining his head in an intermediate direction between the coffin, the Reader, and the icons on the table in a corner of the room. Afterwards, when it seemed to him that this movement of his arm in crossing himself had gone on too long, he stopped and began to look at the corpse.

The dead man lay, as dead men always lie, in a specially heavy way, his rigid limbs sunk in the soft cushions of the coffin, with the head forever bowed on the pillow. His yellow waxen brow with bald patches over his sunken temples was thrust up in the way peculiar to the dead, the protruding nose seeming to press on the upper lip. He was much changed and had grown even thinner since Peter Ivanovich had last seen him, but, as is always the case with the dead, his face was handsomer and above all more dignified than when he was alive. The expression on the face said that what was necessary had been accomplished, and accomplished rightly. Besides this there was in that expression a reproach and a warning to the living. This warning seemed to Peter Ivanovich out of place, or at least not applicable to him. He felt a certain discomfort and so he hurriedly crossed himself once more and turned and went out of the door—too hurriedly and too regardless of propriety, as he himself was aware.

Schwartz was waiting for him in the adjoining room with legs spread wide apart and both hands toying with his top-hat behind his back. The mere sight of that playful, well-groomed, and elegant figure refreshed Peter Ivanovich. He felt that Schwartz was above all these happenings and would not surrender to any depressing influences. His very look said that this incident of a church service for Ivan Ilych could not be a sufficient reason for infringing the order of the session—in other words, that it would certainly not prevent his unwrapping a new pack of cards and shuffling them that evening while a footman placed four fresh candles on the table: in fact, that there was no reason for supposing that this incident would hinder their spending the evening agreeably. Indeed he said this in a whisper as Peter Ivanovich passed him, proposing that they should meet for a game at Fëdor Vasilievich's. But apparently Peter Ivanovich was not destined to play bridge that evening. Praskovya Fëdorovna (a short, fat woman who despite all efforts to the contrary had continued to broaden steadily from her shoulders downwards and who had the same extraordinarily arched eyebrows as the lady who had been standing by the coffin), dressed all in black, her head covered with lace, came out of her own room with some other ladies, conducted them to the room where the dead body lay, and said: "The service will begin immediately. Please go in."

Schwartz, making an indefinite bow, stood still, evidently neither accepting nor declining this invitation. Praskovya Fëdorovna, recognizing Peter Ivanovich, sighed, went close up to him, took his hand, and said: "I know you were a true friend of Ivan Ilych . . ." and looked at him awaiting some suitable response. And Peter Ivanovich knew that, just as it had been the right thing to cross himself in that room, so what he had to do here was to press her hand, sigh, and say, "Believe me. . . ." So he did all this and as he did it felt that the desired result had been achieved: that both he and she were touched.

"Come with me. I want to speak to you before it begins," said the widow. "Give me your arm."

Peter Ivanovich gave her his arm and they went to the inner rooms, passing Schwartz, who winked at Peter Ivanovich compassionately.

"That does for our bridge! Don't object if we find another player. Perhaps you can cut in when you do escape," said his playful look.

Peter Ivanovich sighed still more deeply and despondently, and Praskovya Fëdorovna pressed his arm gratefully. When they reached the drawing-room, upholstered in pink cretonne and lighted by a dim lamp, they sat down at the table—she on a sofa and Peter Ivanovich on a low pouffe, the springs of which yielded spasmodically under his weight. Praskovya Fëdorovna had been on the point of warning him to take another seat, but felt that such a warning was out of keeping with her present condition and so changed her mind. As he sat down on the pouffe Peter Ivanovich recalled how Ivan Ilych had arranged this room and had consulted him regarding this pink cretonne with green leaves. The whole room was full of furniture and knick-knacks, and on her way to the sofa the lace of the widow's black shawl caught on the carved edge of the table. Peter Ivanovich rose to detach it, and the springs of the pouffe, relieved of his weight, rose also and gave him a push. The widow began detaching her shawl herself, and Peter Ivanovich again sat down, suppressing the rebellious springs of the pouffe under him. But the widow had not quite freed herself and Peter Ivanovich got up again, and again the pouffe rebelled and even creaked. When this was all over she took out a clean cambric handkerchief and began to weep. The episode with the shawl and the struggle with the pouffe had cooled Peter Ivanovich's emotions and he sat there with a sullen look on his face. This awkward situation was interrupted by Sokolov, Ivan Ilych's butler, who came to report that the plot in the cemetery that Praskovya Fëdorovna had chosen would cost two hundred rubles. She stopped weeping and, looking at Peter Ivanovich with the air of a victim, remarked in French that it was very hard for her. Peter Ivanovich made a silent gesture signifying his full conviction that it must indeed be so.

"Please smoke," she said in a magnanimous yet crushed voice, and turned to discuss with Sokolov the price of the plot for the grave.

Peter Ivanovich while lighting his cigarette heard her inquiring very circumstantially into the prices of different plots in the cemetery and finally decide which she would take. When that was done she gave instructions about engaging the choir. Sokolov then left the room.

"I look after everything myself," she told Peter Ivanovich, shifting the albums that lay on the table; and noticing that the table was endangered by his cigarette-ash, she immediately passed him an ashtray, saying as she did so: "I consider it an affectation to say that my grief prevents my attending to practical affairs. On the contrary, if anything can—I won't say console me, but—distract me, it is seeing to everything concerning him." She again took out her handkerchief as if preparing to cry, but suddenly, as if mastering her feeling, she shook herself and began to speak calmly. "But there is something I want to talk to you about."

Peter Ivanovich bowed, keeping control of the springs of the pouffe, which immediately began quivering under him.

"He suffered terribly the last few days."

"Did he?" said Peter Ivanovich.

"Oh, terribly! He screamed unceasingly, not for minutes but for hours. For the last three days he screamed incessantly. It was unendurable. I cannot understand how I bore it; you could hear him three rooms off. Oh, what I have suffered!"

"Is it possible that he was conscious all that time?" asked Peter Ivanovich.

"Yes," she whispered. "To the last moment. He took leave of us a quarter of an hour before he died, and asked us to take Volodya away."

The thought of the sufferings of this man he had known so intimately, first as a merry little boy, then as a school-mate, and later as a grown-up colleague, suddenly struck Peter Ivanovich with horror, despite an unpleasant consciousness of his own and this woman's dissimulation. He again saw that brow, and that nose pressing down on the lip, and felt afraid for himself.

"Three days of frightful suffering and then death! Why, that might suddenly, at any time, happen to me," he thought, and for a moment felt terrified. But—he did not himself know how—the customary reflection at once occurred to him that this had happened to Ivan Ilych and not to him, and that it should not and could not happen to him, and that to think that it could would be yielding to depression which he ought not to do, as Schwartz's expression plainly showed. After which reflection Peter Ivanovich felt reassured, and began to ask with interest about the details of Ivan Ilych's death, as though death was an accident natural to Ivan Ilych but certainly not to himself.

After many details of the really dreadful physical sufferings Ivan Ilych had endured (which details he learnt only from the effect those sufferings had produced on Praskovya Fëdorovna's nerves) the widow apparently found it necessary to get to business.

"Oh, Peter Ivanovich, how hard it is! How terribly, terribly hard!" and she again began to weep.

Peter Ivanovich sighed and waited for her to finish blowing her nose. When she had done so he said, "Believe me . . ." and she again began talking and brought out what was evidently her chief concern with him—namely, to question him as to how she could obtain a grant of money from the government on the occasion of her husband's death. She made it appear that she was asking Peter Ivanovich's advice about her pension, but he soon saw that she already knew about that to the minutest detail, more even than he did himself. She knew how much could be got out of the government in consequence of her husband's death, but wanted to find out whether she could not possibly extract something more. Peter Ivanovich tried to think of some means of doing so, but after reflecting for a while and, out of propriety, condemning the government for its niggardliness, he said he thought that nothing more could be got. Then she sighed and evidently began to devise means of getting rid of her visitor. Noticing this, he put out his cigarette, rose, pressed her hand, and went out into the anteroom.

In the dining-room where the clock stood that Ivan Ilych had liked so much and had bought at an antique shop, Peter Ivanovich met a priest and a few acquaintances who had come to attend the service, and he recognized Ivan Ilych's daughter, a handsome young woman. She was in black and her slim figure appeared slimmer than ever. She had a gloomy, determined, almost angry expression, and bowed to Peter Ivanovich as though he were in some way to blame. Behind her, with the same offended look, stood a wealthy young man, an examining magistrate, whom Peter Ivanovich also knew and who was her fiancé, as he had heard. He bowed mournfully to them and was about to pass into the death-chamber, when from under the stairs appeared the figure of Ivan Ilych's schoolboy son, who was extremely like his father. He seemed a little Ivan Ilych, such as Peter Ivanovich remembered when they studied law together. His tear-stained eyes had in them the look that is seen in the eyes of boys of thirteen or fourteen who are not pure-minded. When he saw Peter Ivanovich he scowled morosely and shamefacedly. Peter Ivanovich nodded to him and entered the death-chamber. The service began: candles, groans, incense, tears, and sobs. Peter Ivanovich stood looking gloomily down at his feet. He did not look once at the dead man, did not yield to any depressing influence, and was one of the first to leave the room. There was no one in the anteroom, but Gerasim darted out of the dead man's room, rummaged with his strong hands among the fur coats to find Peter Ivanovich's, and helped him on with it.

"Well, friend Gerasim," said Peter Ivanovich, so as to say something. "It's a sad affair, isn't it?"

"It's God's will. We shall all come to it some day," said Gerasim, displaying his teeth—the even, white teeth of a healthy peasant—and, like a man in the thick of urgent work, he briskly opened the front door, called the coachman, helped Peter Ivanovich into the sledge, and sprang back to the porch as if in readiness for what he had to do next.

Peter Ivanovich found the fresh air particularly pleasant after the smell of incense, the dead body, and carbolic acid.

"Where to, sir?" asked the coachman.

"It's not too late even now. . . . I'll call round on Fëdor Vasilievich."

He accordingly drove there and found them just finishing the first rubber, so that it was quite convenient for him to cut in.

II

Ivan Ilych's life had been most simple and most ordinary and therefore most terrible.

He had been a member of the Court of Justice, and died at the age of forty-five. His father had been an official who after serving in various ministries and departments in Petersburg had made the sort of career which brings men to positions from which by reason of their long service they cannot be dismissed, though they are obviously unfit to hold any responsible position, and for whom therefore posts are specially created, which though fictitious carry salaries of from six to ten thousand rubles that are not fictitious, and in receipt of which they live on to a great age.

Such was the Privy Councillor and superfluous member of various superfluous institutions, Ilya Epimovich Golovin.

He had three sons, of whom Ivan Ilych was the second. The eldest son was following in his father's footsteps only in another department, and was already approaching that stage in the service at which a similar sinecure would be reached. The third son was a failure. He had ruined his prospects in a number of positions and was now serving in the railway department. His father and brothers, and still more their wives, not merely disliked meeting him, but avoided remembering his existence unless compelled to do so. His sister had married Baron Greff, a Petersburg official of her father's type. Ivan Ilych was *le phénix de la famille* as people said. He was neither as cold and formal as his elder brother nor as wild as the younger, but was a happy mean between them—an intelligent, polished, lively, and agreeable man. He had studied with his younger brother at the School of Law, but the latter had failed to complete the course and was expelled when he was in the fifth class. Ivan Ilych finished the course well. Even when he was at the School of Law he was just what he remained for the rest of his life: a capable, cheerful, good-natured, and sociable man, though strict in the fulfilment of what he considered to be his duty: and he considered his duty to be what was so considered by those in authority. Neither as a boy nor as a man was he a toady, but from early youth was by nature attracted to people of high station as a fly is drawn to the light, assimilating their ways and views of life and establishing friendly relations with them. All the enthusiasms of childhood and youth passed without leaving much trace on him; he succumbed to sensuality, to vanity, and lat- terly among the highest classes to liberalism, but always within limits which his instinct unfailingly indicated to him as correct.

At school he had done things which had formerly seemed to him very horrid and made him feel disgusted with himself when he did them; but when later on he saw that such actions were done by peo- ple of good position and that they did not regard them as wrong, he was able not exactly to regard them as right, but to forget about them entirely or not be at all troubled at remembering them.

Having graduated from the School of Law and qualified for the tenth rank of the civil service, and having received money from his father for his equipment, Ivan Ilych ordered himself clothes at Scharmer's, the fashionable tailor, hung a medallion inscribed *res- pice finem* [1] on his watch-chain, took leave of his professor and the prince who was patron of the school, had a farewell dinner with his comrades at Donon's first-class restaurant, and with his new and fashionable portmanteau, linen, clothes, shaving and other toilet ap- pliances, and a travelling rug all purchased at the best shops, he set off for one of the provinces where, through his father's influence, he had been attached to the Governor as an official for special service.

In the province Ivan Ilych soon arranged as easy and agreeable a position for himself as he had had at the School of Law. He per- formed his official tasks, made his career, and at the same time amused himself pleasantly and decorously. Occasionally he paid offi- cial visits to country districts, where he behaved with dignity both to his superiors and inferiors, and performed the duties entrusted to him, which related chiefly to the sectarians, [2] with an exactness and incorruptible honesty of which he could not but feel proud.

In official matters, despite his youth and taste for frivolous gaiety, he was exceedingly reserved, punctilious, and even severe; but in society he was often amusing and witty, and always good-natured, correct in his manner, and *bon enfant*, as the Governor and his

---

[1] "Reflect on your end."
[2] Dissident Christian sects that had broken off from the Russian Orthodox Church.

wife—with whom he was like one of the family—used to say of him.

In the province he had an affair with a lady who made advances to the elegant young lawyer, and there was also a milliner; and there were carousals with aides-de-camp who visited the district, and after-supper visits to a certain outlying street of doubtful reputation; and there was too some obsequiousness to his chief and even to his chief's wife, but all this was done with such a tone of good breeding that no hard names could be applied to it. It all came under the heading of the French saying: *"Il faut que jeunesse se passe."* [3] It was all done with clean hands, in clean linen, with French phrases, and above all among people of the best society and consequently with the approval of people of rank.

So Ivan Ilych served for five years and then came a change in his official life. The new and reformed judicial institutions were introduced, and new men were needed. Ivan Ilych became such a new man. He was offered the post of examining magistrate, and he accepted it though the post was in another province and obliged him to give up the connexions he had formed and to make new ones. His friends met to give him a send-off; they had a group-photograph taken and presented him with a silver cigarette-case, and he set off to his new post.

As examining magistrate Ivan Ilych was just as *comme il faut* and decorous a man, inspiring general respect and capable of separating his official duties from his private life, as he had been when acting as an official on special service. His duties now as examining magistrate were far more interesting and attractive than before. In his former position it had been pleasant to wear an undress uniform made by Scharmer, and to pass through the crowd of petitioners and officials who were timorously awaiting an audience with the Governor, and who envied him as with free and easy gait he went straight into his chief's private room to have a cup of tea and a cigarette with him. But not many people had been directly dependent on him—only police officials and the sectarians when he went on special missions—and he liked to treat them politely, almost as comrades, as if he were letting them feel that he who had the power to crush them was treating them in this simple, friendly way. There were then but few such people. But now, as an examining magistrate, Ivan Ilych felt that everyone without exception, even the most

3 "Youth must have its fling."

important and self-satisfied, was in his power, and that he need only write a few words on a sheet of paper with a certain heading, and this or that important, self-satisfied person would be brought before him in the role of an accused person or a witness, and if he did not choose to allow him to sit down, would have to stand before him and answer his questions. Ivan Ilych never abused his power; he tried on the contrary to soften its expression, but the consciousness of it and of the possibility of softening its effect, supplied the chief interest and attraction of his office. In his work itself, especially in his examinations, he very soon acquired a method of eliminating all considerations irrelevant to the legal aspect of the case, and reducing even the most complicated case to a form in which it would be presented on paper only in its externals, completely excluding his personal opinion of the matter, while above all observing every prescribed formality. The work was new and Ivan Ilych was one of the first men to apply the new Code of 1864.[4]

On taking up the post of examining magistrate in a new town, he made new acquaintances and connexions, placed himself on a new footing, and assumed a somewhat different tone. He took up an attitude of rather dignified aloofness towards the provincial authorities, but picked out the best circle of legal gentlemen and wealthy gentry living in the town and assumed a tone of slight dissatisfaction with the government, of moderate liberalism, and of enlightened citizenship. At the same time, without at all altering the elegance of his toilet, he ceased shaving his chin and allowed his beard to grow as it pleased.

Ivan Ilych settled down very pleasantly in this new town. The society there, which inclined towards opposition to the Governor, was friendly, his salary was larger, and he began to play *vint*,[5] which he found added not a little to the pleasure of life, for he had a capacity for cards, played good-humouredly, and calculated rapidly and astutely, so that he usually won.

After living there for two years he met his future wife, Praskovya Fëdorovna Mikhel, who was the most attractive, clever, and brilliant girl of the set in which he moved, and among other amusements and relaxations from his labours as examining magistrate, Ivan Ilych established light and playful relations with her.

While he had been an official on special service he had been ac-

---

[4] The emancipation of the serfs in 1861 was followed by a thorough all-round reform of judicial proceedings. [TRANS.]
[5] A form of bridge. [TRANS.]

customed to dance, but now as an examining magistrate it was exceptional for him to do so. If he danced now, he did it as if to show that though he served under the reformed order of things, and had reached the fifth official rank, yet when it came to dancing he could do it better than most people. So at the end of an evening he sometimes danced with Praskovya Fëdorovna, and it was chiefly during these dances that he captivated her. She fell in love with him. Ivan Ilych had at first no definite intention of marrying, but when the girl fell in love with him he said to himself: "Really, why shouldn't I marry?"

Praskovya Fëdorovna came of a good family, was not bad-looking, and had some little property. Ivan Ilych might have aspired to a more brilliant match, but even this was good. He had his salary, and she, he hoped, would have an equal income. She was well connected, and was a sweet, pretty, and thoroughly correct young woman. To say that Ivan Ilych married because he fell in love with Praskovya Fëdorovna and found that she sympathized with his views of life would be as incorrect as to say that he married because his social circle approved of the match. He was swayed by both these considerations: the marriage gave him personal satisfaction, and at the same time it was considered the right thing by the most highly placed of his associates.

So Ivan Ilych got married.

The preparations for marriage and the beginning of married life, with its conjugal caresses, the new furniture, new crockery, and new linen, were very pleasant until his wife became pregnant—so that Ivan Ilych had begun to think that marriage would not impair the easy, agreeable, gay, and always decorous character of his life, approved of by society and regarded by himself as natural, but would even improve it. But from the first months of his wife's pregnancy, something new, unpleasant, depressing, and unseemly, and from which there was no way of escape, unexpectedly showed itself.

His wife, without any reason—*de gaieté de cœur* as Ivan Ilych expressed it to himself—began to disturb the pleasure and propriety of their life. She began to be jealous without any cause, expected him to devote his whole attention to her, found fault with everything, and made coarse and ill-mannered scenes.

At first Ivan Ilych hoped to escape from the unpleasantness of this state of affairs by the same easy and decorous relation to life that had served him heretofore: he tried to ignore his wife's disagreeable moods, continued to live in his usual easy and pleasant way, invited friends to his house for a game of cards, and also tried going out to his club or spending his evenings with friends. But one day his wife began upbraiding him so vigorously, using such coarse words, and continued to abuse him every time he did not fulfil her demands, so resolutely and with such evident determination not to give way till he submitted—that is, till he stayed at home and was bored just as she was—that he became alarmed. He now realized that matrimony—at any rate with Praskovya Fëdorovna—was not always conducive to the pleasures and amenities of life, but on the contrary often infringed both comfort and propriety, and that he must therefore entrench himself against such infringement. And Ivan Ilych began to seek for means of doing so. His official duties were the one thing that imposed upon Praskovya Fëdorovna, and by means of his official work and the duties attached to it he began struggling with his wife to secure his own independence.

With the birth of their child, the attempts to feed it and the various failures in doing so, and with the real and imaginary illnesses of mother and child, in which Ivan Ilych's sympathy was demanded but about which he understood nothing, the need of securing for himself an existence outside his family life became still more imperative.

As his wife grew more irritable and exacting and Ivan Ilych transferred the centre of gravity of his life more and more to his official work, so did he grow to like his work better and become more ambitious than before.

Very soon, within a year of his wedding, Ivan Ilych had realized that marriage, though it may add some comforts to life, is in fact a very intricate and difficult affair towards which in order to perform one's duty, that is, to lead a decorous life approved of by society, one must adopt a definite attitude just as towards one's official duties.

And Ivan Ilych evolved such an attitude towards married life. He only required of it those conveniences—dinner at home, housewife, and bed—which it could give him, and above all that propriety of external forms required by public opinion. For the rest he looked for light-hearted pleasure and propriety, and was very thankful when he found them, but if he met with antagonism and querulousness he at once retired into his separate fenced-off world of official duties, where he found satisfaction.

Ivan Ilych was esteemed a good official, and after three years was made Assistant Public Prosecutor. His new duties, their importance, the possibility of indicting and imprisoning anyone he chose, the publicity his speeches received, and the success he had in all these things, made his work still more attractive.

More children came. His wife became more and more querulous and ill-tempered, but the attitude Ivan Ilych had adopted towards his home life rendered him almost impervious to her grumbling.

After seven years' service in that town he was transferred to another province as Public Prosecutor. They moved, but were short of money and his wife did not like the place they moved to. Though the salary was higher the cost of living was greater, besides which two of their children died and family life became still more unpleasant for him.

Praskovya Fëdorovna blamed her husband for every inconvenience they encountered in their new home. Most of the conversations between husband and wife, especially as to the children's education, led to topics which recalled former disputes, and those disputes were apt to flare up again at any moment. There remained only those rare periods of amorousness which still came to them at times but did not last long. These were islets at which they anchored for a while and then again set out upon that ocean of veiled hostility which showed itself in their aloofness from one another. This aloofness might have grieved Ivan Ilych had he considered that it ought not to exist, but he now regarded the position as normal, and even made it the goal at which he aimed in family life. His aim was to free himself more and more from those unpleasantnesses and to give them a semblance of harmlessness and propriety. He attained this by spending less and less time with his family, and when obliged to be at home he tried to safeguard his position by the presence of outsiders. The chief thing however was that he had his official duties. The whole interest of his life now centred in the official world and that interest absorbed him. The consciousness of his power, being able to ruin anybody he wished to ruin, the importance, even the external dignity of his entry into court, or meetings with his subordinates, his success with superiors and inferiors, and above all his masterly handling of cases, of which he was conscious—all this gave him pleasure and filled his life, together with chats with his colleagues, dinners, and bridge. So that on the whole Ivan Ilych's life continued to flow as he considered it should do—pleasantly and properly.

So things continued for another seven years. His eldest daughter was already sixteen, another child had died, and only one son was left, a schoolboy and a subject of dissension. Ivan Ilych wanted to put him in the School of Law, but to spite him Praskovya Fëdorovna entered him at the High School. The daughter had been educated at home and had turned out well: the boy did not learn badly either.

III

So Ivan Ilych lived for seventeen years after his marriage. He was already a Public Prosecutor of long standing, and had declined several proposed transfers while awaiting a more desirable post, when an unanticipated and unpleasant occurrence quite upset the peaceful course of his life. He was expecting to be offered the post of presiding judge in a University town, but Happe somehow came to the front and obtained the appointment instead. Ivan Ilych became irritable, reproached Happe, and quarrelled both with him and with his immediate superiors—who became colder to him and again passed him over when other appointments were made.

This was in 1880, the hardest year of Ivan Ilych's life. It was then that it became evident on the one hand that his salary was insufficient for them to live on, and on the other that he had been forgotten, and not only this, but that what was for him the greatest and most cruel injustice appeared to others a quite ordinary occurrence. Even his father did not consider it his duty to help him. Ivan Ilych felt himself abandoned by everyone, and that they regarded his position with a salary of 3,500 rubles as quite normal and even fortunate. He alone knew that with the consciousness of the injustices done him, with his wife's incessant nagging, and with the debts he had contracted by living beyond his means, his position was far from normal.

In order to save money that summer he obtained leave of absence and went with his wife to live in the country at her brother's place.

In the country, without his work, he experienced *ennui* for the first time in his life, and not only *ennui* but intolerable depression, and he decided that it was impossible to go on living like that, and that it was necessary to take energetic measures.

Having passed a sleepless night pacing up and down the veranda, he decided to go to Petersburg and bestir himself, in order to punish those who had failed to appreciate him and to get transferred to another ministry.

Next day, despite many protests from his wife and her brother, he started for Petersburg with the sole object of obtaining a post with a salary of five thousand rubles a year. He was no longer bent on any particular department, or tendency, or kind of activity. All he now wanted was an appointment to another post with a salary of five thousand rubles, either in the administration, in the banks, with the railways, in one of the Empress Marya's Institutions, or even in the customs—but it had to carry with it a salary of five thousand rubles and be in a ministry other than that in which they had failed to appreciate him.

And this quest of Ivan Ilych's was crowned with remarkable and unexpected success. At Kursk an acquaintance of his, F. I. Ilyin, got into the first-class carriage, sat down beside Ivan Ilych, and told him of a telegram just received by the Governor of Kursk announcing that a change was about to take place in the ministry: Peter Ivanovich was to be superseded by Ivan Semënovich.

The proposed change, apart from its significance for Russia, had a special significance for Ivan Ilych, because by bringing forward a new man, Peter Petrovich, and consequently his friend Zachar Ivanovich, it was highly favourable for Ivan Ilych, since Zachar Ivanovich was a friend and colleague of his.

In Moscow this news was confirmed, and on reaching Petersburg Ivan Ilych found Zachar Ivanovich and received a definite promise of an appointment in his former department of Justice.

A week later he telegraphed to his wife: "Zachar in Miller's place. I shall receive appointment on presentation of report."

Thanks to this change of personnel, Ivan Ilych had unexpectedly obtained an appointment in his former ministry which placed him two stages above his former colleagues besides giving him five thousand rubles salary and three thousand five hundred rubles for expenses connected with his removal. All his ill humour towards his former enemies and the whole department vanished, and Ivan Ilych was completely happy.

He returned to the country more cheerful and contented than he had been for a long time. Praskovya Fëdorovna also cheered up and a truce was arranged between them. Ivan Ilych told of how he had been fêted by everybody in Petersburg, how all those who had been his enemies were put to shame and now fawned on him, how envious they were of his appointment, and how much everybody in Petersburg had liked him.

Praskovya Fëdorovna listened to all this and appeared to believe it. She did not contradict anything, but only made plans for their life in the town to which they were going. Ivan Ilych saw with delight that these plans were his plans, that he and his wife agreed, and that, after a stumble, his life was regaining its due and natural character of pleasant lightheartedness and decorum.

Ivan Ilych had come back for a short time only, for he had to take up his new duties on the 10th of September. Moreover, he needed time to settle into the new place, to move all his belongings from the province, and to buy and order many additional things: in a word, to make such arrangements as he had resolved on, which were almost exactly what Praskovya Fëdorovna too had decided on.

Now that everything had happened so fortunately, and that he and his wife were at one in their aims and moreover saw so little of one another, they got on together better than they had done since the first years of marriage. Ivan Ilych had thought of taking his family away with him at once, but the insistence of his wife's brother and her sister-in-law, who had suddenly become particularly amiable and friendly to him and his family, induced him to depart alone.

So he departed, and the cheerful state of mind induced by his success and by the harmony between his wife and himself, the one intensifying the other, did not leave him. He found a delightful house, just the thing both he and his wife had dreamt of. Spacious, lofty reception rooms in the old style, a convenient and dignified study, rooms for his wife and daughter, a study for his son—it might have been specially built for them. Ivan Ilych himself superintended the arrangements, chose the wallpapers, supplemented the furniture (preferably with antiques which he considered particularly *comme il faut*), and supervised the upholstering. Everything progressed and progressed and approached the ideal he had set himself: even when things were only half completed they exceeded his expectations. He saw what a refined and elegant character, free from vulgarity, it would all have when it was ready. On falling asleep he pictured to himself how the reception-room would look. Looking at the yet unfinished drawing-room he could see the fireplace, the screen, the what-not, the little chairs dotted here and there, the dishes and plates on the walls, and the bronzes, as they would be when everything was in place. He was pleased by the thought of how his wife and daughter, who shared his taste in this matter, would be impressed by it. They were certainly not expecting as much. He had been particularly successful in finding, and buying cheaply, antiques which gave a particularly aristocratic character to the whole place.

But in his letters he intentionally understated everything in order to be able to surprise them. All this so absorbed him that his new duties—though he liked his official work—interested him less than he had expected. Sometimes he even had moments of absent-mindedness during the Court Sessions, and would consider whether he should have straight or curved cornices for his curtains. He was so interested in it all that he often did things himself, rearranging the furniture, or rehanging the curtains. Once when mounting a step-ladder to show the upholsterer, who did not understand, how he wanted the hangings draped, he made a false step and slipped, but being a strong and agile man he clung on and only knocked his side against the knob of the window frame. The bruised place was painful but the pain soon passed, and he felt particularly bright and well just then. He wrote: "I feel fifteen years younger." He thought he would have everything ready by September, but it dragged on till mid-October. But the result was charming not only in his eyes but to everyone who saw it.

In reality it was just what is usually seen in the houses of people of moderate means who want to appear rich, and therefore succeed only in resembling others like themselves: there were damasks, dark wood, plants, rugs, and dull and polished bronzes—all the things people of a certain class have in order to resemble other people of that class. His house was so like the others that it would never have been noticed, but to him it all seemed to be quite exceptional. He was very happy when he met his family at the station and brought them to the newly furnished house all lit up, where a footman in a white tie opened the door into the hall decorated with plants, and when they went on into the drawing-room and the study uttering exclamations of delight. He conducted them everywhere, drank in their praises eagerly, and beamed with pleasure. At tea that evening, when Praskovya Fëdorovna among other things asked him about his fall, he laughed and showed them how he had gone flying and had frightened the upholsterer.

"It's a good thing I'm a bit of an athlete. Another man might have been killed, but I merely knocked myself, just here; it hurts when it's touched, but it's passing off already—it's only a bruise."

So they began living in their new home—in which, as always happens, when they got thoroughly settled in they found they were just one room short—and with the increased income, which as always was just a little (some five hundred rubles) too little, but it was all very nice.

Things went particularly well at first, before everything was finally arranged and while something had still to be done: this thing bought, that thing ordered, another thing moved, and something else adjusted. Though there were some disputes between husband and wife, they were both so well satisfied and had so much to do that it all passed off without any serious quarrels. When nothing was left to arrange it became rather dull and something seemed to be lacking, but they were then making acquaintances, forming habits, and life was growing fuller.

Ivan Ilych spent his mornings at the law courts and came home to dinner, and at first he was generally in a good humour, though he occasionally became irritable just on account of his house. (Every spot on the tablecloth or the upholstery, and every broken window-blind string, irritated him. He had devoted so much trouble to arranging it all that every disturbance of it distressed him.) But on the whole his life ran its course as he believed life should do: easily, pleasantly, and decorously.

He got up at nine, drank his coffee, read the paper, and then put on his undress uniform and went to the law courts. There the harness in which he worked had already been stretched to fit him and he donned it without a hitch: petitioners, inquiries at the chancery, the chancery itself, and the sittings public and administrative. In all this the thing was to exclude everything fresh and vital, which always disturbs the regular course of official business, and to admit only official relations with people, and then only on official grounds. A man would come, for instance, wanting some information. Ivan Ilych, as one in whose sphere the matter did not lie, would have nothing to do with him: but if the man had some business with him in his official capacity, something that could be expressed on officially stamped paper, he would do everything, positively everything he could within the limits of such relations, and in doing so would maintain the semblance of friendly human relations, that is, would observe the courtesies of life. As soon as the official relations ended, so did everything else. Ivan Ilych possessed this capacity to separate his real life from the official side of affairs and not mix the two, in the highest degree, and by long practice and natural aptitude had brought it to such a pitch that sometimes, in the manner of a virtuoso, he would even allow himself to let the human and official relations mingle. He let himself do this just because he felt that he could at any time he chose resume the strictly official attitude again and drop the human relation. And he did it all easily, pleasantly, correctly, and even artistically. In the intervals between the sessions he smoked, drank tea, chatted a little about politics, a little about general topics, a little about cards, but most of all about official appointments. Tired, but with the feelings of a virtuoso—one of the first violins who has played his part in an orchestra with precision —he would return home to find that his wife and daughter had been out paying calls, or had a visitor, and that his son had been to school, had done his homework with his tutor, and was duly learning what is taught at High Schools. Everything was as it should be. After dinner, if they had no visitors, Ivan Ilych sometimes read a book that was being much discussed at the time, and in the evening settled down to work, that is, read official papers, compared the depositions of witnesses, and noted paragraphs of the Code applying to them. This was neither dull nor amusing. It was dull when he might have been playing bridge, but if no bridge was available it was at any rate better than doing nothing or sitting with his wife. Ivan Ilych's chief pleasure was giving little dinners to which he invited men and women of good social position, and just as his drawing-room resembled all other drawing-rooms so did his enjoyable little parties resemble all other such parties.

Once they even gave a dance. Ivan Ilych enjoyed it and everything went off well, except that it led to a violent quarrel with his wife about the cakes and sweets. Praskovya Fëdorovna had made her own plans, but Ivan Ilych insisted on getting everything from an expensive confectioner and ordered too many cakes, and the quarrel occurred because some of those cakes were left over and the confectioner's bill came to forty-five rubles. It was a great and disagreeable quarrel. Praskovya Fëderovna called him "a fool and an imbecile," and he clutched at his head and made angry allusions to divorce.

But the dance itself had been enjoyable. The best people were there, and Ivan Ilych had danced with Princess Trufonova, a sister of the distinguished founder of the Society "Bear my Burden."

The pleasures connected with his work were pleasures of ambition; his social pleasures were those of vanity; but Ivan Ilych's greatest pleasure was playing bridge. He acknowledged that whatever disagreeable incident happened in his life, the pleasure that beamed like a ray of light above everything else was to sit down to bridge with good players, not noisy partners, and of course to four-handed bridge (with five players it was annoying to have to stand out, though one pretended not to mind), to play a clever and serious game (when the cards allowed it), and then to have supper and drink a glass of wine. After a game of bridge, especially if he had won a little (to win a large sum was unpleasant), Ivan Ilych went to bed in specially good humour.

So they lived. They formed a circle of acquaintances among the best people and were visited by people of importance and by young folk. In their views as to their acquaintances, husband, wife, and daughter were entirely agreed, and tacitly and unanimously kept at arm's length and shook off the various shabby friends and relations who, with much show of affection, gushed into the drawing-room with its Japanese plates on the walls. Soon these shabby friends ceased to obtrude themselves and only the best people remained in the Golovins' set.

Young men made up to Lisa, and Petrishchev, an examining magistrate and Dmitri Ivanovich Petrishchev's son and sole heir, began to be so attentive to her that Ivan Ilych had already spoken to Praskovya Fëdorovna about it, and considered whether they should not arrange a party for them, or get up some private theatricals.

So they lived, and all went well, without change, and life flowed pleasantly.

IV

They were all in good health. It could not be called ill health if Ivan Ilych sometimes said that he had a queer taste in his mouth and felt some discomfort in his left side.

But this discomfort increased and, though not exactly painful, grew into a sense of pressure in his side accompanied by ill humour. And his irritability became worse and worse and began to mar the agreeable, easy, and correct life that had established itself in the Golovin family. Quarrels between husband and wife became more and more frequent, and soon the ease and amenity disappeared and even the decorum was barely maintained. Scenes again became frequent, and very few of those islets remained on which husband and wife could meet without an explosion. Praskovya Fëdorovna now had good reason to say that her husband's temper was trying. With characteristic exaggeration she said he had always had a dreadful temper, and that it had needed all her good nature to put up with it for twenty years. It was true that now the quarrels were started by him. His bursts of temper always came just before dinner, often just as he began to eat his soup. Sometimes he noticed that a plate or dish was chipped, or the food was not right, or his son put his elbow on the table, or his daughter's hair was not done as he liked it, and for all this he blamed Praskovya Fëdorovna. At first she retorted and said disagreeable things to him, but once or twice he fell into such a rage at the beginning of dinner that she realized it was due to some physical derangement brought on by taking food, and so she restrained herself and did not answer, but only hurried to get the dinner over. She regarded this self-restraint as highly praiseworthy. Having come to the conclusion that her husband had a dreadful temper and made her life miserable, she began to feel sorry for herself, and the more she pitied herself the more she hated her husband. She began to wish he would die; yet she did not want him to die because then his salary would cease. And this irritated her against him still more. She considered herself dreadfully unhappy just because not even his death could save her, and though she concealed her exasperation, that hidden exasperation of hers increased his irritation also.

After one scene in which Ivan Ilych had been particularly unfair and after which he had said in explanation that he certainly was irritable but that it was due to his not being well, she said that if he was ill it should be attended to, and insisted on his going to see a celebrated doctor.

He went. Everything took place as he had expected and as it always does. There was the usual waiting and the important air assumed by the doctor, with which he was so familiar (resembling that which he himself assumed in court), and the sounding and listening, and the questions which called for answers that were foregone conclusions and were evidently unnecessary, and the look of importance which implied that "if only you put yourself in our hands we will arrange everything—we know indubitably how it has to be done, always in the same way for everybody alike." It was all just as it was in the law courts. The doctor put on just the same air towards him as he himself put on towards an accused person.

The doctor said that so-and-so indicated that there was so-and-so inside the patient, but if the investigation of so-and-so did not confirm this, then he must assume that and that. If he assumed that and that, then . . . and so on. To Ivan Ilych only one question was important: was his case serious or not? But the doctor ignored that inappropriate question. From his point of view it was not the one under consideration, the real question was to decide between a floating kidney, chronic catarrh, or appendicitis. It was not a question of

Ivan Ilych's life or death, but one between a floating kidney and appendicitis. And that question the doctor solved brilliantly, as it seemed to Ivan Ilych, in favour of the appendix, with the reservation that should an examination of the urine give fresh indications the matter would be reconsidered. All this was just what Ivan Ilych had himself brilliantly accomplished a thousand times in dealing with men on trial. The doctor summed up just as brilliantly, looking over his spectacles triumphantly and even gaily at the accused. From the doctor's summing up Ivan Ilych concluded that things were bad, but that for the doctor, and perhaps for everybody else, it was a matter of indifference, though for him it was bad. And this conclusion struck him painfully, arousing in him a great feeling of pity for himself and of bitterness towards the doctor's indifference to a matter of such importance.

He said nothing of this, but rose, placed the doctor's fee on the table, and remarked with a sigh: "We sick people probably often put inappropriate questions. But tell me, in general, is this complaint dangerous, or not? . . ."

The doctor looked at him sternly over his spectacles with one eye, as if to say: "Prisoner, if you will not keep to the questions put to you, I shall be obliged to have you removed from the court."

"I have already told you what I consider necessary and proper. The analysis may show something more." And the doctor bowed.

Ivan Ilych went out slowly, seated himself disconsolately in his sledge, and drove home. All the way home he was going over what the doctor had said, trying to translate those complicated, obscure, scientific phrases into plain language and find in them an answer to the question: "Is my condition bad? Is it very bad? Or is there as yet nothing much wrong?" And it seemed to him that the meaning of what the doctor had said was that it was very bad. Everything in the streets seemed depressing. The cabmen, the houses, the passers-by, and the shops, were dismal. His ache, this dull gnawing ache that never ceased for a moment, seemed to have acquired a new and more serious significance from the doctor's dubious remarks. Ivan Ilych now watched it with a new and oppressive feeling.

He reached home and began to tell his wife about it. She listened, but in the middle of his account his daughter came in with her hat on, ready to go out with her mother. She sat down reluctantly to listen to this tedious story, but could not stand it long, and her mother too did not hear him to the end.

"Well, I am very glad," she said. "Mind now to take your medicine regularly. Give me the prescription and I'll send Gerasim to the chemist's." And she went to get ready to go out.

While she was in the room Ivan Ilych had hardly taken time to breathe, but he sighed deeply when she left it.

"Well," he thought, "perhaps it isn't so bad after all."

He began taking his medicine and following the doctor's directions, which had been altered after the examination of the urine. But then it happened that there was a contradiction between the indications drawn from the examination of the urine and the symptoms that showed themselves. It turned out that what was happening differed from what the doctor had told him, and that he had either forgotten, or blundered, or hidden something from him. He could not, however, be blamed for that, and Ivan Ilych still obeyed his orders implicitly and at first derived some comfort from doing so.

From the time of his visit to the doctor, Ivan Ilych's chief occupation was the exact fulfilment of the doctor's instructions regarding hygiene and the taking of medicine, and the observation of his pain and his excretions. His chief interests came to be people's ailments and people's health. When sickness, deaths, or recoveries were mentioned in his presence, especially when the illness resembled his own, he listened with agitation which he tried to hide, asked questions, and applied what he heard to his own case.

The pain did not grow less, but Ivan Ilych made efforts to force himself to think that he was better. And he could do this so long as nothing agitated him. But as soon as he had any unpleasantness with his wife, any lack of success in his official work, or held bad cards at bridge, he was at once acutely sensible of his disease. He had formerly borne such mischances, hoping soon to adjust what was wrong, to master it and attain success, or make a grand slam. But now every mischance upset him and plunged him into despair. He would say to himself: "There now, just as I was beginning to get better and the medicine had begun to take effect, comes this accursed misfortune, or unpleasantness. . . ." And he was furious with the mishap, or with the people who were causing the unpleasantness and killing him, for he felt that this fury was killing him but could not restrain it. One would have thought that it should have been clear to him that this exasperation with circumstances and people aggravated his illness, and that he ought therefore to ignore unpleasant occurrences. But he drew the very opposite conclusion: he said that he needed peace, and he watched for everything that might disturb it and became irritable at the slightest infringement of it. His condition was rendered worse by the fact that he read medical books and consulted doctors. The progress of his disease was so gradual that he could deceive himself when comparing one day with another—the difference was so slight. But when he consulted the doctors it seemed to him that he was getting worse, and even very rapidly. Yet despite this he was continually consulting them.

That month he went to see another celebrity, who told him almost the same as the first had done but put his questions rather differently, and the interview with this celebrity only increased Ivan Ilych's doubts and fears. A friend of a friend of his, a very good doctor, diagnosed his illness again quite differently from the others, and though he predicted recovery, his questions and suppositions bewildered Ivan Ilych still more and increased his doubts. A homœopathist diagnosed the disease in yet another way, and prescribed medicine which Ivan Ilych took secretly for a week. But after a week, not feeling any improvement and having lost confidence both in the former doctor's treatment and in this one's, he became still more despondent. One day a lady acquaintance mentioned a cure effected by a wonder-working icon. Ivan Ilych caught himself listening attentively and beginning to believe that it had occurred. This incident alarmed him. "Has my mind really weakened to such an extent?" he asked himself. "Nonsense! It's all rubbish. I mustn't give way to nervous fears but having chosen a doctor must keep strictly to his treatment. That is what I will do. Now it's all settled. I won't think about it, but will follow the treatment seriously till summer, and then we shall see. From now there must be no more of this wavering!" This was easy to say but impossible to carry out. The pain in his side oppressed him and seemed to grow worse and more incessant, while the taste in his mouth grew stranger and stranger. It seemed to him that his breath had a disgusting smell, and he was conscious of a loss of appetite and strength. There was no deceiving himself: something terrible, new, and more important than anything before in his life, was taking place within him of which he alone was aware. Those about him did not understand or would not understand it, but thought everything in the world was going on as usual. That tormented Ivan Ilych more than anything. He saw that his household, especially his wife and daughter who were in a perfect whirl of visiting, did not understand anything of it and were annoyed that he was so depressed and so exacting, as if he were to blame for it. Though they tried to disguise it he saw that he was an obstacle in their path, and that his wife had adopted a definite line in regard to his illness and kept to it regardless of anything he said or did. Her attitude was this: "You know," she would say to her friends, "Ivan Ilych can't do as other people do, and keep to the treatment prescribed for him. One day he'll take his drops and keep strictly to his diet and go to bed in good time, but the next day unless I watch him he'll suddenly forget his medicine, eat sturgeon—which is forbidden—and sit up playing cards till one o'clock in the morning."

"Oh, come, when was that?" Ivan Ilych would ask in vexation. "Only once at Peter Ivanovich's."

"And yesterday with Shebek."

"Well, even if I hadn't stayed up, this pain would have kept me awake."

"Be that as it may you'll never get well like that, but will always make us wretched."

Praskovya Fëdorovna's attitude to Ivan Ilych's illness, as she expressed it both to others and to him, was that it was his own fault and was another of the annoyances he caused her. Ivan Ilych felt that this opinion escaped her involuntarily—but that did not make it easier for him.

At the law courts too, Ivan Ilych noticed, or thought he noticed, a strange attitude towards himself. It sometimes seemed to him that people were watching him inquisitively as a man whose place might soon be vacant. Then again, his friends would suddenly begin to chaff him in a friendly way about his low spirits, as if the awful, horrible, and unheard-of thing that was going on within him, incessantly gnawing at him and irresistibly drawing him away, was a very agreeable subject for jests. Schwartz in particular irritated him by his jocularity, vivacity, and *savoir-faire*, which reminded him of what he himself had been ten years ago.

Friends came to make up a set and they sat down to cards. They dealt, bending the new cards to soften them, and he sorted the diamonds in his hand and found he had seven. His partner said "No trumps" and supported him with two diamonds. What more could be wished for? It ought to be jolly and lively. They would make a grand slam. But suddenly Ivan Ilych was conscious of that gnawing pain, that taste in his mouth, and it seemed ridiculous that in such circumstances he should be pleased to make a grand slam.

He looked at his partner Mikhail Mikhaylovich, who rapped the table with his strong hand and instead of snatching up the tricks pushed the cards courteously and indulgently towards Ivan Ilych that he might have the pleasure of gathering them up without the trouble of stretching out his hand for them. "Does he think I am too weak to stretch out my arm?" thought Ivan Ilych, and forgetting what he was doing he over-trumped his partner, missing the grand slam by three tricks. And what was most awful of all was that he saw how upset Mikhail Mikhaylovich was about it but did not himself care. And it was dreadful to realize why he did not care.

They all saw that he was suffering, and said: "We can stop if you are tired. Take a rest." Lie down? No, he was not at all tired, and he finished the rubber. All were gloomy and silent. Ivan Ilych felt that he had diffused this gloom over them and could not dispel it. They had supper and went away, and Ivan Ilych was left alone with the consciousness that his life was poisoned and was poisoning the lives of others, and that this poison did not weaken but penetrated more and more deeply into his whole being.

With this consciousness, and with physical pain besides the terror, he must go to bed, often to lie awake the greater part of the night. Next morning he had to get up again, dress, go to the law courts, speak, and write; or if he did not go out, spend at home those twenty-four hours a day each of which was a torture. And he had to live thus all alone on the brink of an abyss, with no one who understood or pitied him.

V

So one month passed and then another. Just before the New Year his brother-in-law came to town and stayed at their house. Ivan Ilych was at the law courts and Praskovya Fëdorovna had gone shopping. When Ivan Ilych came home and entered his study he found his brother-in-law there—a healthy, florid man—unpacking his portmanteau himself. He raised his head on hearing Ivan Ilych's footsteps and looked up at him for a moment without a word. That stare told Ivan Ilych everything. His brother-in-law opened his mouth to utter an exclamation of surprise but checked himself, and that action confirmed it all.

"I have changed, eh?"

"Yes, there is a change."

And after that, try as he would to get his brother-in-law to return to the subject of his looks, the latter would say nothing about it.

Praskovya Fëdorovna came home and her brother went out to her. Ivan Ilych locked the door and began to examine himself in the glass, first full face, then in profile. He took up a portrait of himself taken with his wife, and compared it with what he saw in the glass. The change in him was immense. Then he bared his arms to the elbow, looked at them, drew the sleeves down again, sat down on an ottoman, and grew blacker than night.

"No, no, this won't do!" he said to himself, and jumped up, went to the table, took up some law papers, and began to read them, but could not continue. He unlocked the door and went into the reception-room. The door leading to the drawing-room was shut. He approached it on tiptoe and listened.

"No, you are exaggerating!" Praskovya Fëdorovna was saying.

"Exaggerating! Don't you see it? Why, he's a dead man! Look at his eyes—there's no light in them. But what is it that is wrong with him?"

"No one knows. Nikolaevich said something, but I don't know what. And Leshchetitsky [6] said quite the contrary. . . ."

Ivan Ilych walked away, went to his own room, lay down, and began musing: "The kidney, a floating kidney." He recalled all the doctors had told him of how it detached itself and swayed about. And by an effort of imagination he tried to catch that kidney and arrest it and support it. So little was needed for this, it seemed to him. "No, I'll go to see Peter Ivanovich again." [7] He rang, ordered the carriage, and got ready to go.

"Where are you going, Jean?" asked his wife, with a specially sad and exceptionally kind look.

This exceptionally kind look irritated him. He looked morosely at her.

"I must go to see Peter Ivanovich."

He went to see Peter Ivanovich, and together they went to see his friend, the doctor. He was in, and Ivan Ilych had a long talk with him.

Reviewing the anatomical and physiological details of what in the doctor's opinion was going on inside him, he understood it all.

There was something, a small thing, in the vermiform appendix. It might all come right. Only stimulate the energy of one organ and check the activity of another, then absorption would take place and everything would come right. He got home rather late for dinner,

---

[6] Nikolaevich, Leshchetitsky, two doctors, the latter a celebrated specialist. [TRANS.]
[7] That was the friend whose friend was a doctor. [TRANS.]

ate his dinner, and conversed cheerfuly, but could not for a long time bring himself to go back to work in his room. At last, however, he went to his study and did what was necessary, but the consciousness that he had put something aside—an important, intimate matter which he would revert to when his work was done—never left him. When he had finished his work he remembered that this intimate matter was the thought of his vermiform appendix. But he did not give himself up to it, and went to the drawing-room for tea. There were callers there, including the examining magistrate who was a desirable match for his daughter, and they were conversing, playing the piano, and singing. Ivan Ilych, as Praskovya Fëdorovna remarked, spent that evening more cheerfully than usual, but he never for a moment forgot that he had postponed the important matter of the appendix. At eleven o'clock he said good-night and went to his bedroom. Since his illness he had slept alone in a small room next to his study. He undressed and took up a novel by Zola, but instead of reading it he fell into thought, and in his imagination that desired improvement in the vermiform appendix occurred. There was the absorption and evacuation and the re-establishment of normal activity. "Yes, that's it!" he said to himself. "One need only assist nature, that's all." He remembered his medicine, rose, took it, and lay down on his back watching for the beneficent action of the medicine and for it to lessen the pain. "I need only take it regularly and avoid all injurious influences. I am already feeling better, much better." He began touching his side: it was not painful to the touch. "There, I really don't feel it. It's much better already." He put out the light and turned on his side. . . . "The appendix is getting better, absorption is occurring." Suddenly he felt the old, familiar, dull, gnawing pain, stubborn and serious. There was the same familiar loathsome taste in his mouth. His heart sank and he felt dazed. "My God! My God!" he muttered. "Again, again! and it will never cease." And suddenly the matter presented itself in a quite different aspect. "Vermiform appendix! Kidney!" he said to himself. "It's not a question of appendix or kidney, but of life and . . . death. Yes, life was there and now it is going, going and I cannot stop it. Yes. Why deceive myself? Isn't it obvious to everyone but me that I'm dying, and that it's only a question of weeks, days . . . it may happen this moment. There was light and now there is darkness. I was here and now I'm going there! Where?" A chill came over him, his breathing ceased, and he felt only the throbbing of his heart.

"When I am not, what will there be? There will be nothing. Then where shall I be when I am no more? Can this be dying? No, I don't want to!" He jumped up and tried to light the candle, felt for it with trembling hands, dropped candle and candlestick on the floor, and fell back on his pillow.

"What's the use? It makes no difference," he said to himself, staring with wide-open eyes into the darkness. "Death. Yes, death. And none of them know or wish to know it, and they have no pity for me. Now they are playing." (He heard through the door the distant sound of a song and its accompaniment.) "It's all the same to them, but they will die too! Fools! I first, and they later, but it will be the same for them. And now they are merry . . . the beasts!"

Anger choked him and he was agonizingly, unbearably miserable. "It is impossible that all men have been doomed to suffer this awful horror!" He raised himself.

"Something must be wrong. I must calm myself—must think it all over from the beginning." And he again began thinking. "Yes, the beginning of my illness: I knocked my side, but I was still quite well that day and the next. It hurt a little, then rather more. I saw the doctors, then followed despondency and anguish, more doctors, and I drew nearer to the abyss. My strength grew less and I kept coming nearer and nearer, and now I have wasted away and there is no light in my eyes. I think of the appendix—but this is death! I think of mending the appendix, and all the while here is death! Can it really be death?" Again terror seized him and he gasped for breath. He leant down and began feeling for the matches, pressing with his elbow on the stand beside the bed. It was in his way and hurt him, he grew furious with it, pressed on it still harder, and upset it. Breathless and in despair he fell on his back, expecting death to come immediately.

Meanwhile the visitors were leaving. Praskovya Fëdorovna was seeing them off. She heard something fall and came in.

"What has happened?"

"Nothing. I knocked it over accidentally."

She went out and returned with a candle. He lay there panting heavily, like a man who has run a thousand yards, and stared upwards at her with a fixed look.

"What is it, Jean?"

"No . . . o . . . thing. I upset it." ("Why speak of it? She won't understand," he thought.)

And in truth she did not understand. She picked up the stand, lit his candle, and hurried away to see another visitor off. When she came back he still lay on his back, looking upwards.

"What is it? Do you feel worse?"

"Yes."

She shook her head and sat down.

"Do you know, Jean, I think we must ask Leshchetitsky to come and see you here."

This meant calling in the famous specialist, regardless of expense. He smiled malignantly and said "No." She remained a little longer and then went up to him and kissed his forehead.

While she was kissing him he hated her from the bottom of his soul and with difficulty refrained from pushing her away.

"Good-night. Please God you'll sleep."

"Yes."

VI

Ivan Ilych saw that he was dying, and he was in continual despair.

In the depth of his heart he knew he was dying, but not only was he not accustomed to the thought, he simply did not and could not grasp it.

The syllogism he had learnt from Kiezewetter's Logic: "Caius is a man, men are mortal, therefore Caius is mortal," had always seemed to him correct as applied to Caius, but certainly not as applied to himself. That Caius—man in the abstract—was mortal, was perfectly correct, but he was not Caius, not an abstract man, but a creature quite, quite separate from all others. He had been little Vanya, with a mamma and a papa, with Mitya and Volodya, with the toys, a coachman and a nurse, afterwards with Katenka and with all the joys, griefs, and delights of childhood, boyhood, and youth. What did Caius know of the smell of that striped leather ball Vanya had been so fond of? Had Caius kissed his mother's hand like that, and did the silk of her dress rustle so for Caius? Had he rioted like that at school when the pastry was bad? Had Caius been in love like that? Could Caius preside at a session as he did? "Caius really was mortal, and it was right for him to die; but for me, little Vanya, Ivan Ilych, with all my thoughts and emotions, it's altogether a different matter. It cannot be that I ought to die. That would be too terrible."

Such was his feeling.

"If I had to die like Caius I should have known it was so. An inner voice would have told me so, but there was nothing of the sort in me and I and all my friends felt that our case was quite different from that of Caius. And now here it is!" he said to himself. "It can't be. It's impossible! But here it is. How is this? How is one to understand it?"

He could not understand it, and tried to drive this false, incorrect, morbid thought away and to replace it by other proper and healthy thoughts. But that thought, and not the thought only but the reality itself, seemed to come and confront him.

And to replace that thought he called up a succession of others, hoping to find in them some support. He tried to get back into the former current of thoughts that had once screened the thought of death from him. But strange to say, all that had formerly shut off, hidden, and destroyed his consciousness of death, no longer had that effect. Ivan Ilych now spent most of his time in attempting to re-establish that old current. He would say to himself: "I will take up my duties again—after all I used to live by them." And banishing all doubts he would go to the law courts, enter into conversation with his colleagues, and sit carelessly as was his wont, scanning the crowd with a thoughtful look and leaning both his emaciated arms on the arms of his oak chair; bending over as usual to a colleague and drawing his papers nearer he would interchange whispers with him, and then suddenly raising his eyes and sitting erect would pronounce certain words and open the proceedings. But suddenly in the midst of those proceedings the pain in his side, regardless of the stage the proceedings had reached, would begin its own gnawing work. Ivan Ilych would turn his attention to it and try to drive the thought of it away, but without success. *It* would come and stand before him and look at him, and he would be petrified and the light would die out of his eyes, and he would again begin asking himself whether *It* alone was true. And his colleagues and subordinates would see with surprise and distress that he, the brilliant and subtle judge, was becoming confused and making mistakes. He would shake himself, try to pull himself together, manage somehow to bring the sitting to a close, and return home with the sorrowful consciousness that his judicial labours could not as formerly hide from him what he wanted them to hide, and could not deliver him from *It*. And what was worst of all was that *It* drew his attention to itself not in order to make him take some action but only that he should look at *It*, look it straight in the face: look at it and, without doing anything, suffer inexpressibly.

And to save himself from this condition Ivan Ilych looked for consolations—new screens—and new screens were found and for a while seemed to save him, but then they immediately fell to pieces or rather became transparent, as if *It* penetrated them and nothing could veil *It*.

In these latter days he would go into the drawing-room he had arranged—that drawing-room where he had fallen and for the sake of which (how bitterly ridiculous it seemed) he had sacrificed his life—for he knew that his illness originated with that knock. He would enter and see that something had scratched the polished table. He would look for the cause of this and find that it was the bronze ornamentation of an album, that had got bent. He would take up the expensive album which he had lovingly arranged, and feel vexed with his daughter and her friends for their untidiness—for the album was torn here and there and some of the photographs turned upside down. He would put it carefully in order and bend the ornamentation back into position. Then it would occur to him to place all those things in another corner of the room, near the plants. He would call the footman, but his daughter or wife would come to help him. They would not agree, and his wife would contradict him, and he would dispute and grow angry. But that was all right, for then he did not think about *It*. *It* was invisible.

But then, when he was moving something himself, his wife would say: "Let the servants do it. You will hurt yourself again." And suddenly *It* would flash through the screen and he would see it. It was just a flash, and he hoped it would disappear, but he would involuntarily pay attention to his side. "It sits there as before, gnawing just the same!" And he could no longer forget *It*, but could distinctly see it looking at him from behind the flowers. "What is it all for?"

"It really is so! I lost my life over that curtain as I might have done when storming a fort. Is that possible? How terrible and how stupid. It can't be true! It can't, but it is."

He would go to his study, lie down, and again be alone with *It*: face to face with *It*. And nothing could be done with *It* except to look at it and shudder.

VII

How it happened it is impossible to say because it came about step by step, unnoticed, but in the third month of Ivan Ilych's illness, his wife, his daughter, his son, his acquaintances, the doctors, the servants, and above all he himself, were aware that the whole interest he had for other people was whether he would soon vacate his place, and at last release the living from the discomfort caused by his presence and be himself released from his sufferings.

He slept less and less. He was given opium and hypodermic injections of morphine, but this did not relieve him. The dull depression he experienced in a somnolent condition at first gave him a little relief, but only as something new, afterwards it became as distressing as the pain itself or even more so.

Special foods were prepared for him by the doctors' orders, but all those foods became increasingly distasteful and disgusting to him.

For his excretions also special arrangements had to be made, and this was a torment to him every time—a torment from the uncleanliness, the unseemliness, and the smell, and from knowing that another person had to take part in it.

But just through this most unpleasant matter, Ivan Ilych obtained comfort. Gerasim, the butler's young assistant, always came in to carry the things out. Gerasim was a clean, fresh peasant lad, grown stout on town food and always cheerful and bright. At first the sight of him, in his clean Russian peasant costume, engaged on that disgusting task embarrassed Ivan Ilych.

Once when he got up from the commode too weak to draw up his trousers, he dropped into a soft armchair and looked with horror at his bare, enfeebled thighs with the muscles so sharply marked on them.

Gerasim with a firm light tread, his heavy boots emitting a pleasant smell of tar and fresh winter air, came in wearing a clean Hessian apron, the sleeves of his print shirt tucked up over his strong, bare young arms; and refraining from looking at his sick master out of consideration for his feelings, and restraining the joy of life that beamed from his face, he went up to the commode.

"Gerasim!" said Ivan Ilych in a weak voice.

Gerasim started, evidently afraid he might have committed some blunder, and with a rapid movement turned his fresh, kind, simple young face which just showed the first downy signs of a beard.

"Yes, sir?"

"That must be very unpleasant for you. You must forgive me. I am helpless."

"Oh, why, sir," and Gerasim's eyes beamed and he showed his glistening white teeth, "what's a little trouble? It's a case of illness with you, sir."

And his deft strong hands did their accustomed task, and he went out of the room stepping lightly. Five minutes later he as lightly returned.

Ivan Ilych was still sitting in the same position in the armchair.

"Gerasim," he said when the latter had replaced the freshly-washed utensil. "Please come here and help me." Gerasim went up to him. "Lift me up. It is hard for me to get up, and I have sent Dmitri away."

Gerasim went up to him, grasped his master with his strong arms deftly but gently, in the same way that he stepped—lifted him, supported him with one hand, and with the other drew up his trousers and would have set him down again, but Ivan Ilych asked to be led to the sofa. Gerasim, without an effort and without apparent pressure, led him, almost lifting him, to the sofa and placed him on it.

"Thank you. How easily and well you do it all!"

Gerasim smiled again and turned to leave the room. But Ivan Ilych felt his presence such a comfort that he did not want to let him go.

"One thing more, please move up that chair. No, the other one—under my feet. It is easier for me when my feet are raised."

Gerasim brought the chair, set it down gently in place, and raised Ivan Ilych's legs on to it. It seemed to Ivan Ilych that he felt better while Gerasim was holding up his legs.

"It's better when my legs are higher," he said. "Place that cushion under them."

Gerasim did so. He again lifted the legs and placed them, and again Ivan Ilych felt better while Gerasim held his legs. When he set them down Ivan Ilych fancied he felt worse.

"Gerasim," he said. "Are you busy now?"

"Not at all, sir," said Gerasim, who had learnt from the towns-folk how to speak to gentlefolk.

"What have you still to do?"

"What have I to do? I've done everything except chopping the logs for tomorrow."

"Then hold my legs up a bit higher, can you?"

"Of course I can. Why not?" And Gerasim raised his master's legs higher and Ivan Ilych thought that in that position he did not feel any pain at all.

"And how about the logs?"

"Don't trouble about that, sir. There's plenty of time."

Ivan Ilych told Gerasim to sit down and hold his legs, and began to talk to him. And strange to say it seemed to him that he felt better while Gerasim held his legs up.

After that Ivan Ilych would sometimes call Gerasim and get him to hold his legs on his shoulders, and he liked talking to him. Gerasim did it all easily, willingly, simply, and with a good nature that touched Ivan Ilych. Health, strength, and vitality in other people were offensive to him, but Gerasim's strength and vitality did not mortify but soothed him.

What tormented Ivan Ilych most was the deception, the lie, which for some reason they all accepted, that he was not dying but was simply ill, and that he only need keep quiet and undergo a treatment and then something very good would result. He however knew that do what they would nothing would come of it, only still more agonizing suffering and death. This deception tortured him— their not wishing to admit what they all knew and what he knew, but wanting to lie to him concerning his terrible condition, and wishing and forcing him to participate in that lie. Those lies—lies enacted over him on the eve of his death and destined to degrade this awful, solemn act to the level of their visitings, their curtains, their sturgeon for dinner—were a terrible agony for Ivan Ilych. And strangely enough, many times when they were going through their antics over him he had been within a hairbreadth of calling out to them: "Stop lying! You know and I know that I am dying. Then at least stop lying about it!" But he had never had the spirit to do it. The awful, terrible act of his dying was, he could see, reduced by those about him to the level of a casual, unpleasant, and almost in-decorous incident (as if someone entered a drawing-room diffusing an unpleasant odour) and this was done by that very decorum which he had served all his life long. He saw that no one felt for him, because no one even wished to grasp his position. Only Gerasim recognized it and pitied him. And so Ivan Ilych felt at ease only with him. He felt comforted when Gerasim supported his legs (sometimes all night long) and refused to go to bed, saying: "Don't you worry, Ivan Ilych. I'll get sleep enough later on," or when he suddenly became familiar and exclaimed: "If you weren't sick it would be another matter, but as it is, why should I grudge a little trouble?" Gerasim alone did not lie; everything showed that he alone understood the facts of the case and did not consider it necessary to disguise them, but simply felt sorry for his emaciated and enfeebled master. Once when Ivan Ilych was sending him away he even said straight out: "We shall all of us die, so why should I grudge a little trouble?"—expressing the fact that he did not think his work burdensome, because he was doing it for a dying man and hoped someone would do the same for him when his time came.

Apart from this lying, or because of it, what most tormented Ivan Ilych was that no one pitied him as he wished to be pitied. At certain moments after prolonged suffering he wished most of all (though he would have been ashamed to confess it) for someone to pity him as a sick child is pitied. He longed to be petted and comforted. He knew he was an important functionary, that he had a beard turning grey, and that therefore what he longed for was impossible, but still he longed for it. And in Gerasim's attitude towards him there was something akin to what he wished for, and so that attitude comforted him. Ivan Ilych wanted to weep, wanted to be petted and cried over, and then his colleague Shebek would come, and instead of weeping and being petted, Ivan Ilych would assume a serious, severe, and profound air, and by force of habit would express his opinion on a decision of the Court of Cassation and would stubbornly insist on that view. This falsity around him and within him did more than anything else to poison his last days.

VIII

It was morning. He knew it was morning because Gerasim had gone, and Peter the footman had come and put out the candles, drawn back one of the curtains, and begun quietly to tidy up. Whether it was morning or evening, Friday or Sunday, made no difference, it was all just the same: the gnawing, unmitigated, agonizing pain, never ceasing for an instant, the consciousness of life inexorably waning but not yet extinguished, the approach of that ever dreaded and hateful Death which was the only reality, and always the same falsity. What were days, weeks, hours, in such a case?

"Will you have some tea, sir?"

"He wants things to be regular, and wishes the gentlefolk to drink tea in the morning," thought Ivan Ilych, and only said "No."

"Wouldn't you like to move onto the sofa, sir?"

"He wants to tidy up the room, and I'm in the way. I am uncleanliness and disorder," he thought, and said only:

"No, leave me alone."

The man went on bustling about. Ivan Ilych stretched out his hand. Peter came up, ready to help.

"What is it, sir?"

"My watch."

Peter took the watch which was close at hand and gave it to his master.

"Half-past eight. Are they up?"

"No, sir, except Vladimir Ivanovich" (the son) "who has gone to school. Praskovya Fëdorovna ordered me to wake her if you asked for her. Shall I do so?"

"No, there's no need to." "Perhaps I'd better have some tea," he thought, and added aloud: "Yes, bring me some tea."

Peter went to the door, but Ivan Ilych dreaded being left alone. "How can I keep him here? Oh yes, my medicine." "Peter, give me my medicine." "Why not? Perhaps it may still do me some good." He took a spoonful and swallowed it. "No, it won't help. It's all tomfoolery, all deception," he decided as soon as he became aware of the familiar, sickly, hopeless taste. "No, I can't believe in it any longer. But the pain, why this pain? If it would only cease just for a moment!" And he moaned. Peter turned towards him. "It's all right. Go and fetch me some tea."

Peter went out. Left alone Ivan Ilych groaned not so much with pain, terrible though that was, as from mental anguish. Always and for ever the same, always these endless days and nights. If only it would come quicker! If only *what* would come quicker? Death, darkness? . . . No, no! Anything rather than death!

When Peter returned with the tea on a tray, Ivan Ilych stared at him for a time in perplexity, not realizing who and what he was. Peter was disconcerted by that look and his embarrassment brought Ivan Ilych to himself.

"Oh, tea! All right, put it down. Only help me to wash and put on a clean shirt."

And Ivan Ilych began to wash. With pauses for rest, he washed his hands and then his face, cleaned his teeth, brushed his hair, and

looked in the glass. He was terrified by what he saw, especially by
the limp way in which his hair clung to his pallid forehead.

While his shirt was being changed he knew that he would be
still more frightened at the sight of his body, so he avoided looking
at it. Finally he was ready. He drew on a dressing-gown, wrapped
himself in a plaid, and sat down in the armchair to take his tea. For
a moment he felt refreshed, but as soon as he began to drink the tea
he was again aware of the same taste, and the pain also returned. He
finished it with an effort, and then lay down stretching out his legs,
and dismissed Peter.

Always the same. Now a spark of hope flashes up, then a sea of
despair rages, and always pain; always pain, always despair, and always the same. When alone he had a dreadful and distressing desire
to call someone, but he knew beforehand that with others present
it would be still worse. "Another dose of morphine—to lose consciousness. I will tell him, the doctor, that he must think of something else. It's impossible, impossible, to go on like this."

An hour and another pass like that. But now there is a ring at
the door bell. Perhaps it's the doctor? It is. He comes in fresh,
hearty, plump, and cheerful, with that look on his face that seems to
say: "There now, you're in a panic about something, but we'll arrange it all for you directly!" The doctor knows this expression is out
of place here, but he has put it on once for all and can't take it off—
like a man who has put on a frock-coat in the morning to pay a
round of calls.

The doctor rubs his hands vigorously and reassuringly.

"Brr! How cold it is! There's such a sharp frost; just let me warm
myself!" he says, as if it were only a matter of waiting till he was
warm, and then he would put everything right.

"Well now, how are you?"

Ivan Ilych feels that the doctor would like to say: "Well, how
are our affairs?" but that even he feels that this would not do, and
says instead: "What sort of a night have you had?"

Ivan Ilych looks at him as much as to say: "Are you really never
ashamed of lying?" But the doctor does not wish to understand this
question, and Ivan Ilych says: "Just as terrible as ever. The pain
never leaves me and never subsides. If only something . . ."

"Yes, you sick people are always like that. . . . There, now I
think I am warm enough. Even Praskovya Fëdorovna, who is so particular, could find no fault with my temperature. Well, now I can
say good-morning," and the doctor presses his patient's hand.

Then, dropping his former playfulness, he begins with a most serious face to examine the patient, feeling his pulse and taking his
temperature, and then begins the sounding and auscultation.

Ivan Ilych knows quite well and definitely that all this is nonsense and pure deception, but when the doctor, getting down on his
knee, leans over him, putting his ear first higher then lower, and
performs various gymnastic movements over him with a significant
expression on his face, Ivan Ilych submits to it all as he used to submit to the speeches of the lawyers, though he knew very well that
they were all lying and why they were lying.

The doctor, kneeling on the sofa, is still sounding him when
Praskovya Fëdorovna's silk dress rustles at the door and she is heard
scolding Peter for not having let her know of the doctor's arrival.

She comes in, kisses her husband, and at once proceeds to prove
that she has been up a long time already, and only owing to a mis-
understanding failed to be there when the doctor arrived.

Ivan Ilych looks at her, scans her all over, sets against her the
whiteness and plumpness and cleanness of her hands and neck, the
gloss of her hair, and the sparkle of her vivacious eyes. He hates her
with his whole soul. And the thrill of hatred he feels for her makes
him suffer from her touch.

Her attitude towards him and his disease is still the same. Just as
the doctor had adopted a certain relation to his patient which he
could not abandon, so had she formed one towards him—that he
was not doing something he ought to do and was himself to blame,
and that she reproached him lovingly for this—and she could not
now change that attitude.

"You see he doesn't listen to me and doesn't take his medicine
at the proper time. And above all he lies in a position that is no
doubt bad for him—with his legs up."

She described how he made Gerasim hold his legs up.

The doctor smiled with a contemptuous affability that said:
"What's to be done? These sick people do have foolish fancies of
that kind, but we must forgive them."

When the examination was over the doctor looked at his watch,
and then Praskovya Fëdorovna announced to Ivan Ilych that it was
of course as he pleased, but she had sent today for a celebrated specialist who would examine him and have a consultation with Michael Danilovich (their regular doctor).

"Please don't raise any objections. I am doing this for my own
sake," she said ironically, letting it be felt that she was doing it all

for his sake and only said this to leave him no right to refuse. He remained silent, knitting his brows. He felt that he was so surrounded and involved in a mesh of falsity that it was hard to unravel anything.

Everything she did for him was entirely for her own sake, and she told him she was doing for herself what she actually was doing for herself, as if that was so incredible that he must understand the opposite.

At half-past eleven the celebrated specialist arrived. Again the sounding began and the significant conversations in his presence and in another room, about the kidneys and the appendix, and the questions and answers, with such an air of importance that again, instead of the real question of life and death which now alone confronted him, the question arose of the kidney and appendix which were not behaving as they ought to and would now be attacked by Michael Danilovich and the specialist and forced to amend their ways.

The celebrated specialist took leave of him with a serious though not hopeless look, and in reply to the timid question Ivan Ilych, with eyes glistening with fear and hope, put to him as to whether there was a chance of recovery, said that he could not vouch for it but there was a possibility. The look of hope with which Ivan Ilych watched the doctor out was so pathetic that Praskovya Fëdorovna, seeing it, even wept as she left the room to hand the doctor his fee.

The gleam of hope kindled by the doctor's encouragement did not last long. The same room, the same pictures, curtains, wallpaper, medicine bottles, were all there, and the same aching suffering body, and Ivan Ilych began to moan. They gave him a subcutaneous injection and he sank into oblivion.

It was twilight when he came to. They brought him his dinner and he swallowed some beef tea with difficulty, and then everything was the same again and night was coming on.

After dinner, at seven o'clock, Praskovya Fëdorovna came into the room in evening dress, her full bosom pushed up by her corset, and with traces of powder on her face. She had reminded him in the morning that they were going to the theatre. Sarah Bernhardt was visiting the town and they had a box, which he had insisted on their taking. Now he had forgotten about it and her toilet offended him, but he concealed his vexation when he remembered that he had himself insisted on their securing a box and going because it would be an instructive and aesthetic pleasure for the children.

Praskovya Fëdorovna came in, self-satisfied but yet with a rather guilty air. She sat down and asked how he was, but, as he saw, only for the sake of asking and not in order to learn about it, knowing that there was nothing to learn—and then went on to what she really wanted to say: that she would not on any account have gone but that the box had been taken and Helen and their daughter were going, as well as Petrishchev (the examining magistrate, their daughter's fiancé), and that it was out of the question to let them go alone; but that she would have much preferred to sit with him for a while; and he must be sure to follow the doctor's orders while she was away.

"Oh, and Fëdor Petrovich" (the fiancé) "would like to come in. May he? And Lisa?"

"All right."

Their daughter came in in full evening dress, her fresh young flesh exposed (making a show of that very flesh which in his own case caused so much suffering), strong, healthy, evidently in love, and impatient with illness, suffering, and death, because they interfered with her happiness.

Fëdor Petrovich came in too, in evening dress, his hair curled *à la Capoul*, a tight stiff collar round his long sinewy neck, an enormous white shirt-front, and narrow black trousers tightly stretched over his strong thighs. He had one white glove tightly drawn on, and was holding his opera hat in his hand.

Following him the schoolboy crept in unnoticed, in a new uniform, poor little fellow, and wearing gloves. Terribly dark shadows showed under his eyes, the meaning of which Ivan Ilych knew well.

His son had always seemed pathetic to him, and now it was dreadful to see the boy's frightened look of pity. It seemed to Ivan Ilych that Vasya was the only one besides Gerasim who understood and pitied him.

They all sat down and again asked how he was. A silence followed. Lisa asked her mother about the opera-glasses, and there was an altercation between mother and daughter as to who had taken them and where they had been put. This occasioned some unpleasantness.

Fëdor Petrovich inquired of Ivan Ilych whether he had ever seen Sarah Bernhardt. Ivan Ilych did not at first catch the question, but then replied: "No, have you seen her before?"

"Yes, in *Adrienne Lecouvreur*."

Praskovya Fëdorovna mentioned some rôles in which Sarah

Bernhardt was particularly good. Her daughter disagreed. Conversation sprang up as to the elegance and realism of her acting—the sort of conversation that is always repeated and is always the same.

In the midst of the conversation Fëdor Petrovich glanced at Ivan Ilych and became silent. The others also looked at him and grew silent. Ivan Ilych was staring with glittering eyes straight before him, evidently indignant with them. This had to be rectified, but it was impossible to do so. The silence had to be broken, but for a time no one dared to break it and they all became afraid that the conventional deception would suddenly become obvious and the truth become plain to all. Lisa was the first to pluck up courage and break that silence, but by trying to hide what everybody was feeling, she betrayed it.

"Well, if we are going it's time to start," she said, looking at her watch, a present from her father, and with a faint and significant smile at Fëdor Petrovich relating to something known only to them. She got up with a rustle of her dress.

They all rose, said good-night, and went away.

When they had gone it seemed to Ivan Ilych that he felt better; the falsity had gone with them. But the pain remained—that same pain and that same fear that made everything monotonously alike, nothing harder and nothing easier. Everything was worse.

Again minute followed minute and hour followed hour. Everything remained the same and there was no cessation. And the inevitable end of it all became more and more terrible.

"Yes, send Gerasim here," he replied to a question Peter asked.

IX

His wife returned late at night. She came in on tiptoe, but he heard her, opened his eyes, and made haste to close them again. She wished to send Gerasim away and to sit with him herself, but he opened his eyes and said: "No, go away."

"Are you in great pain?"

"Always the same."

"Take some opium."

He agreed and took some. She went away.

Till about three in the morning he was in a state of stupefied misery. It seemed to him that he and his pain were being thrust into a narrow, deep black sack, but though they were pushed further and further in they could not be pushed to the bottom. And this, terrible enough in itself, was accompanied by suffering. He was frightened yet wanted to fall through the sack, he struggled but yet cooperated. And suddenly he broke through, fell, and regained consciousness. Gerasim was sitting at the foot of the bed dozing quietly and patiently, while he himself lay with his emaciated stockinged legs resting on Gerasim's shoulders; the same shaded candle was there and the same unceasing pain.

"Go away, Gerasim," he whispered.

"It's all right, sir. I'll stay a while."

"No. Go away."

He removed his legs from Gerasim's shoulders, turned sideways onto his arm, and felt sorry for himself. He only waited till Gerasim had gone into the next room and then restrained himself no longer but wept like a child. He wept on account of his helplessness, his terrible loneliness, the cruelty of man, the cruelty of God, and the absence of God.

"Why hast Thou done all this? Why hast Thou brought me here? Why, why dost Thou torment me so terribly?"

He did not expect an answer and yet wept because there was no answer and could be none. The pain again grew more acute, but he did not stir and did not call. He said to himself: "Go on! Strike me! But what is it for? What have I done to Thee? What is it for?"

Then he grew quiet and not only ceased weeping but even held his breath and became all attention. It was as though he were listening not to an audible voice but to the voice of his soul, to the current of thoughts arising within him.

"What is it you want?" was the first clear conception capable of expression in words, that he heard.

"What do you want? What do you want?" he repeated to himself.

"What do I want? To live and not to suffer," he answered.

And again he listened with such concentrated attention that even his pain did not distract him.

"To live? How?" asked his inner voice.

"Why, to live as I used to—well and pleasantly."

"As you lived before, well and pleasantly?" the voice repeated.

And in imagination he began to recall the best moments of his pleasant life. But strange to say none of those best moments of his pleasant life now seemed at all what they had then seemed—none of them except the first recollections of childhood. There, in childhood, there had been something really pleasant with which it would be possible to live if it could return. But the child who had experienced that happiness existed no longer, it was like a reminiscence of somebody else.

As soon as the period began which had produced the present Ivan Ilych, all that had then seemed joys now melted before his sight and turned into something trivial and often nasty.

And the further he departed from childhood and the nearer he came to the present the more worthless and doubtful were the joys. This began with the School of Law. A little that was really good was still found there—there was lightheartedness, friendship, and hope. But in the upper classes there had already been fewer of such good moments. Then during the first years of his official career, when he was in the service of the Governor, some pleasant moments again occurred; they were the memories of love for a woman. Then all became confused and there was still less of what was good; later on again there was still less that was good, and the further he went the less there was. His marriage, a mere accident, then the disenchantment that followed it, his wife's bad breath and the sensuality and hypocrisy: then that deadly official life and those preoccupations about money, a year of it, and two, and ten, and twenty, and always the same thing. And the longer it lasted the more deadly it became. "It is as if I had been going downhill while I imagined I was going up. And that is really what it was. I was going up in public opinion, but to the same extent life was ebbing away from me. And now it is all done and there is only death."

"Then what does it mean? Why? It can't be that life is so senseless and horrible. But if it really has been so horrible and senseless, why must I die and die in agony? There is something wrong!"

"Maybe I did not live as I ought to have done," it suddenly occurred to him. "But how could that be, when I did everything properly?" he replied, and immediately dismissed from his mind this, the sole solution of all the riddles of life and death, as something quite impossible.

"Then what do you want now? To live? Live how? Live as you lived in the law courts when the usher proclaimed 'The judge is coming!' The judge is coming, the judge!" he repeated to himself. "Here he is, the judge. But I am not guilty!" he exclaimed angrily. "What is it for?" And he ceased crying, but turning his face to the wall continued to ponder on the same question: Why, and for what purpose, is there all this horror? But however much he pondered he found no answer. And whenever the thought occurred to him, as it often did, that it all resulted from his not having lived as he ought to have done, he at once recalled the correctness of his whole life and dismissed so strange an idea.

X

Another fortnight passed. Ivan Ilych now no longer left his sofa. He would not lie in bed but lay on the sofa, facing the wall nearly all the time. He suffered ever the same unceasing agonies and in his loneliness pondered always on the same insoluble question: "What is this? Can it be that it is Death?" And the inner voice answered: "Yes, it is Death."

"Why these sufferings?" And the voice answered, "For no reason—they just are so." Beyond and besides this there was nothing.

From the very beginning of his illness, ever since he had first been to see the doctor, Ivan Ilych's life had been divided between two contrary and alternating moods: now it was despair and the expectation of this uncomprehended and terrible death, and now hope and an intently interested observation of the functioning of his organs. Now before his eyes there was only a kidney or an intestine that temporarily evaded its duty, and now only that incomprehensible and dreadful death from which it was impossible to escape.

These two states of mind had alternated from the very beginning of his illness, but the further it progressed the more doubtful and fantastic became the conception of the kidney, and the more real the sense of impending death.

He had but to call to mind what he had been three months before and what he was now, to call to mind with what regularity he had been going downhill, for every possibility of hope to be shattered.

Latterly during that loneliness in which he found himself as he lay facing the back of the sofa, a loneliness in the midst of a populous town and surrounded by numerous acquaintances and relations but that yet could not have been more complete anywhere—either at the bottom of the sea or under the earth—during that terrible loneliness Ivan Ilych had lived only in memories of the past. Pictures of his past rose before him one after another. They always began with what was nearest in time and then went back to what was most remote—to his childhood—and rested there. If he thought of the stewed prunes that had been offered him that day, his mind went back to the raw shrivelled French plums of his childhood, their peculiar flavour and the flow of saliva when he sucked their stones, and along with the memory of that taste came a whole series of memories of those days: his nurse, his brother, and their toys. "No, I mustn't think of that. . . . It is too painful," Ivan Ilych said to himself, and brought himself back to the present—to the button on the back of the sofa and the creases in its morocco. "Morocco is expensive, but it does not wear well: there had been a quarrel about it. It was a different kind of quarrel and a different kind of morocco that time when we tore father's portfolio and were punished, and mamma brought us some tarts. . . ." And again his thoughts dwelt on his childhood, and again it was painful and he tried to banish them and fix his mind on something else.

Then again together with that chain of memories another series passed through his mind—of how his illness had progressed and grown worse. There also the further back he looked the more life there had been. There had been more of what was good in life and more of life itself. The two merged together. "Just as the pain went on getting worse and worse, so my life grew worse and worse," he thought. "There is one bright spot there at the back, at the beginning of life, and afterwards all becomes blacker and blacker and proceeds more and more rapidly—in inverse ratio to the square of the distance from death," thought Ivan Ilych. And the example of a stone falling downwards with increasing velocity entered his mind. Life, a series of increasing sufferings, flies further and further towards its end—the most terrible suffering. "I am flying. . . ." He shuddered, shifted himself, and tried to resist, but was already aware that resistance was impossible, and again, with eyes weary of gazing but unable to cease seeing what was before them, he stared at the back of the sofa and waited—awaiting that dreadful fall and shock and destruction.

"Resistance is impossible!" he said to himself. "If I could only understand what it is all for! But that too is impossible. An explanation would be possible if it could be said that I have not lived as I ought to. But it is impossible to say that," and he remembered all the legality, correctitude, and propriety of his life. "That at any rate can certainly not be admitted," he thought, and his lips smiled ironically as if someone could see that smile and be taken in by it. "There is no explanation! Agony, death . . . What for?"

XI

Another two weeks went by in this way and during that fortnight an event occurred that Ivan Ilych and his wife had desired. Petrishchev formally proposed. It happened in the evening. The next day Praskovya Fëdorovna came into her husband's room considering how best to inform him of it, but that very night there had been a fresh change for the worse in his condition. She found him still lying on the sofa but in a different position. He lay on his back, groaning and staring fixedly straight in front of him.

She began to remind him of his medicines, but he turned his eyes towards her with such a look that she did not finish what she was saying; so great an animosity, to her in particular, did that look express.

"For Christ's sake let me die in peace!" he said.

She would have gone away, but just then their daughter came in and went up to say good morning. He looked at her as he had done at his wife, and in reply to her inquiry about his health said dryly that he would soon free them all of himself. They were both silent and after sitting with him for a while went away.

"Is it our fault?" Lisa said to her mother. "It's as if we were to blame! I am sorry for papa, but why should we be tortured?"

The doctor came at his usual time. Ivan Ilych answered "Yes" and "No," never taking his angry eyes from him, and at last said: "You know you can do nothing for me, so leave me alone."

"We can ease your sufferings."

"You can't even do that. Let me be."

The doctor went into the drawing-room and told Praskovya Fëdorovna that the case was very serious and that the only resource left was opium to allay her husband's sufferings, which must be terrible.

It was true, as the doctor said, that Ivan Ilych's physical sufferings were terrible, but worse than the physical sufferings were his mental sufferings, which were his chief torture.

His mental sufferings were due to the fact that that night, as he looked at Gerasim's sleepy, good-natured face with its prominent cheekbones, the question suddenly occurred to him: "What if my whole life has really been wrong?"

It occurred to him that what had appeared perfectly impossible before, namely that he had not spent his life as he should have done, might after all be true. It occurred to him that his scarcely perceptible attempts to struggle against what was considered good by the most highly placed people, those scarcely noticeable impulses which he had immediately suppressed, might have been the real thing, and all the rest false. And his professional duties and the whole arrangement of his life and of his family, and all his social and official interests, might all have been false. He tried to defend all those things to himself and suddenly felt the weakness of what he was defending. There was nothing to defend.

"But if that is so," he said to himself, "and I am leaving this life with the consciousness that I have lost all that was given me and it is impossible to rectify it—what then?"

He lay on his back and began to pass his life in review in quite a new way. In the morning when he saw first his footman, then his wife, then his daughter, and then the doctor, their every word and movement confirmed to him the awful truth that had been revealed to him during the night. In them he saw himself—all that for which he had lived—and saw clearly that it was not real at all, but a terrible and huge deception which had hidden both life and death. This consciousness intensified his physical suffering tenfold. He groaned and tossed about, and pulled at his clothing which choked and stifled him. And he hated them on that account.

He was given a large dose of opium and became unconscious, but at noon his sufferings began again. He drove everybody away and tossed from side to side.

His wife came to him and said:

"Jean, my dear, do this for me. It can't do any harm and often helps. Healthy people often do it."

He opened his eyes wide.

"What? Take communion? Why? It's unnecessary! However . . ."

She began to cry.

"Yes, do, my dear. I'll send for our priest. He is such a nice man."

"All right. Very well," he muttered.

When the priest came and heard his confession, Ivan Ilych was softened and seemed to feel a relief from his doubts and consequently from his sufferings, and for a moment there came a ray of hope. He again began to think of the vermiform appendix and the possibility of correcting it. He received the sacrament with tears in his eyes.

When they laid him down again afterwards he felt a moment's ease, and the hope that he might live awoke in him again. He began to think of the operation that had been suggested to him. "To live! I want to live!" he said to himself.

His wife came in to congratulate him after his communion, and when uttering the usual conventional words she added:

"You feel better, don't you?"

Without looking at her he said "Yes."

Her dress, her figure, the expression of her face, the tone of her voice, all revealed the same thing. "This is wrong, it is not as it should be. All you have lived for and still live for is falsehood and deception, hiding life and death from you." And as soon as he admitted that thought, his hatred and his agonizing physical suffering again sprang up, and with that suffering a consciousness of the unavoidable, approaching end. And to this was added a new sensation of grinding shooting pain and a feeling of suffocation.

The expression of his face when he uttered that "yes" was dreadful. Having uttered it, he looked her straight in the eyes, turned on his face with a rapidity extraordinary in his weak state and shouted:

"Go away! Go away and leave me alone!"

XII

From that moment the screaming began that continued for three days, and was so terrible that one could not hear it through two closed doors without horror. At the moment he answered his wife he realized that he was lost, that there was no return, that the end had come, the very end, and his doubts were still unsolved and remained doubts.

"Oh! Oh! Oh!" he cried in various intonations. He had begun by screaming "I won't!" and continued screaming on the letter O.

For three whole days, during which time did not exist for him, he struggled in that black sack into which he was being thrust by an invisible, resistless force. He struggled as a man condemned to death struggles in the hands of the executioner, knowing that he cannot save himself. And every moment he felt that despite all his efforts he was drawing nearer and nearer to what terrified him. He felt that his agony was due to his being thrust into that black hole and still more to his not being able to get right into it. He was hindered from getting into it by his conviction that his life had been a good one. That very justification of his life held him fast and prevented his moving forward, and it caused him most torment of all.

Suddenly some force struck him in the chest and side, making it still harder to breathe, and he fell through the hole and there at the bottom was a light. What had happened to him was like the sensation one sometimes experiences in a railway carriage when one thinks one is going backwards while one is really going forwards and suddenly becomes aware of the real direction.

"Yes, it was all not the right thing," he said to himself, "but that's no matter. It can be done. But what *is* the right thing?" he asked himself, and suddenly grew quiet.

This occurred at the end of the third day, two hours before his death. Just then his schoolboy son had crept softly in and gone up to the bedside. The dying man was still screaming desperately and waving his arms. His hand fell on the boy's head, and the boy caught it, pressed it to his lips, and began to cry.

At that very moment Ivan Ilych fell through and caught sight of the light, and it was revealed to him that though his life had not been what it should have been, this could still be rectified. He asked himself, "What *is* the right thing?" and grew still, listening. Then he felt that someone was kissing his hand. He opened his eyes, looked at his son, and felt sorry for him. His wife came up to him and he glanced at her. She was gazing at him open-mouthed, with undried tears on her nose and cheek and a despairing look on her face. He felt sorry for her too.

"Yes, I am making them wretched," he thought. "They are sorry, but it will be better for them when I die." He wished to say this but had not the strength to utter it. "Besides, why speak? I must act," he thought. With a look at his wife he indicated his son and said: "Take him away . . . sorry for him . . . sorry for you too. . . ." He tried to add, "Forgive me," but said "forgo" and waved his hand, knowing that He whose understanding mattered would understand.

And suddenly it grew clear to him that what had been oppressing him and would not leave him was all dropping away at once from two sides, from ten sides, and from all sides. He was sorry for them, he must act so as not to hurt them: release them and free himself from these sufferings. "How good and how simple!" he thought. "And the pain?" he asked himself. "What has become of it? Where are you, pain?"

He turned his attention to it.

"Yes, here it is. Well, what of it? Let the pain be."

"And death . . . where is it?"

He sought his former accustomed fear of death and did not find it. "Where is it? What death?" There was no fear because there was no death.

In place of death there was light.

"So that's what it is!" he suddenly exclaimed aloud. "What joy!"

To him all this happened in a single instant, and the meaning of that instant did not change. For those present his agony continued for another two hours. Something rattled in his throat, his emaciated body twitched, then the gasping and rattle became less and less frequent.

"It is finished!" said someone near him.

He heard these words and repeated them in his soul.

"Death is finished," he said to himself. "It is no more!"

He drew in a breath, stopped in the midst of a sigh, stretched out, and died.

E. M. FORSTER

The Machine Stops

Introduction

"I have discovered," remarked the great French philosopher Blaise Pascal, "that all the unhappiness of men arises from one single fact, that they cannot stay quietly in their own room."

This striking observation is not to be grasped quickly or casually. A devout Christian, Pascal was aware of that demon of restlessness which eats away at the human soul, that demon which will not let us be content but keeps driving us toward further effort, further mischief, out into the treacherous world and away from the security of our own room. Since Pascal was a very subtle psychologist, we must assume that he was aware of the double interpretation to which his sentence lends itself. He must have seen that precisely this demon of restlessness which will not let us "stay quietly in our own room" is also the source of the best in human experience: it is what makes us work toward achievement and discovery. Pascal thus brings together the two sides of human nature, forever locked in tension, forever at war with each other.

In the world imagined by E. M. Forster in *The Machine Stops*, a fundamental change seems to have occurred in the nature of man: he is now able to stay quietly in his own room. Indeed, that is the dominant style of existence in the ghastly underground utopia Forster envisions, a world in which all needs and wants are provided for through machines summoned by buttons and in which the few remaining situations that require human contact, like procreation, are programed by an unseen, all-powerful Central Committee. The utopia, or really anti-utopia, described by Forster is a world gone insane through an excess of rationalism; the passions of restlessness and unsated desire seem to have been suppressed or bred out of existence.

Did Forster have in mind Pascal's great sentence when he wrote *The Machine Stops*? It seems quite possible. But whether calculated or accidental, it surely is a marvelous touch that in this hell of perfection Pascal's observation no longer applies. That is why we feel about the creatures presented by Forster, especially at the outset of his story, that they are not quite human. Indeed, the main thrust of the story concerns Kuno's struggle to rediscover his humanity. And the token of his humanity? That he is no longer content to remain quietly in his own room.

Written in 1909, before such famous anti-utopian novels as Aldous Huxley's *Brave New World* and George Orwell's *1984*, *The Machine Stops* is a brief, highly concentrated example of what has become in our time a major form of literary expression. The very conciseness of Forster's novella is an important reason for its success, since most novels that try to show how terrible it would be to live in a dehumanized and overly rationalistic world have a tendency to collapse midway from an excess of predictable detail. We soon learn that the imagined utopia is dreadful and that anyone who dares to rebel against it will be crushed; as a result, there are not many possibilities for suspense or drama. But in *The Machine Stops* all the satirical and didactic points are quickly established. This compression, together with Forster's cleverness of detail and his unobtrusively refined style, help to account for the ease with which *The Machine Stops* can be read and for the impact it is likely to have. Later we shall consider in a more general way the nature and limitations of anti-utopian fiction, but let us first look at some of the details of Forster's story.

The very first paragraph offers a vital sequence of references and images. The room in which we find Vashti is "like the cell of a bee," a simile that immediately invites us to draw the familiar but still urgent comparison between a beehive and the kind of mechanized society Forster portrays. There is light in Vashti's room, but neither window nor lamp; there is air, but no connection with the outdoors.

Everything is artificial, machine-made; the term of highest praise in this world is "mechanical." As we soon learn, physical exertion has become as subversive as intellectual distinctiveness, for both are seen as the mark of an outmoded, "atavistic" personal will.

There is one other detail in this first paragraph that is important but easy to miss: the author speaks of "my meditation," a phrase that alerts us at the outset to the probability that he is not just telling a story but has some purpose in mind—to warn, to teach.

As the story begins, Vashti's son Kuno is calling from the other side of the globe. "I can give you fully five minutes," she tells him, for she has to lecture on Australian music—obviously a more important activity than talking to one's own son. The conversation between mother and son is written with great force, and it tells us almost everything we need to know about the remainder of the story. So depersonalized has this world become that it seems normal for a mother to say to her son, "I can give you fully five minutes." He, by contrast, asks to meet "face to face." He has become a heretic who takes exercise, who dares to say that "man is the measure of all things"—and as a result he has been threatened with Homelessness (exile to the surface of the earth). As they talk, Forster notes, the machine transmitting their pictures "did not transmit *nuances* of expression. It only gave a general idea of people—an idea that was good enough for all practical purposes." Indeed, practical purposes rule this world: what does it matter whether a face thousands of miles away registers shades of sadness or crinkles of happiness? What counts is function, not feeling.

Two other key points should be noted about this opening conversation between Vashti and Kuno:

1. Forster allows himself a powerful generalization, one that he will repeat a bit later: "Vashti was seized with the terrors of direct experience." Anything unpredictable or incapable of being programed, anything that brings the risks of unforeseen emotions, has become a source of terror for these creatures.

2. In explaining why she does not like to journey by air, Vashti says, "I get no ideas in an air-ship." Throughout *The Machine Stops* there are references to these "ideas," and they form one of the most intriguing elements in the narrative. By "ideas" is meant here something utterly abstract and disconnected, something that has no connection with sensual experience or with human relationships. In this

world the "idea" is cut off from humanity, as is the god-like Machine that rules humanity. The idea becomes alienated from life, without substance, color, tension. It is rationalism gone berserk.

Forster ends Part I with a clever touch: as Vashti travels to see her son, she passes across the majesty and terror of the earth, precisely what in all previous human history has stimulated men to their most noble ideas. But "these mountains," she says, "give me no ideas." She repeats, " 'No ideas here,' and hid Greece behind a metal blind"—Greece, in the old days of unimproved humanity the land acknowledged to be the cradle of mankind's greatest thought.

Part II divides into two sections: first, the story of Kuno's discovery of air, freedom, and selfhood, and the punishment he receives from the Mending Apparatus; and, second, the gradual disintegration of the Machine itself, that process of breakdown which seems to follow from the logic of mechanization, a process that people living in American cities at this moment can recognize as painfully familiar. The story ends cleverly, on an ambiguous note. Vashti, now struggling to regain her humanity, says that "some fool will start the Machine again, tomorrow," and Kuno replies, "never. Humanity has learnt its lesson." But who can be sure that humanity ever does?

The Machine Stops anticipates the whole genre of anti-utopian fiction, which derives from a writer's discovery that the prospect of the future he has been trained to desire fills him with horror. To a mind raised on the assumption of nineteenth-century philosophies of history that there is an inherent purposiveness, a necessary impulse toward progress, in the human enterprise, there now occurs the fear that history itself is proving to be a cheat—and a cheat not because it has thwarted man's expectations, but because it has perversely fulfilled them. Not progress denied but progress realized is the nightmare haunting anti-utopian fiction. Progress realized means a world in which there is no longer an organic relation between what men do and what they are; a world in which technique and values lose all connection: while technique spins ahead with a mad fecundity, values become debased into mere slogans of an all-powerful state.

The central, terrifying question posed by anti-utopian fiction is this: can human nature be manufactured? Not merely transformed or manipulated or debased, since these it obviously can be, but manufactured by will and decision, to the point where men can "stay quietly in their own room"?

This is a question that Forster—and after him Huxley, Orwell, and others—must face but cannot answer. They tend to assume that there *are* strivings in men toward candor, freedom, truth, and love which cannot be suppressed indefinitely; otherwise, how explain Kuno's wish to return to those traits we would recognize as human? Yet such writers have no choice but to acknowledge that at any particular moment in history these strivings can be suppressed effectively. Modern technology has provided a whole new apparatus for violating human nature: brainwashing and torture, artificial biological selection, protracted "reeducation." The materials of anti-utopian fiction are necessarily exaggerations, but they are exaggerations of tendencies already present in our own life: that is how we recognize them, that is why they frighten us.

Inevitably, anti-utopian fiction keeps returning to the choice posed so brilliantly by the legend of the Grand Inquisitor in Dostoevsky's *Brothers Karamazov:* the misery of the human being who must bear his burden of independence against the contentment of the human creature at rest in his obedience. What makes this contrast between freedom and happiness particularly sharp in our day is the fact that through refinements of technology Dostoevsky's vision can now be realized in social practice. Recall the prophetic speculation of the nineteenth-century historian Alexis de Tocqueville that "a kind of virtuous materialism may ultimately be established in the world which would not corrupt but enervate the soul, and noiselessly unbend its springs of action."

A central fact about an anti-utopian fiction such as *The Machine Stops* is that it deals less with people in their complexity than with mental attitudes. The characters in such a fiction are likely to be lacking in individual consciousness, psychological richness, intimate relationships—all that we have in mind when we speak of "three-dimensional characters." In fact, characters must lack those traits in anti-utopian fiction, since its premise is that a world has been created in which such traits are no longer permissible. The human relations that form the premise of ordinary fiction are the wistful possibilities toward which anti-utopian fiction strains. The necessity of dealing with a world in which man has been absorbed by his social function presents the writer of anti-utopian fiction with many difficulties. His material lacks almost all the usual advantages of fiction:

it must confine itself to an elementary kind of characterization, it cannot provide much in the way of psychological nuance, it hardly pretends to a large accumulation of suspense. Yet, as we all can testify, anti-utopian fiction achieves its impact, and it does this through a variety of ways:

1. *It posits a "flaw" in the perfection of the perfect.* Society has presumably reached a point of perfection, but it still suffers from a "flaw," a weakness: the remembered or yearned-for human. And this "flaw" functions dramatically in anti-utopian fiction quite as the assumption of original sin or a socially induced tendency toward evil functions in the ordinary novel. The "flaw"—in *The Machine Stops* it is Kuno's rebelliousness—provides the possibility for and the particulars of the conflict, while at the same time it ensures that the outcome will be disastrous. Since the ending of an anti-utopian fiction is predictable at its beginning, its dramatic tension depends less on the working out of a developed plot than on the working out of an intellectual conception. And so,

2. *It must be in the grip of an idea at once dramatically simple and historically complex, an idea that has become a commanding passion.* This idea consists, finally, in a catastrophic transmutation of values, a stoppage of history at the expense of human beings (they can now stay quietly in their own room). In reading an anti-utopian fiction we respond less to the world it projects (the mechanical awfulness of Vashti's life) than to the urgency with which it is projected (the mixture of alarm and cleverness with which Forster portrays that life).

3. *As a result, the writer must be clever in the management of substantiating detail.* Since we know all too well that a single rebel against the authoritarian state is doomed to failure and death, we can be surprised only by the ingenuity with which the writer shows the details of the rebel's fate. Thus, in *The Machine Stops* we are horrified by the Mending Apparatus, we are intrigued by the way Kuno struggles to accustom himself to natural air, we are charmed by his rediscovery of the most basic human emotions.

4. *Anti-utopian fiction must strain our sense of the probable while not violating our attachment to the plausible.* If Forster had adhered too closely to the probable—that is, to what he could see in the society of his day—he would not have been able to paint the world of anti-utopia. If he had merely depicted the implausible—that is, a world that had no connection with anything we know—he would

have lost the power to shock us. He met this difficulty by employing what I would call the dramatic strategy and narrative psychology of "one more step." The totalitarian state that he projects in *The Machine Stops* bears many elements of similarity to what we already know in our own experience, but his story takes one crucial step, and no more than one, beyond what we know. It shows human beings virtually stripped of their human traits; they have lost all strivings toward individuality, personality, distinctive achievement.

5. *In presenting the nightmare of anti-utopia, the writer must depend on the ability of his readers to engage in an act of historical recollection.* This means to remember, above all, the power that the idea of Utopia, the hope for a Golden Age, has had in Western society, to remember that this is the enchanted dream for which people have made enormous sacrifices and committed dreadful crimes. "The Golden Age," wrote Dostoevsky, "is the most unlikely of all the dreams that have been, but for it men have given up their life and their strength. . . . Without it the people will not live and cannot die."

These, then, are some of the distinctive elements of anti-utopian fiction, and again one must marvel at the fact that E. M. Forster, a novelist whose main interest lay elsewhere, managed, in one novella, to bring all these elements together. But what needs to be stressed still more is that, in the end, whatever may be distinctive about anti-utopian fiction matters only insofar as it contributes toward the goals at which all serious fiction aims: illumination of the human lot, a deeper understanding of our impulses and psychology, and furtherance of the unending quest for the terms of our freedom.

The Machine Stops

PART I · THE AIR-SHIP

Imagine, if you can, a small room, hexagonal in shape, like the cell of a bee. It is lighted neither by window nor by lamp, yet it is filled with a soft radiance. There are no apertures for ventilation, yet the air is fresh. There are no musical instruments, and yet, at the moment that my meditation opens, this room is throbbing with melodious sounds. An arm-chair is in the centre, by its side a reading-desk—that is all the furniture. And in the arm-chair there sits a swaddled lump of flesh—a woman, about five feet high, with a face as white as a fungus. It is to her that the little room belongs.

An electric bell rang.

The woman touched a switch and the music was silent.

"I suppose I must see who it is," she thought, and set her chair in motion. The chair, like the music, was worked by machinery, and it rolled her to the other side of the room, where the bell still rang importunately.

"Who is it?" she called. Her voice was irritable, for she had been interrupted often since the music began. She knew several thousand people; in certain directions human intercourse had advanced enormously.

But when she listened into the receiver, her white face wrinkled into smiles, and she said:

"Very well. Let us talk, I will isolate myself. I do not expect anything important will happen for the next five minutes—for I can give you fully five minutes, Kuno. Then I must deliver my lecture on 'Music during the Australian Period.'"

She touched the isolation knob, so that no one else could speak to her. Then she touched the lighting apparatus, and the little room was plunged into darkness.

"Be quick!" she called, her irritation returning. "Be quick, Kuno; here I am in the dark wasting my time."

But it was fully fifteen seconds before the round plate that she held in her hands began to glow. A faint blue light shot across it, darkening to purple, and presently she could see the image of her son, who lived on the other side of the earth, and he could see her.

"Kuno, how slow you are."

He smiled gravely.

"I really believe you enjoy dawdling."

"I have called you before, mother, but you were always busy or isolated. I have something particular to say."

"What is it, dearest boy? Be quick. Why could you not send it by pneumatic post?"

"Because I prefer saying such a thing. I want——"

"Well?"

"I want you to come and see me."

Vashti watched his face in the blue plate.

"But I can see you!" she exclaimed. "What more do you want?"

"I want to see you not through the Machine," said Kuno. "I want to speak to you not through the wearisome Machine."

"Oh, hush!" said his mother, vaguely shocked. "You mustn't say anything against the Machine."

"Why not?"

"One mustn't."

"You talk as if a god had made the Machine," cried the other. "I believe that you pray to it when you are unhappy. Men made it, do not forget that. Great men, but men. The Machine is much, but it is not everything. I see something like you in this plate, but I do not see you. I hear something like you through this telephone, but I do not hear you. That is why I want you to come. Come and stop with me. Pay me a visit, so that we can meet face to face, and talk about the hopes that are in my mind."

She replied that she could scarcely spare the time for a visit.

"The air-ship barely takes two days to fly between me and you."

"I dislike air-ships."

"Why?"

"I dislike seeing the horrible brown earth, and the sea, and the stars when it is dark. I get no ideas in an air-ship."

"I do not get them anywhere else."

"What kind of ideas can the air give you?"

He paused for an instant.

"Do you not know four big stars that form an oblong, and three stars close together in the middle of the oblong, and hanging from these stars, three other stars?"

"No, I do not. I dislike the stars. But did they give you an idea? How interesting; tell me."

"I had an idea that they were like a man."

"I do not understand."

"The four big stars are the man's shoulders and his knees. The three stars in the middle are like the belts that men wore once, and the three stars hanging are like a sword."

"A sword?"

"Men carried swords about with them, to kill animals and other men."

"It does not strike me as a very good idea, but it is certainly original. When did it come to you first?"

"In the air-ship——" He broke off, and she fancied that he looked sad. She could not be sure, for the Machine did not transmit *nuances* of expression. It only gave a general idea of people—an idea that was good enough for all practical purposes, Vashti thought. The imponderable bloom, declared by a discredited philosophy to be the actual essence of intercourse, was rightly ignored by the Machine, just as the imponderable bloom of the grape was ignored by the manufacturers of artificial fruit. Something "good enough" had long since been accepted by our race.

"The truth is," he continued, "that I want to see these stars again. They are curious stars. I want to see them not from the air-ship, but from the surface of the earth, as our ancestors did, thousands of years ago. I want to visit the surface of the earth."

She was shocked again.

"Mother, you must come, if only to explain to me what is the harm of visiting the surface of the earth."

"No harm," she replied, controlling herself. "But no advantage. The surface of the earth is only dust and mud, no life remains on it, and you would need a respirator, or the cold of the outer air would kill you. One dies immediately in the outer air."

"I know; of course I shall take all precautions."

"And besides——"

"Well?"

She considered, and chose her words with care. Her son had a
queer temper, and she wished to dissuade him from the expedition.

"It is contrary to the spirit of the age," she asserted.

"Do you mean by that, contrary to the Machine?"

"In a sense, but——"

His image in the blue plate faded.

"Kuno!"

He had isolated himself.

For a moment Vashti felt lonely.

Then she generated the light, and the sight of her room, flooded
with radiance and studded with electric buttons, revived her. There
were buttons and switches everywhere—buttons to call for food, for
music, for clothing. There was the hot-bath button, by pressure of
which a basin of (imitation) marble rose out of the floor, filled to
the brim with a warm deodorised liquid. There was the cold-bath
button. There was the button that produced literature. And there
were of course the buttons by which she communicated with her
friends. The room, though it contained nothing, was in touch with
all that she cared for in the world.

Vashti's next move was to turn off the isolation-switch, and all
the accumulations of the last three minutes burst upon her. The
room was filled with the noise of bells, and speaking-tubes. What was
the new food like? Could she recommend it? Had she had any ideas
lately? Might one tell her one's own ideas? Would she make an engagement to visit the public nurseries at an early date?—say this day
month.

To most of these questions she replied with irritation—a growing
quality in that accelerated age. She said that the new food was horrible. That she could not visit the public nurseries through press of
engagements. That she had no ideas of her own but had just been
told one—that four stars and three in the middle were like a man:
she doubted there was much in it. Then she switched off her cor-
respondents, for it was time to deliver her lecture on Australian music.

The clumsy system of public gatherings had been long since
abandoned; neither Vashti nor her audience stirred from their rooms.
Seated in her arm-chair she spoke, while they in their arm-chairs
heard her, fairly well, and saw her, fairly well. She opened with a
humorous account of music in the pre-Mongolian epoch, and went

on to describe the great outburst of song that followed the Chinese conquest. Remote and primæval as were the methods of I-San-So and the Brisbane school, she yet felt (she said) that study of them might repay the musician of today: they had freshness; they had, above all, ideas.

Her lecture, which lasted ten minutes, was well received, and at its conclusion she and many of her audience listened to a lecture on the sea; there were ideas to be got from the sea; the speaker had donned a respirator and visited it lately. Then she fed, talked to many friends, had a bath, talked again, and summoned her bed.

The bed was not to her liking. It was too large, and she had a feeling for a small bed. Complaint was useless, for beds were of the same dimension all over the world, and to have had an alternative size would have involved vast alterations in the Machine. Vashti isolated herself—it was necessary, for neither day nor night existed under the ground—and reviewed all that had happened since she had summoned the bed last. Ideas? Scarcely any. Events—was Kuno's invitation an event?

By her side, on the little reading-desk, was a survival from the ages of litter—one book. This was the Book of the Machine. In it were instructions against every possible contingency. If she was hot or cold or dyspeptic or at loss for a word, she went to the book, and it told her which button to press. The Central Committee published it. In accordance with a growing habit, it was richly bound.

Sitting up in the bed, she took it reverently in her hands. She glanced round the glowing room as if some one might be watching her. Then, half ashamed, half joyful, she murmured "O Machine! O Machine!" and raised the volume to her lips. Thrice she kissed it, thrice inclined her head, thrice she felt the delirium of acquiescence. Her ritual performed, she turned to page 1367, which gave the times of the departure of the air-ships from the island in the southern hemisphere, under whose soil she lived, to the island in the northern hemisphere, whereunder lived her son.

She thought, "I have not the time."

She made the room dark and slept; she awoke and made the room light; she ate and exchanged ideas with her friends, and listened to music and attended lectures; she made the room dark and slept. Above her, beneath her, and around her, the Machine hummed eternally; she did not notice the noise, for she had been born with it in her ears. The earth, carrying her, hummed as it sped through silence, turning her now to the invisible sun, now to the invisible stars. She awoke and made the room light.

"Kuno!"

"I will not talk to you," he answered, "until you come."

"Have you been on the surface of the earth since we spoke last?"

His image faded.

Again she consulted the book. She became very nervous and lay back in her chair palpitating. Think of her as without teeth or hair. Presently she directed the chair to the wall, and pressed an unfamiliar button. The wall swung apart slowly. Through the opening she saw a tunnel that curved slightly, so that its goal was not visible. Should she go to see her son, here was the beginning of the journey.

Of course she knew all about the communication-system. There was nothing mysterious in it. She would summon a car and it would fly with her down the tunnel until it reached the lift that communicated with the air-ship station: the system had been in use for many, many years, long before the universal establishment of the Machine. And of course she had studied the civilisation that had immediately preceded her own—the civilisation that had mistaken the functions of the system, and had used it for bringing people to things, instead of for bringing things to people. Those funny old days, when men went for change of air instead of changing the air in their rooms! And yet—she was frightened of the tunnel: she had not seen it since her last child was born. It curved—but not quite as she remembered; it was brilliant—but not quite as brilliant as a lecturer had suggested. Vashti was seized with the terrors of direct experience. She shrank back into the room, and the wall closed up again. "Kuno," she said, "I cannot come to see you. I am not well."

Immediately an enormous apparatus fell on to her out of the ceiling, a thermometer was automatically inserted between her lips, a stethoscope was automatically laid upon her heart. She lay powerless. Cool pads soothed her forehead. Kuno had telegraphed to her doctor.

So the human passions still blundered up and down in the Machine. Vashti drank the medicine that the doctor projected into her mouth, and the machinery retired into the ceiling. The voice of Kuno was heard asking how she felt.

"Better." Then with irritation: "But why do you not come to me instead?"

"Because I cannot leave this place."

"Why?"

"Because, any moment, something tremendous may happen."

"Have you been on the surface of the earth yet?"

"Not yet."

"Then what is it?"

"I will not tell you through the Machine."

She resumed her life. . .

But she thought of Kuno as a baby, his birth, his removal to the public nurseries, her one visit to him there, his visits to her—visits which stopped when the Machine had assigned him a room on the other side of the earth. "Parents, duties of," said the Book of the Machine, "cease at the moment of birth. P. 422327483." True, but there was something special about Kuno—indeed there had been something special about all her children—and, after all, she must brave the journey if he desired it. And "something tremendous might happen." What did that mean? The nonsense of a youthful man, no doubt, but she must go. Again she pressed the unfamiliar button, again the wall swung back, and she saw the tunnel that curved out of sight. Clasping the Book, she rose, tottered on to the platform, and summoned the car. Her room closed behind her: the journey to the northern hemisphere had begun.

Of course it was perfectly easy. The car approached and in it she found arm-chairs exactly like her own. When she signalled, it stopped, and she tottered into the lift. One other passenger was in the lift, the first fellow creature she had seen face to face for months. Few travelled in these days, for, thanks to the advance of science, the earth was exactly alike all over. Rapid intercourse, from which the previous civilisation had hoped so much, had ended by defeating itself. What was the good of going to Pekin when it was just like Shrewsbury? Why return to Shrewsbury when it would be just like Pekin? Men seldom moved their bodies; all unrest was concentrated in the soul.

The air-ship service was a relic from the former age. It was kept up, because it was easier to keep it up than to stop it or to diminish it, but it now far exceeded the wants of the population. Vessel after vessel would rise from the vomitories of Rye or of Christchurch (I use the antique names), would sail into the crowded sky, and would draw up at the wharves of the south—empty. So nicely adjusted was the system, so independent of meteorology, that the sky, whether calm or cloudy, resembled a vast kaleidoscope whereon the same patterns periodically recurred. The ship on which Vashti sailed started now at sunset, now at dawn. But always, as it passed above Rheims, it would neighbour the ship that served between Helsingfors and the Brazils, and, every third time it surmounted the Alps, the fleet of Palermo would cross its track behind. Night and day, wind and storm, tide and earthquake, impeded man no longer. He had harnessed Leviathan. All the old literature, with its praise of Nature, and its fear of Nature, rang false as the prattle of a child.

Yet as Vashti saw the vast flank of the ship, stained with exposure to the outer air, her horror of direct experience returned. It was not quite like the air-ship in the cinematophote. For one thing it smelt— not strongly or unpleasantly, but it did smell, and with her eyes shut she should have known that a new thing was close to her. Then she had to walk to it from the lift, had to submit to glances from the other passengers. The man in front dropped his Book—no great matter, but it disquieted them all. In the rooms, if the Book was dropped, the floor raised it mechanically, but the gangway to the air-ship was not so prepared, and the sacred volume lay motionless. They stopped—the thing was unforeseen—and the man, instead of picking up his property, felt the muscles of his arm to see how they had failed him. Then some one actually said with direct utterance: "We shall be late"—and they trooped on board, Vashti treading on the pages as she did so.

Inside, her anxiety increased. The arrangements were old-fashioned and rough. There was even a female attendant, to whom she would have to announce her wants during the voyage. Of course a revolving platform ran the length of the boat, but she was expected to walk from it to her cabin. Some cabins were better than others, and she did not get the best. She thought the attendant had been unfair, and spasms of rage shook her. The glass valves had closed, she could not go back. She saw, at the end of the vestibule, the lift in which she had ascended going quietly up and down, empty. Beneath those corridors of shining tiles were rooms, tier below tier, reaching far into the earth, and in each room there sat a human being, eating, or sleeping, or producing ideas. And buried deep in the hive was her own room. Vashti was afraid.

"O Machine! O Machine!" she murmured, and caressed her Book, and was comforted.

Then the sides of the vestibule seemed to melt together, as do the passages that we see in dreams, the lift vanished, the Book that had been dropped slid to the left and vanished, polished tiles rushed by like a stream of water, there was a slight jar, and the air-ship, issuing from its tunnel, soared above the waters of a tropical ocean.

It was night. For a moment she saw the coast of Sumatra edged by the phosphorescence of waves, and crowned by lighthouses, still sending forth their disregarded beams. These also vanished, and only the stars distracted her. They were not motionless, but swayed to and fro above her head, thronging out of one skylight into another, as if the universe and not the air-ship was careening. And, as often happens on clear nights, they seemed now to be in perspective, now on a plane; now piled tier beyond tier into the infinite heavens, now concealing infinity, a roof limiting for ever the visions of men. In either case they seemed intolerable. "Are we to travel in the dark?" called the passengers angrily, and the attendant, who had been careless, generated the light, and pulled down the blinds of pliable metal. When the air-ships had been built, the desire to look direct at things still lingered in the world. Hence the extraordinary number of skylights and windows, and the proportionate discomfort to those who were civilised and refined. Even in Vashti's cabin one star peeped through a flaw in the blind, and after a few hours' uneasy slumber, she was disturbed by an unfamiliar glow, which was the dawn.

Quick as the ship had sped westwards, the earth had rolled eastwards quicker still, and had dragged back Vashti and her companions towards the sun. Science could prolong the night, but only for a little, and those high hopes of neutralising the earth's diurnal revolution had passed, together with hopes that were possibly higher. To "keep pace with the sun," or even to outstrip it, had been the aim of the civilisation preceding this. Racing aeroplanes had been built for the purpose, capable of enormous speed, and steered by the greatest intellects of the epoch. Round the globe they went, round and round, westward, westward, round and round, amidst humanity's applause. In vain. The globe went eastward quicker still, horrible accidents occurred, and the Committee of the Machine, at the time rising into prominence, declared the pursuit illegal, unmechanical, and punishable by Homelessness.

Of Homelessness more will be said later.

Doubtless the Committee was right. Yet the attempt to "defeat the sun" aroused the last common interest that our race experienced about the heavenly bodies, or indeed about anything. It was the last time that men were compacted by thinking of a power outside the world. The sun had conquered, yet it was the end of his spiritual dominion. Dawn, midday, twilight, the zodiacal path, touched neither men's lives nor their hearts, and science retreated into the ground, to concentrate herself upon problems that she was certain of solving.

So when Vashti found her cabin invaded by a rosy finger of light, she was annoyed, and tried to adjust the blind. But the blind flew up altogether, and she saw through the skylight small pink clouds, swaying against a background of blue, and as the sun crept higher, its radiance entered direct, brimming down the wall, like a golden sea. It rose and fell with the air-ship's motion, just as waves rise and fall, but it advanced steadily, as a tide advances. Unless she was careful, it would strike her face. A spasm of horror shook her and she rang for the attendant. The attendant too was horrified, but she could do nothing; it was not her place to mend the blind. She could only suggest that the lady should change her cabin, which she accordingly prepared to do.

People were almost exactly alike all over the world, but the attendant of the air-ship, perhaps owing to her exceptional duties, had grown a little out of the common. She had often to address passengers with direct speech, and this had given her a certain roughness and originality of manner. When Vashti swerved away from the sunbeams with a cry, she behaved barbarically—she put out her hand to steady her.

"How dare you!" exclaimed the passenger. "You forget yourself!"

The woman was confused, and apologised for not having let her fall. People never touched one another. The custom had become obsolete, owing to the Machine.

"Where are we now?" asked Vashti haughtily.

"We are over Asia," said the attendant, anxious to be polite.

"Asia?"

"You must excuse my common way of speaking. I have got into the habit of calling places over which I pass by their unmechanical names."

"Oh, I remember Asia. The Mongols came from it."

"Beneath us, in the open air, stood a city that was once called Simla."

"Have you ever heard of the Mongols and of the Brisbane school?"

"No."

"Brisbane also stood in the open air."

"Those mountains to the right—let me show you them." She pushed back a metal blind. The main chain of the Himalayas was revealed. "They were once called the Roof of the World, those mountains."

"What a foolish name!"

"You must remember that, before the dawn of civilisation, they seemed to be an impenetrable wall that touched the stars. It was supposed that no one but the gods could exist above their summits. How we have advanced, thanks to the Machine!"

"How we have advanced, thanks to the Machine!" said Vashti.

"How we have advanced, thanks to the Machine!" echoed the passenger who had dropped his Book the night before, and who was standing in the passage.

"And that white stuff in the cracks?—what is it?"

"I have forgotten its name."

"Cover the window, please. These mountains give me no ideas."

The northern aspect of the Himalayas was in deep shadow: on the Indian slope the sun had just prevailed. The forests had been destroyed during the literature epoch for the purpose of making newspaper-pulp, but the snows were awakening to their morning glory, and clouds still hung on the breasts of Kinchinjunga. In the plain were seen the ruins of cities, with diminished rivers creeping by their walls, and by the sides of these were sometimes the signs of vomitories, marking the cities of today. Over the whole prospect air-ships rushed, crossing and intercrossing with incredible *aplomb*, and rising nonchalantly when they desired to escape the perturbations of the lower atmosphere and to traverse the Roof of the World.

"We have indeed advanced, thanks to the Machine," repeated the attendant, and hid the Himalayas behind a metal blind.

The day dragged wearily forward. The passengers sat each in his cabin, avoiding one another with an almost physical repulsion and longing to be once more under the surface of the earth. There were eight or ten of them, mostly young males, sent out from the public nurseries to inhabit the rooms of those who had died in various parts of the earth. The man who had dropped his Book was on the homeward journey. He had been sent to Sumatra for the purpose of propagating the race. Vashti alone was travelling by her private will.

At midday she took a second glance at the earth. The air-ship was crossing another range of mountains, but she could see little, owing to clouds. Masses of black rock hovered below her, and merged

indistinctly into grey. Their shapes were fantastic; one of them resembled a prostrate man.

"No ideas here," murmured Vashti, and hid the Caucasus behind
a metal blind.

In the evening she looked again. They were crossing a golden
sea, in which lay many small islands and one peninsula.

She repeated, "No ideas here," and hid Greece behind a metal
blind.

PART II · THE MENDING APPARATUS

By a vestibule, by a lift, by a tubular railway, by a platform, by a
sliding door—by reversing all the steps of her departure did Vashti
arrive at her son's room, which exactly resembled her own. She might
well declare that the visit was superfluous. The buttons, the knobs,
the reading-desk with the Book, the temperature, the atmosphere,
the illumination—all were exactly the same. And if Kuno himself,
flesh of her flesh, stood close beside her at last, what profit was there
in that? She was too well-bred to shake him by the hand.

Averting her eyes, she spoke as follows:

"Here I am. I have had the most terrible journey and greatly re-
tarded the development of my soul. It is not worth it, Kuno, it is not
worth it. My time is too precious. The sunlight almost touched me,
and I have met with the rudest people. I can only stop a few minutes.
Say what you want to say, and then I must return."

"I have been threatened with Homelessness," said Kuno.

She looked at him now.

"I have been threatened with Homelessness, and I could not tell
you such a thing through the Machine."

Homelessness means death. The victim is exposed to the air,
which kills him.

"I have been outside since I spoke to you last. The tremendous
thing has happened, and they have discovered me."

"But why shouldn't you go outside!" she exclaimed. "It is perfectly legal, perfectly mechanical, to visit the surface of the earth. I
have lately been to a lecture on the sea; there is no objection to that;

one simply summons a respirator and gets an Egression-permit. It is not the kind of thing that spiritually-minded people do, and I begged you not to do it, but there is no legal objection to it."

"I did not get an Egression-permit."

"Then how did you get out?"

"I found out a way of my own."

The phrase conveyed no meaning to her, and he had to repeat it.

"A way of your own?" she whispered. "But that would be wrong."

"Why?"

The question shocked her beyond measure.

"You are beginning to worship the Machine," he said coldly. "You think it irreligious of me to have found out a way of my own. It was just what the Committee thought, when they threatened me with Homelessness."

At this she grew angry. "I worship nothing!" she cried. "I am most advanced. I don't think you irreligious, for there is no such thing as religion left. All the fear and the superstition that existed once have been destroyed by the Machine. I only meant that to find out a way of your own was—— Besides, there is no new way out."

"So it is always supposed."

"Except through the vomitories, for which one must have an Egression-permit, it is impossible to get out. The Book says so."

"Well, the Book's wrong, for I have been out on my feet."

For Kuno was possessed of a certain physical strength.

By these days it was a demerit to be muscular. Each infant was examined at birth, and all who promised undue strength were destroyed. Humanitarians may protest, but it would have been no true kindness to let an athlete live; he would never have been happy in that state of life to which the Machine had called him; he would have yearned for trees to climb, rivers to bathe in, meadows and hills against which he might measure his body. Man must be adapted to his surroundings, must he not? In the dawn of the world our weakly must be exposed on Mount Taygetus, in its twilight our strong will suffer euthanasia, that the Machine may progress, that the Machine may progress, that the Machine may progress eternally.

"You know that we have lost the sense of space. We say 'space is annihilated,' but we have annihilated not space, but the sense thereof. We have lost a part of ourselves. I determined to recover it, and I began by walking up and down the platform of the railway outside my room. Up and down, until I was tired, and so did recapture the meaning of 'Near' and 'Far.' 'Near' is a place to which I can get quickly *on my feet*, not a place to which the train or the airship will take me quickly. 'Far' is a place to which I cannot get quickly on my feet; the vomitory is 'far,' though I could be there in thirty-eight seconds by summoning the train. Man is the measure. That was my first lesson. Man's feet are the measure for distance, his hands are the measure for ownership, his body is the measure for all that is lovable and desirable and strong. Then I went further: it was then that I called to you for the first time, and you would not come.

"This city, as you know, is built deep beneath the surface of the earth, with only the vomitories protruding. Having paced the platform outside my own room, I took the lift to the next platform and paced that also, and so with each in turn, until I came to the topmost, above which begins the earth. All the platforms were exactly alike, and all that I gained by visiting them was to develop my sense of space and my muscles. I think I should have been content with this—it is not a little thing—but as I walked and brooded, it occurred to me that our cities had been built in the days when men still breathed the outer air, and that there had been ventilation shafts for the workmen. I could think of nothing but these ventilation shafts. Had they been destroyed by all the food-tubes and medicine-tubes and music-tubes that the Machine has evolved lately? Or did traces of them remain? One thing was certain. If I came upon them anywhere, it would be in the railway-tunnels of the topmost story. Everywhere else, all space was accounted for.

"I am telling my story quickly, but don't think that I was not a coward or that your answers never depressed me. It is not the proper thing, it is not mechanical, it is not decent to walk along a railway-tunnel. I did not fear that I might tread upon a live rail and be killed. I feared something far more intangible—doing what was not contemplated by the Machine. Then I said to myself, 'Man is the measure,' and I went, and after many visits I found an opening.

"The tunnels, of course, were lighted. Everything is light, artificial light; darkness is the exception. So when I saw a black gap in the tiles, I knew that it was an exception, and rejoiced. I put in my arm—I could put in no more at first—and waved it round and round in ecstasy. I loosened another tile, and put in my head, and shouted into the darkness: 'I am coming, I shall do it yet,' and my voice reverberated down endless passages. I seemed to hear the spirits of those dead workmen who had returned each evening to the star-light and to their wives, and all the generations who had lived in the open air called back to me, 'You will do it yet, you are coming.'"

He paused, and, absurd as he was, his last words moved her. For Kuno had lately asked to be a father, and his request had been refused by the Committee. His was not a type that the Machine desired to hand on.

"Then a train passed. It brushed by me, but I thrust my head and arms into the hole. I had done enough for one day, so I crawled back to the platform, went down in the lift, and summoned my bed. Ah, what dreams! And again I called you, and again you refused."

She shook her head and said:

"Don't. Don't talk of these terrible things. You make me miserable. You are throwing civilisation away."

"But I had got back the sense of space and a man cannot rest then. I determined to get in at the hole and climb the shaft. And so I exercised my arms. Day after day I went through ridiculous movements, until my flesh ached, and I could hang by my hands and hold the pillow of my bed outstretched for many minutes. Then I summoned a respirator, and started.

"It was easy at first. The mortar had somehow rotted, and I soon pushed some more tiles in, and clambered after them into the darkness, and the spirits of the dead comforted me. I don't know what I mean by that. I just say what I felt. I felt, for the first time, that a protest had been lodged against corruption, and that even as the dead were comforting me, so I was comforting the unborn. I felt that humanity existed, and that it existed without clothes. How can I possibly explain this? It was naked, humanity seemed naked, and all these tubes and buttons and machineries neither came into the world with us, nor will they follow us out, nor do they matter supremely while we are here. Had I been strong, I would have torn off every garment I had, and gone out into the outer air unswaddled. But this is not for me, nor perhaps for my generation. I climbed with my respirator and my hygienic clothes and my dietetic tabloids! Better thus than not at all.

"There was a ladder, made of some primaeval metal. The light from the railway fell upon its lowest rungs, and I saw that it led straight upwards out of the rubble at the bottom of the shaft. Perhaps our ancestors ran up and down it a dozen times daily, in their building. As I climbed, the rough edges cut through my gloves so that my hands bled. The light helped me for a little, and then came darkness and, worse still, silence which pierced my ears like a sword. The Machine hums! Did you know that? Its hum penetrates our blood, and may even guide our thoughts. Who knows! I was getting beyond its power. Then I thought: 'This silence means that I am doing wrong.' But I heard voices in the silence, and again they strengthened me." He laughed. "I had need of them. The next moment I cracked my head against something."

She sighed.

"I had reached one of those pneumatic stoppers that defend us from the outer air. You may have noticed them on the air-ship. Pitch dark, my feet on the rungs of an invisible ladder, my hands cut; I cannot explain how I lived through this part, but the voices still comforted me, and I felt for fastenings. The stopper, I suppose, was about eight feet across. I passed my hand over it as far as I could reach. It was perfectly smooth. I felt it almost to the centre. Not quite to the centre, for my arm was too short. Then the voice said: 'Jump. It is worth it. There may be a handle in the centre, and you may catch hold of it and so come to us your own way. And if there is no handle, so that you may fall and are dashed to pieces— it is still worth it: you will still come to us your own way.' So I jumped. There was a handle, and——"

He paused. Tears gathered in his mother's eyes. She knew that he was fated. If he did not die today he would die tomorrow. There was not room for such a person in the world. And with her pity disgust mingled. She was ashamed at having borne such a son, she who had always been so respectable and so full of ideas. Was he really the little boy to whom she had taught the use of his stops and buttons, and to whom she had given his first lessons in the Book? The very hair that disfigured his lip showed that he was reverting to some savage type. On atavism the Machine can have no mercy.

"There was a handle, and I did catch it. I hung tranced over the darkness and heard the hum of these workings as the last whisper in a dying dream. All the things I had cared about and all the people I had spoken to through tubes appeared infinitely little. Meanwhile the handle revolved. My weight had set something in motion and I span slowly, and then——

"I cannot describe it. I was lying with my face to the sunshine. Blood poured from my nose and ears and I heard a tremendous roaring. The stopper, with me clinging to it, had simply been blown out of the earth, and the air that we make down here was escaping through the vent into the air above. It burst up like a fountain. I crawled back to it—for the upper air hurts—and, as it were, I took great sips from the edge. My respirator had flown goodness knows where, my clothes were torn. I just lay with my lips close to the hole, and I sipped until the bleeding stopped. You can imagine nothing so curious. This hollow in the grass—I will speak of it in a minute,—the sun shining into it, not brilliantly but through marbled clouds,—the peace, the nonchalance, the sense of space, and, brushing my cheek, the roaring fountain of our artificial air! Soon I spied my respirator, bobbing up and down in the current high above my head, and higher still were many air-ships. But no one ever looks out of air-ships, and in my case they could not have picked me up. There I was, stranded. The sun shone a little way down the shaft, and revealed the topmost rung of the ladder, but it was hopeless trying to reach it. I should either have been tossed up again by the escape, or else have fallen in, and died. I could only lie on the grass, sipping and sipping, and from time to time glancing around me.

"I knew that I was in Wessex, for I had taken care to go to a lecture on the subject before starting. Wessex lies above the room in which we are talking now. It was once an important state. Its kings held all the southern coast from the Andredswald to Cornwall, while the Wansdyke protected them on the north, running over the high ground. The lecturer was only concerned with the rise of Wessex, so I do not know how long it remained an international power, nor would the knowledge have assisted me. To tell the truth I could do nothing but laugh, during this part. There was I, with a pneumatic stopper by my side and a respirator bobbing over my head, imprisoned, all three of us, in a grass-grown hollow that was edged with fern."

Then he grew grave again.

"Lucky for me that it was a hollow. For the air began to fall back into it and to fill it as water fills a bowl. I could crawl about. Presently I stood. I breathed a mixture, in which the air that hurts predominated whenever I tried to climb the sides. This was not so bad. I had not lost my tabloids and remained ridiculously cheerful, and as for the Machine, I forgot about it altogether. My one aim now was to get to the top, where the ferns were, and to view whatever objects lay beyond.

"I rushed the slope. The new air was still too bitter for me and

I came rolling back, after a momentary vision of something grey. The sun grew very feeble, and I remembered that he was in Scorpio— I had been to a lecture on that too. If the sun is in Scorpio and you are in Wessex, it means that you must be as quick as you can, or it will get too dark. (This is the first bit of useful information I have ever got from a lecture, and I expect it will be the last.) It made me try frantically to breathe the new air, and to advance as far as I dared out of my pond. The hollow filled so slowly. At times I thought that the fountain played with less vigour. My respirator seemed to dance nearer the earth; the roar was decreasing."

He broke off.

"I don't think this is interesting you. The rest will interest you even less. There are no ideas in it, and I wish that I had not troubled you to come. We are too different, mother."

She told him to continue.

"It was evening before I climbed the bank. The sun had very nearly slipped out of the sky by this time, and I could not get a good view. You, who have just crossed the Roof of the World, will not want to hear an account of the little hills that I saw—low colourless hills. But to me they were living and the turf that covered them was a skin, under which their muscles rippled, and I felt that those hills had called with incalculable force to men in the past, and that men had loved them. Now they sleep—perhaps for ever. They commune with humanity in dreams. Happy the man, happy the woman, who awakes the hills of Wessex. For though they sleep, they will never die."

His voice rose passionately.

"Cannot you see, cannot all your lecturers see, that it is we who are dying, and that down here the only thing that really lives is the Machine? We created the Machine, to do our will, but we cannot make it do our will now. It has robbed us of the sense of space and of the sense of touch, it has blurred every human relation and narrowed down love to a carnal act, it has paralysed our bodies and our wills, and now it compels us to worship it. The Machine develops —but not on our lines. The Machine proceeds—but not to our goal. We only exist as the blood corpuscles that course through its arteries, and if it could work without us, it would let us die. Oh, I have no remedy—or, at least, only one—to tell men again and again that I have seen the hills of Wessex as Ælfrid saw them when he overthrew the Danes.

"So the sun set. I forgot to mention that a belt of mist lay between my hill and other hills, and that it was the colour of pearl."

He broke off for the second time.

"Go on," said his mother wearily.

He shook his head.

"Go on. Nothing that you say can distress me now. I am hardened."

"I had meant to tell you the rest, but I cannot: I know that I cannot: good-bye."

Vashti stood irresolute. All her nerves were tingling with his blasphemies. But she was also inquisitive.

"This is unfair," she complained. "You have called me across the world to hear your story, and hear it I will. Tell me—as briefly as possible, for this is a disastrous waste of time—tell me how you returned to civilisation."

"Oh—that!" he said, starting. "You would like to hear about civilisation. Certainly. Had I got to where my respirator fell down?"

"No—but I understand everything now. You put on your respirator, and managed to walk along the surface of the earth to a vomitory, and there your conduct was reported to the Central Committee."

"By no means."

He passed his hand over his forehead, as if dispelling some strong impression. Then, resuming his narrative, he warmed to it again.

"My respirator fell about sunset. I had mentioned that the fountain seemed feebler, had I not."

"Yes."

"About sunset, it let the respirator fall. As I said, I had entirely forgotten about the Machine, and I paid no great attention at the time, being occupied with other things. I had my pool of air, into which I could dip when the outer keenness became intolerable, and which would possibly remain for days, provided that no wind sprang up to disperse it. Not until it was too late, did I realize what the stoppage of the escape implied. You see—the gap in the tunnel had been mended; the Mending Apparatus; the Mending Apparatus, was after me.

"One other warning I had, but I neglected it. The sky at night was clearer than it had been in the day, and the moon, which was about half the sky behind the sun, shone into the dell at moments quite brightly. I was in my usual place—on the boundary between the two atmospheres—when I thought I saw something dark move across the bottom of the dell, and vanish into the shaft. In my folly, I ran down. I bent over and listened, and I thought I heard a faint scraping noise in the depths.

"At this—but it was too late—I took alarm. I determined to put on my respirator and to walk right out of the dell. But my respirator had gone. I knew exactly where it had fallen—between the stopper and the aperture—and I could even feel the mark that it had made in the turf. It had gone, and I realized that something evil was at work, and I had better escape to the other air, and, if I must die, die running towards the cloud that had been the colour of a pearl. I never started. Out of the shaft—it is too horrible. A worm, a long white worm, had crawled out of the shaft and was gliding over the moonlit grass.

"I screamed. I did everything that I should not have done, I stamped upon the creature instead of flying from it, and it at once curled round the ankle. Then we fought. The worm let me run all over the dell, but edged up my leg as I ran. 'Help!' I cried. (That part is too awful. It belongs to the part that you will never know.) 'Help!' I cried. (Why cannot we suffer in silence?) 'Help!' I cried. Then my feet were wound together, I fell, I was dragged away from the dear ferns and the living hills, and past the great metal stopper (I can tell you this part), and I thought it might save me again if I caught hold of the handle. It also was enwrapped, it also. Oh, the whole dell was full of the things. They were searching it in all directions, they were denuding it, and the white snouts of others peeped out of the hole, ready if needed. Everything that could be moved they brought—brushwood, bundles of fern, everything, and down we all went intertwined into hell. The last things that I saw, ere the stopper closed after us, were certain stars, and I felt that a man of my sort lived in the sky. For I did fight, I fought till the very end, and it was only my head hitting against the ladder that quieted me. I woke up in this room. The worms had vanished. I was surrounded by artificial air, artificial light, artificial peace, and my friends were calling to me down speaking-tubes to know whether I had come across any new ideas lately."

Here his story ended. Discussion of it was impossible, and Vashti turned to go.

"It will end in Homelessness," she said quietly.

"I wish it would," retorted Kuno.

"The Machine has been most merciful."

"I prefer the mercy of God."

"By that superstitious phrase, do you mean that you could live in the outer air?"

"Yes."

"Have you ever seen, round the vomitories, the bones of those who were extruded after the Great Rebellion?"

"Yes."

"They were left where they perished for our edification. A few crawled away, but they perished, too—who can doubt it? And so with the Homeless of our own day. The surface of the earth supports life no longer."

"Indeed."

"Ferns and a little grass may survive, but all higher forms have perished. Has any air-ship detected them?"

"No."

"Has any lecturer dealt with them?"

"No."

"Then why this obstinacy?"

"Because I have seen them," he exploded.

"Seen *what?*"

"Because I have seen her in the twilight—because she came to my help when I called—because she, too, was entangled by the worms, and, luckier than I, was killed by one of them piercing her throat."

He was mad. Vashti departed, nor, in the troubles that followed, did she ever see his face again.

PART III · THE HOMELESS

During the years that followed Kuno's escapade, two important developments took place in the Machine. On the surface they were revolutionary, but in either case men's minds had been prepared beforehand, and they did but express tendencies that were latent already.

The first of these was the abolition of respirators.

Advanced thinkers, like Vashti, had always held it foolish to visit the surface of the earth. Air-ships might be necessary, but what was the good of going out for mere curiosity and crawling along for a mile or two in a terrestrial motor? The habit was vulgar and perhaps faintly improper: it was unproductive of ideas, and had no connection with the habits that really mattered. So respirators were abolished, and with them, of course, the terrestrial motors, and except for a few lecturers, who complained that they were debarred access to their subject-matter, the development was accepted quietly. Those who still wanted to know what the earth was like had after all only to listen to some gramophone, or to look into some cinematophote. And even the lecturers acquiesced when they found that a lecture on the sea was none the less stimulating when compiled out of other lectures that had already been delivered on the same subject. "Beware of first-hand ideas!" exclaimed one of the most advanced of them. "First-hand ideas do not really exist. They are but the physical impressions produced by love and fear, and on this gross foundation who could erect a philosophy? Let your ideas be second-hand, and if possible tenth-hand, for then they will be far removed from that disturbing element—direct observation. Do not learn anything about this subject of mine—the French Revolution. Learn instead what I think that Enicharmon thought Urizen thought Gutch thought Ho-Yung thought Chi-Bo-Sing thought Lafcadio Hearn thought Carlyle thought Mirabeau said about the French Revolution. Through the medium of these eight great minds, the blood that was shed at Paris and the windows that were broken at Versailles will be clarified to an idea which you may employ most profitably in your daily lives. But be sure that the intermediates are many and varied, for in history one authority exists to counteract another. Urizen must counteract the scepticism of Ho-Yung and Enicharmon, I must myself counteract the impetuosity of Gutch. You who listen to me are in a better position to judge about the French Revolution than I am. Your descendants will be even in a better position than you, for they will learn what you think I think, and yet another intermediate will be added to the chain. And in time"—his voice rose—"there will come a generation that has got beyond facts, beyond impressions, a generation absolutely colourless, a generation

'seraphically free
From taint of personality,'

which will see the French Revolution not as it happened, nor as they would like it to have happened, but as it would have happened, had it taken place in the days of the Machine."

Tremendous applause greeted this lecture, which did but voice a feeling already latent in the minds of men—a feeling that terrestrial facts must be ignored, and that the abolition of respirators was a positive gain. It was even suggested that air-ships should be abolished too. This was not done, because air-ships had somehow worked themselves into the Machine's system. But year by year they were used less, and mentioned less by thoughtful men.

The second great development was the re-establishment of religion.

This, too, had been voiced in the celebrated lecture. No one could mistake the reverent tone in which the peroration had concluded, and it awakened a responsive echo in the heart of each. Those who had long worshipped silently, now began to talk. They described the strange feeling of peace that came over them when they handled the Book of the Machine, the pleasure that it was to repeat certain numerals out of it, however little meaning those numerals conveyed to the outward ear, the ecstasy of touching a button, however unimportant, or of ringing an electric bell, however superfluously.

"The Machine," they exclaimed, "feeds us and clothes us and houses us; through it we speak to one another, through it we see one another, in it we have our being. The Machine is the friend of ideas and the enemy of superstition: the Machine is omnipotent, eternal; blessed is the Machine." And before long this allocution was printed on the first page of the Book, and in subsequent editions the ritual swelled into a complicated system of praise and prayer. The word "religion" was sedulously avoided, and in theory the Machine was still the creation and the implement of man. But in practice all, save a few retrogrades, worshipped it as divine. Nor was it worshipped in unity. One believer would be chiefly impressed by the blue optic plates, through which he saw other believers; another by the mending apparatus, which sinful Kuno had compared to worms; another by the lifts, another by the Book. And each would pray to this or to that, and ask it to intercede for him with the Machine as a whole. Persecution—that also was present. It did not break out, for reasons that will be set forward shortly. But it was latent, and all who did not accept the minimum known as "undenominational Mechanism" lived in danger of Homelessness, which means death, as we know.

To attribute these two great developments to the Central Committee, is to take a very narrow view of civilisation. The Central Committee announced the developments, it is true, but they were no more the cause of them than were the kings of the imperialistic period the cause of war. Rather did they yield to some invincible pressure, which came no one knew whither, and which, when gratified, was succeeded by some new pressure equally invincible. To such a state of affairs it is convenient to give the name of progress. No one confessed the Machine was out of hand. Year by year it was served with increased efficiency and decreased intelligence. The better a man knew his own duties upon it, the less he understood the duties of his neighbour, and in all the world there was not one who understood the monster as a whole. Those master brains had perished. They had left full directions, it is true, and their successors had each of them mastered a portion of those directions. But Humanity, in its desire for comfort, had over-reached itself. It had exploited the riches of nature too far. Quietly and complacently, it was sinking into decadence, and progress had come to mean the progress of the Machine.

As for Vashti, her life went peacefully forward until the final disaster. She made her room dark and slept; she awoke and made the room light. She lectured and attended lectures. She exchanged ideas with her innumerable friends and believed she was growing more spiritual. At times a friend was granted Euthanasia, and left his or her room for the homelessness that is beyond all human conception. Vashti did not much mind. After an unsuccessful lecture, she would sometimes ask for Euthanasia herself. But the death-rate was not permitted to exceed the birth-rate, and the Machine had hitherto refused it to her.

The troubles began quietly, long before she was conscious of them.

One day she was astonished at receiving a message from her son. They never communicated, having nothing in common, and she had only heard indirectly that he was still alive, and had been transferred from the northern hemisphere, where he had behaved so mischievously, to the southern—indeed, to a room not far from her own.

"Does he want me to visit him?" she thought. "Never again, never. And I have not the time."

No, it was madness of another kind.

He refused to visualize his face upon the blue plate, and speaking out of the darkness with solemnity said:

"The Machine stops."

"What do you say?"

"The Machine is stopping, I know it, I know the signs."

She burst into a peal of laughter. He heard her and was angry, and they spoke no more.

"Can you imagine anything more absurd?" she cried to a friend. "A man who was my son believes that the Machine is stopping. It would be impious if it was not mad."

"The Machine is stopping?" her friend replied. "What does that mean? The phrase conveys nothing to me."

"Nor to me."

"He does not refer, I suppose, to the trouble there has been lately with the music?"

"Oh no, of course not. Let us talk about music."

"Have you complained to the authorities?"

"Yes, and they say it wants mending, and referred me to the Committee of the Mending Apparatus. I complained of those curious gasping sighs that disfigure the symphonies of the Brisbane school. They sound like some one in pain. The Committee of the Mending Apparatus say that it shall be remedied shortly."

Obscurely worried, she resumed her life. For one thing, the defect in the music irritated her. For another thing, she could not forget Kuno's speech. If he had known that the music was out of repair— he could not know it, for he detested music—if he had known that it was wrong, "the Machine stops" was exactly the venomous sort of remark he would have made. Of course he had made it as a venture, but the coincidence annoyed her, and she spoke with some petulance to the Committee of the Mending Apparatus.

They replied, as before, that the defect would be set right shortly.

"Shortly! At once!" she retorted. "Why should I be worried by imperfect music? Things are always put right at once. If you do not mend it at once, I shall complain to the Central Committee."

"No personal complaints are received by the Central Committee," the Committee of the Mending Apparatus replied.

"Through whom am I to make my complaint, then?"

"Through us."

"I complain then."

"Your complaint shall be forwarded in its turn."

"Have others complained?"

This question was unmechanical, and the Committee of the Mending Apparatus refused to answer it.

"It is too bad!" she exclaimed to another of her friends. "There never was such an unfortunate woman as myself. I can never be sure of my music now. It gets worse and worse each time I summon it."

"I too have my troubles," the friend replied. "Sometimes my ideas are interrupted by a slight jarring noise."

"What is it?"

"I do not know whether it is inside my head, or inside the wall."

"Complain, in either case."

"I have complained, and my complaint will be forwarded in its turn to the Central Committee."

Time passed, and they resented the defects no longer. The defects had not been remedied, but the human tissues in that latter day had become so subservient, that they readily adapted themselves to every caprice of the Machine. The sigh at the crisis of the Brisbane symphony no longer irritated Vashti; she accepted it as part of the melody. The jarring noise, whether in the head or in the wall, was no longer resented by her friend. And so with the mouldy artificial fruit, so with the bath water that began to stink, so with the defective rhymes that the poetry machine had taken to emit. All were bitterly complained of at first, and then acquiesced in and forgotten. Things went from bad to worse unchallenged.

It was otherwise with the failure of the sleeping apparatus. That was a more serious stoppage. There came a day when over the whole world—in Sumatra, in Wessex, in the innumerable cities of Courland and Brazil—the beds, when summoned by their tired owners, failed to appear. It may seem a ludicrous matter, but from it we may date the collapse of humanity. The Committee responsible for the failure was assailed by complainants, whom it referred, as usual, to the Committee of the Mending Apparatus, who in its turn assured them that their complaints would be forwarded to the Central Committee. But the discontent grew, for mankind was not yet sufficiently adaptable to do without sleeping.

"Some one is meddling with the Machine——" they began.

"Some one is trying to make himself king, to reintroduce the personal element."

"Punish that man with Homelessness."

"To the rescue! Avenge the Machine! Avenge the Machine!"

"War! Kill the man!"

But the Committee of the Mending Apparatus now came forward, and allayed the panic with well-chosen words. It confessed that the Mending Apparatus was itself in need of repair.

The effect of this frank confession was admirable.

"Of course," said a famous lecturer—he of the French Revolution, who gilded each new decay with splendour—"of course we shall not press our complaints now. The Mending Apparatus has treated us so well in the past that we all sympathize with it, and will wait patiently for its recovery. In its own good time it will resume its duties. Meanwhile let us do without our beds, our tabloids, our other little wants. Such, I feel sure, would be the wish of the Machine."

Thousands of miles away his audience applauded. The Machine still linked them. Under the seas, beneath the roots of the mountains, ran the wires through which they saw and heard, the enormous eyes and ears that were their heritage, and the hum of many workings clothed their thoughts in one garment of subserviency. Only the old and the sick remained ungrateful, for it was rumoured that Euthanasia, too, was out of order, and that pain had reappeared among men.

It became difficult to read. A blight entered the atmosphere and dulled its luminosity. At times Vashti could scarcely see across her room. The air, too, was foul. Loud were the complaints, impotent the remedies, heroic the tone of the lecturer as he cried: "Courage, courage! What matter so long as the Machine goes on? To it the darkness and the light are one." And though things improved again after a time, the old brilliancy was never recaptured, and humanity never recovered from its entrance into twilight. There was an hysterical talk of "measures," of "provisional dictatorship," and the inhabitants of Sumatra were asked to familiarize themselves with the workings of the central power station, the said power station being situated in France. But for the most part panic reigned, and men spent their strength praying to their Books, tangible proofs of the Machine's omnipotence. There were gradations of terror—at times came rumours of hope—the Mending Apparatus was almost mended—the enemies of the Machine had been got under—new "nerve-centres" were evolving which would do the work even more magnificently than before. But there came a day when, without the slightest warning, without any previous hint of feebleness, the entire communication-system broke down, all over the world, and the world, as they understood it, ended.

Vashti was lecturing at the time and her earlier remarks had been punctuated with applause. As she proceeded the audience became silent, and at the conclusion there was no sound. Somewhat displeased, she called to a friend who was a specialist in sympathy. No sound: doubtless the friend was sleeping. And so with the next friend whom she tried to summon, and so with the next, until she remembered Kuno's cryptic remark, "The Machine stops."

The phrase still conveyed nothing. If Eternity was stopping it would of course be set going shortly.

For example, there was still a little light and air—the atmosphere had improved a few hours previously. There was still the Book, and while there was the Book there was security.

Then she broke down, for with the cessation of activity came an unexpected terror—silence.

She had never known silence, and the coming of it nearly killed her—it did kill many thousands of people outright. Ever since her birth she had been surrounded by the steady hum. It was to the ear what artificial air was to the lungs, and agonizing pains shot across her head. And scarcely knowing what she did, she stumbled forward and pressed the unfamiliar button, the one that opened the door of her cell.

Now the door of the cell worked on a simple hinge of its own. It was not connected with the central power station, dying far away in France. It opened, rousing immoderate hopes in Vashti, for she thought that the Machine had been mended. It opened, and she saw the dim tunnel that curved far away towards freedom. One look, and then she shrank back. For the tunnel was full of people—she was almost the last in that city to have taken alarm.

People at any time repelled her, and these were nightmares from her worst dreams. People were crawling about, people were screaming, whimpering, gasping for breath, touching each other, vanishing in the dark, and ever and anon being pushed off the platform on to the live rail. Some were fighting round the electric bells, trying to summon trains which could not be summoned. Others were yelling for Euthanasia or for respirators, or blaspheming the Machine. Others stood at the doors of their cells fearing, like herself, either to stop in them or to leave them. And behind all the uproar was silence—the silence which is the voice of the earth and of the generations who have gone.

No—it was worse than solitude. She closed the door again and sat down to wait for the end. The disintegration went on, accompanied by horrible cracks and rumbling. The valves that restrained the Medical Apparatus must have been weakened, for it ruptured and hung hideously from the ceiling. The floor heaved and fell and flung her from her chair. A tube oozed towards her serpent fashion. And at last the final horror approached—light began to ebb, and she knew that civilisation's long day was closing.

She whirled round, praying to be saved from this, at any rate, kissing the Book, pressing button after button. The uproar outside was increasing, and even penetrated the wall. Slowly the brilliancy of her cell was dimmed, the reflections faded from her metal switches. Now she could not see the reading-stand, now not the Book, though she held it in her hand. Light followed the flight of sound, air was following light, and the original void returned to the cavern from which it had been so long excluded. Vashti continued to whirl, like the devotees of an earlier religion, screaming, praying, striking at the buttons with bleeding hands.

It was thus that she opened her prison and escaped—escaped in the spirit: at least so it seems to me, ere my meditation closes. That she escapes in the body—I cannot perceive that. She struck, by chance, the switch that released the door, and the rush of foul air on her skin, the loud throbbing whispers in her ears, told her that she was facing the tunnel again, and that tremendous platform on which she had seen men fighting. They were not fighting now. Only the whispers remained, and the little whimpering groans. They were dying by hundreds out in the dark.

She burst into tears.

Tears answered her.

They wept for humanity, those two, not for themselves. They could not bear that this should be the end. Ere silence was completed their hearts were opened, and they knew what had been important on the earth. Man, the flower of all flesh, the noblest of all creatures visible, man who had once made god in his image, and had mirrored his strength on the constellations, beautiful naked man was dying, strangled in the garments that he had woven. Century after century had he toiled, and here was his reward. Truly the garment had seemed heavenly at first, shot with the colours of culture, sewn with the threads of self-denial. And heavenly it had been so long as it was a garment and no more, so long as man could shed it at will and live by the essence that is his soul, and the essence, equally divine, that is his body. The sin against the body—it was for that they wept in chief; the centuries of wrong against the muscles and the nerves, and those five portals by which we can alone apprehend— glozing it over with talk of evolution, until the body was white pap, the home of ideas as colourless, last sloshy stirrings of a spirit that had grasped the stars.

"Where are you?" she sobbed.

His voice in the darkness said, "Here."

"Is there any hope, Kuno?"

"None for us."

"Where are you?"

She crawled towards him over the bodies of the dead. His blood spurted over her hands.

"Quicker," he gasped, "I am dying—but we touch, we talk, not through the Machine."

He kissed her.

"We have come back to our own. We die, but we have recaptured life, as it was in Wessex, when Ælfrid overthrew the Danes. We know what they know outside, they who dwelt in the cloud that is the colour of a pearl."

"But, Kuno, is it true? Are there still men on the surface of the earth? Is this—this tunnel, this poisoned darkness—really not the end?"

He replied:

"I have seen them, spoken to them, loved them. They are hiding in the mist and the ferns until our civilisation stops. Today they are the Homeless—tomorrow——"

"Oh, tomorrow—some fool will start the Machine again, tomorrow."

"Never," said Kuno, "never. Humanity has learnt its lesson."

As he spoke, the whole city was broken like a honeycomb. An air-ship had sailed in through the vomitory into a ruined wharf. It crashed downwards, exploding as it went, rending gallery after gallery with its wings of steel. For a moment they saw the nations of the dead, and, before they joined them, scraps of the untainted sky.

JOSEPH CONRAD

The Secret Sharer

AN EPISODE FROM THE COAST

Introduction

Almost everyone would agree that *The Secret Sharer* is not only subtle and complex but, in the end, very elusive. It is a work of fiction that cannot—and, we soon decide, should not—be pinned down to a simple or unambiguous meaning.

Yet, even as we feel the presence of difficulty, we may not be able to locate it immediately or precisely. The main line of action is certainly not hard to follow, nor is it hard to apprehend clearly the two or three central characters. Only in trying to form a balanced evaluation of what it is all about, only in working out our evaluation of the story as a whole, do we run into problems. For Conrad knew that there is a considerable distance between the abstract realm of moral ideas and the human stage on which those ideas come into play. He created situations in which the usual standards of moral judgment are tested under the greatest possible stress. We are subtly educated, as we read *The Secret Sharer*, about the difficulty of applying even the most valid moral standards and the particular difficulty of applying them in the kind of extreme situation—a crisis at sea—in which the protagonist finds himself. As a result, we are left feeling anxious and uncertain; we are not sure how to distribute our sympathies; and we may even come to question whether the usual moral standards are themselves valid.

We read *The Secret Sharer* with mounting interest and intensity; but we begin to flounder once we are forced to confront some perplexing questions:

✦ Does Conrad wish us to conclude that the narrator's action in hiding Leggatt and thereby endangering his ship is admirable, a deplorable error in judgment, a young man's folly, or a risk of the kind that recurs in human experience?

✦ What moral valuation does Conrad wish to place upon the relationship between the narrator and Leggatt?

✦ Is the captain of the Sephora to be seen as mostly a comic dullard unable so much as to imagine the grounds for exonerating Leggatt's act of killing, or is he to be seen as an agent of firm traditional values that have been violated, or neglected, by the narrator?

Further questions of this kind will occur to anyone reading *The Secret Sharer*. Instead of trying to answer them directly, let me dramatize the problem of reading and interpreting this novella by making up three miniature compositions such as some students might compose. Each will take a different point of view. Let us call the three imaginary authors The Lover of Adventure, The Moral Realist, and The Depth Psychologist.

1. *The Lover of Adventure*

What strikes me most forcibly in reading *The Secret Sharer* is that it is a story of action, a story meant to create suspense and excitement. Two men are thrust into difficult circumstances. One must fulfill his responsibilities of command; the other is trying to avoid the consequences of a failure in responsibility. Because Leggatt rouses feelings of sympathy in the young captain, the captain hides him in his stateroom—even though he knows that Leggatt has broken the law. So far, this may seem like a fairly routine idea for a story, but Conrad employs great skill in creating a mixture of feverish intensity and nervous humor, so as to wring from the situation all the suspense it can yield.

One technique he repeatedly employs, somewhat similar to that used by skillful movie directors, is to have a minor character blunder unwittingly and innocently into the center of danger or trouble. We, together with the captain, realize that everything may suddenly blow up; our nerves are therefore on edge; but the figure who brings us to the danger point is himself entirely unaware or merely puzzled. What follows is the humor of incongruity. Take, for example, the steward—that poor, decent fellow who fears the captain has gone a little crazy because he, the steward, can't understand all the captain's weird maneuvers designed to prevent Leggatt from being discovered. The steward's dismay turns, after a while, into fear and horror, since he suspects some dreadful but unexplainable disaster; and thereby we are given a compressed version of the effect the captain's odd behavior must have on the crew as a whole. Thus the steward is used by Conrad for the mixed effects of comic byplay, mounting tension, and symbolic economy.

When the captain of the *Sephora* comes to visit, he is used by Conrad for similar purposes. He too, without any awareness or intent, almost blows up the whole situation. This nice old man who sticks to the letter of the law is notable for a lack of imagination; he sticks to the tried and true moralities of the sea, which the young captain is now beginning to suspect are not adequate for all circumstances. Yet Conrad is shrewd enough not simply to make the *Sephora*'s captain into a mere butt, for we are always left with the possible conclusion that his very limitations of moral imagination explain his ability to perform his duties so faithfully. And, as with the steward, the result is a kind of shivery comedy—a little like that created in movies by showing characters perched on a ledge of a building. When the young captain pretends to be deaf so as to force the *Sephora*'s captain to shout and thereby signal Leggatt to take cover, the effect is at once amusing and unnerving. Emotionally we side with the narrator, but at the same time we feel a bit uneasy because he has played this kind of trick on a decent old man.

Incidents such as these seem to me prime examples of what Conrad himself believed to be the novelist's major obligation. "My task," he wrote, "is, by the power of the written word, to make you hear, to make you feel—it is, before all, to make you *see*. That—and no more, and it is everything." Conrad understood that the job of the storyteller is to tell a story, and to tell it with economy and force. "It is everything."

That Conrad generates the excitement and suspense to which I referred earlier is proved by the fact that we are continually wondering what will happen next. We care because the fate of human beings is involved, the fate of imaginary figures who have been made to seem real. A whole community—the community of the ship—is at stake. The young captain is not completely admirable, and a seaman's board of examiners would probably regard him as not quite "sound"; but as Conrad cleverly bares the mind of the young captain, we share in his risks. We are held captive by the thrust of the narrative, which is primarily—I would insist—about the adventures of a man at sea. The young captain takes on a new responsibility and because he indulges himself in the sentimental yet not unattractive gesture of hiding Leggatt, he risks the destruction of his ship. We therefore become intensely eager to learn the outcome: will Leggatt escape? will the ship emerge safely?

Meanwhile the sense of adventure is heightened because there is a force at work in *The Secret Sharer* that is quite as powerful as the characters themselves—the sea. In Conrad's books the sea often represents the presence, at once threatening and beautiful, of everything that lies beyond human will or desire. The sea is not susceptible to human entreaties, inducements, or fantasies. The sea is simply there, a force with which men have to contend. As such, the sea has a humbling effect on Conrad's characters; if they are clever it persuades them (and if they are stubborn it coerces them) into understanding that there are severe limits to what men can want and even more severe limits to what they can get. At certain moments the sea is calm and beautiful, lulling Conrad's characters into the false security of supposing there is a basic harmony between nature and man. At other moments the sea is turbulent and ugly, teaching Conrad's characters that the physical world is made for neither our comfort nor our survival; it is simply the stage upon which we act out our adventures. The excitement created by Conrad stems not merely from the conflict between man and man, but also from another and deeper conflict: that between man and nature. All great adventure stories touch, at some point, upon the struggle of men to survive in the natural world.

In conclusion, I believe that we should give our major attention, in the reading of fiction, to the outer events, the visible places and atmospheres presented by the authors. I know this is not a fashionable opinion these days. Still, let me quote from Irving Howe, who has recently said, "Good literature is mostly surface, bad criticism mostly depths." What I am saying here does not imply that *The Secret Sharer* is without its emotional complexities and psychological profundities. It implies rather that the "meanings" and "implications" of a piece of fiction do not exist apart from, and should not be abstracted too far from, the surface events. We register the impact of the story, and gather in all its nuances of suggestion, by responding directly to its action. And in that way our reading remains a unified experience—not something artificially split between story and meaning.

2. *The Moral Realist*

Regardless of how exciting the narrative is or how exotic the setting may seem, Conrad's story is concerned primarily with human beings. Since *The Secret Sharer* deals with the problems of men, it must also deal with problems of morality. For human existence always involves choices, perhaps ultimately between good and evil, but immediately between shades of good and evil. Sometimes one is forced to choose what one knows or suspects is the lesser of two evils. And to refuse to make a choice can be an indirect way of making one. By its nature, the moral life is extremely complicated, if only because one can never be sure what the consequences of a particular choice will be. But choose one must.

That is the moral dilemma confronting the young captain in *The Secret Sharer*. He starts his first command with soaring hopes. He wishes to leave behind him the land, which he identifies with "unrest" and messy complications. He looks upon the sea as "untempted life"—and that is his first mistake. For he does not realize that wherever men come together, wherever human wills must clash and one man exert authority over another, life cannot be "untempted."

As Leggatt, exhausted and helpless, swims to the side of his ship, the captain must make a moral decision immediately. To pull a man out of the water is elementary humanity. But to hide this same man after he blandly admits to having committed murder is something else. And the young captain must choose quickly: he cannot gain time by saying that he will think about it.

Is the captain wrong? I am not sure, though I am certain that it is the greatness of Conrad's art that makes the captain's dilemma so vivid. On the one hand, Leggatt seems to be a characteristically decent and clean-cut young Englishman, who, in background, manner, and speech, is very much like the captain himself. Leggatt's act was not unambiguously reprehensible—or so the captain feels. There certainly were extenuating circumstances. It can even be argued that what Leggatt did saved the lives of the entire crew. But on the other hand, the captain has a primary responsibility to *his* ship, *his* men, *his* command.

It is here that the sea becomes important, not as a mysterious pseudo-philosophical "force," but simply as a place where all issues must be confronted in the bluntest and most extreme terms. The captain of a ship must assume absolute responsibility. The welfare of his community (the ship and its men) rests with him alone. The moral issues appear stripped of their usual complications.

Editor's interruption:
As our Moral Realist was writing his composition, there occurred an incident that suggests that sometimes life seems to copy art. An Italian tanker had been grounded near England and her cargo of crude oil was spilling over, thereby contaminating the coastal waters. The captain of the ship was quoted by the *New York Times* of March 30, 1967, as crying out:

I must answer for everything, for everyone!

Continued Captain Pastrengo Rugiati, who probably had never read a Conrad novel yet who spoke like a Conrad character:

I must carry the cross alone!

The young captain is undergoing an initiation in command, a moral test of his capacity for judgment. "I wondered," he had said to himself at the outset of the journey, "how far I should turn out faithful to that ideal conception of one's own personality every man sets up for himself secretly."

It is a situation, as Albert Guerard writes, that "Conrad will dramatize again and again: the act of a sympathetic identification with a suspect or outlaw figure, and the ensuing conflict between loyalty to the individual and loyalty to the community." And what gives the novella its tone of haunting irresolution is the fact that we cannot really be sure how we would—or should—act in similar circumstances. Conrad arranges the novella so that the captain is driven further and further into a corner. He is visited by the elderly captain of the *Sephora*, who is a quite old-fashioned figure: he believes in the traditional codes of moral judgment; he has an unswerving respect for the law; he lives entirely by the standards of duty. Conrad elaborates:

> To the law. His obscure tenacity on that point had in it something incomprehensible and a little awful; something, as it were, mystical, quite apart from his anxiety that he should not be suspected of "countenancing any doings of that sort." Seven-and-thirty virtuous years at sea, of which over twenty of immaculate command, and the last fifteen in the *Sephora*, seemed to have laid him under some pitiless obligation.

The young captain is inclined to mock this worthy man, but we are by no means sure that Conrad intends us entirely to share in that response. For there really is something impressive about the older man's rocklike determination to live by the letter of the law; after all, it is only the presence of such men setting an absolute standard that makes possible the moral imaginativeness, or moral deviations, of the young captain.

At the end, by taking an enormous risk, which endangers the life of his men and the survival of his ship, the young captain manages to scrape through. He helps Leggatt to escape and then he emerges securely in command. Only now can he begin to enjoy his ship: "And I was alone with her. Nothing! no one in the world should stand now between us, throwing a shadow on the way of silent knowledge and mute affection, the perfect communion of a seaman with his first command."

At least this once, he has succeeded in reconciling the obligation he felt toward a trapped human being and the obligation he had to his social role. But I am not sure how, in the end, Conrad wishes us to see the entire story. Is Conrad suggesting that the fact of hiding Leggatt was a temporary aberration, a young man's forgiveable rashness, which as he grows in maturity and experience he will never again risk? Is Conrad suggesting that the young captain has validated his humanity by not allowing his official burdens to keep him from helping a fellow creature in distress? Or is Conrad suggesting that there can be no simple answer to the moral dilemma that he has himself imagined, and that men must somehow struggle within themselves to find ways of fulfilling those moral responsibilities that may clash with one another but that seem, at any given moment, equally urgent?

I am not sure what Conrad's answer to these questions would be.

I suspect that he could not give a simple and unqualified answer. But I do believe that Conrad has, in this brilliant novella, given us a moral action that has endless ramifications. Few of us are likely to become sea captains, but all of us are likely to face choices like that of the hero in *The Secret Sharer*.

3. The Depth Psychologist

Nothing in *The Secret Sharer* is merely, or simply, what it seems. This is a symbolic novella, in which we have to dig beneath the surface for meanings and implications. The clue to it all, which I offer as a defense against the charge of reading things "into" the novella, is a single word. Throughout the story the young captain keeps referring to Leggatt as his "double," thereby meaning to suggest some sort of hidden or half-visible relationship between the two men. The crisis evoked by Leggatt's appearance makes the captain aware of potential aspects of his own self.

From the outset Conrad establishes a dreamlike atmosphere. The language of the very first sentence—*mysterious, half-submerged, incomprehensible, crazy of aspect, abandoned, nomad tribe, no sign of human habitation*—points to something eerie, something uncanny. Conrad's stress on "stillness" in the opening paragraphs reinforces this impression. Clearly, we are in the presence of a tale that means more than it says and that uses external events mainly as clues to the psychic life, even the subconscious wishes and fantasies, of the characters.

The idea of a "double" goes back to nineteenth-century Russian literature, especially to Gogol and Dostoevsky. For example, Ivan Karamazov, in Dostoevsky's great novel *The Brothers Karamazov*, is a serious man, a thoughtful intellectual. Behind Ivan, however, there is another character, his half-brother Smerdyakov, who is morally odious and in fact turns out to have committed a murder. As the novel progresses it becomes clear that Smerdyakov is meant to bring out, with an exaggerated stress, certain unattractive qualities of Ivan Karamazov—qualities that Ivan might repudiate with horror but that Dostoevsky means us to see as at least *possibilities* within Ivan. This kind of relationship is partly a moral one: we all have a devil within us. But it is also psychological.

The captain immediately recognizes a kinship between himself and Leggatt: "a mysterious communication was established already between us two." And Leggatt says later that it was "as if you had expected me." Exactly what the nature of their kinship is we do not yet know, except for such superficial similarities as speech and national background. The central action of the novella is then developed to make clear that between the two men there is a psychological relationship involving guilt—indeed, that the captain and Leggatt could even be regarded as two halves of a human character split between surface and depth, appearance and reality, respectability and sin. The captain gives Leggatt his "sleeping-suit," the clothing men use when they dream and slip back into unconscious life. Later the captain himself also walks about in a sleeping-suit, as if he were implicitly recognizing his slide back into the depths of the psyche. For what the young captain recognizes in Leggatt are latent qualities of his own—urges which, in his highly disciplined life, he has suppressed, but which now stir interest and sympathy within him. He hides Leggatt in his own room, and Leggatt thus becomes his "secret sharer" quite in the way our guilt shares in our conscious life. Perhaps too (I am not sure) the captain can be seen as Leggatt's secret sharer, in the way our conscious life can become vulnerable to the claims of the unconscious.

I do not think that this is a fanciful reading of *The Secret Sharer*. How else can we account for the young captain's intense fascination with Leggatt and for the fact that he keeps noticing similarities in their character and background? For Conrad is trying, through these physical devices, to suggest a psychic partnership: it is a way of making the young captain, at first glance the typical boy scout, recognize that he too might kill, that he too has instincts for violence, and that even on the "untempting" sea he is open to all the failings of humanity.

When the captain first sees Leggatt, he observes, "He was complete but for the head. A headless corpse!"—which is to say that he sees Leggatt as representing the part of man that is beneath the head, beneath the mind, beneath consciousness. Psychologists tell us that water is a universal symbol in our dreams and stands for the unconscious, and it is notable that Leggatt emerges from and returns to the water in the dark of night. The young captain is thus undertaking an interior or night journey; he is probing into the depths of his self and there discovering, under the pressures of his first great responsibility, that he too has inclinations to criminality and sinfulness. This process of self-discovery ("I was somewhat of a stranger to myself," he says early in the story), does not weaken him; it endows him with strength to go ahead with his work.

Albert Guerard, in his fine book, *Conrad the Novelist*, substantiates the ideas I am advancing:

> as double Leggatt is also very inwardly a secret self. He provokes a crippling division of the narrator's personality, and one that interferes with his seamanship. On the first night the captain intends to pin together the curtains across the bed in which Leggatt is lying. But he cannot. He is too tired, in "a peculiarly intimate way." He feels less "torn in two" when he is with Leggatt in the cabin, but this naturally involves neglect of his duties. As for other times—"I was constantly watching myself, my secret self, as dependent on my actions as my own personality, sleeping in that bed, behind that door which faced me as I sat at the head table." . . . He has been seriously disoriented, and even begins to doubt Leggatt's bodily existence. "I think I had come creeping quietly as near insanity as any man who has not actually gone over the border." The whispering communion of the narrator and his double—of the seaman-self and some darker, more interior, and outlaw self—must have been necessary and rewarding, since the story ends as positively as it does. But it is obvious to both men that the arrangement cannot be permanent.

If I were to stretch a point, I would say that the young captain represents the ego, as it is being buffetted about in a new and difficult situation, the kind of situation in which we all become more open than usual to feelings of vulnerability. In the novella those feelings are symbolized by Leggatt, the shameful twin of the young captain, whom we might call, in Freudian terms, the id. At the opposite extreme, the *Sephora*'s captain represents the claims of conscience or the superego. When the young captain makes the *Sephora*'s captain shout so that Leggatt can overhear the conversation, this is, on the level of plot, a way of signaling to Leggatt to make himself scarce; on the level of significance, it is a way by which the ego keeps in touch with the id at a moment when it is being heavily pressured by the superego. I have no special interest in defending this Freudian terminology, but I am convinced that something like this does occur in the novella Conrad wrote.

Here, then, are expressions of three points of view. And these "papers" are only preliminary explorations of the novella. For the reader who would like to compare the three treatments, a few notes may be helpful:

+ *People may use different vocabularies and yet be saying quite similar things. You will probably find many points of harmony among the three interpretations.*

+ *But don't try to make the three readings absolutely harmonious. Each may provide insights that the others lack. And if there are contradictions among them, perhaps they should be left unresolved, the way the novella itself may leave matters unresolved.*

+ *The French philosopher Pascal once said: "There are two errors. (1) To take everything literally. (2) To take everything spiritually." Perhaps that is the thought to have uppermost in mind when you read fiction like* The Secret Sharer.

The Secret Sharer

AN EPISODE FROM THE COAST

I

On my right hand there were lines of fishing-stakes resembling a mysterious system of half-submerged bamboo fences, incomprehensible in its division of the domain of tropical fishes, and crazy of aspect as if abandoned for ever by some nomad tribe of fishermen now gone to the other end of the ocean; for there was no sign of human habitation as far as the eye could reach. To the left a group of barren islets, suggesting ruins of stone walls, towers, and blockhouses, had its foundations set in a blue sea that itself looked solid, so still and stable did it lie below my feet; even the track of light from the westering sun shone smoothly, without that animated glitter which tells of an imperceptible ripple. And when I turned my head to take a parting glance at the tug which had just left us anchored outside the bar, I saw the straight line of the flat shore joined to the stable sea, edge to edge, with a perfect and unmarked closeness, in one levelled floor half brown, half blue under the enormous dome of the sky. Corresponding in their insignificance to the islets of the sea, two small clumps of trees, one on each side of the only fault in the impeccable joint, marked the mouth of the river Meinam we had just left on the first preparatory stage of our homeward journey; and, far back on the inland level, a larger and loftier mass, the grove surrounding the great Paknam pagoda, was the only thing on which the eye could rest from the vain task of exploring the monotonous sweep of the horizon. Here and there gleams as of a few scattered pieces of silver marked the windings of the great river; and on the nearest of them, just within the bar, the tug steaming right into the land became lost to my sight, hull and funnel and masts, as though the impassive earth had swallowed her up without an effort, without a tremor. My eye followed the light cloud of her smoke, now here, now there, above the plain, according to the devious curves of the stream, but always fainter and farther away, till I lost it at last behind the mitre-shaped hill of the great pagoda. And then I was left alone with my ship, anchored at the head of the Gulf of Siam.

She floated at the starting-point of a long journey, very still in an immense stillness, the shadows of her spars flung far to the eastward by the setting sun. At that moment I was alone on her decks. There was not a sound in her—and around us nothing moved, nothing lived, not a canoe on the water, not a bird in the air, not a cloud in the sky. In this breathless pause at the threshold of a long passage we seemed to be measuring our fitness for a long and arduous enterprise, the appointed task of both our existences to be carried out, far from all human eyes, with only sky and sea for spectators and for judges.

There must have been some glare in the air to interfere with one's sight, because it was only just before the sun left us that my roaming eyes made out beyond the highest ridge of the principal islet of the group something which did away with the solemnity of perfect solitude. The tide of darkness flowed on swiftly; and with tropical suddenness a swarm of stars came out above the shadowy earth, while I lingered yet, my hand resting lightly on my ship's rail as if on the shoulder of a trusted friend. But, with all that multitude of celestial bodies staring down at one, the comfort of quiet communion with her was gone for good. And there were also disturbing sounds by this time—voices, footsteps forward; the steward flitted along the main-deck, a busily ministering spirit; a hand-bell tinkled urgently under the poop-deck. . . .

I found my two officers waiting for me near the supper table, in the lighted cuddy. We sat down at once, and as I helped the chief mate, I said:

"Are you aware that there is a ship anchored inside the islands? I saw her mastheads above the ridge as the sun went down."

He raised sharply his simple face, overcharged by a terrible growth of whisker, and emitted his usual ejaculations: "Bless my soul, sir! You don't say so!"

My second mate was a round-cheeked, silent young man, grave beyond his years, I thought; but as our eyes happened to meet I detected a slight quiver on his lips. I looked down at once. It was not my part to encourage sneering on board my ship. It must be said, too, that I knew very little of my officers. In consequence of certain events of no particular significance, except to myself, I had been appointed to the command only a fortnight before. Neither did I know much of the hands forward. All these people had been together for eighteen months or so, and my position was that of the only stranger on board. I mention this because it has some bearing on what is to follow. But what I felt most was my being a stranger to the ship; and if all the truth must be told, I was somewhat of a stranger to myself. The youngest man on board (barring the second mate), and untried as yet by a position of the fullest responsibility, I was willing to take the adequacy of the others for granted. They had simply to be equal to their tasks; but I wondered how far I should turn out faithful to that ideal conception of one's own personality every man sets up for himself secretly.

Meantime the chief mate, with an almost visible effect of collaboration on the part of his round eyes and frightful whiskers, was trying to evolve a theory of the anchored ship. His dominant trait was to take all things into earnest consideration. He was of a painstaking turn of mind. As he used to say, he "liked to account to himself" for practically everything that came in his way, down to a miserable scorpion he had found in his cabin a week before. The why and the wherefore of that scorpion—how it got on board and came to select his room rather than the pantry (which was a dark place and more what a scorpion would be partial to), and how on earth it managed to drown itself in the inkwell of his writing-desk—had exercised him infinitely. The ship within the islands was much more easily accounted for; and just as we were about to rise from table he made his pronouncement. She was, he doubted not, a ship from home lately arrived. Probably she drew too much water to cross the bar except at the top of spring tides. Therefore she went into that natural harbour to wait for a few days in preference to remaining in an open roadstead.

"That's so," confirmed the second mate, suddenly, in his slightly hoarse voice. "She draws over twenty feet. She's the Liverpool ship

Sephora with a cargo of coal. Hundred and twenty-three days from Cardiff."

We looked at him in surprise.

"The tugboat skipper told me when he came on board for your letters, sir," explained the young man. "He expects to take her up the river the day after to-morrow."

After thus overwhelming us with the extent of his information he slipped out of the cabin. The mate observed regretfully that he "could not account for that young fellow's whims." What prevented him telling us all about it at once, he wanted to know.

I detained him as he was making a move. For the last two days the crew had had plenty of hard work, and the night before they had very little sleep. I felt painfully that I—a stranger—was doing something unusual when I directed him to let all hands turn in without setting an anchor-watch. I proposed to keep on deck myself till one o'clock or thereabouts. I would get the second mate to relieve me at that hour.

"He will turn out the cook and the steward at four," I concluded, "and then give you a call. Of course at the slightest sign of any sort of wind we'll have the hands up and make a start at once."

He concealed his astonishment. "Very well, sir." Outside the cuddy he put his head in the second mate's door to inform him of my unheard-of caprice to take a five hours' anchor-watch on myself. I heard the other raise his voice incredulously—"What? The Captain himself?" Then a few more murmurs, a door closed, then another. A few moments later I went on deck.

My strangeness, which had made me sleepless, had prompted that unconventional arrangement, as if I had expected in those solitary hours of the night to get on terms with the ship of which I knew nothing, manned by men of whom I knew very little more. Fast alongside a wharf, littered like any ship in port with a tangle of unrelated things, invaded by unrelated shore people, I had hardly seen her yet properly. Now, as she lay cleared for sea, the stretch of her main-deck seemed to me very fine under the stars. Very fine, very roomy for her size, and very inviting. I descended the poop and paced the waist, my mind picturing to myself the coming passage through the Malay Archipelago, down the Indian Ocean, and up the Atlantic. All its phases were familiar enough to me, every characteristic, all the alternatives which were likely to face me on the high seas—everything! . . . except the novel responsibility of command. But I took heart from the reasonable thought that the ship was like

other ships, the men like other men, and that the sea was not likely
to keep any special surprises expressly for my discomfiture.

Arrived at that comforting conclusion, I bethought myself of a
cigar and went below to get it. All was still down there. Everybody
at the after end of the ship was sleeping profoundly. I came out
again on the quarter-deck, agreeably at ease in my sleeping-suit on
that warm breathless night, barefooted, a glowing cigar in my teeth,
and, going forward, I was met by the profound silence of the fore
end of the ship. Only as I passed the door of the forecastle I heard a
deep, quiet, trustful sigh of some sleeper inside. And suddenly I rejoiced in the great security of the sea as compared with the unrest of
the land, in my choice of that untempted life presenting no disquieting problems, invested with an elementary moral beauty by the
absolute straightforwardness of its appeal and by the singleness of its
purpose.

The riding-light in the fore-rigging burned with a clear, un-
troubled, as if symbolic, flame, confident and bright in the mysterious shades of the night. Passing on my way aft along the other side
of the ship, I observed that the rope side-ladder, put over, no doubt,
for the master of the tug when he came to fetch away our letters, had
not been hauled in as it should have been. I became annoyed at this,
for exactitude in small matters is the very soul of discipline. Then I
reflected that I had myself peremptorily dismissed my officers from
duty, and by my own act had prevented the anchor-watch being formally set and things properly attended to. I asked myself whether it
was wise ever to interfere with the established routine of duties even
from the kindest of motives. My action might have made me appear
eccentric. Goodness only knew how that absurdly whiskered mate
would "account" for my conduct, and what the whole ship thought
of that informality of their new captain. I was vexed with myself.

Not from compunction certainly, but, as it were mechanically, I
proceeded to get the ladder in myself. Now a side-ladder of that sort
is a light affair and comes in easily, yet my vigorous tug, which
should have brought it flying on board, merely recoiled upon my
body in a totally unexpected jerk. What the devil! . . . I was so astounded by the immovableness of that ladder that I remained stock-
still, trying to account for it to myself like that imbecile mate of
mine. In the end, of course, I put my head over the rail.

The side of the ship made an opaque belt of shadow on the
darkling glassy shimmer of the sea. But I saw at once something
elongated and pale floating very close to the ladder. Before I could

form a guess a faint flash of phosphorescent light, which seemed to issue suddenly from the naked body of a man, flickered in the sleeping water with the elusive, silent play of summer lightning in a night sky. With a gasp I saw revealed to my stare a pair of feet, the long legs, a broad livid back immersed right up to the neck in a greenish cadaverous glow. One hand, awash, clutched the bottom rung of the ladder. He was complete but for the head. A headless corpse! The cigar dropped out of my gaping mouth with a tiny plop and a short hiss quite audible in the absolute stillness of all things under heaven. At that I suppose he raised up his face, a dimly pale oval in the shadow of the ship's side. But even then I could only barely make out down there the shape of his black-haired head. However, it was enough for the horrid, frost-bound sensation which had gripped me about the chest to pass off. The moment of vain exclamations was past, too. I only climbed on the spare spar and leaned over the rail as far as I could, to bring my eyes nearer to that mystery floating alongside.

As he hung by the ladder, like a resting swimmer, the sea-lightning played about his limbs at every stir; and he appeared in it ghastly, silvery, fish-like. He remained as mute as a fish, too. He made no motion to get out of the water, either. It was inconceivable that he should not attempt to come on board, and strangely troubling to suspect that perhaps he did not want to. And my first words were prompted by just that troubled incertitude.

"What's the matter?" I asked in my ordinary tone, speaking down to the face upturned exactly under mine.

"Cramp," it answered, no louder. Then slightly anxious, "I say, no need to call any one."

"I was not going to," I said.

"Are you alone on deck?"

"Yes."

I had somehow the impression that he was on the point of letting go the ladder to swim away beyond my ken—mysterious as he came. But, for the moment, this being appearing as if he had risen from the bottom of the sea (it was certainly the nearest land to the ship) wanted only to know the time. I told him. And he, down there, tentatively:

"I suppose your captain's turned in?"

"I am sure he isn't," I said.

He seemed to struggle with himself, for I heard something like the low, bitter murmur of doubt. "What's the good?" His next words came out with a hesitating effort.

"Look here, my man. Could you call him out quietly?"

I thought the time had come to declare myself.

"I am the captain."

I heard a "By Jove!" whispered at the level of the water. The phosphorescence flashed in the swirl of the water all about his limbs, his other hand seized the ladder.

"My name's Leggatt."

The voice was calm and resolute. A good voice. The self-possession of that man had somehow induced a corresponding state in myself. It was very quietly that I remarked:

"You must be a good swimmer."

"Yes. I've been in the water practically since nine o'clock. The question for me now is whether I am to let go this ladder and go on swimming till I sink from exhaustion, or—to come on board here."

I felt this was no mere formula of desperate speech, but a real alternative in the view of a strong soul. I should have gathered from this that he was young; indeed, it is only the young who are ever confronted by such clear issues. But at the time it was pure intuition on my part. A mysterious communication was established already between us two—in the face of that silent, darkened tropical sea. I was young, too; young enough to make no comment. The man in the water began suddenly to climb up the ladder, and I hastened away from the rail to fetch some clothes.

Before entering the cabin I stood still, listening in the lobby at the foot of the stairs. A faint snore came through the closed door of the chief mate's room. The second mate's door was on the hook, but the darkness in there was absolutely soundless. He, too, was young and could sleep like a stone. Remained the steward, but he was not likely to wake up before he was called. I got a sleeping-suit out of my room and, coming back on deck, saw the naked man from the sea sitting on the main-hatch, glimmering white in the darkness, his elbows on his knees and his head in his hands. In a moment he had concealed his damp body in a sleeping-suit of the same grey-stripe pattern as the one I was wearing and followed me like my double on the poop. Together we moved right aft, barefooted, silent.

"What is it?" I asked in a deadened voice, taking the lighted lamp out of the binnacle, and raising it to his face.

"An ugly business."

He had rather regular features; a good mouth; light eyes under somewhat heavy, dark eyebrows; a smooth, square forehead; no growth on his cheeks; a small, brown moustache, and a well-shaped, round chin. His expression was concentrated, meditative, under the inspecting light of the lamp I held up to his face; such as a man thinking hard in solitude might wear. My sleeping-suit was just right for his size. A well-knit young fellow of twenty-five at most. He caught his lower lip with the edge of white, even teeth.

"Yes," I said, replacing the lamp in the binnacle. The warm, heavy tropical night closed upon his head again.

"There's a ship over there," he murmured.

"Yes, I know. The *Sephora*. Did you know of us?"

"Hadn't the slightest idea. I am the mate of her—" He paused and corrected himself. "I should say I *was*."

"Aha! Something wrong?"

"Yes. Very wrong indeed. I've killed a man."

"What do you mean? Just now?"

"No, on the passage. Weeks ago. Thirty-nine south. When I say a man—"

"Fit of temper," I suggested, confidently.

The shadowy, dark head, like mine, seemed to nod imperceptibly above the ghostly grey of my sleeping-suit. It was, in the night, as though I had been faced by my own reflection in the depths of a sombre and immense mirror.

"A pretty thing to have to own up to for a Conway boy," murmured my double, distinctly.

"You're a Conway boy?"

"I am," he said, as if startled. Then, slowly . . . "Perhaps you too—"

It was so; but being a couple of years older I had left before he joined. After a quick interchange of dates a silence fell; and I thought suddenly of my absurd mate with his terrific whiskers and the "Bless my soul—you don't say so" type of intellect. My double gave me an inkling of his thoughts by saying: "My father's a parson in Norfolk. Do you see me before a judge and jury on that charge? For myself I can't see the necessity. There are fellows that an angel from heaven— And I am not that. He was one of those creatures that are just simmering all the time with a silly sort of wickedness. Miserable devils that have no business to live at all. He wouldn't do his duty and wouldn't let anybody else do theirs. But what's the good of talking! You know well enough the sort of ill-conditioned snarling cur—"

He appealed to me as if our experiences had been as identical as our clothes. And I knew well enough the pestiferous danger of such a character where there are no means of legal repression. And I knew well enough also that my double there was no homicidal ruffian. I did not think of asking him for details, and he told me the story roughly in brusque, disconnected sentences. I needed no more. I saw it all going on as though I were myself inside that other sleeping suit.

"It happened while we were setting a reefed foresail, at dusk. Reefed foresail! You understand the sort of weather. The only sail we had left to keep the ship running; so you may guess what it had been like for days. Anxious sort of job, that. He gave me some of his cursed insolence at the sheet. I tell you I was overdone with this terrific weather that seemed to have no end to it. Terrific, I tell you— and a deep ship. I believe the fellow himself was half crazed with funk. It was no time for gentlemanly reproof, so I turned round and felled him like an ox. He up and at me. We closed just as an awful sea made for the ship. All hands saw it coming and took to the rigging, but I had him by the throat, and went on shaking him like a rat, the men above us yelling, 'Look out! look out!' Then a crash as if the sky had fallen on my head. They say that for over ten minutes hardly anything was to be seen of the ship—just the three masts and a bit of the forecastle head and of the poop all awash driving along in a smother of foam. It was a miracle that they found us, jammed together behind the forebits. It's clear that I meant business, because I was holding him by the throat still when they picked us up. He was black in the face. It was too much for them. It seems they rushed us aft together, gripped as we were, screaming 'Murder!' like a lot of lunatics, and broke into the cuddy. And the ship running for her life, touch and go all the time, any minute her last in a sea fit to turn your hair grey only a-looking at it. I understand that the skipper, too, started raving like the rest of them. The man had been deprived of sleep for more than a week, and to have this sprung on him at the height of a furious gale nearly drove him out of his mind. I wonder they didn't fling me overboard after getting the carcass of their precious ship-mate out of my fingers. They had rather a job to separate us, I've been told. A sufficiently fierce story to make an old judge and a respectable jury sit up a bit. The first thing I heard when I came to myself was the maddening howling of that endless gale, and on that the voice of the old man. He was hanging on to my bunk, staring into my face out of his sou'wester.

" 'Mr. Leggatt, you have killed a man. You can act no longer as chief mate of this ship.' "

His care to subdue his voice made it sound monotonous. He rested a hand on the end of the skylight to steady himself with, and all that time did not stir a limb, so far as I could see. "Nice little tale for a quiet tea-party," he concluded in the same tone.

One of my hands, too, rested on the end of the skylight; neither did I stir a limb, so far as I knew. We stood less than a foot from each other. It occurred to me that if old "Bless my soul—you don't say so" were to put his head up the companion and catch sight of us, he would think he was seeing double, or imagine himself come upon a scene of weird witchcraft; the strange captain having a quiet confabulation by the wheel with his own grey ghost. I became very much concerned to prevent anything of the sort. I heard the other's soothing undertone.

"My father's a parson in Norfolk," it said. Evidently he had forgotten he had told me this important fact before. Truly a nice little tale.

"You had better slip down into my stateroom now," I said, moving off stealthily. My double followed my movements; our bare feet made no sound; I let him in, closed the door with care, and, after giving a call to the second mate, returned on deck for my relief.

"Not much sign of any wind yet," I remarked when he approached.

"No, sir. Not much," he assented, sleepily, in his hoarse voice, with just enough deference, no more, and barely suppressing a yawn.

"Well, that's all you have to look out for. You have got your orders."

"Yes, sir."

I paced a turn or two on the poop and saw him take up his position face forward with his elbow in the ratlines of the mizzen-rigging before I went below. The mate's faint snoring was still going on peacefully. The cuddy lamp was burning over the table on which stood a vase with flowers, a polite attention from the ship's provision merchant—the last flowers we should see for the next three months at the very least. Two bunches of bananas hung from the beam symmetrically, one on each side of the rudder-casing. Everything was as before in the ship—except that two of her captain's sleeping-suits were simultaneously in use, one motionless in the cuddy, the other keeping very still in the captain's stateroom.

It must be explained here that my cabin had the form of the capital letter L, the door being within the angle and opening into the short part of the letter. A couch was to the left, the bed-place to the right; my writing-desk and the chronometers' table faced the door. But any one opening it, unless he stepped right inside, had no view of what I call the long (or vertical) part of the letter. It contained some lockers surmounted by a bookcase; and a few clothes, a thick jacket or two, caps, oilskin coat, and such like, hung on hooks. There was at the bottom of that part a door opening into my bathroom, which could be entered also directly from the saloon. But that way was never used.

The mysterious arrival had discovered the advantage of this particular shape. Entering my room, lighted strongly by a big bulkhead lamp swung on gimbals above my writing-desk, I did not see him anywhere till he stepped out quietly from behind the coats hung in the recessed part.

"I heard somebody moving about, and went in there at once," he whispered.

I, too, spoke under my breath.

"Nobody is likely to come in here without knocking and getting permission."

He nodded. His face was thin and the sunburn faded, as though he had been ill. And no wonder. He had been, I heard presently, kept under arrest in his cabin for nearly seven weeks. But there was nothing sickly in his eyes or in his expression. He was not a bit like me, really; yet, as we stood leaning over my bed-place, whispering side by side, with our dark heads together and our backs to the door, anybody bold enough to open it stealthily would have been treated to the uncanny sight of a double captain busy talking in whispers with his other self.

"But all this doesn't tell me how you came to hang on to our side-ladder," I inquired, in the hardly audible murmurs we used, after he had told me something more of the proceedings on board the *Sephora* once the bad weather was over.

"When we sighted Java Head I had had time to think all those matters out several times over. I had six weeks of doing nothing else, and with only an hour or so every evening for a tramp on the quarter-deck."

He whispered, his arms folded on the side of my bed-place, staring through the open port. And I could imagine perfectly the manner of this thinking out—a stubborn if not a steadfast operation; something of which I should have been perfectly incapable.

"I reckoned it would be dark before we closed with the land," he continued, so low that I had to strain my hearing, near as we were to each other, shoulder touching shoulder almost. "So I asked to speak to the old man. He always seemed very sick when he came to see me—as if he could not look me in the face. You know, that foresail saved the ship. She was too deep to have run long under bare poles. And it was I that managed to set it for him. Anyway, he came. When I had him in my cabin—he stood by the door looking at me as if I had the halter round my neck already—I asked him right away to leave my cabin door unlocked at night while the ship was going through Sunda Straits. There would be the Java coast within two or three miles, off Angier Point. I wanted nothing more. I've had a prize for swimming my second year in the Conway."

"I can believe it," I breathed out.

"God only knows why they locked me in every night. To see some of their faces you'd have thought they were afraid I'd go about at night strangling people. Am I a murdering brute? Do I look it? By Jove! if I had been he wouldn't have trusted himself like that into my room. You'll say I might have chucked him aside and bolted out, there and then—it was dark already. Well, no. And for the same reason I wouldn't think of trying to smash the door. There would have been a rush to stop me at the noise, and I did not mean to get into a confounded scrimmage. Somebody else might have got killed—for I would not have broken out only to get chucked back, and I did not want any more of that work. He refused, looking more sick than ever. He was afraid of the men, and also of that old second mate of his who had been sailing with him for years—a grey-headed old humbug; and his steward, too, had been with him devil knows how long—seventeen years or more—a dogmatic sort of loafer who hated me like poison, just because I was the chief mate. No chief mate ever made more than one voyage in the *Sephora*, you know. Those two old chaps ran the ship. Devil only knows what the skipper wasn't afraid of (all his nerve went to pieces altogether in that hellish spell of bad weather we had)—of what the law would do to him—of his wife, perhaps. Oh, yes! she's on board. Though I don't think she would have meddled. She would have been only too glad to have me out of the ship in any way. The 'brand of Cain' business, don't you see. That's all right. I was ready enough to go off wandering on the face of the earth—and that was price enough to pay for an Abel of that sort. Anyhow, he wouldn't listen to me. 'This thing must take its course. I represent the law here.' He was shaking like a leaf. 'So you won't?' 'No!' 'Then I hope you will be able to sleep on that,' I said, and turned my back on him. 'I wonder that *you* can,' cries he, and locks the door.

"Well, after that, I couldn't. Not very well. That was three weeks ago. We have had a slow passage through the Java Sea; drifted about Carimata for ten days. When we anchored here they thought, I suppose, it was all right. The nearest land (and that's five miles) is the ship's destination; the consul would soon set about catching me; and there would have been no object in bolting to these islets there. I don't suppose there's a drop of water on them. I don't know how it was, but to-night that steward, after bringing me my supper, went out to let me eat it, and left the door unlocked. And I ate it—all there was, too. After I had finished I strolled out on the quarter-deck. I don't know that I meant to do anything. A breath of fresh air was all I wanted, I believe. Then a sudden temptation came over me. I kicked off my slippers and was in the water before I had made up my mind fairly. Somebody heard the splash and they raised an awful hullabaloo. 'He's gone! Lower the boats! He's committed suicide! No, he's swimming.' Certainly I was swimming. It's not so easy for a swimmer like me to commit suicide by drowning. I landed on the nearest islet before the boat left the ship's side. I heard them pulling about in the dark, hailing, and so on, but after a bit they gave up. Everything quieted down and the anchorage became as still as death. I sat down on a stone and began to think. I felt certain they would start searching for me at daylight. There was no place to hide on those stony things—and if there had been, what would have been the good? But now I was clear of that ship, I was not going back. So after a while I took off all my clothes, tied them up in a bundle with a stone inside, and dropped them in the deep water on the outer side of that islet. That was suicide enough for me. Let them think what they liked, but I didn't mean to drown myself. I meant to swim till I sank—but that's not the same thing. I struck out for another of these little islands, and it was from that one that I first saw your riding-light. Something to swim for. I went on easily, and on the way I came upon a flat rock a foot or two above water. In the daytime, I dare say, you might make it out with a glass from your poop. I scrambled up on it and rested myself for a bit. Then I made another start. That last spell must have been over a mile."

His whisper was getting fainter and fainter, and all the time he stared straight out through the port-hole, in which there was not even a star to be seen. I had not interrupted him. There was something that made comment impossible in his narrative, or perhaps in himself; a sort of feeling, a quality, which I can't find a name for. And when he ceased, all I found was a futile whisper: "So you swam for our light?"

"Yes—straight for it. It was something to swim for. I couldn't see any stars low down because the coast was in the way, and I couldn't see the land, either. The water was like glass. One might have been swimming in a confounded thousand-feet deep cistern with no place for scrambling out anywhere; but what I didn't like was the notion of swimming round and round like a crazed bullock before I gave out; and as I didn't mean to go back . . . No. Do you see me being hauled back, stark naked, off one of these little islands by the scruff of the neck and fighting like a wild beast? Somebody would have got killed for certain, and I did not want any of that. So I went on. Then your ladder—"

"Why didn't you hail the ship?" I asked, a little louder.

He touched my shoulder lightly. Lazy footsteps came right over our heads and stopped. The second mate had crossed from the other side of the poop and might have been hanging over the rail, for all we knew.

"He couldn't hear us talking—could he?" My double breathed into my very ear, anxiously.

His anxiety was an answer, a sufficient answer, to the question I had put to him. An answer containing all the difficulty of that situation. I closed the porthole quietly, to make sure. A louder word might have been overheard.

"Who's that?" he whispered then.

"My second mate. But I don't know much more of the fellow than you do."

And I told him a little about myself. I had been appointed to take charge while I least expected anything of the sort, not quite a fortnight ago. I didn't know either the ship or the people. Hadn't had the time in port to look about me or size anybody up. And as to the crew, all they knew was that I was appointed to take the ship home. For the rest, I was almost as much of a stranger on board as himself, I said. And at the moment I felt it most acutely. I felt that it would take very little to make me a suspect person in the eyes of the ship's company.

He had turned about meantime; and we, the two strangers in the ship, faced each other in identical attitudes.

"Your ladder—" he murmured, after a silence. "Who'd have thought of finding a ladder hanging over at night in a ship anchored out here! I felt just then a very unpleasant faintness. After the life I've been leading for nine weeks, anybody would have got out of condition. I wasn't capable of swimming round as far as your rudder-chains. And, lo and behold! there was a ladder to get hold of. After I gripped it I said to myself, 'What's the good?' When I saw a man's head looking over I thought I would swim away presently and leave him shouting—in whatever language it was. I didn't mind being looked at. I—I liked it. And then you speaking to me so quietly —as if you had expected me—made me hold on a little longer. It had been a confounded lonely time—I don't mean while swimming. I was glad to talk a little to somebody that didn't belong to the *Sephora*. As to asking for the captain, that was a mere impulse. It could have been no use, with all the ship knowing about me and the other people pretty certain to be round here in the morning. I don't know—I wanted to be seen, to talk with somebody, before I went on. I don't know what I would have said. . . . 'Fine night, isn't it?' or something of the sort."

"Do you think they will be round here presently?" I asked with some incredulity.

"Quite likely," he said, faintly.

He looked extremely haggard all of a sudden. His head rolled on his shoulders.

"H'm. We shall see then. Meantime get into that bed," I whispered. "Want help? There."

It was a rather high bed-place with a set of drawers underneath. This amazing swimmer really needed the lift I gave him by seizing his leg. He tumbled in, rolled over on his back, and flung one arm across his eyes. And then, with his face nearly hidden, he must have looked exactly as I used to look in that bed. I gazed upon my other self for a while before drawing across carefully the two green serge curtains which ran on a brass rod. I thought for a moment of pinning them together for greater safety, but I sat down on the couch, and once there I felt unwilling to rise and hunt for a pin. I would do it in a moment. I was extremely tired, in a peculiarly intimate way, by the strain of stealthiness, by the effort of whispering and the general secrecy of this excitement. It was three o'clock by now and I had been on my feet since nine, but I was not sleepy; I could not have gone to sleep. I sat there, fagged out, looking at the curtains, trying to clear my mind of the confused sensation of being in two places at once, and greatly bothered by an exasperating knocking in my head. It was a relief to discover suddenly that it was not in my head at all, but on the outside of the door. Before I could collect myself the words "Come in" were out of my mouth, and the steward entered with a tray, bringing in my morning coffee. I had slept, after all, and I was so frightened that I shouted, "This way! I am here, steward," as though he had been miles away. He put down the tray on the table next the couch and only then said, very quietly, "I can see you are here, sir." I felt him give me a keen look, but I dared not meet his eyes just then. He must have wondered why I had drawn the curtains of my bed before going to sleep on the couch. He went out, hooking the door open as usual.

I heard the crew washing decks above me. I knew I would have been told at once if there had been any wind. Calm, I thought, and I was doubly vexed. Indeed, I felt dual more than ever. The steward reappeared suddenly in the doorway. I jumped up from the couch so quickly that he gave a start.

"What do you want here?"

"Close your port, sir—they are washing decks."

"It is closed," I said, reddening.

"Very well, sir." But he did not move from the doorway and returned my stare in an extraordinary, equivocal manner for a time. Then his eyes wavered, all his expression changed, and in a voice unusually gentle, almost coaxingly:

"May I come in to take the empty cup away, sir?"

"Of course!" I turned my back on him while he popped in and out. Then I unhooked and closed the door and even pushed the bolt. This sort of thing could not go on very long. The cabin was as hot as an oven, too. I took a peep at my double, and discovered that he had not moved, his arm was still over his eyes; but his chest heaved; his hair was wet; his chin glistened with perspiration. I reached over him and opened the port.

"I must show myself on deck," I reflected.

Of course, theoretically, I could do what I liked, with no one to say nay to me within the whole circle of the horizon; but to lock my cabin door and take the key away I did not dare. Directly I put my head out of the companion I saw the group of my two officers, the second mate barefooted, the chief mate in long india-rubber boots, near the break of the poop, and the steward half-way down the poop-ladder talking to them eagerly. He happened to catch sight of me and dived, the second ran down on the main-deck shouting some order or other, and the chief mate came to meet me, touching his cap.

There was a sort of curiosity in his eye that I did not like. I don't know whether the steward had told them that I was "queer" only, or downright drunk, but I know the man meant to have a good look at me. I watched him coming with a smile which, as he got into point-blank range, took effect and froze his very whiskers. I did not give him time to open his lips.

"Square the yards by lifts and braces before the hands go to breakfast."

It was the first particular order I had given on board that ship; and I stayed on deck to see it executed, too. I had felt the need of asserting myself without loss of time. That sneering young cub got taken down a peg or two on that occasion, and I also seized the opportunity of having a good look at the face of every foremast man as they filed past me to go to the after braces. At breakfast time, eating nothing myself, I presided with such frigid dignity that the two mates were only too glad to escape from the cabin as soon as decency permitted; and all the time the dual working of my mind distracted me almost to the point of insanity. I was constantly watching myself, my secret self, as dependent on my actions as my own personality, sleeping in that bed, behind that door which faced me as I sat at the head of the table. It was very much like being mad, only it was worse because one was aware of it.

I had to shake him for a solid minute, but when at last he opened his eyes it was in the full possession of his senses, with an inquiring look.

"All's well so far," I whispered. "Now you must vanish into the bath-room."

He did so, as noiseless as a ghost, and then I rang for the steward, and facing him boldly, directed him to tidy up my stateroom while I was having my bath—"and be quick about it." As my tone admitted of no excuses, he said, "Yes, sir," and ran off to fetch his dust-pan and brushes. I took a bath and did most of my dressing, splashing, and whistling softly for the steward's edification, while the secret sharer of my life stood drawn up bolt upright in that little space, his face looking very sunken in daylight, his eyelids lowered under the stern, dark line of his eyebrows drawn together by a slight frown.

When I left him there to go back to my room the steward was finishing dusting. I sent for the mate and engaged him in some insignificant conversation. It was, as it were, trifling with the terrific character of his whiskers; but my object was to give him an opportunity for a good look at my cabin. And then I could at last shut, with a clear conscience, the door of my stateroom and get my double back into the recessed part. There was nothing else for it. He had to sit still on a small folding stool, half smothered by the heavy coats hanging there. We listened to the steward going into the bathroom out of the saloon, filling the water-bottles there, scrubbing the bath, setting things to rights, whisk, bang, clatter—out again into the saloon—turn the key—click. Such was my scheme for keeping my second self invisible. Nothing better could be contrived under the circumstances. And there we sat; I at my writing-desk ready to appear busy with some papers, he behind me out of sight of the door. It would not have been prudent to talk in day-time; and I could not have stood the excitement of that queer sense of whispering to myself. Now and then, glancing over my shoulder, I saw him far back there, sitting rigidly on the low stool, his bare feet close together, his arms folded, his head hanging on his breast—and perfectly still. Anybody would have taken him for me.

I was fascinated by it myself. Every moment I had to glance over my shoulder. I was looking at him when a voice outside the door said:

"Beg pardon, sir."

"Well!" . . . I kept my eyes on him, and so when the voice outside the door announced, "There's a ship's boat coming our way, sir," I saw him give a start—the first movement he had made for hours. But he did not raise his bowed head.

"All right. Get the ladder over."

I hesitated. Should I whisper something to him? But what? His immobility seemed to have been never disturbed. What could I tell him he did not know already? . . . Finally I went on deck.

II

The skipper of the *Sephora* had a thin red whisker all round his face, and the sort of complexion that goes with hair of that colour;

also the particular, rather smeary shade of blue in the eyes. He was not exactly a showy figure; his shoulders were high, his stature but middling—one leg slightly more bandy than the other. He shook hands, looking vaguely around. A spiritless tenacity was his main characteristic, I judged. I behaved with a politeness which seemed to disconcert him. Perhaps he was shy. He mumbled to me as if he were ashamed of what he was saying; gave his name (it was something like Archbold—but at this distance of years I hardly am sure), his ship's name, and a few other particulars of that sort, in the manner of a criminal making a reluctant and doleful confession. He had had terrible weather on the passage out—terrible—terrible—wife aboard, too.

By this time we were seated in the cabin and the steward brought in a tray with a bottle and glasses. "Thanks! No." Never took liquor. Would have some water, though. He drank two tumblerfuls. Terrible thirsty work. Ever since daylight had been exploring the islands round his ship.

"What was that for—fun?" I asked, with an appearance of polite interest.

"No!" He sighed. "Painful duty."

As he persisted in his mumbling and I wanted my double to hear every word, I hit upon the notion of informing him that I regretted to say I was hard of hearing.

"Such a young man, too!" he nodded, keeping his smeary blue, unintelligent eyes fastened upon me. What was the cause of it— some disease? he inquired, without the least sympathy and as if he thought that, if so, I'd got no more than I deserved.

"Yes; disease," I admitted in a cheerful tone which seemed to shock him. But my point was gained, because he had to raise his voice to give me his tale. It is not worth while to record that version. It was just over two months since all this had happened, and he had thought so much about it that he seemed completely muddled as to its bearings, but still immensely impressed.

"What would you think of such a thing happening on board your own ship? I've had the *Sephora* for these fifteen years. I am a well-known shipmaster."

He was densely distressed—and perhaps I should have sympathised with him if I had been able to detach my mental vision from the unsuspected sharer of my cabin as though he were my second self. There he was on the other side of the bulkhead, four or five feet from us, no more, as we sat in the saloon. I looked politely at

Captain Archbold (if that was his name), but it was the other I saw, in a grey sleeping-suit, seated on a low stool, his bare feet close together, his arms folded, and every word said between us falling into the ears of his dark head bowed on his chest.

"I have been at sea now, man and boy, for seven-and-thirty years, and I've never heard of such a thing happening in an English ship. And that it should be my ship. Wife on board, too."

I was hardly listening to him.

"Don't you think," I said, "that the heavy sea which, you told me, came aboard just then might have killed the man? I have seen the sheer weight of a sea kill a man very neatly, by simply breaking his neck."

"Good God!" he uttered, impressively, fixing his smeary blue eyes on me. "The sea! No man killed by the sea ever looked like that." He seemed positively scandalised at my suggestion. And as I gazed at him, certainly not prepared for anything original on his part, he advanced his head close to mine and thrust his tongue out at me so suddenly that I couldn't help starting back.

After scoring over my calmness in this graphic way he nodded wisely. If I had seen the sight, he assured me, I would never forget it as long as I lived. The weather was too bad to give the corpse a proper sea burial. So next day at dawn they took it up on the poop, covering its face with a bit of bunting; he read a short prayer, and then, just as it was, in its oilskins and long boots, they launched it amongst those mountainous seas that seemed ready every moment to swallow up the ship herself and the terrified lives on board of her.

"That reefed foresail saved you," I threw in.

"Under God—it did," he exclaimed fervently. "It was by a special mercy, I firmly believe, that it stood some of those hurricane squalls."

"It was the setting of that sail which—" I began.

"God's own hand in it," he interrupted me. "Nothing less could have done it. I don't mind telling you that I hardly dared give the order. It seemed impossible that we could touch anything without losing it, and then our last hope would have been gone."

The terror of that gale was on him yet. I let him go on for a bit, then said, casually—as if returning to a minor subject:

"You were very anxious to give up your mate to the shore people, I believe?"

He was. To the law. His obscure tenacity on that point had in it something incomprehensible and a little awful; something, as it were, mystical, quite apart from his anxiety that he should not be suspected of "countenancing any doings of that sort." Seven-and-thirty virtuous years at sea, of which over twenty of immaculate command, and the last fifteen in the *Sephora*, seemed to have laid him under some pitiless obligation.

"And you know," he went on, groping shamefacedly amongst his feelings, "I did not engage that young fellow. His people had some interest with my owners. I was in a way forced to take him on. He looked very smart, very gentlemanly, and all that. But do you know —I never liked him, somehow. I am a plain man. You see, he wasn't exactly the sort for the chief mate of a ship like the *Sephora*."

I had become so connected in thoughts and impressions with the secret sharer of my cabin that I felt as if I, personally, were being given to understand that I, too, was not the sort that would have done for the chief mate of a ship like the *Sephora*. I had no doubt of it in my mind.

"Not at all the style of man. You understand," he insisted, superfluously, looking hard at me.

I smiled urbanely. He seemed at a loss for a while.

"I suppose I must report a suicide."

"Beg pardon?"

"Sui-cide! That's what I'll have to write to my owners directly I get in."

"Unless you manage to recover him before to-morrow," I assented, dispassionately. . . . "I mean, alive."

He mumbled something which I really did not catch, and I turned my ear to him in a puzzled manner. He fairly bawled:

"The land—I say, the mainland is at least seven miles off my anchorage."

"About that."

My lack of excitement, of curiosity, of surprise, of any sort of pronounced interest, began to arouse his distrust. But except for the felicitous pretence of deafness I had not tried to pretend anything. I had felt utterly incapable of playing the part of ignorance properly, and therefore was afraid to try. It is also certain that he had brought some ready-made suspicions with him, and that he viewed my politeness as a strange and unnatural phenomenon. And yet how else could I have received him? Not heartily! That was impossible for psychological reasons, which I need not state here. My only object was to keep off his inquiries. Surlily? Yes, but surliness might have provoked a point-blank question. From its novelty to him and from its nature, punctilious courtesy was the manner best calculated to restrain the man. But there was the danger of his breaking through my defence bluntly. I could not, I think, have met him by a direct lie, also for psychological (not moral) reasons. If he had only known how afraid I was of his putting my feeling of identity with the other to the test! But, strangely enough—(I thought of it only afterwards)—I believe that he was not a little disconcerted by the reverse side of that weird situation, by something in me that reminded him of the man he was seeking—suggested a mysterious similitude to the young fellow he had distrusted and disliked from the first.

However that might have been, the silence was not very prolonged. He took another oblique step.

"I reckon I had no more than a two-mile pull to your ship. Not a bit more."

"And quite enough, too, in this awful heat," I said.

Another pause full of mistrust followed. Necessity, they say, is mother of invention, but fear, too, is not barren of ingenious suggestions. And I was afraid he would ask me point-blank for news of my other self.

"Nice little saloon, isn't it?" I remarked, as if noticing for the first time the way his eyes roamed from one closed door to the other. "And very well fitted out, too. Here, for instance," I continued, reaching over the back of my seat negligently and flinging the door open, "is my bath-room."

He made an eager movement, but hardly gave it a glance. I got up, shut the door of the bath-room, and invited him to have a look round, as if I were very proud of my accommodation. He had to rise and be shown round, but he went through the business without any raptures whatever.

"And now we'll have a look at my stateroom," I declared, in a voice as loud as I dared to make it, crossing the cabin to the starboard side with purposely heavy steps.

He followed me in and gazed around. My intelligent double had vanished. I played my part.

"Very convenient—isn't it?"

"Very nice. Very comf . . ." He didn't finish and went out brusquely as if to escape from some unrighteous wiles of mine. But it was not to be. I had been too frightened not to feel vengeful; I felt I had him on the run, and I meant to keep him on the run. My polite insistence must have had something menacing in it, because he gave in suddenly. And I did not let him off a single item; mate's room, pantry, storerooms, the very sail-locker which was also under the poop—he had to look into them all. When at last I showed him out on the quarter-deck he drew a long, spiritless sigh, and mumbled dismally that he must really be going back to his ship now. I desired my mate, who had joined us, to see to the captain's boat.

The man of whiskers gave a blast on the whistle which he used to wear hanging round his neck, and yelled, *"Sephora's* away!" My double down there in my cabin must have heard, and certainly could not feel more relieved than I. Four fellows came running out from somewhere forward and went over the side, while my own men, appearing on deck too, lined the rail. I escorted my visitor to the gangway ceremoniously, and nearly overdid it. He was a tenacious beast. On the very ladder he lingered, and in that unique, guiltily conscientious manner of sticking to the point:

"I say . . . you . . . you don't think that—"

I covered his voice loudly:

"Certainly not. . . . I am delighted. Good-bye."

I had an idea of what he meant to say, and just saved myself by the privilege of defective hearing. He was too shaken generally to insist, but my mate, close witness of that parting, looked mystified and his face took on a thoughtful cast. As I did not want to appear as if I wished to avoid all communication with my officers, he had the opportunity to address me.

"Seems a very nice man. His boat's crew told our chaps a very extraordinary story, if what I am told by the steward is true. I suppose you had it from the captain, sir?"

"Yes. I had a story from the captain."

"A very horrible affair—isn't it, sir?"

"It is."

"Beats all these tales we hear about murders in Yankee ships."

"I don't think it beats them. I don't think it resembles them in the least."

"Bless my soul—you don't say so! But of course I've no acquaintance whatever with American ships, not I, so I couldn't go against your knowledge. It's horrible enough for me. . . . But the queerest part is that those fellows seemed to have some idea the man was hidden aboard here. They had really. Did you ever hear of such a thing?"

"Preposterous—isn't it?"

We were walking to and fro athwart the quarter-deck. No one of the crew forward could be seen (the day was Sunday), and the mate pursued:

"There was some little dispute about it. Our chaps took offence. 'As if we would harbour a thing like that,' they said. 'Wouldn't you like to look for him in our coal-hold?" Quite a tiff. But they made it up in the end. I suppose he did drown himself. Don't you, sir?"

"I don't suppose anything."

"You have no doubt in the matter, sir?"

"None whatever."

I left him suddenly. I felt I was producing a bad impression, but with my double down there it was most trying to be on deck. And it was almost as trying to be below. Altogether a nerve-trying situation. But on the whole I felt less torn in two when I was with him. There was no one in the whole ship whom I dared take into my confidence. Since the hands had got to know his story, it would have been impossible to pass him off for any one else, and an accidental discovery was to be dreaded now more than ever. . . .

The steward being engaged in laying the table for dinner, we could talk only with our eyes when I first went down. Later in the afternoon we had a cautious try at whispering. The Sunday quietness of the ship was against us; the stillness of air and water around her was against us; the elements, the men were against us—everything was against us in our secret partnership; time itself—for this could not go on forever. The very trust in Providence was, I suppose, denied to his guilt. Shall I confess that this thought cast me down very much? And as to the chapter of accidents which counts for so much in the book of success, I could only hope that it was closed. For what favourable accident could be expected?

"Did you hear everything?" were my first words as soon as we took up our position side by side, leaning over my bed-place.

He had. And the proof of it was his earnest whisper, "The man told you he hardly dared to give the order."

I understood the reference to be to that saving foresail.

"Yes. He was afraid of it being lost in the setting."

"I assure you he never gave the order. He may think he did, but he never gave it. He stood there with me on the break of the poop after the maintopsail blew away, and whimpered about our last hope—positively whimpered about it and nothing else—and the night coming on! To hear one's skipper go on like that in such weather was enough to drive any fellow out of his mind. It worked me up into a sort of desperation. I just took it into my own hands and

went away from him, boiling, and— But what's the use telling you?
You know! . . . Do you think that if I had not been pretty fierce
with them I should have got the men to do anything? Not it! The
bo's'n perhaps? Perhaps! It wasn't a heavy sea—it was a sea gone
mad! I suppose the end of the world will be something like that;
and a man may have the heart to see it coming once and be done
with it—but to have to face it day after day— I don't blame anybody. I was precious little better than the rest. Only—I was an
officer of that old coal-wagon, anyhow—"

"I quite understand," I conveyed that sincere assurance into his
ear. He was out of breath with whispering; I could hear him pant
slightly. It was all very simple. The same strung-up force which had
given twenty-four men a chance, at least, for their lives, had, in a
sort of recoil, crushed an unworthy mutinous existence.

But I had no leisure to weigh the merits of the matter—footsteps in the saloon, a heavy knock. "There's enough wind to get
under way with, sir." Here was the call of a new claim upon my
thoughts and even upon my feelings.

"Turn the hands up," I cried through the door. "I'll be on deck
directly."

I was going out to make the acquaintance of my ship. Before I
left the cabin our eyes met—the eyes of the only two strangers on
board. I pointed to the recessed part where the little camp-stool
awaited him and laid my finger on my lips. He made a gesture—
somewhat vague—a little mysterious, accompanied by a faint smile,
as if of regret.

This is not the place to enlarge upon the sensations of a man
who feels for the first time a ship move under his feet to his own independent word. In my case they were not unalloyed. I was not
wholly alone with my command; for there was that stranger in my
cabin. Or rather, I was not completely and wholly with her. Part of
me was absent. That mental feeling of being in two places at once
affected me physically as if the mood of secrecy had penetrated my
very soul. Before an hour had elapsed since the ship had begun to
move, having occasion to ask the mate (he stood by my side) to
take a compass bearing of the Pagoda, I caught myself reaching up
to his ear in whispers. I say I caught myself, but enough had escaped
to startle the man. I can't describe it otherwise than by saying that
he shied. A grave, preoccupied manner, as though he were in possession of some perplexing intelligence, did not leave him henceforth.
A little later I moved away from the rail to look at the compass with

such a stealthy gait that the helmsman noticed it—and I could not help noticing the unusual roundness of his eyes. These are trifling instances, though it's to no commander's advantage to be suspected of ludicrous eccentricities. But I was also more seriously affected. There are to a seaman certain words, gestures, that should in given conditions come as naturally, as instinctively as the winking of a menaced eye. A certain order should spring on to his lips without thinking; a certain sign should get itself made, so to speak, without reflection. But all unconscious alertness had abandoned me. I had to make an effort of will to recall myself back (from the cabin) to the conditions of the moment. I felt that I was appearing an irresolute commander to those people who were watching me more or less critically.

And, besides, there were the scares. On the second day out, for instance, coming off the deck in the afternoon (I had straw slippers on my bare feet) I stopped at the open pantry door and spoke to the steward. He was doing something there with his back to me. At the sound of my voice he nearly jumped out of his skin, as the saying is, and incidentally broke a cup.

"What on earth's the matter with you?" I asked, astonished.

He was extremely confused. "Beg your pardon, sir. I made sure you were in your cabin."

"You see I wasn't."

"No, sir. I could have sworn I had heard you moving in there not a moment ago. It's most extraordinary . . . very sorry, sir."

I passed on with an inward shudder. I was so identified with my secret double that I did not even mention the fact in those scanty, fearful whispers we exchanged. I suppose he had made some slight noise of some kind or other. It would have been miraculous if he hadn't at one time or another. And yet, haggard as he appeared, he looked always perfectly self-controlled, more than calm—almost invulnerable. On my suggestion he remained almost entirely in the bath-room, which, upon the whole, was the safest place. There could be really no shadow of an excuse for any one ever wanting to go in there, once the steward had done with it. It was a very tiny place. Sometimes he reclined on the floor, his legs bent, his head sustained on one elbow. At others I would find him on the camp-stool, sitting in his grey sleeping-suit and with his cropped dark hair like a patient, unmoved convict. At night I would smuggle him into my bed-place, and we would whisper together, with the regular footfalls of the officer of the watch passing and repassing over our heads. It was an infinitely miserable time. It was lucky that some tins of fine preserves were stowed in a locker in my stateroom; hard bread I could always get hold of; and so he lived on stewed chicken, paté de foie gras, asparagus, cooked oysters, sardines—on all sorts of abominable sham delicacies out of tins. My early morning coffee he always drank; and it was all I dared do for him in that respect.

Every day there was the horrible manœuvring to go through so that my room and then the bath-room should be done in the usual way. I came to hate the sight of the steward, to abhor the voice of that harmless man. I felt that it was he who would bring on the disaster of discovery. It hung like a sword over our heads.

The fourth day out, I think (we were then working down the east side of the Gulf of Siam, tack for tack, in light winds and smooth water)—the fourth day, I say, of this miserable juggling with the unavoidable, as we sat at our evening meal, that man, whose slightest movement I dreaded, after putting down the dishes ran up on deck busily. This could not be dangerous. Presently he came down again; and then it appeared that he had remembered a coat of mine which I had thrown over a rail to dry after having been wetted in a shower which had passed over the ship in the afternoon. Sitting stolidly at the head of the table I became terrified at the sight of the garment on his arm. Of course he made for my door. There was no time to lose.

"Steward," I thundered. My nerves were so shaken that I could not govern my voice and conceal my agitation. This was the sort of thing that made my terrifically whiskered mate tap his forehead with his forefinger. I had detected him using that gesture while talking on deck with a confidential air to the carpenter. It was too far to hear a word, but I had no doubt that this pantomime could only refer to the strange new captain.

"Yes, sir," the pale-faced steward turned resignedly to me. It was this maddening course of being shouted at, checked without rhyme or reason, arbitrarily chased out of my cabin, suddenly called into it, sent flying out of his pantry on incomprehensible errands, that accounted for the growing wretchedness of his expression.

"Where are you going with that coat?"

"To your room, sir."

"Is there another shower coming?"

"I'm sure I don't know, sir. Shall I go up again and see, sir?"

"No! never mind."

My object was attained, as of course my other self in there would

have heard everything that passed. During this interlude my two
officers never raised their eyes off their respective plates; but the lip
of that confounded cub, the second mate, quivered visibly.

I expected the steward to hook my coat on and come out at
once. He was very slow about it; but I dominated my nervousness
sufficiently not to shout after him. Suddenly I became aware (it
could be heard plainly enough) that the fellow for some reason or
other was opening the door of the bath-room. It was the end. The
place was literally not big enough to swing a cat in. My voice died in
my throat and I went stony all over. I expected to hear a yell of surprise and terror, and made a movement, but had not the strength to
get on my legs. Everything remained still. Had my second self taken
the poor wretch by the throat? I don't know what I could have done
next moment if I had not seen the steward come out of my room,
close the door, and then stand quietly by the sideboard.

"Saved," I thought. "But, no! Lost! Gone! He was gone!"

I laid my knife and fork down and leaned back in my chair. My
head swam. After a while, when sufficiently recovered to speak in a
steady voice, I instructed my mate to put the ship round at eight
o'clock himself.

"I won't come on deck," I went on. "I think I'll turn in, and unless the wind shifts I don't want to be disturbed before midnight. I
feel a bit seedy."

"You did look middling bad a little while ago," the chief mate
remarked without showing any great concern.

They both went out, and I stared at the steward clearing the
table. There was nothing to be read on that wretched man's face.
But why did he avoid my eyes I asked myself. Then I thought I
should like to hear the sound of his voice.

"Steward!"

"Sir!" Startled as usual.

"Where did you hang up that coat?"

"In the bath-room, sir." The usual anxious tone. "It's not quite
dry yet, sir."

For some time longer I sat in the cuddy. Had my double vanished as he had come? But of his coming there was an explanation,
whereas his disappearance would be inexplicable. . . . I went slowly
into my dark room, shut the door, lighted the lamp, and for a time
dared not turn round. When at last I did I saw him standing bolt-
upright in the narrow recessed part. It would not be true to say I
had a shock, but an irresistible doubt of his bodily existence flitted

through my mind. Can it be, I asked myself, that he is not visible to other eyes than mine? It was like being haunted. Motionless, with a grave face, he raised his hands slightly at me in a gesture which meant clearly, "Heavens! what a narrow escape!" Narrow indeed. I think I had come creeping quietly as near insanity as any man who has not actually gone over the border. That gesture restrained me, so to speak.

The mate with the terrific whiskers was now putting the ship on the other tack. In the moment of profound silence which follows upon the hands going to their stations I heard on the poop his raised voice: "Hard alee!" and the distant shout of the order repeated on the maindeck. The sails, in that light breeze, made but a faint fluttering noise. It ceased. The ship was coming round slowly; I held my breath in the renewed stillness of expectation; one wouldn't have thought that there was a single living soul on her decks. A sudden brisk shout, "Mainsail haul!" broke the spell, and in the noisy cries and rush overhead of the men running away with the mainbrace we two, down in my cabin, came together in our usual position by the bed-place.

He did not wait for my question. "I heard him fumbling here and just managed to squat myself down in the bath," he whispered to me. "The fellow only opened the door and put his arm in to hang the coat up. All the same—"

"I never thought of that," I whispered back, even more appalled than before at the closeness of the shave, and marvelling at that something unyielding in his character which was carrying him through so finely. There was no agitation in his whisper. Whoever was being driven distracted, it was not he. He was sane. And the proof of his sanity was continued when he took up the whispering again.

"It would never do for me to come to life again."

It was something that a ghost might have said. But what he was alluding to was his old captain's reluctant admission of the theory of suicide. It would obviously serve his turn—if I had understood at all the view which seemed to govern the unalterable purpose of his action.

"You must maroon me as soon as ever you can get amongst these islands off the Cambodje shore," he went on.

"Maroon you! We are not living in a boy's adventure tale," I protested. His scornful whispering took me up.

"We aren't indeed! There's nothing of a boy's tale in this. But there's nothing else for it. I want no more. You don't suppose I am afraid of what can be done to me? Prison or gallows or whatever they may please. But you don't see me coming back to explain such things to an old fellow in a wig and twelve respectable tradesmen, do you? What can they know whether I am guilty or not—or of *what* I am guilty, either? That's my affair. What does the Bible say? 'Driven off the face of the earth.' Very well. I am off the face of the earth now. As I came at night so I shall go."

"Impossible!" I murmured. "You can't."

"Can't? . . . Not naked like a soul on the Day of Judgment. I shall freeze on to this sleeping-suit. The Last Day is not yet—and . . . you have understood thoroughly. Didn't you?"

I felt suddenly ashamed of myself. I may say truly that I under-stood—and my hesitation in letting that man swim away from my ship's side had been a mere sham sentiment, a sort of cowardice.

"It can't be done now till next night," I breathed out. "The ship is on the off-shore tack and the wind may fail us."

"As long as I know that you understand," he whispered. "But of course you do. It's a great satisfaction to have got somebody to un-derstand. You seem to have been there on purpose." And in the same whisper, as if we two whenever we talked had to say things to each other which were not fit for the world to hear, he added, "It's very wonderful."

We remained side by side talking in our secret way—but some-times silent or just exchanging a whispered word or two at long in-tervals. And as usual he stared through the port. A breath of wind came now and again into our faces. The ship might have been moored in dock, so gently and on an even keel she slipped through the water, that did not murmur even at our passage, shadowy and si-lent like a phantom sea.

At midnight I went on deck, and to my mate's great surprise put the ship round on the other tack. His terrible whiskers flitted round me in silent criticism. I certainly should not have done it if it had been only a question of getting out of that sleepy gulf as quickly as possible. I believe he told the second mate, who relieved him, that it was a great want of judgment. The other only yawned. That intoler-able cub shuffled about so sleepily and lolled against the rails in such a slack, improper fashion that I came down on him sharply.

"Aren't you properly awake yet?"

"Yes, sir! I am awake."

"Well, then, be good enough to hold yourself as if you were. And keep a look-out. If there's any current we'll be closing with some islands before daylight."

The east side of the gulf is fringed with islands, some solitary, others in groups. On the blue background of the high coast they seem to float on silvery patches of calm water, arid and grey, or dark green and rounded like clumps of evergreen bushes, with the larger ones, a mile or two long, showing the outlines of ridges, ribs of grey rock under the dank mantle of matted leafage. Unknown to trade, to travel, almost to geography, the manner of life they harbour is an unsolved secret. There must be villages—settlements of fishermen at least—on the largest of them, and some communication with the world is probably kept up by native craft. But all that forenoon, as we headed for them, fanned along by the faintest of breezes, I saw no sign of man or canoe in the field of the telescope I kept on pointing at the scattered group.

At noon I gave no orders for a change of course, and the mate's whiskers became much concerned and seemed to be offering themselves unduly to my notice. At last I said:

"I am going to stand right in. Quite in—as far as I can take her."

The stare of extreme surprise imparted an air of ferocity also to his eyes, and he looked truly terrific for a moment.

"We're not doing well in the middle of the gulf," I continued, casually. "I am going to look for the land breezes to-night."

"Bless my soul! Do you mean, sir, in the dark amongst the lot of all them islands and reefs and shoals?"

"Well—if there are any regular land breezes at all on this coast one must get close inshore to find them, mustn't one?"

"Bless my soul!" he exclaimed again under his breath. All that afternoon he wore a dreamy, contemplative appearance which in him was a mark of perplexity. After dinner I went into my stateroom as if I meant to take some rest. There we two bent our dark heads over a half-unrolled chart lying on my bed.

"There," I said. "It's got to be Koh-ring. I've been looking at it ever since sunrise. It has got two hills and a low point. It must be inhabited. And on the coast opposite there is what looks like the mouth of a biggish river—with some town, no doubt, not far up. It's the best chance for you that I can see."

"Anything. Koh-ring let it be."

He looked thoughtfully at the chart as if surveying chances and distances from a lofty height—and following with his eyes his own

figure wandering on the blank land of Cochin-China, and then passing off that piece of paper clean out of sight into uncharted regions.
And it was as if the ship had two captains to plan her course for her.
I had been so worried and restless running up and down that I had
not had the patience to dress that day. I had remained in my sleeping-suit, with straw slippers and a soft floppy hat. The closeness of
the heat in the gulf had been most oppressive, and the crew were
used to see me wandering in that airy attire.

"She will clear the south point as she heads now," I whispered
into his ear. "Goodness only knows when, though, but certainly
after dark. I'll edge her in to half a mile, as far as I may be able to
judge in the dark—"

"Be careful," he murmured, warningly—and I realised suddenly
that all my future, the only future for which I was fit, would perhaps go irretrievably to pieces in any mishap to my first command.

I could not stop a moment longer in the room. I motioned him
to get out of sight and made my way on the poop. That unplayful
cub had the watch. I walked up and down for a while thinking
things out, then beckoned him over.

"Send a couple of hands to open the two quarter-deck ports," I
said, mildly.

He actually had the impudence, or else so forgot himself in his
wonder at such an incomprehensible order, as to repeat:

"Open the quarter-deck ports! What for, sir?"

"The only reason you need concern yourself about is because I
tell you to do so. Have them open wide and fastened properly."

He reddened and went off, but I believe made some jeering remark to the carpenter as to the sensible practice of ventilating a
ship's quarter-deck. I know he popped into the mate's cabin to impart the fact to him because the whiskers came on deck, as it were
by chance, and stole glances at me from below—for signs of lunacy
or drunkenness, I suppose.

A little before supper, feeling more restless than ever, I rejoined,
for a moment, my second self. And to find him sitting so quietly was
surprising, like something against nature, inhuman.

I developed my plan in a hurried whisper.

"I shall stand in as close as I dare and then put her round. I will
presently find means to smuggle you out of here into the sail-locker,
which communicates with the lobby. But there is an opening, a sort
of square for hauling the sails out, which gives straight on the quarter-deck and which is never closed in fine weather, so as to give air

to the sails. When the ship's way is deadened in stays and all the hands are aft at the main-braces you will have a clear road to slip out and get overboard through the open quarter-deck port. I've had them both fastened up. Use a rope's end to lower yourself into the water so as to avoid a splash—you know. It could be heard and cause some beastly complication."

He kept silent for a while, then whispered, "I understand."

"I won't be there to see you go," I began with an effort. "The rest . . . I only hope I have understood, too."

"You have. From first to last"—and for the first time there seemed to be a faltering, something strained in his whisper. He caught hold of my arm, but the ringing of the supper bell made me start. He didn't, though; he only released his grip.

After supper I didn't come below again till well past eight o'clock. The faint, steady breeze was loaded with dew; and the wet, darkened sails held all there was of propelling power in it. The night, clear and starry, sparkled darkly, and the opaque, lightless patches shifting slowly against the low stars were the drifting islets. On the port bow there was a big one more distant and shadowily imposing by the great space of sky it eclipsed.

On opening the door I had a back view of my very own self looking at a chart. He had come out of the recess and was standing near the table.

"Quite dark enough," I whispered.

He stepped back and leaned against my bed with a level, quiet glance. I sat on the couch. We had nothing to say to each other. Over our heads the officer of the watch moved here and there. Then I heard him move quickly. I knew what that meant. He was making for the companion; and presently his voice was outside my door.

"We are drawing in pretty fast, sir. Land looks rather close."

"Very well," I answered. "I am coming on deck directly."

I waited till he was gone out of the cuddy, then rose. My double moved too. The time had come to exchange our last whispers, for neither of us was ever to hear each other's natural voice.

"Look here!" I opened a drawer and took out three sovereigns. "Take this anyhow. I've got six and I'd give you the lot, only I must keep a little money to buy some fruit and vegetables for the crew from native boats as we go through Sunda Straits."

He shook his head.

"Take it," I urged him, whispering desperately. "No one can tell what—"

He smiled and slapped meaningly the only pocket of the sleeping-jacket. It was not safe, certainly. But I produced a large old silk handkerchief of mine, and tying the three pieces of gold in a corner, pressed it on him. He was touched, I suppose, because he took it at last, and tied it quickly round his waist under the jacket, on his bare skin.

Our eyes met; several seconds elapsed, till, our glances still mingled, I extended my hand and turned the lamp out. Then I passed through the cuddy, leaving the door of my room wide open. . . . "Steward!"

He was still lingering in the pantry in the greatness of his zeal, giving a rub-up to a plated cruet stand the last thing before going to bed. Being careful not to wake up the mate, whose room was opposite, I spoke in an undertone.

He looked round anxiously. "Sir!"

"Can you get me a little hot water from the galley?"

"I am afraid, sir, the galley fire's been out for some time now."

"Go and see."

He flew up the stairs.

"Now," I whispered, loudly, into the saloon—too loudly, perhaps, but I was afraid I couldn't make a sound. He was by my side in an instant—the double captain slipped past the stairs—through a tiny dark passage . . . a sliding door. We were in the sail-locker, scrambling on our knees over the sails. A sudden thought struck me. I saw myself wandering barefooted, bareheaded, the sun beating on my dark poll. I snatched off my floppy hat and tried hurriedly in the dark to ram it on my other self. He dodged and fended off silently. I wonder what he thought had come to me before he understood and suddenly desisted. Our hands met gropingly, lingered united in a steady, motionless clasp for a second. . . . No word was breathed by either of us when they separated.

I was standing quietly by the pantry door when the steward returned.

"Sorry, sir. Kettle barely warm. Shall I light the spirit-lamp?"

"Never mind."

I came out on deck slowly. It was now a matter of conscience to shave the land as close as possible—for now he must go overboard whenever the ship was put in stays. Must! There could be no going back for him. After a moment I walked over to leeward and my heart flew into my mouth at the nearness of the land on the bow.

Under any other circumstances I would not have held on a minute longer. The second mate had followed me anxiously.

I looked on till I felt I could command my voice.

"She may weather," I said then in a quiet tone.

"Are you going to try that, sir?" he stammered out incredulously.

I took no notice of him and raised my tone just enough to be heard by the helmsman.

"Keep her good full."

"Good full, sir."

The wind fanned my cheek, the sails slept, the world was silent. The strain of watching the dark loom of the land grow bigger and denser was too much for me. I had shut my eyes—because the ship must go closer. She must! The stillness was intolerable. Were we standing still?

When I opened my eyes the second view started my heart with a thump. The black southern hill of Koh-ring seemed to hang right over the ship like a towering fragment of the everlasting night. On that enormous mass of blackness there was not a gleam to be seen, not a sound to be heard. It was gliding irresistibly towards us and yet seemed already within reach of the hand. I saw the vague figures of the watch grouped in the waist, gazing in awed silence.

"Are you going on, sir?" inquired an unsteady voice at my elbow.

I ignored it. I had to go on.

"Keep her full. Don't check her way. That won't do now," I said, warningly.

"I can't see the sails very well," the helmsman answered me, in strange, quavering tones.

Was she close enough? Already she was, I won't say in the shadow of the land, but in the very blackness of it, already swallowed up as it were, gone too close to be recalled, gone from me altogether.

"Give the mate a call," I said to the young man who stood at my elbow as still as death. "And turn all hands up."

My tone had a borrowed loudness reverberated from the height of the land. Several voices cried out together: "We are all on deck, sir."

Then stillness again, with the great shadow gliding closer, towering higher, without light, without a sound. Such a hush had fallen on the ship that she might have been a bark of the dead floating in slowly under the very gate of Erebus.

"My God! Where are we?"

It was the mate moaning at my elbow. He was thunderstruck, and as it were deprived of the moral support of his whiskers. He clapped his hands and absolutely cried out, "Lost!"

"Be quiet," I said, sternly.

He lowered his tone, but I saw the shadowy gesture of his despair. "What are we doing here?"

"Looking for the land wind."

He made as if to tear his hair, and addressed me recklessly.

"She will never get out. You have done it, sir. I knew it'd end in something like this. She will never weather, and you are too close now to stay. She'll drift ashore before she's round. O my God!"

I caught his arm as he was raising it to batter his poor devoted head, and shook it violently.

"She's ashore already," he wailed, trying to tear himself away.

"Is she? . . . Keep good full there!"

"Good full, sir," cried the helmsman in a frightened, thin, child-like voice.

I hadn't let go the mate's arm and went on shaking it. "Ready about, do you hear? You go forward"—shake—"and stop there" —shake—"and hold your noise"—shake—"and see these head-sheets properly overhauled"—shake, shake—shake.

And all the time I dared not look towards the land lest my heart should fail me. I released my grip at last and he ran forward as if fleeing for dear life.

I wondered what my double there in the sail-locker thought of this commotion. He was able to hear everything—and perhaps he was able to understand why, on my conscience, it had to be thus close—no less. My first order "Hard alee!" re-echoed ominously under the towering shadow of Koh-ring as if I had shouted in a mountain gorge. And then I watched the land intently. In that smooth water and light wind it was impossible to feel the ship coming-to. No! I could not feel her. And my second self was making now ready to slip out and lower himself overboard. Perhaps he was gone already . . . ?

The great black mass brooding over our very mastheads began to pivot away from the ship's side silently. And now I forgot the secret stranger ready to depart, and remembered only that I was a total stranger to the ship. I did not know her. Would she do it? How was she to be handled?

I swung the mainyard and waited helplessly. She was perhaps stopped, and her very fate hung in the balance, with the black mass of Koh-ring like the gate of the everlasting night towering over her taffrail. What would she do now? Had she way on her yet? I stepped to the side swiftly, and on the shadowy water I could see nothing except a faint phosphorescent flash revealing the glassy smoothness of the sleeping surface. It was impossible to tell—and I had not learned yet the feel of my ship. Was she moving? What I needed was something easily seen, a piece of paper, which I could throw overboard and watch. I had nothing on me. To run down for it I didn't dare. There was no time. All at once my strained, yearning stare distinguished a white object floating within a yard of the ship's side. White on the black water. A phosphorescent flash passed under it. What was that thing? . . . I recognised my own floppy hat. It must have fallen off his head . . . and he didn't bother. Now I had what I wanted—the saving mark for my eyes. But I hardly thought of my other self, now gone from the ship, to be hidden for ever from all friendly faces, to be a fugitive and a vagabond on the earth, with no brand of the curse on his sane forehead to stay a slaying hand . . . too proud to explain.

And I watched the hat—the expression of my sudden pity for his mere flesh. It had been meant to save his homeless head from the dangers of the sun. And now—behold—it was saving the ship, by serving me for a mark to help out the ignorance of my strangeness. Ha! It was drifting forward, warning me just in time that the ship had gathered sternway.

"Shift the helm," I said in a low voice to the seaman standing still like a statue.

The man's eyes glistened wildly in the binnacle light as he jumped round to the other side and spun round the wheel.

I walked to the break of the poop. On the over-shadowed deck all hands stood by the forebraces waiting for my order. The stars ahead seemed to be gliding from right to left. And all was so still in the world that I heard the quiet remark "She's round," passed in a tone of intense relief between two seamen.

"Let go and haul."

The foreyards ran round with a great noise, amidst cheery cries. And now the frightful whiskers made themselves heard giving various orders. Already the ship was drawing ahead. And I was alone with her. Nothing! no one in the world should stand now between us, throwing a shadow on the way of silent knowledge and mute affection, the perfect communion of a seaman with his first command.

Walking to the taffrail, I was in time to make out, on the very edge of a darkness thrown by a towering black mass like the very gateway of Erebus—yes, I was in time to catch an evanescent glimpse of my white hat left behind to mark the spot where the secret sharer of my cabin and of my thoughts, as though he were my second self, had lowered himself into the water to take his punishment: a free man, a proud swimmer striking out for a new destiny.

THOMAS MANN

Death in Venice

Translated by H. T. Lowe-Porter

Introduction

(Scene: A professor's office in an American university. It is a brilliant spring day, and the idea of beauty, which runs through Death in Venice *both as lure and threat, seems to be vibrating in the atmosphere. Occasionally both speakers impatiently stare out the window at the green of the campus. The professor is in his mid-forties, old enough both to have experienced the shock of modernist literature and to be uncomfortable with the present cultural tastes of the young. The student is bright but not "literary" in the narrow sense. Most of the time both speakers seem to be enjoying themselves, and they seem to like each other.)*

STUDENT Yes, of course I enjoyed *Death in Venice*. After all your raving about it in class and all your warnings that we would find it tricky, I felt it a personal challenge to "get" the story. But I'm not sure I know *why* I enjoyed it. There's something insidious about this story. I mean, I had the sense that Mann was "working" on me all the time, like an expert magician—so that I couldn't respond with the simple direct excitement I felt when I read some Conrad stories.

TEACHER That seems to me pretty much the right reaction. Mann writes in a way that is meant to stir up a maximum of self-consciousness and self-doubt. Tolstoy wants to absorb you into his world; Conrad wants to entangle you in the suspense of his narrative. But Mann wants to get you absorbed into his devices and strategies as a writer—you are always supposed to be watching not just what he does but also his act of doing it. He posits a tacit arrangement between writer and reader by which they are to share an ironic and problematic attitude to the materials of the story. After all, Mann himself said that the style of *Death in Venice* is "parodistic"—

STUDENT Wait, I don't get that. Parody of what? Aschenbach? But I had the impression Mann wanted us to sympathize with Aschenbach and that he was sympathetic too.

TEACHER I have the same impression. But isn't that just where the complexity, or "trickiness," comes in? We are meant to sympathize with Aschenbach, even while we recognize that, in some sense, he is making a fool of himself. I'd even say, perhaps *because* he is making a fool of himself, since we all have the potentiality of foolishness within us and may even miss something essential in life if we never risk foolishness. After all, a great writer, rather stuffy and official—

STUDENT But how do we really know that Aschenbach is a great writer? Just because Mann says so?

TEACHER Hold on, we'll come back to that. As I was saying: a great writer, rather stuffy and official, falling in love with a beautiful youth and sacrificing his life in order to be near the youth—isn't that, by every ordinary judgment, pretty foolish? I suppose Mann wants us partly to share that judgment, or at least he doesn't entirely dismiss it. But if that were the only or the main judgment proposed by Mann, there wouldn't be much of a story. He sees other and perhaps stronger elements in Aschenbach's final deed. He wants us to recognize Aschenbach's decision to stay in Venice as a repudiation of the puritanical or bourgeois ethic of work, the notion that work is somehow sacred; as an abandonment of his self to long-suppressed desires and energies; as a realization of the *a*moral potentialities always present in the career of an artist; and as a climax, half heroic and half comic—a sort of love-in-death apotheosis reached in his old age.

At the same time, it's important to notice that Mann does not abandon himself to Aschenbach in the way that Aschenbach abandons himself to Tadzio. Mann keeps an ironic distance from Aschenbach; he writes with exactly the control, the restraint, the discipline that Aschenbach gives up. So I'd say that Mann is both imitating and mimicking Aschenbach's style, both copying it and making fun of it. This style, as Mann says toward the beginning of the story, is that of an "official" writer—

STUDENT What's that?

TEACHER A writer whom the entire society honors and who, in

some way, speaks for the entire society. Perhaps the closest we've had to it recently in the United States is Robert Frost. Anyway, Aschenbach's style is that of an "official" writer who has left behind him, as unworthy remnants of his youthful effort, all evidence of bohemianism, radicalism, experimentalism, and so on. Now it happens that this style is pretty much Mann's own, both before and after the composition of *Death in Venice*. So, quite knowingly and with considerable slyness, Mann seems to be parodying himself also.

STUDENT   But you still haven't really told me what "parody" means here.

TEACHER   I'd say that parody—in *this* story—signifies an imitation so close to the mark, so maliciously literal, that what comes out reads like a kind of deadpan put-down. Take the sentence that ends the "overture" to the story. (*He finds the passage in the book before him and reads it aloud.*)

> Yes, personally speaking too, art heightens life. She gives deeper joy, she consumes more swiftly. She engraves adventures of the spirit and the mind in the faces of her votaries; let them lead outwardly a life of the most cloistered calm, she will in the end produce in them a fastidiousness, an over-refinement, a nervous fever and exhaustion, such as a career of extravagant passions and pleasures can hardly show.

You heard how I read that—with a kind of exaggerated gravity, an underscored ponderosity. But I hope I didn't sound completely absurd, for what Mann is saying here is not at all absurd; it makes sense. Yet I think Mann is also, here as throughout the story, poking some sly fun—wait a minute— (*He gets up to rummage through his bookshelves and finds what he wants. The student glances at his watch.*)

Here it is, one of the best critical books on Mann, *The Ironic German* by Erich Heller. He writes:

> What the English translation invariably misses is the ironical elegance and the overtone of mockery, subtly ridiculing the habitual posturing of the German language. In English, alas, the ironically draped velvet and silk often looks like solemnly donned corduroy and tweed.

Well, I don't think the English translation *always* misses Mann's "ironical elegance," but certainly that comes through less clearly than it does in the German. Even if you don't know German you can see in the translation that Mann writes with tongue in cheek, even as he still expects us to take Aschenbach as a serious and perhaps even tragic figure.

STUDENT That brings us back, I guess, to the question I asked: how can we know that Aschenbach is the great writer Mann says he is? Are we just supposed to take his word for it?

TEACHER Well, let me in turn ask you: how do you know Anna Karenina is the beautiful woman Tolstoy says she is? Are we supposed simply to take his word for it?

STUDENT No; there's evidence. First, Tolstoy describes her beauty and second, he shows how her beauty affects other people.

(During the speech that follows, the student, while listening more or less intently, picks up the book by Erich Heller, begins to thumb his way through it, and then, noticing something, folds down a page.)

TEACHER That's right. And in principle the portrayal of a literary genius is not different from the portrayal of a beautiful woman —it's only more difficult. Neither can be shown directly, not the beauty of the woman or the genius of the writer. You can show a clever man through his speech, as James does in *The Tragic Muse*; you can show a villain through his conduct, as Melville does in *Billy Budd*; you can show a weakling through his indecision, as Conrad does in *Lord Jim*. But you cannot "prove" that a character said to be a great novelist actually is a great novelist—short of the impractical (and hazardous) method of including his novel within your own.

But you can show the *impact* a great writer has on other characters (something Mann hardly does in this story) or the problems a great writer faces at certain critical moments of his life. What enables us to believe that Aschenbach is indeed a great writer is that the breakdown of will from which he suffers is of a kind that an overworked and rigidly disciplined writer might really suffer from— though, to be fair about it, other people who do highly concentrated intellectual work could also suffer from it. So I'd say that while Mann can never "completely" demonstrate that Aschenbach is a great writer, he gradually increases what might be called the increment of probability—the piling on of little touches that makes us accept his claims for Aschenbach—from his early listing of Aschenbach's work (a characteristic mixture of respect and irony in its tone) to his detailed presentation of Aschenbach's culminating experience.

And another thing: to the extent that we are persuaded that Aschenbach's final days in Venice are significant and moving, to that extent we are inclined to accept as a premise that he must be a major, if not a "great," writer. Otherwise, his crisis could not take on all the ramifications that in fact it does. The breakdown of a mere fool or a mere stuffed shirt could not move us as much as Aschenbach's breakdown actually does. And since it moves us, we tend to conclude that he is a good deal more than a mere fool or a mere stuffed shirt. How's that?

STUDENT   Fairly convincing. But I have another question, and it goes beyond *Death in Venice*. You keep talking, about this story and the others, as if irony and complexity were ikons we should bow down before. But why should we?

TEACHER   If you keep asking questions like that, we'll be sitting here till the end of summer. They're easier to ask than to answer. Still, I guess you're right. English teachers and literary people in general do tend to make irony and complexity into ikons. But not without reason. Life really is very complex, and the more you examine it, the more you become convinced that the truth about experience is always likely to be problematic, ambiguous, enigmatic. And an essential part of that complexity is the attitude we designate as ironic—by which I mean, roughly speaking, the capacity for taking a self-critical and self-deflating distance from one's own convictions, a capacity for seeing the ridiculous in one's serious beliefs while nevertheless holding them with great seriousness. I think a healthy mind is always a little ironic about its own passions.

STUDENT   But aren't some of you literary people awfully solemn in your constant harping on irony?

TEACHER   No defense!

(A *short break, for coffee and leg-stretching. The student seems to be getting more involved, and therefore more articulate*.)

STUDENT   I have my doubts about something I said in class Tuesday. I talked about Aschenbach's discipline as a writer, all those years he kept himself chained to his desk, the way he would spend his summers in the mountains, lonely and devoted to his work. Then I said that he must have stored up a lot of unused emotion, a lot of unlived life, and that it finally burst out. It's almost an accident that the pretty boy Tadzio brought it out—somebody else or even some *thing*, as long as it suggested or embodied the idea of beauty, might have evoked it just as well. And then I worked out a sort of scheme, more or less Freudian, about a conflict between discipline and passion in Aschenbach's life.

It's still true, I guess, but not true enough. Because now it seems to me that any man who works the way Aschenbach has, who gives himself so completely to the discipline of his craft, must also be expressing his passion through that discipline. You can't get anything worthwhile done just by proclaiming your "creativity"—you have to work. And Aschenbach did that. He deserves our respect because—

TEACHER Keep talking like that and you'll soon be accused of being over thirty! But I'm glad to hear you say those things and I think it shows you're getting more and more from the story. With Aschenbach, there *was* a conflict between discipline and passion. Yet, at the same time, his discipline *was* his passion. Most readers are inclined to think of him as merely "repressed," while the truth is that he is a man who has lived. Only—

STUDENT Only, I guess, if you give yourself to one thing, you miss out on something else. Maybe that's what you meant a few weeks ago when you said about George Eliot that sometimes, in reading her novels, it seemed as if tragedy consisted in the mere need to make choices. Aschenbach made his choice, and now as he plunges into Venice, the time has come to pay.

TEACHER Yes. Speaking of Venice, you know that the city has always been identified with beautiful corruption, or I suppose one could say, the corruption of beauty. Recently I came across this remark of Lord Byron: "been at Venice, which was much visited by the young English gentlemen of those [Elizabethan] times, and was then what Paris is now—the seat of all dissoluteness." So when Mann chose Venice as the place to which Aschenbach, to his own surprise, decides to go, he was using a city that had these connotations of vice for the European reader.

STUDENT Yes, and I think it's pretty marvelous the way Mann creates an atmosphere of foreboding—something dark, even a little creepy—when Aschenbach first comes to Venice. I think we feel that Aschenbach has yielded himself to some sort of descent or collapse—maybe into the corruption of the world which in recent years he has not allowed himself to notice, or maybe into the secret depths of his own self which he has kept so tightly bottled up. And then the atmosphere of the city marvelously parallels Aschenbach's own disintegration—

TEACHER   Or is it a liberation?

STUDENT   Well, as you'd say, do we have to choose? It's a disintegration, insofar as Aschenbach abandons his responsibilities as a writer and a citizen, even abandons the human responsibility for self-preservation. But it's also a liberation, insofar as Aschenbach heeds his own desires, even his whims, so that he becomes "loose." He becomes free and honest with himself, once he no longer cares about his place in society or his reputation as a literary man. But it's not clear to me that Mann wants us to make a choice here—

TEACHER   Or that a choice really can be made. Except, of course, by people who bring to their reading a fixed and ready-made morality that nothing can change, or by those who have decided, as a matter of principle, not to have any ideas about morality. But most of us wish to have moral principles and also to recognize how difficult it is to apply them, and for us the story of Aschenbach achieves what another of Mann's critics, Kenneth Burke, says: it "makes us at home in indecision . . . it humanizes the state of doubt." And that, I'd say, is where our sympathy for Aschenbach comes in: not so much for what he does but for all those crisscrossing pressures of desire and responsibility that assault him almost until his end.

STUDENT   OK. While you were talking before, I looked through the Heller book and found his description of Aschenbach's end. I think it's good:

> before the story of Aschenbach reaches this dissolute climax, Thomas Mann traces with consummate skill all the stages of passion: how the aesthetic enjoyment [of Tadzio] changes to infatuation, infatuation to love, love to degrading abandon, abandon to death. And Venice joins in: the temperature on the beach rises from day to day, the blue sky turns leaden, a sirocco sets in, the streets begin to smell of carbolic acid, nothing can any longer stop the spreading disease. At one point, before he has acknowledged to himself the nature and power of his passion, Aschenbach, suffering badly from the sirocco, determines to leave. It is the last exercise of his moral will; and it fails. The virtuosity of the narrator is at its highest in the delineation of this incident: how Aschenbach, resentful at being hurried over breakfast, but in fact only desirous of seeing Tadzio once more, allows his luggage to be taken to the station ahead of him on the hotel's private motorboat, while he himself will follow later—for there is plenty of time—on the public vaporetto; how his sadness mounts, sadness at losing Venice forever, as he travels along the

palaces of the *Canal Grande;* how he curses his rash decision as the weather seems to improve; how at the station he finds that his luggage has gone on the wrong train; how he is easily persuaded to await its return on the Lido; how his innermost soul rejoices at the accident as if secretly celebrating the successful conclusion of a subtle maneuver; and how, as he settles down again in the hotel, he realizes that he will be in no haste to leave again, for it is Tadzio to whom he has come back. And indeed, the weather changes, the sky is clear, and the prose itself seems now to worship the sun god with Homeric metaphors and rhythms which are yet disquietingly upset by adjectives and inflections announcing the wilder deity.

TEACHER Yes, that's a vivid description. And while we're talking about Mann's techniques, what do you make of those ominous "strangers," those dark and silent figures who appear several times in the story?

STUDENT I assume they are meant to be symbolic messengers of death. Or maybe, "messenger" is the wrong word. They are more like portents, warnings or signs, which Aschenbach only half understands, though he senses they mean disaster.

First, there is the stranger in Munich standing silently near "the mortuary chapel," who says nothing but gives Aschenbach's thoughts "a fresh turn"—as if this specter persuades the old writer that time is running out and that if he's ever going to have pleasure, he'd better look for it now. When he sees this figure, who strikes me like an engraving of Death, Aschenbach has that terrific vision of a tropical landscape, "a kind of primeval wilderness-world" in which "the eyes of a crouching tiger gleamed"—Mann's description of the vision is overpowering. The point here is not hard to get. Aschenbach, who has dedicated himself to rationality and clarity, all the daylight virtues, is now going to yield himself to orgy and darkness. He is going to yield himself to death, but he sees death as a seed-ground of creation and pleasure, the place where finally his passions will burst out.

TEACHER That's good. Let me take it a little further. Aschenbach keeps meeting those agents of death, sinister figures who say nothing but remind him—or suggest to us—that he is taking a one-way journey. There's the old man on the boat to Venice, who fills Aschenbach with nausea. There's the gondolier, who rows Aschenbach to the Lido, first against the writer's will and then with his resigned acceptance. There's the ballad singer at the end of the story, who has the same features of death and is associated in Aschenbach's imagination with the hourglass—that's a traditional symbol of death. Mann is simply uncanny in his gift for placing these figures at strategic points, as chill reminders of what lies ahead.

STUDENT   But all this brings us back to the most important question: what does Mann intend finally to suggest about the relationship between art and morality, beauty and goodness—since I assume the story is written with the idea of making suggestions about that?

TEACHER   Not if you mean a series of little points that can be ticked off. . . .

STUDENT   OK, granted; I understand that a work of fiction doesn't end up, in our minds, as a set of didactic ideas; but still, if we're going to talk about it at all, we have to be able to infer certain attitudes. . . . Anyway, why should I go on making this point? You've said it yourself often enough.

TEACHER   All right, forgive me. I'd say, for one thing, that Mann is composing a great imaginative footnote to Plato—showing how art and morality, the quest for the beautiful and the quest for the good, *can* come into conflict. The artist may start with an "idea" of the beautiful—a Platonic essence—but in order to create his picture, he has to embody that idea in a sensual medium, that is, in color or sound or words. Once he does that, he can easily give way to the lure of the medium itself, so that he slowly and perhaps unwittingly abandons the pure "idea" with which be began and yields himself to the texture of his painting, the rhetoric of his language, the harmony of his sound. Soon enough, all considerations of good and evil, all considerations of human relevance, can be left behind. Not that this always has to happen. But it can; and, as Mann suggests, it can happen to the "classical" writer, like the older Aschenbach who supposes he has left behind him all such enticements, just as much as it could happen to the "romantic" writer, like the young Aschenbach.

STUDENT   Would you say, then, that Aschenbach's falling in love with Tadzio is meant as a parallel, or a sort of allegory, of the artist in relation to his materials? At first, after all, Aschenbach is simply intrigued by Tadzio's beauty; he still keeps an impersonal attitude toward him; he even sees Tadzio as an embodiment of the Greek god of love, Eros. But then Tadzio becomes transformed in his imagination from an "idea" into a tempting human creature, and Mann describes very wonderfully how Aschenbach sinks into the forbidden, giving way to his homosexual—

TEACHER   Yes, but wait a minute. I resist any impulse to "allegor-

ize" this· wonderful story. My main notion as a teacher of literature
is to stick closely to the surface of the story, to get the greatest richness out of the events and figures the author gives us. *Death in Venice* is about a man named Aschenbach who goes through certain experiences. As a kind of shadow-play behind those experiences we detect the pattern of ideas you've described. But we mustn't let the experience be pushed aside by the pattern.

STUDENT Yes, agreed; I already said I see that point. But suppose you let me go ahead abstracting from the story, with the understanding that we have to return to the surface of the story at the
end.

I think Mann is trying to suggest that in all art—and *perhaps*
thereby in all human experience—there is a doubleness, a mixture of
potentialities. Art strains for purity, form, structure. But art deals
with ugliness, chaos, evil. Aschenbach is destroyed by what Mann
calls "the triumph of drunken disorder over the forces of a life con-
secrated to rule and discipline." But we have to remember: (a) that
Aschenbach *has* already written his books and (b) that Mann, in
writing about Aschenbach's "drunken disorder," clearly rises above
Aschenbach's final views and feelings. Furthermore, Aschenbach has
become a certain special kind of writer, what you called an "official"
writer or what I'd call an Establishment writer—with the understanding that that's a way to describe a writer and not necessarily a
way to dismiss him. So in a sense Aschenbach aligns himself with
the bourgeois values of prudence, restraint, order, duty—what I suppose you'd call Apollonian art. But just as bourgeois culture can be
exposed to disintegrating pressures (like the plague, which corrupts
the Venetian authorities), so the Apollonian artist is vulnerable to
the destructive forces of passion and death, Dionysian wildness. The
last section of the story is based on a parallel—just suggested—
between Aschenbach and Venice; Aschenbach's moral collapse, his
coming close to crime, lawlessness, the "monstrous and perverse,"
corresponds to a collapse in the social structure of Venice. Of course,
criticism of the bourgeoisie isn't the main point of *Death in Venice.*
What I think Mann is most concerned with is the equivocal nature
of art, the contradictions inherent in the artistic nature and the
possibilities of maybe reconciling them. The artist has to deal with
opposing tendencies in his own personality, the demands of will and
the demands of passion. Aschenbach demands and practices an ascetic allegiance to form which implies repression and the wearing-
down of internal resources; he values self-conquest at any price. He

rejects the possibility of moral ambiguities, of needs that go beyond morality. He yields to the absolute of moralism, and therefore suffers a collapse of his moral existence. For to Mann, "the singleminded cult of one exclusive perspective is tantamount to a self-hypnosis which [leads] to death or to a 'dignified state of petrifaction.'" Aschenbach "had outgrown the ironic pose"—and this involves a kind of death for the writer. Yet through his very self-discipline he develops an enormous respect for and sensitivity to beauty, and because, as Mann ironically says, "beauty alone is lovely and visible at once," that is, beauty has both a spiritual and a physical existence, he becomes prey to Tadzio's "perfection of form." The cult of form leads to the chaos of abandonment.

TEACHER   That's a nice epigrammatic way of rounding it out, and I pretty much agree. But since it's getting late, let me add one more small point. You remember those passages in which Mann invokes the name of Phaedrus—

STUDENT   I think I'm on to that also, or at least I think I see the point in general. Aschenbach is remembering the dialogue of Plato in which Socrates and the young Phaedrus discuss the nature of love. There's that vivid story Socrates tells about love, in which it is compared to a chariot drawn by two horses, one of them rational, steady, and clear; the other wild, capricious, and murky. These two horses seem to represent two sides of human nature, fighting for domination within us and suggesting the two kinds of love man is capable of. I guess Aschenbach invokes Plato's dialogue to tell himself that he too is vulnerable to the kind of conflict Socrates describes through the story of the two horses, that he too must give way to his "lower" nature after having held it in check so sternly and for such a long time.

TEACHER   Yes, I'm glad you looked it up. But there's one more point that seems to me the slyest of all—characteristic Mann slyness and playfulness. Mann has Aschenbach remember that Socrates, after telling the story of the horses, "said the subtlest thing of all: that the lover was nearer the divine than the beloved; for the god [of Love] was in the one but not in the other—perhaps the tenderest, most mocking thought that ever was thought, and source of all the guile and secret bliss the lover knows."

By recalling this thought of Socrates, Aschenbach is not only acknowledging, as you say, that he too is susceptible to the lure of the senses and the corruption that can follow. He is also, in some final way, justifying himself! Justifying himself in the style classical to lovers. He is saying that what is in him, the feeling of devotion he has for Tadzio, transcends all the ridiculousness and ugliness of what he is doing. By invoking Socrates, Aschenbach also compares himself to Socrates—puts himself in the same light. . . . I think it's a remarkably clever touch and one that must have amused Mann as he watched his story spinning irony within irony.

STUDENT   Well, I'll admit I hadn't thought of that. But there's one more point . . .

TEACHER   No, enough! Because there are too many more points! That's the kind of story it is, one idea or impression giving rise to another. But we can stop here.

Death in Venice

Gustave Aschenbach—or von Aschenbach, as he had been known officially since his fiftieth birthday—had set out alone from his house in Prince Regent Street, Munich, for an extended walk. It was a spring afternoon in that year of grace 19—, when Europe sat upon the anxious seat beneath a menace that hung over its head for months. Aschenbach had sought the open soon after tea. He was overwrought by a morning of hard, nerve-taxing work, work which had not ceased to exact his uttermost in the way of sustained concentration, conscientiousness, and tact; and after the noon meal found himself powerless to check the onward sweep of the productive mechanism within him, that *motus animi continuus* [1] in which, according to Cicero, eloquence resides. He had sought but not found relaxation in sleep—though the wear and tear upon his system had come to make a daily nap more and more imperative—and now undertook a walk, in the hope that air and exercise might send him back refreshed to a good evening's work.

May had begun, and after weeks of cold and wet a mock summer had set in. The English Gardens, though in tenderest leaf, felt as sultry as in August and were full of vehicles and pedestrians near the city. But towards Aumeister the paths were solitary and still, and

[1] Uninterrupted motion of thought.

Aschenbach strolled thither, stopping awhile to watch the lively crowds in the restaurant garden with its fringe of carriages and cabs. Thence he took his homeward way outside the park and across the sunset fields. By the time he reached the North Cemetery, however, he felt tired, and a storm was brewing above Föhring; so he waited at the stopping-place for a tram to carry him back to the city.

He found the neighborhood quite empty. Not a wagon in sight, either on the paved Ungererstrasse, with its gleaming tram-lines stretching off towards Schwabing, nor on the Föhring highway. Nothing stirred behind the hedge in the stone-mason's yard, where crosses, monuments, and commemorative tablets made a supernumerary and untenanted graveyard opposite the real one. The mortuary chapel, a structure in Byzantine style, stood facing it, silent in the gleam of the ebbing day. Its façade was adorned with Greek crosses and tinted hieratic designs, and displayed a symmetrically arranged selection of scriptural texts in gilded letters, all of them with a bearing upon the future life, such as: "They are entering into the House of the Lord" and "May the Light Everlasting shine upon them." Aschenbach beguiled some minutes of his waiting with reading these formulas and letting his mind's eye lose itself in their mystical meaning. He was brought back to reality by the sight of a man standing in the portico, above the two apocalyptic beasts that guarded the staircase, and something not quite usual in this man's appearance gave his thoughts a fresh turn.

Whether he had come out of the hall through the bronze doors or mounted unnoticed from outside, it was impossible to tell. Aschenbach casually inclined to the first idea. He was of medium height, thin, beardless, and strikingly snub-nosed; he belonged to the red-haired type and possessed its milky, freckled skin. He was obviously not Bavarian; and the broad, straight-brimmed straw hat he had on even made him look distinctly exotic. True, he had the indigenous rucksack buckled on his back, wore a belted suit of yellowish woollen stuff, apparently frieze, and carried a grey mackintosh cape across his left forearm, which was propped against his waist. In his right hand, slantwise to the ground, he held an iron-shod stick, and braced himself against its crook, with his legs crossed. His chin was up, so that the Adam's apple looked very bald in the lean neck rising from the loose shirt; and he stood there sharply peering up into space out of colourless, red-lashed eyes, while two pronounced perpendicular furrows showed on his forehead in curious contrast to his little turned-up nose. Perhaps his heightened and heightening position helped out the impression Aschenbach received. At any rate, standing there as though at survey, the man had a bold and domineering, even a ruthless, air, and his lips completed the picture by seeming to curl back, either by reason of some deformity or else because he grimaced, being blinded by the sun in his face; they laid bare the long, white, glistening teeth to the gums.

Aschenbach's gaze, though unawares, had very likely been inquisitive and tactless; for he became suddenly conscious that the stranger was returning it, and indeed so directly, with such hostility, such plain intent to force the withdrawal of the other's eyes, that Aschenbach felt an unpleasant twinge and, turning his back, began to walk along the hedge, hastily resolving to give the man no further heed. He had forgotten him the next minute. Yet whether the pilgrim air the stranger wore kindled his fantasy or whether some other physical or psychical influence came in play, he could not tell; but he felt the most surprising consciousness of a widening of inward barriers, a kind of vaulting unrest, a youthful ardent thirst for distant scenes—a feeling so lively and so new, or at least so long ago outgrown and forgot, that he stood there rooted to the spot, his eyes on the ground and his hands clasped behind him, exploring these sentiments of his, their bearing and scope.

True, what he felt was no more than a longing to travel; yet coming upon him with such suddenness and passion as to resemble a seizure, almost a hallucination. Desire projected itself visually: his fancy, not quite yet lulled since morning, imaged the marvels and terrors of the manifold earth. He saw. He beheld a landscape, a tropical marshland, beneath a reeking sky, steaming, monstrous, rank—a kind of primeval wilderness-world of islands, morasses, and alluvial channels. Hairy palm-trunks rose near and far out of lush brakes of fern, out of bottoms of crass vegetation, fat, swollen, thick with incredible bloom. There were trees, misshapen as a dream, that dropped their naked roots straight through the air into the ground or into water that was stagnant and shadowy and glassy-green, where mammoth milk-white blossoms floated, and strange high-shouldered birds with curious bills stood gazing sidewise without sound or stir. Among the knotted joints of a bamboo thicket the eyes of a crouching tiger gleamed—and he felt his heart throb with terror, yet with a longing inexplicable. Then the vision vanished. Aschenbach, shaking his head, took up his march once more along the hedge of the stone-mason's yard.

He had, at least ever since he commanded means to get about

the world at will, regarded travel as a necessary evil, to be endured now and again willy-nilly for the sake of one's health. Too busy with the tasks imposed upon him by his own ego and the European soul, too laden with the care and duty to create, too preoccupied to be an amateur of the gay outer world, he had been content to know as much of the earth's surface as he could without stirring far outside his own sphere—had, indeed, never even been tempted to leave Europe. Now more than ever, since his life was on the wane, since he could no longer brush aside as fanciful his artist fear of not having done, of not being finished before the works ran down, he had confined himself to close range, had hardly stepped outside the charming city which he had made his home and the rude country house he had built in the mountains, whither he went to spend the rainy summers.

And so the new impulse which thus late and suddenly swept over him was speedily made to conform to the pattern of self-discipline he had followed from his youth up. He had meant to bring his work, for which he lived, to a certain point before leaving for the country, and the thought of a leisurely ramble across the globe, which should take him away from his desk for months, was too fantastic and upsetting to be seriously entertained. Yet the source of the unexpected contagion was known to him only too well. This yearning for new and distant scenes, this craving for freedom, release, forgetfulness—they were, he admitted to himself, an impulse towards flight, flight from the spot which was the daily theatre of a rigid, cold, and passionate service. That service he loved, had even almost come to love the enervating daily struggle between a proud, tenacious, well-tried will and this growing fatigue, which no one must suspect, nor the finished product betray by any faintest sign that his inspiration could ever flag or miss fire. On the other hand, it seemed the part of common sense not to span the bow too far, not to suppress summarily a need that so unequivocally asserted itself. He thought of his work, and the place where yesterday and again today he had been forced to lay it down, since it would not yield either to patient effort or a swift *coup de main*. Again and again he had tried to break or untie the knot—only to retire at last from the attack with a shiver of repugnance. Yet the difficulty was actually not a great one; what sapped his strength was distaste for the task, betrayed by a fastidiousness he could no longer satisfy. In his youth, indeed, the nature and inmost essence of the literary gift had been, to him, this very scrupulosity; for it had bridled and tempered his sensibilities, knowing full well that feeling is prone to be content with easy gains and blithe half-perfection. So now, perhaps, feeling, thus tyrannized, avenged itself by leaving him, refusing from now on to carry and wing his art and taking away with it all the ecstasy he had known in form and expression. Not that he was doing bad work. So much, at least, the years had brought him, that at any moment he might feel tranquilly assured of mastery. But he got no joy of it—not though a nation paid it homage. To him it seemed his work had ceased to be marked by that fiery play of fancy which is the product of joy, and more, and more potently, than any intrinsic content, forms in turn the joy of the receiving world. He dreaded the summer in the country, alone with the maid who prepared his food and the man who served him; dreaded to see the familiar mountain peaks and walls that would shut him up again with his heavy discontent. What he needed was a break, an interim existence, a means of passing time, other air and a new stock of blood, to make the summer tolerable and productive. Good, then, he would go on a journey. Not far—not all the way to the tigers. A night in a *wagon-lit*, three or four weeks of lotus-eating at some one of the gay world's playgrounds in the lovely south. . . .

So ran his thoughts, while the clang of the electric tram drew nearer down the Ungererstrasse; and as he mounted the platform he decided to devote the evening to a study of maps and railway guides. Once in, he bethought him to look back after the man in the straw hat, the companion of this brief interval which had after all been so fruitful. But he was not in his former place, nor in the tram itself, nor yet at the next stop; in short, his whereabouts remained a mystery.

Gustave Aschenbach was born at L—, a country town in the province of Silesia. He was the son of an upper official in the judicature, and his forbears had all been officers, judges, departmental functionaries—men who lived their strict, decent, sparing lives in the service of king and state. Only once before had a livelier mentality—in the quality of a clergyman—turned up among them; but swifter, more perceptive blood had in the generation before the poet's flowed into the stock from the mother's side, she being the daughter of a Bohemian musical conductor. It was from her he had the foreign traits that betrayed themselves in his appearance. The union of dry, conscientious officialdom and ardent, obscure impulse, produced an artist—and this particular artist: author of the lucid and vigorous prose epic on the life of Frederick the Great; careful, tireless weaver of the richly patterned tapestry entitled *Maia*, a novel that gathers up the threads of many human destinies in the warp of a single idea; creator of that powerful narrative *The Abject*, which taught a whole grateful generation that a man can still be capable of moral resolution even after he has plumbed the depths of knowledge; and lastly—to complete the tale of works of his mature period —the writer of that impassioned discourse on the theme of Mind and Art whose ordered force and antithetic eloquence led serious critics to rank it with Schiller's *Simple and Sentimental Poetry.*

Aschenbach's whole soul, from the very beginning, was bent on fame—and thus, while not precisely precocious, yet thanks to the unmistakable trenchancy of his personal accent he was early ripe and ready for a career. Almost before he was out of high school he had a name. Ten years later he had learned to sit at his desk and sustain and live up to his growing reputation, to write gracious and pregnant phrases in letters that must needs be brief, for many claims press upon the solid and successful man. At forty, worn down by the strains and stresses of his actual task, he had to deal with a daily post heavy with tributes from his own and foreign countries.

Remote on one hand from the banal, on the other from the eccentric, his genius was calculated to win at once the adhesion of the general public and the admiration, both sympathetic and stimulating, of the connoisseur. From childhood up he was pushed on·every side to achievement, and achievement of no ordinary kind; and so his young days never knew the sweet idleness and blithe *laisse aller* [2] that belong to youth. A nice observer once said of him in company—it was at the time when he fell ill in Vienna in his thirty-fifth year: "You see, Aschenbach has always lived like this"—here the speaker closed the fingers of his left hand to a fist—"never like this"—and he let his open hand hang relaxed from the back of his chair. It was apt. And this attitude was the more morally valiant in that Aschenbach was not by nature robust—he was only called to the constant tension of his career, not actually born to it.

By medical advice he had been kept from school and educated at home. He had grown up solitary, without comradeship; yet had early been driven to see that he belonged to those whose talent is not so much out of the common as is the physical basis on which talent relies for its fulfilment. It is a seed that gives early of its fruit, whose

_____
[2] To take life as it comes.

powers seldom reach a ripe old age. But his favourite motto was "Hold fast"; indeed, in his novel on the life of Frederick the Great he envisaged nothing else than the apotheosis of the old hero's word of command, *"Durchhalten,"* which seemed to him the epitome of fortitude under suffering. Besides, he deeply desired to live to a good old age, for it was his conviction that only the artist to whom it has been granted to be fruitful on all stages of our human scene can be truly great, or universal, or worthy of honour.

Bearing the burden of his genius, then, upon such slender shoulders and resolved to go so far, he had the more need of discipline—and discipline, fortunately, was his native inheritance from the father's side. At forty, at fifty, he was still living as he had commenced to live in the years when others are prone to waste and revel, dream high thoughts and postpone fulfilment. He began his day with a cold shower over chest and back; then, setting a pair of tall wax candles in silver holders at the head of his manuscript, he sacrificed to art, in two or three hours of almost religious fervour, the powers he had assembled in sleep. Outsiders might be pardoned for believing that his *Maia* world and the epic amplitude revealed by the life of Frederick were a manifestation of great power working under high pressure, that they came forth, as it were, all in one breath. It was the more triumph for his morale; for the truth was that they were heaped up to greatness in layer after layer, in long days of work, out of hundreds and hundreds of single inspirations; they owed their excellence, both of mass and detail, to one thing and one alone: that their creator could hold out for years under the strain of the same piece of work, with an endurance and a tenacity of purpose like that which had conquerered his native province of Silesia, devoting to actual composition none but his best and freshest hours.

For an intellectual product of any value to exert an immediate influence which shall also be deep and lasting, it must rest on an inner harmony, yes, an affinity, between the personal destiny of its author and that of his contemporaries in general. Men do not know why they award fame to one work of art rather than another. Without being in the faintest connoisseurs, they think to justify the warmth of their commendations by discovering in it a hundred virtues, whereas the real ground of their applause is inexplicable—it is sympathy. Aschenbach had once given direct expression—though in an unobtrusive place—to the idea that almost everything conspicuously great is great in despite: has come into being in defiance of affliction and pain, poverty, destitution, bodily weakness, vice, passion, and a thousand other obstructions. And that was more than observation—it was the fruit of experience, it was precisely the formula of his life and fame, it was the key to his work. What wonder, then, if it was also the fixed character, the outward gesture, of his most individual figures?

The new type of hero favoured by Aschenbach, and recurring many times in his works, had early been analysed by a shrewd critic: "The conception of an intellectual and virginal manliness, which clenches its teeth and stands in modest defiance of the swords and spears that pierce its side." That was beautiful, it was *spirituel*, it was exact, despite the suggestion of too great passivity it held. Forbearance in the face of fate, beauty constant under torture, are not merely passive. They are a positive achievement, an explicit triumph; and the figure of Sebastian is the most beautiful symbol, if not of art as a whole, yet certainly of the art we speak of here. Within that world of Aschenbach's creation were exhibited many phases of this theme: there was the aristocratic self-command that is eaten out within and for as long as it can conceals its biologic decline from the eyes of the world; the sere and ugly outside, hiding the embers of smouldering fire—and having power to fan them to so pure a flame as to challenge supremacy in the domain of beauty itself; the pallid languors of the flesh, contrasted with the fiery ardours of the spirit within, which can fling a whole proud people down at the foot of the Cross, at the feet of its own sheer self-abnegation; the gracious bearing preserved in the stern, stark service of form; the unreal, precarious existence of the born intrigant with its swiftly enervating alternation of schemes and desires—all these human fates and many more of their like one read in Aschenbach's pages, and reading them might doubt the existence of any other kind of heroism than the heroism born of weakness. And, after all, what kind could be truer to the spirit of the times? Gustave Aschenbach was the poet-spokesman of all those who labour at the edge of exhaustion; of the overburdened, of those who are already worn out but still hold themselves upright; of all our modern moralizers of accomplishment, with stunted growth and scanty resources, who yet contrive by skilful husbanding and prodigious spasms of will to produce, at least for a while, the effect of greatness. There are many such, they are the heroes of the age. And in Aschenbach's pages they saw themselves; he justified, he exalted them, he sang their praise—and they, they were grateful, they heralded his fame.

He had been young and crude with the times and by them badly counselled. He had taken false steps, blundered, exposed himself, offended in speech and writing against tact and good sense. But he had attained to honour, and honour, he used to say, is the natural goal towards which every considerable talent presses with whip and spur. Yes, one might put it that his whole career had been one conscious and overweening ascent to honour, which left in the rear all the misgivings or self-derogation which might have hampered him.

What pleases the public is lively and vivid delineation which makes no demands on the intellect; but passionate and absolutist youth can only be enthralled by a problem. And Aschenbach was as absolute, as problematist, as any youth of them all. He had done homage to intellect, had overworked the soil of knowledge and ground up her seed-corn; had turned his back on the "mysteries," called genius itself in question, held up art to scorn—yes, even while his faithful following revelled in the characters he created, he, the young artist, was taking away the breath of the twenty-year-olds with his cynic utterances on the nature of art and the artist life.

But it seems that a noble and active mind blunts itself against nothing so quickly as the sharp and bitter irritant of knowledge. And certain it is that the youth's constancy of purpose, no matter how painfully conscientious, was shallow beside the mature resolution of the master of his craft, who made a right-about-face, turned his back on the realm of knowledge, and passed it by with averted face, lest it lame his will or power of action, paralyse his feelings or his passions, deprive any of these of their conviction or utility. How else interpret the oft-cited story of *The Abject* than as a rebuke to the excesses of psychology-ridden age, embodied in the delineation of the weak and silly fool who manages to lead fate by the nose; driving his wife, out of sheer innate pusillanimity, into the arms of a beardless youth, and making this disaster an excuse for trifling away the rest of his life?

With rage the author here rejects the rejected, casts out the outcast—and the measure of his fury is the measure of his condemnation of all moral shilly-shallying. Explicitly he renounces sympathy with the abyss, explicitly he refutes the flabby humanitarianism of the phrase: *"Tout comprendre c'est tout pardonner."* [3] What was here unfolding, or rather was already in full bloom, was the "miracle of regained detachment," which a little later became the theme of one of the author's dialogues, dwelt upon not without a certain oracular emphasis. Strange sequence of thought! Was it perhaps an in-

[3] "To understand everything is to forgive everything."

tellectual consequence of this rebirth, this new austerity, that from now on his style showed an almost exaggerated sense of beauty, a lofty purity, symmetry, and simplicity, which gave his productions a stamp of the classic, of conscious and deliberate mastery? And yet: this moral fibre, surviving the hampering and disintegrating effect of knowledge, does it not result in its turn in a dangerous simplification, in a tendency to equate the world and the human soul, and thus to strengthen the hold of the evil, the forbidden, and the ethically impossible? And has not form two aspects? Is it not moral and immoral at once: moral in so far as it is the expression and result of discipline, immoral—yes, actually hostile to morality—in that of its very essence it is indifferent to good and evil, and deliberately concerned to make the moral world stoop beneath its proud and undivided sceptre?

Be that as it may. Development is destiny; and why should a career attended by the applause and adulation of the masses necessarily take the same course as one which does not share the glamour and the obligations of fame? Only the incorrigible bohemian smiles or scoffs when a man of transcendent gifts outgrows his carefree prentice stage, recognizes his own worth and forces the world to recognize it too and pay it homage, though he puts on a courtly bearing to hide his bitter struggles and his loneliness. Again, the play of a developing talent must give its possessor joy, if of a wilful, defiant kind. With time, an official note, something almost expository, crept into Gustave Aschenbach's method. His later style gave up the old sheer audacities, the fresh and subtle nuances—it became fixed and exemplary, conservative, formal, even formulated. Like Louis XIV—or as tradition has it of him—Aschenbach, as he went on in years, banished from his style every common word. It was at this time that the school authorities adopted selections from his works into their text-books. And he found it only fitting—and had no thought but to accept—when a German prince signalized his accession to the throne by conferring upon the poet-author of the life of Frederick the Great on his fiftieth birthday the letters-patent of nobility.

He had roved about for a few years, trying this place and that as a place of residence, before choosing, as he soon did, the city of Munich for his permanent home. And there he lived, enjoying among his fellow-citizens the honour which is in rare cases the reward of intellectual eminence. He married young, the daughter of a university family; but after a brief term of wedded happiness his wife had died. A daughter, already married, remained to him. A son he never had.

Gustave von Aschenbach was somewhat below middle height, dark and smooth-shaven, with a head that looked rather too large for his almost delicate figure. He wore his hair brushed back; it was thin at the parting, bushy and grey on the temples, framing a lofty, rugged, knotty brow—if one may so characterize it. The nose-piece of his rimless gold spectacles cut into the base of his thick, aristocratically hooked nose. The mouth was large, often lax, often suddenly narrow and tense; the cheeks lean and furrowed, the pronounced chin slightly cleft. The vicissitudes of fate, it seemed, must have passed over this head, for he held it, plaintively, rather on one side; yet it was art, not the stern discipline of an active career, that had taken over the office of modelling these features. Behind this brow were born the flashing thrust and parry of the dialogue between Frederick and Voltaire on the theme of war; these eyes, weary and sunken, gazing through their glasses, had beheld the bloodstained inferno of the hospitals in the Seven Years' War. Yes, personally speaking too, art heightens life. She gives deeper joy, she consumes more swiftly. She engraves adventures of the spirit and the mind in the faces of votaries; let them lead outwardly a life of the most cloistered calm, she will in the end produce in them a fastidiousness, an over-refinement, a nervous fever and exhaustion, such as a career of extravagant passions and pleasures can hardly show.

Eager though he was to be off, Aschenbach was kept in Munich by affairs both literary and practical for some two weeks after that walk of his. But at length he ordered his country home put ready against his return within the next few weeks, and on a day between the middle and the end of May took the evening train for Trieste, where he stopped only twenty-four hours, embarking for Pola the next morning but one.

What he sought was a fresh scene, without associations, which should yet be not too out-of-the-way; and accordingly he chose an island in the Adriatic, not far off the Istrian coast. It had been well known some years, for its splendidly rugged cliff formations on the side next to the open sea, and its population, clad in a bright flutter of rags and speaking an outlandish tongue. But there was rain and heavy air, the society at the hotel was provincial Austrian, and limited; besides, it annoyed him not to be able to get at the sea—he missed the close and soothing contact which only a gentle sandy slope affords. He could not feel this was the place he sought; an inner impulse made him wretched, urging him on he knew not whither; he racked his brains, he looked up boats, then all at once his goal stood plain before his eyes. But of course! When one wanted to arrive overnight at the incomparable, the fabulous, the like-nothing-else-in-the-world, where was it one went? Why, obviously; he had intended to go there, what ever was he doing here? A blunder. He made all haste to correct it, announcing his departure at once. Ten days after his arrival on the island a swift motor-boat bore him and his luggage in the misty dawning back across the water to the naval station, where he landed only to pass over the landing-stage and on to the wet decks of a ship lying there with steam up for the passage to Venice.

It was an ancient hulk belonging to an Italian line, obsolete, dingy, grimed with soot. A dirty hunchbacked sailor, smirkingly polite, conducted him at once belowships to a cavernous, lamplit cabin. There behind a table sat a man with a beard like a goat's; he had his hat on the back of his head, a cigar-stump in the corner of his mouth; he reminded Aschenbach of an old-fashioned circus-director. This person put the usual questions and wrote out a ticket to Venice, which he issued to the traveller with many commercial flourishes.

"A ticket for Venice," repeated he, stretching out his arm to dip the pen into the thick ink in a tilted ink-stand. "One first-class to Venice! Here you are, *signore mio*." He made some scrawls on the paper, strewed bluish sand on it out of a box, thereafter letting the sand run off into an earthen vessel, folded the paper with bony yellow fingers, and wrote on the outside. "An excellent choice," he rattled on. "Ah, Venice! What a glorious city! Irresistibly attractive to the cultured man for her past history as well as her present charm." His copious gesturings and empty phrases gave the odd impression that he feared the traveller might alter his mind. He changed Aschenbach's note, laying the money on the spotted tablecover with the glibness of a croupier. "A pleasant visit to you, signore," he said, with a melodramatic bow. "Delighted to serve you." Then he beckoned and called out: "Next" as though a stream of passengers stood waiting to be served, though in point of fact there was not one. Aschenbach returned to the upper deck.

He leaned an arm on the railing and looked at the idlers lounging along the quay to watch the boat go out. Then he turned his attention to his fellow-passengers. Those of the second class, both men and women, were squatted on their bundles of luggage on the forward deck. The first cabin consisted of a group of lively youths, clerks from Pola, evidently, who had made up a pleasure excursion to Italy and were not a little thrilled at the prospect, bustling about and laughing with satisfaction at the stir they made. They leaned over the railings and shouted, with a glib command of epithet, derisory remarks at such of their fellow-clerks as they saw going to business along the quay; and these in turn shook their sticks and shouted as good back again. One of the party, in a dandified buff suit, a rakish panama with a coloured scarf, and a red cravat, was loudest of the loud: he outcrowed all the rest. Aschenbach's eyes dwelt on him, and he was shocked to see that the apparent youth was no youth at all. He was an old man, beyond a doubt, with wrinkles and crow's-feet round eyes and mouth; the dull carmine of the cheeks was rouge, the brown hair a wig. His neck was shrunken and sinewy, his turned-up moustaches and small imperial were dyed, and the unbroken double row of yellow teeth he showed when he laughed were but too obviously a cheapish false set. He wore a seal ring on each forefinger, but the hands were those of an old man. Aschenbach was moved to shudder as he watched the creature and his association with the rest of the group. Could they not see he was old, that he had no right to wear the clothes they wore or pretend to be one of them? But they were used to him, it seemed; they suffered him among them, they paid back his jokes in kind and playful pokes in the ribs he gave them. How could they? Aschenbach put his hand to his brow, he covered his eyes, for he had slept little, and they smarted. He felt not quite canny, as though the world were suffering a dreamlike distortion of perspective which he might arrest by shutting it all out for a few minutes and then looking at it afresh. But instead he felt a floating sensation, and opened his eyes with unreasoning alarm to find that the ship's dark sluggish bulk was slowly leaving the jetty. Inch by inch, with the to-and-fro motion of her machinery, the strip of iridescent dirty water widened, the boat manœuvred clumsily and turned her bow to the open sea. Aschenbach moved over to the starboard side, where the hunchbacked sailor had set up a deck-chair for him, and a steward in a greasy dress-coat asked for orders.

The sky was grey, the wind humid. Harbour and island dropped behind, all sight of land soon vanished in mist. Flakes of sodden, clammy soot fell upon the still undried deck. Before the boat was an hour out a canvas had to be spread as a shelter from the rain.

Wrapped in his cloak, a book in his lap, our traveller rested; the hours slipped by unawares. It stopped raining, the canvas was taken down. The horizon was visible right round: beneath the sombre dome of the sky stretched the vast plain of empty sea. But immeasurable unarticulated space weakens our power to measure time as well: the time-sense falters and grows dim. Strange, shadowy figures passed and repassed—the elderly coxcomb, the goat-bearded man from the bowels of the ship—with vague gesturings and mutterings through the traveller's mind as he lay. He fell asleep.

At midday he was summoned to luncheon in a corridor-like saloon with the sleeping-cabins giving off it. He ate at the head of the long table; the party of clerks, including the old man, sat with the jolly captain at the other end, where they had been carousing since ten o'clock. The meal was wretched, and soon done. Aschenbach was driven to seek the open and look at the sky—perhaps it would lighten presently above Venice.

He had not dreamed it could be otherwise, for the city had ever given him a brilliant welcome. But sky and sea remained leaden, with spurts of fine, mistlike rain; he reconciled himself to the idea of seeing a different Venice from that he had always approached on the landward side. He stood by the foremast, his gaze on the distance, alert for the first glimpse of the coast. And he thought of the melancholy and susceptible poet who had once seen the towers and turrets of his dreams rise out of these waves; repeated the rhythms born of his awe, his mingled emotions of joy and suffering—and easily susceptible to a prescience already shaped within him, he asked his own sober, weary heart if a new enthusiasm, a new preoccupation, some late adventure of the feelings could still be in store for the idle traveller.

The flat coast showed on the right, the sea was soon populous with fishing-boats. The Lido appeared and was left behind as the ship glided at half speed through the narrow harbour of the same name, coming to a full stop on the lagoon in sight of garish, badly built houses. Here it waited for the boat bringing the sanitary inspector.

An hour passed. One had arrived—and yet not. There was no conceivable haste—yet one felt harried. The youths from Pola were on deck, drawn hither by the martial sound of horns coming across the water from the direction of the Public Gardens. They had drunk a good deal of Asti and were moved to shout and hurrah at the drilling *bersaglieri*. But the young-old man was a truly repulsive sight in the condition to which his company with youth had brought him. He could not carry his wine like them: he was pitiably drunk. He swayed as he stood—watery-eyed, a cigarette between his shaking fingers, keeping upright with difficulty. He could not have taken a step without falling and knew better than to stir, but his spirits were deplorably high. He buttonholed anyone who came within reach, he stuttered, he giggled, he leered, he fatuously shook his beringed old forefinger; his tongue kept seeking the corner of his mouth in a suggestive motion ugly to behold. Aschenbach's brow darkened as he looked, and there came over him once more a dazed sense, as though things about him were just slightly losing their ordinary perspective, beginning to show a distortion that might merge into the gortesque. He was prevented from dwelling on the feeling, for now the machinery began to thud again, and the ship took up its passage through the Canale di San Marco which had been interrupted so near the goal.

He saw it once more, that landing-place that takes the breath away, that amazing group of incredible structures the Republic set up to meet the awe-struck eye of the approaching seafarer: the airy splendour of the palace and Bridge of Sighs, the columns of lion and saint on the shore, the glory of the projecting flank of the fairy temple, the vista of gateway and clock. Looking, he thought that to come to Venice by the station is like entering a palace by the back door. No one should approach, save by the high seas as he was doing now, this most improbable of cities.

The engines stopped. Gondolas pressed alongside, the landing-stairs were let down, customs officials came on board and did their office, people began to go ashore. Aschenbach ordered a gondola. He meant to take up his abode by the sea and needed to be conveyed with his luggage to the landing-stage of the little steamers that ply between the city and the Lido. They called down his order to the surface of the water where the gondoliers were quarreling in dialect. Then came another delay while his trunk was worried down the ladder-like stairs. Thus he was forced to endure the importunities of the ghastly young-old man, whose drunken state obscurely urged him to pay the stranger the honour of a formal farewell. "We wish you a very pleasant sojourn," he babbled, bowing and scraping. "Pray keep us in mind. *Au revoir, excusez et bon jour, votre Excellence.*" He drooled, he blinked, he licked the corner of his mouth, the little imperial bristled on his elderly chin. He put the tips of two fingers to his mouth and said thickly: "Give her our love, will you, the pretty little dear"—here his upper plate came away and fell down on the lower one. . . . Aschenbach escaped. "Little sweety-sweety-sweetheart" he heard behind him, gurgled and stuttered, as he climbed down the rope stair into the boat.

Is there anyone but must repress a secret thrill, on arriving in Venice for the first time—or returning thither after long absence—and stepping into a Venetian gondola? That singular conveyance, come down unchanged from ballad times, black as nothing else on earth except a coffin—what pictures it calls up of lawless, silent adventures in the plashing night; or even more, what visions of death itself, the bier and solemn rites and last soundless voyage! And has anyone remarked that the seat in such a bark, the armchair lacquered in coffin-black and dully black-upholstered, is the softest, most luxurious, most relaxing seat in the world? Aschenbach realized it when he had let himself down at the gondolier's feet, opposite his luggage, which lay neatly composed on the vessel's beak. The rowers still gestured fiercely; he heard their harsh, incoherent tones. But the strange stillness of the water-city seemed to take up their voices gently, to disembody and scatter them over the sea. It was warm here in the harbour. The lukewarm air of the sirocco breathed upon him, he leaned back among his cushions and gave himself to the yielding element, closing his eyes for very pleasure in an indolence as unaccustomed as sweet. "The trip will be short," he thought, and wished it might last forever. They gently swayed away from the boat with its bustle and clamour of voices.

It grew still and stiller all about. No sound but the splash of the oars, the hollow slap of the wave against the steep, black, halbert-shaped beak of the vessel, and one sound more—a muttering by fits and starts, expressed as it were by the motion of his arms, from the lips of the gondolier. He was talking to himself, between his teeth. Aschenbach glanced up and saw with surprise that the lagoon was widening, his vessel was headed for the open sea. Evidently it would not do to give himself up to sweet *far niente*; he must see his wishes carried out.

"You are to take me to the steamboat landing, you know," he said, half turning round towards it. The muttering stopped. There was no reply.

"Take me to the steamboat landing," he repeated, and this time turned quite round and looked up into the face of the gondolier as he stood there on his little elevated deck, high against the pale grey sky. The man had an unpleasing, even brutish face, and wore blue clothes like a sailor's, with a yellow sash; a shapeless straw hat with the braid torn at the brim perched rakishly on his head. His facial structure, as well as the curling blond moustache under the short snub nose, showed him to be of non-Italian stock. Physically rather undersized, so that one would have expected him to be very muscular, he pulled vigorously at the oar, putting all his body-weight behind each stroke. Now and then the effort he made curled back his lips and bared his white teeth to the gums. He spoke in a decided, almost curt voice, looking out to sea over his fare's head: "The signore is going to the Lido."

Aschenbach answered: "Yes, I am. But I only took the gondola to cross over to San Marco. I am using the *vaporetto* from there."

"But the signore cannot use the *vaporetto*."

"And why not?"

"Because the *vaporetto* does not take luggage."

It was true. Aschenbach remembered it. He made no answer. But the man's gruff, overbearing manner, so unlike the usual courtesy of his countrymen towards the stranger, was intolerable. Aschenbach spoke again: "That is my own affair. I may want to give my luggage in deposit. You will turn round."

No answer. The oar splashed, the wave struck dull against the prow. And the muttering began anew, the gondolier talked to himself, between his teeth.

What should the traveller do? Alone on the water with this tongue-tied, obstinate, uncanny man, he saw no way of enforcing his will. And if only he did not excite himself, how pleasantly he might rest! Had he not wished the voyage might last forever? The wisest thing—and how much the pleasantest!—was to let matters take their own course. A spell of indolence was upon him; it came from the chair he sat in—this low, black-upholstered arm-chair, so gently rocked at the hands of the despotic boatman in his rear. The thought passed dreamily through Aschenbach's brain that perhaps he had fallen into the clutches of a criminal; it had not power to rouse him to action. More annoying was the simpler explanation: that the man was only trying to extort money. A sense of duty, a recollection, as it were, that this ought to be prevented, made him collect himself to say:

"How much do you ask for the trip?"

And the gondolier, gazing out over his head, replied: "The signore will pay."

There was an established reply to this; Aschenbach made it, mechanically:

"I will pay nothing whatever if you do not take me where I want to go."

"The signore wants to go to the Lido."

"But not with you."

"I am a good rower, signore. I will row you well."

"So much is true," thought Aschenbach, and again he relaxed. "That is true, you row me well. Even if you mean to rob me, even if you hit me in the back with your oar and send me down to the kingdom of Hades, even then you will have rowed me well."

But nothing of the sort happened. Instead, they fell in with company: a boat came alongside and waylaid them, full of men and women singing to guitar and mandolin. They rowed persistently bow for bow with the gondola and filled the silence that had rested on the waters with their lyric love of gain. Aschenbach tossed money into the hat they held out. The music stopped at once, they rowed away. And once more the gondolier's mutter became audible as he talked to himself in fits and snatches.

Thus they rowed on, rocked by the wash of a steamer returning citywards. At the landing two municipal officials were walking up and down with their hands behind their backs and their faces turned towards the lagoon. Aschenbach was helped on shore by the old man with a boat-hook who is the permanent feature of every landing-stage in Venice; and having no small change to pay the boatman, crossed over into the hotel opposite. His wants were supplied in the lobby; but when he came back his possessions were already on a hand-car on the quay, and gondola and gondolier were gone.

"He ran away, signore," said the old boatman. "A bad lot, a man without a licence. He is the only gondolier without one. The others telephoned over, and he knew we were on the look-out, so he made off."

Aschenbach shrugged.

"The signore has had a ride for nothing," said the old man, and held out his hat. Aschenbach dropped some coins. He directed that his luggage be taken to the Hôtel des Bains and followed the hand-car through the avenue, that white-blossoming avenue with taverns, booths, and pensions on either side it, which runs across the island diagonally to the beach.

He entered the hotel from the garden terrace at the back and passed through the vestibule and hall into the office. His arrival was expected, and he was served with courtesy and dispatch. The manager, a small, soft, dapper man with a black moustache and a caressing way with him, wearing a French frock-coat, himself took him up in the lift and showed him his room. It was a pleasant chamber, furnished in cherry-wood, with lofty windows looking out to sea. It was decorated with strong-scented flowers. Aschenbach, as soon as he was alone, and while they brought in his trunk and bags and disposed them in the room, went up to one of the windows and stood looking out upon the beach in its afternoon emptiness, and at the sunless sea, now full and sending long, low waves with rhythmic beat upon the sand.

A solitary, unused to speaking of what he sees and feels, has mental experiences which are at once more intense and less articulate than those of a gregarious man. They are sluggish, yet more wayward, and never without a melancholy tinge. Sights and impressions which others brush aside with a glance, a light comment, a smile, occupy him more than their due; they sink silently in, they take on meaning, they become experience, emotion, adventure. Solitude gives birth to the original in us, to beauty unfamiliar and perilous—to poetry. But also, it gives birth to the opposite: to the perverse, the illicit, the absurd. Thus the traveller's mind still dwelt with disquiet on the episodes of his journey hither: on the horrible old fop with his drivel about a mistress, on the outlaw boatman and his lost tip. They did not offend his reason, they hardly afforded food for thought; yet they seemed by their very nature fundamentally strange, and thereby vaguely disquieting. Yet here was the sea; even in the midst of such thoughts he saluted it with his eyes, exulting that Venice was near and accessible. At length he turned round, disposed his personal belongings and made certain arrangements with the chambermaid for his comfort, washed up, and was conveyed to the ground floor by the green-uniformed Swiss who ran the lift.

He took tea on the terrace facing the sea and afterwards went down and walked some distance along the shore promenade in the direction of Hôtel Excelsior. When he came back it seemed to be time to change for dinner. He did so, slowly and methodically as his way was, for he was accustomed to work while he dressed; but even so found himself a little early when he entered the hall, where a large number of guests had collected—strangers to each other and affecting mutual indifference, yet united in expectancy of the meal. He picked up a paper, sat down in a leather arm-chair, and took stock of the company, which compared most favourably with that he had just left.

This was a broad and tolerant atmosphere, of wide horizons. Subdued voices were speaking most of the principal European tongues. That uniform of civilization, the conventional evening dress, gave outward conformity to the varied types. There were long, dry Americans, large-familied Russians, English ladies, German children with French *bonnes*. The Slavic element predominated, it seemed. In Aschenbach's neighbourhood Polish was being spoken.

Round a wicker table next to him was gathered a group of young folk in charge of a governess or companion—three young girls; perhaps fifteen to seventeen years old, and a long-haired boy of about fourteen. Aschenbach noticed with astonishment the lad's perfect beauty. His face recalled the noblest moment of Greek sculpture —pale, with a sweet reserve, with clustering honey-coloured ringlets, the brow and nose descending in one line, the winning mouth, the expression of pure and godlike serenity. Yet with all this chaste perfection of form it was of such unique personal charm that the observer thought he had never seen, either in nature or art, anything so utterly happy and consummate. What struck him further was the strange contrast the group afforded, a difference in educational method, so to speak, shown in the way the brother and sisters were clothed and treated. The girls, the eldest of whom was practically grown up, were dressed with an almost disfiguring austerity. All three wore half-length slate-coloured frocks of cloister-like plainness, arbitrarily unbecoming in cut, with white turn-over collars as their only adornment. Every grace of outline was wilfully suppressed; their hair lay smoothly plastered to their heads, giving them a vacant expression, like a nun's. All this could only be by the mother's orders; but there was no trace of the same pedagogic severity in the case of the boy. Tenderness and softness, it was plain, conditioned his existence. No scissors had been put to the lovely hair that (like the Spinnario's) curled about his brows, above his ears, longer still in the neck. He wore an English sailor suit, with quilted sleeves that narrowed round the delicate wrists of his long and slender though still childish hands. And this suit, with its breast-knot, lacings, and embroideries, lent the slight figure something "rich and strange," a spoilt, exquisite air. The observer saw him in half profile, with one foot in its black patent leather advanced, one elbow resting on the arm of his basket-chair, the cheek nestled into the closed hand in a pose of easy grace, quite unlike the stiff subservient mien which was evidently habitual to his sisters. Was he delicate? His facial tint was ivory-white against the golden darkness of his clustering locks. Or was he simply a pampered darling, the object of a self-willed and partial love? Aschenbach inclined to think the latter. For in almost every artist nature is inborn a wanton and treacherous proneness to side with the beauty that breaks hearts, to single out aristocratic pretensions and pay them homage.

A waiter announced, in English, that dinner was served. Gradually the company dispersed through the glass doors into the dining-room. Latecomers entered from the vestibule or the lifts. Inside, dinner was being served; but the young Poles still sat and waited about their wicker table. Aschenbach felt comfortable in his deep arm-chair, he enjoyed the beauty before his eyes, he waited with them.

The governess, a short, stout, red-faced person, at length gave the signal. With lifted brows she pushed back her chair and made a bow to the tall woman, dressed in palest grey, who now entered the hall. This lady's abundant jewels were pearls, her manner was cool and measured; the fashion of her gown and the arrangement of her lightly powdered hair had the simplicity prescribed in certain circles whose piety and aristocracy are equally marked. She might have been, in Germany, the wife of some high official. But there was something faintly fabulous, after all, in her appearance, though lent it solely by the pearls she wore: they were well-nigh priceless, and consisted of ear-rings and a three-stranded necklace, very long, with gems the size of cherries.

The brother and sisters had risen briskly. They bowed over their mother's hand to kiss it, she turning away from them, with a slight smile on her face, which was carefully preserved but rather sharp-nosed and worn. She addressed a few words in French to the governess, then moved towards the glass door. The children followed, the girls in order of age, then the governess, and last the boy. He chanced to turn before he crossed the threshold, and as there was no one else in the room, his strange, twilit grey eyes met Aschenbach's, as our traveller sat there with the paper on his knee, absorbed in looking after the group.

There was nothing singular, of course, in what he had seen. They had not gone in to dinner before their mother, they had waited, given her a respectful salute, and but observed the right and proper forms on entering the room. Yet they had done all this so expressly, with such self-respecting dignity, discipline, and sense of duty that Aschenbach was impressed. He lingered still a few minutes, then he, too, went into the dining-room, where he was shown a table far off the Polish family, as he noted at once, with a stirring of regret.

Tired, yet mentally alert, he beguiled the long, tedious meal with abstract, even with transcendent matters: pondered the mysterious harmony that must come to subsist between the individual human being and the universal law, in order that human beauty may result; passed on to general problems of form and art, and came at length to the conclusion that what seemed to him fresh and happy thoughts were like the flattering inventions of a dream, which the waking sense proves worthless and insubstantial. He spent the evening in the park, that was sweet with odours of evening—sitting, smoking, wandering about; went to bed betimes, and passed the night in deep, unbroken sleep, visited, however, by varied and lively dreams.

The weather next day was no more promising. A land breeze blew. Beneath a colourless, overcast sky the sea lay sluggish, and as it were shrunken, so far withdrawn as to leave bare several rows of long sand-banks. The horizon looked close and prosaic. When Aschenbach opened his window he thought he smelt the stagnant odour of the lagoons.

He felt suddenly out of sorts and already began to think of leaving. Once, years before, after weeks of bright spring weather, this wind had found him out; it had been so bad as to force him to flee from the city like a fugitive. And now it seemed beginning again— the same feverish distaste, the pressure on his temples, the heavy eyelids. It would be a nuisance to change again; but if the wind did not turn, this was no place for him. To be on the safe side, he did not entirely unpack. At nine o'clock he went down to the buffet, which lay between the hall and the dining-room and served as breakfast-room.

A solemn stillness reigned here, such as it is the ambition of all large hotels to achieve. The waiters moved on noiseless feet. A rattling of tea-things, a whispered word—and no other sounds. In a corner diagonally to the door, two tables off his own, Aschenbach saw the Polish girls with their governess. They sat there very straight, in their stiff blue linen frocks with little turn-over collars and cuffs, their ash-blond hair newly brushed flat, their eyelids red from sleep; and handed each other the marmalade. They had nearly finished their meal. The boy was not there.

Aschenbach smiled. "Aha, little Phæax," he thought. "It seems you are privileged to sleep yourself out." With sudden gaiety he quoted:

Oft veränderten Schmuck und warme Bäder und Ruhe.[4]

He took a leisurely breakfast. The porter came up with his braided cap in his hand, to deliver some letters that had been sent on. Aschenbach lighted a cigarette and opened a few letters and thus was still seated to witness the arrival of the sluggard.

He entered through the glass doors and passed diagonally across the room to his sisters at their table. He walked with extraordinary grace—the carriage of the body, the action of the knee, the way he set down his foot in its white shoe—it was all so light, it was at once dainty and proud, it wore an added charm in the childish shyness which made him twice turn his head as he crossed the room, made him give a quick glance and then drop his eyes. He took his seat, with a smile and a murmured word in his soft and blurry tongue; and Aschenbach, sitting so that he could see him in profile, was astonished anew, yes, startled, at the godlike beauty of the human being. The lad had on a light sailor suit of blue and white striped cotton, with a red silk breast-knot and a simple white standing collar round the neck—a not very elegant effect—yet above this collar the head was poised like a flower, in incomparable loveliness. It was the head of Eros, with the yellowish bloom of Parian marble, with fine serious brows, and dusky clustering ringlets standing out in soft plenteousness over temples and ears.

"Good, oh, very good indeed!" thought Aschenbach, assuming the patronizing air of the connoisseur to hide, as artists will, their ravishment over a masterpiece. "Yes," he went on to himself, "if it were not that sea and beach were waiting for me, I should sit here as long as you do." But he went out on that, passing through the hall, beneath the watchful eye of the functionaries, down the steps and directly across the board walk to the section of the beach reserved for the guests of the hotel. The bathing-master, a barefoot old man in linen trousers and sailor blouse, with a straw hat, showed him the cabin that had been rented for him, and Aschenbach had him set up table and chair on the sandy platform before it. Then he

[4] "Newly decorated rooms, warm baths, and repose."

dragged the reclining-chair through the pale yellow sand, closer to the sea, sat down, and composed himself.

He delighted, as always, in the scene on the beach, the sight of sophisticated society giving itself over to a simple life at the edge of the element. The shallow grey sea was already gay with children wading, with swimmers, with figures in bright colours lying on the sand-banks with arms behind their heads. Some were rowing in little keelless boats painted red and blue, and laughing when they capsized. A long row of *capanne* ran down the beach, with platforms, where people sat as on verandas, and there was social life, with bustle and with indolent repose; visits were paid, amid much chatter, punctilious morning toilettes hob-nobbed with comfortable and privileged dishabille. On the hard wet sand close to the sea figures in white bath-robes or loose wrappings in garish colours strolled up and down. A mammoth sandhill had been built up on Aschenbach's right, the work of children, who had stuck it full of tiny flags. Vendors of sea-shells, fruit, and cakes knelt beside their wares spread out on the sand. A row of cabins on the left stood obliquely to the others and to the sea, thus forming the boundary of the enclosure on this side; and on the little veranda in front of one of these a Russian family was encamped; bearded men with strong white teeth, ripe, indolent women, a Fräulein from the Baltic provinces, who sat at an easel painting the sea and tearing her hair in despair; two ugly but good-natured children and an old maidservant in a head-cloth, with the caressing, servile manner of the born dependent. There they sat together in grateful enjoyment of their blessings: constantly shouting at their romping children, who paid not the slightest heed; making jokes in broken Italian to the funny old man who sold them sweetmeats, kissing each other on the cheeks—no jot concerned that their domesticity was overlooked.

"I'll stop," thought Aschenbach. "Where could it be better than here?" With his hands clasped in his lap he let his eyes swim in the wideness of the sea, his gaze lose focus, blur, and grow vague in the misty immensity of space. His love of the ocean had profound sources: the hard-worked artist's longing for rest, his yearning to seek refuge from the thronging manifold shapes of his fancy in the bosom of the simple and vast; and another yearning, opposed to his art and perhaps for that very reason a lure, for the unorganized, the immeasurable, the eternal—in short, for nothingness. He whose preoccupation is with excellence longs fervently to find rest in perfection; and is not nothingness a form of perfection? As he sat there dreaming thus, deep, deep into the void, suddenly the margin line of the shore was cut by a human form. He gathered up his gaze and withdrew it from the illimitable, and lo, it was the lovely boy who crossed his vision coming from the left along the sand. He was barefoot, ready for wading, the slender legs uncovered above the knee, and moved slowly, yet with such a proud, light tread as to make it seem he had never worn shoes. He looked towards the diagonal row of cabins; and the sight of the Russian family, leading their lives there in joyous simplicity, distorted his features in a spasm of angry disgust. His brow darkened, his lips curled, one corner of the mouth was drawn down in a harsh line that marred the curve of the cheek, his frown was so heavy that the eyes seemed to sink in as they uttered beneath the black and vicious language of hate. He looked down, looked threateningly back once more; then giving it up with a violent and contemptuous shoulder-shrug, he left his enemies in the rear.

A feeling of delicacy, a qualm, almost like a sense of shame, made Aschenbach turn away as though he had not seen; he felt unwilling to take advantage of having been, by chance, privy to this passionate reaction. But he was in truth both moved and exhilarated—that is to say, he was delighted. This childish exhibition of fanaticism, directed against the good-naturedest simplicity in the world—it gave to the godlike and inexpressive the final human touch. The figure of the half-grown lad, a masterpiece from nature's own hand, had been significant enough when it gratified the eye alone; and now it evoked sympathy as well—the little episode had set it off, lent it a dignity in the onlooker's eyes that was beyond its years.

Aschenbach listened with still averted head to the boy's voice announcing his coming to his companions at the sand-heap. The voice was clear, though a little weak, but they answered, shouting his name—or his nickname—again and again. Aschenbach was not without curiosity to learn it, but could make out nothing more exact than two musical syllables, something like Adgio—or, oftener still, Adjiu, with a long-drawn-out *u* at the end. He liked the melodious sound, and found it fitting; said it over to himself a few times and turned back with satisfaction to his papers.

Holding his travelling-pad on his knees, he took his fountain-pen and began to answer various items of his correspondence. But presently he felt it too great a pity to turn his back, and the eyes of his mind, for the sake of mere commonplace correspondence, to this scene which was, after all, the most rewarding one he knew. He put aside his papers and swung round to the sea; in no long time, beguiled by the voices of the children at play, he had turned his head and sat resting it against the chair-back, while he gave himself up to contemplating the activities of the exquisite Adgio.

His eye found him out at once, the red breast-knot was unmistakable. With some nine or ten companions, boys and girls of his own age and younger, he was busy putting in place an old plank to serve as a bridge across the ditches between the sand-piles. He directed the work by shouting and motioning with his head, and they were all chattering in many tongues—French, Polish, and even some of the Balkan languages. But his was the name oftenest on their lips, he was plainly sought after, wooed, admired. One lad in particular, a Pole like himself, with a name that sounded something like Jaschiu, a sturdy lad with brilliantined black hair, in a belted linen suit, was his particular liegeman and friend. Operations at the sand-pile being ended for the time, they two walked away along the beach, with their arms round each other's waists, and once the lad Jaschiu gave Adgio a kiss.

Aschenbach felt like shaking a finger at him. "But you, Critobulus," he thought with a smile, "you I advise to take a year's leave. That long, at least, you will need for complete recovery." A vendor came by with strawberries, and Aschenbach made his second breakfast of the great luscious, dead-ripe fruit. It had grown very warm, although the sun had not availed to pierce the heavy layer of mist. His mind felt relaxed, his senses revelled in this vast and soothing communion with the silence of the sea. The grave and serious man found sufficient occupation in speculating what name it could be that sounded like Adgio. And with the help of a few Polish memories he at length fixed on Tadzio, a shortened form of Thaddeus, which sounded, when called, like Tadziu or Adziu.

Tadzio was bathing. Aschenbach had lost sight of him for a moment, then descried him far out in the water, which was shallow for a very long way—saw his head, and his arm striking out like an oar. But his watchful family were already on the alert; the mother and governess called from the veranda in front of their bathing-cabin, until the lad's name, with its softened consonants and long-drawn u-sound, seemed to possess the beach like a rallying-cry; the cadence had something sweet and wild: "Tadziu! Tadziu!" He turned and ran back against the water, churning the waves to a foam, his head flung high. The sight of this living figure, virginally pure and austere, with dripping locks, beautiful as a tender young god, emerging from the depths of sea and sky, outrunning the element—it conjured up mythologies, it was like a primeval legend, handed down from the beginning of time, of the birth of form, of the origin of the gods. With closed lids Aschenbach listened to this poesy hymning itself silently within him, and anon he thought it was good to be here and that he would stop awhile.

Afterwards Tadzio lay on the sand and rested from his bathe, wrapped in his white sheet, which he wore drawn underneath the right shoulder, so that his head was cradled on his bare right arm. And even when Aschenbach read, without looking up, he was conscious that the lad was there; that it would cost him but the slightest turn of the head to have the rewarding vision once more in his purview. Indeed, it was almost as though he sat there to guard the youth's repose; occupied, of course, with his own affairs, yet alive to the presence of that noble human creature close at hand. And his heart was stirred, it felt a father's kindness: such an emotion as the possessor of beauty can inspire in one who has offered himself up in spirit to create beauty.

At midday he left the beach, returned to the hotel, and was carried up in the lift to his room. There he lingered a little time before the glass and looked at his own grey hair, his keen and weary face. And he thought of his fame, and how people gazed respectfully at him in the streets, on account of his unerring gift of words and their power to charm. He called up all the worldly successes his genius had reaped, all he could remember, even his patent of nobility. Then went to luncheon down in the dining-room, sat at his little table and ate. Afterwards he mounted again in the lift, and a group of young folk, Tadzio among them, pressed with him into the little compartment. It was the first time Aschenbach had seen him close at hand, not merely in perspective, and could see and take account of the details of his humanity. Someone spoke to the lad, and he, answering, with an indescribably lovely smile, stepped out again, as they had come to the first floor, backwards, with his eyes cast down. "Beauty makes people self-conscious," Aschenbach thought, and considered within himself imperatively why this should be. He had noted, further, that Tadzio's teeth were imperfect, rather jagged and bluish, without a healthy glaze, and of that peculiar brittle transparency which the teeth of chlorotic people often show. "He is delicate, he is sickly," Aschenbach thought. "He will most likely not live to grow old." He did not try to account for the pleasure the idea gave him.

In the afternoon he spent two hours in his room, then took the *vaporetto* to Venice, across the foul-smelling lagoon. He got out at San Marco, had his tea in the Piazza, and then, as his custom was, took a walk through the streets. But this walk of his brought about nothing less than a revolution in his mood and an entire change in all his plans.

There was a hateful sultriness in the narrow streets. The air was so heavy that all the manifold smells wafted out of houses, shops, and cook-shops—smells of oil, perfumery, and so forth—hung low, like exhalations, not dissipating. Cigarette smoke seemed to stand in the air, it drifted so slowly away. Today the crowd in these narrow lanes oppressed the stroller instead of diverting him. The longer he walked, the more was he in tortures under that state, which is the product of the sea air and the sirocco and which excites and enervates at once. He perspired painfully. His eyes rebelled, his chest was heavy, he felt feverish, the blood throbbed in his temples. He fled from the huddled, narrow streets of the commercial city, crossed many bridges, and came into the poor quarter of Venice. Beggars waylaid him, the canals sickened him with their evil exhalations. He reached a quiet square, one of those that exist at the city's heart, forsaken of God and man; there he rested awhile on the margin of a fountain, wiped his brow, and admitted to himself that he must be gone.

For the second time, and now quite definitely, the city proved that in certain weathers it could be directly inimical to his health. Nothing but sheer unreasoning obstinacy would linger on, hoping for an unprophesiable change in the wind. A quick decision was in place. He could not go home at this stage, neither summer nor winter quarters would be ready. But Venice had not a monopoly of sea and shore: there were other spots where these were to be had without the evil concomitants of lagoon and fever-breeding vapours. He remembered a little bathing-place not far from Trieste of which he had had a good report. Why not go thither? At once, of course, in order that this second change might be worth the making. He resolved, he rose to his feet and sought the nearest gondola-landing, where he took a boat and was conveyed to San Marco through the gloomy windings of many canals, beneath balconies of delicate marble traceries flanked by carven lions; round slippery corners of wall, past melancholy façades with ancient business shields reflected in the rocking water. It was not too easy to arrive at his destination, for his gondolier, being in league with various lace-makers and glass-blowers, did his best to persuade his fare to pause, look, and be tempted to buy. Thus the charm of this bizarre passage through the heart of Venice, even while it played upon his spirit, yet was sensibly cooled by the predatory commercial spirit of the fallen queen of the seas.

Once back in his hotel, he announced at the office, even before dinner, that circumstances unforeseen obliged him to leave early next morning. The management expressed its regret, it changed his money and receipted his bill. He dined, and spent the lukewarm evening in a rocking-chair on the rear terrace, reading the newspapers. Before he went to bed, he made his luggage ready against the morning.

His sleep was not of the best, for the prospect of another journey made him restless. When he opened his window next morning, the sky was still overcast, but the air seemed fresher—and there and then his rue began. Had he not given notice too soon? Had he not let himself be swayed by a slight and momentary indisposition? If he had only been patient, not lost heart so quickly, tried to adapt himself to the climate, or even waited for a change in the weather before deciding! Then, instead of the hurry and flurry of departure, he would have before him now a morning like yesterday's on the beach. Too late! He must go on wanting what he had wanted yesterday. He dressed and at eight o'clock went down to breakfast.

When he entered the breakfast-room it was empty. Guests came in while he sat waiting for his order to be filled. As he sipped his tea he saw the Polish girls enter with their governess, chaste and morning-fresh, with sleep-reddened eyelids. They crossed the room and sat down at their table in the window. Behind them came the porter, cap in hand, to announce that it was time for him to go. The car was waiting to convey him and other travellers to the Hôtel Excelsior, whence they would go by motor-boat through the company's private canal to the station. Time pressed. But Aschenbach found it did nothing of the sort. There still lacked more than an hour of train-time. He felt irritated at the hotel habit of getting the guests out of the house earlier than necessary; and requested the porter to let him breakfast in peace. The man hesitated and withdrew, only to come back again five minutes later. The car could wait no longer. Good, then it might go, and take his trunk with it, Aschenbach answered with some heat. He would use the public conveyance, in his

own time; he begged them to leave the choice of it to him. The
functionary bowed. Aschenbach, pleased to be rid of him, made a
leisurely meal, and even had a newspaper of the waiter. When at
length he rose, the time was grown very short. And it so happened
that at that moment Tadzio came through the glass doors into the
room.

To reach his own table he crossed the traveller's path, and mod-
estly cast down his eyes before the grey-haired man of the lofty
brows—only to lift them again in that sweet way he had and direct
his full soft gaze upon Aschenbach's face. Then he was past. "For
the last time, Tadzio," thought the elder man. "It was all too brief!"
Quite unusually for him, he shaped a farewell with his lips, he actually uttered it, and added: "May God bless you!" Then he went
out, distributed tips, exchanged farewells with the mild little manager in the frock-coat, and, followed by the porter with his hand-
luggage, left the hotel. On foot as he had come, he passed through
the white-blossoming avenue, diagonally across the island to the boat-
landing. He went on board at once—but the tale of his journey
across the lagoon was a tale of woe, a passage through the very valley
of regrets.

It was the well-known route: through the lagoon, past San Marco, up the Grand Canal. Aschenbach sat on the circular bench in
the bows, with his elbow on the railing, one hand shading his eyes.
They passed the Public Gardens, once more the princely charm of
the Piazzetta rose up before him and then dropped behind, next
came the great row of palaces, the canal curved, and the splendid
marble arches of the Rialto came in sight. The traveller gazed—and
his bosom was torn. The atmosphere of the city, the faintly rotten
scent of swamp and sea, which had driven him to leave—in what
deep, tender, almost painful draughts he breathed it in! How was it
he had not known, had not thought, how much his heart was set
upon it all! What this morning had been slight regret, some little
doubt of his own wisdom, turned now to grief, to actual wretchedness, a mental agony so sharp that it repeatedly brought tears to his
eyes, while he questioned himself how he could have foreseen it.
The hardest part, the part that more than once it seemed he could
not bear, was the thought that he should never more see Venice
again. Since now for the second time the place had made him ill,
since for the second time he had had to flee for his life, he must
henceforth regard it as a forbidden spot, to be forever shunned;
senseless to try it again, after he had proved himself unfit. Yes, if he

fled it now, he felt that wounded pride must prevent his return to this spot where twice he had made actual bodily surrender. And this conflict between inclination and capacity all at once assumed, in this middle-aged man's mind, immense weight and importance; the physical defeat seemed a shameful thing, to be avoided at whatever cost; and he stood amazed at the ease with which on the day before he had yielded to it.

Meanwhile the steamer neared the station landing; his anguish of irresolution amounted almost to panic. To leave seemed to the sufferer impossible, to remain not less so. Torn thus between two alternatives, he entered the station. It was very late, he had not a moment to lose. Time pressed, it scourged him onward. He hastened to buy his ticket and looked round in the crowd to find the hotel porter. The man appeared and said that the trunk had already gone off. "Gone already?" "Yes, it has gone to Como." "To Como?" A hasty exchange of words—angry questions from Aschenbach, and puzzled replies from the porter—at length made it clear that the trunk had been put with the wrong luggage even before leaving the hotel, and in company with other trunks was now well on its way in precisely the wrong direction.

Aschenbach found it hard to wear the right expression as he heard this news. A reckless joy, a deep incredible mirthfulness shook him almost as with a spasm. The porter dashed off after the lost trunk, returning very soon, of course, to announce that his efforts were unavailing. Aschenbach said he would not travel without his luggage; that he would go back and wait at the Hôtel des Bains until it turned up. Was the company's motor-boat still outside? The man said yes, it was at the door. With his native eloquence he prevailed upon the ticket-agent to take back the ticket already purchased; he swore that he would wire, that no pains should be spared, that the trunk would be restored in the twinkling of an eye. And the unbelievable thing came to pass: the traveller, twenty minutes after he had reached the station, found himself once more on the Grand Canal on his way back to the Lido.

What a strange adventure indeed, this right-about face of destiny—incredible, humiliating, whimsical as any dream! To be passing again, within the hour, these scenes from which in profoundest grief he had but now taken leave forever! The little swift-moving vessel, a furrow of foam at its prow, tacking with droll agility between steamboats and gondolas, went like a shot to its goal; and he, its sole passenger, sat hiding the panic and thrills of a truant schoolboy beneath

314 / THOMAS MANN

a mask of forced resignation. His breast still heaved from time to time with a burst of laughter over the contretemps. Things could not, he told himself, have fallen out more luckily. There would be the necessary explanations, a few astonished faces—then all would be well once more, a mischance prevented, a grievous error set right; and all he had thought to have left forever was his own once more, his for as long as he liked. . . . And did the boat's swift motion deceive him, or was the wind now coming from the sea?

The waves struck against the tiled sides of the narrow canal. At Hôtel Excelsior the automobile omnibus awaited the returned traveller and bore him along by the crisping waves back to the Hôtel des Bains. The little mustachioed manager in the frock-coat came down the steps to greet him.

In dulcet tones he deplored the mistake, said how painful it was to the management and himself; applauded Aschenbach's resolve to stop on until the errant trunk came back; his former room, alas, was already taken, but another as good awaited his approval. "*Pas de chance, monsieur*," said the Swiss lift-porter, with a smile, as he conveyed him upstairs. And the fugitive was soon quartered in another room which in situation and furnishings almost precisely resembled the first.

He laid out the contents of his hand-bag in their wonted places; then, tired out, dazed by the whirl of the extraordinary forenoon, subsided into the arm-chair by the open window. The sea wore a pale-green cast, the air felt thinner and purer, the beach with its cabins and boats had more colour, notwithstanding the sky was still grey. Aschenbach, his hands folded in his lap, looked out. He felt rejoiced to be back, yet displeased with his vacillating moods, his ignorance of his own real desires. Thus for nearly an hour he sat, dreaming, resting, barely thinking. At midday he saw Tadzio, in his striped sailor suit with red breast-knot, coming up from the sea, across the barrier and along the board walk to the hotel. Aschenbach recognized him, even at this height, knew it was he before he actually saw him, had it in mind to say to himself: "Well, Tadzio, so here you are again too!" But the casual greeting died away before it reached his lips, slain by the truth in his heart. He felt the rapture of his blood, the poignant pleasure, and realized that it was for Tadzio's sake the leavetaking had been so hard.

He sat quite still, unseen at his high post, and looked within himself. His features were lively, he lifted his brows; a smile, alert, inquiring, vivid, widened the mouth. Then he raised his head, and with both hands, hanging limp over the chair-arms, he described a slow motion, palms outward, a lifting and turning movement, as though to indicate a wide embrace. It was a gesture of welcome, a calm and deliberate acceptance of what might come.

Now daily the naked god with cheeks aflame drove his four fire-breathing steeds through heaven's spaces; and with him streamed the strong east wind that fluttered his yellow locks. A sheen, like white satin, lay over all the idly rolling sea's expanse. The sand was burning hot. Awnings of rust-coloured canvas were spanned before the bathing-huts, under the ether's quivering silver-blue; one spent the morning hours within the small, sharp square of shadow they purveyed. But evening too was rarely lovely: balsamic with the breath of flowers and shrubs from the near-by park, while overhead the constellations circled in their spheres, and the murmuring of the night-girted sea swelled softly up and whispered to the soul. Such nights as these contained the joyful promise of a sunlit morrow, brim-full of sweetly ordered idleness, studded thick with countless precious possibilities.

The guest detained here by so happy a mischance was far from finding the return of his luggage a ground for setting out anew. For two days he had suffered slight inconvenience and had to dine in the large salon in his travelling-clothes. Then the lost trunk was set down in his room, and he hastened to unpack, filling presses and drawers with his possessions. He meant to stay on—and on; he rejoiced in the prospect of wearing a silk suit for the hot morning hours on the beach and appearing in acceptable evening dress at dinner.

He was quick to fall in with the pleasing monotony of this manner of life, readily enchanted by its mild soft brilliance and ease. And what a spot it is, indeed!—uniting the charms of a luxurious bathing-resort by a southern sea with the immediate nearness of a unique and marvellous city. Aschenbach was not pleasure-loving. Always, wherever and whenever it was the order of the day to be merry, to refrain from labour and make glad the heart, he would soon be conscious of the imperative summons—and especially was this so in his youth—back to the high fatigues, the sacred and fasting service that consumed his days. This spot and this alone had power to beguile him, to relax his resolution, to make him glad. At times—of a forenoon perhaps, as he lay in the shadow of his awning, gazing out dreamily over the blue of the southern sea, or in the mildness of the night, beneath the wide starry sky, ensconced among the cushions of the gondola that bore him Lido-wards after an evening on the Piazza, while the gay lights faded and the melting music of the serenades died away on his ear—he would think of his mountain home, the theatre of his summer labours. There clouds hung low and trailed through the garden, violent storms extinguished the lights of the house at night, and the ravens he fed swung in the tops of the fir trees. And he would feel transported to Elysium, to the ends of the earth, to a spot more carefree for the sons of men, where no snow is, and no winter, no storms or downpours of rain; where Oceanus sends a mild and cooling breath, and days flow on in blissful idleness, without effort or struggle, entirely dedicated to the sun and the feasts of the sun.

Aschenbach saw the boy Tadzio almost constantly. The narrow confines of their world of hotel and beach, the daily round followed by all alike, brought him in close, almost uninterrupted touch with the beautiful lad. He encountered him everywhere—in the salons of the hotel, on the cooling rides to the city and back, among the splendours of the Piazza, and besides all this in many another going and coming as chance vouchsafed. But it was the regular morning hours on the beach which gave him his happiest opportunity to study and admire the lovely apparition. Yes, this immediate happiness, this daily recurring boon at the hand of circumstance, this it was that filled him with content, with joy in life, enriched his stay, and lingered out the row of sunny days that fell into place so pleasantly one behind the other.

He rose early—as early as though he had a panting press of work—and was among the first on the beach, when the sun lay dazzling white in its morning slumber. He gave the watchman a friendly good-morning and chatted with the barefoot, white-haired old man who prepared his place, spread the awning, trundled out the chair and table onto the little platform. Then he settled down; he had three or four hours before the sun reached its height and the fearful climax of its power; three or four hours while the sea went deeper and deeper blue; three or four hours in which to watch Tadzio.

He would see him come up, on the left, along the margin of the sea; or from behind, between the cabins; or, with a start of joyful surprise, would discover that he himself was late, and Tadzio already down, in the blue and white bathing-suit that was now his only wear on the beach; there and engrossed in his usual activities in the sand, beneath the sun. It was a sweetly idle, trifling, fitful life, of play and rest, of strolling, wading, digging, fishing, swimming, lying on the sand. Often the women sitting on the platform would call out to him in their high voices: "Tadziu! Tadziu!" and he would come running and waving his arms, eager to tell them what he had done, show them what he had found, what caught—shells, sea-horses, jelly-fish, and sidewards-running crabs. Aschenbach understood not a word he said; it might be the sheerest commonplace, in his ear it became mingled harmonies. Thus the lad's foreign birth raised his speech to music; a wanton sun showered splendour on him and the noble distances of the sea formed the background which set off his figure.

Soon the observer knew every line and pose of this form that limned itself so freely against sea and sky; its every loveliness, though conned by heart, yet thrilled him each day afresh; his admiration knew no bounds, the delight of his eyes was unending. Once the lad was summoned to speak to a guest who was waiting for his mother at their cabin. He ran up, ran dripping wet out of the sea, tossing his curls, and put out his hand, standing with his weight on one leg, resting the other foot on the toes; as he stood there in a posture of suspense the turn of his body was enchanting, while his features wore a look half shamefaced, half conscious of the duty breeding laid upon him to please. Or he would lie at full length, with his bath-robe around him, one slender young arm resting on the sand, his chin in the hollow of his hand; the lad they called Jaschiu squatting beside him, paying him court. There could be nothing lovelier on earth than the smile and look with which the playmate thus singled out rewarded his humble friend and vassal. Again, he might be at the water's edge, alone, removed from his family, quite close to Aschenbach; standing erect, his hands clasped at the back of his neck, rocking slowly on the balls of his feet, day-dreaming away into blue space, while little waves ran up and bathed his toes. The ringlets of honey-coloured hair clung to his temples and neck, the fine down along the upper vertebrae was yellow in the sunlight; the thin envelope of flesh covering the torso betrayed the delicate outlines of the ribs and the symmetry of the breast-structure. His armpits were still as smooth as a statue's, smooth the glistening hollows behind the knees, where the blue network of veins suggested that the body was formed of some stuff more transparent than mere flesh. What discipline, what precision of thought were expressed by the tense youthful perfection of this form! And yet the pure, strong will which had laboured in darkness and succeeded in bringing this godlike work of art to the light of day—was it not known and familiar to him, the artist? Was not the same force at work in himself when he strove in cold fury to liberate from the marble mass of language the slender forms of his art which he saw with the eye of his mind and would body forth to men as the mirror and image of spiritual beauty?

Mirror and image! His eyes took in the proud bearing of that figure there at the blue water's edge; with an outburst of rapture he told himself that what he saw was beauty's very essence; form as divine thought, the single and pure perfection which resides in the mind, of which an image and likeness, rare and holy, was here raised up for adoration. This was very frenzy—and without a scruple, nay, eagerly, the aging artist bade it come. His mind was in travail, his whole mental background in a state of flux. Memory flung up in him the primitive thoughts which are youth's inheritance, but which with him had remained latent, never leaping up into a blaze. Has it not been written that the sun beguiles our attention from things of the intellect to fix it on things of the sense? The sun, they say, dazzles; so bewitching reason and memory that the soul for very pleasure forgets its actual state, to cling with doting on the loveliest of all the objects she shines on. Yes, and then it is only through the medium of some corporeal being that it can raise itself again to contemplation of higher things. Amor, in sooth, is like the mathematician who in order to give children a knowledge of pure form must do so in the language of pictures; so, too, the god, in order to make visible the spirit, avails himself of the forms and colours of human youth, gilding it with all imaginable beauty that it may serve memory as a tool, the very sight of which then sets us afire with pain and longing.

Such were the devotee's thoughts, such the power of his emotions. And the sea, so bright with glancing sunbeams, wove in his mind a spell and summoned up a lovely picture: there was the ancient planetree outside the walls of Athens, a hallowed, shady spot, fragrant with willow-blossom and adorned with images and votive offerings in honour of the nymphs and Achelous. Clear ran the smooth-pebbled stream at the foot of the spreading tree. Crickets were fiddling. But on the gentle grassy slope, where one could lie yet hold the head erect, and shelter from the scorching heat, two men reclined, an elder with a younger, ugliness paired with beauty and wisdom with grace. Here Socrates held forth to youthful Phædrus upon the nature of virtue and desire, wooing him with insinuating wit and charming turns of phrase. He told him of the shuddering and unwonted heat that comes upon him whose heart is open, when his eye beholds an image of eternal beauty; spoke of the impious and corrupt, who cannot conceive beauty though they see its image, and are incapable of awe; and of the fear and reverence felt by the noble soul when he beholds a godlike face or a form which is a good image of beauty: how as he gazes he worships the beautiful one and scarcely dares to look upon him, but would offer sacrifice as to an idol or a god, did he not fear to be thought stark mad. "For beauty, my Phædrus, beauty alone, is lovely and visible at once. For, mark you, it is the sole aspect of the spiritual which we can perceive through our senses, or bear so to perceive. Else what should become of us, if the divine, if reason and virtue and truth, were to speak to us through the senses? Should we not perish and be consumed by love, as Semele aforetime was by Zeus? So beauty, then, is the beauty-lover's way to the spirit—but only the way, only the means, my little Phædrus." . . . And then, sly arch-lover that he was, he said the subtlest thing of all: that the lover was nearer the divine than the beloved; for the god was in the one but not in the other —perhaps the tenderest, most mocking thought that ever was thought, and source of all the guile and secret bliss the lover knows.

Thought that can merge wholly into feeling, feeling that can merge wholly into thought—these are the artist's highest joy. And our solitary felt in himself at this moment power to command and wield a thought that thrilled with emotion, an emotion as precise and concentrated as thought: namely, that nature herself shivers with ecstasy when the mind bows down in homage before beauty. He felt a sudden desire to write. Eros, indeed, we are told, loves idleness, and for idle hours alone was he created. But in this crisis the violence of our sufferer's seizure was directed almost wholly towards production, its occasion almost a matter of indifference. News had reached him on his travels that a certain problem had been raised, the intellectual world challenged for its opinion on a great and burning question of art and taste. By nature and experience the theme was his own; and he could not resist the temptation to set it off in the glistening foil of his words. He would write, and moreover he would write in Tadzio's presence. This lad should be in a sense his model, his style should follow the lines of this figure that seemed to him divine; he would snatch up this beauty into the realms of the mind, as once the eagle bore the Trojan shepherd aloft. Never had the pride of the word been so sweet to him, never had he known so well that Eros is in the word, as in those perilous and precious hours when he sat at his rude table, within the shade of his awning, his idol full in his view and the music of his voice in his ears, and fashioned his little essay after the model Tadzio's beauty set: that page and a half of choicest prose, so chaste, so lofty, so poignant with feeling, which would shortly be the wonder and admiration of the multitude. Verily it is well for the world that it sees only the beauty of the completed work and not its origins nor the conditions whence it sprang; since knowledge of the artist's inspiration might often but confuse and alarm and so prevent the full effect of its excellence. Strange hours, indeed, these were, and strangely unnerving the labour that filled them! Strangely fruitful intercourse this, between one body and another mind! When Aschenbach put aside his work and left the beach he felt exhausted, he felt broken—conscience reproached him, as it were after a debauch.

Next morning on leaving the hotel he stood at the top of the stairs leading down from the terrace and saw Tadzio in front of him on his way to the beach. The lad had just reached the gate in the railings, and he was alone. Aschenbach felt, quite simply, a wish to overtake him, to address him and have the pleasure of his reply and answering look; to put upon a blithe and friendly footing his relation with this being who all unconsciously had so greatly heightened and quickened his emotions. The lovely youth moved at a loitering pace—he might easily be overtaken; and Aschenbach hastened his own step. He reached him on the board walk that ran behind the bathing-cabins, and all but put out his hand to lay it on shoulder or head, while his lips parted to utter a friendly salutation in French. But—perhaps from the swift pace of his last few steps—he found his heart throbbing unpleasantly fast, while his breath came in such quick pants that he could only have gasped had he tried to speak. He hesitated, sought after self-control, was suddenly panic-stricken lest the boy notice him hanging there behind him and look round. Then he gave up, abandoned his plan, and passed him with bent head and hurried step.

"Too late! Too late!" he thought as he went by. But was it too late? This step he had delayed to take might so easily have put everything in a lighter key, have led to a sane recovery from his folly. But the truth may have been that the aging man did not want to be cured, that his illusion was far too dear to him. Who shall unriddle the puzzle of the artist nature? Who understands that mingling of discipline and licence in which it stands so deeply rooted? For not to be able to want sobriety is licentious folly. Aschenbach was no longer disposed to self-analysis. He had no taste for it; his self-esteem, the attitude of mind proper to his years, his maturity and single-mindedness, disinclined him to look within himself and decide whether it was constraint or puerile sensuality that had prevented him from carrying out his project. He felt confused, he was afraid someone, if only the watchman, might have been observing his behaviour and final surrender—very much he feared being ridiculous. And all the time he was laughing at himself for his serio-comic seizure. "Quite crestfallen," he thought. "I was like the gamecock that lets his wings droop in the battle. That must be the Love-God himself, that makes us hang our heads at sight of beauty and weighs our proud spirits low as the ground." Thus he played with the idea —he embroidered upon it, and was too arrogant to admit fear of an emotion.

The term he had set for his holiday passed by unheeded; he had no thought of going home. Ample funds had been sent him. His sole concern was that the Polish family might leave, and a chance question put to the hotel barber elicited the information that they had come only very shortly before himself. The sun browned his face and hands, the invigorating salty air heightened his emotional energies. Heretofore he had been wont to give out at once, in some new effort, the powers accumulated by sleep or food or outdoor air; but now the strength that flowed in upon him with each day of sun and sea and idleness he let go up in one extravagant gush of emotional intoxication.

His sleep was fitful; the priceless, equable days were divided one from the next by brief nights filled with happy unrest. He went, indeed, early to bed, for at nine o'clock, with the departure of Tadzio from the scene, the day was over for him. But in the faint greyness of the morning a tender pang would go through him as his heart was minded of its adventure; he could no longer bear his pillow and, rising, would wrap himself against the early chill and sit down by the window to await the sunrise. Awe of the miracle filled his soul new-risen from its sleep. Heaven, earth, and its waters yet lay enfolded in the ghostly, glassy pallor of dawn; one paling star still swam in the shadowy vast. But there came a breath, a winged word from far and inaccessible abodes, that Eos was rising from the side of her spouse; and there was that first sweet reddening of the farthest strip of sea and sky that manifests creation to man's sense. She neared, the goddess, ravisher of youth, who stole away Cleitos and Cephalus and, defying all the envious Olympians, tasted beautiful Orion's love. At the world's edge began a strewing of roses, a shining and a blooming ineffably pure; baby cloudlets hung illumined, like attendant amoretti, in the blue and blushful haze; purple effulgence fell upon the sea, that seemed to heave it forward on its welling waves; from horizon to zenith went great quivering thrusts like golden lances, the gleam became a glare; without a sound, with godlike violence, glow and glare and rolling flames streamed upwards, and with flying hoof-beats the steeds of the sun-god mounted the sky. The lonely watcher sat, the splendour of the god shone on him, he closed his eyes and let the glory kiss his lids. Forgotten feelings, precious pangs of his youth, quenched long since by the stern service that had been his life and now returned so strangely metamorphosed—he recognized them with a puzzled, wondering smile. He mused, he dreamed, his lips slowly shaped a name; still smiling, his face turned seawards and his hands lying folded in his lap, he fell asleep once more as he sat.

But that day, which began so fierily and festally, was not like other days; it was transmuted and gilded with mythical significance. For whence could come the breath, so mild and meaningful, like a whisper from higher spheres, that played about temple and ear? Troops of small feathery white clouds ranged over the sky, like grazing herds of the gods. A stronger wind arose and Poseidon's horses ran up, arching their manes, among them too the steers of him with the purpled locks, who lowered their horns and bellowed as they came on; while like prancing goats the waves on the farther strand leaped among the craggy rocks. It was a world possessed, peopled by Pan, that closed round the spellbound man, and his doting heart conceived the most delicate fancies. When the sun was going down behind Venice, he would sometimes sit on a bench in the park and watch Tadzio, white-clad, with gay-coloured sash, at play there on the rolled gravel with his ball; and at such times it was not Tadzio whom he saw, but Hyacinthus, doomed to die because two gods were rivals for his love. Ah, yes, he tasted the envious pangs that Zephyr knew when his rival, bow and cithara, oracle and all forgot, played with the beauteous youth; he watched the discus, guided by torturing jealousy, strike the beloved head; paled as he received the broken body in his arms, and saw the flower spring up, watered by that sweet blood and signed forevermore with his lament.

There can be no relation more strange, more critical, than that between two beings who know each other only with their eyes, who meet daily, yes, even hourly, eye each other with a fixed regard, and yet by some whim or freak of convention feel constrained to act like strangers. Uneasiness rules between them, unslaked curiosity, a hysterical desire to give rein to their suppressed impulse to recognize and address each other; even, actually, a sort of strained but mutual regard. For one human being instinctively feels respect and love for another human being so long as he does not know him well enough to judge him; and that he does not, the craving he feels is evidence.

Some sort of relation and acquaintanceship was perforce set up between Aschenbach and the youthful Tadzio; it was with a thrill of joy the older man perceived that the lad was not entirely unresponsive to all the tender notice lavished on him. For instance, what should move the lovely youth, nowadays when he descended to the beach, always to avoid the board walk behind the bathing-huts and saunter along the sand, passing Aschenbach's tent in front, sometimes so unnecessarily close as almost to graze his table or chair? Could the power of an emotion so beyond his own so draw, so fascinate its innocent object? Daily Aschenbach would wait for Tadzio. Then sometimes, on his approach, he would pretend to be preoccupied and let the charmer pass unregarded by. But sometimes he looked up, and their glances met; when that happened both were profoundly serious. The elder's dignified and cultured mien let nothing appear of his inward state; but in Tadzio's eyes a question lay— he faltered in his step, gazed on the ground, then up again with that ineffably sweet look he had; and when he was past, something in his bearing seemed to say that only good breeding hindered him from turning round.

But once, one evening, it fell out differently. The Polish brother and sisters, with their governess, had missed the evening meal, and Aschenbach had noted the fact with concern. He was restive over their absence, and after dinner walked up and down in front of the hotel, in evening dress and a straw hat; when suddenly he saw the nunlike sisters with their companion appear in the light of the arc-lamps, and four paces behind them Tadzio. Evidently they came from the steamer-landing, having dined for some reason in Venice. It had been chilly on the lagoon, for Tadzio wore a dark-blue reefer-jacket with gilt buttons, and a cap to match. Sun and sea air could not burn his skin, it was the same creamy hue as at first—though he did look a little pale, either from the cold or in the bluish moonlight of the arc-lamps. The shapely brows were so delicately drawn, the

324 / THOMAS MANN

eyes so deeply dark—lovelier he was than words could say, and as often the thought visited Aschenbach, and brought its own pang, that language could but extol, not reproduce, the beauties of the sense.

The sight of that dear form was unexpected, it had appeared un-hoped-for, without giving him time to compose his features. Joy, surprise, and admiration might have painted themselves quite openly upon his face—and just at this second it happened that Tadzio smiled. Smiled at Aschenbach, unabashed and friendly, a speaking, winning, captivating smile, with slowly parting lips. With such a smile it might be that Narcissus bent over the mirroring pool, a smile profound, infatuated, lingering, as he put out his arms to the reflection of his own beauty; the lips just slightly pursed, perhaps half-realizing his own folly in trying to kiss the cold lips of his shad-ow—with a mingling of coquetry and curiosity and a faint unease, enthralling and enthralled.

Aschenbach received that smile and turned away with it as though entrusted with a fatal gift. So shaken was he that he had to flee from the lighted terrace and front gardens and seek out with hurried steps the darkness of the park at the rear. Reproaches strangely mixed of tenderness and remonstrance burst from him: "How dare you smile like that! No one is allowed to smile like that!" He flung himself on a bench, his composure gone to the winds, and breathed in the nocturnal fragrance of the garden. He leaned back, with hanging arms, quivering from head to foot, and quite unmanned he whispered the hackneyed phrase of love and longing—impossible in these circumstances, absurd, abject, ridicu-lous enough, yet sacred too, and not unworthy of honour even here: "I love you!"

In the fourth week of his stay on the Lido, Gustave von Aschen-bach made certain singular observations touching the world about him. He noticed, in the first place, that though the season was approaching its height, yet the number of guests declined and, in particular, that the German tongue had suffered a rout, being scarce-ly or never heard in the land. At table and on the beach he caught nothing but foreign words. One day at the barber's—where he was now a frequent visitor—he heard something rather startling. The bar-ber mentioned a German family who had just left the Lido after a brief stay, and rattled on in his obsequious way: "The signore is not leaving—he has no fear of the sickness, has he?" Aschenbach looked at him. "The sickness?" he repeated. Whereat the prattler fell silent, became very busy all at once, affected not to hear. When Aschenbach persisted he said he really knew nothing at all about it, and tried in a fresh burst of eloquence to drown the embarrassing subject.

That was one afternoon. After luncheon Aschenbach had himself ferried across to Venice, in a dead calm, under a burning sun; driven by his mania, he was following the Polish young folk, whom he had seen with their companion, taking the way to the landing-stage. He did not find his idol on the Piazza. But as he sat there at tea, at a little round table on the shady side, suddenly he noticed a peculiar odour, which, it seemed to him now, had been in the air for days without his being aware: a sweetish, medicinal smell, associated with wounds and disease and suspect cleanliness. He sniffed and pondered and at length recognized it; finished his tea and left the square at the end facing the cathedral. In the narrow space the stench grew stronger. At the street corners placards were stuck up, in which the city authorities warned the population against the danger of certain infections of the gastric system, prevalent during the heated season; advising them not to eat oysters or other shell-fish and not to use the canal waters. The ordinance showed every sign of minimizing an existing situation. Little groups of people stood about silently in the squares and on the bridges; the traveller moved among them, watched and listened and thought.

He spoke to a shopkeeper lounging at his door among dangling coral necklaces and trinkets of artificial amethyst, and asked him about the disagreeable odour. The man looked at him, heavy-eyed, and hastily pulled himself together. "Just a formal precaution, signore," he said, with a gesture. "A police regulation we have to put up with. The air is sultry—the sirocco is not wholesome, as the signore knows. Just a precautionary measure, you understand—probably unnecessary. . . ." Aschenbach thanked him and passed on. And on the boat that bore him back to the Lido he smelt the germicide again.

On reaching his hotel he sought the table in the lobby and buried himself in the newspapers. The foreign-language sheets had nothing. But in the German papers certain rumours were mentioned, statistics given, then officially denied, then the good faith of the denials called in question. The departure of the German and Austrian contingent was thus made plain. As for other nationals, they knew or suspected nothing—they were still undisturbed.

Aschenbach tossed the newspapers back on the table. "It ought to be kept quiet," he thought, aroused. "It should not be talked about." And he felt in his heart a curious elation at these events impending in the world about him. Passion is like crime: it does not thrive on the established order and the common round; it welcomes every blow dealt the bourgeois structure, every weakening of the social fabric, because therein it feels a sure hope of its own advantage. These things that were going on in the unclean alleys of Venice, under cover of an official hushing-up policy—they gave Aschenbach a dark satisfaction. The city's evil secret mingled with the one in the depths of his heart—and he would have staked all he possessed to keep it, since in his infatuation he cared for nothing but to keep Tadzio here, and owned to himself, not without horror, that he could not exist were the lad to pass from his sight.

He was no longer satisfied to owe his communion with his charmer to chance and the routine of hotel life; he had begun to follow and waylay him. On Sundays, for example, the Polish family never appeared on the beach. Aschenbach guessed they went to mass at San Marco and pursued them thither. He passed from the glare of the Piazza into the golden twilight of the holy place and found him he sought bowed in worship over a prie-dieu. He kept in the background, standing on the fissured mosaic pavement among the devout populace, that knelt and muttered and made the sign of the cross; and the crowded splendour of the oriental temple weighed voluptuously on his sense. A heavily ornate priest intoned and gesticulated before the altar, where little candle-flames flickered helplessly in the reek of incense-breathing smoke; and with that cloying sacrificial smell another seemed to mingle—the odour of the sickened city. But through all the glamour and glitter Aschenbach saw the exquisite creature there in front turn his head, seek out and meet his lover's eye.

The crowd streamed out through the portals into the brilliant square thick with fluttering doves, and the fond fool stood aside in the vestibule on the watch. He saw the Polish family leave the church. The children took ceremonial leave of their mother, and she turned towards the Piazzetta on her way home, while his charmer and the cloistered sisters, with their governess, passed beneath the clock tower into the Merceria. When they were a few paces on, he followed—he stole behind them on their walk through the city. When they paused, he did so too; when they turned round, he fled into inns and courtyards to let them pass. Once he lost them from view, hunted feverishly over bridges and in filthy *culs-de-sac*, only to confront them suddenly in a narrow passage whence there was no escape, and experience a moment of panic fear. Yet it would be untrue to say he suffered. Mind and heart were drunk with passion, his footsteps guided by the dæmonic power whose pastime it is to trample on human reason and dignity.

Tadzio and his sisters at length took a gondola. Aschenbach hid behind a portico or fountain while they embarked, and directly they pushed off did the same. In a furtive whisper he told the boatman he would tip him well to follow at a little distance the other gondola, just rounding a corner, and fairly sickened at the man's quick, sly grasp and ready acceptance of the go-between's rôle.

Leaning back among soft, black cushions, he swayed gently in the wake of the other black-snouted bark, to which the strength of his passion chained him. Sometimes it passed from his view, and then he was assailed by an anguish of unrest. But his guide appeared to have long practice in affairs like these; always, by dint of short cuts or deft manœuvres, he contrived to overtake the coveted sight. The air was heavy and foul, the sun burnt down through a slate-coloured haze. Water slapped gurgling against wood and stone. The gondolier's cry, half warning, half salute, was answered with singular accord from far within the silence of the labyrinth. They passed little gardens, high up the crumbling wall, hung with clustering white and purple flowers that sent down an odour of almonds. Moorish lattices showed shadowy in the gloom. The marble steps of a church descended into the canal, and on them a beggar squatted, displaying his misery to view, showing the whites of his eyes, holding out his hat for alms. Farther on a dealer in antiquities cringed before his lair, inviting the passer-by to enter and be duped. Yes, this was Venice, this the fair frailty that fawned and that betrayed, half fairy-tale, half snare; the city in whose stagnating air the art of painting once put forth so lusty a growth, and where musicians were moved to accords so weirdly lulling and lascivious. Our adventurer felt his senses wooed by this voluptuousness of sight and sound, tasted his secret knowledge that the city sickened and had its sickness for love of gain, and bent an ever more unbridled leer on the gondola that glided on before him.

It came at last to this—that his frenzy left him capacity for nothing else but to pursue his flame; to dream of him absent, to lavish, lover-like, endearing terms on his mere shadow. He was alone, he was a foreigner, he was sunk deep in this belated bliss of his—all of which enabled him to pass unblushing through experiences well-nigh unbelievable. One night, returning late from Venice, he paused by his beloved's chamber door in the second storey, leaned his head against the panel, and remained there long, in utter drunkenness, powerless to tear himself away, blind to the danger of being caught in so mad an attitude.

And yet there were not wholly lacking moments when he paused and reflected, when in consternation he asked himself what path was this on which he had set his foot. Like most other men of parts and attainments, he had an aristocratic interest in his forbears, and when he achieved a success he liked to think he had gratified them, compelled their admiration and regard. He thought of them now, involved as he was in this illicit adventure, seized of these exotic excesses of feeling; thought of their stern self-command and decent manliness, and gave a melancholy smile. What would they have said? What, indeed, would they have said to his entire life, that varied to the point of degeneracy from theirs? This life in the bonds of art, had not he himself, in the days of his youth and in the very spirit of those bourgeois forefathers, pronounced mocking judgment upon it? And yet, at bottom, it had been so like their own! It had been a service, and he a soldier, like some of them; and art was war —a grilling, exhausting struggle that nowadays wore one out before one could grow old. It had been a life of self-conquest, a life against odds, dour, steadfast, abstinent; he had made it symbolical of the kind of overstrained heroism the time admired, and he was entitled to call it manly, even courageous. He wondered if such a life might not be somehow specially pleasing in the eyes of the god who had him in his power. For Eros had received most countenance among the most valiant nations—yes, were we not told that in their cities prowess made him flourish exceedingly? And many heroes of olden time had willingly borne his yoke, not counting any humiliation such if it happened by the god's decree; vows, prostrations, self-abasements, these were no source of shame to the lover; rather they reaped him praise and honour.

Thus did the fond man's folly condition his thoughts; thus did he seek to hold his dignity upright in his own eyes. And all the while he kept doggedly on the traces of the disreputable secret the city kept hidden at its heart, just as he kept his own—and all that he learned fed his passion with vague, lawless hopes. He turned over newspapers at cafés, bent on finding a report on the progress of the disease; and in the German sheets, which had ceased to appear on the hotel table, he found a series of contradictory statements. The deaths, it was variously asserted, ran to twenty, to forty, to a hundred or more; yet in the next day's issue the existence of the pestilence was, if not roundly denied, reported as a matter of a few sporadic cases such as might be brought into a seaport town. After that the warnings would break out again, and the protests against the unscrupulous game the authorities were playing. No definite information was to be had.

And yet our solitary felt he had a sort of first claim on a share in the unwholesome secret; he took a fantastic satisfaction in putting leading questions to such persons as were interested to conceal it, and forcing them to explicit untruths by way of denial. One day he attacked the manager, that small, soft-stepping man in the French frock-coat, who was moving about among the guests at luncheon, supervising the service and making himself socially agreeable. He paused at Aschenbach's table to exchange a greeting, and the guest put a question, with a negligent, casual air: "Why in the world are they forever disinfecting the city of Venice?" "A police regulation," the adroit one replied; "a precautionary measure, intended to protect the health of the public during this unseasonably warm and sultry weather." "Very praiseworthy of the police," Aschenbach gravely responded. After a further exchange of meteorological commonplaces the manager passed on.

It happened that a band of street musicians came to perform in the hotel gardens that evening after dinner. They grouped themselves beneath an iron stanchion supporting an arc-light, two women and two men, and turned their faces, that shone white in the glare, up towards the guests who sat on the hotel terrace enjoying this popular entertainment along with their coffee and iced drinks. The hotel lift-boys, waiters, and office staff stood in the doorway and listened; the Russian family displayd the usual Russian absorption in their enjoyment—they had their chairs put down into the garden to be nearer the singers and sat there in a half-circle with gratitude painted on their features, the old serf in her turban erect behind their chairs.

These strolling players were adepts at mandolin, guitar, harmonica, even compassing a reedy violin. Vocal numbers alternated with instrumental, the younger woman, who had a high shrill voice, joining in a love-duet with the sweetly falsettoing tenor. The actual head of the company, however, and incontestably its most gifted member, was the other man, who played the guitar. He was a sort of baritone buffo; with no voice to speak of, but possessed of a pantomimic gift and remarkable burlesque *élan*. Often he stepped out of the group and advanced towards the terrace, guitar in hand, and his audience rewarded his sallies with bursts of laughter. The Russians in their parterre seats were beside themselves with delight over this display of southern vivacity; their shouts and screams of applause encouraged him to bolder and bolder flights.

Aschenbach sat near the balustrade, a glass of pomegranate-juice and soda-water sparkling ruby-red before him, with which he now and then moistened his lips. His nerves drank in thirstily the unlovely sounds, the vulgar and sentimental tunes, for passion paralyses good taste and makes its victims accept with rapture what a man in his senses would either laugh at or turn from with disgust. Idly he sat and watched the antics of the buffoon with his face set in a fixed and painful smile, while inwardly his whole being was rigid with the intensity of the regard he bent on Tadzio, leaning over the railing six paces off.

He lounged there, in the white belted suit he sometimes wore at dinner, in all his innate, inevitable grace, with his left arm on the balustrade, his legs crossed, the right hand on the supporting hip; and looked down on the strolling singers with an expression that was hardly a smile, but rather a distant curiosity and polite toleration. Now and then he straightened himself and with a charming movement of both arms drew down his white blouse through his leather belt, throwing out his chest. And sometimes—Aschenbach saw it with triumph, with horror, and a sense that his reason was tottering —the lad would cast a glance, that might be slow and cautious, or might be sudden and swift, as though to take him by surprise, to the place where his lover sat. Aschenbach did not meet the glance. An ignoble caution made him keep his eyes in leash. For in the rear of the terrace sat Tadzio's mother and governess; and matters had gone so far that he feared to make himself conspicuous. Several times, on the beach, in the hotel lobby, on the Piazza, he had seen, with a stealing numbness, that they called Tadzio away from his neighbourhood. And his pride revolted at the affront, even while conscience told him it was deserved.

The performer below presently began a solo, with guitar accompaniment, a street song in several stanzas, just then the rage all over Italy. He delivered it in a striking and dramatic recitative, and his company joined in the refrain. He was a man of slight build, with a thin, undernourished face; his shabby felt hat rested on the back of his neck, a great mop of red hair sticking out in front; and he stood there on the gravel in advance of his troupe, in an impudent, swaggering posture, twanging the strings of his instrument and flinging a witty and rollicking recitative up to the terrace, while the veins on his forehead swelled with the violence of his effort. He was scarcely a Venetian type, belonging rather to the race of the Neapolitan jesters, half bully, half comedian, brutal, blustering, an unpleasant customer, and entertaining to the last degree. The words of his song were trivial and silly, but on his lips, accompanied with gestures of head, hands, arms, and body, with leers and winks and the loose play of the tongue in the corner of his mouth, they took on meaning; an equivocal meaning, yet vaguely offensive. He wore a white sport shirt with a suit of ordinary clothes, and a strikingly large and naked-looking Adam's apple rose out of the open collar. From that pale, snub-nosed face it was hard to judge of his age; vice sat on it, it was furrowed with grimacing, and two deep wrinkles of defiance and self-will, almost of desperation, stood oddly between the red brows, above the grinning, mobile mouth. But what more than all drew upon him the profound scrutiny of our solitary watcher was that this suspicious figure seemed to carry with it its own suspicious odour. For whenever the refrain occurred and the singer, with waving arms and antic gestures, passed in his grotesque march immediately beneath Aschenbach's seat, a strong smell of carbolic was wafted up to the terrace.

After the song he began to take up money, beginning with the Russian family, who gave liberally, and then mounting the steps to the terrace. But here he became as cringing as he had before been forward. He glided between the tables, bowing and scraping, showing his strong white teeth in a servile smile, though the two deep furrows on the brow were still very marked. His audience looked at the strange creature as he went about collecting his livelihood, and their curiosity was not unmixed with disfavour. They tossed coins with their fingertips into his hat and took care not to touch it. Let the enjoyment be never so great, a sort of embarrassment always comes when the comedian oversteps the physical distance between himself and respectable people. This man felt it and sought to make his peace by fawning. He came along the railing to Aschenbach, and with him came the smell no one else seemed to notice.

"Listen!" said the solitary, in a low voice, almost mechanically; "they are disinfecting Venice—why?" The mountebank answered hoarsely: "Because of the police. Orders, signore. On account of the heat and the sirocco. The sirocco is oppressive. Not good for the health." He spoke as though surprised that anyone could ask, and with the flat of his hand he demonstrated how oppressive the sirocco was. "So there is no plague in Venice?" Aschenbach asked the question between his teeth, very low. The man's expressive face fell, he put on a look of comical innocence. "A plague? What sort of plague? Is the sirocco a plague? Or perhaps our police are a plague! You are making fun of us, signore! A plague! Why should there be? The police make regulations on account of the heat and the weather. . . ." He gestured. "Quite," said Aschenbach, once more, soft and low; and dropping an unduly large coin into the man's hat dismissed him with a sign. He bowed very low and left. But he had not reached the steps when two of the hotel servants flung themselves on him and began to whisper, their faces close to his. He shrugged, seemed to be giving assurances, to be swearing he had said nothing. It was not hard to guess the import of his words. They let him go at last and he went back into the garden, where he conferred briefly with his troupe and then stepped forward for a farewell song.

It was one Aschenbach had never to his knowledge heard before, a rowdy air, with words in impossible dialect. It had a laughing-refrain in which the other three artists joined at the top of their lungs. The refrain had neither words nor accompaniment, it was nothing but rhythmical, modulated, natural laughter, which the soloist in particular knew how to render with most deceptive realism. Now that he was farther off his audience, his self-assurance had come back, and this laughter of his rang with a mocking note. He would be overtaken, before he reached the end of the last line of each stanza; he would catch his breath, lay his hand over his mouth, his voice would quaver and his shoulders shake, he would lose power to contain himself longer. Just at the right moment each time, it came whooping, bawling, crashing out of him, with a verisimilitude that never failed to set his audience off in profuse and unpremeditated mirth that seemed to add gusto to his own. He bent his knees, he clapped his thigh, he held his sides, he looked ripe for bursting. He no longer laughed, but yelled, pointing his finger at the company there above as though there could be in all the world nothing so comic as they; until at last they laughed in hotel, terrace, and garden, down to the waiters, lift-boys, and servants—laughed as though possessed.

Aschenbach could no longer rest in his chair, he sat poised for flight. But the combined effect of the laughing, the hospital odour in his nostrils, and the nearness of the beloved was to hold him in a spell; he felt unable to stir. Under cover of the general commotion he looked across at Tadzio and saw that the lovely boy returned his gaze with a seriousness that seemed the copy of his own; the general hilarity, it seemed to say, had no power over him, he kept aloof. The grey-haired man was overpowered, disarmed by this docile, childlike deference; with difficulty he refrained from hiding his face in his hands. Tadzio's habit, too, of drawing himself up and taking a deep sighing breath struck him as being due to an oppression of the chest. "He is sickly, he will never live to grow up," he thought once again, with that dispassionate vision to which his madness of desire sometimes so strangely gave way. And compassion struggled with the reckless exultation of his heart.

The players, meanwhile, had finished and gone; their leader bowing and scraping, kissing his hands and adorning his leave-taking with antics that grew madder with the applause they evoked. After all the others were outside, he pretended to run backwards full tilt against a lamp-post and slunk to the gate apparently doubled over with pain. But there he threw off his buffoon's mask, stood erect, with an elastic straightening of his whole figure, ran out his tongue impudently at the guests on the terrace, and vanished in the night. The company dispersed. Tadzio had long since left the balustrade. But he, the lonely man, sat for long, to the waiters' annoyance, before the dregs of pomegranate-juice in his glass. Time passed, the night went on. Long ago, in his parental home, he had watched the sand filter through an hour-glass—he could still see, as though it stood before him, the fragile, pregnant little toy. Soundless and fine the rust-red streamlet ran through the narrow neck, and made, as it declined in the upper cavity, an exquisite little vortex.

The very next afternoon the solitary took another step in pursuit of his fixed policy of baiting the outer world. This time he had all possible success. He went, that is, into the English travel bureau in the Piazza, changed some money at the desk, and posing as the suspicious foreigner, put his fateful question. The clerk was a tweed-clad young Britisher, with his eyes set close together, his hair parted in the middle, and radiating that steady reliability which makes his like so strange a phenomenon in the *gamin*, agile-witted south. He began: "No ground for alarm, sir. A mere formality. Quite regular in view of the unhealthy climatic conditions." But then, looking up, he chanced to meet with his own blue eyes the stranger's weary, melancholy gaze, fixed on his face. The Englishman coloured. He continued in a lower voice, rather confused: "At least, that is the official explanation, which they see fit to stick to. I may tell you there's a bit more to it than that." And then, in his good, straightforward way, he told the truth.

For the past several years Asiatic cholera had shown a strong tendency to spread. Its source was the hot, moist swamps of the delta of the Ganges, where it bred in the mephitic air of that primeval island-jungle, among whose bamboo thickets the tiger crouches, where life of every sort flourishes in rankest abundance, and only man avoids the spot. Thence the pestilence had spread throughout Hindustan, raging with great violence; moved eastwards to China, westward to Afghanistan and Persia; following the great caravan routes, it brought terror to Astrakhan, terror to Moscow. Even while Europe trembled lest the spectre be seen striding westward across country, it was carried by sea from Syrian ports and appeared simultaneously at several points on the Mediterranean littoral; raised its head in Toulon and Malaga, Palermo and Naples, and soon got a firm hold in Calabria and Apulia. Northern Italy had been spared— so far. But in May the horrible vibrions were found on the same day in two bodies: the emaciated, blackened corpses of a bargee and a woman who kept a greengrocer's shop. Both cases were hushed up. But in a week there were ten more—twenty, thirty in different quarters of the town. An Austrian provincial, having come to Venice on a few days' pleasure trip, went home and died with all the symptoms of the plague. Thus was explained the fact that the German-language papers were the first to print the news of the Venetian outbreak. The Venetian authorities published in reply a statement to the effect that the state of the city's health had never been better; at the same time instituting the most necessary precautions. But by that time the food supplies—milk, meat, or vegetables—had probably been contaminated, for death unseen and unacknowledged was devouring and laying waste in the narrow streets, while a brooding unseasonable heat warmed the waters of the canals and encouraged the spread of the pestilence. Yes, the disease seemed to flourish and wax strong, to redouble its generative powers. Recoveries were rare. Eighty out of every hundred died, and horribly, for the onslaught was of the extremest violence, and not infrequently of the "dry" type, the most malignant form of the contagion. In this form the victim's body loses power to expel the water secreted by the blood-vessels, it shrivels up, he passes with hoarse cries from convulsion to convulsion, his blood grows thick like pitch, and he suffocates in a few hours. He is fortunate indeed, if, as sometimes happens, the disease, after a slight *malaise*, takes the form of a profound unconsciousness, from which the sufferer seldom or never rouses. By the beginning of June the quarantine buildings of the *ospedale civico* had quietly filled up, the two orphan asylums were entirely occupied, and there was a hideously brisk traffic between the *Nuovo Fundamento* and the island of San Michele, where the cemetery was. But the city was not swayed by high-minded motives or regard for international agreements. The authorities were more actuated by fear of being out of pocket, by regard for the new exhibition of paintings just opened in the Public Gardens, or by apprehension of the large losses the hotels and the shops that catered to foreigners would suffer in case of panic and blockade. And the fears of the people supported the persistent official policy of silence and denial. The city's first medical officer, an honest and competent man, had indignantly resigned his office and been privily replaced by a more compliant person. The fact was known; and this corruption in high places played its part, together with the suspense as to where the walking terror might strike next, to demoralize the baser elements in the city and encourage those antisocial forces which shun the light of day. There was intemperance, indecency, increase of crime. Evenings one saw many drunken people, which was unusual. Gangs of men in surly mood made the streets unsafe, theft and assault were said to be frequent, even murder; for in two cases persons supposedly victims of the plague were proved to have been poisoned by their own families. And professional vice was rampant, displaying excesses heretofore unknown and only at home much farther south and in the east.

Such was the substance of the Englishman's tale. "You would do well," he concluded, "to leave today instead of tomorrow. The blockade cannot be more than a few days off."

"Thank you," said Aschenbach, and left the office.

The Piazza lay in sweltering sunshine. Innocent foreigners sat before the cafés or stood in front of the cathedral, the centre of clouds of doves that, with fluttering wings, tried to shoulder each other away and pick the kernels of maize from the extended hand. Aschenbach strode up and down the spacious flags, feverishly excited, triumphant in possession of the truth at last, but with a sickening taste in his mouth and a fantastic horror at his heart. One decent, expiatory course lay open to him; he considered it. Tonight, after dinner, he might approach the lady of the pearls and address her in words which he precisely formulated in his mind: "Madame, will you permit an entire stranger to serve you with a word of advice and warning which self-interest prevents others from uttering? Go away. Leave here at once, without delay, with Tadzio and your daughters. Venice is in the grip of pestilence." Then might he lay his hand in farewell upon the head of that instrument of a mocking deity; and thereafter himself flee the accursed morass. But he knew that he was far indeed from any serious desire to take such a step. It would restore him, would give him back himself once more; but he who is beside himself revolts at the idea of self-possession. There crossed his mind the vision of a white building with inscriptions on it, glittering in the sinking sun—he recalled how his mind had dreamed away into their transparent mysticism; recalled the strange pilgrim apparition that had wakened in the aging man a lust for strange countries and fresh sights. And these memories, again, brought in their train the thought of returning home, returning to reason, self-mastery, an ordered existence, to the old life of effort. Alas! the bare thought made him wince with a revulsion that was like physical nausea. "It must be kept quiet," he whispered fiercely. "I will not speak!" The knowledge that he shared the city's secret, the city's guilt—it put him beside himself, intoxicated him as a small quantity of wine will a man suffering from brain-fag. His thoughts dwelt upon the image of the desolate and calamitous city, and he was giddy with fugitive, mad, unreasoning hopes and visions of monstrous sweetness. That tender sentiment he had a moment ago evoked, what was it compared with such images as these? His art, his moral sense, what were they in the balance beside the boons that chaos might confer? He kept silence, he stopped on.

That night he had a fearful dream—if dream be the right word for a mental and physical experience which did indeed befall him in deep sleep, as a thing quite apart and real to his senses, yet without his seeing himself as present in it. Rather its theatre seemed to be his own soul, and the events burst in from outside, violently over-coming the profound resistance of his spirit; passed him through and left him, left the whole cultural structure of a lifetime trampled on, ravaged, and destroyed.

The beginning was fear; fear and desire, with a shuddering curi-osity. Night reigned, and his senses were on the alert; he heard loud, confused noises from far away, clamour and hubbub. There was a rattling, a crashing, a low dull thunder; shrill halloos and a kind of howl with a long-drawn *u*-sound at the end. And with all these, dominating them all, flute-notes of the cruellest sweetness, deep and cooing, keeping shamelessly on until the listener felt his very entrails bewitched. He heard a voice, naming, though darkly, that which was to come: "The stranger god!" A glow lighted up the surrounding mist and by it he recognized a mountain scene like that about his country home. From the wooded heights, from among the tree-trunks and crumbling moss-covered rocks, a troop came tumbling and raging down, a whirling rout of men and animals, and over-flowed the hillside with flames and human forms, with clamour and the reeling dance. The females stumbled over the long, hairy pelts that dangled from their girdles; with heads flung back they uttered loud hoarse cries and shook their tambourines high in air; bran-dished naked daggers or torches vomiting trails of sparks. They shrieked, holding their breasts in both hands; coiling snakes with quivering tongues they clutched about their waists. Horned and hairy males, girt about the loins with hides, drooped heads and lifted arms and thighs in unison, as they beat on brazen vessels that gave out droning thunder, or thumped madly on drums. There were troops of beardless youths armed with garlanded staves; these ran after goats and thrust their staves against the creatures' flanks, then clung to the plunging horns and let themselves be borne off with triumphant shouts. And one and all the mad rout yelled that cry, composed of soft consonants with a long-drawn *u*-sound at the end, so sweet and wild it was together, and like nothing ever heard before! It would ring through the air like the bellow of a challenging stag, and be given back many-tongued; or they would use it to goad each other on to dance with wild excess of tossing limbs—they never let it die. But the deep, beguiling notes of the flute wove in and out and over all. Beguiling too it was to him who struggled in the grip of these sights and sounds, shamelessly awaiting the coming feast and the ut-termost surrender. He trembled, he shrank, his will was steadfast to preserve and uphold his own god against this stranger who was sworn enemy to dignity and self-control. But the mountain wall took up the noise and howling and gave it back manifold; it rose high, swelled to a madness that carried him away. His senses reeled in the steam of panting bodies, the acrid stench from the goats, the odour as of stagnant waters—and another, too familiar smell—of wounds, uncleanness, and disease. His heart throbbed to the drums, his brain reeled, a blind rage seized him, a whirling lust, he craved with all his soul to join the ring that formed about the obscene symbol of the godhead, which they were unveiling and elevating, monstrous and wooden, while from full throats they yelled their rallying-cry. Foam dripped from their lips, they drove each other on with lewd gesturings and beckoning hands. They laughed, they howled, they thrust their pointed staves into each other's flesh and licked the blood as it ran down. But now the dreamer was in them and of them, the stranger god was his own. Yes, it was he who was flinging himself upon the animals, who bit and tore and swallowed smoking gobbets of flesh—while on the trampled moss there now began the rites in honour of the god, an orgy of promiscuous embraces—and in his very soul he tasted the bestial degradation of his fall.

The unhappy man woke from this dream shattered, unhinged, powerless in the demon's grip. He no longer avoided men's eyes nor cared whether he exposed himself to suspicion. And anyhow, people were leaving; many of the bathing-cabins stood empty, there were many vacant places in the dining-room, scarcely any foreigners were seen in the streets. The truth seemed to have leaked out; despite all efforts to the contrary, panic was in the air. But the lady of the pearls stopped on with her family; whether because the rumours had not reached her or because she was too proud and fearless to heed them. Tadzio remained; and it seemed at times to Aschenbach, in his obsessed state, that death and fear together might clear the island of all other souls and leave him there alone with him he coveted. In the long mornings on the beach his heavy gaze would rest, a fixed and reckless stare, upon the lad; towards nightfall, lost to shame, he would follow him through the city's narrow streets where horrid death stalked too, and at such time it seemed to him as though the moral law were fallen in ruins and only the monstrous and perverse held out a hope.

Like any lover, he desired to please; suffered agonies at the thought of failure, and brightened his dress with smart ties and handkerchiefs and other youthful touches. He added jewellery and perfumes and spent hours each day over his toilette, appearing at dinner elaborately arrayed and tensely excited. The presence of the youthful beauty that had bewitched him filled him with disgust of his own aging body; the sight of his own sharp features and grey hair plunged him in hopeless mortification; he made desperate efforts to recover the appearance and freshness of his youth and began paying frequent visits to the hotel barber. Enveloped in the white sheet, beneath the hands of that garrulous personage, he would lean back in the chair and look at himself in the glass with misgiving.

"Grey," he said, with a grimace.

"Slightly," answered the man. "Entirely due to neglect, to a lack of regard for appearances. Very natural, of course, in men of affairs, but, after all, not very sensible, for it is just such people who ought to be above vulgar prejudice in matters like these. Some folk have very strict ideas about the use of cosmetics; but they never extend them to the teeth, as they logically should. And very disgusted other people would be if they did. No, we are all as old as we feel, but no older, and grey hair can misrepresent a man worse than dyed. You, for instance, signore, have a right to your natural colour. Surely you will permit me to restore what belongs to you?"

"How?" asked Aschenbach.

For answer the oily one washed his client's hair in two waters, one clear and one dark, and lo, it was as black as in the days of his youth. He waved it with the tongs in wide, flat undulations, and stepped back to admire the effect.

"Now if we were just to freshen up the skin a little," he said.

And with that he went on from one thing to another, his enthusiasm waxing with each new idea. Aschenbach sat there comfortably; he was incapable of objecting to the process—rather as it went forward it roused his hopes. He watched it in the mirror and saw his eyebrows grow more even and arching, the eyes gain in size and brilliance, by dint of a little application below the lids. A delicate carmine glowed on his cheeks where the skin had been so brown and leathery. The dry, anæmic lips grew full, they turned the colour of ripe strawberries, the lines round eyes and mouth were treated with a facial cream and gave place to youthful bloom. It was a young man who looked back at him from the glass—Aschenbach's heart leaped at the sight. The artist in cosmetic at last professed himself satisfied; after the manner of such people, he thanked his client profusely for what he had done himself. "The merest trifle, the merest, signore," he said as he added the final touches. "Now the signore can fall in love as soon as he likes." Aschenbach went off as in a dream, dazed between joy and fear, in his red neck-tie and broad straw hat with its gay striped band.

A lukewarm storm-wind had come up. It rained a little now and then, the air was heavy and turbid and smelt of decay. Aschenbach, with fevered cheeks beneath the rouge, seemed to hear rushing and flapping sounds in his ears, as though storm-spirits were abroad— unhallowed ocean harpies who follow those devoted to destruction, snatch away and defile their viands. For the heat took away his appetite and thus he was haunted with the idea that his food was infected.

One afternoon he pursued his charmer deep into the stricken city's huddled heart. The labyrinthine little streets, squares, canals, and bridges, each one so like the next, at length quite made him lose his bearings. He did not even know the points of the compass; all his care was not to lose sight of the figure after which his eyes thirsted. He slunk under walls, he lurked behind buildings or people's backs; and the sustained tension of his senses and emotions exhausted him more and more, though for a long time he was unconscious of fatigue. Tadzio walked behind the others, he let them pass ahead in the narrow alleys, and as he sauntered slowly after, he would turn his head and assure himself with a glance of his strange, twilit grey eyes that his lover was still following. He saw him—and he did not betray him. The knowledge enraptured Aschenbach. Lured by those eyes, led on the leading-string of his own passion and folly, utterly lovesick, he stole upon the footsteps of his unseemly hope—and at the end found himself cheated. The Polish family crossed a small vaulted bridge, the height of whose archway hid them from his sight, and when he climbed it himself they were nowhere to be seen. He hunted in three directions—straight ahead and on both sides of the narrow, dirty quay—in vain. Worn quite out and unnerved, he had to give over the search.

His head burned, his body was wet with clammy sweat, he was plagued by intolerable thirst. He looked about for refreshment, of whatever sort, and found a little fruit-shop where he bought some strawberries. They were overripe and soft; he ate them as he went. The street he was on opened out into a little square, one of those charmed, forsaken spots he liked; he recognized it as the very one where he had sat weeks ago and conceived his abortive plan of flight. He sank down on the steps of the well and leaned his head against its stone rim. It was quiet here. Grass grew between the stones, and rubbish lay about. Tall, weather-beaten houses bordered the square, one of them rather palatial, with vaulted windows, gaping now, and little lion balconies. In the ground floor of another was an apothecary's shop. A waft of carbolic acid was borne on a warm gust of wind.

There he sat, the master: this was he who had found a way to reconcile art and honours; who had written *The Abject*, and in a style of classic purity renounced bohemianism and all its works, all sympathy with the abyss and the troubled depths of the outcast

human soul. This was he who had put knowledge underfoot to
climb so high; who had outgrown the ironic pose and adjusted himself to the burdens and obligations of fame; whose renown had been
officially recognized and his name ennobled, whose style was set for
a model in the schools. There he sat. His eyelids were closed, there
was only a swift, sidelong glint of the eyeballs now and again, something between a question and a leer; while the rouged and flabby
mouth uttered single words of the sentences shaped in his disordered brain by the fantastic logic that governs our dreams.

"For mark you, Phædrus, beauty alone is both divine and visible;
and so it is the sense way, the artist's way, little Phædrus, to the spirit. But, now tell me, my dear boy, do you believe that such a man
can ever attain wisdom and true manly worth, for whom the path to
the spirit must lead through the senses? Or do you rather think—for
I leave the point to you—that it is a path of perilous sweetness, a
way of transgression, and must surely lead him who walks in it
astray? For you know that we poets cannot walk the way of beauty
without Eros as our companion and guide. We may be heroic after
our fashion, disciplined warriors of our craft, yet are we all like
women, for we exult in passion, and love is still our desire—our craving and our shame. And from this you will perceive that we poets
can be neither wise nor worthy citizens. We must needs be wanton,
must needs rove at large in the realm of feeling. Our magisterial style
is all folly and pretence, our honourable repute a farce, the crowd's
belief in us is merely laughable. And to teach youth, or the populace,
by means of art is a dangerous practice and ought to be forbidden.
For what good can an artist be as a teacher, when from his birth up
he is headed direct for the pit? We may want to shun it and attain
to honour in the world; but however we turn, it draws us still. So,
then, since knowledge might destroy us, we will have none of it. For
knowledge, Phædrus, does not make him who possesses it dignified
or austere. Knowledge is all-knowing, understanding, forgiving; it
takes up no position, sets no store by form. It has compassion with
the abyss—it *is* the abyss. So we reject it, firmly, and henceforward
our concern shall be with beauty alone. And by beauty we mean
simplicity, largeness, and renewed severity of discipline; we mean a
return to detachment and to form. But detachment, Phædrus, and
preoccupation with form lead to intoxication and desire, they may
lead the noblest among us to frightful emotional excesses, which his
own stern cult of the beautiful would make him the first to condemn. So they too, they too, lead to the bottomless pit. Yes, they

lead us thither, I say, us who are poets—who by our natures are prone not to excellence but to excess. And now, Phædrus, I will go. Remain here; and only when you can no longer see me, then do you depart also."

A few days later Gustave Aschenbach left his hotel rather later than usual in the morning. He was not feeling well and had to struggle against spells of giddiness only half physical in their nature, accompanied by a swiftly mounting dread, a sense of futility and hopelessness—but whether this referred to himself or to the outer world he could not tell. In the lobby he saw a quantity of luggage lying strapped and ready; asked the porter whose it was, and received in answer the name he already knew he should hear—that of the Polish family. The expression of his ravaged features did not change; he only gave that quick lift of the head with which we sometimes receive the uninteresting answer to a casual query. But he put another: "When?" "After luncheon," the man replied. He nodded, and went down to the beach.

It was an unfriendly scene. Little crisping shivers ran all across the wide stretch of shallow water between the shore and the first sand-bank. The whole beach, once so full of colour and life, looked now autumnal, out of season; it was nearly deserted and not even very clean. A camera on a tripod stood at the edge of the water, apparently abandoned; its black cloth snapped in the freshening wind.

Tadzio was there, in front of his cabin, with the three or four playfellows still left him. Aschenbach set up his chair some half-way between the cabins and the water, spread a rug over his knees, and sat looking on. The game this time was unsupervised, the elders being probably busy with their packing, and it looked rather lawless and out-of-hand. Jaschiu, the sturdy lad in the belted suit, with the black, brilliantined hair, became angry at a handful of sand thrown in his eyes; he challenged Tadzio to a fight, which quickly ended in the downfall of the weaker. And perhaps the coarser nature saw here a chance to avenge himself at last, by one cruel act, for his long weeks of subserviency: the victor would not let the vanquished get up, but remained kneeling on Tadzio's back, pressing Tadzio's face into the sand—for so long a time that it seemed the exhausted lad might even suffocate. He made spasmodic efforts to shake the other off, lay still, and then began a feeble twitching. Just as Aschenbach was about to spring indignantly to the rescue, Jaschiu let his victim go. Tadzio, very pale, half sat up, and remained so, leaning on one arm, for several minutes, with darkening eyes and rumpled hair.

Then he rose and walked slowly away. The others called him, at first gaily, then imploringly; he would not hear. Jaschiu was evidently overtaken by swift remorse; he followed his friend and tried to make his peace, but Tadzio motioned him back with a jerk of one shoulder and went down to the water's edge. He was barefoot and wore his striped linen suit with the red breast-knot.

There he stayed a little, with bent head, tracing figures in the wet sand with one toe; then stepped into the shallow water, which at its deepest did not wet his knees; waded idly through it and reached the sand-bar. Now he paused again, with his face turned seaward; and next began to move slowly leftwards along the narrow strip of sand the sea left bare. He paced there, divided by an expanse of water from the shore, from his mates by his moody pride; a remote and isolated figure, with floating locks, out there in sea and wind, against the misty inane. Once more he paused to look: with a sudden recollection, or by an impulse, he turned from the waist up, in an exquisite movement, one hand resting on his hip, and looked over his shoulder at the shore. The watcher sat just as he had sat that time in the lobby of the hotel when first the twilit grey eyes had met his own. He rested his head against the chair-back and followed the movements of the figure out there, then lifted it, as it were in answer to Tadzio's gaze. It sank on his breast, the eyes looked out beneath their lids, while his whole face took on the relaxed and brooding expression of deep slumber. It seemed to him the pale and lovely Summoner out there smiled at him and beckoned; as though, with the hand he lifted from his hip, he pointed outward as he hovered on before into an immensity of richest expectation.

Some minutes passed before anyone hastened to the aid of the elderly man sitting there collapsed in his chair. They bore him to his room. And before nightfall a shocked and respectful world received the news of his decease.

FRANZ KAFKA

The Metamorphosis

Translated by Willa and Edwin Muir

Introduction

I have powerfully assumed the
negativity of my times.
KAFKA, *Diaries*

Man cannot live without a permanent trust
in something indestructible in himself,
and at the same time that indestructible
something as well as his trust in it may
remain permanently concealed from him.
KAFKA, *Diaries*

Habitually we describe human character in terms of animals
and the personalities we attribute to them. Rapacious? A
wolf. Nasty? A rat. Heroic? A lion. Proud? An eagle.

Suppose, however, you are the characteristic figure of twentieth-
century urban life, or what may come to the same thing, the characteristic "anti-hero" of twentieth-century literature. Suppose you
are the poor and harassed little man, a clerk or salesman trembling
before your superiors, living always in fear of losing your wretched
job, and wishing mainly to creep through life unnoticed and unre-
buked. What are you then? A worm, an insect, a cockroach.

It is from this imagery of folklore, this reservoir of unexamined
human attitudes, that Franz Kafka starts his remarkable novella *The
Metamorphosis*. What we casually employ in our speech as a simile
or metaphor Kafka presents with a flat and terrifying literalness. The
harassed clerk (in this story, as it happens, a traveling salesman) is
not *like* a cockroach; nor *is* he, *figuratively*, a bedbug. Rather, he

347

wakes up one morning and discovers that he *is, literally,* an insect,
though still burdened with his human consciousness. What flares up
horribly in our nightmares is here transformed into a detail of realism. A conventional nineteenth-century novelist might have begun
his story by writing, "As William Chamberlain awoke one morning
from uneasy dreams he discovered he had lost his fortune and had
been transformed into a rather poor man"; Kafka opens in the same
way but ends the sentence with a shock that would have been inconceivable to the conventional nineteenth-century novelist: "As
Gregor Samsa awoke one morning from uneasy dreams he found
himself transformed in his bed into a gigantic insect."

Writing about this extraordinary opening, Martin Greenberg, one
of Kafka's best critics, remarks:

> Kafka's *Metamorphosis* is peculiar as a narrative in having its climax
> in the very first sentence: "As Gregor Samsa awoke one morning
> from uneasy dreams he found himself transformed in his bed into a
> gigantic insect." The rest of the *novella* falls away from this high
> point of astonishment in one long expiring sigh, punctuated by three
> sub-climaxes (the three eruptions of the bug from the bedroom).
> How is it possible, one may ask, for a story to start at the climax and
> then merely subside? What kind of story is that? The answer to this
> question is—a story for which the traditional Aristotelian form of
> narrative (complication and denouement) has lost any intrinsic
> necessity and which has therefore evolved its own peculiar form out
> of the very matter it seeks to tell. *The Metamorphosis* produces its
> own form out of itself. The traditional kind of narrative based on the
> drama of denouement—on the "unknotting" of complications and
> the coming to a conclusion—could not serve Kafka because it is just
> exactly the absence of denouement and conclusions that is his subject
> matter. His story is about death, but death that is without denoue-
> ment, death that is merely a spiritually inconclusive petering out.

The traditional kind of story, following the pattern described by
Aristotle in his *Poetics,* assumes the possibility and indeed proposes
the likelihood that there will be a major change in the experience of
the central character. This change can be tragic, comic, heroic, or a
mixture of these; but it is assumed to be both meaningful and dramatic. Hence, there follow in the story complications of plot and
then the denouement (realization, conclusion, a winding up of the
plot and its meanings). But Kafka, expressing the vision of twentieth-century modernism, sees no such possibility in the life of
Gregor Samsa; he is writing about a man who has reached dead-end

and perhaps has always been there; he therefore opens the story at the beginning of Gregor's end. Nothing but death is possible to Gregor once he becomes (or is revealed to be) an insect. No complications or denouement are possible. "Gregor Samsa is an insect" —once the extension of that metaphor has been established, everything else follows with the necessity of a mathematical proof; the story must move steadily downward, showing Gregor's disintegration and suggesting what it means.

The action of Gregor as he awakens in the morning, discovers that he has undergone a physical transformation, and yet continues to behave as if he were still the traveling salesman, enslaved to his company, his habits, his family—all this serves a purpose. It reenacts with grotesque emphasis the earlier life of Gregor. We see him trying once again to go to his miserable job: "Traveling about day in, day out. . . . The devil take it all!" And as soon as he is late, for the first time in five years, the chief clerk of his firm, like a warden of a jail, accuses him of laziness, neglect, and possible theft. "What a fate, to be condemned to work for a firm where the smallest omission at once gave rise to the gravest suspicion! Were all employees in a body nothing but scoundrels . . . ?" Gregor has been sacrificing his life to pay off a debt incurred by his parents—yet later he will learn that he had been deceived by his father. If not for that obligation, he thinks, "I'd have given notice long ago, I'd have gone to the chief and told him exactly what I think of him"—a characteristic fantasy of the meek underling.

In these few pages, where the insect-salesman tries to behave as if nothing important had occurred, Kafka presents vividly and memorably the utter sadness of a man at the mercy of his circumstances, a man who in youth has already been trapped by life. For Gregor Samsa is not meant to be a strongly individualized character whom we remember for his unique traits, appearance, and attitudes. Quite the contrary. What matters about Gregor is the whole complex of circumstances and conduct which he shares with millions of other Gregors. He is meant to strike us as an image of humanity in an extreme state: man at the end of his rope.

Yet there is a side to Gregor's metamorphosis which we may be inclined to overlook. On the one hand, Gregor tries to deny his situation, for how can a man, and a man who has to support a family, become an insect? But within Gregor's humiliating transformation there is also rebellion—desperate and dispirited, but rebellion nonetheless. By turning into an insect he need no longer bow and scrape before his bosses, he need no longer turn over his money to his small-souled and selfish family. Becoming an insect, Gregor Samsa ceases to live the life of a machine. For the first time Gregor feels able to express, with whatever futility, his "rage" against his circumstances; for the first time, he pays attention to the needs of his own body—something a man can ignore more easily than an insect. His rebellion, in extreme symbolic terms, is like that of a man who refuses to get up in the morning and says in effect, *to hell with it, I'm through.* Martin Greenberg develops this point carefully: "the human self whose claims Gregor always postponed and continues to postpone, is past being put off, having declared itself negatively by changing him from a human being into an insect. His metamorphosis is a judgment on himself by his defeated humanity." At one and the same time, the metamorphosis comes to seem a humiliation, a rebellion, a "cop-out," and, finally, a preparation for death. Still, because the will to survive flickers in Gregor Samsa, there continue to stir within him those human impulses and desires which mingle, so pathetically and incongruously, with his physical needs as an insect.

The novella is organized into three sections or panels, each of which is brought to a little climax when Gregor tries to reestablish some token of connectedness with his family and the outer world:

1. It is Gregor's habit to lock himself into his room each night. (Even in his own home, Gregor behaves as if he were among strangers—this man has become cut off from every ordinary human tie and in turn has cut himself off from those near to him. Mistrust and deceit characterize the relationships within his family.) After he has awakened, Gregor faces the problem of opening his door. Painfully he unlocks it with his jaws, shows himself to his family, tries to speak but cannot be understood by anyone, and then is driven back into the room by his angry father. Note here three significant points:

✦ *Gregor's voice has altered, so that the others cannot understand what he says. Yet he understands them as well as ever. This illustrates with considerable poignancy Gregor's dilemma: he is the outsider, the man who understands but is not understood, the man who wishes to reach out but cannot make himself heard. His loneliness and isolation are terrifying.*

✦ *The father, writes Kafka, drives Gregor back into his room "pitilessly." "From behind his father gave him a strong push which was literally a deliverance and he flew far into the room, bleeding freely. The door was slammed behind him with the stick, and then at last there was silence." A dominant theme in Kafka's fiction is here being announced: the struggle between an insecure young man and his overbearing and unsympathetic father, in which the father comes to symbolize or suggest the heartlessness of circumstances, the pressures of fate, the coldness and unresponsiveness of the world. As the story develops, it will become clearer still that this is a dominant motif.*

✦ *Yet Gregor still refuses to face the reality of his situation and keeps trying to reassure himself that it is all a temporary misfortune: "he must lie low for the present and, by exercising patience and the utmost consideration, help the family to bear the inconvenience he was bound to cause them in his present condition." All of his life Gregor has been trained to blame himself when things went wrong, and now he continues in quite the same way.*

2. The second part describes a temporary "stabilization" of Gregor's metamorphosis. He settles down to live as an animal and slowly to "forget" that he must continue to suffer from his human awareness. His sister, who still has a certain affection for him, brings Gregor food—though after a time the repugnance she experiences at the sight of him overcomes her feelings and she can no longer bear to look at him. Utter isolation becomes his accepted way of life, and gradually he accepts the physical habits of an insect—*as if*, implies Kafka, *a man can get used to anything, any disaster, any humiliation.* He is slowly but inexorably regressing to the animal level. Yet he also retains human sentiments, for example, the shame he feels when a member of his family sees him.

A conflict breaks out over an apparently trivial matter. Gregor has not protested the removal of furniture from his room, but now he fastens himself upon a photograph that is hanging on the wall. At the beginning of the story Kafka, with seeming casualness, had described this picture: it shows a woman in furs, nondescript, impersonal, signifying little in itself. Yet here Gregor makes his last stand, trying to prevent the picture from being taken away from him. The pathos is unbearable: all that remains to him of a lifetime is a drab pin-up. Yet Gregor keeps struggling between the side of him that is human and the side that is insect, between his wish to remain a man and his resignation at the prospect of becoming mere vermin.

His mother, who until now has shown him some sympathy, faints upon seeing what has become of him; his father attacks him with an apple. The fruit lodges in the insect's back and begins to fester.

3. Given a little time, people, it seems, can accept anything. The family is no longer so concerned about keeping Gregor out of sight; they neglect him increasingly; they take in boarders; and all of them become more active, finding jobs and work. Gregor's room becomes a storehouse for old junk, including himself. Gregor's will to live is ebbing, since the possibility of being able to return to the human community seems also to be disappearing. Which is it that Gregor really suffers from—banishment or self-banishment? Both; the two are inseparable.

And now there occurs the most unnerving incident in the story. Gregor hears his sister playing the violin and, strangely moved by the music, comes out to listen—quite as a brother might. Hysteria follows, and in final despair Gregor crawls backs to his junk-room, free of the last delusion of hope.

These are the crucial episodes of the novella, and on the face of it, they form a steady downward slope, from shock to rejection, from rejection to humiliation, from humiliation to despair, and from despair to death. Yet there is another rhythm in the story, not nearly so powerful as that of Gregor's disintegration but still requiring our notice: Gregor's hesitant discovery of the possibilities of salvation. Martin Greenberg writes acutely about this:

> Gregor, unable to accept his transformation into a bug and automatically trying to walk like a man, inadvertently falls down on his insect legs and feels an instantaneous sense of comfort which he takes as a promise of future relief from his sufferings—with supreme illogic he derives a hope of release from his animal condition from the very comfort he gets by adapting himself to that condition: so divided is his self-consciousness from his true self. But there is a second meaning, which piles irony upon the irony: precisely as a noisome outcast from the human world Gregor feels the possibility of relief, of *final* relief. Only as an outcast does he sense the possibility of an ultimate salvation rather than just a restoration of the *status quo*.

There begins to well up in Gregor a new hunger, at the very time that he turns away from food:

> "I'm hungry enough," said Gregor sadly to himself, "but not for that kind of food. How these lodgers are stuffing themselves, and here am I dying of starvation!"

He is starved for some way of escaping the death-in-life that has been symbolized by his metamorphosis. When he hears the music, some deep yearning stirs within him: "Was he an animal, that music had such an effect upon him? He felt as if the way were opening before him to the unknown nourishment he craved." But what way could be open to someone in his situation? Once he has heard his sister's demand that he be destroyed, Gregor simply gives up:

> "And what now?" said Gregor to himself, looking round in the darkness. . . . He thought of his family with tenderness and love. The decision that he must disappear was one that he held to even more strongly than his sister, if that were possible. In this state of vacant and peaceful meditation he remained until the tower clock struck three in the morning. The first broadening of light in the world outside the window entered his consciousness once more. Then his head sank to the floor of its own accord and from his nostrils came the last faint flicker of his breath.

There remains the most important and most difficult question concerning *The Metamorphosis.* Why does it create such a powerful and haunting impression? How does Kafka manage to make an apparently simple story seem representative of fundamental aspects of human existence?

These questions should be struggled with by each reader. But let me offer a few remarks, first in the hope they will be helpful and second because I want to say a few more things about this remarkable story.

Literary critics speak about the gift of *invention*, the gift for conceiving remarkable or profound situations, vivid or archetypal characters. Kafka's greatest feat in this story was simply to imagine its central idea. Before he started writing, he must have experienced a remarkable moment of vision, the moment in which he saw for the first time Gregor Samsa transformed into a bug. Upon this revelation the story rests.

To imagine is not yet to achieve. Only a little less brilliant than the conception is the way Kafka avoids all the mistakes that might have followed. These would primarily have been deficiencies in tact. Kafka could have yielded to the impulse to make his story sensationalistic, sentimental, or gruesome. A self-pitying phrase, an overwrought adjective, a pedantic drop into moralism could have ruined the story. For artistic discipline consists not merely in what a writer puts in, but also in what he manages to leave out. Throughout *The Metamorphosis* Kafka remains faithful to the purity of his original idea. Once Gregor Samsa has been metamorphosed, all that follows is as commonplace as the dullest day in the dullest life. Kafka is not concerned here with display and dazzle. He is trying to probe the depths of a human situation: the vulnerability we all share.

The subject of *The Metamorphosis* is profoundly serious; it can be seen as a claim for the essential hopelessness of human existence. But what save the story from lugubriousness are, first, the dryness of Kafka's style and, second, the humor that he weaves into his narrative.

About Kafka's style I will say only that it is undecorative, devoted to exact description, and free of all the vanities of rhetoric that afflict most writers. The prose is meant to function as a transparent glass, through which we see the world of Gregor Samsa; but at no point does Kafka want us to pay attention—as Thomas Mann obviously does in *Death in Venice*—to the writing as such. And because the prose is so matter-of-fact, it controls and contains the terribleness of what it presents. So disarmingly mild does the writing seem that we almost forget we are witnessing the disintegration of a human being.

Kafka's humor is essentially the humor of incongruity, depending on a contrast between the terribleness of the depicted events and the moderateness of the tone of voice with which they are told. One of Kafka's critics, F. D. Luke, writes about his "humorous distance" as

an essential feature of Kafka's technique and of his greatness. As a storyteller, it is this that enables him to exploit every possible effect of understatement, to accentuate horror by reporting it with terrible detachment: Gregor's situation, for example, is "his mishap" or "his present condition," and his family suffer "inconvenience" and "anxieties." Kafka's attitude is essentially a species of *Galgenhumor* [gallows humor], the humor, on a vaster scale, of the criminal who, led out to execution on a Monday, remarked, "Well, this is a good beginning to the week."

And then the ending of *The Metamorphosis*. Gregor Samsa has expired, and his family seems to thrive. They take an excursion into the country; things don't look so bad for them after all; they can move to a smaller, less expensive house; and the daughter is visibly beginning to bloom. The concluding sentence describes how she springs to her feet and stretches "her young body." Forgotten is Gregor the man and forgotten Gregor the insect; forgotten the sufferings of the son; forgotten all suffering. In its cruel and heedless rhythm, life continues.

The Metamorphosis

I

As Gregor Samsa awoke one morning from uneasy dreams he found himself transformed in his bed into a gigantic insect. He was lying on his hard, as it were armor-plated, back and when he lifted his head a little he could see his dome-like brown belly divided into stiff arched segments on top of which the bed quilt could hardly keep in position and was about to slide off completely. His numerous legs, which were pitifully thin compared to the rest of his bulk, waved helplessly before his eyes.

What has happened to me? he thought. It was no dream. His room, a regular human bedroom, only rather too small, lay quiet between the four familiar walls. Above the table on which a collection of cloth samples was unpacked and spread out—Samsa was a commercial traveler—hung the picture which he had recently cut out of an illustrated magazine and put into a pretty gilt frame. It showed a lady, with a fur cap on and a fur stole, sitting upright and holding out to the spectator a huge fur muff into which the whole of her forearm had vanished!

Gregor's eyes turned next to the window, and the overcast sky —one could hear rain drops beating on the window gutter—made him quite melancholy. What about sleeping a little longer and forgetting all this nonsense, he thought, but it could not be done, for he was accustomed to sleep on his right side and in his present condition he could not turn himself over. However violently he forced himself towards his right side he always rolled on to his back again. He tried it at least a hundred times, shutting his eyes to keep from seeing his struggling legs, and only desisted when he began to feel in his side a faint dull ache he had never experienced before.

Oh God, he thought, what an exhausting job I've picked on! Traveling about day in, day out. It's much more irritating work than doing the actual business in the office, and on top of that there's the trouble of constant traveling, of worrying about train connections, the bed and irregular meals, casual acquaintances that are always new and never become intimate friends. The devil take it all! He felt a slight itching up on his belly; slowly pushed himself on his back nearer to the top of the bed so that he could lift his head more easily; identified the itching place which was surrounded by many small white spots the nature of which he could not understand and made to touch it with a leg, but drew the leg back immediately, for the contact made a cold shiver run through him.

He slid down again into his former position. This getting up early, he thought, makes one quite stupid. A man needs his sleep. Other commercials live like harem women. For instance, when I come back to the hotel of a morning to write up the orders I've got, these others are only sitting down to breakfast. Let me just try that with my chief; I'd be sacked on the spot. Anyhow, that might be quite a good thing for me, who can tell? If I didn't have to hold my hand because of my parents I'd have given notice long ago, I'd have gone to the chief and told him exactly what I think of him. That would knock him endways from his desk! It's a queer way of doing, too, this sitting on high at a desk and talking down to employees, especially when they have to come quite near because the chief is hard of hearing. Well, there's still hope; once I've saved enough money to pay back my parents' debts to him—that should take another five or six years—I'll do it without fail. I'll cut myself completely loose then. For the moment, though, I'd better get up, since my train goes at five.

He looked at the alarm clock ticking on the chest. Heavenly Father! he thought. It was half-past six o'clock and the hands were quietly moving on, it was even past the half-hour, it was getting on toward a quarter to seven. Had the alarm clock not gone off? From the bed one could see that it had been properly set for four o'clock; of course it must have gone off. Yes, but was it possible to sleep quietly through that ear-splitting noise? Well, he had not slept quietly, yet apparently all the more soundly for that. But what was he to do now? The next train went at seven o'clock; to catch that he would need to hurry like mad and his samples weren't even packed up, and he himself wasn't feeling particularly fresh and active. And even if he did catch the train he wouldn't avoid a row with the chief, since the firm's porter would have been waiting for the five o'clock train and would have long since reported his failure to turn up. The porter was a creature of the chief's, spineless and stupid. Well, supposing he were to say he was sick? But that would be most unpleasant and would look suspicious, since during his five years' employment he had not been ill once. The chief himself would be sure to come with the sick-insurance doctor, would reproach his parents with their son's laziness and would cut all excuses short by referring to the insurance doctor, who of course regarded all mankind as perfectly healthy malingerers. And would he be so far wrong on this occasion? Gregor really felt quite well, apart from a drowsiness that was utterly superfluous after such a long sleep, and he was even unusually hungry.

As all this was running through his mind at top speed without his being able to decide to leave his bed— the alarm clock had just struck a quarter to seven—there came a cautious tap at the door behind the head of his bed. "Gregor," said a voice—it was his mother's—"it's a quarter to seven. Hadn't you a train to catch?" That gentle voice! Gregor had a shock as he heard his own voice answering hers, unmistakably his own voice, it was true, but with a persistent horrible twittering squeak behind it like an undertone, that left the words in their clear shape only for the first moment and then rose up reverberating round them to destroy their sense, so that one could not be sure one had heard them rightly. Gregor wanted to answer at length and explain everything, but in the circumstances he confined himself to saying: "Yes, yes, thank you, Mother, I'm getting up now." The wooden door between them must have kept the change in his voice from being noticeable outside, for his mother contented herself with this statement and shuffled away. Yet this brief exchange of words had made the other members of the family aware that Gregor was still in the house, as they had not expected, and at one of the side doors his father was already knocking, gently, yet with his fist. "Gregor, Gregor," he called, "what's the matter with you?" And after a little while he called again in a deeper voice: "Gregor! Gregor!" At the other side door his sister was saying in a low, plaintive tone: "Gregor? Aren't you well? Are you needing anything?" He answered them both at once: "I'm just ready," and did his best to make his voice sound as normal as possible by enunciating the words very clearly and leaving long pauses between them. So his father went back to his breakfast, but his sister whispered: "Gregor, open the door, do." However, he was not thinking of opening the door, and felt thankful for the prudent habit he had acquired in traveling of locking all doors during the night, even at home.

His immediate intention was to get up quietly without being disturbed, to put on his clothes and above all eat his breakfast, and only then to consider what else was to be done, since in bed, he was well aware, his meditations would come to no sensible conclusion. He remembered that often enough in bed he had felt small aches and pains, probably caused by awkward postures, which had proved purely imaginary once he got up, and he looked forward eagerly to seeing this morning's delusions gradually fall away. That the change in his voice was nothing but the precursor of a severe chill, a standing ailment of commercial travelers, he had not the least possible doubt.

To get rid of the quilt was quite easy; he had only to inflate himself a little and it fell off by itself. But the next move was difficult, especially because he was so uncommonly broad. He would have needed arms and hands to hoist himself up; instead he had only the numerous little legs which never stopped waving in all directions and which he could not control in the least. When he tried to bend one of them it was the first to stretch itself straight; and did he succeed at last in making it do what he wanted, all the other legs meanwhile waved the more wildly in a high degree of unpleasant agitation. "But what's the use of lying idle in bed," said Gregor to himself.

He thought that he might get out of bed with the lower part of his body first, but this lower part, which he had not yet seen and of which he could form no clear conception, proved too difficult to move; it shifted so slowly; and when finally, almost wild with annoyance, he gathered his forces together and thrust out recklessly, he had miscalculated the direction and bumped heavily against the lower end of the bed, and the stinging pain he felt informed him that precisely this lower part of his body was at the moment probably the most sensitive.

So he tried to get the top part of himself out first, and cautiously moved his head towards the edge of the bed. That proved easy enough, and despite its breadth and mass the bulk of his body at last slowly followed the movement of his head. Still, when he finally got his head free over the edge of the bed he felt too scared to go on advancing, for after all if he let himself fall in this way it would take a miracle to keep his head from being injured. And at all costs he must not lose consciousness now, precisely now; he would rather stay in bed.

But when after a repetition of the same efforts he lay in his former position again, sighing, and watched his little legs struggling against each other more wildly than ever, if that were possible, and saw no way of bringing any order into this arbitrary confusion, he told himself again that it was impossible to stay in bed and that the most sensible course was to risk everything for the smallest hope of getting away from it. At the same time he did not forget meanwhile to remind himself that cool reflection, the coolest possible, was much better than desperate resolves. In such moments he focused his eyes as sharply as possible on the window, but, unfortunately, the prospect of the morning fog, which muffled even the other side of the narrow street, brought him little encouragement and comfort. "Seven o'clock already," he said to himself when the alarm clock chimed again, "seven o'clock already and still such a thick fog." And for a little while he lay quiet, breathing lightly, as if perhaps expecting such complete repose to restore all things to their real and normal condition.

But then he said to himself: "Before it strikes a quarter past seven I must be quite out of this bed, without fail. Anyhow, by that time someone will have come from the office to ask for me, since it opens before seven." And he set himself to rocking his whole body at once in a regular rhythm, with the idea of swinging it out of the bed. If he tipped himself out in that way he could keep his head from injury by lifting it at an acute angle when he fell. His back seemed to be hard and was not likely to suffer from a fall on the carpet. His biggest worry was the loud crash he would not be able to help making, which would probably cause anxiety, if not terror, behind all the doors. Still, he must take the risk.

When he was already half out of the bed—the new method was

more a game than an effort, for he needed only to hitch himself across by rocking to and fro—it struck him how simple it would be if he could get help. Two strong people—he thought of his father and the servant girl—would be amply sufficient; they would only have to thrust their arms under his convex back, lever him out of the bed, bend down with their burden and then be patient enough to let him turn himself right over on to the floor, where it was to be hoped his legs would then find their proper function. Well, ignoring the fact that the doors were all locked, ought he really to call for help? In spite of his misery he could not suppress a smile at the very idea of it.

He had got so far that he could barely keep his equilibrium when he rocked himself strongly, and he would have to nerve himself very soon for the final decision since in five minutes' time it would be a quarter past seven—when the front door bell rang. "That's someone from the office," he said to himself, and grew almost rigid, while his little legs only jigged about all the faster. For a moment everything stayed quiet. "They're not going to open the door," said Gregor to himself, catching at some kind of irrational hope. But then of course the servant girl went as usual to the door with her heavy tread and opened it. Gregor needed only to hear the first good morning of the visitor to know immediately who it was— the chief clerk himself. What a fate, to be condemned to work for a firm where the smallest omission at once gave rise to the gravest suspicion! Were all employees in a body nothing but scoundrels, was there not among them one single loyal devoted man who, had he wasted only an hour or so of the firm's time in a morning, was so tormented by conscience as to be driven out of his mind and actually incapable of leaving his bed? Wouldn't it really have been sufficient to send an apprentice to inquire—if any inquiry were necessary at all—did the chief clerk himself have to come and thus indicate to the entire family, an innocent family, that this suspicious circumstance could be investigated by no one less versed in affairs than himself? And more through the agitation caused by these reflections than through any act of will Gregor swung himself out of bed with all his strength. There was a loud thump, but it was not really a crash. His fall was broken to some extent by the carpet, his back, too, was less stiff than he thought, and so there was merely a dull thud, not so very startling. Only he had not lifted his head carefully enough and had hit it; he turned it and rubbed it on the carpet in pain and irritation.

"That was something falling down in there," said the chief clerk in the next room to the left. Gregor tried to suppose to himself that something like what had happened to him today might some day happen to the chief clerk; one really could not deny that it was possible. But as if in brusque reply to this supposition the chief clerk took a couple of firm steps in the next-door room and his patent leather boots creaked. From the right-hand room his sister was whispering to inform him of the situation: "Gregor, the chief clerk's here." "I know," muttered Gregor to himself; but he didn't dare to make his voice loud enough for his sister to hear it.

"Gregor," said his father now from the left-hand room, "the chief clerk has come and wants to know why you didn't catch the early train. We don't know what to say to him. Besides, he wants to talk to you in person. So open the door, please. He will be good enough to excuse the untidiness of your room." "Good morning, Mr. Samsa," the chief clerk was calling amiably meanwhile. "He's not well," said his mother to the visitor, while his father was still speaking through the door, "he's not well, sir, believe me. What else would make him miss a train! The boy thinks about nothing but his work. It makes me almost cross the way he never goes out in the evenings; he's been here the last eight days and has stayed at home every single evening. He just sits there quietly at the table reading a newspaper or looking through railway timetables. The only amusement he gets is doing fretwork. For instance, he spent two or three evenings cutting out a little picture frame; you would be surprised to see how pretty it is; it's hanging in his room; you'll see it in a minute when Gregor opens the door. I must say I'm glad you've come, sir; we should never have got him to unlock the door by ourselves; he's so obstinate; and I'm sure he's unwell, though he wouldn't have it to be so this morning." "I'm just coming," said Gregor slowly and carefully, not moving an inch for fear of losing one word of the conversation. "I can't think of any other explanation, madam," said the chief clerk, "I hope it's nothing serious. Although on the other hand I must say that we men of business—fortunately or unfortunately— very often simply have to ignore any slight indisposition, since business must be attended to." "Well, can the chief clerk come in now?" asked Gregor's father impatiently, again knocking on the door. "No," said Gregor. In the left-hand room a painful silence followed this refusal, in the right-hand room his sister began to sob.

Why didn't his sister join the others? She was probably newly out of bed and hadn't even begun to put on her clothes yet. Well, why was she crying? Because he wouldn't get up and let the chief clerk in, because he was in danger of losing his job, and because the chief would begin dunning his parents again for the old debts? Surely these were things one didn't need to worry about for the present. Gregor was still at home and not in the least thinking of deserting the family. At the moment, true, he was lying on the carpet and no one who knew the condition he was in could seriously expect him to admit the chief clerk. But for such a small discourtesy, which could plausibly be explained away somehow later on, Gregor could hardly be dismissed on the spot. And it seemed to Gregor that it would be much more sensible to leave him in peace for the present than to trouble him with tears and entreaties. Still, of course, their uncertainty bewildered them all and excused their behavior.

"Mr. Samsa," the chief clerk called now in a louder voice, "what's the matter with you? Here you are, barricading yourself in your room, giving only 'yes' and 'no' for answers, causing your parents a lot of unnecessary trouble and neglecting—I mention this only in passing—neglecting your business duties in an incredible fashion. I am speaking here in the name of your parents and of your chief, and I beg you quite seriously to give me an immediate and precise explanation. You amaze me, you amaze me. I thought you were a quiet, dependable person, and now all at once you seem bent on making a disgraceful exhibition of yourself. The chief did hint to me early this morning a possible explanation for your disappearance —with reference to the cash payments that were entrusted to you recently—but I almost pledged my solemn word of honor that this could not be so. But now that I see how incredibly obstinate you are, I no longer have the slightest desire to take your part at all. And your position in the firm is not so unassailable. I came with the intention of telling you all this in private, but since you are wasting my time so needlessly I don't see why your parents shouldn't hear it too. For some time past your work has been most unsatisfactory; this is not the season of the year for a business boom, of course, we admit that, but a season of the year for doing no business at all, that does not exist, Mr. Samsa, must not exist."

"But, sir," cried Gregor, beside himself and in his agitation forgetting everything else, "I'm just going to open the door this very minute. A slight illness, an attack of giddiness, has kept me from getting up. I'm still lying in bed. But I feel all right again. I'm getting out of bed now. Just give me a moment or two longer! I'm not quite so well as I thought. But I'm all right, really. How a thing

like that can suddenly strike one down! Only last night I was quite
well, my parents can tell you, or rather I did have a slight presentiment. I must have showed some sign of it. Why didn't I report
it at the office! But one always thinks that an indisposition can be
got over without staying in the house. Oh sir, do spare my parents!
All that you're reproaching me with now has no foundation; no one
has ever said a word to me about it. Perhaps you haven't looked at
the last orders I sent in. Anyhow, I can still catch the eight o'clock
train, I'm much the better for my few hours' rest. Don't let me de-
tain you here, sir; I'll be attending to business very soon, and do be
good enough to tell the chief so and to make my excuses to him!"

And while all this was tumbling out pell-mell and Gregor hardly
knew what he was saying, he had reached the chest quite easily, perhaps because of the practice he had had in bed, and was now trying
to lever himself upright by means of it. He meant actually to open
the door, actually to show himself and speak to the chief clerk; he
was eager to find out what the others, after all their insistence,
would say at the sight of him. If they were horrified then the responsibility was no longer his and he could stay quiet. But if they
took it calmly, then he had no reason either to be upset, and could
really get to the station for the eight o'clock train if he hurried. At
first he slipped down a few times from the polished surface of the
chest, but at length with a last heave he stood upright; he paid no
more attention to the pains in the lower part of his body, however
they smarted. Then he let himself fall against the back of a near-by
chair, and clung with his little legs to the edges of it. That brought
him into control of himself again and he stopped speaking, for now
he could listen to what the chief clerk was saying.

"Did you understand a word of it?" the chief clerk was asking;
"surely he can't be trying to make fools of us?" "Oh dear," cried his
mother, in tears, "perhaps he's terribly ill and we're tormenting him.
Grete! Grete!" she called out then. "Yes Mother?" called his sister
from the other side. They were calling to each other across Gregor's
room. "You must go this minute for the doctor. Gregor is ill. Go for
the doctor, quick. Did you hear how he was speaking?" "That was
no human voice," said the chief clerk in a voice noticeably low beside the shrillness of the mother's. "Anna! Anna!" his father was
calling through the hall to the kitchen, clapping his hands, "get a
locksmith at once!" And the two girls were already running through
the hall with a swish of skirts—how could his sister have got dressed
so quickly?—and were tearing the front door open. There was no

sound of its closing again; they had evidently left it open, as one does in houses where some great misfortune has happened.

But Gregor was now much calmer. The words he uttered were no longer understandable, apparently, although they seemed clear enough to him, even clearer than before, perhaps because his ear had grown accustomed to the sound of them. Yet at any rate people now believed that something was wrong with him, and were ready to help him. The positive certainty with which these first measures had been taken comforted him. He felt himself drawn once more into the human circle and hoped for great and remarkable results from both the doctor and the locksmith, without really distinguishing precisely between them. To make his voice as clear as possible for the decisive conversation that was now imminent he coughed a little, as quietly as he could, of course, since this noise too might not sound like a human cough for all he was able to judge. In the next room meanwhile there was complete silence. Perhaps his parents were sitting at the table with the chief clerk, whispering, perhaps they were all leaning against the door and listening.

Slowly Gregor pushed the chair towards the door, then let go of it, caught hold of the door for support—the soles at the end of his little legs were somewhat sticky—and rested against it for a moment after his efforts. Then he set himself to turning the key in the lock with his mouth. It seemed, unhappily, that he hadn't really any teeth—what could he grip the key with?—but on the other hand his jaws were certainly very strong; with their help he did manage to set the key in motion, heedless of the fact that he was undoubtedly damaging them somewhere, since a brown fluid issued from his mouth, flowed over the key and dripped on the floor. "Just listen to that," said the chief clerk next door; "he's turning the key." That was a great encouragement to Gregor; but they should all have shouted encouragement to him, his father and mother too: "Go on, Gregor," they should have called out, "keep going, hold on to that key!" And in the belief that they were all following his efforts intently, he clenched his jaws recklessly on the key with all the force at his command. As the turning of the key progressed he circled round the lock, holding on now only with his mouth, pushing on the key, as required, or pulling it down again with all the weight of his body. The louder click of the finally yielding lock literally quickened Gregor. With a deep breath of relief he said to himself: "So I didn't need the locksmith," and laid his head on the handle to open the door wide.

Since he had to pull the door towards him, he was still invisible when it was really wide open. He had to edge himself slowly round the near half of the double door, and to do it very carefully if he was not to fall plump upon his back just on the threshold. He was still carrying out this difficult manoeuvre, with no time to observe anything else, when he heard the chief clerk utter a loud "Oh!"—it sounded like a gust of wind—and now he could see the man, standing as he was nearest to the door, clapping one hand before his open mouth and slowly backing away as if driven by some invisible steady pressure. His mother—in spite of the chief clerk's being there her hair was still undone and sticking up in all directions—first clasped her hands and looked at his father, then took two steps towards Gregor and fell on the floor among her outspread skirts, her face quite hidden on her breast. His father knotted his fist with a fierce expression on his face as if he meant to knock Gregor back into his room, then looked uncertainly round the living room, covered his eyes with his hands and wept till his great chest heaved.

Gregor did not go now into the living room, but leaned against the inside of the firmly shut wing of the door, so that only half his body was visible and his head above it bending sideways to look at the others. The light had meanwhile strengthened; on the other side of the street one could see clearly a section of the endlessly long, dark gray building opposite—it was a hospital—abruptly punctuated by its row of regular windows; the rain was still falling, but only in large singly discernible and literally singly splashing drops. The breakfast dishes were set out on the table lavishly, for breakfast was the most important meal of the day to Gregor's father, who lingered it out for hours over various newspapers. Right opposite Gregor on the wall hung a photograph of himself on military service, as a lieutenant, hand on sword, a carefree smile on his face, inviting one to respect his uniform and military bearing. The door leading to the hall was open, and one could see that the front door stood open too, showing the landing beyond and the beginning of the stairs going down.

"Well," said Gregor, knowing perfectly that he was the only one who had retained any composure, "I'll put my clothes on at once, pack up my samples and start off. Will you only let me go? You see, sir, I'm not obstinate, and I'm willing to work; traveling is a hard life, but I couldn't live without it. Where are you going, sir? To the office? Yes? Will you give a true account of all this? One can be temporarily incapacitated, but that's just the moment for remembering former services and bearing in mind that later on, when the incapacity has been got over, one will certainly work with all the more industry and concentration. I'm loyally bound to serve the chief, you know that very well. Besides, I have to provide for my parents and my sister. I'm in great difficulties, but I'll get out of them again. Don't make things any worse for me than they are. Stand up for me in the firm. Travelers are not popular there, I know. People think they earn sacks of money and just have a good time. A prejudice there's no particular reason for revising. But you, sir, have a more comprehensive view of affairs than the rest of the staff, yes, let me tell you in confidence, a more comprehensive view than the chief himself, who, being the owner, lets his judgment easily be swayed against one of his employees. And you know very well that the traveler, who is never seen in the office almost the whole year round, can so easily fall a victim to gossip and ill luck and unfounded complaints, which he mostly knows nothing about, except when he comes back exhausted from his rounds, and only then suffers in person from their evil consequences, which he can no longer trace back to the original causes. Sir, sir, don't go away without a word to me to show that you think me in the right at least to some extent!"

But at Gregor's very first words the chief clerk had already backed away and only stared at him with parted lips over one twitching shoulder. And while Gregor was speaking he did not stand still one moment but stole away towards the door, without taking his eyes off Gregor, yet only an inch at a time, as if obeying some secret injunction to leave the room. He was already at the hall, and the suddenness with which he took his last step out of the living room would have made one believe he had burned the sole of his foot. Once in the hall he stretched his right arm before him towards the staircase, as if some supernatural power were waiting there to deliver him.

Gregor perceived that the chief clerk must on no account be allowed to go away in this frame of mind if his position in the firm were not to be endangered to the utmost. His parents did not understand this so well; they had convinced themselves in the course of years that Gregor was settled for life in this firm, and besides they were so occupied with their immediate troubles that all foresight had forsaken them. Yet Gregor had this foresight. The chief clerk must be detained, soothed, persuaded and finally won over; the whole future of Gregor and his family depended on it! If only his sister had been there! She was intelligent; she had begun to cry while Gregor was still lying quietly on his back. And no doubt the chief clerk, so partial to ladies, would have been guided by her; she would have shut the door of the flat and in the hall talked him out of his horror. But she was not there, and Gregor would have to handle the situation himself. And without remembering that he was still unaware what powers of movement he possessed, without even remembering that his words in all possibility, indeed in all likelihood, would again be unintelligible, he let go the wing of the door, pushed himself through the opening, started to walk towards the chief clerk, who was already ridiculously clinging with both hands to the railing on the landing; but immediately, as he was feeling for a support, he fell down with a little cry upon all his numerous legs. Hardly was he down when he experienced for the first time this morning a sense of physical comfort; his legs had firm ground under them; they were completely obedient, as he noted with joy; they even strove to carry him forward in whatever direction he chose; and he was inclined to believe that a final relief from all his sufferings was at hand. But in the same moment as he found himself on the floor, rocking with suppressed eagerness to move, not far from his mother, indeed just in front of her, she, who had seemed so completely crushed, sprang all at once to her feet, her arms and fingers outspread, cried: "Help, for God's sake, help!" bent her head down as if to see Gregor better, yet on the contrary kept backing senselessly away; had quite forgotten that the laden table stood behind her; sat upon it hastily, as if in absence of mind, when she bumped into it; and seemed altogether unaware that the big coffee pot beside her was upset and pouring coffee in a flood over the carpet.

"Mother, Mother," said Gregor in a low voice, and looked up at her. The chief clerk, for the moment, had quite slipped from his mind; instead, he could not resist snapping his jaws together at the sight of the streaming coffee. That made his mother scream again, she fled from the table and fell into the arms of his father, who hastened to catch her. But Gregor had now no time to spare for his parents; the chief clerk was already on the stairs; with his chin on the banisters he was taking one last backward look. Gregor made a spring, to be as sure as possible of overtaking him; the chief clerk must have divined his intention, for he leaped down several steps and vanished; he was still yelling "Ugh!" and it echoed through the whole staircase.

Unfortunately, the flight of the chief clerk seemed completely to upset Gregor's father, who had remained relatively calm until now, for instead of running after the man himself, or at least not hindering Gregor in his pursuit, he seized in his right hand the walking stick which the chief clerk had left behind on a chair, together with a hat and greatcoat, snatched in his left hand a large newspaper from the table and began stamping his feet and flourishing the stick and the newspaper to drive Gregor back into his room. No entreaty of Gregor's availed, indeed no entreaty was even understood, however humbly he bent his head his father only stamped on the floor the more loudly. Behind his father his mother had torn open a window, despite the cold weather, and was leaning far out of it with her face in her hands. A strong draught set in from the street to the staircase, the window curtains blew in, the newspapers on the table fluttered, stray pages whisked over the floor. Pitilessly Gregor's father drove him back, hissing and crying "Shoo!" like a savage. But Gregor was quite unpracticed in walking backwards, it really was a slow business. If he only had a chance to turn round he could get back to his room at once, but he was afraid of exasperating his father by the slowness of such a rotation and at any moment the stick in his father's hand might hit him a fatal blow on the back or on the head. In the end, however, nothing else was left for him to do since to his horror he observed that in moving backwards he could not even control the direction he took; and so, keeping an anxious eye on his father all the time over his shoulder, he began to turn round as quickly as he could, which was in reality very slowly. Perhaps his father noted his good intentions, for he did not interfere except every now and then to help him in the manoeuvre from a distance with the point of the stick. If only he would have stopped making that unbearable hissing noise! It made Gregor quite lose his head. He had turned almost completely round when the hissing noise so distracted him that he even turned a little the wrong way again. But when at last his head was fortunately right in front of the doorway, it appeared that his body was too broad simply to get through the opening. His father, of course, in his present mood was far from thinking of such a thing as opening the other half of the door, to let Gregor have enough space. He had merely the fixed idea of driving Gregor back into his room as quickly as possible. He would never have suffered Gregor to make the circumstantial preparations for standing up on end and perhaps slipping his way through the door. Maybe he was now making more noise than ever to urge Gregor forward, as if no obstacle impeded him; to Gregor, anyhow, the noise in his rear sounded no longer like the voice of one single father; this was really no joke, and Gregor thrust himself—come what might—into the doorway. One side of his body rose up, he was tilted at an angle in the doorway, his flank was quite bruised, horrid blotches stained the white door, soon he was stuck fast and, left to himself, could not have moved at all, his legs on one side fluttered trembling in the air, those on the other were crushed painfully to the floor—when from behind his father gave him a strong push which was literally a deliverance and he flew far into the room, bleeding freely. The door was slammed behind him with the stick, and then at last there was silence.

II

Not until it was twilight did Gregor awake out of a deep sleep, more like a swoon than a sleep. He would certainly have waked up of his own accord not much later, for he felt himself sufficiently rested and well-slept, but it seemed to him as if a fleeting step and a cautious shutting of the door leading into the hall had aroused him. The electric lights in the street cast a pale sheen here and there on the ceiling and the upper surfaces of the furniture, but down below, where he lay, it was dark. Slowly, awkwardly trying out his feelers, which he now first learned to appreciate, he pushed his way to the door to see what had been happening there. His left side felt like one single long, unpleasantly tense scar, and he had actually to limp on his two rows of legs. One little leg, moreover, had been severely damaged in the course of that morning's events—it was almost a miracle that only one had been damaged—and trailed uselessly behind him.

He had reached the door before he discovered what had really drawn him to it: the smell of food. For there stood a basin filled with fresh milk in which floated little sops of white bread. He could almost have laughed with joy, since he was now still hungrier than in the morning, and he dipped his head almost over the eyes straight into the milk. But soon in disappointment he withdrew it again; not only did he find it difficult to feed because of his tender left side—and he could only feed with the palpitating collaboration of his whole body—he did not like the milk either, although milk had been his favorite drink and that was certainly why his sister had set it there for him, indeed it was almost with repulsion that he turned away from the basin and crawled back to the middle of the room.

He could see through the crack of the door that the gas was turned on in the living room, but while usually at this time his father made a habit of reading the afternoon newspaper in a loud voice to his mother and occasionally to his sister as well, not a sound was now to be heard. Well, perhaps his father had recently given up this habit of reading aloud, which his sister had mentioned so often in conversation and in her letters. But there was the same silence all around, although the flat was certainly not empty of occupants. "What a quiet life our family has been leading," said Gregor to himself, and as he sat there motionless staring into the darkness he felt great pride in the fact that he had been able to provide such a life for his parents and sister in such a fine flat. But what if all the quiet, the comfort, the contentment were now to end in horror? To keep himself from being lost in such thoughts Gregor took refuge in movement and crawled up and down the room.

Once during the long evening one of the side doors was opened a little and quickly shut again, later the other side door too; some-one had apparently wanted to come in and then thought better of it. Gregor now stationed himself immediately before the living room door, determined to persuade any hesitating visitor to come in or at least to discover who it might be; but the door was not opened again and he waited in vain. In the early morning, when the doors were locked, they had all wanted to come in, now that he had opened one door and the other had apparently been opened during the day, no one came in and even the keys were on the other side of the doors.

It was late at night before the gas went out in the living room, and Gregor could easily tell that his parents and his sister had all stayed awake until then, for he could clearly hear the three of them stealing away on tiptoe. No one was likely to visit him, not until the morning, that was certain; so he had plenty of time to meditate at his leisure on how he was to arrange his life afresh. But the lofty, empty room in which he had to lie flat on the floor filled him with an apprehension he could not account for, since it had been his very own room for the past five years—and with a half-unconscious action, not without a slight feeling of shame, he scuttled under the sofa, where he felt comfortable at once, although his back was a little cramped and he could not lift his head up, and his only regret was that his body was too broad to get the whole of it under the sofa.

He stayed there all night, spending the time partly in a light slumber, from which his hunger kept waking him up with a start, and partly in worrying and sketching vague hopes, which all led to the same conclusion, that he must lie low for the present and, by exercising patience and the utmost consideration, help the family to bear the inconvenience he was bound to cause them in his present condition.

Very early in the morning, it was still almost night, Gregor had the chance to test the strength of his new resolutions, for his sister, nearly fully dressed, opened the door from the hall and peered in. She did not see him at once, yet when she caught sight of him under the sofa—well, he had to be somewhere, he couldn't have flown away, could he?—she was so startled that without being able to help it she slammed the door shut again. But as if regretting her behavior she opened the door again immediately and came in on tiptoe, as if she were visiting an invalid or even a stranger. Gregor had pushed his head forward to the very edge of the sofa and watched her. Would she notice that he had left the milk standing, and not for lack of hunger, and would she bring in some other kind of food more to his taste? If she did not do it of her own accord, he would rather starve than draw her attention to the fact, although he felt a wild impulse to dart out from under the sofa, throw himself at her feet and beg her for something to eat. But his sister at once noticed, with surprise, that the basin was still full, except for a little milk that had been spilt all around it, she lifted it immediately, not with her bare hands, true, but with a cloth and carried it away. Gregor was wildly curious to know what she would bring instead, and made various speculations about it. Yet what she actually did next, in the goodness of her heart, he could never have guessed at. To find out what he liked she brought him a whole selection of food, all set out on an old newspaper. There were old, half-decayed vegetables, bones from last night's supper covered with a white sauce that had thickened; some raisins and almonds; a piece of cheese that Gregor would have called uneatable two days ago; a dry roll of bread, a buttered roll, and a roll both buttered and salted. Besides all that, she set down again the same basin, into which she had poured some water, and which was apparently to be reserved for his exclusive use. And with fine tact, knowing that Gregor would not eat in her presence, she withdrew quickly and even turned the key, to let him understand that he could take his ease as much as he liked. Gregor's legs all whizzed towards the food. His wounds must have healed completely, moreover, for he felt no disability, which amazed him and made him reflect how more than a month ago he had cut one finger a little with a knife and had still suffered pain from the wound only the day before yesterday. Am I less sensitive now? he thought, and sucked greedily at the cheese, which above all the other edibles attracted him at once and strongly. One after another and with tears of satisfaction in his eyes he quickly devoured the cheese, the vegetables and the sauce; the fresh food, on the other hand, had no charms for him, he could not even stand the smell of it and actually dragged away to some little distance the things he could eat. He had long finished his meal and was only lying lazily on the same spot when his sister turned the key slowly as a sign for him to retreat. That roused him at once, although he was nearly asleep, and he hurried under the sofa again. But it took considerable self-control for him to stay under the sofa, even for the short time his sister was in the room, since the large meal had swollen his body somewhat and he was so cramped he could hardly breathe. Slight attacks of breathlessness afflicted him and his eyes were starting a little out of his head as he watched his unsuspecting sister sweeping together with a broom not only the remains of what he had eaten but even the things he had not touched, as if these were now of no use to anyone, and hastily shoveling it all into a bucket, which she covered with a wooden lid and carried away. Hardly had she turned her back when Gregor came from under the sofa and stretched and puffed himself out.

In this manner Gregor was fed, once in the early morning while his parents and the servant girl were still asleep, and a second time after they had all had their midday dinner, for then his parents took a short nap and the servant girl could be sent out on some errand or other by his sister. Not that they would have wanted him to starve, of course, but perhaps they could not have borne to know more about his feeding than from hearsay, perhaps too his sister wanted to spare them such little anxieties wherever possible, since they had quite enough to bear as it was.

Under what pretext the doctor and the locksmith had been got rid of on that first morning Gregor could not discover, for since what he said was not understood by the others it never struck any of them, not even his sister, that he could understand what they said, and so whenever his sister came into his room he had to content himself with hearing her utter only a sigh now and then and an occasional appeal to the saints. Later on, when she had got a little used to the situation—of course she could never get completely used to it—she sometimes threw out a remark which was kindly meant or could be so interpreted. "Well, he liked his dinner today," she would say when Gregor had made a good clearance of his food; and when he had not eaten, which gradually happened more and more often, she would say almost sadly: "Everything's been left standing again."

But although Gregor could get no news directly, he overheard a lot from the neighboring rooms, and as soon as voices were audible, he would run to the door of the room concerned and press his whole body against it. In the first few days especially there was no conversation that did not refer to him somehow, even if only indirectly. For two whole days there were family consultations at every mealtime about what should be done; but also between meals the same subject was discussed, for there were always at least two members of the family at home, since no one wanted to be alone in the flat and to leave it quite empty was unthinkable. And on the very first of these days the household cook—it was not quite clear what and how much she knew of the situation—went down on her knees to his mother and begged leave to go, and when she departed, a quarter of an hour later, gave thanks for her dismissal with tears in her eyes as if for the greatest benefit that could have been conferred on her, and without any prompting swore a solemn oath that she would never say a single word to anyone about what had happened.

Now Gregor's sister had to cook too, helping her mother; true, the cooking did not amount to much, for they ate scarcely anything. Gregor was always hearing one of the family vainly urging another to eat and getting no answer but: "Thanks, I've had all I want," or something similar. Perhaps they drank nothing either. Time and again his sister kept asking his father if he wouldn't like some beer and offered kindly to go and fetch it herself, and when he made no answer suggested that she could ask the concierge to fetch it, so that he need feel no sense of obligation, but then a round "No" came from his father and no more was said about it.

In the course of that very first day Gregor's father explained the family's financial position and prospects to both his mother and his sister. Now and then he rose from the table to get some voucher or memorandum out of the small safe he had rescued from the collapse of his business five years earlier. One could hear him opening the complicated lock and rustling papers out and shutting it again. This statement made by his father was the first cheerful information

Gregor had heard since his imprisonment. He had been of the opinion that nothing at all was left over from his father's business, at least his father had never said anything to the contrary, and of course he had not asked him directly. At that time Gregor's sole desire was to do his utmost to help the family to forget as soon as possible the catastrophe which had overwhelmed the business and thrown them all into a state of complete despair. And so he had set to work with unusual ardor and almost overnight had become a commercial traveler instead of a little clerk, with of course much greater chances of earning money, and his success was immediately translated into good round coin which he could lay on the table for his amazed and happy family. These had been fine times, and they had never recurred, at least not with the same sense of glory, although later on Gregor had earned so much money that he was able to meet the expenses of the whole household and did so. They had simply got used to it, both the family and Gregor; the money was gratefully accepted and gladly given, but there was no special uprush of warm feeling. With his sister alone had he remained intimate, and it was a secret plan of his that she, who loved music, unlike himself, and could play movingly on the violin, should be sent next year to study at the Conservatorium, despite the great expense that would entail, which must be made up in some other way. During his brief visits home the Conservatorium was often mentioned in the talks he had with his sister, but always merely as a beautiful dream which could never come true, and his parents discouraged even these innocent references to it; yet Gregor had made up his mind firmly about it and meant to announce the fact with due solemnity on Christmas Day.

Such were the thoughts, completely futile in his present condition, that went through his head as he stood clinging upright to the door and listening. Sometimes out of sheer weariness he had to give up listening and let his head fall negligently against the door, but he always had to pull himself together again at once, for even the slight sound his head made was audible next door and brought all conversation to a stop. "What can he be doing now?" his father would say after a while, obviously turning towards the door, and only then would the interrupted conversation gradually be set going again.

Gregor was now informed as amply as he could wish—for his father tended to repeat himself in his explanations, partly because it was a long time since he had handled such matters and partly because his mother could not always grasp things at once—that a certain amount of investments, a very small amount it was true, had survived the wreck of their fortunes and had even increased a little because the dividends had not been touched meanwhile. And besides that, the money Gregor brought home every month—he had kept only a few dollars for himself—had never been quite used up and now amounted to a small capital sum. Behind the door Gregor nodded his head eagerly, rejoiced at this evidence of unexpected thrift and foresight. True, he could really have paid off some more of his father's debts to the chief with his extra money, and so brought much nearer the day on which he could quit his job, but doubtless it was better the way his father had arranged it.

Yet this capital was by no means sufficient to let the family live on the interest of it; for one year, perhaps, or at the most two, they could live on the principal, that was all. It was simply a sum that ought not to be touched and should be kept for a rainy day; money for living expenses would have to be earned. Now his father was still hale enough but an old man, and he had done no work for the past five years and could not be expected to do much; during these five years, the first years of leisure in his laborious though unsuccessful life, he had grown rather fat and become sluggish. And Gregor's old mother, how was she to earn a living with her asthma, which troubled her even when she walked through the flat and kept her lying on a sofa every other day panting for breath beside an open window? And was his sister to earn her bread, she who was still a child of seventeen and whose life hitherto had been so pleasant, consisting as it did in dressing herself nicely, sleeping long, helping in the housekeeping, going out to a few modest entertainments and above all playing the violin? At first whenever the need for earning money was mentioned Gregor let go his hold on the door and threw himself down on the cool leather sofa beside it, he felt so hot with shame and grief.

Often he just lay there the long nights through without sleeping at all, scrabbling for hours on the leather. Or he nerved himself to the great effort of pushing an armchair to the window, then crawled up over the window sill and, braced against the chair, leaned against the window panes, obviously in some recollection of the sense of freedom that looking out of a window always used to give him. For in reality day by day things that were even a little way off were growing dimmer to his sight; the hospital across the street, which he used to execrate for being all too often before his eyes, was now quite beyond his range of vision, and if he had not known that he lived in

Charlotte Street, a quiet street but still a city street, he might have believed that his window gave on a desert waste where gray sky and gray land blended indistinguishably into each other. His quick-witted sister only needed to observe twice that the armchair stood by the window; after that whenever she had tidied the room she always pushed the chair back to the same place at the window and even left the inner casements open.

If he could have spoken to her and thanked her for all she had to do for him, he could have borne her ministrations better; as it was, they oppressed him. She certainly tried to make as light as possible of whatever was disagreeable in her task, and as time went on she succeeded, of course, more and more, but time brought more enlightenment to Gregor too. The very way she came in distressed him. Hardly was she in the room when she rushed to the window, without even taking time to shut the door, careful as she was usually to shield the sight of Gregor's room from the others, and as if she were almost suffocating tore the casements open with hasty fingers, standing then in the open draught for a while even in the bitterest cold and drawing deep breaths. This noisy scurry of hers upset Gregor twice a day; he would crouch trembling under the sofa all the time, knowing quite well that she would certainly have spared him such a disturbance had she found it at all possible to stay in his presence without opening the window.

On one occasion, about a month after Gregor's metamorphosis, when there was surely no reason for her to be still startled at his appearance, she came a little earlier than usual and found him gazing out of the window, quite motionless, and thus well placed to look like a bogey. Gregor would not have been surprised had she not come in at all, for she could not immediately open the window while he was there, but not only did she retreat, she jumped back as if in alarm and banged the door shut; a stranger might well have thought that he had been lying in wait for her there meaning to bite her. Of course he hid himself under the sofa at once, but he had to wait until midday before she came again, and she seemed more ill at ease than usual. This made him realize how repulsive the sight of him still was to her, and that it was bound to go on being repulsive, and what an effort it must cost her not to run away even from the sight of the small portion of his body that stuck out from under the sofa. In order to spare her that, therefore, one day he carried a sheet on his back to the sofa—it cost him four hours' labor—and arranged it there in such a way as to hide him completely, so that even if she were to bend down she could not see him. Had she considered the sheet unnecessary, she would certainly have stripped it off the sofa again, for it was clear enough that this curtaining and confining of himself was not likely to conduce Gregor's comfort, but she left it where it was, and Gregor even fancied that he caught a thankful glance from her eye when he lifted the sheet carefully a very little with his head to see how she was taking the new arrangement.

For the first fortnight his parents could not bring themselves to the point of entering his room, and he often heard them expressing their appreciation of his sister's activities, whereas formerly they had frequently scolded her for being as they thought a somewhat useless daughter. But now, both of them often waited outside the door, his father and his mother, while his sister tidied his room, and as soon as she came out she had to tell them exactly how things were in the room, what Gregor had eaten, how he had conducted himself this time and whether there was not perhaps some slight improvement in his condition. His mother, moreover, began relatively soon to want to visit him, but his father and sister dissuaded her at first with arguments which Gregor listened to very attentively and altogether approved. Later, however, she had to be held back by main force, and when she cried out: "Do let me in to Gregor, he is my unfortunate son! Can't you understand that I must go to him?" Gregor thought that it might be well to have her come in, not every day, of course, but perhaps once a week; she understood things, after all, much better than his sister, who was only a child despite the efforts she was making and had perhaps taken on so difficult a task merely out of childish thoughtlessness.

Gregor's desire to see his mother was soon fulfilled. During the daytime he did not want to show himself at the window, out of consideration for his parents, but he could not crawl very far around the few square yards of floor space he had, nor could he bear lying quietly at rest all during the night, while he was fast losing any interest he had ever taken in food, so that for mere recreation he had formed the habit of crawling crisscross over the walls and ceiling. He especially enjoyed hanging suspended from the ceiling; it was much better than lying on the floor; one could breathe more freely; one's body swung and rocked lightly; and in the almost blissful absorption induced by this suspension it could happen to his own surprise that he let go and fell plump on the floor. Yet he now had his body much better under control than formerly, and even such a big fall did him no harm. His sister at once remarked the new distraction

Gregor had found for himself—he left traces behind him of the sticky stuff on his soles wherever he crawled—and she got the idea in her head of giving him as wide a field as possible to crawl in and of removing the pieces of furniture that hindered him, above all the chest of drawers and the writing desk. But that was more than she could manage all by herself; she did not dare ask her father to help her; and as for the servant girl, a young creature of sixteen who had had the courage to stay on after the cook's departure, she could not be asked to help, for she had begged as an especial favor that she might keep the kitchen door locked and open it only on a definite summons; so there was nothing left but to apply to her mother at an hour when her father was out. And the old lady did come, with exclamations of joyful eagerness, which, however, died away at the door of Gregor's room. Gregor's sister, of course, went in first, to see that everything was in order before letting his mother enter. In great haste Gregor pulled the sheet lower and rucked it more in folds so that it really looked as if it had been thrown accidentally over the sofa. And this time he did not peer out from under it; he renounced the pleasure of seeing his mother on this occasion and was only glad that she had come at all. "Come in, he's out of sight," said his sister, obviously leading her mother in by the hand. Gregor could now hear the two women struggling to shift the heavy old chest from its place, and his sister claiming the greater part of the labor for herself, without listening to the admonitions of her mother who feared she might overstrain herself. It took a long time. After at least a quarter of an hour's tugging his mother objected that the chest had better be left where it was, for in the first place it was too heavy and could never be got out before his father came home, and standing in the middle of the room like that it would only hamper Gregor's movements, while in the second place it was not at all certain that removing the furniture would be doing a service to Gregor. She was inclined to think to the contrary; the sight of the naked walls made her own heart heavy, and why shouldn't Gregor have the same feeling, considering that he had been used to his furniture for so long and might feel forlorn without it. "And doesn't it look," she concluded in a low voice—in fact she had been almost whispering all the time as if to avoid letting Gregor, whose exact whereabouts she did not know, hear even the tones of her voice, for she was convinced that he could not understand her words—"doesn't it look as if we were showing him, by taking away his furniture, that we have given up hope of his ever getting better and are just leaving him coldly to himself? I think it would be best to keep his room exactly as it has always been, so that when he comes back to us he will find everything unchanged and be able all the more easily to forget what has happened in between."

On hearing these words from his mother Gregor realized that the lack of all direct human speech for the past two months together with the monotony of family life must have confused his mind, otherwise he could not account for the fact that he had quite earnestly looked forward to having his room emptied of furnishing. Did he really want his warm room, so comfortably fitted with old family furniture, to be turned into a naked den in which he would certainly be able to crawl unhampered in all directions but at the price of shedding simultaneously all recollection of his human background? He had indeed been so near the brink of forgetfulness that only the voice of his mother, which he had not heard for so long, had drawn him back from it. Nothing should be taken out of his room; everything must stay as it was; he could not dispense with the good influence of the furniture on his state of mind; and even if the furniture did hamper him in his senseless crawling round and round, that was no drawback but a great advantage.

Unfortunately his sister was of the contrary opinion; she had grown accustomed, and not without reason, to consider herself an expert in Gregor's affairs as against her parents, and so her mother's advice was now enough to make her determined on the removal not only of the chest and the writing desk, which had been her first intention, but of all the furniture except the indispensable sofa. This determination was not, of course, merely the outcome of childish recalcitrance and of the self-confidence she had recently developed so unexpectedly and at such cost; she had in fact perceived that Gregor needed a lot of space to crawl about in, while on the other hand he never used the furniture at all, so far as could be seen. Another factor might have been also the enthusiastic temperament of an adolescent girl, which seeks to indulge itself on every opportunity and which now tempted Grete to exaggerate the horror of her brother's circumstances in order that she might do all the more for him. In a room where Gregor lorded it all alone over empty walls no one save herself was likely ever to set foot.

And so she was not to be moved from her resolve by her mother who seemed moreover to be ill at ease in Gregor's room and therefore unsure of herself, was soon reduced to silence and helped her daughter as best she could to push the chest outside. Now, Gregor could do without the chest, if need be, but the writing desk he must retain. As soon as the two women had got the chest out of his room, groaning as they pushed it, Gregor stuck his head out from under the sofa to see how he might intervene as kindly and cautiously as possible. But as bad luck would have it, his mother was the first to return, leaving Grete clasping the chest in the room next door where she was trying to shift it all by herself, without of course moving it from the spot. His mother however was not accustomed to the sight of him, it might sicken her and so in alarm Gregor backed quickly to the other end of the sofa, yet could not prevent the sheet from swaying a little in front. That was enough to put her on the alert. She paused, stood still for a moment and then went back to Grete.

Although Gregor kept reassuring himself that nothing out of the way was happening, but only a few bits of furniture were being changed round, he soon had to admit that all this trotting to and fro of the two women, their little ejaculations and the scraping of furniture along the floor affected him like a vast disturbance coming from all sides at once, and however much he tucked in his head and legs and cowered to the very floor he was bound to confess that he would not be able to stand it for long. They were clearing his room out; taking away everything he loved; the chest in which he kept his fret saw and other tools was already dragged off; they were now loosening the writing desk which had almost sunk into the floor, the desk at which he had done all his homework when he was at the commercial academy, at the grammar school before that, and, yes, even at the primary school—he had no more time to waste in weighing the good intentions of the two women, whose existence he had by now almost forgotten, for they were so exhausted that they were laboring in silence and nothing could be heard but the heavy scuffling of their feet.

And so he rushed out—the women were just leaning against the writing desk in the next room to give themselves a breather—and four times changed his direction, since he really did not know what to rescue first, then on the wall opposite, which was already otherwise cleared, he was struck by the picture of the lady muffled in so much fur and quickly crawled up to it and pressed himself to the glass, which was a good surface to hold on to and comforted his hot belly. This picture at least, which was entirely hidden beneath him, was going to be removed by nobody. He turned his head towards the door of the living room so as to observe the women when they came back.

They had not allowed themselves much of a rest and were already coming; Grete had twined her arm round her mother and was almost supporting her. "Well, what shall we take now?" said Grete, looking round. Her eyes met Gregor's from the wall. She kept her composure, presumably because of her mother, bent her head down to her mother, to keep her from looking up, and said, although in a fluttering, unpremeditated voice: "Come, hadn't we better go back to the living room for a moment?" Her intentions were clear enough to Gregor, she wanted to bestow her mother in safety and then chase him down from the wall. Well, just let her try it! He clung to his picture and would not give it up. He would rather fly in Grete's face.

But Grete's words had succeeded in disquieting her mother, who took a step to one side, caught sight of the huge brown mass on the flowered wallpaper, and before she was really conscious that what she saw was Gregor screamed in a loud, hoarse voice: "Oh God, oh God!" fell with outspread arms over the sofa as if giving up and did not move. "Gregor!" cried his sister, shaking her fist and glaring at him. This was the first time she had directly addressed him since his metamorphosis. She ran into the next room for some aromatic essence with which to rouse her mother from her fainting fit. Gregor wanted to help too—there was still time to rescue the picture—but he was stuck fast to the glass and had to tear himself loose; he then ran after his sister into the next room as if he could advise her, as he used to do; but then had to stand helplessly behind her; she meanwhile searched among various small bottles and when she turned round started in alarm at the sight of him; one bottle fell on the floor and broke; a splinter of glass cut Gregor's face and some kind of corrosive medicine splashed him; without pausing a moment longer Grete gathered up all the bottles she could carry and ran to her mother with them; she banged the door shut with her foot. Gregor was now cut off from his mother, who was perhaps nearly dying because of him; he dared not open the door for fear of frightening away his sister, who had to stay with her mother; there was nothing he could do but wait; and harassed by self-reproach and worry he began now to crawl to and fro, over everything, walls, furniture and ceiling, and finally in his despair, when the whole room seemed to be reeling round him, fell down on to the middle of the big table.

A little while elapsed, Gregor was still lying there feebly and all around was quiet, perhaps that was a good omen. Then the doorbell rang. The servant girl was of course locked in her kitchen, and Grete would have to open the door. It was his father. "What's been happening?" were his first words; Grete's face must have told him everything. Grete answered in a muffled voice, apparently hiding her head on his breast: "Mother has been fainting, but she's better now. Gregor's broken loose." "Just what I expected," said his father, "just what I've been telling you, but you women would never listen." It was clear to Gregor that his father had taken the worst interpretation of Grete's all too brief statement and was assuming that Gregor had been guilty of some violent act. Therefore Gregor must now try to propitiate his father, since he had neither time nor means for an explanation. And so he fled to the door of his own room and crouched against it, to let his father see as soon as he came in from the hall that his son had the good intention of getting back into his room immediately and that it was not necessary to drive him there, but that if only the door were opened he would disappear at once.

Yet his father was not in the mood to perceive such fine distinctions. "Ah!" he cried as soon as he appeared, in a tone which sounded at once angry and exultant. Gregor drew his head back from the door and lifted it to look at his father. Truly, this was not the father he had imagined to himself; admittedly he had been too absorbed of late in his new recreation of crawling over the ceiling to take the same interest as before in what was happening elsewhere in the flat, and he ought really to be prepared for some changes. And yet, and yet, could that be his father? The man who used to lie wearily sunk in bed whenever Gregor set out on a business journey; who welcomed him back of an evening lying in a long chair in a dressing gown; who could not really rise to his feet but only lifted his arms in greeting, and on the rare occasions when he did go out with his family, on one or two Sundays a year and on high holidays, walked between Gregor and his mother, who were slow walkers anyhow, even more slowly than they did, muffled in his old greatcoat, shuffling laboriously forward with the help of his crook-handled stick which he set down most cautiously at every step and, whenever he wanted to say anything, nearly always came to a full stop and gathered his escort around him? Now he was standing there in fine shape; dressed in a smart blue uniform with gold buttons, such as bank messengers wear; his strong double chin bulged over the stiff high collar of his jacket; from under his bushy eyebrows his black eyes darted fresh and penetrating glances; his onetime tangled white hair had been combed flat on either side of a shining and carefully exact parting. He pitched his cap, which bore a gold monogram, probably the badge of some bank, in a wide sweep across the whole room on to a sofa and with the tail-ends of his jacket thrown back, his hands in his trouser pockets, advanced with a grim visage towards Gregor. Likely enough he did not himself know what he meant to do; at any rate he lifted his feet uncommonly high, and Gregor was dumbfounded at the enormous size of his shoe soles. But Gregor could not risk standing up to him, aware as he had been from the very first day of his new life that his father believed only the severest measures suitable for dealing with him. And so he ran before his father, stopping when he stopped and scuttling forward again when his father made any kind of move. In this way they circled the room several times without anything decisive happening; indeed the whole operation did not even look like a pursuit because it was carried out so slowly. And so Gregor did not leave the floor, for he feared that his father might take as a piece of peculiar wickedness any excursion of his over the walls or the ceiling. All the same, he could not stay this course much longer, for while his father took one step he had to carry out a whole series of movements. He was already beginning to feel breathless, just as in his former life his lungs had not been very dependable. As he was staggering along, trying to concentrate his energy on running, hardly keeping his eyes open; in his dazed state never even thinking of any other escape than simply going forward; and having almost forgotten that the walls were free to him, which in this room were well provided with finely carved pieces of furniture full of knobs and crevices—suddenly something lightly flung landed close behind him and rolled before him. It was an apple; a second apple followed immediately; Gregor came to a stop in alarm; there was no point in running on, for his father was determined to bombard him. He had filled his pockets with fruit from the dish on the sideboard and was now shying apple after apple, without taking particularly good aim for the moment. The small red apples rolled about the floor as if magnetized and cannoned into each other. An apple thrown without much force grazed Gregor's back and glanced off harmlessly. But another following immediately landed right on his back and sank in; Gregor wanted to drag himself forward, as if this startling, incredible pain could be left behind him; but he felt as if nailed to the spot and flattened himself out in a complete derangement of all his senses. With his last conscious look he saw the door of his room being torn open and his mother rushing out ahead of his screaming sister, in her underbodice, for her daughter had loosened her clothing to let her breathe more freely and recover from her swoon, he saw his mother rushing towards his father, leaving one after another behind her on the floor her loosened petticoats, stumbling over her petticoats straight to his father and embracing him, in complete union with him—but here Gregor's sight began to fail—with her hands clasped round his father's neck as she begged for her son's life.

III

The serious injury done to Gregor, which disabled him for more than a month—the apple went on sticking in his body as a visible reminder, since no one ventured to remove it—seemed to have made even his father recollect that Gregor was a member of the family, despite his present unfortunate and repulsive shape, and ought not to be treated as an enemy, that, on the contrary, family duty required the suppression of disgust and the exercise of patience, nothing but patience.

And although his injury had impaired, probably for ever, his power of movement, and for the time being it took him long, long minutes to creep across his room like an old invalid—there was no question now of crawling up the wall—yet in his own opinion he was sufficiently compensated for this worsening of his condition by the fact that towards evening the living-room door, which he used to watch intently for an hour or two beforehand, was always thrown open, so that lying in the darkness of his room, invisible to the family, he could see them all at the lamp-lit table and listen to their talk, by general consent as it were, very different from his earlier eavesdropping.

True, their intercourse lacked the lively character of former times, which he had always called to mind with a certain wistfulness in the small hotel bedrooms where he had been wont to throw himself down, tired out, on damp bedding. They were now mostly very silent. Soon after supper his father would fall asleep in his armchair; his mother and sister would admonish each other to be silent; his mother, bending low over the lamp, stitched at fine sewing for an underwear firm; his sister, who had taken a job as a salesgirl, was learning shorthand and French in the evenings on the chance of bettering herself. Sometimes his father woke up, and as if quite unaware that he had been sleeping said to his mother: "What a lot of sewing you're doing today!" and at once fell asleep again, while the two women exchanged a tired smile.

With a kind of mulishness his father persisted in keeping his uniform on even in the house; his dressing gown hung uselessly on its peg and he slept fully dressed where he sat, as if he were ready for service at any moment and even here only at the beck and call of his superior. As a result, his uniform, which was not brand-new to start with, began to look dirty, despite all the loving care of the mother and sister to keep it clean, and Gregor often spent whole evenings gazing at the many greasy spots on the garment, gleaming with gold buttons always in a high state of polish, in which the old man sat sleeping in extreme discomfort and yet quite peacefully.

As soon as the clock struck ten his mother tried to rouse his father with gentle words and to persuade him after that to get into bed, for sitting there he could not have a proper sleep and that was what he needed most, since he had to go to duty at six. But with the mulishness that had obsessed him since he became a bank messenger he always insisted on staying longer at the table, although he regularly fell asleep again and in the end only with the greatest trouble could be got out of his armchair and into his bed. However insistently Gregor's mother and sister kept urging him with gentle reminders, he would go on slowly shaking his head for a quarter of an hour, keeping his eyes shut, and refuse to get to his feet. The mother plucked at his sleeve, whispering endearments in his ear, the sister left her lessons to come to her mother's help, but Gregor's father was not to be caught. He would only sink down deeper in his chair. Not until the two women hoisted him up by the armpits did he open his eyes and look at them both, one after the other, usually with the remark: "This is a life. This is the peace and quiet of my old age." And leaning on the two of them he would heave himself up, with difficulty, as if he were a great burden to himself, suffer them to lead him as far as the door and then wave them off and go on alone, while the mother abandoned her needlework and the sister her pen in order to run after him and help him farther.

Who could find time, in this overworked and tired-out family, to bother about Gregor more than was absolutely needful? The household was reduced more and more; the servant girl was turned off; a gigantic bony charwoman with white hair flying round her head came in morning and evening to do the rough work; everything else was done by Gregor's mother, as well as great piles of sewing. Even various family ornaments, which his mother and sister used to wear with pride at parties and celebrations, had to be sold, as Gregor discovered of an evening from hearing them all discuss the prices obtained. But what they lamented most was the fact that they could not leave the flat which was much too big for their present circumstances, because they could not think of any way to shift Gregor. Yet Gregor saw well enough that consideration for him was not the main difficulty preventing the removal, for they could have easily shifted him in some suitable box with a few air holes in it; what really kept them from moving into another flat was rather their own complete hopelessness and the belief that they had been singled out for a misfortune such as had never happened to any of their relations or acquaintances. They fulfilled to the uttermost all that the world demands of poor people, the father fetched breakfast for the small clerks in the bank, the mother devoted her energy to making underwear for strangers, the sister trotted to and fro behind the counter at the behest of customers, but more than this they had not the strength to do. And the wound in Gregor's back began to nag at him afresh when his mother and sister, after getting his father into bed, came back again, left their work lying, drew close to each other and sat cheek by cheek; when his mother, pointing towards his room, said: "Shut that door now, Grete," and he was left again in darkness, while next door the women mingled their tears or perhaps sat dry-eyed staring at the table.

Gregor hardly slept at all by night or by day. He was often haunted by the idea that next time the door opened he would take the family's affairs in hand again just as he used to do; once more, after this long interval, there appeared in his thoughts the figures of the chief and the chief clerk, the commercial travelers and the apprentices, the porter who was so dull-witted, two or three friends in other firms, a chambermaid in one of the rural hotels, a sweet and fleeting memory, a cashier in a milliner's shop, whom he had wooed earnestly but too slowly—they all appeared, together with strangers or people he had quite forgotten, but instead of helping him and his family they were one and all unapproachable and he was glad when they vanished. At other times he would not be in the mood to bother about his family, he was only filled with rage at the way they were neglecting him, and although he had no clear idea of what he might care to eat he would make plans for getting into the larder to take the food that was after all his due, even if he were not hungry. His sister no longer took thought to bring him what might especially please him, but in the morning and at noon before she went to business hurriedly pushed into his room with her foot any food that was available, and in the evening cleared it out again with one sweep of the broom, heedless of whether it had been merely tasted, or—as most frequently happened—left untouched. The cleaning of his room, which she now did always in the evenings, could not have been more hastily done. Streaks of dirt stretched along the walls, here and there lay balls of dust and filth. At first Gregor used to station himself in some particularly filthy corner when his sister arrived, in order to reproach her with it, so to speak. But he could have sat there for weeks without getting her to make any improvements; she could see the dirt as well as he did, but she had simply made up her mind to leave it alone. And yet, with a touchiness that was new to her, which seemed anyhow to have infected the whole family, she jealously guarded her claim to be the sole caretaker of Gregor's room. His mother once subjected his room to a thorough cleaning, which was achieved only by means of several buckets of water—all this dampness of course upset Gregor too and he lay widespread, sulky and motionless on the sofa—but she was well punished for it. Hardly had his sister noticed the changed aspect of his room that evening than she rushed in high dudgeon into the living room and, despite the imploringly raised hands of her mother, burst into a storm of weeping, while her parents—her father had of course been startled out of his chair—looked on at first in helpless amazement; then they too began to go into action; the father reproached the mother on his right for not having left the cleaning of Gregor's room to his sister; shrieked at the sister on his left that never again was she to be allowed to clean Gregor's room; while the mother tried to pull the father into his bedroom, since he was beyond himself with agitation; the sister, shaken with sobs, then beat upon the table with her small fists; and Gregor hissed loudly with rage because not one of them thought of shutting the door to spare him such a spectacle and so much noise.

Still, even if the sister, exhausted by her daily work, had grown tired of looking after Gregor as she did formerly, there was no need for his mother's intervention or for Gregor's being neglected at all. The charwoman was there. This old widow, whose strong bony frame had enabled her to survive the worst a long life could offer, by no means recoiled from Gregor. Without being in the least curious she had once by chance opened the door of his room and at the sight of Gregor, who, taken by surprise, began to rush to and fro although no one was chasing him, merely stood there with her arms folded. From that time she never failed to open his door a little for a moment, morning and evening, to have a look at him. At first she even used to call him to her, with words which apparently she took to be friendly, such as: "Come along, then, you old dung beetle!" or "Look at the old dung beetle, then!" To such allocutions Gregor made no answer, but stayed motionless where he was, as if the door had never been opened. Instead of being allowed to disturb him so senselessly whenever the whim took her, she should rather have been ordered to clean out his room daily, that charwoman! Once, early in the morning—heavy rain was lashing on the windowpanes, perhaps a sign that spring was on the way—Gregor was so exasperated when she began addressing him again that he ran at her, as if to attack her, although slowly and feebly enough. But the charwoman instead of showing fright merely lifted high a chair that happened to be beside the door, and as she stood there with her mouth wide open it was clear that she meant to shut it only when she brought the chair down on Gregor's back. "So you're not coming any nearer?" she asked, as Gregor turned away again, and quietly put the chair back into the corner.

Gregor was now eating hardly anything. Only when he happened to pass the food laid out for him did he take a bit of something in his mouth as a pastime, kept it there for an hour at a time and usually spat it out again. At first he thought it was chagrin over the state of his room that prevented him from eating, yet he soon got used to the various changes in his room. It had become a habit in the family to push into his room things there was no room for elsewhere, and there were plenty of these now, since one of the rooms had been let to three lodgers. These serious gentlemen—all three of them with full beards, as Gregor once observed through a crack in the door—had a passion for order, not only in their own room but, since they were now members of the household, in all its arrangements, especially in the kitchen. Superfluous, not to say dirty, objects they could not bear. Besides, they had brought with them most of the furnishings they needed. For this reason many things could be dispensed with that it was no use trying to sell but that should not be thrown away either. All of them found their way into Gregor's room. The ash can likewise and the kitchen garbage can. Anything that was not needed for the moment was simply flung into Gregor's room by the charwoman, who did everything in a hurry; fortunately Gregor usually saw only the object, whatever it was, and the hand that held it. Perhaps she intended to take the things away again as time and opportunity offered, or to collect them until she could throw them all out in a heap, but in fact they just lay wherever she happened to throw them, except when Gregor pushed his way through the junk heap and shifted it somewhat, at first out of necessity, because he had not room enough to crawl, but later with increasing enjoyment, although after such excursions, being sad and weary to death, he would lie motionless for hours. And since the lodgers often ate their supper at home in the common living room, the living-room door stayed shut many an evening, yet Gregor reconciled himself quite easily to the shutting of the door, for often enough on evenings when it was opened he had disregarded it entirely and lain in the darkest corner of his room, quite unnoticed by the family. But on one occasion the charwoman left the door open a little and it stayed ajar even when the lodgers came in for supper and the lamp was lit. They set themselves at the top end of the table where formerly Gregor and his father and mother had eaten their meals, unfolded their napkins and took knife and fork in hand. At once his mother appeared in the other doorway with a dish of meat and close behind her his sister with a dish of potatoes piled high. The food steamed with a thick vapor. The lodgers bent over the food set before them as if to scrutinize it before eating, in fact the man in the middle, who seemed to pass for an authority with the other two, cut a piece of meat as it lay on the dish, obviously to discover if it were tender or should be sent back to the kitchen. He showed satisfaction, and Gregor's mother and sister, who had been watching anxiously, breathed freely and began to smile.

The family itself took its meals in the kitchen. None the less, Gregor's father came into the living room before going into the kitchen and with one prolonged bow, cap in hand, made a round of the table. The lodgers all stood up and murmured something in their beards. When they were alone again they ate their food in almost complete silence. It seemed remarkable to Gregor that among the various noises coming from the table he could always distinguish the sound of their masticating teeth, as if this were a sign to Gregor that one needed teeth in order to eat, and that with toothless jaws even of the finest make one could do nothing. "I'm hungry enough," said Gregor sadly to himself, "but not for that kind of food. How these lodgers are stuffing themselves, and here am I dying of starvation!"

On that very evening—during the whole of his time there Gregor could not remember ever having heard the violin—the sound of violin-playing came from the kitchen. The lodgers had already finished their supper, the one in the middle had brought out a newspaper and given the other two a page apiece, and now they were leaning back at ease reading and smoking. When the violin began to play they pricked up their ears, got to their feet, and went on tiptoe to the hall door where they stood huddled together. Their movements must have been heard in the kitchen, for Gregor's father called out: "Is the violin-playing disturbing you, gentlemen? It can be stopped at once." "On the contrary," said the middle lodger, "could not Fräulein Samsa come and play in this room, beside us, where it is much more convenient and comfortable?" "Oh certainly," cried Gregor's father, as if he were the violin-player. The lodgers came back into the living room and waited. Presently Gregor's father arrived with the music stand, his mother carrying the music and his sister with the violin. His sister quietly made everything ready to start playing; his parents, who had never let rooms before and so had an exaggerated idea of the courtesy due to lodgers, did not venture to sit down on their own chairs; his father leaned against the door, the right hand thrust between two buttons of his livery coat, which was formally buttoned up; but his mother was offered a chair by one of the lodgers and, since she left the chair just where he had happened to put it, sat down in a corner to one side.

Gregor's sister began to play; the father and mother, from either side, intently watched the movements of her hands. Gregor, attracted by the playing, ventured to move forward a little until his head was actually inside the living room. He felt hardly any surprise at his growing lack of consideration for the others; there had been a time when he prided himself on being considerate. And yet just on this occasion he had more reason than ever to hide himself, since owing to the amount of dust which lay thick in his room and rose into the air at the slightest movement, he too was covered with dust; fluff and hair and remnants of food trailed with him, caught on his back and along his sides; his indifference to everything was much too great for him to turn on his back and scrape himself clean on the carpet, as once he had done several times a day. And in spite of his condition, no shame deterred him from advancing a little over the spotless floor of the living room.

To be sure, no one was aware of him. The family was entirely absorbed in the violin-playing; the lodgers, however, who first of all had stationed themselves, hands in pockets, much too close behind the music stand so that they could all have read the music, which must have bothered his sister, had soon retreated to the window, half-whispering with downbent heads, and stayed there while his father turned an anxious eye on them. Indeed, they were making it more than obvious that they had been disappointed in their expectation of hearing good or enjoyable violin-playing, that they had had more than enough of the performance and only out of courtesy suffered a continued disturbance of their peace. From the way they all kept blowing the smoke of their cigars high in the air through nose and mouth one could divine their irritation. And yet Gregor's sister was playing so beautifully. Her face leaned sideways, intently and sadly her eyes followed the notes of music. Gregor crawled a little farther forward and lowered his head to the ground so that it might be possible for his eyes to meet hers. Was he an animal, that music had such an effect upon him? He felt as if the way were opening before him to the unknown nourishment he craved. He was determined to push forward till he reached his sister, to pull at her skirt and so let her know that she was to come into his room with her violin, for no one here appreciated her playing as he would appreciate it. He would never let her out of his room, at least, not so long as he lived; his frightful appearance would become, for the first time, useful to him; he would watch all the doors of his room at once and spit at intruders; but his sister should need no constraint, she should stay with him of her own free will; she should sit beside him on the sofa, bend down her ear to him and hear him confide that he had had the firm intention of sending her to the Conservatorium, and that, but for his mishap, last Christmas—surely Christmas was long past?—he would have announced it to everybody without allowing a single objection. After this confession his sister would be so touched that she would burst into tears, and Gregor would then raise himself to her shoulder and kiss her on the neck, which, now that she went to business, she kept free of any ribbon or collar.

"Mr. Samsa!" cried the middle lodger, to Gregor's father, and pointed, without wasting any more words, at Gregor, now working himself slowly forwards. The violin fell silent, the middle lodger first smiled to his friends with a shake of the head and then looked at Gregor again. Instead of driving Gregor out, his father seemed to think it more needful to begin by soothing down the lodgers, although they were not at all agitated and apparently found Gregor more entertaining than the violin-playing. He hurried towards them and, spreading out his arms, tried to urge them back into their own room and at the same time to block their view of Gregor. They now began to be really a little angry, one could not tell whether because of the old man's behavior or because it had just dawned on them that all unwittingly they had such a neighbor as Gregor next door. They demanded explanations of his father, they waved their arms like him, tugged uneasily at their beards, and only with reluctance backed towards their room. Meanwhile Gregor's sister, who stood there as if lost when her playing was so abruptly broken off, came to life again, pulled herself together all at once after standing for a while holding violin and bow in nervelessly hanging hands and staring at her music, pushed her violin into the lap of her mother, who was still sitting in her chair fighting asthmatically for breath, and ran into the lodgers' room to which they were now being shepherded by her father rather more quickly than before. One could see the pillows and blankets on the beds flying under her accustomed fingers and being laid in order. Before the lodgers had actually reached their room she had finished making the beds and slipped out.

The old man seemed once more to be so possessed by his mulish self-assertiveness that he was forgetting all the respect he should show to his lodgers. He kept driving them on and driving them on until in the very door of the bedroom the middle lodger stamped his foot loudly on the floor and so brought him to a halt. "I beg to announce," said the lodger, lifting one hand and looking also at Gregor's mother and sister, "that because of the disgusting conditions prevailing in this household and family"—here he spat on the floor with emphatic brevity—"I give you notice on the spot. Naturally I won't pay you a penny for the days I have lived here, on the contrary I shall consider bringing an action for damages against you, based on claims—believe me—that will be easily susceptible of proof." He ceased and stared straight in front of him, as if he expected something. In fact his two friends at once rushed into the breach with these words: "And we too give notice on the spot." On that he seized the door-handle and shut the door with a slam.

Gregor's father, groping with his hands, staggered forward and fell into his chair; it looked as if he were stretching himself there for his ordinary evening nap, but the marked jerkings of his head, which was as if uncontrollable, showed that he was far from asleep. Gregor had simply stayed quietly all the time on the spot where the lodgers had espied him. Disappointment at the failure of his plan, perhaps also the weakness arising from extreme hunger, made it impossible for him to move. He feared, with a fair degree of certainty, that at any moment the general tension would discharge itself in a combined attack upon him, and he lay waiting. He did not react even to the noise made by the violin as it fell off his mother's lap from under her trembling fingers and gave out a resonant note.

"My dear parents," said his sister, slapping her hand on the table by way of introduction, "things can't go on like this. Perhaps you don't realize that, but I do. I won't utter my brother's name in the presence of this creature, and so all I say is: we must try to get rid of it. We've tried to look after it and to put up with it as far as is humanly possible, and I don't think anyone could reproach us in the slightest."

"She is more than right," said Gregor's father to himself. His mother, who was still choking for lack of breath, began to cough hollowly into her hand with a wild look in her eyes.

His sister rushed over to her and held her forehead. His father's thoughts seemed to have lost their vagueness at Grete's words, he sat more upright, fingering his service cap that lay among the plates still lying on the table from the lodgers' supper, and from time to time looked at the still form of Gregor.

"We must try to get rid of it," his sister now said explicitly to her father, since her mother was coughing too much to hear a word, "it will be the death of both of you, I can see that coming. When one has to work as hard as we do, all of us, one can't stand this continual torment at home on top of it. At least I can't stand it any longer." And she burst into such a passion of sobbing that her tears dropped on her mother's face, where she wiped them off mechanically.

"My dear," said the old man sympathetically, and with evident understanding, "but what can we do?"

Gregor's sister merely shrugged her shoulders to indicate the feeling of helplessness that had now overmastered her during her weeping fit, in contrast to her former confidence.

"If he could understand us," said her father, half questioningly; Grete, still sobbing, vehemently waved a hand to show how unthinkable that was.

"If he could understand us," repeated the old man, shutting his eyes to consider his daughter's conviction that understanding was impossible, "then perhaps we might come to some agreement with him. But as it is—"

"He must go," cried Gregor's sister, "that's the only solution, Father. You must just try to get rid of the idea that this is Gregor. The fact that we've believed it for so long is the root of all our trouble. But how can it be Gregor? If this were Gregor, he would have realized long ago that human beings can't live with such a creature, and he'd have gone away on his own accord. Then we wouldn't have any brother, but we'd be able to go on living and keep his memory in honor. As it is, this creature persecutes us, drives away our lodgers, obviously wants the whole apartment to himself and would have us all sleep in the gutter. Just look, Father," she shrieked all at once, "he's at it again!" And in an access of panic that was quite incomprehensible to Gregor she even quitted her mother, literally thrusting the chair from her as if she would rather sacrifice her mother than stay so near to Gregor, and rushed behind her father, who also rose up, being simply upset by her agitation, and half-spread his arms out as if to protect her.

Yet Gregor had not the slightest intention of frightening anyone, far less his sister. He had only begun to turn round in order to crawl back to his room, but it was certainly a startling operation to watch, since because of his disabled condition he could not execute the difficult turning movements except by lifting his head and then bracing it against the floor over and over again. He paused and looked round. His good intentions seemed to have been recognized; the alarm had only been momentary. Now they were all watching him in melancholy silence. His mother lay in her chair, her legs stiffly outstretched and pressed together, her eyes almost closing for sheer weariness; his father and his sister were sitting beside each other, his sister's arm around the old man's neck.

Perhaps I can go on turning round now, thought Gregor, and began his labors again. He could not stop himself from panting with the effort, and had to pause now and then to take breath. Nor did anyone harass him, he was left entirely to himself. When he had completed the turn-round he began at once to crawl straight back. He was amazed at the distance separating him from his room and could not understand how in his weak state he had managed to accomplish the same journey so recently, almost without remarking it. Intent on crawling as fast as possible, he barely noticed that not a single word, not an ejaculation from his family, interfered with his progress. Only when he was already in the doorway did he turn his head round, not completely, for his neck muscles were getting stiff, but enough to see that nothing had changed behind him except that his sister had risen to her feet. His last glance fell on his mother, who was not quite overcome by sleep.

Hardly was he well inside his room when the door was hastily pushed shut, bolted and locked. The sudden noise in his rear startled him so much that his little legs gave beneath him. It was his sister who had shown such haste. She had been standing ready waiting and had made a light spring forward, Gregor had not even heard her coming, and she cried "At last!" to her parents as she turned the key in the lock.

"And what now?" said Gregor to himself, looking round in the darkness. Soon he made the discovery that he was now unable to stir a limb. This did not surprise him, rather it seemed unnatural that he should ever actually have been able to move on these feeble little legs. Otherwise he felt relatively comfortable. True, his whole body was aching, but it seemed that the pain was gradually growing less and would finally pass away. The rotting apple in his back and the inflamed area around it, all covered with soft dust, already hardly troubled him. He thought of his family with tenderness and love. The decision that he must disappear was one that he held to even more strongly than his sister, if that were possible. In this state of vacant and peaceful meditation he remained until the tower clock struck three in the morning. The first broadening of light in the world outside the window entered his consciousness once more. Then his head sank to the floor of its own accord and from his nostrils came the last faint flicker of his breath.

When the charwoman arrived early in the morning—what between her strength and her impatience she slammed all the doors so loudly, never mind how often she had been begged not to do so, that no one in the whole apartment could enjoy any quiet sleep after her arrival—she noticed nothing unusual as she took her customary peep into Gregor's room. She thought he was lying motionless on purpose, pretending to be in the sulks; she credited him with every kind of intelligence. Since she happened to have the long-handled broom in her hand she tried to tickle him up with it from the doorway. When that too produced no reaction she felt provoked and poked at him a little harder, and only when she had pushed him along the floor without meeting any resistance was her attention aroused. It did not take her long to establish the truth of the matter, and her eyes widened, she let out a whistle, yet did not waste much time over it but tore open the door of the Samsas' bedroom and yelled into the darkness at the top of her voice: "Just look at this, it's dead; it's lying here dead and done for!"

Mr. and Mrs. Samsa started up in their double bed and before they realized the nature of the charwoman's announcement had some difficulty in overcoming the shock of it. But then they got out of bed quickly, one on either side, Mr. Samsa throwing a blanket over his shoulders, Mrs. Samsa in nothing but her nightgown; in this array they entered Gregor's room. Meanwhile the door of the living room opened, too, where Grete had been sleeping since the advent of the lodgers; she was completely dressed as if she had not been to bed, which seemed to be confirmed also by the paleness of her face. "Dead?" said Mrs. Samsa, looking questioningly at the charwoman, although she could have investigated for herself, and the fact was obvious enough without investigation. "I should say so," said the charwoman, proving her words by pushing Gregor's corpse a long way to one side with her broomstick. Mrs. Samsa made a movement as if to stop her, but checked it. "Well," said Mr. Samsa, "now thanks be to God." He crossed himself, and the three women followed his example. Grete, whose eyes never left the corpse, said: "Just see how thin he was. It's such a long time since he's eaten anything. The food came out again just as it went in." Indeed, Gregor's body was completely flat and dry, as could only now be seen when it was no longer supported by the legs and nothing prevented one from looking closely at it.

"Come in beside us, Grete, for a little while," said Mrs. Samsa with a tremulous smile, and Grete, not without looking back at the corpse, followed her parents into their bedroom. The charwoman shut the door and opened the window wide. Although it was so early in the morning a certain softness was perceptible in the fresh air. After all, it was already the end of March.

The three lodgers emerged from their room and were surprised to see no breakfast; they had been forgotten. "Where's our breakfast?" said the middle lodger peevishly to the charwoman. But she put her finger to her lips and hastily, without a word, indicated by gestures that they should go into Gregor's room. They did so and stood, their hands in the pockets of their somewhat shabby coats, around Gregor's corpse in the room where it was now fully light.

At that the door of the Samsas' bedroom opened and Mr. Samsa appeared in his uniform, his wife on one arm, his daughter on the other. They all looked a little as if they had been crying; from time to time Grete hid her face on her father's arm.

"Leave my house at once!" said Mr. Samsa, and pointed to the door without disengaging himself from the women. "What do you mean by that?" said the middle lodger, taken somewhat aback, with a feeble smile. The two others put their hands behind them and kept rubbing them together, as if in gleeful expectation of a fine set-to in which they were bound to come off the winners. "I mean just what I say," answered Mr. Samsa, and advanced in a straight line with his two companions towards the lodger. He stood his ground at first quietly, looking at the floor as if his thoughts were taking a new pattern in his head. "Then let us go, by all means," he said, and looked up at Mr. Samsa as if in a sudden access of humility he were expecting some renewed sanction for this decision. Mr. Samsa merely nodded briefly once or twice with meaning eyes. Upon that the lodger really did go with long strides into the hall, his two friends had been listening and had quite stopped rubbing their hands for some moments and now went scuttling after him as if afraid that Mr. Samsa might get into the hall before them and cut them off from their leader. In the hall they all three took their hats from the rack, their sticks from the umbrella stand, bowed in silence and quitted the apartment. With a suspiciousness which proved quite unfounded Mr. Samsa and the two women followed them out to the landing; leaning over the banister they watched the three figures slowly but surely going down the long stairs, vanishing from sight at a certain turn of the staircase on every floor and coming into view again after a moment or so; the more they dwindled, the more the Samsa family's interest in them dwindled, and when a butcher's boy met them and passed them on the stairs coming up proudly with a tray on his head, Mr. Samsa and the two women soon left the landing and as if a burden had been lifted from them went back into their apartment.

They decided to spend this day in resting and going for a stroll; they had not only deserved such a respite from work, but absolutely needed it. And so they sat down at the table and wrote three notes of excuse, Mr. Samsa to his board of management, Mrs. Samsa to her employer and Grete to the head of her firm. While they were writing, the charwoman came in to say that she was going now, since her morning's work was finished. At first they only nodded without looking up, but as she kept hovering there they eyed her irritably. "Well?" said Mr. Samsa. The charwoman stood grinning in the doorway as if she had good news to impart to the family but meant not to say a word unless properly questioned. The small ostrich feather standing upright on her hat, which had annoyed Mr. Samsa ever since she was engaged, was waving gaily in all directions. "Well, what is it then?" asked Mrs. Samsa, who obtained more respect from the charwoman than the others. "Oh," said the charwoman, giggling so amiably that she could not at once continue, "just this, you don't need to bother about how to get rid of the thing next door. It's been seen to already." Mrs. Samsa and Grete bent over their letters again, as if preoccupied; Mr. Samsa, who perceived that she was eager to begin describing it all in detail, stopped her with a decisive hand. But since she was not allowed to tell her story, she remembered the great hurry she was in, being obviously deeply huffed: "Bye, everybody," she said, whirling off violently, and departed with a frightful slamming of doors.

"She'll be given notice tonight," said Mr. Samsa, but neither from his wife nor his daughter did he get any answer, for the charwoman seemed to have shattered again the composure they had barely achieved. They rose, went to the window and stayed there, clasping each other tight. Mr. Samsa turned in his chair to look at them and quietly observed them for a little. Then he called out: "Come along, now, do. Let bygones be bygones. And you might have some consideration for me." The two of them complied at once, hastened to him, caressed him and quickly finished their letters.

Then they all three left the apartment together, which was more than they had done for months, and went by tram into the open country outside the town. The tram, in which they were the only passengers, was filled with warm sunshine. Leaning comfortably back in their seats they canvassed their prospects for the future, and it appeared on closer inspection that these were not at all bad, for the jobs they had got, which so far they had never really discussed with each other, were all three admirable and likely to lead to better things later on. The greatest immediate improvement in their condition would of course arise from moving to another house; they wanted to take a smaller and cheaper but also better situated and more easily run apartment than the one they had, which Gregor had selected. While they were thus conversing, it struck both Mr. and Mrs. Samsa, almost at the same moment, as they became aware of their daughter's increasing vivacity, that in spite of all the sorrow of recent times, which had made her cheeks pale, she had bloomed into a pretty girl with a good figure. They grew quieter and half unconsciously exchanged glances of complete agreement, having come to the conclusion that it would soon be time to find a good husband for her. And it was like a confirmation of their new dreams and excellent intentions that at the end of their journey their daughter sprang to her feet first and stretched her young body.

FLANNERY O'CONNOR

The Displaced Person

Introduction

Critics of American literature regard Flannery O'Connor as one of the most gifted writers we have had in the twentieth century. Her stories (more than her novels) are brilliantly constructed, sharp-edged in meaning and language, witty, complex, often very moving. She wrote almost exclusively about the South, the one patch of the world she knew best, and like many other Southern writers, she created characters who sometimes come out looking like grotesques. And she was a Catholic, which in the South means to be in a minority. She took her religion seriously, so that traces of Christian symbolism and elements of Christian belief can be found in many of her writings. Catholicism, she once said, affects the work of the writer "primarily by guaranteeing his respect for mystery."

Part of the mystery, and the pleasure, of a great work of art is that it is open to a variety of readings and that any sensitive person, whether a professional critic or a private reader, can add something to the common store of understanding. By now you have acquired some ideas about and experience in the art of reading fiction, so instead of presenting a detailed analysis of *The Displaced Person* in this introduction, I shall concentrate on a few questions that are likely to trouble readers.

✦ *What is Flannery O'Connor's attitude toward the Negro characters in* The Displaced Person? *Do you feel some uneasiness at what seems to be her acceptance of stereotypes about blacks who "know their place"?*

The Displaced Person was first published in 1954, a few years before the upsurge of black protest in both South and North. Flannery O'Connor seems not to have been greatly interested in politics, and this story was not meant to be read as a reflection, one way or another, on the condition of black rural workers in the South. Nor should it be read as a recommendation, one way or another, about the possibility or need for black revolt in the South. Whatever she herself may have thought about these matters, they are beyond the bounds of the action and meaning of this novella; and whatever we ourselves may think about these matters, it would be a mistake to put them in the forefront of our response to *The Displaced Person*.

Yet there they are, Astor and Sulk. What are we to make of them? What does O'Connor want us to make of them?

The main stress of *The Displaced Person* is not a social one, though it clearly has social implications. Through a terrible accumulation of comedy, it shows how xenophobia can have disastrous consequences. More generally, it portrays a society without a moral center.

Like any other writer, O'Connor had to work with what she knew. She had to use the familiar elements, the grainy particulars of the world in which she had grown up, in order to dramatize her general insights into the human situation. (Some critics would say, instead, that only by dramatizing these particulars can a writer reach general insights of any validity.) What Flannery O'Connor knew best was a piece of the South in her time, and in that South the blacks were in fact relegated to an inferior socio-economic position. Now, in the hands of another writer, this could have and sometimes did become the material for a fiction of outrage or protest; but in this novella O'Connor's main concern was not with that view of things. We simply have to grant each writer the privilege of writing about what he or she wants. We can judge his skill, his insight, his honesty; but we cannot dictate his material or angle of vision.

Still, we have the right to ask: Is the treatment of the blacks in *The Displaced Person* condescending, as some readers might feel it to be? In my judgment, no. The two black characters are shown as occupying the lowest social level in the rural South: which is true to the facts. They are shown as accepting this position or at least not rebelling against it: which, like it or not, is also true to the facts in many instances and at certain times. But they are also shown as decidedly critical in their view of the whites, at times sardonic and hostile. The two black characters are not at the center of this novella, though they play a significant role in its development; but to the extent that it is relevant to her story, O'Connor shows that the blacks have a life and opinions of their own, which the whites barely glimpse and still less understand.

Astor, the old black man, is clearly a figure of some strength. He plays the social game as defined in his corner of the world: he has to. But his eye is sharp, his tongue sharper still. When Mrs. Shortley tells the two black men that "the Displaced Person" might take over their jobs, Astor comes back with a brilliant remark to Sulk: "Never mind, your place too low for anybody to dispute with you for it." Astor knows precisely where he stands. Even Sulk has his moments of sharp perception. In a comic exchange with Mr. Shortley, Sulk has decidedly the better of it:

> "Whyn't you go back to Africa?" he asked Sulk one morning as they were cleaning out the silo. "That's your country, ain't it?"
> "I ain't going there," the boy said. "They might eat me up."
> "Well, if you behave yourself it isn't any reason you can't stay here," Mr. Shortley said kindly. "Because you didn't run away from nowhere. . . . It's the people that run away from where they come from that I ain't got any use for."
> "I never felt no need to travel," the Negro said.

Sulk's answers can be taken as ingenuous and thereby unwittingly amusing or as a kind of put-on and thereby implicitly sarcastic. Either way, O'Connor shows a cool, controlled sympathy for his situation.

There is another important fact concerning the black characters in *The Displaced Person*. When Mr. Guizac is killed at the end, everyone on the farm is implicated in the deed—everyone but Astor. This omission is not accidental. We have been persuaded by the preceding action that, in his stubborn and grumbling way, Astor is a man of some integrity: he makes no speeches but his judgments are telling, and he would not be the kind of person to allow racial feeling to lure him into the dreadful act that climaxes *The Displaced Person*. In fact, Astor seems a brilliant portrait of the kind of black

man who has to play the distasteful social role of the shuffling old
eccentric, but who nevertheless retains his humanity behind the mask.
A remark Flannery O'Connor once made in an interview is very
much to the point here: "The uneducated Southern Negro is not
the clown he's often made out to be. He's a man of very elaborate
manners and great formality which he uses superbly for his own
protection and to insure his own privacy." This seems to apply
exactly to Astor.

We may therefore conclude: this novella shows the black characters in the stereotyped situation to which the South has confined
them, it even shows some of the stereotyped responses they have
to act out, but by the end of the action, major and subtle differentia-
tions have been made both between whites and blacks and between
the blacks themselves. No sensitive reader can see Astor and Sulk
as the Shortleys and Mrs. McIntyre do.

✦ *What is the purpose of the by-play concerning the Shortleys in the first part of the novella? What attitude does
the author invite us to take toward them?*

Our first response to the comic by-play about the Shortleys ought,
I think, to be sheer delight. They are very funny, though in their
slothful way also somehow endearing. What O'Connor does with
them is never nasty or mean-spirited, for she knows them well, takes
an undeluded view of them, and still rather likes them.

The comedy is of a kind that has often been used in Southern
writing, especially in the works of William Faulkner and Erskine
Caldwell: it is the comedy of the far-fetched, tall tales about little
people, meant to get at the absurdity of life, and it is also the comedy
of social incongruity, the way standards of judgment become scrambled when radically different styles of life are juxtaposed. Nothing
could be more delicious, for example, than the business at the outset where Mr. Guizac kisses Mrs. McIntyre's hand. To the mountainous Mrs. Shortley, all provincial self-certainty and no fancy notions about life, Mr. Guizac's gesture seems outlandish. She has no
way of knowing that in Europe it is quite conventional, nor does
she care. Kissing Mrs. McIntyre's hand seems to Mrs. Shortley the
kind of thing "those Europeans" would do, those no-account and
unaccountable foreigners who overrun this country by the millions.
Mrs. Shortley "jerked her own hand up toward her mouth," as if
threatened by the prospect that someone might try that sort of out-

rage with her, and then, in a gesture so wildly preposterous it almost defies explanation, "brought it down and rubbed it vigorously on her seat." The comedy is broad, so to say, but not malicious. To add absurdity to absurdity, Mrs. Shortley reflects that if Mr. Shortley had tried to kiss Mrs. McIntyre's hand, the landlady "would have knocked him into the middle of next week." The paragraph is then topped off with the reflection that Mr. Shortley "didn't have time to mess around"—which takes its full humorous impact as we come to see how inefficient and slow-moving Mr. Shortley actually is.

The comedy continues—though here an ominous note creeps in—with Mrs. Shortley's reflections about the DP's who come from "Europe where they had not advanced as in this country." It is a comedy of low-life ignorance, the provincial mind comfortably fixed in its absolute limitations and never troubled by self-doubt or imagination. The point comes through again with lovely ironic force, when Mrs. Shortley reflects on Catholicism:

> Mrs. Shortley looked at the priest and was reminded that these people did not have an advanced religion. There was no telling what all they believed since none of the foolishness had been reformed out of it.

That phrase about "the foolishness reformed out of it" ought to be remembered, because later it will take on a much more serious implication.

Mrs. Shortley is not an evil woman. She has, we come to see, her own version of pride: she packs up her family in the old jalopy and flees before dawn so as not to allow her husband to be fired. In a crazy way she even has a sense of fairness: she avers that between the impossible Guizacs overrunning the country and the blacks, "I'll stand up for the niggers." And she shows touches of sentiment, as when she chuckles, "Aw Chancey," in appreciation of his trick of seeming to swallow a cigarette, which "was actually his way of making love to her." But essentially she is immovable, rock-like in her refusal to be affected by experience. O'Connor has some easygoing fun in suggesting this through exaggerated physical equivalents: "She stood on two tremendous legs, with the grand self-confidence of a mountain, and rose, up narrowing bulges of granite, to two icy blue points of light that pierced forward, surveying everything."

In part what O'Connor is doing here is engaging in a kind of shrewd playfulness, or by-playfulness, for its own sake—the sort of thing often found in a Dickens novel when all his hijinks are going full blast and he simply invites the reader to marvel and enjoy.

That is, O'Connor takes a distinct pleasure in recording the craziness of human conduct, and she does this in a tone of sardonic affection. Mrs. Shortley comes to be one of the great comic figures in American literature, decidedly larger than life, archetypal and unforgettable. There are characters in fiction who seem to step out of the page and to live on their own, beyond the context in which they were first imagined. Mrs. Shortley is one of these rare wonders, and if you respond to her as I do, you are likely to feel some chagrin at the artistic necessity that dooms her to death before the story is finished.

At the same time, since O'Connor is a very tidy and economical writer, she is using Mrs. Shortley to prepare for the main point or theme of the story. That preparation comes through in a contrast of moral style between the priest and the peacock, on one side, and the Shortleys and Mrs. McIntyre, on the other. Mr. Guizac, in a literal sense the displaced person, barely figures as a character in his own right; he is there mostly as a convenience to keep the drama in motion. A traditional, indeed an inevitable, way to create a conflict between characters, and between the values they represent, is to introduce a stranger into a fixed community. Precisely because he is a stranger, his intrusion can seem threatening; the writer can then take this threat and develop it in either comic or tragic terms. O'Connor does both: *The Displaced Person* moves from comic beginning to tragic conclusion. The comedy appears, for instance, in Mr. Shortley's manly assertion, "I ain't going to have the Pope of Rome tell me how to run no dairy." The tragedy comes with Mr. Guizac's death at the climax of the story.

✦ *Toward what discoveries of feeling, what revelation of vision, does* The Displaced Person *finally move?*

The first, and most immediately accessible, materials that O'Connor provides us with are social in character. But as we read we begin to sense that she is after bigger game: she wants to make implications that can only be described as religious.

The social material of this novella is fairly easy to grasp. Mr. Guizac's silent intrusion threatens the slothful arrangements of the Shortleys. His work pleases Mrs. McIntyre, but it also leaves her somewhat uneasy. She appreciates the advantages of having a worker as efficient as Mr. Guizac, but she is thoroughly part of the social world that has produced the Shortleys and she is therefore put off by the strangeness of all that Mr. Guizac represents. Mrs. Shortley has fantasies in which the blacks are displaced by "them," those European refugees who "did not have an advanced religion." She "was seeing the ten million billion of them pushing their way into new places over here and herself, a giant angel with wings as wide as a house, telling the Negroes that they would have to find another place." And then, her mind a little confused by memories of those hideous "Time Marches On" newsreels,* Mrs. Shortley wonders, "If they [the Guizacs] had come from where that kind of thing [the killing of concentration camp prisoners] was done to them, who was to say they were not the kind that would also do it to others?"

At a first look, what we have here is simply an instance, comic in manifestation but mean in consequences, of provincial narrowness of spirit, a kind of xenophobia that automatically suspects strangers. At first Mrs. McIntyre does not share this feeling, since she's delighted finally to have efficient help. Though they live by the same essential values and bear the marks of the same constricting culture, Mrs. Shortley and Mrs. McIntyre are different in one major respect: Mrs. Shortley is visionary (she sees things in the sky) and Mrs. McIntyre practical (she has eyes only for dollar bills). Yet in the end, the two of them come together. They share a revulsion against Mr. Guizac's scheme for marrying his cousin to Sulk as a way of saving the girl ("She in camp three year") from the hell of postwar Europe. The most deeply ingrained prejudice dominates the minds of both Mrs. Shortley and Mrs. McIntyre, the shiftless and the efficient, the visionary and the pragmatic. Mrs. McIntyre must acknowledge to herself that she feels more at home with the indolent Shortleys than with the hard-working Mr. Guizac, who has no respect for, indeed hardly any understanding of, the taboos on which her society rests. At first Mrs. Shortley and Mrs. McIntyre are made uneasy by the stranger and then they begin to fear him, for his ways seem to them less and less comprehensible. We remember now Mrs. Shortley's observation that "these people," the Catholics, "did not have an advanced religion" because "none of the foolishness had been reformed out of it." To the parochial Southern mind, whether represented by Mrs. Shortley or by Mrs. McIntyre, the root cause of Mr. Guizac's strangeness is that he is a religious outsider.

---

* "Time Marches On" was a popular newsreel shown in movie theatres in the years before the Second World War. Quick scenes of war, violence, and other disasters would be followed by a pompous voice booming out, "Time marches on!" It was just as awful as it sounds, and apparently Mrs. Shortley's sense of European politics came mostly from her exposure to this newsreel.

Yet as we read *The Displaced Person* we must be struck by the thought that this social aspect of the story, though clearly in the forefront, isn't all that O'Connor has in mind. The continuous religious imagery and references force us to conclude that she is trying to suggest a kind of religious fable. We recognize that Father Flynn, far from being a mere accessory to the main action, is a crucial figure. In his purring, low-keyed way he speaks for the Christian virtue of charity and tries to persuade Mrs. McIntyre that it is not only good business to hire Mr. Guizac, it is also an act of goodness. Mrs. McIntyre's response to the priest's subtle appeals is more ambiguous than Mrs. Shortley's would be, because Mrs. McIntyre, being a rung higher on the social ladder, is more inclined to watch her manners and disguise her feelings. In the end, of course, she acts out in conduct what Mrs. Shortley had anticipated in vision. But meanwhile we come to see that fundamentally *The Displaced Person* involves a contrast in religious outlooks and styles, a contrast between radically conflicting versions or interpretations of Christianity.

In the very first sentence we meet that exotic peacock. What is it doing there, on a small Southern farm? On the level of simple plausibility, it hardly seems likely that you'd find a peacock in such a place; but perhaps that's just the point, perhaps the peacock is there to suggest a radical other possibility for responding to human existence which Mrs. McIntyre and the Shortleys don't or can't see but which Father Flynn immediately does. For the peacock serves throughout the story to emphasize the distinction between the priest's complex, humane, and sensitive version of Christianity and the rigid, impoverished, and joyless sort of fundamentalism that the Shortleys and Mrs. McIntyre exemplify.

> "So beauti-ful," the priest said. "A tail full of suns," and he crept forward on tiptoe and looked down on the bird's back where the polished gold and green design began. The peacock stood still as if he had just come down from some sun-drenched height to be a vision for them all.

A vision of what? Of a faith, a way of life, that responds to the beauties of the world, or, as Father Flynn might say, to the beauties of God's creation and thereby to the possibilities for compassion and grace among its inhabitants.

Mrs. Shortley, to whom the peacock is "nothing but a pea-chicken," finds her esthetic satisfactions in Chancey's game of swallowing a cigarette. Yet she also has a vision of her own. It is a vision she sees as "the sky folded back in two pieces" and a voice directs her to "Prophesy!" Her fists clench, since for her religion is a fierce and wrathful thing, and she says in a loud voice, "The children of wicked nations will be butchered. . . . Legs where arms should be, foot to face, ear in the palm of hand. Who will remain whole? Who?" The images of mangled bodies derive from "Time Marches On," but they eerily anticipate the killing of Mr. Guizac. In that killing Mrs. McIntyre and Mr. Shortley are immediately responsible, though Mrs. Shortley has been a kind of spiritual inciter.

A little before that climactic scene in the farmyard, in a brilliant bit of dialogue, Mrs. McIntyre tries to justify to the old priest her decision to fire Mr. Guizac. The priest appeals tacitly to her better instincts; he is distracted by the beauty of the peacock ("Christ will come like that!"); and when he mentions Christ, Mrs. McIntyre is upset ("Christ in the conversation embarrassed her the way sex had her mother"). On the matter of racial feeling the priest avoids a direct confrontation with Mrs. McIntyre, since he senses, rightly enough, that it is something on which she cannot be budged. They cannot connect. The distance between the two versions of faith, the one morally responsible and esthetically vibrant and the other morally impoverished and esthetically blinded, remains to the very end—with the only possible note of reconciliation the fact that when Mrs. McIntyre is bedridden at the end, Father Flynn comes to see her, after feeding his breadcrumbs to the dazzling peacock.

A few questions remain, which I will raise but not pretend to answer. We surely respond sympathetically to the contrast between versions of faith, indeed versions of life, as represented by Father Flynn on the one side and by the Shortleys and Mrs. McIntyre on the other. But does O'Connor stack the cards a little? That is, by making the contrast between a Catholic priest and fundamentalist Southern Protestants, does she provoke an intrusion of feelings not really necessary to her story? *

---

* In a letter to Sister Mariella Gable, Flannery O'Connor explained why she so frequently used Protestant fanatics in her stories rather than Catholic ones:

"To a lot of Protestants I know, monks and nuns are fanatics, none greater. And to a lot of monks and nuns I know, my Protestant prophets [in her stories] are fanatics. For my part, I think the only difference between them is that if you are a Catholic and have this intensity of belief you join the convent and are heard no more; whereas if you are a Protestant and have it, there is no convent for you to join and you go about the world getting into all sorts of trouble and drawing the wrath of people who don't believe anything much at all down on your head.

"This is one reason why I can write about Protestant believers better than Catholic believers—because they express their belief in diverse kinds of dramatic action which is obvious enough for me to catch."

Another question: We see and respond with pleasure to the foreground action of this novella, and we notice and respond with interest to the symbolic scheme, or the scheme of suggested meanings, that lies behind the foreground action; but are the two harmoniously related? Or are there places where the scheme jostles, bends, and twists the action, so that we feel the illusion of reality is snapped because of the author's doctrinal intentions? My own judgment would be that, by and large, O'Connor is successful in keeping action and scheme in harmony, but there is one place where the relationship is badly strained. It is no more than a sentence, and I think no reader is likely to have any trouble sensing why O'Connor put it in. I refer to the place where the exasperated Mrs. McIntyre bursts out, "Christ was just another D.P." It is possible to justify this remark in terms of the ideas O'Connor is trying to develop. But can it be justified in terms of what she has shown about Mrs. McIntyre, her background and character? I think not. I think it is hard to believe that a woman like Mrs. McIntyre would allow herself a remark so direct, so shocking, so at variance with all she has been brought up to believe, or at least to say.

Are there other such discordant notes in *The Displaced Person*? I leave that to your judgment.

The Displaced Person

The peacock was following Mrs. Shortley up the road to the hill where she meant to stand. Moving one behind the other, they looked like a complete procession. Her arms were folded and as she mounted the prominence, she might have been the giant wife of the countryside, come out at some sign of danger to see what the trouble was. She stood on two tremendous legs, with the grand self-confidence of a mountain, and rose, up narrowing bulges of granite, to two icy blue points of light that pierced forward, surveying everything. She ignored the white afternoon sun which was creeping behind a ragged wall of cloud as if it pretended to be an intruder and cast her gaze down the red clay road that turned off from the highway.

The peacock stopped just behind her, his tail—glittering green-gold and blue in the sunlight—lifted just enough so that it would not touch the ground. It flowed out on either side like a floating train and his head on the long blue reed-like neck was drawn back as if his attention were fixed in the distance on something no one else could see.

Mrs. Shortley was watching a black car turn through the gate from the highway. Over by the toolshed, about fifteen feet away, the two Negroes, Astor and Sulk, had stopped work to watch. They were hidden by a mulberry tree but Mrs. Shortley knew they were there.

Mrs. McIntyre was coming down the steps of her house to meet the car. She had on her largest smile but Mrs. Shortley, even from her distance, could detect a nervous slide in it. These people who were coming were only hired help, like the Shortleys themselves or the Negroes. Yet here was the owner of the place out to welcome them. Here she was, wearing her best clothes and a string of beads, and now bounding forward with her mouth stretched.

The car stopped at the walk just as she did and the priest was the first to get out. He was a long-legged black-suited old man with a white hat on and a collar that he wore backwards, which, Mrs. Shortley knew, was what priests did who wanted to be known as priests. It was this priest who had arranged for these people to come here. He opened the back door of the car and out jumped two children, a boy and a girl, and then, stepping more slowly, a woman in brown, shaped like a peanut. Then the front door opened and out stepped the man, the Displaced Person. He was short and a little sway-backed and wore gold-rimmed spectacles.

Mrs. Shortley's vision narrowed on him and then widened to include the woman and the two children in a group picture. The first thing that struck her as very peculiar was that they looked like other people. Every time she had seen them in her imagination, the image she had got was of the three bears, walking single file, with wooden shoes on like Dutchmen and sailor hats and bright coats with a lot of buttons. But the woman had on a dress she might have worn herself and the children were dressed like anybody from around. The man had on khaki pants and a blue shirt. Suddenly, as Mrs. McIntyre held out her hand to him, he bobbed down from the waist and kissed it.

Mrs. Shortley jerked her own hand up toward her mouth and then after a second brought it down and rubbed it vigorously on her seat. If Mr. Shortley had tried to kiss her hand, Mrs. McIntyre would have knocked him into the middle of next week, but then Mr. Shortley wouldn't have kissed her hand anyway. He didn't have time to mess around.

She looked closer, squinting. The boy was in the center of the group, talking. He was supposed to speak the most English because he had learned some in Poland and so he was to listen to his father's Polish and say it in English and then listen to Mrs. McIntyre's English and say that in Polish. The priest had told Mrs. McIntyre his name was Rudolph and he was twelve and the girl's name was Sledgewig and she was nine. Sledgewig sounded to Mrs. Shortley like something you would name a bug, or vice versa, as if you named a boy Bollweevil. All of them's last name was something that only they themselves and the priest could pronounce. All she could make out of it was Gobblehook. She and Mrs. McIntyre had been calling them the Gobblehooks all week while they got ready for them.

There had been a great deal to do to get ready for them because they didn't have anything of their own, not a stick of furniture or a sheet or a dish, and everything had had to be scraped together out of things that Mrs. McIntyre couldn't use any more herself. They had collected a piece of odd furniture here and a piece there and they had taken some flowered chicken feed sacks and made curtains for the windows, two red and one green, because they had not had enough of the red sacks to go around. Mrs. McIntyre said she was not made of money and she could not afford to buy curtains. "They can't talk," Mrs. Shortley said. "You reckon they'll know what colors even is?" and Mrs. McIntyre had said that after what those people had been through, they should be grateful for anything they could get. She said to think how lucky they were to escape from over there and come to a place like this.

Mrs. Shortley recalled a newsreel she had seen once of a small room piled high with bodies of dead naked people all in a heap, their arms and legs tangled together, a head thrust in here, a head there, a foot, a knee, a part that should have been covered up sticking out, a hand raised clutching nothing. Before you could realize that it was real and take it into your head, the picture changed and a hollow-sounding voice was saying, "Time marches on!" This was the kind of thing that was happening every day in Europe where they had not advanced as in this country, and watching from her vantage point, Mrs. Shortley had the sudden intuition that the Gobblehooks, like rats with typhoid fleas, could have carried all those murderous ways over the water with them directly to this place. If they had come from where that kind of thing was done to them, who was to say they were not the kind that would also do it to others? The width and breadth of this question nearly shook her. Her stomach trembled as if there had been a slight quake in the heart of the mountain and automatically she moved down from her elevation and went forward to be introduced to them, as if she meant to find out at once what they were capable of.

She approached, stomach foremost, head back, arms folded, boots flopping gently against her large legs. About fifteen feet from the gesticulating group, she stopped and made her presence felt by training her gaze on the back of Mrs. McIntyre's neck. Mrs. McIntyre was a small woman of sixty with a round wrinkled face and red bangs that came almost down to two high orange-colored penciled eyebrows. She had a little doll's mouth and eyes that were a soft blue when she opened them wide but more like steel or granite when she narrowed them to inspect a milk can. She had buried one husband and divorced two and Mrs. Shortley respected her as a person nobody had put anything over on yet—except, ha, ha, perhaps the Shortleys. She held out her arm in Mrs. Shortley's direction and said to the Rudolph boy, "And this is Mrs. Shortley. Mr. Shortley is my dairyman. Where's Mr. Shortley?" she asked as his wife began to approach again, her arms still folded. "I want him to meet the Guizacs."

Now it was Guizac. She wasn't calling them Gobblehook to their face. "Chancey's at the barn," Mrs. Shortley said. "He don't have time to rest himself in the bushes like them niggers over there."

Her look first grazed the tops of the displaced people's heads and then revolved downwards slowly, the way a buzzard glides and drops in the air until it alights on the carcass. She stood far enough away so that the man would not be able to kiss her hand. He looked directly at her with little green eyes and gave her a broad grin that was toothless on one side. Mrs. Shortley, without smiling, turned her attention to the little girl who stood by the mother, swinging her shoulders from side to side. She had long braided hair in two looped pigtails and there was no denying she was a pretty child even if she did have a bug's name. She was better looking than either Annie Maude or Sarah Mae, Mrs. Shortley's two girls going on fifteen and seventeen but Annie Maude had never got her growth and Sarah Mae had a cast in her eye. She compared the foreign boy to her son, H. C., and H. C. came out far ahead. H. C. was twenty years old with her build and eye-glasses. He was going to Bible school now and when he finished he was going to start him a church. He had a strong sweet voice for hymns and could sell anything. Mrs. Shortley looked at the priest and was reminded that these people did not have an advanced religion. There was no telling what all they believed since none of the foolishness had been reformed out of it. Again she saw the room piled high with bodies.

The priest spoke in a foreign way himself, English but as if he had a throatful of hay. He had a big nose and a bald rectangular face and head. While she was observing him, his large mouth dropped open and with a stare behind her, he said, "Arrrrrr!" and pointed.

Mrs. Shortley spun around. The peacock was standing a few feet behind her, with his head slightly cocked.

"What a beauti-ful birrrrd!" the priest murmured.

"Another mouth to feed," Mrs. McIntyre said, glancing in the peafowl's direction.

"And when does he raise his splendid tail?" asked the priest.

"Just when it suits him," she said. "There used to be twenty or thirty of those things on the place but I've let them die off. I don't like to hear them scream in the middle of the night."

"So beauti-ful," the priest said. "A tail full of suns," and he crept forward on tiptoe and looked down on the bird's back where the polished gold and green design began. The peacock stood still as if he had just come down from some sun-drenched height to be a vision for them all. The priest's homely red face hung over him, glowing with pleasure.

Mrs. Shortley's mouth had drawn acidly to one side. "Nothing but a peachicken," she muttered.

Mrs. McIntyre raised her orange eyebrows and exchanged a look with her to indicate that the old man was in his second childhood. "Well, we must show the Guizacs their new home," she said impatiently and she herded them into the car again. The peacock stepped off toward the mulberry tree where the two Negroes were hiding and the priest turned his absorbed face away and got in the car and drove the displaced people down to the shack they were to occupy.

Mrs. Shortley waited until the car was out of sight and then she made her way circuitously to the mulberry tree and stood about ten feet behind the two Negroes, one an old man holding a bucket half full of calf feed and the other a yellowish boy with a short woodchuck-like head pushed into a rounded felt hat. "Well," she said slowly, "yawl have looked long enough. What you think about them?"

The old man, Astor, raised himself. "We been watching," he said as if this would be news to her. "Who they now?"

"They come from over the water," Mrs. Shortley said with a wave of her arm. "They're what is called Displaced Persons."

"Displaced Persons," he said. "Well now. I declare. What do that mean?"

"It means they ain't where they were born at and there's nowhere for them to go—like if you was run out of here and wouldn't nobody have you."

"It seem like they here, though," the old man said in a reflective voice. "If they here, they somewhere."

"Sho is," the other agreed. "They here."

The illogic of Negro-thinking always irked Mrs. Shortley. "They ain't where they belong to be at," she said. "They belong to be back over yonder where everything is still like they been used to. Over here it's more advanced than where they come from. But yawl better look out now," she said and nodded her head. "There's about ten million billion more just like them and I know what Mrs. McIntyre said."

"Say what?" the young one asked.

"Places are not easy to get nowadays, for white or black, but I reckon I heard what she stated to me," she said in a sing-song voice.

"You liable to hear most anything," the old man remarked, leaning forward as if he were about to walk off but holding himself suspended.

"I heard her say, 'This is going to put the Fear of the Lord into those shiftless niggers!' " Mrs. Shortley said in a ringing voice.

The old man started off. "She say something like that every now and then," he said. "Ha. Ha. Yes indeed."

"You better get on in that barn and help Mr. Shortley," she said to the other one. "What you reckon she pays you for?"

"He the one sont me out," the Negro muttered. "He the one gimme something else to do."

"Well you better get to doing it then," she said and stood there until he moved off. Then she stood a while longer, reflecting, her unseeing eyes directly in front of the peacock's tail. He had jumped into the tree and his tail hung in front of her, full of fierce planets with eyes that were each ringed in green and set against a sun that was gold in one second's light and salmon-colored in the next. She might have been looking at a map of the universe but she didn't notice it any more than she did the spots of sky that cracked the dull green of the tree. She was having an inner vision instead. She was seeing the ten million billion of them pushing their way into new places over here and herself, a giant angel with wings as wide as a house, telling the Negroes that they would have to find another place. She turned herself in the direction of the barn, musing on this, her expression lofty and satisfied.

She approached the barn from an oblique angle that allowed her a look in the door before she could be seen herself. Mr. Chancey Shortley was adjusting the last milking machine on a large black and white spotted cow near the entrance, squatting at her heels. There was about a half-inch of cigarette adhering to the center of his lower lip. Mrs. Shortley observed it minutely for half a second. "If she seen or heard of you smoking in this barn, she would blow a fuse," she said.

Mr. Shortley raised a sharply rutted face containing a washout under each cheek and two long crevices eaten down both sides of his blistered mouth. "You gonter be the one to tell her?" he asked.

"She's got a nose of her own," Mrs. Shortley said.

Mr. Shortley, without appearing to give the feat any consideration, lifted the cigarette stub with the sharp end of his tongue, drew it into his mouth, closed his lips tightly, rose, stepped out, gave his wife a good round appreciative stare, and spit the smoldering butt into the grass.

"Aw Chancey," she said, "haw haw," and she dug a little hole for it with her toe and covered it up. This trick of Mr. Shortley's was actually his way of making love to her. When he had done his courting, he had not brought a guitar to strum or anything pretty for her to keep, but had sat on her porch steps, not saying a word, imitating a paralyzed man propped up to enjoy a cigarette. When the cigarette got the proper size, he would turn his eyes to her and open his mouth and draw in the butt and then sit there as if he had swallowed it, looking at her with the most loving look anybody could imagine. It nearly drove her wild and every time he did it, she wanted to pull his hat down over his eyes and hug him to death.

"Well," she said, going into the barn after him, "the Gobblehooks have come and she wants you to meet them, says, 'Where's Mr. Shortley?' and I says, 'He don't have time . . .'"

"Tote up them weights," Mr. Shortley said, squatting to the cow again.

"You reckon he can drive a tractor when he don't know English?" she asked. "I don't think she's going to get her money's worth out of them. That boy can talk but he looks delicate. The one can work can't talk and the one can talk can't work. She ain't any better off than if she had more niggers."

"I rather have a nigger if it was me," Mr. Shortley said.

"She says it's ten million more like them, Displaced Persons, she says that there priest can get her all she wants."

"She better quit messin with that there priest," Mr. Shortley said.

"He don't look smart," Mrs. Shortley said, "—kind of foolish."

"I ain't going to have the Pope of Rome tell me how to run no dairy," Mr. Shortley said.

"They ain't Eye-talians, they're Poles," she said. "From Poland where all them bodies were stacked up at. You remember all them bodies?"

"I give them three weeks here," Mr. Shortley said.

Three weeks later Mrs. McIntyre and Mrs. Shortley drove to the cane bottom to see Mr. Guizac start to operate the silage cutter, a new machine that Mrs. McIntyre had just bought because she said, for the first time, she had somebody who could operate it. Mr. Guizac could drive a tractor, use the rotary hay-baler, the silage cutter, the combine, the letz mill, or any other machine she had on the place. He was an expert mechanic, a carpenter, and a mason. He was thrifty and energetic. Mrs. McIntyre said she figured he would save her twenty dollars a month on repair bills alone. She said getting him was the best day's work she had ever done in her life. He could work milking machines and he was scrupulously clean. He did not smoke.

She parked her car on the edge of the cane field and they got out. Sulk, the young Negro, was attaching the wagon to the cutter and Mr. Guizac was attaching the cutter to the tractor. He finished first and pushed the colored boy out of the way and attached the wagon to the cutter himself, gesticulating with a bright angry face when he wanted the hammer or the screwdriver. Nothing was done quick enough to suit him. The Negroes made him nervous.

The week before, he had come upon Sulk at the dinner hour, sneaking with a croker sack into the pen where the young turkeys were. He had watched him take a frying-size turkey from the lot and thrust it in the sack and put the sack under his coat. Then he had followed him around the barn, jumped on him, dragged him to Mrs. McIntyre's back door and had acted out the entire scene for her, while the Negro muttered and grumbled and said God might strike him dead if he had been stealing any turkey, he had only been taking it to put some black shoe polish on its head because it had the sorehead. God might strike him dead if that was not the truth before Jesus. Mrs. McIntyre told him to go put the turkey back and then she was a long time explaining to the Pole that all Negroes would steal. She finally had to call Rudolph and tell him in English and have him tell his father in Polish, and Mr. Guizac had gone off with a startled disappointed face.

Mrs. Shortley stood by hoping there would be trouble with the silage machine but there was none. All of Mr. Guizac's motions were quick and accurate. He jumped on the tractor like a monkey and maneuvered the big orange cutter into the cane; in a second the silage was spurting in a green jet out of the pipe into the wagon. He went jolting down the row until he disappeared from sight and the noise became remote.

Mrs. McIntyre sighed with pleasure. "At last," she said, "I've got somebody I can depend on. For years I've been fooling with sorry people. Sorry people. Poor white trash and niggers," she muttered. "They've drained me dry. Before you all came I had Ringfields and Collins and Jarrells and Perkins and Pinkins and Herrins and God knows what all else and not a one of them left without taking something off this place that didn't belong to them. Not a one!"

Mrs. Shortley could listen to this with composure because she knew that if Mrs. McIntyre had considered her trash, they couldn't have talked about trashy people together. Neither of them approved of trash. Mrs. McIntyre continued with the monologue that Mrs. Shortley had heard oftentimes before. "I've been running this place for thirty years," she said, looking with a deep frown out over the field, "and always just barely making it. People think you're made of money. I have the taxes to pay. I have the insurance to keep up. I have the repair bills. I have the feed bills." It all gathered up and she stood with her chest lifted and her small hands gripped around her elbows. "Ever since the Judge died," she said, "I've barely been making ends meet and they all take something when they leave. The niggers don't leave—they stay and steal. A nigger thinks anybody is rich he can steal from and that white trash thinks anybody is rich who can afford to hire people as sorry as they are. And all I've got is the dirt under my feet!"

You hire and fire, Mrs. Shortley thought, but she didn't always say what she thought. She stood by and let Mrs. McIntyre say it all out to the end but this time it didn't end as usual. "But at last I'm saved!" Mrs. McIntyre said. "One fellow's misery is the other fellow's gain. That man there," and she pointed where the Displaced Person had disappeared, "—he has to work! He wants to work!" She turned to Mrs. Shortley with her bright wrinkled face. "That man is my salvation!" she said.

Mrs. Shortley looked straight ahead as if her vision penetrated the cane and the hill and pierced through to the other side. "I would suspicion salvation got from the devil," she said in a slow detached way.

"Now what do you mean by that?" Mrs. McIntyre asked, looking at her sharply.

Mrs. Shortley wagged her head but would not say anything else. The fact was she had nothing else to say for this intuition had only at that instant come to her. She had never given much thought to the devil for she felt that religion was essentially for those people who didn't have the brains to avoid evil without it. For people like herself, for people of gumption, it was a social occasion providing the opportunity to sing; but if she had ever given it much thought, she would have considered the devil the head of it and God the hanger-on. With the coming of these displaced people, she was obliged to give new thought to a good many things.

"I know what Sledgewig told Annie Maude," she said, and when Mrs. McIntyre carefully did not ask her what but reached down and broke off a sprig of sassafras to chew, she continued in a way to indicate she was not telling all, "that they wouldn't be able to live long, the four of them, on seventy dollars a month."

"He's worth raising," Mrs. McIntyre said. "He saves me money."

This was as much as to say that Chancey had never saved her money. Chancey got up at four in the morning to milk her cows, in winter wind and summer heat, and he had been doing it for the last two years. They had been with her the longest she had ever had anybody. The gratitude they got was these hints that she hadn't been saved any money.

"Is Mr. Shortley feeling better today?" Mrs. McIntyre asked.

Mrs. Shortley thought it was about time she was asking that question. Mr. Shortley had been in bed two days with an attack. Mr. Guizac had taken his place in the dairy in addition to doing his own work. "No he ain't," she said. "That doctor said he was suffering from over-exhaustion."

"If Mr. Shortley is over-exhausted," Mrs. McIntyre said, "then he must have a second job on the side," and she looked at Mrs. Shortley with almost closed eyes as if she were examining the bottom of a milk can.

Mrs. Shortley did not say a word but her dark suspicion grew like a black thunder cloud. The fact was that Mr. Shortley did have a second job on the side and that, in a free country, this was none of Mrs. McIntyre's business. Mr. Shortley made whisky. He had a small still back in the farthest reaches of the place, on Mrs. McIntyre's land to be sure, but on land that she only owned and did not cultivate, on idle land that was not doing anybody any good. Mr. Shortley was not afraid of work. He got up at four in the morning and milked her cows and in the middle of the day when he was supposed to be resting, he was off attending to his still. Not every man would work like that. The Negroes knew about his still but he knew about theirs so there had never been any disagreeableness between them. But with foreigners on the place, with people who were all eyes and no understanding, who had come from a place continually fighting, where the religion had not been reformed—with this kind of people, you had to be on the lookout every minute. She thought there ought to be a law against them. There was no reason they couldn't stay over there and take the places of some of the people who had been killed in their wars and butcherings.

"What's furthermore," she said suddenly, "Sledgewig said as soon as her papa saved the money, he was going to buy him a used car. Once they get them a used car, they'll leave you."

"I can't pay him enough for him to save money," Mrs. McIntyre said. "I'm not worrying about that. Of course," she said then, "if Mr. Shortley got incapacitated, I would have to use Mr. Guizac in the dairy all the time and I would have to pay him more. He doesn't smoke," she said, and it was the fifth time within the week that she had pointed this out.

"It is no man," Mrs. Shortley said emphatically, "that works as hard as Chancey, or is as easy with a cow, or is more of a Christian," and she folded her arms and her gaze pierced the distance. The noise of the tractor and cutter increased and Mr. Guizac appeared coming around the other side of the cane row. "Which can not be said about everybody," she muttered. She wondered whether, if the Pole found Chancey's still, he would know what it was. The trouble with these people was, you couldn't tell what they knew. Every time Mr. Guizac smiled, Europe stretched out in Mrs. Shortley's imagination, mysterious and evil, the devil's experiment station.

The tractor, the cutter, the wagon passed, rattling and rumbling and grinding before them. "Think how long that would have taken with men and mules to do it," Mrs. McIntyre shouted. "We'll get this whole bottom cut within two days at this rate."

"Maybe," Mrs. Shortley muttered, "if don't no terrible accident occur." She thought how the tractor had made mules worthless. Nowadays you couldn't give away a mule. The next thing to go, she reminded herself, will be niggers.

In the afternoon she explained what was going to happen to them to Astor and Sulk who were in the cow lot, filling the manure spreader. She sat down next to the block of salt under a small shed, her stomach in her lap, her arms on top of it. "All you colored people better look out," she said. "You know how much you can get for a mule."

"Nothing, no indeed," the old man said, "not one thing."

"Before it was a tractor," she said, "it could be a mule. And before it was a Displaced Person, it could be a nigger. The time is going to come," she prophesied, "when it won't be no more occasion to speak of a nigger."

The old man laughed politely. "Yes indeed," he said. "Ha ha."

The young one didn't say anything. He only looked sullen but when she had gone in the house, he said, "Big Belly act like she know everything."

"Never mind," the old man said, "your place too low for anybody to dispute with you for it."

She didn't tell her fears about the still to Mr. Shortley until he was back on the job in the dairy. Then one night after they were in bed, she said, "That man prowls."

Mr. Shortley folded his hands on his bony chest and pretended he was a corpse.

"Prowls," she continued and gave him a sharp kick in the side with her knee. "Who's to say what they know and don't know? Who's to say if he found it he wouldn't go right to her and tell? How you know they don't make liquor in Europe? They drive tractors. They got them all kinds of machinery. Answer me."

"Don't worry me now," Mr. Shortley said. "I'm a dead man."

"It's them little eyes of his that's foreign," she muttered. "And that way he's got a shrugging." She drew her shoulders up and shrugged several times. "Howcome he's got anything to shrug about?" she asked.

"If everybody was as dead as I am, nobody would have no trouble," Mr. Shortley said.

"That priest," she muttered and was silent for a minute. Then she said, "In Europe they probably got some different way to make liquor but I reckon they know all the ways. They're full of crooked ways. They never have advanced or reformed. They got the same religion as a thousand years ago. It could only be the devil responsible for that. Always fighting amongst each other. Disputing. And then get us into it. Ain't they got us into it twict already and we ain't got no more sense than to go over there and settle it for them and then they come on back over here and snoop around and find your still and go straight to her. And liable to kiss her hand any minute. Do you hear me?"

"No," Mr. Shortley said.

"And I'll tell you another thing," she said. "I wouldn't be a tall surprised if he don't know everything you say, whether it be in English or not."

"I don't speak no other language," Mr. Shortley murmured.

"I suspect," she said, "that before long there won't be no more niggers on this place. And I tell you what. I'd rather have niggers than them Poles. And what's furthermore, I aim to take up for the niggers when the time comes. When Gobblehook first come here, you recollect how he shook their hands, like he didn't know the difference, like he might have been as black as them, but when it come to finding out Sulk was taking turkeys, he gone on and told her. I known he was taking turkeys. I could have told her myself."

Mr. Shortley was breathing softly as if he were asleep.

"A nigger don't know when he has a friend," she said. "And I'll tell you another thing. I get a heap out of Sledgewig. Sledgewig said that in Poland they lived in a brick house and one night a man come and told them to get out of it before daylight. Do you believe they ever lived in a brick house?

"Airs," she said. "That's just airs. A wooden house is good enough for me. Chancey," she said, "turn thisaway. I hate to see niggers mistreated and run out. I have a heap of pity for niggers and poor folks. Ain't I always had?" she asked. "I say ain't I always been a friend to niggers and poor folks?

"When the time comes," she said, "I'll stand up for the niggers and that's that. I ain't going to see that priest drive out all the niggers."

Mrs. McIntyre bought a new drag harrow and a tractor with a power lift because she said, for the first time, she had someone who could handle machinery. She and Mrs. Shortley had driven to the back field to inspect what he had harrowed the day before. "That's been done beautifully!" Mrs. McIntyre said, looking out over the red undulating ground.

Mrs. McIntyre had changed since the Displaced Person had been working for her and Mrs. Shortley had observed the change very closely: she had begun to act like somebody who was getting rich secretly and she didn't confide in Mrs. Shortley the way she used to. Mrs. Shortley suspected that the priest was at the bottom of the change. They were very slick. First he would get her into his Church and then he would get his hand in her pocketbook. Well, Mrs. Shortley thought, the more fool she! Mrs. Shortley had a secret herself. She knew something the Displaced Person was doing that would floor Mrs. McIntyre. "I still say he ain't going to work forever for seventy dollars a month," she murmured. She intended to keep her secret to herself and Mr. Shortley.

"Well," Mrs. McIntyre said, "I may have to get rid of some of this other help so I can pay him more."

Mrs. Shortley nodded to indicate she had known this for some time. "I'm not saying those niggers ain't had it coming," she said. "But they do the best they know how. You can always tell a nigger what to do and stand by until he does it."

"That's what the Judge said," Mrs. McIntyre said and looked at her with approval. The Judge was her first husband, the one who had left her the place. Mrs. Shortley had heard that she had married him when she was thirty and he was seventy-five, thinking she would be rich as soon as he died, but the old man was a scoundrel and when his estate was settled, they found he didn't have a nickel. All he left her were the fifty acres and the house. But she always spoke of him in a reverent way and quoted his sayings, such as, "One fellow's misery is the other fellow's gain," and "The devil you know is better than the devil you don't."

"However," Mrs. Shortley remarked, "the devil you know is better than the devil you don't," and she had to turn away so that Mrs. McIntyre would not see her smile. She had found out what the Displaced Person was up to through the old man, Astor, and she had not told anybody but Mr. Shortley. Mr. Shortley had risen straight up in bed like Lazarus from the tomb.

"Shut your mouth!" he had said.

"Yes," she had said.

"Naw!" Mr. Shortley had said.

"Yes," she had said.

Mr. Shortley had fallen back flat.

"The Pole don't know any better," Mrs. Shortley had said. "I reckon that priest is putting him up to it is all. I blame the priest."

The priest came frequently to see the Guizacs and he would always stop in and visit Mrs. McIntyre too and they would walk around the place and she would point out her improvements and listen to his rattling talk. It suddenly came to Mrs. Shortley that he was trying to persuade her to bring another Polish family onto the place. With two of them here, there would be almost nothing spoken but Polish! The Negroes would be gone and there would be the two families against Mr. Shortley and herself! She began to imagine a war of words, to see the Polish words and the English words coming at each other, stalking forward, not sentences, just words, gabble gabble gabble, flung out high and shrill and stalking forward and then grappling with each other. She saw the Polish words, dirty and all-knowing and unreformed, flinging mud on the clean English words until everything was equally dirty. She saw them all piled up in a room, all the dead dirty words, theirs and hers too, piled up like the naked bodies in the newsreel. God save me! she cried silently, from the stinking power of Satan! And she started from that day to read her Bible with a new attention. She pored over the Apocalypse and began to quote from the Prophets and before long she had come to a deeper understanding of her existence. She saw plainly that the meaning of the world was a mystery that had been planned and she was not surprised to suspect that she had a special part in the plan because she was strong. She saw that the Lord God Almighty had created the strong people to do what had to be done and she felt that she would be ready when she was called. Right now she felt that her business was to watch the priest.

His visits irked her more and more. On the last one, he went about picking up feathers off the ground. He found two peacock feathers and four or five turkey feathers and an old brown hen feather and took them off with him like a bouquet. This foolish-acting did not deceive Mrs. Shortley any. Here he was: leading foreigners over in hordes to places that were not theirs, to cause disputes, to uproot niggers, to plant the Whore of Babylon in the midst of the righteous! Whenever he came on the place, she hid herself behind something and watched until he left.

It was on a Sunday afternoon that she had her vision. She had gone to drive in the cows for Mr. Shortley who had a pain in his knee and she was walking slowly through the pasture, her arms folded, her eyes on the distant low-lying clouds that looked like rows and rows of white fish washed up on a great blue beach. She paused after an incline to heave a sigh of exhaustion for she had an immense weight to carry around and she was not as young as she used to be.

At times she could feel her heart, like a child's fist, clenching and unclenching inside her chest, and when the feeling came, it stopped her thought altogether and she would go about like a large hull of herself, moving for no reason; but she gained this incline without a tremor and stood at the top of it, pleased with herself. Suddenly while she watched, the sky folded back in two pieces like the curtain to a stage and a gigantic figure stood facing her. It was the color of the sun in the early afternoon, white-gold. It was of no definite shape but there were fiery wheels with fierce dark eyes in them, spinning rapidly all around it. She was not able to tell if the figure was going forward or backward because its magnificence was so great. She shut her eyes in order to look at it and it turned blood-red and the wheels turned white. A voice, very resonant, said the one word, "Prophesy!"

She stood there, tottering slightly but still upright, her eyes shut tight and her fists clenched and her straw sunhat low on her forehead. "The children of wicked nations will be butchered," she said in a loud voice. "Legs where arms should be, foot to face, ear in the palm of hand. Who will remain whole? Who will remain whole? Who?"

Presently she opened her eyes. The sky was full of white fish carried lazily on their sides by some invisible current and pieces of the sun, submerged some distance beyond them, appeared from time to time as if they were being washed in the opposite direction. Woodenly she planted one foot in front of the other until she had crossed the pasture and reached the lot. She walked through the barn like one in a daze and did not speak to Mr. Shortley. She continued up the road until she saw the priest's car parked in front of Mrs. McIntyre's house. "Here again," she muttered. "Come to destroy."

Mrs. McIntyre and the priest were walking in the yard. In order not to meet them face to face, she turned to the left and entered the feed house, a single-room shack piled on one side with flowered sacks of scratch feed. There were spilled oyster shells in one corner and a few old dirty calendars on the wall, advertising calf feed and various patent medicine remedies. One showed a bearded gentleman in a frock coat, holding up a bottle, and beneath his feet was the inscription, "I have been made regular by this marvelous discovery!" Mrs. Shortley had always felt close to this man as if he were some distinguished person she was acquainted with but now her mind was on nothing but the dangerous presence of the priest. She stationed herself at a crack between two boards where she could look out and see him and Mrs. McIntyre strolling toward the turkey brooder, which was placed just outside the feed house.

"Arrrr!" he said as they approached the brooder. "Look at the little biddies!" and he stooped and squinted through the wire.

Mrs. Shortley's mouth twisted.

"Do you think the Guizacs will want to leave me?" Mrs. McIntyre asked. "Do you think they'll go to Chicago or some place like that?"

"And why should they do that now?" asked the priest, wiggling his finger at a turkey, his big nose close to the wire.

"Money," Mrs. McIntyre said.

"Arrrr, give them some morrre then," he said indifferently. "They have to get along."

"So do I," Mrs. McIntyre muttered. "It means I'm going to have to get rid of some of these others."

"And arrre the Shortleys satisfactory?" he inquired, paying more attention to the turkeys than to her.

"Five times in the last month I've found Mr. Shortley smoking in the barn," Mrs. McIntyre said. "Five times."

"And arrre the Negroes any better?"

"They lie and steal and have to be watched all the time," she said.

"Tsk, tsk," he said. "Which will you discharge?"

"I've decided to give Mr. Shortley his month's notice tomorrow," Mrs. McIntyre said.

The priest scarcely seemed to hear her he was so busy wiggling his finger inside the wire. Mrs. Shortley sat down on an open sack of laying mash with a dead thump that sent feed dust clouding up around her. She found herself looking straight ahead at the opposite wall where the gentleman on the calendar was holding up his marvelous discovery but she didn't see him. She looked ahead as if she saw nothing whatsoever. Then she rose and ran to her house. Her face was an almost volcanic red.

She opened all the drawers and dragged out boxes and old battered suitcases from under the bed. She began to unload the drawers into the boxes, all the time without pause, without taking off the sunhat she had on her head. She set the two girls to doing the same. When Mr. Shortley came in, she did not even look at him but merely pointed one arm at him while she packed with the other. "Bring the car around to the back door," she said. "You ain't waiting to be fired!"

Mr. Shortley had never in his life doubted her omniscience. He perceived the entire situation in half a second and, with only a sour scowl, retreated out the door and went to drive the automobile around to the back.

They tied the two iron beds to the top of the car and the two rocking chairs inside the beds and rolled the two mattresses up between the rocking chairs. On top of this they tied a crate of chickens. They loaded the inside of the car with the old suitcases and boxes, leaving a small space for Annie Maude and Sarah Mae. It took them the rest of the afternoon and half the night to do this but Mrs. Shortley was determined that they would leave before four o'clock in the morning, that Mr. Shortley should not adjust another milking machine on this place. All the time she had been working, her face was changing rapidly from red to white and back again.

Just before dawn, as it began to drizzle rain, they were ready to leave. They all got in the car and sat there cramped up between boxes and bundles and rolls of bedding. The square black automobile moved off with more than its customary grinding noises as if it were protesting the load. In the back, the two long bony yellow-haired girls were sitting on a pile of boxes and there was a beagle hound puppy and a cat with two kittens somewhere under the blankets. The car moved slowly, like some overfreighted leaking ark, away from their shack and past the white house where Mrs. McIntyre was sleeping soundly—hardly guessing that her cows would not be milked by Mr. Shortley that morning—and past the Pole's shack on top of the hill and on down the road to the gate where the two Negroes were walking, one behind the other, on their way to help with the milking. They looked straight at the car and its occupants but even as the dim yellow headlights lit up their faces, they politely did not seem to see anything, or anyhow, to attach significance to what was there. The loaded car might have been passing mist in the early morning half-light. They continued up the road at the same even pace without looking back.

A dark yellow sun was beginning to rise in a sky that was the same slick dark gray as the highway. The fields stretched away, stiff and weedy, on either side. "Where we goin?" Mr. Shortley asked for the first time.

Mrs. Shortley sat with one foot on a packing box so that her knee was pushed into her stomach. Mr. Shortley's elbow was almost under her nose and Sara Mae's bare left foot was sticking over the front seat, touching her ear.

"Where we goin?" Mr. Shortley repeated and when she didn't answer again, he turned and looked at her.

Fierce heat seemed to be swelling slowly and fully into her face as if it were welling up now for a final assault. She was sitting in an erect way in spite of the fact that one leg was twisted under her and one knee was almost into her neck, but there was a peculiar lack of light in her icy blue eyes. All the vision in them might have been turned around, looking inside her. She suddenly grabbed Mr. Shortley's elbow and Sarah Mae's foot at the same time and began to tug and pull on them as if she were trying to fit the two extra limbs onto herself.

Mr. Shortley began to curse and quickly stopped the car and Sarah Mae yelled to quit but Mrs. Shortley apparently intended to rearrange the whole car at once. She thrashed forward and backward, clutching at everything she could get her hands on and hugging it to herself, Mr. Shortley's head, Sarah Mae's leg, the cat, a wad of white bedding, her own big moon-like knee; then all at once her fierce expression faded into a look of astonishment and her grip on what she had loosened. One of her eyes drew near to the other and seemed to collapse quietly and she was still.

The two girls, who didn't know what had happened to her, began to say, "Where we goin, Ma? Where we goin?" They thought she was playing a joke and that their father, staring straight ahead at her, was imitating a dead man. They didn't know that she had had a great experience or ever been displaced in the world from all that belonged to her. They were frightened by the gray slick road before them and they kept repeating in higher and higher voices, "Where we goin, Ma? Where we goin?" while their mother, her huge body rolled back still against the seat and her eyes like blue-painted glass, seemed to contemplate for the first time the tremendous frontiers of her true country.

II

"Well," Mrs. McIntyre said to the old Negro, "we can get along without them. We've seen them come and seen them go—black and white." She was standing in the calf barn while he cleaned it and she held a rake in her hand and now and then pulled a corn cob from a corner or pointed to a soggy spot that he had missed. When she discovered the Shortleys were gone, she was delighted as it meant she wouldn't have to fire them. The people she hired always left her—because they were that kind of people. Of all the families she had had, the Shortleys were the best if she didn't count the Displaced Person. They had been not quite trash; Mrs. Shortley was a good woman, and she would miss her but as the Judge used to say, you couldn't have your pie and eat it too, and she was satisfied with the D.P. "We've seen them come and seen them go," she repeated with satisfaction.

"And me and you," the old man said, stooping to drag his hoe under a feed rack, "is still here."

She caught exactly what he meant her to catch in his tone. Bars of sunlight fell from the cracked ceiling across his back and cut him in three distinct parts. She watched his long hands clenched around the hoe and his crooked old profile pushed close to them. You might have been here *before* I was, she said to herself, but it's mighty likely I'll be here when you're gone. "I've spent half my life fooling with worthless people," she said in a severe voice, "but now I'm through."

"Black and white," he said, "is the same."

"I am through," she repeated and gave her dark smock that she had thrown over her shoulders like a cape a quick snatch at the neck. She had on a broad-brimmed black straw hat that had cost her twenty dollars twenty years ago and that she used now for a sunhat. "Money is the root of all evil," she said. "The Judge said so every day. He said he deplored money. He said the reason you niggers were so uppity was because there was so much money in circulation."

The old Negro had known the Judge. "Judge say he long for the day when he be too poor to pay a nigger to work," he said. "Say when that day come, the world be back on its feet."

She leaned forward, her hands on her hips and her neck stretched and said, "Well that day has almost come around here and I'm telling each and every one of you: you better look sharp. I don't have to put up with foolishness any more. I have somebody now who *has* to work!"

The old man knew when to answer and when not. At length he said, "We seen them come and we seen them go."

"However, the Shortleys were not the worst by far," she said. "I well remember those Garrits."

"They was before them Collinses," he said.

"No, before the Ringfields."

"Sweet Lord, them Ringfields!" he murmured.

"None of that kind *want* to work," she said.

"We seen them come and we seen them go," he said as if this were a refrain. "But we ain't never had one before," he said, bending himself up until he faced her, "like what we got now." He was cinnamon-colored with eyes that were so blurred with age that they seemed to be hung behind cobwebs.

She gave him an intense stare and held it until, lowering his hands on the hoe, he bent down again and dragged a pile of shavings alongside the wheelbarrow. She said stiffly, "He can wash out that barn in the time it took Mr. Shortley to make up his mind he had to do it."

"He from Pole," the old man muttered.

"From Poland."

"In Pole it ain't like it is here," he said. "They got different ways of doing," and he began to mumble unintelligibly.

"What are you saying?" she said. "If you have anything to say about him, say it and say it aloud."

He was silent, bending his knees precariously and edging the rake along the underside of the trough.

"If you know anything he's done that he shouldn't, I expect you to report it to me," she said.

"It warn't like it was what he should ought or oughtn't," he muttered. "It was like what nobody else don't do."

"You don't have anything against him," she said shortly, "and he's here to stay."

"We ain't never had one like him before is all," he murmured and gave his polite laugh.

"Times are changing," she said. "Do you know what's happening to this world? It's swelling up. It's getting so full of people that only the smart thrifty energetic ones are going to survive," and she tapped the words, smart, thrifty, and energetic out on the palm of her hand. Through the far end of the stall she could see down the road to where the Displaced Person was standing in the open barn door with the green hose in his hand. There was a certain stiffness about his figure that seemed to make it necessary for her to approach him slowly, even in her thoughts. She had decided this was because she couldn't hold an easy conversation with him. Whenever she said anything to him, she found herself shouting and nodding extravagantly and she would be conscious that one of the Negroes was leaning behind the nearest shed, watching.

"No indeed!" she said, sitting down on one of the feed racks and folding her arms, "I've made up my mind that I've had enough trashy people on this place to last me a lifetime and I'm not going to spend my last years fooling with Shortleys and Ringfields and Collins when the world is full of people who *have* to work."

"Howcome they so many extra?" he asked.

"People are selfish," she said. "They have too many children. There's no sense in it any more."

He had picked up the wheelbarrow handles and was backing out the door and he paused, half in the sunlight and half out, and stood there chewing his gums as if he had forgotten which direction he wanted to move in.

"What you colored people don't realize," she said, "is that I'm the one around here who holds all the strings together. If you don't work, I don't make any money and I can't pay you. You're all dependent on me but you each and every one act like the shoe is on the other foot."

It was not possible to tell from his face if he heard her. Finally he backed out with the wheelbarrow. "Judge say the devil he know is better than the devil he don't," he said in a clear mutter and turned and trundled off.

She got up and followed him, a deep vertical pit appearing suddenly in the center of her forehead, just under the red bangs. "The Judge has long since ceased to pay the bills around here," she called in a piercing voice.

He was the only one of her Negroes who had known the Judge and he thought this gave him title. He had had a low opinion of Mr. Crooms and Mr. McIntyre, her other husbands, and in his veiled polite way, he had congratulated her after each of her divorces. When he thought it necessary, he would work under a window where he knew she was sitting and talk to himself, a careful roundabout discussion, question and answer and then refrain. Once she had got up silently and slammed the window down so hard that he had fallen backwards off his feet. Or occasionally he spoke with the peacock. The cock would follow him around the place, his steady eye on the ear of corn that stuck up from the old man's back pocket or he would sit near him and pick himself. Once from the open kitchen door, she had heard him say to the bird, "I remember when it was twenty of you walking about this place and now it's only you and two hens. Crooms it was twelve. McIntyre it was five. You and two hens now."

And that time she had stepped out of the door onto the porch and said, "MISTER Crooms and MISTER McIntyre! And I don't want to hear you call either of them anything else again. And you can understand this: when that peachicken dies there won't be any replacements."

She kept the peacock only out of a superstitious fear of annoying the Judge in his grave. He had liked to see them walking around the place for he said they made him feel rich. Of her three husbands, the Judge was the one most present to her although he was the only one she had buried. He was in the family graveyard, a little space fenced in the middle of the back cornfield, with his mother and father and grandfather and three great aunts and two infant cousins. Mr. Crooms, her second, was forty miles away in the state asylum and Mr. McIntyre, her last, was intoxicated, she supposed, in some hotel room in Florida. But the Judge, sunk in the cornfield with his family, was always at home.

She had married him when he was an old man and because of his money but there had been another reason that she would not admit then, even to herself: she had liked him. He was a dirty snuff-dipping Court House figure, famous all over the county for being rich, who wore high-top shoes, a string tie, a gray suit with a black stripe in it, and a yellowed panama hat, winter and summer. His teeth and hair were tobacco-colored and his face a clay pink pitted and tracked with mysterious prehistoric-looking marks as if he had been unearthed among fossils. There had been a peculiar odor about him of sweaty fondled bills but he never carried money on him or had a nickel to show. She was his secretary for a few months and the old man with his sharp eye had seen at once that here was a woman who admired him for himself. The three years that he lived after they married were the happiest and most prosperous of Mrs. McIntyre's life, but when he died his estate proved to be bankrupt. He left her a mortgaged house and fifty acres that he had managed to cut the timber off before he died. It was as if, as the final triumph of a successful life, he had been able to take everything with him.

But she had survived. She had survived a succession of tenant farmers and dairymen that the old man himself would have found hard to outdo, and she had been able to meet the constant drain of a tribe of moody unpredictable Negroes, and she had even managed to hold her own against the incidental bloodsuckers, the cattle dealers and lumber men and the buyers and sellers of anything who drove up in pieced-together trucks and honked in the yard.

She stood slightly reared back with her arms folded under her smock and a satisfied expression on her face as she watched the Displaced Person turn off the hose and disappear inside the barn. She was sorry that the poor man had been chased out of Poland and run across Europe and had had to take up in a tenant shack in a strange country, but she had not been responsible for any of this. She had had a hard time herself. She knew what it was to struggle. People ought to have to struggle. Mr. Guizac had probably had everything given to him all the way across Europe and over here. He had probably not had to struggle enough. She had given him a job. She didn't know if he was grateful or not. She didn't know anything about him except that he did the work. The truth was that he was not very real to her yet. He was a kind of miracle that she had seen happen and that she talked about but that she still didn't believe.

She watched as he came out of the barn and motioned to Sulk, who was coming around the back of the lot. He gesticulated and then took something out of his pocket and the two of them stood looking at it. She started down the lane toward them. The Negro's figure was slack and tall and he was craning his round head forward in his usual idiotic way. He was a little better than half-witted but when they were like that they were always good workers. The Judge had said always hire you a half-witted nigger because they don't have sense enough to stop working. The Pole was gesticulating rapidly. He left something with the colored boy and then walked off and before she rounded the turn in the lane, she heard the tractor crank up. He was on his way to the field. The Negro was still hanging there, gaping at whatever he had in his hand.

She entered the lot and walked through the barn, looking with approval at the wet spotless concrete floor. It was only nine-thirty and Mr. Shortley had never got anything washed until eleven. As she came out at the other end, she saw the Negro moving very slowly in a diagonal path across the road in front of her, his eyes still on what Mr. Guizac had given him. He didn't see her and he paused and dipped his knees and leaned over his hand, his tongue describing little circles. He had a photograph. He lifted one finger and traced it lightly over the surface of the picture. Then he looked up and saw her and seemed to freeze, his mouth in a half-grin, his finger lifted.

"Why haven't you gone to the field?" she asked.

He raised one foot and opened his mouth wider while the hand with the photograph edged toward his back pocket.

"What's that?" she said.

"It ain't nothin," he muttered and handed it to her automatically.

It was a photograph of a girl of about twelve in a white dress. She had blond hair with a wreath in it and she looked forward out of light eyes that were bland and composed. "Who is this child?" Mrs. McIntyre asked.

"She his cousin," the boy said in a high voice.

"Well what are you doing with it?" she asked.

"She going to mah me," he said in an even higher voice.

"Marry you!" she shrieked.

"I pays half to get her over here," he said. "I pays him three dollar a week. She bigger now. She his cousin. She don't care who she mah she so glad to get away from there." The high voice seemed to shoot up like a nervous jet of sound and then fall flat as he watched her face. Her eyes were the color of blue granite when the glare falls on it, but she was not looking at him. She was looking down the road where the distant sound of the tractor could be heard.

"I don't reckon she goin to come nohow," the boy murmured.

"I'll see that you get every cent of your money back," she said in a toneless voice and turned and walked off, holding the photograph bent in two. There was nothing about her small stiff figure to indicate that she was shaken.

As soon as she got in the house, she lay down on her bed and shut her eyes and pressed her hand over her heart as if she were trying to keep it in place. Her mouth opened and she made two or three dry little sounds. Then after a minute she sat up and said aloud, "They're all the same. It's always been like this," and she fell back flat again.

"Twenty years of being beaten and done in and they even robbed his grave!" and remembering that, she began to cry quietly, wiping her eyes every now and then with the hem of her smock.

What she had thought of was the angel over the Judge's grave. This had been a naked granite cherub that the old man had seen in the city one day in a tombstone store window. He had been taken with it at once, partly because its face reminded him of his wife and partly because he wanted a genuine work of art over his grave. He had come home with it sitting on the green plush train seat beside him. Mrs. McIntyre had never noticed the resemblance to herself. She had always thought it hideous but when the Herrins left the angel left with them, all but its toes, for the ax old man Herrin had used to break it off with had struck slightly too high. Mrs. McIntyre had never been able to afford to have it replaced.

When she had cried all she could, she got up and went into the back hall, a closet-like space that was dark and quiet as a chapel and sat down on the edge of the Judge's black mechanical chair with her elbow on his desk. This was a giant roll-top piece of furniture pocked with pigeon holes full of dusty papers. Old bankbooks and ledgers were stacked in the half-open drawers and there was a small safe, empty but locked, set like a tabernacle in the center of it. She had left this part of the house unchanged since the old man's time. It was a kind of memorial to him, sacred because he had conducted his business here. With the slightest tilt one way or the other, the chair gave a rusty skeletal groan that sounded something like him when he had complained of his poverty. It had been his first principle to talk as if he were the poorest man in the world and she followed it, not only because he had but because it was true. When she sat with her intense constricted face turned toward the empty safe, she knew there was nobody poorer in the world than she was.

She sat motionless at the desk for ten or fifteen minutes and then as if she had gained some strength, she got up and got in her car and drove to the cornfield.

The road ran through a shadowy pine thicket and ended on top of a hill that rolled fan-wise down and up again in a broad expanse of tasseled green. Mr. Guizac was cutting from the outside of the field in a circular path to the center where the graveyard was all but hidden by the corn, and she could see him on the high far side of the slope, mounted on the tractor with the cutter and wagon behind him. From time to time, he had to get off the tractor and climb in the wagon to spread the silage because the Negro had not arrived.

She watched impatiently, standing in front of her black coupe with her arms folded under her smock, while he progressed slowly around the rim of the field, gradually getting close enough for her to wave to him to get down. He stopped the machine and jumped off and came running forward, wiping his red jaw with a piece of grease rag.

"I want to talk to you," she said and beckoned him to the edge of the thicket where it was shady. He took off the cap and followed her, smiling, but his smile faded when she turned and faced him. Her eyebrows, thin and fierce as a spider's leg, had drawn together ominously and the deep vertical pit had plunged down from under the red bangs into the bridge of her nose. She removed the bent picture from her pocket and handed it to him silently. Then she stepped back and said, "Mr. Guizac! You would bring this poor innocent child over here and try to marry her to a half-witted thieving black stinking nigger! What kind of a monster are you!"

He took the photograph with a slowly returning smile. "My cousin," he said. "She twelve here. First Communion. Six-ten now."

Monster! she said to herself and looked at him as if she were seeing him for the first time. His forehead and skull were white where they had been protected by his cap but the rest of his face was red and bristled with short yellow hairs. His eyes were like two bright nails behind his gold-rimmed spectacles that had been mended over the nose with haywire. His whole face looked as if it might have been patched together out of several others. "Mr. Guizac," she said, beginning slowly and then speaking faster until she ended breathless in the middle of a word, "that nigger cannot have a white wife from Europe. You can't talk to a nigger that way. You'll excite him and besides it can't be done. Maybe it can be done in Poland but it can't be done here and you'll have to stop. It's all foolishness. That nigger don't have a grain of sense and you'll excite . . ."

"She in camp three year," he said.

"Your cousin," she said in a positive voice, "cannot come over here and marry one of my Negroes."

"She six-ten year," he said. "From Poland. Mamma die, pappa die. She wait in camp. Three camp." He pulled a wallet from his pocket and fingered through it and took out another picture of the same girl, a few years older, dressed in something dark and shapeless. She was standing against a wall with a short woman who apparently had no teeth. "She mamma," he said, pointing to the woman. "She die in two camp."

"Mr. Guizac," Mrs. McIntyre said, pushing the picture back at him, "I will not have my niggers upset. I cannot run this place without my niggers. I can run it without you but not without them and if you mention this girl to Sulk again, you won't have a job with me. Do you understand?"

His face showed no comprehension. He seemed to be piecing all these words together in his mind to make a thought.

Mrs. McIntyre remembered Mrs. Shortley's words: "He understands everything, he only pretends he don't so as to do exactly as he pleases," and her face regained the look of shocked wrath she had begun with. "I cannot understand how a man who calls himself a Christian," she said, "could bring a poor innocent girl over here and marry her to something like that. I cannot understand it. I cannot!" and she shook her head and looked into the distance with a pained blue gaze.

After a second he shrugged and let his arms drop as if he were tired. "She no care black," he said. "She in camp three year."

Mrs. McIntyre felt a peculiar weakness behind her knees. "Mr. Guizac," she said, "I don't want to have to speak to you about this again. If I do, you'll have to find another place yourself. Do you understand?"

The patched face did not say. She had the impression that he didn't see her there. "This is my place," she said. "I say who will come here and who won't."

"Ya," he said and put back on his cap.

"I am not responsible for the world's misery," she said as an afterthought.

"Ya," he said.

"You have a good job. You should be grateful to be here," she added, "but I'm not sure you are."

"Ya," he said and gave his little shrug and turned back to the tractor.

She watched him get on and maneuver the machine into the corn again. When he had passed her and rounded the turn, she climbed to the top of the slope and stood with her arms folded and looked out grimly over the field. "They're all the same," she muttered, "whether they come from Poland or Tennessee. I've handled Herrins and Ringfields and Shortleys and I can handle a Guizac," and she narrowed her gaze until it closed entirely around the diminishing figure on the tractor as if she were watching him through a gunsight.

All her life she had been fighting the world's overflow and now she had it in the form of a Pole. "You're just like all the rest of them," she said, "—only smart and thrifty and energetic but so am I. And this is my place," and she stood there, a small black-hatted, black-smocked figure with an aging cherubic face, and folded her arms as if she were equal to anything. But her heart was beating as if some interior violence had already been done to her. She opened her eyes to include the whole field so that the figure on the tractor was no larger than a grasshopper in her widened view.

She stood there for some time. There was a slight breeze and the corn trembled in great waves on both sides of the slope. The big cutter, with its monotonous roar, continued to shoot it pulverized into the wagon in a steady spurt of fodder. By nightfall, the Displaced Person would have worked his way around and around until there would be nothing on either side of the two hills but the stubble, and down in the center, risen like a little island, the graveyard where the Judge lay grinning under his desecrated monument.

III

The priest, with his long bland face supported on one finger, had been talking for ten minutes about Purgatory while Mrs. McIntyre squinted furiously at him from an opposite chair. They were drinking ginger ale on her front porch and she had kept rattling the ice in her glass, rattling her beads, rattling her bracelet like an impatient pony jingling its harness. There is no moral obligation to keep him, she was saying under her breath, there is absolutely no moral obligation. Suddenly she lurched up and her voice fell across his brogue like a drill into a mechanical saw. "Listen!" she said, "I'm not theological. I'm practical! I want to talk to you about something practical!"

"Arrrrrrr," he groaned, grating to a halt.

She had put at least a finger of whisky in her own ginger ale so that she would be able to endure his full-length visit and she sat down awkwardly, finding the chair closer to her than she had expected. "Mr. Guizac is not satisfactory," she said.

The old man raised his eyebrows in mock wonder.

"He's extra," she said. "He doesn't fit in. I have to have somebody who fits in."

The priest carefully turned his hat on his knees. He had a little
trick of waiting a second silently and then swinging the conversation
back into his own paths. He was about eighty. She had never known
a priest until she had gone to see this one on the business of getting
her the Displaced Person. After he had got her the Pole, he had used
the business introduction to try to convert her—just as she had
supposed he would.

"Give him time," the old man said. "He'll learn to fit in. Where
is that beautiful birrrrd of yours?" he asked and then said, "Arrrrr, I
see him!" and stood up and looked out over the lawn where the
peacock and the two hens were stepping at a strained attention,
their long necks ruffled, the cock's violent blue and the hens' silver-
green, glinting in the late afternoon sun.

"Mr. Guizac," Mrs. McIntyre continued, bearing down with a
flat steady voice, "is very efficient. I'll admit that. But he doesn't
understand how to get on with my niggers and they don't like him.
I can't have my niggers run off. And I don't like his attitude. He's
not in the least grateful for being here."

The priest had his hand on the screen door and he opened it,
ready to make his escape. "Arrrr, I must be off," he murmured.

"I tell you if I had a white man who understood the Negroes, I'd
have to let Mr. Guizac go," she said and stood up again.

He turned then and looked her in the face. "He has nowhere
to go," he said. Then he said, "Dear lady, I know you well enough
to know you wouldn't turn him out for a trifle!" and without waiting
for an answer, he raised his hand and gave her his blessing in a
rumbling voice.

She smiled angrily and said, "I didn't create his situation, of
course."

The priest let his eyes wander toward the birds. They had reached
the middle of the lawn. The cock stopped suddenly and curving his
neck backwards, he raised his tail and spread it with a shimmering
timbrous noise. Tiers of small pregnant suns floated in a green-gold
haze over his head. The priest stood transfixed, his jaw slack. Mrs.
McIntyre wondered where she had ever seen such an idiotic old
man. "Christ will come like that!" he said in a loud gay voice and
wiped his hand over his mouth and stood there, gaping.

Mrs. McIntyre's face assumed a set puritanical expression and she
reddened. Christ in the conversation embarrassed her the way sex
had her mother. "It is not my responsibility that Mr. Guizac has no-

where to go," she said. "I don't find myself responsible for all the extra people in the world."

The old man didn't seem to hear her. His attention was fixed on the cock who was taking minute steps backward, his head against the spread tail. "The Transfiguration," he murmured.

She had no idea what he was talking about. "Mr. Guizac didn't have to come here in the first place," she said, giving him a hard look.

The cock lowered his tail and began to pick grass.

"He didn't have to come in the first place," she repeated, emphasizing each word.

The old man smiled absently. "He came to redeem us," he said and blandly reached for her hand and shook it and said he must go.

If Mr. Shortley had not returned a few weeks later, she would have gone out looking for a new man to hire. She had not wanted him back but when she saw the familiar black automobile drive up the road and stop by the side of the house, she had the feeling that she was the one returning, after a long miserable trip, to her own place. She realized all at once that it was Mrs. Shortley she had been missing. She had had no one to talk to since Mrs. Shortley left, and she ran to the door, expecting to see her heaving herself up the steps.

Mr. Shortley stood there alone. He had on a black felt hat and a shirt with red and blue palm trees designed in it but the hollows in his long bitten blistered face were deeper than they had been a month ago.

"Well!" she said. "Where is Mrs. Shortley?"

Mr. Shortley didn't say anything. The change in his face seemed to have come from the inside; he looked like a man who had gone for a long time without water. "She was God's own angel," he said in a loud voice. "She was the sweetest woman in the world."

"Where is she?" Mrs. McIntyre murmured.

"Daid," he said. "She had herself a stroke on the day she left out of here." There was a corpse-like composure about his face. "I figure that Pole killed her," he said. "She seen through him from the first. She known he come from the devil. She told me so."

It took Mrs. McIntyre three days to get over Mrs. Shortley's death. She told herself that anyone would have thought they were kin. She rehired Mr. Shortley to do farm work though actually she didn't want him without his wife. She told him she was going to give thirty days' notice to the Displaced Person at the end of the month and that then he could have his job back in the dairy. Mr. Shortley preferred the dairy job but he was willing to wait. He said it would give him some satisfaction to see the Pole leave the place, and Mrs. McIntyre said it would give her a great deal of satisfaction. She confessed that she should have been content with the help she had in the first place and not have been reaching into other parts of the world for it. Mr. Shortley said he never had cared for foreigners since he had been in the first world's war and seen what they were like. He said he had seen all kinds then but that none of them were like us. He said he recalled the face of one man who had thrown a hand-grenade at him and that the man had had little round eye-glasses exactly like Mr. Guizac's.

"But Mr. Guizac is a Pole, he's not a German," Mrs. McIntyre said.

"It ain't a great deal of difference in them two kinds," Mr. Short-ley had explained.

The Negroes were pleased to see Mr. Shortley back. The Displaced Person had expected them to work as hard as he worked himself, whereas Mr. Shortley recognized their limitations. He had never been a very good worker himself with Mrs. Shortley to keep him in line, but without her, he was even more forgetful and slow. The Pole worked as fiercely as ever and seemed to have no inkling that he was about to be fired. Mrs. McIntyre saw jobs done in a short time that she had thought would never get done at all. Still she was resolved to get rid of him. The sight of his small stiff figure moving quickly here and there had come to be the most irritating sight on the place for her, and she felt she had been tricked by the old priest. He had said there was no legal obligation for her to keep the Displaced Person if he was not satisfactory, but then he had brought up the moral one.

She meant to tell him that *her* moral obligation was to her own people, to Mr. Shortley, who had fought in the world war for his country and not to Mr. Guizac who had merely arrived here to take advantage of whatever he could. She felt she must have this out with the priest before she fired the Displaced Person. When the first of the month came and the priest hadn't called, she put off giving the Pole notice for a little longer.

Mr. Shortley told himself that he should have known all along that no woman was going to do what she said she was when she said she was. He didn't know how long he could afford to put up with her shilly-shallying. He thought himself that she was going soft and was afraid to turn the Pole out for fear he would have a hard time getting another place. He could tell her the truth about this: that if she let him go, in three years he would own his own house and have a television aerial sitting on top of it. As a matter of policy, Mr. Shortley began to come to her back door every evening to put certain facts before her. "A white man sometimes don't get the consideration a nigger gets," he said, "but that don't matter because he's still white, but sometimes," and here he would pause and look off into the distance, "a man that's fought and bled and died in the service of his native land don't get the consideration of one of them like them he was fighting. I ast you: is that right?" When he asked her such questions he could watch her face and tell he was making an impression. She didn't look too well these days. He noticed lines around her eyes that hadn't been there when he and Mrs. Shortley had been the only white help on the place. Whenever he thought of Mrs. Shortley, he felt his heart go down like an old bucket into a dry well.

The old priest kept away as if he had been frightened by his last visit but finally, seeing that the Displaced Person had not been fired, he ventured to call again to take up giving Mrs. McIntyre instructions where he remembered leaving them off. She had not asked to be instructed but he instructed anyway, forcing a little definition of one of the sacraments or of some dogma into each conversation he had, no matter with whom. He sat on her porch, taking no notice of her partly mocking, partly outraged expression as she sat shaking her foot, waiting for an opportunity to drive a wedge into his talk. "For," he was saying, as if he spoke of something that had happened yesterday in town, "when God sent his Only Begotten Son, Jesus Christ Our Lord"—he slightly bowed his head—"as a Redeemer to mankind, He . . ."

"Father Flynn!" she said in a voice that made him jump. "I want to talk to you about something serious!"

The skin under the old man's right eye flinched.

"As far as I'm concerned," she said and glared at him fiercely, "Christ was just another D.P."

He raised his hands slightly and let them drop on his knees. "Arrrrr," he murmured as if he were considering this.

"I'm going to let that man go," she said. "I don't have any obliga-

tion to him. My obligation is to the people who've done something
for their country, not to the ones who've just come over to take advantage of what they can get," and she began to talk rapidly, remembering all her arguments. The priest's attention seemed to retire to
some private oratory to wait until she got through. Once or twice
his gaze roved out onto the lawn as if he were hunting some means
of escape but she didn't stop. She told him how she had been hanging onto this place for thirty years, always just barely making it
against people who came from nowhere and were going nowhere,
who didn't want anything but an automobile. She said she had
found out they were the same whether they came from Poland or
Tennessee. When the Guizacs got ready, she said, they would not
hesitate to leave her. She told him how the people who looked rich
were the poorest of all because they had the most to keep up. She
asked him how he thought she paid her feed bills. She told him
she would like to have her house done over but she couldn't afford
it. She couldn't even afford to have the monument restored over
her husband's grave. She asked him if he would like to guess what
her insurance amounted to for the year. Finally she asked him if
he thought she was made of money and the old man suddenly let
out a great ugly bellow as if this were a comical question.

When the visit was over, she felt let down, though she had clearly
triumphed over him. She made up her mind now that on the first of
the month, she would give the Displaced Person his thirty days'
notice and she told Mr. Shortley so.

Mr. Shortley didn't say anything. His wife had been the only
woman he was ever acquainted with who was never scared off from
doing what she said. She said the Pole had been sent by the devil
and the priest. Mr. Shortley had no doubt that the priest had got
some peculiar control over Mrs. McIntyre and that before long she
would start attending his Masses. She looked as if something was
wearing her down from the inside. She was thinner and more fidgety
and not as sharp as she used to be. She would look at a milk can
now and not see how dirty it was and he had seen her lips move
when she was not talking. The Pole never did anything the wrong
way but all the same he was very irritating to her. Mr. Shortley himself did things as he pleased—not always her way—but she didn't seem
to notice. She had noticed though that the Pole and all his family
were getting fat; she pointed out to Mr. Shortley that the hollows
had come out of their cheeks and that they saved every cent they

made. "Yes'm, and one of these days he'll be able to buy and sell you out," Mr. Shortley had ventured to say, and he could tell that the statement had shaken her.

"I'm just waiting for the first," she had said.

Mr. Shortley waited too and the first came and went and she didn't fire him. He could have told anybody how it would be. He was not a violent man but he hated to see a woman done in by a foreigner. He felt that that was one thing a man couldn't stand by and see happen.

There was no reason Mrs. McIntyre should not fire Mr. Guizac at once but she put it off from day to day. She was worried about her bills and about her health. She didn't sleep at night or when she did she dreamed about the Displaced Person. She had never discharged any one before; they had all left her. One night she dreamed that Mr. Guizac and his family were moving into her house and that she was moving in with Mr. Shortley. This was too much for her and she woke up and didn't sleep again for several nights; and one night she dreamed that the priest came to call and droned on and on, saying, "Dear lady, I know your tender heart won't suffer you to turn the porrrrr man out. Think of the thousands of them, think of the ovens and the boxcars and the camps and the sick children and Christ Our Lord."

"He's extra and he's upset the balance around her," she said, "and I'm a logical practical woman and there are no ovens here and no camps and no Christ Our Lord and when he leaves, he'll make more money. He'll work at the mill and buy a car and don't talk to me— all they want is a car."

"The ovens and the boxcars and the sick children," droned the priest, "and our dear Lord."

"Just one too many," she said.

The next morning, she made up her mind while she was eating her breakfast that she would give him his notice at once, and she stood up and walked out of the kitchen and down the road with her table napkin still in her hand. Mr. Guizac was spraying the barn, standing in his swaybacked way with one hand on his hip. He turned off the hose and gave her an impatient kind of attention as if she were interfering with his work. She had not thought of what she would say to him, she had merely come. She stood in the barn door, looking severely at the wet spotless floor and the dripping stanchions.

"Ya goot?" he said.

"Mr. Guizac," she said, "I can barely meet my obligations now." Then she said in a louder, stronger voice, emphasizing each word, "I have bills to pay."

"I too," Mr. Guizac said. "Much bills, little money," and he shrugged.

At the other end of the barn, she saw a long beak-nosed shadow glide like a snake halfway up the sunlit open door and stop; and somewhere behind her, she was aware of a silence where the sound of the Negroes shoveling had come a minute before. "This is my place," she said angrily. "All of you are extra. Each and every one of you are extra!"

"Ya," Mr. Guizac said and turned on the hose again.

She wiped her mouth with the napkin she had in her hand and walked off, as if she had accomplished what she came for.

Mr. Shortley's shadow withdrew from the door and he leaned against the side of the barn and lit half of a cigarette that he took out of his pocket. There was nothing for him to do now but wait on the hand of God to strike but he knew one thing: he was not going to wait with his mouth shut.

Starting that morning, he began to complain and to state his side of the case to every person he saw, black or white. He complained in the grocery store and at the courthouse and on the street corner and directly to Mrs. McIntyre herself, for there was nothing underhanded about him. If the Pole could have understood what he had to say, he would have said it to him too. "All men was created free and equal," he said to Mrs. McIntyre, "and I risked my life and limb to prove it. Gone over there and fought and bled and died and come back on over here and find out who's got my job—just exactly who I been fighting. It was a hand-grenade come that near to killing me and I seen who throwed it—little man with eye-glasses just like his. Might have bought them at the same store. Small world," and he gave a bitter little laugh. Since he didn't have Mrs. Shortley to do the talking any more, he had started doing it himself and had found that he had a gift for it. He had the power of making other people see his logic. He talked a good deal to the Negroes.

"Whyn't you go back to Africa?" he asked Sulk one morning as they were cleaning out the silo. "That's your country, ain't it?"

"I ain't goin there," the boy said. "They might eat me up."

"Well, if you behave yourself it isn't any reason you can't stay here," Mr. Shortley said kindly. "Because you didn't run away from nowhere. Your granddaddy was brought. He didn't have a thing to do with coming. It's the people that run away from where they come from that I ain't got any use for."

"I never felt no need to travel," the Negro said.

"Well," Mr. Shortley said, "if I was going to travel again, it would be to either China or Africa. You go to either of them two places and you can tell right away what the difference is between you and them. You go to these other places and the only way you can tell is if they say something. And then you can't always tell because about half of them know the English language. That's where we make our mistake," he said, "—letting all them people onto English. There'd be a heap less trouble if everybody only knew his own language. My wife said knowing two languages was like having eyes in the back of your head. You couldn't put nothing over on her."

"You sho couldn't," the boy muttered, and then he added, "She was fine. She was sho fine. I never known a finer white woman than her."

Mr. Shortley turned in the opposite direction and worked silently for a while. After a few minutes he leaned up and tapped the colored boy on the shoulder with the handle of his shovel. For a second he only looked at him while a great deal of meaning gathered in his wet eyes. Then he said softly, "Revenge is mine, saith the Lord."

Mrs. McIntyre found that everybody in town knew Mr. Shortley's version of her business and that everyone was critical of her conduct. She began to understand that she had a moral obligation to fire the Pole and that she was shirking it because she found it hard to do. She could not stand the increasing guilt any longer and on a cold Saturday morning, she started off after breakfast to fire him. She walked down to the machine shed where she heard him cranking up the tractor.

There was a heavy frost on the ground that made the fields look like the rough backs of sheep; the sun was almost silver and the woods stuck up like dry bristles on the sky line. The countryside seemed to be receding from the little circle of noise around the shed. Mr. Guizac was squatting on the ground beside the small tractor, putting in a part. Mrs. McIntyre hoped to get the fields turned over while he still had thirty days to work for her. The colored boy was standing by with some tools in his hand and Mr. Shortley was under the shed about to get up on the large tractor and back it out. She meant to wait until he and the Negro got out of the way before she began her unpleasant duty.

She stood watching Mr. Guizac, stamping her feet on the hard ground, for the cold was climbing like a paralysis up her feet and legs. She had on a heavy black coat and a red head-kerchief with her black hat pulled down on top of it to keep the glare out of her eyes. Under the black brim her face had an abstracted look and once or twice her lips moved silently. Mr. Guizac shouted over the noise of the tractor for the Negro to hand him a screwdriver and when he got it, he turned over on his back on the icy ground and reached up under the machine. She could not see his face, only his feet and legs and trunk sticking impudently out from the side of the tractor. He had on rubber boots that were cracked and splashed with mud. He raised one knee and then lowered it and turned himself slightly. Of all the things she resented about him, she resented most that he hadn't left of his own accord.

Mr. Shortley had got on the large tractor and was backing it out from under the shed. He seemed to be warmed by it as if its heat and strength sent impulses up through him that he obeyed instantly. He had headed it toward the small tractor but he braked it on a slight incline and jumped off and turned back toward the shed. Mrs. McIntyre was looking fixedly at Mr. Guizac's legs lying flat on the ground now. She heard the brake on the large tractor slip and, looking up, she saw it move forward, calculating its own path. Later she remembered that she had seen the Negro jump silently out of the way as if a spring in the earth had released him and that she had seen Mr. Shortley turn his head with incredible slowness and stare silently over his shoulder and that she had started to shout to the Displaced Person but that she had not. She had felt her eyes and Mr. Shortley's eyes and the Negro's eyes come together in one look that froze them in collusion forever, and she had heard the little noise the Pole made as the tractor wheel broke his backbone. The two men ran forward to help and she fainted.

She remembered, when she came to, running somewhere, perhaps into the house and out again but she could not remember what for or if she had fainted again when she got there. When she finally came back to where the tractors were, the ambulance had arrived. Mr. Guizac's body was covered with the bent bodies of his wife and two children and by a black one which hung over him, murmuring words she didn't understand. At first she thought this must be the doctor but then with a feeling of annoyance she recognized the priest, who had come with the ambulance and was slipping something into the crushed man's mouth. After a minute he stood up and she looked first at his bloody pants legs and then at his face which was not averted from her but was as withdrawn and expressionless as the rest of the countryside. She only stared at him for she was too shocked by her experience to be quite herself. Her mind was not taking hold of all that was happening. She felt she was in some foreign country where the people bent over the body were natives, and she watched like a stranger while the dead man was carried away in the ambulance.

That evening Mr. Shortley left without notice to look for a new position and the Negro, Sulk, was taken with a sudden desire to see more of the world and set off for the southern part of the state. The old man Astor could not work without company. Mrs. McIntyre hardly noticed that she had no help left for she came down with a nervous affliction and had to go to the hospital. When she came back, she saw that the place would be too much for her to run now and she turned her cows over to a professional auctioneer (who sold them at a loss) and retired to live on what she had, while she tried to save her declining health. A numbness developed in one of her legs and her hands and head began to jiggle and eventually she had to stay in bed all the time with only a colored woman to wait on her. Her eyesight grew steadily worse and she lost her voice altogether. Not many people remembered to come out to the country to see her except the old priest. He came regularly once a week with a bag of breadcrumbs and, after he had fed these to the peacock, he would come in and sit by the side of her bed and explain the doctrines of the Church.

SAUL BELLOW

Seize the Day

Introduction

> In this republican country, amid the
> fluctuating waves of our social life,
> somebody is always at the drowning point.
>
> NATHANIEL HAWTHORNE,
> *The House of the Seven Gables*

Saul Bellow is surely one of the three or four best novelists we now have in America, and *Seize the Day* strikes me as a masterpiece, a work in which many of the pressures and problems that seem unique to contemporary life are fiercely dramatized. That life in the city is or can be terribly lonely, that modern men are "alienated" (cut off, estranged) from one another as they grapple for status in the commercial jungle, that many people are forced to take on demeaning work in order to survive—all this becomes intensely alive in the pages of Bellow's work. I assume that, as you read these remarks, you have already read Bellow's story. We might now examine its elements.

THE SETTING   The novel as a form of literature is devoted primarily to portraying *this* world, the one in which we live out our daily lives. Ever since the early eighteenth century, when Daniel Defoe described the experience of a clever and resilient streetwalker named Moll Flanders, the novel has been devoted to "circumstantial realism." This means that the novelist sets out to show imaginary human beings in circumstances we can believe are accurate renderings of "what life is really like." Not that the novelist can simply transcribe, the way a tape recorder does; he must be more than a mere reporter. He must employ the details of closely observed reality in some sort of imaginary pattern or scheme. But the material he uses is the material of commonplace reality. In a fine book of literary criticism, *The Rise of the Novel*, Ian Watt writes that the novel rests on

> the premise, or primary convention, that the novel is a full and authentic report of human experience, and is therefore under an obligation to satisfy its reader with such details of the story as the individuality of the actors concerned, the particulars of the times and places of their actions, details which are presented through a more largely referential use of language than is common in other literary forms.

Seize the Day, a novella that shares these attributes of the novel, evokes a neighborhood in New York City—the Upper West Side; and it does this with a precision and vividness of detail that merit comparison with the way Dickens evoked nineteenth-century London. The Upper West Side is rather special in the life of New York City. It is a neighborhood of sharply contrasting economic levels and social types. The main thoroughfare is Broadway. Between roughly 65th and 120th Streets, Broadway is full of busy shops, shabby hotels that have seen better days, decaying but sometimes still grand apartment houses, appalling slums, gourmet food stores, and odd little squares where old people rest in the sun and drug addicts come for their dope. To the west of Broadway run the parallel avenues West End Avenue and Riverside Drive, which for years have been populated by upper-middle-class Jews but to which there has recently come an influx of intellectuals and young couples in search of large apartments. Only a short distance away, mostly east but also west of Broadway, are some of the worst slum buildings in New York City, inhabited mainly by poor Negroes and Puerto Ricans. It is also a neighborhood with a large proportion of old people: sometimes as you walk along Broadway, you think of it as Mortality Row. You see men crippled by strokes; you see addicts hopelessly "high"; you see people mumbling or shouting to themselves; you see various kinds of sharpers getting ready to make a deal; you see very charming adolescents dressed up in the current uniform of rebellion. It is a neighborhood that is slowly going to seed, but one that still has a great deal of vitality in its somewhat hopeful mixture of colors, races, and ethnic groups.

What first gives *Seize the Day* its solidity as a piece of fiction is the acute description, the sharp thrusting bits of observation, with which Bellow captures this neighborhood. All of his characters carry the aroma of this neighborhood; all of them represent aspects of its complex society. The opening of *Seize the Day*, especially the second and fourth paragraphs, shows Bellow cannily preparing his story by anchoring it in the particulars of this little world, in which the Hotel Ansonia, "the neighborhood's great landmark,"

> looks like a baroque palace from Prague or Munich enlarged a hundred times, with towers, domes, huge swells and bubbles of metal gone green from exposure, iron fretwork and festoons. Black television antennae are densely planted on its round summits. Under the changes of weather it may look like marble or like sea water, black as slate in the fog, white as tufa in sunlight.

Later Bellow will add other little touches:

> The traffic seemed to come down Broadway out of the sky, where the hot spokes of the sun rolled from the south. Hot, stony odors rose from the subway grating in the street.

Passages of this kind serve to "validate" Bellow's story; they help persuade us of its reality by setting the events, even those we may think strange, in a world that seems thoroughly familiar, credible, even tangible. It is almost as if, while poor Tommy Wilhelm goes through his wretched day, we could smell the smells and feel the heat of that cement jungle.

But in evoking this neighborhood so vividly, Bellow is not merely placing his fiction in recognizable circumstances. He is also calling upon a tradition of earlier fiction: that is, in the course of describing this part of New York Bellow also makes us aware of the many novels that have evoked the life of man in the city—Dickens' novels set in London, Dreiser's novels set in Chicago, Balzac's in Paris, and many others. The result is emotional enrichment, for even as we respond to the concreteness of Bellow's description we also are aware that behind that description is the *idea* of the modern city that has coursed through so much of the literature and thought of the last one hundred and fifty years.

POETRY   Nothing could be more mundane, more earthbound than what we have thus far noticed. But any work of fiction, no matter how devoted it may be to the principle of realism and no matter how pessimistic its underlying outlook, must also bring into play the recurring human impulses to spiritual fulfillment and personal satisfaction. Bellow does this primarily through his representation of Tommy Wilhelm's character, but there is one special way—both touching and ironic—that deserves a word of analysis. As Tommy Wilhelm wanders through the city, drenched and dazed in his suffering, there come back to him snatches of poetry, lines from Shakespeare, Milton, and Shelley. He is not the kind of man you'd expect to read or quote verse, though it would be jumping to an overhasty conclusion to suppose it entirely out of character for him to remember an occasional passage. His mind wanders back to his college years, to an anthology (Lieder and Lovett) that was widely used in the colleges during the thirties; these were the years that seemed to him full of promise, the years when he was still responsive to notions about beauty and the human spirit—everything, as he might self-pityingly say, that stirred him before he got crushed by wife, job, kids, and aging. The lines Tommy remembers are carefully chosen by Bellow; they represent both dimmed aspirations and, in their specific context, something of the sense of doom that now oppresses him. Especially the lines from Shelley, a writer who epitomizes the hopefulness and expressiveness of romanticism, play a sadly ironic part in the story: they represent a dredging-up from Tommy's psychic life of almost-forgotten dreams and feelings, and they serve also as an ironic counterpoint to what now seems his unavoidable fate.

THE HERO   "One of the key themes in Bellow's fiction," writes the critic Alfred Kazin, "is the attempt of his protagonists to get a grip on existence, to understand not themselves (they know that is impossible) but the infinitely elusive universe in which, as human creatures, they find themselves." But, continues Kazin, it is not merely that Bellow's characters are trapped in a crisis of morale and survival; they are also "burdened by a speculative quest, a need to understand their particular destiny within the general problem of human destiny. This compulsion, even when it is unconscious . . . as is the case of Tommy Wilhelm in *Seize the Day* . . . is the motivating energy of his heroes."

Kazin's description seems to me very helpful. But since he is talking mainly about Bellow's heroes in general, he doesn't get around to the special problem posed by Tommy Wilhelm—namely, that he is a fat and self-pitying slob, a man gone emotionally to seed, in many ways an unattractive specimen of the damage that life can do to a human being and the damage he can do to himself. Yet it is this character, who in the slang of an earlier generation would have been called a "sad sack," that carries the major burden of the action and its significance. We see Tommy in a day of panic, when it seems as if his whole life is falling apart and there is no way out for him, except perhaps to go crawling back to the job he hates and the wife he cannot bear. In his sloppy way Tommy Wilhelm has tried to rebel against the routines of modern life; he has tried to assert his will; and he has failed miserably. How then can we see him as any sort of significant figure or moral example? How can we feel that what happens to him is at all important? And, most crucial of all, how can we suppose that our lives are in any way implicated with that of so pitiful an example of mankind?

The answers to these questions—which are, I think, the key questions faced by a reader of *Seize the Day*—are fairly complex.

Tommy Wilhelm, though splendidly individualized as a character, also comes out of a certain tradition in the development of fiction. It is quite possible that in addition to seeing Tommy as a unique figure, Bellow saw him as a great-grandson of those suffering buffoons who appear and reappear in the novels of Dostoevsky, perhaps even of the "underground man." The buffoon in Dostoevsky's novels is a character who humiliates himself before his fellows, who keeps violating the norms of propriety and decorum, who simply cannot live by the claims of moderation and good sense, and who acts out—in a kind of mocking fashion—the sickness that Dostoevsky believes to be hidden beneath the good middle-class adjustment of other characters. The buffoon, in the novels of Dostoevsky and other writers, functions like an amusement-park mirror: you look in the mirror, you see your face and body horribly distorted; yet when you look more closely, you may find that the very process of distortion reveals something about you (that leer, that grin, that simper, that smirk) which you might not see in an ordinary mirror. In short, the buffoon causes us to see a part of our selves that we do not like to acknowledge. That is why he makes us uncomfortable. Watching the buffoon, one might say: there, but for the grace of social hypocrisy, go I.

But Tommy Wilhelm also comes out of another tradition. Tommy is a *shlemiehl*. That is a Yiddish word applied, with a mixture of affection and contempt, to the kind of person who just cannot do anything right. He means well; his heart may be warm; he is

even capable (like Tommy at one brilliant moment in the story) of
feeling great love for his fellow men. But constantly he acts out the
Yiddish proverb: a *shlemiehl* lands on his back and bruises his nose.
That's Tommy Wilhelm.

And so we return to a problem that was raised in the discussion of Tolstoy's *The Death of Ivan Ilych:* the problem of the
reader's identification with a character. The inexperienced reader
starts out by identifying, as if in a daydream, with those characters
he would most like to resemble: the beautiful, the charming, the
popular, and perhaps even the wise. Yet the experience of literature
does not allow us to rest in this state of amiable self-delusion. It requires us to probe more deeply into human existence, which means,
of course, into the faults and follies of ourselves. Soon we come to
see that the identification with the picture-book hero or heroine
brings us very little profit in the way of moral insight, psychological
self-understanding, or power of mind. We find that, by recognizing
how part of us is indeed like the miser in Ben Jonson's *Volpone* or
the sensualist in Dostoevsky's *The Brothers Karamazov* or the idle
woman in Flaubert's *Madame Bovary*, we can come to a more painful but also more truthful realization of what human life is really
like. To recognize in ourselves something of the fools and failures of
literature is not merely to rein in our vanity and clip our daydreams;
it is also to strengthen ourselves for the difficulties life brings. The
great novelist Flaubert said, *"Emma Bovary, c'est moi."* But if
Emma Bovary had met someone like herself she would not have
been able to say this in the ironic way that Flaubert did. That is one
difference between Flaubert and his character Emma.

I say all this to suggest that if you simply draw away in superiority or disgust from Tommy Wilhelm, you are indulging in a denial
of common humanity. But more: it would be a bad misreading of
Seize the Day to suppose that Tommy is nothing more than a poor
slob, a hopeless *shlemiehl*. For Tommy is a slob who feels, a *shlemiehl* who struggles to understand his failure. Tommy, for all his
unattractiveness, is a man like you and me—which means in part
that he is weak and foolish. He lives, like most urban people, under
the weight of unbearable pressures. Sometimes he displays his grief
in a nasty or exhibitionist way; sometimes he consciously exploits his
misery in order to win the solace or sympathy of those near him.
But what makes Tommy more than a mere passive victim, more
than a bundle of defeats and bruises, is that he does hang on to the

redemptive idea that life can be meaningful and dignified, even morally exalted.

On the day that we see him, everything has gone wrong. All his troubles converge. (That, by the way, is one respect in which the form of the short novel differs from that of the full-scale novel. In a full-scale novel Bellow would probably have spread out these troubles over a longer time and described each of them in greater detail; but in a short novel he must pack them in closely and persuade us that at a certain point in a man's life everything can come crashing down on his head. One of the very few advantages of growing older is that the idea of an overwhelming concentration of troubles comes to seem quite believable.)

Tommy Wilhelm suffers from a "crisis of identity." He does not know who he is, and he does not really know what he would like to be. Only his dissatisfaction redeems him a little. He has changed his name, as if to shake off his Jewish past and the father whom he both adores and dislikes. His father still calls him "Wilky," as if to keep upon the middle-aged Tommy the heavy, tyrannical hand of paternity that has always been there. And in the back of Tommy's mind there is another dimly apprehended self, "Velvel," the Yiddish name by which he had been called as a child. These confusions contribute to, and are surely caused by, the struggle between father and son which forms the underlying action of the book. (A fascinating study could be written comparing *Seize the Day* to Kafka's *Metamorphosis*.)

In the world of the Jews—and, therefore, always in the novels of Saul Bellow—the family plays a central role. It is tight-knit, supportive, and sometimes oppressive. Tommy Wilhelm, however, is a man adrift, no longer part of a sustaining family yet desperately in need of it. The family into which he was born no longer exists for him in any satisfactory way; the family he created through marriage he has himself torn apart. And yet, as he staggers from personal defeat to financial ruin, some glimmer of hope—both a self-delusion and a token of possible recovery—survives in him. What is man's real business in life, writes Bellow, if not "to carry his peculiar burden, to feel shame and impotence, to taste these quelled tears. . . . Maybe the making of mistakes expressed the very purpose of his life and the essence of his being here."

If we can see Tommy Wilhelm in his two-sidedness, we can also grasp the major narrative rhythm of the book. Bellow sets up a series of brief incidents, each of which multiplies the panic to which Tommy is subject. These incidents form a series of panels in which we see Tommy Wilhelm struggling against and surrendering to emotional and physical sloth. That is the external and more visible line of action. But there is also another line of action, one that occurs within Tommy himself, and this consists of his struggle to break out of his own wretchedness. Throughout the story he is at the door of a grief so large it would be liberating to enter; yet he cannot open that door. He is blocked by his vanity, blocked by his fear, blocked by his disintegration. He knows that only love can make human existence bearable, but he is trapped in self-pity. At the end, in one striking moment of concentration, Tommy releases all his grief at the coffin of a stranger. He weeps here—for what? Perhaps for his wasted life, perhaps for the death he feels to be imminent, perhaps for the waste in all humanity. But we sense that he weeps *beyond* the limits of self. In a magnificent sentence Bellow writes that Tommy "sank deeper than sorrow, through torn sobs and cries toward the consummation of his heart's ultimate need." Only, said Augustine, by losing one's self can one find one's self.

MINOR CHARACTERS   What an odd crew—half-people, crippled humanity, grotesques.

Maurice Venice is a "double" of Tommy, an extreme and extremely foolish version of Tommy's hopes and failures. Perls and Rappaport are money-driven crones, selfish and diseased, Dickensian caricatures who live for nothing but the latest stock quotations. But Tommy's father, Dr. Adler, and the enigmatic quack Tamkin are more complex.

Dr. Adler is anything but the usual warm and protective Jewish father who has been so frequent a figure in recent American fiction. He is a hard old man who wishes his son no harm and who even offers advice that, in the abstract, is quite sensible. He is not exactly selfish, but neither is he really unselfish; he is simply a man who has withdrawn his sympathies and lives entirely behind the crust of his ego. Thereby he is guilty of a great sin: he does not care to become involved with the sufferings of his fellow men. The rationalization by means of which he defends himself has considerable truth to it: that old people should not have to bear the burdens of the young, even if the young are their own children. Except that in sticking to this defensible view, he neglects the still more urgent need humanity has for exceptions—namely, the exception dictated by love for one's flesh and blood. Even when he speaks about his son as if Tommy were his patient, he performs only half his task. He displays skill as a diagnostician but refuses to accept the burden of curing. In reality, of course, he can never be a mere doctor in relation to Tommy. For he is a father, and morally speaking, fatherhood is not a role about which one can make choices. By nevertheless refusing the pain of fatherhood, Dr. Adler comes to represent the indifference that the world habitually displays to a man who has begun to lose his grip.

Tamkin, a more complex figure, is difficult to make out. In all of his novels Bellow likes to include this sort of fast-talking sharper, full of information, half-information, and misinformation. A mass of pretensions and inconsistencies, Tamkin is quite ridiculous if viewed only through the lens of rationality. But he has something that no one else in the story has: an overflowing if suspect vitality. He is alive, scheming and kicking. He is a faker and a cheat, but also—perhaps—a bit of a healer and a sage. A con man stuffed with intellectual rubbish, he is also the only one to speak truthfully and urgently to Tommy: "Now, Wilhelm, I'm trying to do you some good. I want to tell you, don't marry suffering. Some people do. They get married to it, and sleep and eat together, just as husband and wife. If they go with joy they think it's adultery." Right. Tamkin represents here the dual principle of temptation-and-conscience which Jewish tradition symbolizes through the idea that every person has his own "good angel" and his own "bad angel." For Tommy Wilhelm, Tamkin is both of these, confusedly and simultaneously. He swindles Tommy but he also tells him a burning truth: "Don't marry suffering."

STYLE   The prose of *Seize the Day* is remarkably varied. It is nervous, full of staccato effects, sometimes rising to high eloquence and sometimes dropping to street colloquialism. Bellow never allows his writing to settle to a single flat level; he keeps it jumping and turning, shifting and breaking, in accordance with the discordant rhythms of the life he portrays. He is, first of all, quite marvelous at capturing the movement of New York speech, that strange mixture of gutter vitality, Broadway sharpness, dead jargon, and Yiddish melody. Listen to Maurice Venice speaking:

"Finally, finally I got her number and phoned her and said, 'This is Maurice Venice, scout for Kaskaskia Films.' So right away she says, 'Yah, so's your old lady.' Well, when I saw I wasn't getting nowhere with her I said to her, 'Well, miss. I don't blame you. You're a very beautiful thing and must have a dozen admirers after you all the time, boy friends who like to call and pull your leg and give a tease.

But as I happen to be a very busy fellow and don't have the time to horse around or argue, I tell you what to do. Here's my number, and here's the number of the Kaskaskia Distributors, Inc. Ask them who am I, Maurice Venice. The scout.' She did it. A little while later she phoned me back, all apologies and excuses, but I didn't want to embarrass her and get off on the wrong foot with an artist. . . . Because I seldom am wrong about talent. If I see it, it's there."

Sometimes Bellow himself turns to that sharp, nervous prose that American Jewish writers have made their hallmark in recent years, a prose that depends upon the heightening and tensing of speech rhythms:

Fair-haired hippopotamus!—that was how he looked to himself. He saw a big round face, a wide, flourishing red mouth, stump teeth. And the hat, too; and the cigar, too. I should have done hard labor all my life, he reflected. Hard honest labor that tires you out and makes you sleep. I'd have worked off my energy and felt better. Instead, I had to distinguish myself—yet.

And there are crucial moments in which Bellow allows himself a more elevated and formal style, as in the closing paragraphs. It is a style that approaches the condition of eloquence, an interval of direct statement amid parody, mimicked dialogue, and verbal play. And it comes when all that has been held back throughout the story is finally released and the torrent of blocked grief pours out.

Seize the Day

I

When it came to concealing his troubles, Tommy Wilhelm was
not less capable than the next fellow. So at least he thought, and
there was a certain amount of evidence to back him up. He had
once been an actor—no, not quite, an extra—and he knew what acting should be. Also, he was smoking a cigar, and when a man is
smoking a cigar, wearing a hat, he has an advantage; it is harder to
find out how he feels. He came from the twenty-third floor down to
the lobby on the mezzanine to collect his mail before breakfast, and
he believed—he hoped—that he looked passably well: doing all
right. It was a matter of sheer hope, because there was not much
that he could add to his present effort. On the fourteenth floor he
looked for his father to enter the elevator; they often met at this
hour, on the way to breakfast. If he worried about his appearance it
was mainly for his old father's sake. But there was no stop on the
fourteenth, and the elevator sank and sank. Then the smooth door
opened and the great dark red uneven carpet that covered the lobby
billowed toward Wilhelm's feet. In the foreground the lobby was
dark, sleepy. French drapes like sails kept out the sun, but three
high, narrow windows were open, and in the blue air Wilhelm saw a

pigeon about to light on the great chain that supported the marquee of the movie house directly underneath the lobby. For one moment he heard the wings beating strongly.

Most of the guests at the Hotel Gloriana were past the age of retirement. Along Broadway in the Seventies, Eighties, and Nineties, a great part of New York's vast population of old men and women lives. Unless the weather is too cold or wet they fill the benches about the tiny railed parks and along the subway gratings from Verdi Square to Columbia University, they crowd the shops and cafeterias, the dime stores, the tea-rooms, the bakeries, the beauty parlors, the reading rooms and club rooms. Among these old people at the Gloriana, Wilhelm felt out of place. He was comparatively young, in his middle forties, large and blond, with big shoulders; his back was heavy and strong, if already a little stooped or thickened. After breakfast the old guests sat down on the green leather armchairs and sofas in the lobby and began to gossip and look into the papers; they had nothing to do but wait out the day. But Wilhelm was used to an active life and liked to go out energetically in the morning. And for several months, because he had no position, he had kept up his morale by rising early; he was shaved and in the lobby by eight o'clock. He bought the paper and some cigars and drank a Coca-Cola or two before he went in to breakfast with his father. After breakfast—out, out to attend to business. The getting out had in itself become the chief business. But he had realized that he could not keep this up much longer, and today he was afraid. He was aware that his routine was about to break up and he sensed that a huge trouble long presaged but till now formless was due. Before evening, he'd know.

Nevertheless he followed his daily course and crossed the lobby.

Rubin, the man at the newsstand, had poor eyes. They may not have been actually weak but they were poor in expression, with lacy lids that furled down at the corners. He dressed well. It didn't seem necessary—he was behind the counter most of the time—but he dressed very well. He had on a rich brown suit; the cuffs embarrassed the hairs on his small hands. He wore a Countess Mara painted necktie. As Wilhelm approached, Rubin did not see him; he was looking out dreamily at the Hotel Ansonia, which was visible from his corner, several blocks away. The Ansonia, the neighborhood's great landmark, was built by Stanford White. It looks like a baroque palace from Prague or Munich enlarged a hundred times, with towers, domes, huge swells and bubbles of metal gone green from exposure, iron fretwork and festoons. Black television antennae are densely planted on its round summits. Under the changes of weather it may look like marble or like sea water, black as slate in the fog, white as tufa in sunlight. This morning it looked like the image of itself reflected in deep water, white and cumulous above, with cavernous distortions underneath. Together, the two men gazed at it.

Then Rubin said, "Your dad is in to breakfast already, the old gentleman."

"Oh, yes? Ahead of me today?"

"That's a real knocked-out shirt you got on," said Rubin. "Where's it from, Saks?"

"No, it's a Jack Fagman—Chicago."

Even when his spirits were low, Wilhelm could still wrinkle his forehead in a pleasing way. Some of the slow, silent movements of his face were very attractive. He went back a step, as if to stand away from himself and get a better look at his shirt. His glance was comic, a comment upon his untidiness. He liked to wear good clothes, but once he had put it on each article appeared to go its own way. Wilhelm, laughing, panted a little; his teeth were small; his cheeks when he laughed and puffed grew round, and he looked much younger than his years. In the old days when he was a college freshman and wore a raccoon coat and a beanie on his large blond head his father used to say that, big as he was, he could charm a bird out of a tree. Wilhelm had great charm still.

"I like this dove-gray color," he said in his sociable, good-natured way. "It isn't washable. You have to send it to the cleaner. It never smells as good as washed. But it's a nice shirt. It cost sixteen, eighteen bucks."

This shirt had not been bought by Wilhelm; it was a present from his boss—his former boss, with whom he had had a falling out. But there was no reason why he should tell Rubin the history of it. Although perhaps Rubin knew—Rubin was the kind of man who knew, and knew and knew. Wilhelm also knew many things about Rubin, for that matter, about Rubin's wife and Rubin's business, Rubin's health. None of these could be mentioned, and the great weight of the unspoken left them little to talk about.

"Well, y'lookin' pretty sharp today," Rubin said.

And Wilhelm said gladly, "Am I? Do you really think so?" He

could not believe it. He saw his reflection in the glass cupboard full
of cigar boxes, among the grand seals and paper damask and the
gold-embossed portraits of famous men, García, Edward the Sev-
enth, Cyrus the Great. You had to allow for the darkness and de-
formations of the glass, but he thought he didn't look too good. A
wide wrinkle like a comprehensive bracket sign was written upon his
forehead, the point between his brows, and there were patches of
brown on his dark blond skin. He began to be half amused at the
shadow of his own marveling, troubled, desirous eyes, and his nostrils and his lips. Fair-haired hippopotamus!—that was how he
looked to himself. He saw a big round face, a wide, flourishing red
mouth, stump teeth. And the hat, too; and the cigar, too. I should
have done hard labor all my life, he reflected. Hard honest labor
that tires you out and makes you sleep. I'd have worked off my
energy and felt better. Instead, I had to distinguish myself—yet.

He had put forth plenty of effort, but that was not the same as
working hard, was it? And if as a young man he had got off to a bad
start it was due to this very same face. Early in the nineteen-thirties,
because of his striking looks, he had been very briefly considered star
material, and he had gone to Hollywood. There for seven years,
stubbornly, he had tried to become a screen artist. Long before that
time his ambition or delusion had ended, but through pride and
perhaps also through laziness he had remained in California. At last
he turned to other things, but those seven years of persistence and
defeat had unfitted him somehow for trades and businesses, and
then it was too late to go into one of the professions. He had been
slow to mature, and he had lost ground, and so he hadn't been able
to get rid of his energy and he was convinced that this energy itself
had done him the greatest harm.

"I didn't see you at the gin game last night," said Rubin.

"I had to miss it. How did it go?"

For the last few weeks Wilhelm had played gin almost nightly,
but yesterday he had felt that he couldn't afford to lose any more.
He had never won. Not once. And while the losses were small they
weren't gains, were they? They were losses. He was tired of losing,
and tired also of the company, and so he had gone by himself to the
movies.

"Oh," said Rubin, "it went okay. Carl made a chump of himself
yelling at the guys. This time Doctor Tamkin didn't let him get
away with it. He told him the psychological reason why."

"What was the reason?"

Rubin said, "I can't quote him. Who could? You know the way Tamkin talks. Don't ask me. Do you want the *Trib?* Aren't you going to look at the closing quotations?"

"It won't help much to look. I know what they were yesterday at three," said Wilhelm. "But I suppose I better had get the paper." It seemed necessary for him to lift one shoulder in order to put his hand into his jacket pocket. There, among little packets of pills and crushed cigarette butts and strings of cellophane, the red tapes of packages which he sometimes used as dental floss, he recalled that he had dropped some pennies.

"That doesn't sound so good," said Rubin. He meant to be conversationally playful, but his voice had no tone and his eyes, slack and lid-blinded, turned elsewhere. He didn't want to hear. It was all the same to him. Maybe he already knew, being the sort of man who knew and knew.

No, it wasn't good. Wilhelm held three orders of lard in the commodities market. He and Dr. Tamkin had bought this lard together four days ago at 12.96, and the price at once began to fall and was still falling. In the mail this morning there was sure to be a call for additional margin payment. One came every day.

The psychologist, Dr. Tamkin, had got him into this. Tamkin lived at the Gloriana and attended the card game. He had explained to Wilhelm that you could speculate in commodities at one of the uptown branches of a good Wall Street house without making the full deposit of margin legally required. It was up to the branch manager. If he knew you—and all the branch managers knew Tamkin —he would allow you to make short-term purchases. You needed only to open a small account.

"The whole secret of this type of speculation," Tamkin had told him, "is in the alertness. You have to act fast—buy it and sell it; sell it and buy in again. But quick! Get to the window and have them wire Chicago at just the right second. Strike and strike again! Then get out the same day. In no time at all you turn over fifteen, twenty thousand dollars' worth of soy beans, coffee, corn, hides, wheat, cotton." Obviously the doctor understood the market well. Otherwise he could not make it sound so simple. "People lose because they are greedy and can't get out when it starts to go up. They gamble, but I do it scientifically. This is not guesswork. You must take a few points and get out. Why, ye gods!" said Dr. Tamkin with his bulging eyes, his bald head, and his drooping lip. "Have you stopped to think how much dough people are making in the market?"

Wilhelm with a quick shift from gloomy attention to the panting laugh which entirely changed his face had said, "Ho, have I ever! What do you think? Who doesn't know it's way beyond nineteen-twenty-eight—twenty-nine and still on the rise? Who hasn't read the Fulbright investigation? There's money everywhere. Everyone is shoveling it in. Money is—is—"

"And can you rest—can you sit still while this is going on?" said Dr. Tamkin. "I confess to you I can't. I think about people, just because they have a few bucks to invest, making fortunes. They have no sense, they have no talent, they just have the extra dough and it makes them more dough. I get so worked up and tormented and restless, so restless! I haven't even been able to practice my profession. With all this money around you don't want to be a fool while everyone else is making. I know guys who make five, ten thousand a week just by fooling around. I know a guy at the Hotel Pierre. There's nothing to him, but he has a whole case of Mumm's champagne at lunch. I know another guy on Central Park South— But what's the use of talking. They make millions. They have smart lawyers who get them out of taxes by a thousand schemes."

"Whereas I got taken," said Wilhelm. "My wife refused to sign a joint return. One fairly good year and I got into the thirty-two-percent bracket and was stripped bare. What of all my bad years?"

"It's a businessmen's government," said Dr. Tamkin. "You can be sure that these men making five thousand a week—"

"I don't need that sort of money," Wilhelm had said. "But oh! if I could only work out a little steady income from this. Not much. I don't ask much. But how badly I need—! I'd be so grateful if you'd show me how to work it."

"Sure I will. I do it regularly. I'll bring you my receipts if you like. And do you want to know something? I approve of your attitude very much. You want to avoid catching the money fever. This type of activity is filled with hostile feeling and lust. You should see what it does to some of these fellows. They go on the market with murder in their hearts."

"What's that I once heard a guy say?" Wilhelm remarked. "A man is only as good as what he loves."

"That's it—just it," Tamkin said. "You don't have to go about it their way. There's also a calm and rational, a psychological approach."

Wilhelm's father, old Dr. Adler, lived in an entirely different world from his son, but he had warned him once against Dr. Tamkin. Rather casually—he was a very bland old man—he said, "Wilky, perhaps you listen too much to this Tamkin. He's interesting to talk to. I don't doubt it. I think he's pretty common but he's a persuasive man. However, I don't know how reliable he may be."

It made Wilhelm profoundly bitter that his father should speak to him with such detachment about his welfare. Dr. Adler liked to appear affable. Affable! His own son, his one and only son, could not speak his mind or ease his heart to him. I wouldn't turn to Tamkin, he thought, if I could turn to him. At least Tamkin sympathizes with me and tries to give me a hand, whereas Dad doesn't want to be disturbed.

Old Dr. Adler had retired from practice; he had a considerable fortune and could easily have helped his son. Recently Wilhelm had told him, "Father—it so happens that I'm in a bad way now. I hate to have to say it. You realize that I'd rather have good news to bring you. But it's true. And since it's true, Dad— What else am I supposed to say? It's true."

Another father might have appreciated how difficult this confession was—so much bad luck, weariness, weakness, and failure. Wilhelm had tried to copy the old man's tone and made himself sound gentlemanly, low-voiced, tasteful. He didn't allow his voice to tremble; he made no stupid gesture. But the doctor had no answer. He only nodded. You might have told him that Seattle was near Puget Sound, or that the Giants and Dodgers were playing a night game, so little was he moved from his expression of healthy, handsome, good-humored old age. He behaved toward his son as he had formerly done toward his patients, and it was a great grief to Wilhelm; it was almost too much to bear. Couldn't he see—couldn't he feel? Had he lost his family sense?

Greatly hurt, Wilhelm struggled however to be fair. Old people are bound to change, he said. They have hard things to think about. They must prepare for where they are going. They can't live by the old schedule any longer and all their perspectives change, and other people become alike, kin and acquaintances. Dad is no longer the same person, Wilhelm reflected. He was thirty-two when I was born, and now he's going on eighty. Furthermore, it's time I stopped feeling like a kid toward him, a small son.

The handsome old doctor stood well above the other old people in the hotel. He was idolized by everyone. This was what people said: "That's old Professor Adler, who used to teach internal medicine. He was a diagnostician, one of the best in New York, and had a tremendous practice. Isn't he a wonderful-looking old guy? It's a pleasure to see such a fine old scientist, clean and immaculate. He stands straight and understands every single thing you say. He still has all his buttons. You can discuss any subject with him." The clerks, the elevator operators, the telephone girls and waitresses and chambermaids, and management flattered and pampered him. That was what he wanted. He had always been a vain man. To see how his father loved himself sometimes made Wilhelm madly indignant.

He folded over the *Tribune* with its heavy, black, crashing sensational print and read without recognizing any of the words, for his mind was still on his father's vanity. The doctor had created his own praise. People were primed and did not know it. And what did he need praise for? In a hotel where everyone was busy and contacts were so brief and had such small weight, how could it satisfy him? He could be in people's thoughts here and there for a moment; in and then out. He could never matter much to them. Wilhelm let out a long, hard breath and raised the brows of his round and somewhat circular eyes. He stared beyond the thick borders of the paper.

. . . love that well which thou must leave ere long.

Involuntary memory brought him this line. At first he thought it referred to his father, but then he understood that it was for himself, rather. *He* should love that well. "This thou perceivest, which makes *thy* love more strong." Under Dr. Tamkin's influence Wilhelm had recently begun to remember the poems he used to read. Dr. Tamkin knew, or said he knew, the great English poets and once in a while he mentioned a poem of his own. It was a long time since anyone had spoken to Wilhelm about this sort of thing. He didn't like to think about his college days, but if there was one course that now made sense it was Literature I. The textbook was Lieder and Lovett's *British Poetry and Prose,* a black heavy book with thin pages. Did I read that? he asked himself. Yes, he had read it and there was one accomplishment at least he could recall with pleasure. He had read "Yet once more, O ye laurels." How pure this was to say! It was beautiful.

Sunk though he be beneath the wat'ry floor . . .

Such things had always swayed him, and now the power of such words was far, far greater.

Wilhelm respected the truth, but he could lie and one of the things he lied often about was his education. He said he was an alumnus of Penn State; in fact he had left school before his sophomore year was finished. His sister Catherine had a B.S. degree. Wilhelm's late mother was a graduate of Bryn Mawr. He was the only member of the family who had no education. This was another sore point. His father was ashamed of him.

But he had heard the old man bragging to another old man, saying, "My son is a sales executive. He didn't have the patience to finish school. But he does all right for himself. His income is up in the five figures somewhere."

"What—thirty, forty thousand?" said his stooped old friend.

"Well, he needs at least that much for his style of life. Yes, he needs that."

Despite his troubles, Wilhelm almost laughed. Why, that boasting old hypocrite. He knew the sales executive was no more. For many weeks there had been no executive, no sales, no income. But how we love looking fine in the eyes of the world—how beautiful are the old when they are doing a snow job! It's Dad, thought Wilhelm, who is the salesman. He's selling me. *He* should have gone on the road.

But what of the truth? Ah, the truth was that there were problems, and of these problems his father wanted no part. His father was ashamed of him. The truth, Wilhelm thought, was very awkward. He pressed his lips together, and his tongue went soft; it pained him far at the back, in the cords and throat, and a knot of ill formed in his chest. Dad never was a pal to me when I was young, he reflected. He was at the office or the hospital, or lecturing. He expected me to look out for myself and never gave me much thought. Now he looks down on me. And maybe in some respects he's right.

No wonder Wilhelm delayed the moment when he would have to go into the dining room. He had moved to the end of Rubin's counter. He had opened the *Tribune*; the fresh pages drooped from his hands; the cigar was smoked out and the hat did not defend him. He was wrong to suppose that he was more capable than the next fellow when it came to concealing his troubles. They were clearly written out upon his face. He wasn't even aware of it.

There was the matter of the different names, which, in the hotel, came up frequently. "Are you Doctor Adler's son?" "Yes, but my name is Tommy Wilhelm." And the doctor would say, "My son and I use different monickers. I uphold tradition. He's for the new." The Tommy was Wilhelm's own invention. He adopted it when he went to Hollywood, and dropped the Adler. Hollywood was his own idea, too. He used to pretend that it had all been the doing of a certain talent scout named Maurice Venice. But the scout had never made him a definite offer of a studio connection. He had approached him, but the results of the screen tests had not been good. After the test Wilhelm took the initiative and pressed Maurice Venice until he got him to say, "Well, I suppose you might make it out there." On the strength of this Wilhelm had left college and had gone to California.

Someone had said, and Wilhelm agreed with the saying, that in Los Angeles all the loose objects in the country were collected, as if America had been tilted and everything that wasn't tightly screwed down had slid into Southern California. He himself had been one of these loose objects. Sometimes he told people, "I was too mature for college. I was a big boy, you see. Well, I thought, when do you start to become a man?" After he had driven a painted flivver and had worn a yellow slicker with slogans on it, and played illegal poker, and gone out on Coke dates, he had *had* college. He wanted to try something new and quarreled with his parents about his career. And then a letter came from Maurice Venice.

The story of the scout was long and intricate and there were several versions of it. The truth about it was never told. Wilhelm had lied first boastfully and then out of charity to himself. But his memory was good, he could still separate what he had invented from the actual happenings, and this morning he found it necessary as he stood by Rubin's showcase with his *Tribune* to recall the crazy course of the true events.

I didn't seem even to realize that there was a depression. How could I have been such a jerk as not to prepare for anything and just go on luck and inspiration? With round gray eyes expanded and his large shapely lips closed in severity toward himself he forced open all that had been hidden. Dad I couldn't affect one way or another. Mama was the one who tried to stop me, and we carried on and yelled and pleaded. The more I lied the louder I raised my voice, and charged—like a hippopotamus. Poor Mother! How I disappointed her. Rubin heard Wilhelm give a broken sigh as he stood with the forgotten *Tribune* crushed under his arm.

When Wilhelm was aware that Rubin watched him, loitering and idle, apparently not knowing what to do with himself this morning, he turned to the Coca-Cola machine. He swallowed hard at the Coke bottle and coughed over it, but he ignored his coughing, for he was still thinking, his eyes upcast and his lips closed behind his hand. By a peculiar twist of habit he wore his coat collar turned up always, as though there were a wind. It never lay flat. But on his broad back, stooped with its own weight, its strength warped almost into deformity, the collar of his sports coat appeared anyway to be no wider than a ribbon.

He was listening to the sound of his own voice as he explained, twenty-five years ago in the living room on West End Avenue, "But Mother, if I don't pan out as an actor I can still go back to school."

But she was afraid he was going to destroy himself. She said, "Wilky, Dad could make it easy for you if you wanted to go into medicine." To remember this stifled him.

"I can't bear hospitals. Besides, I might make a mistake and hurt someone or even kill a patient. I couldn't stand that. Besides, I haven't got that sort of brains."

Then his mother had made the mistake of mentioning her nephew Artie, Wilhelm's cousin, who was an honor student at Columbia in math and languages. That dark little gloomy Artie with his disgusting narrow face, and his moles and self-sniffing ways and his unclean table manners, the boring habit he had of conjugating verbs when you went for a walk with him. "Roumanian is an easy language. You just add a *tl* to everything." He was now a professor, this same Artie with whom Wilhelm had played near the soldiers' and sailors' monument on Riverside Drive. Not that to be a professor was in itself so great. How could anyone bear to know so many languages? And Artie also had to remain Artie, which was a bad deal. But perhaps success had changed him. Now that he had a place in the world perhaps he was better. Did Artie love his languages, and live for them, or was he also, in his heart, cynical? So many people nowadays were. No one seemed satisfied, and Wilhelm was especially horrified by the cynicism of successful people. Cynicism was bread and meat to everyone. And irony, too. Maybe it couldn't be helped. It was probably even necessary. Wilhelm, however, feared it intensely. Whenever at the end of the day he was unusually fatigued he attributed it to cynicism. Too much of the world's business done. Too much falsity. He had various words to express the effect this had on him. Chicken! Unclean! Congestion! he exclaimed in his heart. Rat race! Phony! Murder! Play the Game! Buggers!

At first the letter from the talent scout was nothing but a flattering sort of joke. Wilhelm's picture in the college paper when he was running for class treasurer was seen by Maurice Venice, who wrote to him about a screen test. Wilhelm at once took the train to New York. He found the scout to be huge and oxlike, so stout that his arms seemed caught from beneath in a grip of flesh and fat; it looked as though it must be positively painful. He had little hair. Yet he enjoyed a healthy complexion. His breath was noisy and his voice rather difficult and husky because of the fat in his throat. He had on a double-breasted suit of the type then known as the pillbox; it was chalk-striped, pink on blue; the trousers hugged his ankles.

They met and shook hands and sat down. Together these two big men dwarfed the tiny Broadway office and made the furnishings look like toys. Wilhelm had the color of a Golden Grimes apple when he was well, and then his thick blond hair had been vigorous and his wide shoulders unwarped; he was leaner in the jaws, his eyes fresher and wider; his legs were then still awkward but he was impressively handsome. And he was about to make his first great mistake. Like, he sometimes thought, I was going to pick up a weapon and strike myself a blow with it.

Looming over the desk in the small office darkened by overbuilt midtown—sheer walls, gray spaces, dry lagoons of tar and pebbles—Maurice Venice proceeded to establish his credentials. He said, "My letter was on the regular stationery, but maybe you want to check on me?"

"Who, *me?*" said Wilhelm. "Why?"

"There's guys who think I'm in a racket and make a charge for the test. I don't ask a cent. I'm no agent. There ain't no commission."

"I never even thought of it," said Wilhelm. Was there perhaps something fishy about this Maurice Venice? He protested too much.

In his husky, fat-weakened voice he finally challenged Wilhelm, "If you're not sure, you can call the distributor and find out who I am, Maurice Venice."

Wilhelm wondered at him. "Why shouldn't I be sure? Of course I am."

"Because I can see the way you size me up, and because this is a dinky office. Like you don't believe me. Go ahead. Call. I won't care if you're cautious. I mean it. There's quite a few people who doubt me at first. They can't really believe that fame and fortune are going to hit 'em."

"But I tell you I do believe you," Wilhelm had said, and bent inward to accommodate the pressure of his warm, panting laugh. It was purely nervous. His neck was ruddy and neatly shaved about the ears—he was fresh from the barbershop; his face anxiously glowed with his desire to make a pleasing impression. It was all wasted on Venice, who was just as concerned about the impression *he* was making.

"If you're surprised, I'll just show you what I mean," Venice had said. "It was about fifteen months ago right in this identical same office when I saw a beautiful thing in the paper. It wasn't even a photo but a drawing, a brassière ad, but I knew right away that this was star material. I called up the paper to ask who the girl was, they gave me the name of the advertising agency; I phoned the agency and they gave me the name of the artist; I got hold of the artist and he gave me the number of the model agency. Finally, finally I got her number and phoned her and said, 'This is Maurice Venice, scout for Kaskaskia Films.' So right away she says, 'Yah, so's your old lady.' Well, when I saw I wasn't getting nowhere with her I said to her, 'Well, miss. I don't blame you. You're a very beautiful thing and must have a dozen admirers after you all the time, boy friends who like to call and pull your leg and give a tease. But as I happen to be a very busy fellow and don't have the time to horse around or argue, I tell you what to do. Here's my number, and here's the number of the Kaskaskia Distributors, Inc. Ask them who am I, Maurice Venice. The scout.' She did it. A little while later she phoned me back, all apologies and excuses, but I didn't want to embarrass her and get off on the wrong foot with an artist. I know better than to do that. So I told her it was a natural precaution, never mind. I wanted to run a screen test right away. Because I seldom am wrong about talent. If I see it, it's there. Get that, please. And do you know who that little girl is today?"

"No," Wilhelm said eagerly. "Who is she?"

Venice said impressively, " 'Nita Christenberry."

Wilhelm sat utterly blank. This was failure. He didn't know the name, and Venice was waiting for his response and would be angry.

And in fact Venice had been offended. He said, "What's the matter with you! Don't you read a magazine? She's a starlet."

"I'm sorry," Wilhelm answered. "I'm at school and don't have time to keep up. If I don't know her, it doesn't mean a thing. She made a big hit, I'll bet."

"You can say that again. Here's a photo of her." He handed Wilhelm some pictures. She was a bathing beauty—short, the usual breasts, hips, and smooth thighs. Yes, quite good, as Wilhelm recalled. She stood on high heels and wore a Spanish comb and mantilla. In her hand was a fan.

He had said, "She looks awfully peppy."

"Isn't she a divine girl? And what personality! Not just another broad in the show business, believe me." He had a surprise for Wilhelm. "I have found happiness with her," he said.

"You have?" said Wilhelm, slow to understand.

"Yes, boy, we're engaged."

Wilhelm saw another photograph, taken on the beach. Venice was dressed in a terry-cloth beach outfit, and he and the girl, cheek to cheek, were looking into the camera. Below, in white ink, was written "Love at Malibu Colony."

"I'm sure you'll be very happy. I wish you—"

"I *know*," said Venice firmly, "I'm going to be happy. When I saw that drawing, the breath of fate breathed on me. I felt it over my entire body."

"Say, it strikes a bell suddenly," Wilhelm had said. "Aren't you related to Martial Venice the producer?"

Venice was either a nephew of the producer or the son of a first cousin. Decidedly he had not made good. It was easy enough for Wilhelm to see this now. The office was so poor, and Venice bragged so nervously and identified himself so scrupulously—the poor guy. He was the obscure failure of an aggressive and powerful clan. As such he had the greatest sympathy from Wilhelm.

Venice had said, "Now I suppose you want to know where you come in. I seen your school paper, by accident. You take quite a remarkable picture."

"It can't be so much," said Wilhelm, more panting than laughing.

"You don't want to tell me my business," Venice said. "Leave it to me. I studied up on this."

"I never imagined— Well, what kind of roles do you think I'd fit?"

"All this time that we've been talking, I've been watching. Don't think I haven't. You remind me of someone. Let's see who it can be—one of the great old-timers. Is it Milton Sills? No, that's not the one. Conway Tearle, Jack Mulhall? George Bancroft? No, his face was ruggeder. One thing I can tell you, though, a George Raft type you're not—those tough, smooth, black little characters."

"No, I wouldn't seem to be."

"No, you're not that flyweight type, with the fists, from a night-club, and the glamorous sideburns, doing the tango or the bolero. Not Edward G. Robinson, either—I'm thinking aloud. Or the Cagney fly-in-your-face role, a cabbie, with that mouth and those punches."

"I realize that."

"Not suave like William Powell, or a lyric juvenile like Buddy Rogers. I suppose you don't play the sax? No. But—"

"But what?"

"I have you placed as the type that loses the girl to the George Raft type or the William Powell type. You are steady, faithful, you get stood up. The older women would know better. The mothers are on your side. With what they been through, if it was up to them, they'd take you in a minute. You're very sympathetic, even the young girls feel that. You'd make a good provider. But they go more for the other types. It's as clear as anything."

This was not how Wilhelm saw himself. And as he surveyed the old ground he recognized now that he had been not only confused but hurt. Why, he thought, he cast me even then for a loser.

Wilhelm had said, with half a mind to be defiant, "Is that your opinion?"

It never occurred to Venice that a man might object to stardom in such a role. "Here is your chance," he said. "Now you're just in college. What are you studying?" He snapped his fingers. "Stuff." Wilhelm himself felt this way about it. "You may plug along fifty years before you get anywheres. This way, in one jump, the world knows who you are. You become a name like Roosevelt, Swanson. From east to west, out to China, into South America. This is no bunk. You become a lover to the whole world. The world wants it, needs it. One fellow smiles, a billion people also smile. One fellow cries, the other billion sob with him. Listen, bud—" Venice had pulled himself together to make an effort. On his imagination there was some great weight which he could not discharge. He wanted Wilhelm, too, to feel it. He twisted his large, clean, well-meaning, rather foolish features as though he were their unwilling captive, and said in his choked, fat-obstructed voice, "Listen, everywhere there are people trying hard, miserable, in trouble, downcast, tired, trying and trying. They need a break, right? A break through, a help, luck or sympathy."

"That certainly is the truth," said Wilhelm. He had seized the feeling and he waited for Venice to go on. But Venice had no more to say; he had concluded. He gave Wilhelm several pages of blue hectographed script, stapled together, and told him to prepare for the screen test. "Study your lines in front of a mirror," he said. "Let yourself go. The part should take ahold of you. Don't be afraid to make faces and be emotional. Shoot the works. Because when you start to act you're no more an ordinary person, and those things don't apply to you. You don't behave the same way as the average."

And so Wilhelm had never returned to Penn State. His roommate sent his things to New York for him, and the school authorities had to write to Dr. Adler to find out what had happened.

Still, for three months Wilhelm delayed his trip to California. He wanted to start out with the blessings of his family, but they were never given. He quarreled with his parents and his sister. And then, when he was best aware of the risks and knew a hundred reasons against going and had made himself sick with fear, he left home. This was typical of Wilhelm. After much thought and hesitation and debate he invariably took the course he had rejected innumerable times. Ten such decisions made up the history of his life. He had decided that it would be a bad mistake to go to Hollywood, and then he went. He had made up his mind not to marry his wife, but ran off and got married. He had resolved not to invest money with Tamkin, and then had given him a check.

But Wilhelm had been eager for life to start. College was merely another delay. Venice had approached him and said that the world had named Wilhelm to shine before it. He was to be freed from the anxious and narrow life of the average. Moreover, Venice had claimed that he never made a mistake. His instinct for talent was infallible, he said.

But when Venice saw the results of the screen test he did a quick about-face. In those days Wilhelm had had a speech difficulty. It was not a true stammer, it was a thickness of speech which the sound track exaggerated. The film showed that he had many peculiarities, otherwise unnoticeable. When he shrugged, his hands drew up within his sleeves. The vault of his chest was huge, but he really didn't look strong under the lights. Though he called himself a hippopotamus, he more nearly resembled a bear. His walk was bearlike, quick and rather soft, toes turned inward, as though his shoes were an impediment. About one thing Venice had been right. Wilhelm was photogenic, and his wavy blond hair (now graying) came out well, but after the test Venice refused to encourage him. He tried to get rid of him. He couldn't afford to take a chance on him, he had made too many mistakes already and lived in fear of his powerful relatives.

Wilhelm had told his parents, "Venice says I owe it to myself to go." How ashamed he was now of this lie! He had begged Venice not to give him up. He had said, "Can't you help me out? It would kill me to get back to school now."

Then when he reached the Coast he learned that a recommendation from Maurice Venice was the kiss of death. Venice needed help and charity more than he, Wilhelm, ever had. A few years later when Wilhelm was down on his luck and working as an orderly in a Los Angeles hospital, he saw Venice's picture in the papers. He was under indictment for pandering. Closely following the trial, Wilhelm found out that Venice had indeed been employed by Kaskaskia Films but that he had evidently made use of the connection to organize a ring of call girls. Then what did he want with me? Wilhelm had cried to himself. He was unwilling to believe anything very bad about Venice. Perhaps he was foolish and unlucky, a fall guy, a dupe, a sucker. You didn't give a man fifteen years in prison for that. Wilhelm often thought that he might write him a letter to say how sorry he was. He remembered the breath of fate and Venice's certainty that he would be happy. 'Nita Christenberry was sentenced to three years. Wilhelm recognized her although she had changed her name.

By that time Wilhelm too had taken his new name. In California he became Tommy Wilhelm. Dr. Adler would not accept the change. Today he still called his son Wilky, as he had done for more than forty years. Well, now, Wilhelm was thinking, the paper crowded in disarray under his arm, there's really very little that a man can change at will. He can't change his lungs, or nerves, or constitution or temperament. They're not under his control. When he's young and strong and impulsive and dissatisfied with the way things are he wants to rearrange them to assert his freedom. He can't over-throw the government or be differently born; he only has a little scope and maybe a foreboding, too, that essentially you can't change. Nevertheless, he makes a gesture and becomes Tommy Wilhelm. Wilhelm had always had a great longing to be Tommy. He had never, however, succeeded in feeling like Tommy, and in his soul had always remained Wilky. When he was drunk he reproached himself horribly as Wilky. "You fool, you clunk, you Wilky!" he called himself. He thought that it was a good thing perhaps that he had not become a success as Tommy since that would not have been a genuine success. Wilhelm would have feared that not he but Tommy had brought it off, cheating Wilky of his birthright. Yes, it had been a stupid thing to do, but it was his imperfect judgment at the age of twenty which should be blamed. He had cast off his fa-ther's name, and with it his father's opinion of him. It was, he knew it was, his bid for liberty, Adler being in his mind the title of the species, Tommy the freedom of the person. But Wilky was his ines-capable self.

In middle age you no longer thought such thoughts about free choice. Then it came over you that from one grandfather you had inherited such and such a head of hair which looked like honey when it whitens or sugars in the jar; from another, broad thick shoulders; an oddity of speech from one uncle, and small teeth from another, and the gray eyes with darkness diffused even into the whites, and a wide-lipped mouth like a statue from Peru. Wan-dering races have such looks, the bones of one tribe, the skin of another. From his mother he had gotten sensitive feelings, a soft heart, a brooding nature, a tendency to be confused under pressure.

The changed name was a mistake, and he would admit it as freely as you liked. But this mistake couldn't be undone now, so why must his father continually remind him how he had sinned? It was too late. He would have to go back to the pathetic day when the sin was committed. And where was that day? Past and dead. Whose humiliating memories were these? His and not his father's. What had he to think back on that he could call good? Very, very little. You had to forgive. First, to forgive yourself, and then general for-giveness. Didn't he suffer from his mistakes far more than his father could?

"Oh, God," Wilhelm prayed. "Let me out of my trouble. Let me out of my thoughts, and let me do something better with myself. For all the time I have wasted I am very sorry. Let me out of the clutch and into a different life. For I am all balled up. Have mercy."

II

The mail.

The clerk who gave it to him did not care what sort of appearance he made this morning. He only glanced at him from under his brows, upward, as the letters changed hands. Why should the hotel people waste courtesies on him? They had his number. The clerk knew that he was handing him, along with the letters, a bill for his rent. Wilhelm assumed a look that removed him from all such things. But it was bad. To pay the bill he would have to withdraw money from his brokerage account, and the account was being watched because of the drop in lard. According to the *Tribune*'s figures lard was still twenty points below last year's level. There were government price supports. Wilhelm didn't know how these worked but he understood that the farmer was protected and that the SEC kept an eye on the market and therefore he believed that lard would rise again and he wasn't greatly worried as yet. But in the meantime his father might have offered to pick up his hotel tab. Why didn't he? What a selfish old man he was! He saw his son's hardships; he could so easily help him. How little it would mean to him, and how much to Wilhelm! Where was the old man's heart? Maybe, thought Wilhelm, I was sentimental in the past and exaggerated his kindliness—warm family life. It may never have been there.

Not long ago his father had said to him in his usual affable, pleasant way, "Well, Wilky, here we are under the same roof again, after all these years."

Wilhelm was glad for an instant. At last they would talk over old times. But he was also on guard against insinuations. Wasn't his father saying, "Why are you here in a hotel with me and not at home in Brooklyn with your wife and two boys? You're neither a widower nor a bachelor. You have brought me all your confusions. What do you expect me to do with them?"

So Wilhelm studied the remark for a bit, then said, "The roof is twenty-six stories up. But how many years has it been?"

"That's what I was asking you."

"Gosh, Dad, I'm not sure. Wasn't it the year Mother died? What year was that?"

He asked this question with an innocent frown on his Golden Grimes, dark blond face. *What year was it!* As though he didn't know the year, the month, the day, the very hour of his mother's death.

"Wasn't it nineteen-thirty-one?" said Dr. Adler.

"Oh, was it?" said Wilhelm. And in hiding the sadness and the overwhelming irony of the question he gave a nervous shiver and wagged his head and felt the ends of his collar rapidly.

"Do you know?" his father said. "You must realize, an old fellow's memory becomes unreliable. It was in winter, that I'm sure of. Nineteen-thirty-two?"

Yes, it was age. Don't make an issue of it, Wilhelm advised himself. If you were to ask the old doctor in what year he had interned, he'd tell you correctly. All the same, don't make an issue. Don't quarrel with your own father. Have pity on an old man's failings.

"I believe the year was closer to nineteen-thirty-four, Dad," he said.

But Dr. Adler was thinking, Why the devil can't he stand still when we're talking? He's either hoisting his pants up and down by the pockets or jittering with his feet. A regular mountain of tics, he's getting to be. Wilhelm had a habit of moving his feet back and forth as though, hurrying into a house, he had to clean his shoes first on the doormat.

Then Wilhelm had said, "Yes, that was the beginning of the end, wasn't it, Father?"

Wilhelm often astonished Dr. Adler. Beginning of the end? What could he mean—what was he fishing for? Whose end? The end of family life? The old man was puzzled but he would not give Wilhelm an opening to introduce his complaints. He had learned that it was better not to take up Wilhelm's strange challenges. So he merely agreed pleasantly, for he was a master of social behavior, and said, "It was an awful misfortune for us all."

He thought, What business has he to complain to *me* of his mother's death?

Face to face they had stood, each declaring himself silently after his own way. It was: it was not, the beginning of the end—*some* end.

Unaware of anything odd in his doing it, for he did it all the time, Wilhelm had pinched out the coal of his cigarette and dropped the butt in his pocket, where there were many more. And as he gazed at his father the little finger of his right hand began to twitch and tremble; of that he was unconscious, too.

And yet Wilhelm believed that when he put his mind to it he could have perfect and even distinguished manners, outdoing his father. Despite the slight thickness in his speech—it amounted almost to a stammer when he started the same phrase over several times in his effort to eliminate the thick sound—he could be fluent. Otherwise he would never have made a good salesman. He claimed also that he was a good listener. When he listened he made a tight mouth and rolled his eyes thoughtfully. He would soon tire and begin to utter short, loud, impatient breaths, and he would say, "Oh yes . . . yes . . . yes. I couldn't agree more." When he was forced to differ he would declare, "Well, I'm not sure. I don't really see it that way. I'm of two minds about it." He would never willingly hurt any man's feelings.

But in conversation with his father he was apt to lose control of himself. After any talk with Dr. Adler, Wilhelm generally felt dissatisfied, and his dissatisfaction reached its greatest intensity when they discussed family matters. Ostensibly he had been trying to help the old man to remember a date, but in reality he meant to tell him, "You were set free when Ma died. You wanted to forget her. You'd like to get rid of Catherine, too. Me, too. You're not kidding anyone"—Wilhelm striving to put this across, and the old man not having it. In the end he was left struggling, while his father seemed unmoved.

And then once more Wilhelm had said to himself, "But man! you're not a kid. Even then you weren't a kid!" He looked down over the front of his big, indecently big, spoiled body. He was beginning to lose his shape, his gut was fat, and he looked like a hippopotamus. His younger son called him "a hummuspotamus"; that was little Paul. And here he was still struggling with his old dad, filled with ancient grievances. Instead of saying, "Good-by, youth! Oh, good-by those marvelous, foolish wasted days. What a big clunk I was—I *am*."

Wilhelm was still paying heavily for his mistakes. His wife Margaret would not give him a divorce, and he had to support her and the two children. She would regularly agree to divorce him, and then think things over again and set new and more difficult conditions. No court would have awarded her the amounts he paid. One of today's letters, as he had expected, was from her. For the first time he had sent her a postdated check, and she protested. She also enclosed bills for the boys' educational insurance policies, due next week. Wilhelm's mother-in-law had taken out these policies in Beverly Hills, and since her death two years ago he had to pay the premiums. Why couldn't she have minded her own business! They were his kids, and he took care of them and always would. He had planned to set up a trust fund. But that was on his former expectations. Now he had to rethink the future, because of the money problem. Meanwhile, here were the bills to be paid. When he saw the two sums punched out so neatly on the cards he cursed the company and its IBM equipment. His heart and his head were congested with anger. Everyone was supposed to have money. It was nothing to the company. It published pictures of funerals in the magazines and frightened the suckers, and then punched out little holes, and the customers would lie awake to think out ways to raise the dough. They'd be ashamed not to have it. They couldn't let a great company down, either, and they got the scratch. In the old days a man was put in prison for debt, but there were subtler things now. They made it a shame not to have money and set everybody to work.

Well, and what else had Margaret sent him? He tore the envelope open with his thumb, swearing that he would send any other bills back to her. There was, luckily, nothing more. He put the hole-punched cards in his pocket. Didn't Margaret know that he was nearly at the end of his rope? Of course. Her instinct told her that this was her opportunity, and she was giving him the works.

He went into the dining room, which was under Austro-Hungarian management at the Hotel Gloriana. It was run like a European establishment. The pastries were excellent, especially the strudel. He often had apple strudel and coffee in the afternoon.

As soon as he entered he saw his father's small head in the sunny bay at the farther end, and heard his precise voice. It was with an odd sort of perilous expression that Wilhelm crossed the dining room.

Dr. Adler liked to sit in a corner that looked across Broadway down to the Hudson and New Jersey. On the other side of the street was a supermodern cafeteria with gold and purple mosaic columns. On the second floor a private-eye school, a dental laboratory, a reducing parlor, a veteran's club, and a Hebrew school shared the space. The old man was sprinkling sugar on his strawberries. Small hoops of brilliance were cast by the water glasses on the white tablecloth, despite a faint murkiness in the sunshine. It was early summer, and the long window was turned inward; a moth was on the pane; the putty was broken and the white enamel on the frames was streaming with wrinkles.

"Ha, Wilky," said the old man to his tardy son. "You haven't met our neighbor Mr. Perls, have you? From the fifteenth floor."

"How d'do," Wilhelm said. He did not welcome this stranger; he began at once to find fault with him. Mr. Perls carried a heavy cane with a crutch tip. Dyed hair, a skinny forehead—these were not reasons for bias. Nor was it Mr. Perls's fault that Dr. Adler was using him, not wishing to have breakfast with his son alone. But a gruffer voice within Wilhelm spoke, asking, "Who is this damn frazzle-faced herring with his dyed hair and his fish teeth and this drippy mustache? Another one of Dad's German friends. Where does he collect all these guys? What is the stuff on his teeth? I never saw such pointed crowns. Are they stainless steel, or a kind of silver? How can a human face get into this condition. Uch!" Staring with his widely spaced gray eyes, Wilhelm sat, his broad back stooped under the sports jacket. He clasped his hands on the table with an implication of suppliance. Then he began to relent a little toward Mr. Perls, beginning at the teeth. Each of those crowns represented a tooth ground to the quick, and estimating a man's grief with his teeth as two per cent of the total, and adding to that his flight from Germany and the probable origin of his wincing wrinkles, not to be confused with the wrinkles of his smile, it came to a sizable load.

"Mr. Perls was a hosiery wholesaler," said Dr. Adler.

"Is this the son you told me was in the selling line?" said Mr. Perls.

Dr. Adler replied, "I have only this one son. One daughter. She was a medical technician before she got married—anesthetist. At one time she had an important position in Mount Sinai."

He couldn't mention his children without boasting. In Wilhelm's opinion, there was little to boast of. Catherine, like Wilhelm, was big and fair-haired. She had married a court reporter who had a pretty hard time of it. She had taken a professional name, too— Philippa. At forty she was still ambitious to become a painter. Wilhelm didn't venture to criticize her work. It didn't do much to him, he said, but then he was no critic. Anyway, he and his sister were generally on the outs and he didn't often see her paintings. She worked very hard, but there were fifty thousand people in New York with paints and brushes, each practically a law unto himself. It was the Tower of Babel in paint. *He* didn't want to go far into this. Things were chaotic all over.

Dr. Adler thought that Wilhelm looked particularly untidy this morning—unrested, too, his eyes red-rimmed from excessive smoking. He was breathing through his mouth and he was evidently much distracted and rolled his red-shot eyes barbarously. As usual, his coat collar was turned up as though he had had to go out in the rain. When he went to business he pulled himself together a little; otherwise he let himself go and looked like hell.

"What's the matter, Wilky, didn't you sleep last night?"

"Not very much."

"You take too many pills of every kind—first stimulants and then depressants, anodynes followed by analeptics, until the poor organism doesn't know what's happened. Then the luminal won't put people to sleep, and the Pervitin or Benzedrine won't wake them. God knows! These things get to be as serious as poisons, and yet everyone puts all their faith in them."

"No, Dad, it's not the pills. It's that I'm not used to New York any more. For a native, that's very peculiar, isn't it? It was never so noisy at night as now, and every little thing is a strain. Like the alternate parking. You have to run out at eight to move your car. And where can you put it? If you forget for a minute they tow you away. Then some fool puts advertising leaflets under your windshield wiper and you have heart failure a block away because you think you've got a ticket. When you do get stung with a ticket, you can't argue. You haven't got a chance in court and the city wants the revenue."

"But in your line you have to have a car, eh?" said Mr. Perls.

"Lord knows why any lunatic would want one in the city who didn't need it for his livelihood."

Wilhelm's old Pontiac was parked in the street. Formerly, when on an expense account, he had always put it up in a garage. Now he was afraid to move the car from Riverside Drive lest he lose his space, and he used it only on Saturdays when the Dodgers were playing in Ebbets Field and he took his boys to the game. Last Saturday, when the Dodgers were out of town, he had gone out to visit his mother's grave.

Dr. Adler had refused to go along. He couldn't bear his son's driving. Forgetfully, Wilhelm traveled for miles in second gear; he was seldom in the right lane and he neither gave signals nor watched for lights. The upholstery of his Pontiac was filthy with grease and ashes. One cigarette burned in the ashtray, another in his hand, a third on the floor with maps and other waste paper and Coca-Cola bottles. He dreamed at the wheel or argued and gestured, and therefore the old doctor would not ride with him.

Then Wilhelm had come back from the cemetery angry because the stone bench between his mother's and his grandmother's graves had been overturned and broken by vandals. "Those damn teen-age hoodlums get worse and worse," he said. "Why, they must have used a sledge-hammer to break the seat smack in half like that. If I could catch one of them!" He wanted the doctor to pay for a new seat, but his father was cool to the idea. He said he was going to have himself cremated.

Mr. Perls said, "I don't blame you if you get no sleep up where you are." His voice was tuned somewhat sharp, as though he were slightly deaf. "Don't you have Parigi the singing teacher there? God, they have some queer elements in this hotel. On which floor is that Estonian woman with all her cats and dogs? They should have made her leave long ago."

"They've moved her down to twelve," said Dr. Adler.

Wilhelm ordered a large Coca-Cola with his breakfast. Working in secret at the small envelopes in his pocket, he found two pills by touch. Much fingering had worn and weakened the paper. Under cover of a napkin he swallowed a Phenaphen sedative and a Unicap, but the doctor was sharp-eyed and said, "Wilky, what are you taking now?"

"Just my vitamin pills." He put his cigar butt in an ashtray on the table behind him, for his father did not like the odor. Then he drank his Coca-Cola.

"That's what you drink for breakfast, and not orange juice?" said Mr. Perls. He seemed to sense that he would not lose Dr. Adler's favor by taking an ironic tone with his son.

"The caffeine stimulates brain activity," said the old doctor. "It does all kinds of things to the respiratory center."

"It's just a habit of the road, that's all," Wilhelm said. "If you drive around long enough it turns your brains, your stomach, and everything else."

His father explained, "Wilky used to be with the Rojax Corporation. He was their northeastern sales representative for a good many years but recently ended the connection."

"Yes," said Wilhelm, "I was with them from the end of the

war." He sipped the Coca-Cola and chewed the ice, glancing at one and the other with his attitude of large, shaky, patient dignity. The waitress set two boiled eggs before him.

"What kind of line does this Rojax company manufacture?" said Mr. Perls.

"Kiddies' furniture. Little chairs, rockers, tables, Jungle-Gyms, slides, swings, seesaws."

Wilhelm let his father do the explaining. Large and stiff-backed, he tried to sit patiently, but his feet were abnormally restless. All right! His father had to impress Mr. Perls? He would go along once more, and play his part. Fine! He would play along and help his father maintain his style. Style was the main consideration. That was just fine!

"I was with the Rojax Corporation for almost ten years," he said. "We parted ways because they wanted me to share my territory. They took a son-in-law into the business—a new fellow. It was his idea."

To himself, Wilhelm said, Now God alone can tell why I have to lay my whole life bare to this blasted herring here. I'm sure nobody else does it. Other people keep their business to themselves. Not me.

He continued, "But the rationalization was that it was too big a territory for one man. I had a monopoly. That wasn't so. The real reason was that they had gotten to the place where they would have to make me an officer of the corporation. Vice presidency. I was in line for it, but instead this son-in-law got in, and—"

Dr. Adler thought Wilhelm was discussing his grievances much too openly and said, "My son's income was up in the five figures."

As soon as money was mentioned, Mr. Perls's voice grew eagerly sharper. "Yes? What, the thirty-two-per-cent bracket? Higher even, I guess?" He asked for a hint, and he named the figures not idly but with a sort of hugging relish. Uch! How they love money, thought Wilhelm. They adore money! Holy money! Beautiful money! It was getting so that people were feeble-minded about everything except money. While if you didn't have it you were a dummy, a dummy! You had to excuse yourself from the face of the earth. Chicken! that's what it was. The world's business. If only he could find a way out of it.

Such thinking brought on the usual congestion. It would grow into a fit of passion if he allowed it to continue. Therefore he stopped talking and began to eat.

Before he struck the egg with his spoon he dried the moisture with his napkin. Then he battered it (in his father's opinion) more than was necessary. A faint grime was left by his fingers on the white of the egg after he had picked away the shell. Dr. Adler saw it with silent repugnance. What a Wilky he had given to the world! Why, he didn't even wash his hands in the morning. He used an electric razor so that he didn't have to touch water. The doctor couldn't bear Wilky's dirty habits. Only once—and never again, he swore—had he visited his room. Wilhelm, in pajamas and stockings had sat on his bed, drinking gin from a coffee mug and rooting for the Dodgers on television. "That's two and two on you, Duke. Come on—hit it, now." He came down on the mattress—bam! The bed looked kicked to pieces. Then he drank the gin as though it were tea, and urged his team on with his fist. The smell of dirty clothes was outrageous. By the bedside lay a quart bottle and foolish magazines and mystery stories for the hours of insomnia. Wilhelm lived in worse filth than a savage. When the Doctor spoke to him about this he answered, "Well, I have no wife to look after my things." And who—*who!*—had done the leaving? Not Margaret. The Doctor was certain that she wanted him back.

Wilhelm drank his coffee with a trembling hand. In his full face his abused bloodshot gray eyes moved back and forth. Jerkily he set his cup back and put half the length of a cigarette into his mouth; he seemed to hold it with his teeth, as though it were a cigar.

"I can't let them get away with it," he said. "It's also a question of morale."

His father corrected him. "Don't you mean a moral question, Wilky?"

"I mean that, too. I have to do something to protect myself. I was promised executive standing." Correction before a stranger mortified him, and his dark blond face changed color, more pale, and then more dark. He went on talking to Perls but his eyes spied on his father. "I was the one who opened the territory for them. I could go back for one of their competitors and take away their customers. *My* customers. Morale enters into it because they've tried to take away my confidence."

"Would you offer a different line to the same people?" Mr. Perls wondered.

"Why not? I know what's wrong with the Rojax product."

"Nonsense," said his father. "Just nonsense and kid's talk, Wilky. You're only looking for trouble and embarrassment that way.

What would you gain by such a silly feud? You have to think about making a living and meeting your obligations."

Hot and bitter, Wilhelm said with pride, while his feet moved angrily under the table, "I don't have to be told about my obligations. I've been meeting them for years. In more than twenty years I've never had a penny of help from anybody. I preferred to dig a ditch on the WPA but never asked anyone to meet my obligations for me."

"Wilky has had all kinds of experiences," said Dr. Adler.

The old doctor's face had a wholesome reddish and almost translucent color, like a ripe apricot. The wrinkles beside his ears were deep because the skin conformed so tightly to his bones. With all his might, he was a healthy and fine small old man. He wore a white vest of a light check pattern. His hearing-aid doodad was in the pocket. An unusual shirt of red and black stripes covered his chest. He bought his clothes in a college shop farther uptown. Wilhelm thought he had no business to get himself up like a jockey, out of respect for his profession.

"Well," said Mr. Perls. "I can understand how you feel. You want to fight it out. By a certain time of life, to have to start all over again can't be a pleasure, though a good man can always do it. But anyway you want to keep on with a business you know already, and not have to meet a whole lot of new contacts."

Wilhelm again thought, Why does it have to be me and my life that's discussed, and not him and his life? He would never allow it. But I am an idiot. I have no reserve. To me it can be done. I talk. I must ask for it. Everybody wants to have intimate conversations, but the smart fellows don't give out, only the fools. The smart fellows talk intimately about the fools, and examine them all over and give them advice. Why do I allow it? The hint about his age had hurt him. No, you can't admit it's as good as ever, he conceded. Things do give out.

"In the meanwhile," Dr. Adler said, "Wilky is taking it easy and considering various propositions. Isn't that so?"

"More or less," said Wilhelm. He suffered his father to increase Mr. Perls's respect for him. The WPA ditch had brought the family into contempt. He was a little tired. The spirit, the peculiar burden of his existence lay upon him like an accretion, a load, a hump. In any moment of quiet, when sheer fatigue prevented him from struggling, he was apt to feel this mysterious weight, this growth or collection of nameless things which it was the business of his life to carry about. That must be what a man was for. This large, odd, excited, fleshy, blond, abrupt personality named Wilhelm, or Tommy, was here, present, in the present—Dr. Tamkin had been putting into his mind many suggestions about the present moment, the here and now—this Wilky, or Tommy Wilhelm, forty-four years old, father of two sons, at present living in the Hotel Gloriana, was assigned to be the carrier of a load which was his own self, his characteristic self. There was no figure or estimate for the value of his load. But it is probably exaggerated by the subject, T. W. Who is a visionary sort of animal. Who has to believe that he can know why he exists. Though he has never seriously tried to find out why.

Mr. Perls said, "If he wants time to think things over and have a rest, why doesn't he run down to Florida for a while? Off season it's cheap and quiet. Fairyland. The mangoes are just coming in. I got two acres down there. You'd think you were in India."

Mr. Perls utterly astonished Wilhelm when he spoke of fairyland with a foreign accent. Mangoes—India? What did he mean, India?

"Once upon a time," said Wilhelm, "I did some public-relations work for a big hotel down in Cuba. If I could get them a notice in Leonard Lyons or one of the other columns it might be good for another holiday there, gratis. I haven't had a vacation for a long time, and I could stand a rest after going so hard. You know that's true, Father." He meant that his father knew how deep the crisis was becoming; how badly he was strapped for money; and that he could not rest but would be crushed if he stumbled; and that his obligations would destroy him. He couldn't falter. He thought, The money! When I had it, I flowed money. They bled it away from me. I hemorrhaged money. But now it's almost all gone, and where am I supposed to turn for more?

He said, "As a matter of fact, Father, I am tired as hell."

But Mr. Perls began to smile and said, "I understand from Doctor Tamkin that you're going into some kind of investment with him, partners."

"You know, he's a very ingenious fellow," said Dr. Adler. "I really enjoy hearing him go on. I wonder if he really is a medical doctor."

"Isn't he?" said Perls. "Everybody thinks he is. He talks about his patients. Doesn't he write prescriptions?"

"I don't really know what he does," said Dr. Adler. "He's a cunning man."

"He's a psychologist, I understand," said Wilhelm.

"I don't know what sort of psychologist or psychiatrist he may be," said his father. "He's a little vague. It's growing into a major industry, and a very expensive one. Fellows have to hold down very big jobs in order to pay those fees. Anyway, this Tamkin is clever. He never said he practiced here, but I believe he was a doctor in California. They don't seem to have much legislation out there to cover these things, and I hear a thousand dollars will get you a degree from a Los Angeles correspondence school. He gives the impression of knowing something about chemistry, and things like hypnotism. I wouldn't trust him, though."

"And why wouldn't you?" Wilhelm demanded.

"Because he's probably a liar. Do you believe he invented all the things he claims?"

Mr. Perls was grinning.

"He was written up in *Fortune*," said Wilhelm. "Yes, in *Fortune* magazine. He showed me the article. I've seen his clippings."

"That doesn't make him legitimate," said Dr. Adler. "It might have been another Tamkin. Make no mistake, he's an operator. Perhaps even crazy."

"Crazy, you say?"

Mr. Perls put in, "He could be both sane and crazy. In these days nobody can tell for sure which is which."

"An electrical device for truck drivers to wear in their caps," said Dr. Adler, describing one of Tamkin's proposed inventions. "To wake them with a shock when they begin to be drowsy at the wheel. It's triggered by the change in blood-pressure when they start to doze."

"It doesn't sound like such an impossible thing to me," said Wilhelm.

Mr. Perls said, "To me he described an underwater suit so a man could walk on the bed of the Hudson in case of an atomic attack. He said he could walk to Albany in it."

"Ha, ha, ha, ha, ha!" cried Dr. Adler in his old man's voice. "Tamkin's Folly. You could go on a camping trip under Niagara Falls."

"This is just his kind of fantasy," said Wilhelm. "It doesn't mean a thing. Inventors are supposed to be like that. I get funny ideas myself. Everybody wants to make something. Any American does."

But his father ignored this and said to Perls, "What other inventions did he describe?"

While the frazzle-faced Mr. Perls and his father in the unseemly, monkey-striped shirt were laughing, Wilhelm could not restrain himself and joined in with his own panting laugh. But he was in despair. They were laughing at the man to whom he had given a power of attorney over his last seven hundred dollars to speculate for him in the commodities market. They had bought all that lard. It had to rise today. By ten o'clock, or half-past ten, trading would be active, and he would see.

III

Between white tablecloths and glassware and glancing silverware, through overfull light, the long figure of Mr. Perls went away into the darkness of the lobby. He thrust with his cane, and dragged a large built-up shoe which Wilhelm had not included in his estimate of troubles. Dr. Adler wanted to talk about him. "There's a poor man," he said, "with a bone condition which is gradually breaking him up."

"One of those progressive diseases?" said Wilhelm.

"Very bad. I've learned," the doctor told him, "to keep my sympathy for the real ailments. This Perls is more to be pitied than any man I know."

Wilhelm understood he was being put on notice and did not express his opinion. He ate and ate. He did not hurry but kept putting food on his plate until he had gone through the muffins and his father's strawberries, and then some pieces of bacon that were left; he had several cups of coffee, and when he was finished he sat gigantically in a state of arrest and didn't seem to know what he should do next.

For a while father and son were uncommonly still. Wilhelm's preparations to please Dr. Adler had failed completely, for the old man kept thinking, You'd never guess he had a clean upbringing, and, What a dirty devil this son of mine is. Why can't he try to sweeten his appearance a little? Why does he want to drag himself like this? And he makes himself look so idealistic.

Wilhelm sat, mountainous. He was not really so slovenly as his father found him to be. In some aspects he even had a certain delicacy. His mouth, though broad, had a fine outline, and his brow and his gradually incurved nose, dignity, and in his blond hair there was white but there were also shades of gold and chestnut. When he

was with the Rojax Corporation Wilhelm had kept a small apartment in Roxbury, two rooms in a large house with a small porch and
garden, and on mornings of leisure, in late spring weather like this,
he used to sit expanded in a wicker chair with the sunlight pouring
through the weave, and sunlight through the slug-eaten holes of the
young hollyhocks and as deeply as the grass allowed into small flowers. This peace (he forgot that that time had had its troubles, too),
this peace was gone. It must not have belonged to him, really, for to
be here in New York with his old father was more genuinely like his
life. He was well aware that he didn't stand a chance of getting
sympathy from his father, who said he kept his for real ailments.
Moreover, he advised himself repeatedly not to discuss his vexatious
problems with him, for his father, with some justice, wanted to be
left in peace. Wilhelm also knew that when he began to talk about
these things he made himself feel worse, he became congested with
them and worked himself into a clutch. Therefore he warned himself, Lay off, pal. It'll only be an aggravation. From a deeper source,
however, came other promptings. If he didn't keep his troubles before him he risked losing them altogether, and he knew by experience that this was worse. And furthermore, he could not succeed in
excusing his father on the ground of old age. No. No, he could not.
I am his son, he thought. He is my father. He is as much father as I
am son—old or not. Affirming this, though in complete silence, he
sat, and, sitting, he kept his father at the table with him.

"Wilky," said the old man, "have you gone down to the baths
here yet?"

"No, Dad, not yet."

"Well, you know the Gloriana has one of the finest pools in
New York. Eighty feet, blue tile. It's a beauty."

Wilhelm had seen it. On the way to the gin game you passed the
stairway to the pool. He did not care for the odor of the wall-locked
and chlorinated water.

"You ought to investigate the Russian and Turkish baths, and
the sunlamps and massage. I don't hold with sunlamps. But the
massage does a world of good, and there's nothing better than
hydrotherapy when you come right down to it. Simple water has a
calming effect and would do you more good than all the barbiturates
and alcohol in the world."

Wilhelm reflected that this advice was as far as his father's help
and sympathy would extend.

"I thought," he said, "that the water cure was for lunatics."

The doctor received this as one of his son's jokes and said with a smile, "Well, it won't turn a sane man into a lunatic. It does a great deal for me. I couldn't live without my massages and steam."

"You're probably right. I ought to try it one of these days. Yesterday, late in the afternoon, my head was about to bust and I just had to have a little air, so I walked around the reservoir, and I sat down for a while in a playground. It rests me to watch the kids play potsy and skiprope."

The doctor said with approval, "Well, now, that's more like the idea."

"It's the end of the lilacs," said Wilhelm. "When they burn it's the beginning of summer. At least, in the city. Around the time of year when the candy stores take down the windows and start to sell sodas on the sidewalk. But even though I was raised here, Dad, I can't take city life any more, and I miss the country. There's too much push here for me. It works me up too much. I take things too hard. I wonder why you never retired to a quieter place."

The doctor opened his small hand on the table in a gesture so old and so typical that Wilhelm felt it like an actual touch upon the foundations of his life. "I am a city boy myself, you must remember," Dr. Adler explained. "But if you find the city so hard on you, you ought to get out."

"I'll do that," said Wilhelm, "as soon as I can make the right connection. Meanwhile—"

His father interrupted, "Meanwhile I suggest you cut down on drugs."

"You exaggerate that, Dad. I don't really— I give myself a little boost against—" He almost pronounced the word "misery" but he kept his resolution not to complain.

The doctor, however, fell into the error of pushing his advice too hard. It was all he had to give his son and he gave it once more. "Water and exercise," he said.

He wants a young, smart, successful son, thought Wilhelm, and he said, "Oh, Father, it's nice of you to give me this medical advice, but steam isn't going to cure what ails me."

The doctor measurably drew back, warned by the sudden weak strain of Wilhelm's voice and all that the droop of his face, the swell of his belly against the restraint of his belt intimated.

"Some new business?" he asked unwillingly.

Wilhelm made a great preliminary summary which involved the whole of his body. He drew and held a long breath, and his color changed and his eyes swam. "New?" he said.

"You make too much of your problems," said the doctor. "They ought not to be turned into a career. Concentrate on real troubles —fatal sickness, accidents." The old man's whole manner said, Wilky, don't start this on me. I have a right to be spared.

Wilhelm himself prayed for restraint; he knew this weakness of his and fought it. He knew, also, his father's character. And he began mildly, "As far as the fatal part of it goes, everyone on this side of the grave is the same distance from death. No, I guess my trouble is not exactly new. I've got to pay premiums on two policies for the boys. Margaret sent them to me. She unloads everything on me. Her mother left her an income. She won't even file a joint tax return. I get stuck. Etcetera. But you've heard the whole story before."

"I certainly have," said the old man. "And I've told you to stop giving her so much money."

Wilhelm worked his lips in silence before he could speak. The congestion was growing. "Oh, but my kids, Father. My kids. I love them. I don't want them to lack anything."

The doctor said with a half-deaf benevolence, "Well, naturally. And she, I'll bet, is the beneficiary of that policy."

"Let her be. I'd sooner die myself before I collected a cent of such money."

"Ah yes." The old man sighed. He did not like the mention of death. "Did I tell you that your sister Catherine—Philippa—is after me again."

"What for?"

"She wants to rent a gallery for an exhibition."

Stiffly fair-minded, Wilhelm said, "Well, of course that's up to you, Father."

The round-headed old man with his fine, feather-white, ferny hair said, "No, Wilky. There's not a thing on those canvases. I don't believe it; it's a case of the emperor's clothes. I may be old enough for my second childhood, but at least the first is well behind me. I was glad enough to buy crayons for her when she was four. But now she's a woman of forty and too old to be encouraged in her delusions. She's no painter."

"I wouldn't go so far as to call her a born artist," said Wilhelm, "but you can't blame her for trying something worth while."

"Let her husband pamper her."

Wilhelm had done his best to be just to his sister, and he had sincerely meant to spare his father, but the old man's tight, benevolent deafness had its usual effect on him. He said, "When it comes to women and money, I'm completely in the dark. What makes Margaret act like this?"

"She's showing you that you can't make it without her," said the doctor. "She aims to bring you back by financial force."

"But if she ruins me, Dad, how can she expect me to come back? No, I have a sense of honor. What you don't see is that she's trying to put an end to me."

His father stared. To him this was absurd. And Wilhelm thought, Once a guy starts to slip, he figures he might as well be a clunk. A real big clunk. He even takes pride in it. But there's nothing to be proud of—hey, boy? Nothing. I don't blame Dad for his attitude. And it's no cause for pride.

"I don't understand that. But if you feel like this why don't you settle with her once and for all?"

"What do you mean, Dad?" said Wilhelm, surprised. "I thought I told you. Do you think I'm not willing to settle? Four years ago when we broke up I gave her everything—goods, furniture, savings. I tried to show good will, but I didn't get anywhere. Why when I wanted Scissors, the dog, because the animal and I were so attached to each other—it was bad enough to leave the kids—she absolutely refused me. Not that she cared a damn about the animal. I don't think you've seen him. He's an Australian sheep dog. They usually have one blank or whitish eye which gives a misleading look, but they're the gentlest dogs and have unusual delicacy about eating or talking. Let me at least have the companionship of this animal. Never." Wilhelm was greatly moved. He wiped his face at all corners with his napkin. Dr. Adler felt that his son was indulging himself too much in his emotions.

"Whenever she can hit me, she hits, and she seems to live for that alone. And she demands more and more, and still more. Two years ago she wanted to go back to college and get another degree. It increased my burden but I thought it would be wiser in the end if she got a better job through it. But still she takes as much from me as before. Next thing she'll want to be a Doctor of Philosophy. She says the women in her family live long, and I'll have to pay and pay for the rest of my life."

The doctor said impatiently, "Well, these are details, not principles. Just details which you can leave out. The dog! You're mixing up all kinds of irrelevant things. Go to a good lawyer."

"But I've already told you, Dad. I got a lawyer, and she got one, too, and both of them talk and send me bills, and I eat my heart out. Oh, Dad, Dad, what a hole I'm in!" said Wilhelm in utter misery. "The lawyers—see?—draw up an agreement, and she says okay on Monday and wants more money on Tuesday. And it begins again."

"I always thought she was a strange kind of woman," said Dr. Adler. He felt that by disliking Margaret from the first and disapproving of the marriage he had done all that he could be expected to do.

"Strange, Father? I'll show you what she's like." Wilhelm took hold of his broad throat with brown-stained fingers and bitten nails and began to choke himself.

"What are you doing?" cried the old man.

"I'm showing you what she does to me."

"Stop that—stop it!" the old man said and tapped the table commandingly.

"Well, Dad, she hates me. I feel that she's strangling me. I can't catch my breath. She just has fixed herself on me to kill me. She can do it at long distance. One of these days I'll be struck down by suffocation or apoplexy because of her. I just can't catch my breath."

"Take your hands off your throat, you foolish man," said his father. "Stop this bunk. Don't expect me to believe in all kinds of voodoo."

"If that's what you want to call it, all right." His face flamed and paled and swelled and his breath was laborious.

"But I'm telling you that from the time I met her I've been a slave. The Emancipation Proclamation was only for colored people. A husband like me is a slave, with an iron collar. The churches go up to Albany and supervise the law. They won't have divorces. The court says, 'You want to be free. Then you have to work twice as hard—twice, at least! Work! you bum.' So then guys kill each other for the buck, and they may be free of a wife who hates them but they are sold to the company. The company knows a guy has got to have his salary, and takes full advantage of him. Don't talk to me about being free. A rich man may be free on an income of a million net. A poor man may be free because nobody cares what he does.

But a fellow in my position has to sweat it out until he drops dead."

His father replied to this, "Wilky, it's entirely your own fault. You don't have to allow it."

Stopped in his eloquence, Wilhelm could not speak for a while. Dumb and incompetent, he struggled for breath and frowned with effort into his father's face.

"I don't understand your problems," said the old man. "I never had any like them."

By now Wilhelm had lost his head and he waved his hands and said over and over, "Oh, Dad, don't give me that stuff, don't give me that. Please don't give me that sort of thing."

"It's true," said his father. "I come from a different world. Your mother and I led an entirely different life."

"Oh, how can you compare Mother," Wilhelm said. "Mother was a help to you. Did she harm you ever?"

"There's no need to carry on like an opera, Wilky," said the doctor. "This is only your side of things."

"What? It's the truth," said Wilhelm.

The old man could not be persuaded and shook his round head and drew his vest down over the gilded shirt, and leaned back with a completeness of style that made this look, to anyone out of hearing, like an ordinary conversation between a middle-aged man and his respected father. Wilhelm towered and swayed, big and sloven, with his gray eyes red-shot and his honey-colored hair twisted in flaming shapes upward. Injustice made him angry, made him beg. But he wanted an understanding with his father, and he tried to capitulate to him. He said, "You can't compare Mother and Margaret, and neither can you and I be compared, because you, Dad, were a success. And a success—is a success. I never made a success."

The doctor's old face lost all of its composure and became hard and angry. His small breast rose sharply under the red and black shirt and he said, "Yes. Because of hard work. I was not self-indulgent, not lazy. My old man sold dry goods in Williamsburg. We were nothing, do you understand? I knew I couldn't afford to waste my chances."

"I wouldn't admit for one minute that I was lazy," said Wilhelm. "If anything, I tried too hard. I admit I made many mistakes. Like I thought I shouldn't do things you had done already. Study chemistry. You had done it already. It was in the family."

His father continued, "I didn't run around with fifty women, either. I was not a Hollywood star. I didn't have time to go to Cuba for a vacation. I stayed at home and took care of my children."

Oh, thought Wilhelm, eyes turning upward. Why did I come here in the first place, to live near him? New York is like a gas. The colors are running. My head feels so tight, I don't know what I'm doing. He thinks I want to take away his money or that I envy him. He doesn't see what I want.

"Dad," Wilhelm said aloud, "you're being very unfair. It's true the movies was a false step. But I love my boys. I didn't abandon them. I left Margaret because I had to."

"Why did you have to?"

"Well—" said Wilhelm, struggling to condense his many reasons into a few plain words. "I had to—I had to."

With sudden and surprising bluntness his father said, "Did you have bed-trouble with her? Then you should have stuck it out. Sooner or later everyone has it. Normal people stay with it. It passes. But you wouldn't, so now you pay for your stupid romantic notions. Have I made my view clear?"

It was very clear. Wilhelm seemed to hear it repeated from various sides and inclined his head different ways, and listened and thought. Finally he said, "I guess that's the medical standpoint. You may be right. I just couldn't live with Margaret. I wanted to stick it out, but I was getting very sick. She was one way and I was another. She wouldn't be like me, so I tried to be like her, and I couldn't do it."

"Are you sure she didn't tell *you* to go?" the doctor said.

"I wish she had. I'd be in a better position now. No, it was me. I didn't want to leave, but I couldn't stay. Somebody had to take the initiative. I did. Now I'm the fall guy too."

Pushing aside in advance all the objections that his son would make, the doctor said, "Why did you lose your job with Rojax?"

"I didn't, I've told you."

"You're lying. You wouldn't have ended the connection. You need the money too badly. But you must have got into trouble." The small old man spoke concisely and with great strength. "Since you have to talk and can't let it alone, tell the truth. Was there a scandal—a woman?"

Wilhelm fiercely defended himself. "No, Dad, there wasn't any woman. I told you how it was."

"Maybe it was a man, then," the old man said wickedly.

Shocked, Wilhelm stared at him with burning pallor and dry

lips. His skin looked a little yellow. "I don't think you know what you're talking about," he answered after a moment. "You shouldn't let your imagination run so free. Since you've been living here on Broadway you must think you understand life, up to date. You ought to know your own son a little better. Let's drop that, now."

"All right, Wilky, I'll withdraw it. But something must have happened in Roxbury nevertheless. You'll never go back. You're just talking wildly about representing a rival company. You won't. You've done something to spoil your reputation, I think. But you've got girl friends who are expecting you back, isn't that so?"

"I take a lady out now and then while on the road," said Wilhelm. "I'm not a monk."

"No one special? Are you sure you haven't gotten into complications?"

He had tried to unburden himself and instead, Wilhelm thought, he had to undergo an inquisition to prove himself worthy of a sympathetic word. Because his father believed that he did all kinds of gross things.

"There is a woman in Roxbury that I went with. We fell in love and wanted to marry, but she got tired of waiting for my divorce. Margaret figured that. On top of which the girl was a Catholic and I had to go with her to the priest and make an explanation."

Neither did this last confession touch Dr. Adler's sympathies or sway his calm old head or affect the color of his complexion.

"No, no, no, no; all wrong," he said.

Again Wilhelm cautioned himself. Remember his age. He is no longer the same person. He can't bear trouble. I'm so choked up and congested anyway I can't see straight. Will I ever get out of the woods, and recover my balance? You're never the same afterward. Trouble rusts out the system.

"You really *want* a divorce?" said the old man.

"For the price I pay I should be getting something."

"In that case," Dr. Adler said, "it seems to me no normal person would stand for such treatment from a woman."

"Ah, Father, Father!" said Wilhelm. "It's always the same thing with you. Look how you lead me on. You always start out to help me with my problems, and be sympathetic and so forth. It gets my hopes up and I begin to be grateful. But before we're through I'm a hundred times more depressed than before. Why is that? You have no sympathy. You want to shift all the blame on to me. Maybe you're wise to do it." Wilhelm was beginning to lose himself. "All

you seem to think about is your death. Well, I'm sorry. But I'm going to die too. And I'm your son. It isn't my fault in the first place.
There ought to be a right way to do this, and be fair to each other.
But what I want to know is, why do you start up with me if you're
not going to help me? What do you want to know about my problems
for, Father? So you can lay the whole responsibility on me—so that
you won't have to help me? D'you want me to comfort you for having
such a son?" Wilhelm had a great knot of wrong tied tight within his
chest, and tears approached his eyes but he didn't let them out. He
looked shabby enough as it was. His voice was thick and hazy, and
he was stammering and could not bring his awful feelings forth.

"You have some purpose of your own," said the doctor, "in acting so unreasonable. What do you want from me? What do you expect?"

"What do I expect?" said Wilhelm. He felt as though he were
unable to recover something. Like a ball in the surf, washed beyond
reach, his self-control was going out. "I expect *help!*" The words escaped him in a loud, wild, frantic cry and startled the old man, and
two or three breakfasters within hearing glanced their way. Wilhelm's hair, the color of whitened honey, rose dense and tall with
the expansion of his face, and he said, "When I suffer—you aren't
even sorry. That's because you have no affection for me, and you
don't want any part of me."

"Why must I like the way you behave? No, I don't like it," said
Dr. Adler.

"All right. You want me to change myself. But suppose I could
do it—what would I become? What could I? Let's suppose that all
my life I have had the wrong ideas about myself and wasn't what I
thought I was. And wasn't even careful to take a few precautions, as
most people do—like a woodchuck has a few exits to his tunnel. But
what shall I do now? More than half my life is over. More than half.
And now you tell me I'm not even normal."

The old man too had lost his calm. "You cry about being
helped," he said. "When you thought you had to go into the service
I sent a check to Margaret every month. As a family man you could
have had an exemption. But no! The war couldn't be fought without you and you had to get yourself drafted and be an office-boy in
the Pacific theater. Any clerk could have done what you did. You
could find nothing better to become than a GI."

Wilhelm was going to reply, and half raised his bearish figure from the chair, his fingers spread and whitened by their grip on the table, but the old man would not let him begin. He said, "I see other elderly people here with children who aren't much good, and they keep backing them and holding them up at a great sacrifice. But I'm not going to make that mistake. It doesn't enter your mind that when I die—a year, two years from now—you'll still be here. I do think of it."

He had intended to say that he had a right to be left in peace. Instead he gave Wilhelm the impression that he meant it was not fair for the better man of the two, and the more useful, the more admired, to leave the world first. Perhaps he meant that, too—a little; but he would not under other circumstances have come out with it so flatly.

"Father," said Wilhelm with an unusual openness of appeal. "Don't you think I know how you feel? I have pity. I want you to live on and on. If you outlive me, that's perfectly okay by me." As his father did not answer this avowal and turned away his glance, Wilhelm suddenly burst out, "No, but you hate me. And if I had money you wouldn't. By God, you have to admit it. The money makes the difference. Then we would be a fine father and son, if I was a credit to you—so you could boast and brag about me all over the hotel. But I'm not the right type of son. I'm too old, I'm too old and too unlucky."

His father said, "I can't give you any money. There would be no end to it if I started. You and your sister would take every last buck from me. I'm still alive, not dead. I am still here. Life isn't over yet. I am as much alive as you or anyone. And I want nobody on my back. Get off! And I give you the same advice, Wilky. Carry nobody on your back."

"Just keep your money," said Wilhelm miserably. "Keep it and enjoy it yourself. That's the ticket!"

IV

Ass! Idiot! Wild boar! Dumb mule! Slave! Lousy, wallowing hippopotamus! Wilhelm called himself as his bending legs carried him from the dining room. His pride! His inflamed feelings! His begging and feebleness! And trading insults with his old father—and spreading confusion over everything. Oh, how poor, contemptible, and

ridiculous he was! When he remembered how he had said, with
great reproof, "You ought to know your own son"—why, how corny
and abominable it was.

He could not get out of the sharply brilliant dining room fast
enough. He was horribly worked up; his neck and shoulders, his
entire chest ached as though they had been tightly tied with ropes.
He smelled the salt odor of tears in his nose.

But at the same time, since there were depths in Wilhelm not
unsuspected by himself, he received a suggestion from some remote
element in his thoughts that the business of life, the real business—
to carry his peculiar burden, to feel shame and impotence, to taste
these quelled tears—the only important business, the highest business was being done. Maybe the making of mistakes expressed the
very purpose of his life and the essence of his being here. Maybe he
was supposed to make them and suffer from them on this earth.
And though he had raised himself above Mr. Perls and his father
because they adored money, still they were called to act energetically
and this was better than to yell and cry, pray and beg, poke and
blunder and go by fits and starts and fall upon the thorns of life.
And finally sink beneath that watery floor—would that be tough
luck, or would it be good riddance?

But he raged once more against his father. Other people with
money, while they're still alive, want to see it do some good.
Granted, he shouldn't support me. But have I ever asked him to do
that? Have I ever asked for dough at all, either for Margaret or for
the kids or for myself? It isn't the money, but only the assistance;
not even assistance, but just the feeling. But he may be trying to
teach me that a grown man should be cured of such feeling. Feeling
got me in dutch at Rojax. I had the *feeling* that I belonged to the
firm, and my *feelings* were hurt when they put Gerber in over me.
Dad thinks I'm too simple. But I'm not so simple as he thinks.
What about his feelings? He doesn't forget death for one single second, and that's what makes him like this. And not only is death on
his mind but through money he forces me to think about it, too. It
gives him power over me. He forces me that way, he himself, and
then he's sore. If he was poor, I could care for him and show it. The
way I *could* care, too, if I only had a chance. He'd see how much
love and respect I had in me. It would make him a different man,
too. He'd put his hands on me and give me his blessing.

Someone in a gray straw hat with a wide cocoa-colored band
spoke to Wilhelm in the lobby. The light was dusky, splotched with

red underfoot; green, the leather furniture; yellow, the indirect lighting.

"Hey, Tommy. Say, there."

"Excuse me," said Wilhelm, trying to reach a house phone. But this was Dr. Tamkin, whom he was just about to call.

"You have a very obsessional look on your face," said Dr. Tamkin.

Wilhelm thought, Here he is, Here he is. If I could only figure this guy out.

"Oh," he said to Tamkin. "Have I got such a look? Well, whatever it is, you name it and I'm sure to have it."

The sight of Dr. Tamkin brought his quarrel with his father to a close. He found himself flowing into another channel.

"What are we doing?" he said. "What's going to happen to lard today?"

"Don't worry yourself about that. All we have to do is hold on to it and it's sure to go up. But what's made you so hot under the collar, Wilhelm?"

"Oh, one of those family situations." This was the moment to take a new look at Tamkin, and he viewed him closely but gained nothing by the new effort. It was conceivable that Tamkin was everything that he claimed to be, and all the gossip false. But was he a scientific man, or not? If he was not, this might be a case for the district attorney's office to investigate. Was he a liar? That was a delicate question. Even a liar might be trustworthy in some ways. Could he trust Tamkin—could he? He feverishly, fruitlessly sought an answer.

But the time for this question was past, and he had to trust him now. After a long struggle to come to a decision, he had given him the money. Practical judgment was in abeyance. He had worn himself out, and the decision was no decision. How had this happened? But how had his Hollywood career begun? It was not because of Maurice Venice, who turned out to be a pimp. It was because Wilhelm himself was ripe for the mistake. His marriage, too, had been like that. Through such decisions somehow his life had taken form. And so, from the moment when he tasted the peculiar flavor of fatality in Dr. Tamkin, he could no longer keep back the money.

Five days ago Tamkin had said, "Meet me tomorrow, and we'll go to the market." Wilhelm, therefore, had had to go. At eleven o'clock they had walked to the brokerage office. On the way, Tam-

kin broke the news to Wilhelm that though this was an equal partnership he couldn't put up his half of the money just yet; it was tied
up for a week or so in one of his patents. Today he would be two
hundred dollars short; next week, he'd make it up. But neither of
them needed an income from the market, of course. This was only a
sporting proposition anyhow, Tamkin said. Wilhelm had to answer,
"Of course." It was too late to withdraw. What else could he do?
Then came the formal part of the transaction, and it was frightening. The very shade of green of Tamkin's check looked wrong; it was
a false, disheartening color. His handwriting was peculiar, even monstrous; the e's were like i's, the t's and l's the same, and the h's like
wasps' bellies. He wrote like a fourth-grader. Scientists, however, dealt
mostly in symbols they printed. This was Wilhelm's explanation.

Dr. Tamkin had given him his check for three hundred dollars.
Wilhelm, in a blinded and convulsed aberration, pressed and pressed
to try to kill the trembling of his hand as he wrote out his check for
a thousand. He set his lips tight, crouched with his huge back over
the table, and wrote with crumbling, terrified fingers, knowing that
if Tamkin's check bounced his own would not be honored either. His
sole cleverness was to set the date ahead by one day to give the
green check time to clear.

Next he had signed a power of attorney, allowing Tamkin to
speculate with his money, and this was an even more frightening
document. Tamkin never said a word about it, but here they were
and it had to be done.

After delivering his signatures, the only precaution Wilhelm took
was to come back to the manager of the brokerage office and ask
him privately, "Uh, about Doctor Tamkin. We were in here a few
minutes ago, remember?"

That day had been a weeping, smoky one and Wilhelm had gotten away from Tamkin on the pretext of having to run to the post
office. Tamkin had gone to lunch alone, and here was Wilhelm,
back again, breathless, his hat dripping, needlessly asking the manager if he remembered.

"Yes, sir, I know," the manager had said. He was a cold, mild,
lean German who dressed correctly and around his neck wore a pair
of opera glasses with which he read the board. He was an extremely
correct person except that he never shaved in the morning, not car-
ing, probably, how he looked to the fumblers and the old people
and the operators and the gamblers and the idlers of Broadway up-

town. The market closed at three. Maybe, Wilhelm guessed, he had a thick beard and took a lady out to dinner later and wanted to look fresh-shaven.

"Just a question," said Wilhelm. "A few minutes ago I signed a power of attorney so Doctor Tamkin could invest for me. You gave me the blanks."

"Yes, sir, I remember."

"Now this is what I want to know," Wilhelm had said. "I'm no lawyer and I only gave the paper a glance. Does this give Doctor Tamkin power of attorney over any other assets of mine—money, or property?"

The rain had dribbled from Wilhelm's deformed, transparent raincoat; the buttons of his shirt, which always seemed tiny, were partly broken, in pearly quarters of the moon, and some of the dark, thick golden hairs that grew on his belly stood out. It was the manager's business to conceal his opinion of him; he was shrewd, gray, correct (although unshaven) and had little to say except on matters that came to his desk. He must have recognized in Wilhelm a man who reflected long and then made the decision he had rejected twenty separate times. Silvery, cool, level, long-profiled, experienced, indifferent, observant, with unshaven refinement, he scarcely looked at Wilhelm, who trembled with fearful awkwardness. The manager's face, low-colored, long-nostriled, acted as a unit of perception; his eyes merely did their reduced share. Here was a man, like Rubin, who knew and knew and knew. He, a foreigner, knew; Wilhelm, in the city of his birth, was ignorant.

The manager had said, "No, sir, it does not give him."

"Only over the funds I deposited with you?"

"Yes, that is right, sir."

"Thank you, that's what I wanted to find out," Wilhelm had said, grateful.

The answer comforted him. However, the question had no value. None at all. For Wilhelm had no other assets. He had given Tamkin his last money. There wasn't enough of it to cover his obligations anyway, and Wilhelm had reckoned that he might as well go bankrupt now as next month. "Either broke or rich," was how he had figured, and that formula had encouraged him to make the gamble. Well, not rich; he did not expect that, but perhaps Tamkin might really show him how to earn what he needed in the market. By now, however, he had forgotten his own reckoning and was aware only that he stood to lose his seven hundred dollars to the last cent.

Dr. Tamkin took the attitude that they were a pair of gentlemen experimenting with lard and grain futures. The money, a few hundred dollars, meant nothing much to either of them. He said to Wilhelm, "Watch. You'll get a big kick out of this and wonder why more people don't go into it. You think the Wall Street guys are so smart—geniuses? That's because most of us are psychologically afraid to think about the details. Tell me this. When you're on the road, and you don't understand what goes on under the hood of your car, you'll worry what'll happen if something goes wrong with the engine. Am I wrong?" No, he was right. "Well," said Dr. Tamkin with an expression of quiet triumph about his mouth, almost the suggestion of a jeer. "It's the same psychological principle, Wilhelm. They are rich because you don't understand what goes on. But it's no mystery, and by putting in a little money and applying certain principles of observation, you begin to grasp it. It can't be studied in the abstract. You have to take a specimen risk so that you feel the process, the money-flow, the whole complex. To know how it feels to be a seaweed you have to get in the water. In a very short time we'll take out a hundred-per-cent profit." Thus Wilhelm had had to pretend at the outset that his interest in the market was theoretical.

"Well," said Tamkin when he met him now in the lobby, "what's the problem, what is this family situation? Tell me." He put himself forward as the keen mental scientist. Whenever this happened Wilhelm didn't know what to reply. No matter what he said or did it seemed that Dr. Tamkin saw through him.

"I had some words with my dad."

Dr. Tamkin found nothing extraordinary in this. "It's the eternal same story," he said. "The elemental conflict of parent and child. It won't end, ever. Even with a fine old gentleman like your dad."

"I don't suppose it will. I've never been able to get anywhere with him. He objects to my feelings. He thinks they're sordid. I upset him and he gets mad at me. But maybe all old men are alike."

"Sons, too. Take it from one of them," said Dr. Tamkin. "All the same, you should be proud of such a fine old patriarch of a father. It should give you hope. The longer he lives, the longer your life-expectancy becomes."

Wilhelm answered, brooding, "I guess so. But I think I inherit more from my mother's side, and she died in her fifties."

"A problem arose between a young fellow I'm treating and his dad—I just had a consultation," said Dr. Tamkin as he removed his dark gray hat.

"So early in the morning?" said Wilhelm with suspicion.

"Over the telephone, of course."

What a creature Tamkin was when he took off his hat! The indirect light showed the many complexities of his bald skull, his gull's nose, his rather handsome eyebrows, his vain mustache, his deceiver's brown eyes. His figure was stocky, rigid, short in the neck, so that the large ball of the occiput touched his collar. His bones were peculiarly formed, as though twisted twice where the ordinary human bone was turned only once, and his shoulders rose in two pagoda-like points. At mid-body he was thick. He stood pigeon-toed, a sign perhaps that he was devious or had much to hide. The skin of his hands was aging, and his nails were moonless, concave, clawlike, and they appeared loose. His eyes were as brown as beaver fur and full of strange lines. The two large brown naked balls looked thoughtful—but were they? And honest—but was Dr. Tamkin honest? There was a hypnotic power in his eyes, but this was not always of the same strength, nor was Wilhelm convinced that it was completely natural. He felt that Tamkin tried to make his eyes deliberately conspicuous, with studied art, and that he brought forth his hypnotic effect by an exertion. Occasionally it failed or drooped, and when this happened the sense of his face passed downward to his heavy (possibly foolish?) red underlip.

Wilhelm wanted to talk about the lard holdings, but Dr. Tamkin said, "This father-and-son case of mine would be instructive to you. It's a different psychological type completely than your dad. This man's father thinks that he isn't his son."

"Why not?"

"Because he has found out something about the mother carrying on with a friend of the family for twenty-five years."

"Well, what do you know!" said Wilhelm. His silent thought was, Pure bull. Nothing but bull!

"You must note how interesting the woman is, too. She has two husbands. Whose are the kids? The fellow detected her and she gave a signed confession that two of the four children were not the father's."

"It's amazing," said Wilhelm, but he said it in a rather distant way. He was always hearing such stories from Dr. Tamkin. If you were to believe Tamkin, most of the world was like this. Everybody in the hotel had a mental disorder, a secret history, a concealed disease. The wife of Rubin at the newsstand was supposed to be kept by Carl, the yelling, loud-mouthed gin-rummy player. The wife of Frank in the barbershop had disappeared with a GI while he was waiting for her to disembark at the French Lines pier. Everyone was like the faces on a playing card, upside down either way. Every public figure had a character-neurosis. Maddest of all were the businessmen, the heartless, flaunting, boisterous business class who ruled this country with their hard manners and their bold lies and their absurd words that nobody could believe. They were crazier than anyone. They spread the plague. Wilhelm, thinking of the Rojax Corporation, was inclined to agree that many businessmen were insane. And he supposed that Tamkin, for all his peculiarities, spoke a kind of truth and did some people a sort of good. It confirmed Wilhelm's suspicions to hear that there was a plague, and he said, "I couldn't agree with you more. They trade on anything, they steal everything, they're cynical right to the bones."

"You have to realize," said Tamkin, speaking of his patient, or his client, "that the mother's confession isn't good. It's a confession of duress. I try to tell the young fellow he shouldn't worry about a phony confession. But what does it help him if I am rational with him?"

"No?" said Wilhelm, intensely nervous. "I think we ought to go over to the market. It'll be opening pretty soon."

"Oh, come on," said Tamkin. "It isn't even nine o'clock, and there isn't much trading the first hour anyway. Things don't get hot in Chicago until half-past ten, and they're an hour behind us, don't forget. Anyway, I say lard will go up, and it will. Take my word. I've made a study of the guilt-aggression cycle which is behind it. I ought to know *something* about that. Straighten your collar."

"But meantime," said Wilhelm, "we have taken a licking this week. Are you sure your insight is at its best? Maybe when it isn't we should lay off and wait."

"Don't you realize," Dr. Tamkin told him, "you can't march in a straight line to the victory? You fluctuate toward it. From Euclid to Newton there was straight lines. The modern age analyzes the wavers. On my own accounts, I took a licking in hides and coffee. But I have confidence. I'm sure I'll outguess them." He gave Wilhelm a narrow smile, friendly, calming, shrewd, and wizard-like, patronizing, secret, potent. He saw his fears and smiled at them.

"It's something," he remarked, "to see how the competition-factor will manifest itself in different individuals."

"So? Let's go over."

"But I haven't had my breakfast yet."

"I've had mine."

"Come, have a cup of coffee."

"I wouldn't want to meet my dad." Looking through the glass doors, Wilhelm saw that his father had left by the other exit. Wilhelm thought, He didn't want to run into me, either. He said to Dr. Tamkin, "Okay, I'll sit with you, but let's hurry it up because I'd like to get to the market while there's still a place to sit. Everybody and his uncle gets in ahead of you."

"I want to tell you about this boy and his dad. It's highly absorbing. The father was a nudist. Everybody went naked in the house. Maybe the woman found men *with* clothes attractive. Her husband didn't believe in cutting his hair, either. He practiced dentistry. In his office he wore riding pants and a pair of boots, and he wore a green eyeshade."

"Oh, come off it," said Wilhelm.

"This is a true case history."

Without warning, Wilhelm began to laugh. He himself had had no premonition of his change of humor. His face became warm and pleasant, and he forgot his father, his anxieties; he panted bearlike, happily, through his teeth. "This sounds like a horse-dentist. He wouldn't have to put on pants to treat a horse. Now what else are you going to tell me? Did the wife play the mandolin? Does the boy join the cavalry? Oh, Tamkin, you really are a killer-diller."

"Oh, you think I'm try to amuse you," said Tamkin. "That's because you aren't familiar with my outlook. I deal in facts. Facts always are sensational. I'll say that a second time. Facts *always!* are sensational."

Wilhelm was reluctant to part with his good mood. The doctor had little sense of humor. He was looking at him earnestly.

"I'd bet you any amount of money," said Tamkin, "that the facts about you are sensational."

"Oh—ha, ha! You want them? You can sell them to a true confession magazine."

"People forget how sensational the things are that they do. They don't see it on themselves. It blends into the background of their daily life."

Wilhelm smiled. "Are you sure this boy tells you the truth?"

"Yes, because I've known the whole family for years."

"And you do psychological work with your own friends? I didn't know that was allowed."

"Well, I'm a radical in the profession. I have to do good wherever I can."

Wilhelm's face became ponderous again and pale. His whitened gold hair lay heavy on his head, and he clasped uneasy fingers on the table. Sensational, but oddly enough, dull, too. Now how do you figure that out? It blends with the background. Funny but unfunny. True but false. Casual but laborious, Tamkin was. Wilhelm was most suspicious of him when he took his driest tone.

"With me," said Dr. Tamkin, "I am at my most efficient when I don't need the fee. When I only love. Without a financial reward. I remove myself from the social influence. Especially money. The spiritual compensation is what I look for. Bringing people into the here-and-now. The real universe. That's the present moment. The past is no good to us. The future is full of anxiety. Only the present is real —the here-and-now. Seize the day."

"Well," said Wilhelm, his earnestness returning. "I know you are a very unusual man. I like what you say about here-and-now. Are all the people who come to see you personal friends and patients too? Like that tall handsome girl, the one who always wears those beautiful broomstick skirts and belts?"

"She was an epileptic, and a most bad and serious pathology, too. I'm curing her successfully. She hasn't had a seizure in six months, and she used to have one every week."

"And that young cameraman, the one who showed us those movies from the jungles of Brazil, isn't he related to her?"

"Her brother. He's under my care, too. He has some terrible tendencies, which are to be expected when you have an epileptic sibling. I came into their lives when they needed help desperately, and took hold of them. A certain man forty years older than she had her in his control and used to give her fits by suggestion whenever she tried to leave him. If you only knew one per cent of what goes on in the city of New York! You see, I understand what it is when the lonely person begins to feel like an animal. When the night comes and he feels like howling from his window like a wolf. I'm taking complete care of that young fellow and his sister. I have to steady him down or he'll go from Brazil to Australia the next day. The way I keep him in the here-and-now is by teaching him Greek."

This was a complete surprise! "What, do you know Greek?"

"A friend of mine taught me when I was in Cairo. I studied Aristotle with him to keep from being idle."

Wilhelm tried to take in these new claims and examine them. Howling from the window like a wolf when night comes sounded genuine to him. That was something really to think about. But the Greek! He realized that Tamkin was watching to see how he took it. More elements were continually being added. A few days ago Tamkin had hinted that he had once been in the underworld, one of the Detroit Purple Gang. He was once head of a mental clinic in Toledo. He had worked with a Polish inventor on an unsinkable ship. He was a technical consultant in the field of television. In the life of a man of genius, all of these things might happen. But had they happened to Tamkin? Was he a genius? He often said that he had attended some of the Egyptian royal family as a psychiatrist. "But everybody is alike, common or aristocrat," he told Wilhelm. "The aristocrat knows less about life."

An Egyptian princess whom he had treated in California, for horrible disorders he had described to Wilhelm, retained him to come back to the old country with her, and there he had had many of her friends and relatives under his care. They turned over a villa on the Nile to him. "For ethical reasons, I can't tell you many of the details about them," he said—but Wilhelm had already heard all these details, and strange and shocking they were, if true. *If* true —he could not be free from doubt. For instance, the general who had to wear ladies' silk stockings and stand otherwise naked before the mirror—and all the rest. Listening to the doctor when he was so strangely factual, Wilhelm had to translate his words into his own language, and he could not translate fast enough or find terms to fit what he heard.

"Those Egyptian big shots invested in the market, too, for the heck of it. What did they need extra money for? By association, I almost became a millionaire myself, and if I had played it smart there's no telling what might have happened. I could have been the ambassador." The American? The Egyptian ambassador? "A friend of mine tipped me off on the cotton. I made a heavy purchase of it. I didn't have that kind of money, but everybody there knew me. It never entered their minds that a person of their social circle didn't have dough. The sale was made on the phone. Then, while the cotton shipment was at sea, the price tripled. When the stuff suddenly became so valuable all hell broke loose on the world cotton market, they looked to see who was the owner of this big shipment. Me!

They investigated my credit and found out I was a mere doctor, and they canceled. This was illegal. I sued them. But as I didn't have the money to fight them I sold the suit to a Wall Street lawyer for twenty thousand dollars. He fought it and was winning. They settled with him out of court for more than a million. But on the way back from Cairo, flying, there was a crash. All on board died. I have this guilt on my conscience, of being the murderer of that lawyer. Although he was a crook."

Wilhelm thought, I must be a real jerk to sit and listen to such impossible stories. I guess I am a sucker for people who talk about the deeper things of life, even the way he does.

"We scientific men speak of irrational guilt, Wilhelm," said Dr. Tamkin, as if Wilhelm were a pupil in his class. "But in such a situation, because of the money, I wished him harm. I realize it. This isn't the time to describe all the details, but the money made me guilty. Money and Murder both begin with M. Machinery. Mischief."

Wilhelm, his mind thinking for him at random, said, "What about Mercy? Milk-of-human-kindness?"

"One fact should be clear to you by now. Money-making is aggression. That's the whole thing. The functionalistic explanation is the only one. People come to the market to kill. They say, 'I'm going to make a killing.' It's not accidental. Only they haven't got the genuine courage to kill, and they erect a symbol of it. The money. They make a killing by a fantasy. Now, counting and number is always a sadistic activity. Like hitting. In the Bible, the Jews wouldn't allow you to count them. They knew it was sadistic."

"I don't understand what you mean," said Wilhelm. A strange uneasiness tore at him. The day was growing too warm and his head felt dim. "What makes them want to kill?"

"By and by, you'll get the drift," Dr. Tamkin assured him. His amazing eyes had some of the rich dryness of a brown fur. Innumerable crystalline hairs or spicules of light glittered in their bold surfaces. "You can't understand without first spending years on the study of the ultimates of human and animal behavior, the deep chemical, organismic, and spiritual secrets of life. I am a psychological poet."

"If you're this kind of poet," said Wilhelm, whose fingers in his pocket were feeling in the little envelopes for the Phenaphen capsules, "what are you doing on the market?"

"That's a good question. Maybe I am better at speculation because I don't care. Basically, I don't wish hard enough for money,
and therefore I come with a cool head to it."

Wilhelm thought, Oh, sure! That's an answer, is it? I bet that if
I took a strong attitude he'd back down on everything. He'd grovel
in front of me. The way he looks at me on the sly, to see if I'm being taken in! He swallowed his Phenaphen pill with a long gulp of
water. The rims of his eyes grew red as it went down. And then he
felt calmer.

"Let me see if I can give you an answer that will satisfy you,"
said Dr. Tamkin. His flapjacks were set before him. He spread the
butter on them, poured on brown maple syrup, quartered them, and
began to eat with hard, active, muscular jaws which sometimes gave
a creak at the hinges. He pressed the handle of his knife against his
chest and said, "In here, the human bosom—mine, yours, everybody's—there isn't just one soul. There's a lot of souls. But there are
two main ones, the real soul and a pretender soul. Now! Every man
realizes that he has to love something or somebody. He feels that he
must go outward. 'If thou canst not love, what art thou?' Are you
with me?"

"Yes, Doc, I think so," said Wilhelm listening—a little skepti-
cally but nonetheless hard.

" 'What art thou?' Nothing. That's the answer. Nothing. In the
heart of hearts—Nothing! So of course you can't stand that and
want to be Something, and you try. But instead of being this Something, the man puts it over on everybody instead. You can't be that
strict to yourself. You love a *little*. Like you have a dog" (*Scissors!*)
"or give some money to a charity drive. Now that isn't love, is it?
What is it? Egotism, pure and simple. It's a way to love the pretender soul. Vanity. Only vanity, is what it is. And social control.
The interest of the pretender soul is the same as the interest of the
social life, the society mechanism. This is the main tragedy of human life. Oh, it is terrible! Terrible! You are not free. Your own be-
trayer is inside of you and sells you out. You have to obey him like a
slave. He makes you work like a horse. And for what? For who?"

"Yes, for what?" The doctor's words caught Wilhelm's heart. "I
couldn't agree more," he said. "When do we get free?"

"The purpose is to keep the whole thing going. The true soul is
the one that pays the price. It suffers and gets sick, and it realizes
that the pretender can't be loved. Because the pretender is a lie. The

true soul loves the truth. And when the true soul feels like this, it wants to kill the pretender. The love has turned into hate. Then you become dangerous. A killer. You have to kill the deceiver."

"Does this happen to everybody?"

The doctor answered simply, "Yes, to everybody. Of course, for simplification purposes, I have spoken of the soul; it isn't a scientific term, but it helps you to understand it. Whenever the slayer slays, he wants to slay the soul in him which has gypped and deceived him. Who is his enemy? Him. And his lover? Also. Therefore, all suicide is murder, and all murder is suicide. It's the one and identical phenomenon. Biologically, the pretender soul takes away the energy of the true soul and makes it feeble, like a parasite. It happens unconsciously, unawaringly, in the depths of the organism. Ever take up parasitology?"

"No, it's my dad who's the doctor."

"You should read a book about it."

Wilhelm said, "But this means that the world is full of murderers. So it's not the world. It's a kind of hell."

"Sure," the doctor said. "At least a kind of purgatory. You walk on the bodies. They are all around. I can hear them cry de profundis and wring their hands. I hear them, poor human beasts. I can't help hearing. And my eyes are open to it. I have to cry, too. This is the human tragedy-comedy."

Wilhelm tried to capture his vision. And again the doctor looked untrustworthy to him, and he doubted him. "Well," he said, "there are also kind, ordinary, helpful people. They're—out in the country. All over. What kind of morbid stuff do you read, anyway?" The doctor's room was full of books.

"I read the best of literature, science and philosophy," Dr. Tamkin said. Wilhelm had observed that in his room even the TV aerial was set upon a pile of volumes. "Korzybski, Aristotle, Freud, W. H. Sheldon, and all the great poets. You answer me like a layman. You haven't applied your mind strictly to this."

"Very interesting," said Wilhelm. He was aware that he hadn't applied his mind strictly to anything. "You don't have to think I'm a dummy, though. I have ideas, too." A glance at the clock told him that the market would soon open. They could spare a few minutes yet. There were still more things he wanted to hear from Tamkin. He realized that Tamkin spoke faultily, but then scientific men were not always strictly literate. It was the description of the two souls that had awed him. In Tommy he saw the pretender. And even

Wilky might not be himself. Might the name of his true soul be the one by which his old grandfather had called him—Velvel? The name of a soul, however, must be only that—soul. What did it look like? Does my soul look like me? Is there a soul that looks like Dad? Like Tamkin? Where does the true soul get its strength? Why does it have to love truth? Wilhelm was tormented, but tried to be oblivious to his torment. Secretly, he prayed the doctor would give him some useful advice and transform his life. "Yes, I understand you," he said. "It isn't lost on me."

"I never said you weren't intelligent, but only you just haven't made a study of it all. As a matter of fact you're a profound personality with very profound creative capacities but also disturbances. I've been concerned with you, and for some time I've been treating you."

"Without my knowing it? I haven't felt you doing anything. What do you mean? I don't think I like being treated without my knowledge. I'm of two minds. What's the matter, don't you think I'm normal?" And he really was divided in mind. That the doctor cared about him pleased him. This was what he craved, that someone should care about him, wish him well. Kindness, mercy, he wanted. But—and here he retracted his heavy shoulders in his peculiar way, drawing his hands up into his sleeves; his feet moved uneasily under the table—but he was worried, too, and even somewhat indignant. For what right had Tamkin to meddle without being asked? What kind of privileged life did this man lead? He took other people's money and speculated with it. Everybody came under his care. No one could have secrets from him.

The doctor looked at him with his deadly brown, heavy, impenetrable eyes, his naked shining head, his red hanging underlip, and said, "You have lots of guilt in you."

Wilhelm helplessly admitted, as he felt the heat rise to his wide face, "Yes, I think so too. But personally," he added, "I don't feel like a murderer. I always try to lay off. It's the others who get me. You know—make me feel oppressed. And if you don't mind, and it's all the same to you, I would rather know it when you start to treat me. And now, Tamkin, for Christ's sake, they're putting out the lunch menus already. Will you sign the check, and let's go!"

Tamkin did as he asked, and they rose. They were passing the bookkeeper's desk when he took out a substantial bundle of onion-skin papers and said, "These are receipts of the transactions. Duplicates. You'd better keep them as the account is in your name and you'll need them for income taxes. And here is a copy of a poem I wrote yesterday."

"I have to leave something at the desk for my father," Wilhelm said, and he put his hotel bill in an envelope with a note. *Dear Dad, Please carry me this month, Yours, W.* He watched the clerk with his sullen pug's profile and his stiff-necked look push the envelope into his father's box.

"May I ask you really why you and your dad had words?" said Dr. Tamkin, who had hung back, waiting.

"It was about my future," said Wilhelm. He hurried down the stairs with swift steps, like a tower in motion, his hands in his trousers pockets. He was ashamed to discuss the matter. "He says there's a reason why I can't go back to my old territory, and there is. I told everybody I was going to be an officer of the corporation. And I was supposed to. It was promised. But then they welshed because of the son-in-law. I bragged and made myself look big."

"If you was humble enough, you could go back. But it doesn't make much difference. We'll make you a good living on the market."

They came into the sunshine of upper Broadway, not clear but throbbing through the dust and fumes, a false air of gas visible at eye-level as it spurted from the bursting buses. From old habit, Wilhelm turned up the collar of his jacket.

"Just a technical question," Wilhelm said. "What happens if your losses are bigger than your deposit?"

"Don't worry. They have ultra-modern electronic bookkeeping machinery, and it won't let you get in debt. It puts you out automatically. But I want you to read this poem. You haven't read it yet."

Light as a locust, a helicopter bringing mail from Newark Airport to La Guardia sprang over the city in a long leap.

The paper Wilhelm unfolded had ruled borders in red ink. He read:

Mechanism vs Functionalism
Ism vs Hism

If thee thyself couldst only see
Thy greatness that is and yet to be,
Thou would feel joy-beauty-what ecstasy.
They are at thy feet, earth-moon-sea, the trinity.

Why-forth then dost thou tarry
And partake thee only of the crust
And skim the earth's surface narry
When all creations art thy just?

Seek ye then that which art not there
In thine own glory let thyself rest.
Witness. Thy power is not bare.
Thou art King. Thou art at thy best.

Look then right before thee.
Open thine eyes and see.
At the foot of Mt. Serenity
Is thy cradle to eternity.

Utterly confused, Wilhelm said to himself explosively, What kind of mishmash, claptrap is this! What does he want from me? Damn him to hell, he might as well hit me on the head, and lay me out, kill me. What does he give me this for? What's the purpose? Is it a deliberate test? Does he want to mix me up? He's already got me mixed up completely. I was never good at riddles. Kiss those seven hundred bucks good-by, and call it one more mistake in a long line of mistakes— Oh, Mama, what a line! He stood near the shining window of a fancy fruit store, holding Tamkin's paper, rather dazed, as though a charge of photographer's flash powder had gone up in his eyes.

But he's waiting for my reaction. I have to say something to him about his poem. It really is no joke. What will I tell him? Who is this King? The poem is written *to* someone. But who? I can't even bring myself to talk. I feel too choked and strangled. With all the books he reads, how come the guy is so illiterate? And why do people just naturally assume that you'll know what they're talking about? No. I don't know, and nobody knows. The planets don't, the stars don't, infinite space doesn't. It doesn't square with Planck's Constant or anything else. So what's the good of it? Where's the need of it? What does he mean here by Mount Serenity? Could it be a figure of speech for Mount Everest? As he says people are all committing suicide, maybe those guys who climbed Everest were only trying to kill themselves, and if we want peace we should stay at the foot of the mountain. In the here-and-now. But it's also here-and-now on the slope, and on the top, where they climbed to seize the day. Surface narry is something he can't mean, I don't believe. I'm about to start foaming at the mouth. "Thy cradle . . ." Who is resting in his cradle—in his glory? My thoughts are at an end. I feel the wall. No more. So ——k it all! The money and everything. Take it away! When I have the money they eat me alive, like those piranha fish in the movie about the Brazilian jungle. It was hideous when they ate up that Brahma bull in the river. He turned pale, just like clay, and in five minutes nothing was left except the skeleton still in one piece, floating away. When I haven't got it any more, at least they'll let me alone.

"Well, what do you think of this?" said Dr. Tamkin. He gave a special sort of wise smile, as though Wilhelm must now see what kind of man he was dealing with.

"Nice. Very nice. Have you been writing long?"

"I've been developing this line of thought for years and years. You follow it all the way?"

"I'm trying to figure out who this Thou is."

"Thou? Thou is you."

"Me! Why? This applies to me?"

"Why shouldn't it apply to you. You were in my mind when I composed it. Of course, the hero of the poem is sick humanity. If it would open its eyes it would be great."

"Yes, but how do I get into this?"

"The main idea of the poem is construct or destruct. There is no ground in between. Mechanism is destruct. Money of course is destruct. When the last grave is dug, the gravedigger will have to be paid. If you could have confidence in nature you would not have to fear. It would keep you up. Creative is nature. Rapid. Lavish. Inspirational. It shapes leaves. It rolls the waters of the earth. Man is the chief of this. All creations are his just inheritance. You don't know what you've got within you. A person either creates or he destroys. There is no neutrality . . ."

"I realized you were no beginner," said Wilhelm with propriety. "I have only one criticism to make. I think 'why-forth' is wrong. You should write 'Wherefore then dost thou . . .'" And he reflected, So? I took a gamble. It'll have to be a miracle, though, to save me. My money will be gone, then it won't be able to destruct me. He can't just take and lose it, though. He's in it, too. I think he's in a bad way himself. He must be. I'm sure because, come to think of it, he sweated blood when he signed that check. But what have I let myself in for? The waters of the earth are going to roll over me.

V

Patiently, in the window of the fruit store, a man with a scoop spread crushed ice between his rows of vegetables. There were also Persian melons, lilacs, tulips with radiant black at the middle. The many street noises came back after a little while from the caves of the sky. Crossing the tide of Broadway traffic, Wilhelm was saying to himself, The reason Tamkin lectures me is that somebody has lectured him, and the reason for the poem is that he wants to give me good advice. Everybody seems to know something. Even fellows like Tamkin. Many people know what to do, but how many can do it?

He believed that he must, that he could and would recover the good things, the happy things, the easy tranquil things of life. He had made mistakes, but he could overlook these. He had been a fool, but that could be forgiven. The time wasted—must be relinquished. What else could one do about it? Things were too complex, but they might be reduced to simplicity again. Recovery was possible. First he had to get out of the city. No, first he had to pull out his money. . . .

From the carnival of the street—pushcarts, accordion and fiddle, shoeshine, begging, the dust going round like a woman on stilts —they entered the narrow crowded theater of the brokerage office. From front to back it was filled with the Broadway crowd. But how was lard doing this morning? From the rear of the hall Wilhelm tried to read the tiny figures. The German manager was looking through his binoculars. Tamkin placed himself on Wilhelm's left and covered his conspicuous bald head. "The guy'll ask me about the margin," he muttered. They passed, however, unobserved. "Look, the lard has held its place," he said.

Tamkin's eyes must be very sharp to read the figures over so many heads and at this distance—another respect in which he was unusual.

The room was always crowded. Everyone talked. Only at the front could you hear the flutter of the wheels within the board. Teletyped news items crossed the illuminated screen above.

"Lard. Now what about rye?" said Tamkin, rising on his toes. Here he was a different man, active and impatient. He parted people who stood in his way. His face turned resolute, and on either side of his mouth odd bulges formed under his mustache. Already he was pointing out to Wilhelm the appearance of a new pattern on the board. "There's something up today," he said.

"Then why'd you take so long with breakfast?" said Wilhelm.

There were no reserved seats in the room, only customary ones. Tamkin always sat in the second row, on the commodities side of the aisle. Some of his acquaintances kept their hats on the chairs for him.

"Thanks. Thanks," said Tamkin, and he told Wilhelm, "I fixed it up yesterday."

"That was a smart thought," said Wilhelm. They sat down.

With folded hands, by the wall, sat an old Chinese businessman in a seersucker coat. Smooth and fat, he wore a white Vandyke. One day Wilhelm had seen him on Riverside Drive pushing two little girls along in a baby carriage—his grandchildren. Then there were two women in their fifties, supposed to be sisters, shrewd and able money-makers, according to Tamkin. They had never a word to say to Wilhelm. But they would chat with Tamkin. Tamkin talked to everyone.

Wilhelm sat between Mr. Rowland, who was elderly, and Mr. Rappaport, who was very old. Yesterday Rowland had told him that in the year 1908, when he was a junior at Harvard, his mother had given him twenty shares of steel for his birthday, and then he had started to read the financial news and had never practiced law but instead followed the market for the rest of his life. Now he speculated only in soy beans, of which he had made a specialty. By his conservative method, said Tamkin, he cleared two hundred a week. Small potatoes, but then he was a bachelor, retired, and didn't need money.

"Without dependents," said Tamkin. "He doesn't have the problems that you and I do."

Did Tamkin have dependents? He had everything that it was possible for a man to have—science, Greek, chemistry, poetry, and now dependents too. That beautiful girl with epilepsy, perhaps. He often said that she was a pure, marvelous, spiritual child who had no knowledge of the world. He protected her, and, if he was not lying, adored her. And if you encouraged Tamkin by believing him, or even if you refrained from questioning him, his hints became more daring. Sometimes he said that he paid for her music lessons. Sometimes he seemed to have footed the bill for the brother's camera expedition to Brazil. And he spoke of paying for the support of the orphaned child of a dead sweetheart. These hints, made dully as asides, grew by repetition into sensational claims.

"For myself, I don't need much," said Tamkin. "But a man can't live for himself and I need the money for certain important things. What do you figure you have to have, to get by?"

"Not less than fifteen grand, after taxes. That's for my wife and the two boys."

"Isn't there anybody else?" said Tamkin with a shrewdness almost cruel. But his look grew more sympathetic as Wilhelm stumbled, not willing to recall another grief.

"Well—there was. But it wasn't a money matter."

"I should hope!" said Tamkin. "If love is love, it's free. Fifteen grand, though, isn't too much for a man of your intelligence to ask out of life. Fools, hard-hearted criminals, and murderers have millions to squander. They burn up the world—oil, coal, wood, metal, and soil, and suck even the air and the sky. They consume, and they give back no benefit. A man like you, humble for life, who wants to feel and live, has trouble—not wanting," said Tamkin in his parenthetical fashion, "to exchange an ounce of soul for a pound of social power—he'll never make it without help in a world like this. But don't you worry." Wilhelm grasped at this assurance. "Just you never mind. We'll go easily beyond your figure."

Dr. Tamkin gave Wilhelm comfort. He often said that he had made as much as a thousand a week in commodities. Wilhelm had examined the receipts, but until this moment it had never occurred to him that there must be debit slips too; he had been shown only the credits.

"But fifteen grand is not an ambitious figure," Tamkin was telling him. "For that you don't have to wear yourself out on the road, dealing with narrow-minded people. A lot of them don't like Jews, either, I suppose?"

"I can't afford to notice. I'm lucky when I have my occupation. Tamkin, do you mean you can save our money?"

"Oh, did I forget to mention what I did before closing yesterday? You see, I closed out one of the lard contracts and bought a hedge of December rye. The rye is up three points already and takes some of the sting out. But lard will go up, too."

"Where? God, yes, you're right," said Wilhelm, eager, and got to his feet to look. New hope freshened his heart. "Why didn't you tell me before?"

And Tamkin, smiling like a benevolent magician, said, "You

must learn to have trust. The slump in lard can't last. And just take a look at eggs. Didn't I predict they couldn't go any lower? They're rising and rising. If we had taken eggs we'd be far ahead."

"Then why didn't we take them?"

"We were just about to. I had a buying order in at .24, but the tide turned at .26¼ and we barely missed. Never mind. Lard will go back to last year's levels."

Maybe. But when? Wilhelm could not allow his hopes to grow too strong. However, for a little while he could breathe more easily. Late-morning trading was getting active. The shining numbers whirred on the board, which sounded like a huge cage of artificial birds. Lard fluctuated between two points, but rye slowly climbed.

He closed his strained, greatly earnest eyes briefly and nodded his Buddha's head, too large to suffer such uncertainties. For several moments of peace he was removed to his small yard in Roxbury.

He breathed in the sugar of the pure morning.

He heard the long phrases of the birds.

No enemy wanted his life.

Wilhelm thought, I will get out of here. I don't belong in New York any more. And he sighed like a sleeper.

Tamkin said, "Excuse me," and left his seat. He could not sit still in the room but passed back and forth between the stocks and commodities sections. He knew dozens of people and was continually engaging in discussions. Was he giving advice, gathering information, or giving it, or practicing—whatever mysterious profession he practiced? Hypnotism? Perhaps he could put people in a trance while he talked to them. What a rare, peculiar bird he was, with those pointed shoulders, that bare head, his loose nails, almost claws, and those brown, soft, deadly, heavy eyes.

He spoke of things that mattered, and as very few people did this he could take you by surprise, excite you, move you. Maybe he wished to do good, maybe give himself a lift to a higher level, maybe believe his own prophecies, maybe touch his own heart. Who could tell? He had picked up a lot of strange ideas; Wilhelm could only suspect, he could not say with certainty, that Tamkin hadn't made them his own.

Now Tamkin and he were equal partners, but Tamkin had put up only three hundred dollars. Suppose he did this not only once but five times; then an investment of fifteen hundred dollars gave him five thousand to speculate with. If he had power of attorney in every case, he could shift the money from one account to another.

No, the German probably kept an eye on him. Nevertheless it was possible. Calculations like this made Wilhelm feel ill. Obviously Tamkin was a plunger. But how did he get by? He must be in his fifties. How did he support himself? Five years in Egypt; Hollywood before that; Michigan; Ohio; Chicago. A man of fifty has supported himself for at least thirty years. You could be sure that Tamkin had never worked in a factory or in an office. How did he make it? His taste in clothes was horrible, but he didn't buy cheap things. He wore corduroy or velvet shirts from Clyde's, painted neckties, striped socks. There was a slightly acid or pasty smell about his person; for a doctor, he didn't bathe much. Also, Dr. Tamkin had a good room at the Gloriana and had had it for about a year. But so was Wilhelm himself a guest, with an unpaid bill at present in his father's box. Did the beautiful girl with the skirts and belts pay him? Was he defrauding his so-called patients? So many questions impossible to answer could not be asked about an honest man. Nor perhaps about a sane man. Was Tamkin a lunatic, then? That sick Mr. Perls at breakfast had said that there was no easy way to tell the sane from the mad, and he was right about that in any big city and especially in New York—the end of the world, with its complexity and machinery, bricks and tubes, wires and stones, holes and heights. And was everybody crazy here? What sort of people did you see? Every other man spoke a language entirely his own, which he had figured out by private thinking; he had his own ideas and peculiar ways. If you wanted to talk about a glass of water, you had to start back with God creating the heavens and earth; the apple; Abraham; Moses and Jesus; Rome; the Middle Ages; gunpowder; the Revolution; back to Newton; up to Einstein; then war and Lenin and Hitler. After reviewing this and getting it all straight again you could proceed to talk about a glass of water. "I'm fainting, please get me a little water." You were lucky even then to make yourself understood. And this happened over and over and over with everyone you met. You had to translate and translate, explain and explain, back and forth, and it was the punishment of hell itself not to understand or be understood, not to know the crazy from the sane, the wise from the fools, the young from the old or the sick from the well. The fathers were no fathers and the sons no sons. You had to talk with yourself in the daytime and reason with yourself at night. Who else was there to talk to in a city like New York?

A queer look came over Wilhelm's face with its eyes turned up and his silent mouth with its high upper lip. He went several degrees further—when you are like this, dreaming that everybody is outcast, you realize that this must be one of the small matters. There is a larger body, and from this you cannot be separated. The glass of water fades out. You do not go from simple *a* and simple *b* to the great *x* and *y*, nor does it matter whether you agree about the glass but, far beneath such details, what Tamkin would call the real soul says plain and understandable things to everyone. There sons and fathers are themselves, and a glass of water is only an ornament; it makes a hoop of brightness on the cloth; it is an angel's mouth. There truth for everybody may be found, and confusion is only— only temporary, thought Wilhelm.

The idea of this larger body had been planted in him a few days ago beneath Times Square, when he had gone downtown to pick up tickets for the baseball game on Saturday (a double-header at the Polo Grounds). He was going through an underground corridor, a place he had always hated and hated more than ever now. On the walls between the advertisements were words in chalk: "Sin No More," and "Do Not Eat the Pig," he had particularly noticed. And in the dark tunnel, in the haste, heat, and darkness which disfigure and make freaks and fragments of nose and eyes and teeth, all of a sudden, unsought, a general love for all these imperfect and lurid-looking people burst out in Wilhelm's breast. He loved them. One and all, he passionately loved them. They were his brothers and his sisters. He was imperfect and disfigured himself, but what difference did that make if he was united with them by this blaze of love? And as he walked he began to say, "Oh my brothers—my brothers and my sisters," blessing them all as well as himself.

So what did it matter how many languages there were, or how hard it was to describe a glass of water? Or matter that a few minutes later he didn't feel anything like a brother toward the man who sold him the tickets?

On that very same afternoon he didn't hold so high an opinion of this same onrush of loving kindness. What did it come to? As they had the capacity and must use it once in a while, people were bound to have such involuntary feelings. It was only another one of those subway things. Like having a hard-on at random. But today, his day of reckoning, he consulted his memory again and thought, I must go back to that. That's the right clue and may do me the most good. Something very big. Truth, like.

The old fellow on the right, Mr. Rappaport, was nearly blind and kept asking Wilhelm, "What's the new figure on November wheat? Give me July soy beans too." When you told him he didn't say thank you. He said, "Okay," instead, or, "Check," and turned away until he needed you again. He was very old, older even than Dr. Adler, and if you believed Tamkin he had once been the Rockefeller of the chicken business and had retired with a large fortune.

Wilhelm had a queer feeling about the chicken industry, that it was sinister. On the road, he frequently passed chicken farms. Those big, rambling, wooden buildings out in the neglected fields; they were like prisons. The lights burned all night in them to cheat the poor hens into laying. Then the slaughter. Pile all the coops of the slaughtered on end, and in one week they'd go higher than Mount Everest or Mount Serenity. The blood filling the Gulf of Mexico. The chicken shit, acid, burning the earth.

How old—old this Mr. Rappaport was! Purple stains were buried in the flesh of his nose, and the cartilage of his ear was twisted like a cabbage heart. Beyond remedy by glasses, his eyes were smoky and faded.

"Read me that soy-bean figure now, boy," he said, and Wilhelm did. He thought perhaps the old man might give him a tip, or some useful advice or information about Tamkin. But no. He only wrote memoranda on a pad, and put the pad in his pocket. He let no one see what he had written. And Wilhelm thought this was the way a man who had grown rich by the murder of millions of animals, little chickens, would act. If there was a life to come he might have to answer for the killing of all those chickens. What if they all were waiting? But if there was a life to come, everybody would have to answer. But if there was a life to come, the chickens themselves would be all right.

Well! What stupid ideas he was having this morning. Phooey!

Finally old Rappaport did address a few remarks to Wilhelm. He asked him whether he had reserved his seat in the synagogue for Yom Kippur.

"No," said Wilhelm.

"Well, you better hurry up if you expect to say *Yiskor* for your parents. I never miss."

And Wilhelm thought, Yes, I suppose I should say a prayer for Mother once in a while. His mother had belonged to the Reform congregation. His father had no religion. At the cemetery Wilhelm had paid a man to say a prayer for her. He was among the tombs and he wanted to be tipped for the *El molai rachamin*. "Thou God of Mercy," Wilhelm thought that meant. *B'gan Aden*—"in Paradise." Singing, they drew it out. *B'gan Ay–den*. The broken bench beside the grave made him wish to do something. Wilhelm often prayed in his own manner. He did not go to the synagogue but he would occasionally perform certain devotions, according to his feelings. Now he reflected, In Dad's eyes I am the wrong kind of Jew. He doesn't like the way I act. Only he is the right kind of Jew. Whatever you are, it always turns out to be the wrong kind.

Mr. Rappaport grumbled and whiffed at his long cigar, and the board, like a swarm of electrical bees, whirred.

"Since you were in the chicken business, I thought you'd speculate in eggs, Mr. Rappaport." Wilhelm, with his warm, panting laugh, sought to charm the old man.

"Oh. Yeah. Loyalty, hey?" said old Rappaport. "I should stick to them. I spent a lot of time amongst chickens. I got to be an expert chicken-sexer. When the chick hatches you have to tell the boys from the girls. It's not easy. You need long, long experience. What do you think, it's a joke? A whole industry depends on it. Yes, now and then I buy a contract eggs. What have you got today?"

Wilhelm said anxiously, "Lard. Rye."

"Buy? Sell?"

"Bought."

"Uh," said the old man. Wilhelm could not determine what he meant by this. But of course you couldn't expect him to make himself any clearer. It was not in the code to give information to anyone. Sick with desire, Wilhelm waited for Mr. Rappaport to make an exception in his case. Just this once! Because it was critical. Silently, by a sort of telepathic concentration, he begged the old man to speak the single word that would save him, give him the merest sign. "Oh, please—please help," he nearly said. If Rappaport would close one eye, or lay his head to one side, or raise his finger and point to a column in the paper or to a figure on his pad. A hint! A hint!

A long perfect ash formed on the end of the cigar, the white ghost of the leaf with all its veins and its fainter pungency. It was ignored, in its beauty, by the old man. For it was beautiful. Wilhelm he ignored as well.

Then Tamkin said to him, "Wilhelm, look at the jump our rye just took."

December rye climbed three points as they tensely watched; the tumblers raced and the machine's lights buzzed.

"A point and a half more, and we can cover the lard losses," said

Tamkin. He showed him his calculations on the margin of the *Times*.

"I think you should put in the selling order now. Let's get out with a small loss."

"Get out now? Nothing doing."

"Why not? Why should we wait?"

"Because," said Tamkin with a smiling, almost openly scoffing look, "you've got to keep your nerve when the market starts to go places. Now's when you can make something."

"I'd get out while the getting's good."

"No, you shouldn't lose your head like this. It's obvious to me what the mechanism is, back in the Chicago market. There's a short supply of December rye. Look, it's just gone up another quarter. We should ride it."

"I'm losing my taste for the gamble," said Wilhelm. "You can't feel safe when it goes up so fast. It's liable to come down just as quick."

Dryly, as though he were dealing with a child, Tamkin told him in a tone of tiring patience, "Now listen, Tommy. I have it diagnosed right. If you wish I should sell I can give the sell order. But this is the difference between healthiness and pathology. One is objective, doesn't change his mind every minute, enjoys the risk element. But that's not the neurotic character. The neurotic character—"

"Damn it, Tamkin!" said Wilhelm roughly. "Cut that out. I don't like it. Leave my character out of consideration. Don't pull any more of that stuff on me. I tell you I don't like it."

Tamkin therefore went no further; he backed down. "I meant," he said, softer, "that as a salesman you are basically an artist type. The seller is in the visionary sphere of the business function. And then you're an actor, too."

"No matter what type I am—" An angry and yet weak sweetness rose into Wilhelm's throat. He coughed as though he had the flu. It was twenty years since he had appeared on the screen as an extra. He blew the bagpipes in a film called *Annie Laurie*. Annie had come to warn the young Laird; he would not believe her and called the bagpipers to drown her out. He made fun of her while she wrung her hands. Wilhelm, in a kilt, barelegged, blew and blew and blew and not a sound came out. Of course all the music was recorded. He fell sick with the flu after that and still suffered sometimes from chest weakness.

"Something stuck in your throat?" said Tamkin. "I think maybe you are too disturbed to think clearly. You should try some of my 'here-and-now' mental exercises. It stops you from thinking so much about the future and the past and cuts down confusion."

"Yes, yes, yes, yes," said Wilhelm, his eyes fixed on December rye.

"Nature only knows one thing, and that's the present. Present, present, eternal present, like a big, huge, giant wave—colossal, bright and beautiful, full of life and death, climbing into the sky, standing in the seas. You must go along with the actual, the Here-and-Now, the glory—"

. . . chest weakness, Wilhelm's recollection went on. Margaret nursed him. They had had two rooms of furniture, which was later seized. She sat on the bed and read to him. He made her read for days, and she read stories, poetry, everything in the house. He felt dizzy, stifled when he tried to smoke. They had him wear a flannel vest.

> Come then, Sorrow!
> Sweetest Sorrow!
> Like an own babe I nurse thee on my breast!

Why did he remember that? Why?

"You have to pick out something that's in the actual, immediate present moment," said Tamkin. "And say to yourself here-and-now, here-and-now, here-and-now. 'Where am I?' 'Here.' 'When is it?' 'Now.' Take an object or a person. Anybody. 'Here and now I see a person.' 'Here and now I see a man.' 'Here and now I see a man sitting on a chair.' Take me, for instance. Don't let your mind wander. 'Here and now I see a man in a brown suit. Here and now I see a corduroy shirt.' You have to narrow it down, one item at a time, and not let your imagination shoot ahead. Be in the present. Grasp the hour, the moment, the instant."

Is he trying to hypnotize or con me? Wilhelm wondered. To take my mind off selling? But even if I'm back at seven hundred bucks, then where am I?

As if in prayer, his lids coming down with raised veins, frayed out, on his significant eyes. Tamkin said, " 'Here and now I see a button. Here and now I see the thread that sews the button. Here and now I see the green thread.' " Inch by inch he contemplated himself in order to show Wilhelm how calm it would make him. But Wilhelm was hearing Margaret's voice as she read, somewhat unwillingly,

Come then, Sorrow!

      •   •   •

I thought to leave thee,
And deceive thee,
But now of all the world I love thee best.

Then Mr. Rappaport's old hand pressed his thigh, and he said, "What's my wheat? Those damn guys are blocking the way. I can't see."

VI

Rye was still ahead when they went out to lunch, and lard was holding its own.

They ate in the cafeteria with the gilded front. There was the same art inside as outside. The food looked sumptuous. Whole fishes were framed like pictures with carrots, and the salads were like terraced landscapes or like Mexican pyramids; slices of lemon and onion and radishes were like sun and moon and stars; the cream pies were about a foot thick and the cakes swollen as if sleepers had baked them in their dreams.

"What'll you have?" said Tamkin.

"Not much. I ate a big breakfast. I'll find a table. Bring me some yogurt and crackers and a cup of tea. I don't want to spend much time over lunch."

Tamkin said, "You've got to eat."

Finding an empty place at this hour was not easy. The old people idled and gossiped over their coffee. The elderly ladies were rouged and mascaraed and hennaed and used blue hair rinse and eye shadow and wore costume jewelry, and many of them were proud and stared at you with expressions that did not belong to their age. Were there no longer any respectable old ladies who knitted and cooked and looked after their grandchildren? Wilhelm's grandmother had dressed him in a sailor suit and danced him on her knee, blew on the porridge for him and said, "Admiral, you must eat." But what was the use of remembering this so late in the day?

He managed to find a table, and Dr. Tamkin came along with a tray piled with plates and cups. He had Yankee pot roast, purple cabbage, potatoes, a big slice of watermelon, and two cups of coffee. Wilhelm could not even swallow his yogurt. His chest pained him still.

At once Tamkin involved him in a lengthy discussion. Did he do it to stall Wilhelm and prevent him from selling out the rye—or to recover the ground lost when he had made Wilhelm angry by hints about the neurotic character? Or did he have no purpose except to talk?

"I think you worry a lot too much about what your wife and your father will say. Do they matter so much?"

Wilhelm replied, "A person can become tired of looking himself over and trying to fix himself up. You can spend the entire second half of your life recovering from the mistakes of the first half."

"I believe your dad told me he had some money to leave you."

"He probably does have something."

"A lot?"

"Who can tell," said Wilhelm guardedly.

"You ought to think over what you'll do with it."

"I may be too feeble to do anything by the time I get it. If I get anything."

"A thing like this you ought to plan out carefully. Invest it properly." He began to unfold the schemes whereby you bought bonds, and used the bonds as security to buy something else and thereby earned twelve per cent safely on your money. Wilhelm failed to follow the details. Tamkin said, "If he made you a gift now, you wouldn't have to pay the inheritance taxes."

Bitterly, Wilhelm told him, "My father's death blots out all other considerations from his mind. He forces me to think about it, too. Then he hates me because he succeeds. When I get desperate —of course I think about money. But I don't want anything to happen to him. I certainly don't want him to die." Tamkin's brown eyes glittered shrewdly at him. "You don't believe it. Maybe it's not psychological. But on my word of honor. A joke is a joke, but I don't want to joke about stuff like this. When he dies, I'll be robbed, like. I'll have no more father."

"You love your old man?"

Wilhelm grasped at this. "Of course, of course I love him. My father. My mother—" As he said this there was a great pull at the very center of his soul. When a fish strikes the line you feel the live force in your hand. A mysterious being beneath the water, driven by hunger, has taken the hook and rushes away and fights, writhing. Wilhelm never identified what struck within him. It did not reveal itself. It got away.

And Tamkin, the confuser of the imagination, began to tell, or to fabricate, the strange history of *his* father. "He was a great singer," he said. "He left us five kids because he fell in love with an opera soprano. I never held it against him, but admired the way he followed the life-principle. I wanted to do the same. Because of unhappiness, at a certain age, the brain starts to die back." (True, true! thought Wilhelm.) "Twenty years later I was doing experiments in Eastman Kodak, Rochester, and I found the old fellow. He had five more children." (False, false!) "He wept; he was ashamed. I had nothing against him. I naturally felt strange."

"My dad is something of a stranger to me, too," said Wilhelm, and he began to muse. Where is the familiar person he used to be? Or I used to be? Catherine—she won't even talk to me any more, my own sister. It may not be so much my trouble that Papa turns his back on as my confusion. It's too much. The ruins of life, and on top of that confusion—chaos and old night. Is it an easier farewell for Dad if we don't part friends? He should maybe do it angrily— "Blast you with my curse!" And why, Wilhelm further asked, should he or anybody else pity me; or why should I be pitied sooner than another fellow? It is my childish mind that thinks people are ready to give it just because you need it.

Then Wilhelm began to think about his own two sons and to wonder how he appeared to them, and what they would think of him. Right now he had an advantage through baseball. When he went to fetch them, to go to Ebbets Field, though, he was not himself. He put on a front but he felt as if he had swallowed a fistful of sand. The strange, familiar house, horribly awkward; the dog, Scissors, rolled over on his back and barked and whined. Wilhelm acted as if there were nothing irregular, but a weary heaviness came over him. On the way to Flatbush he would think up anecdotes about old Pigtown and Charlie Ebbets for the boys and reminiscences of the old stars, but it was very heavy going. They did not know how much he cared for them. No. It hurt him greatly and he blamed Margaret for turning them against him. She wanted to ruin him, while she wore the mask of kindness. Up in Roxbury he had to go and explain to the priest, who was not sympathetic. They don't care about individuals, their rules come first. Olive said she would marry him outside the Church when he was divorced. But Margaret would not let go. Olive's father was a pretty decent old guy, an osteopath, and he understood what it was all about. Finally he said, "See here, I have to advise Olive. She is asking me. I am mostly a freethinker myself, but the girl has to live in this town." And by now Wilhelm and

Olive had had a great many troubles and she was beginning to dread his days in Roxbury, she said. He trembled at offending this small, pretty, dark girl whom he adored. When she would get up late on Sunday morning she would wake him almost in tears at being late for Mass. He would try to help her hitch her garters and smooth out her slip and dress and even put on her hat with shaky hands; then he would rush her to church and drive in second gear in his forgetful way, trying to apologize and to calm her. She got out a block from church to avoid gossip. Even so she loved him, and she would have married him if he had obtained the divorce. But Margaret must have sensed this. Margaret would tell him he did not really want a divorce; he was afraid of it. He cried, "Take everything I've got, Margaret. Let me go to Reno. Don't you want to marry again?" No. She went out with other men, but took his money. She lived in order to punish him.

Dr. Tamkin told Wilhelm, "Your dad is jealous of you."

Wilhelm smiled. "Of *me*? That's rich."

"Sure. People are always jealous of a man who leaves his wife."

"Oh," said Wilhelm scornfully. "When it comes to wives he wouldn't have to envy me."

"Yes, and your wife envies you, too. She thinks, He's free and goes with young women. Is she getting old?"

"Not exactly old," said Wilhelm, whom the mention of his wife made sad. Twenty years ago, in a neat blue wool suit, in a soft hat made of the same cloth—he could plainly see her. He stooped his yellow head and looked under the hat at her clear, simple face, her living eyes moving, her straight small nose, her jaw beautifully, painfully clear in its form. It was a cool day, but he smelled the odor of pines in the sun, in the granite canyon. Just south of Santa Barbara, this was.

"She's forty-some years old," he said.

"I was married to a lush," said Tamkin. "A painful alcoholic. I couldn't take her out to dinner because she'd say she was going to the ladies' toilet and disappear into the bar. I'd ask the bartenders they shouldn't serve her. But I loved her deeply. She was the most spiritual woman of my entire experience."

"Where is she now?"

"Drowned," said Tamkin. "At Provincetown, Cape Cod. It must have been a suicide. She was that way—suicidal. I tried everything in my power to cure her. Because," said Tamkin, "my real calling is to be a healer. I get wounded. I suffer from it. I would like to escape from the sicknesses of others, but I can't. I am only on loan to myself, so to speak. I belong to humanity."

Liar! Wilhelm inwardly called him. Nasty lies. He invented a woman and killed her off and then called himself a healer, and made himself so earnest he looked like a bad-natured sheep. He's a puffed-up little bogus and humbug with smelly feet. A doctor! A doctor would wash himself. He believes he's making a terrific impression, and he practically invites you to take off your hat when he talks about himself; and he thinks he has an imagination, but he hasn't, neither is he smart.

Then what am I doing with him here, and why did I give him the seven hundred dollars? thought Wilhelm.

Oh, this was a day of reckoning. It was a day, he thought, on which, willing or not, he would take a good close look at the truth. He breathed hard and his misshapen hat came low upon his congested dark blond face. A rude look. Tamkin was a charlatan, and furthermore he was desperate. And furthermore, Wilhelm had always known this about him. But he appeared to have worked it out at the back of his mind that Tamkin for thirty or forty years had gotten through many a tight place, that he would get through this crisis too and bring him, Wilhelm, to safety also. And Wilhelm realized that he was on Tamkin's back. It made him feel that he had virtually left the ground and was riding upon the other man. He was in the air. It was for Tamkin to take the steps.

The doctor, if he was a doctor, did not look anxious. But then his face did not have much variety. Talking always about spontaneous emotion and open receptors and free impulses, he was about as expressive as a pincushion. When his hypnotic spell failed, his big underlip made him look weak-minded. Fear stared from his eyes, sometimes, so humble as to make you sorry for him. Once or twice Wilhelm had seen that look. Like a dog, he thought. Perhaps he didn't look it now, but he was very nervous. Wilhelm knew, but he could not afford to recognize this too openly. The doctor needed a little room, a little time. He should not be pressed now. So Tamkin went on, telling his tales.

Wilhelm said to himself, I am on his back—his back. I gambled seven hundred bucks, so I must take this ride. I have to go along with him. It's too late. I can't get off.

"You know," Tamkin said, "that blind old man Rappaport—he's pretty close to totally blind—is one of the most interesting personalities around here. If you could only get him to tell his true story. It's fascinating. This is what he told me. You often hear about bigamists with a secret life. But this old man never hid anything from anybody. He's a regular patriarch. Now, I'll tell you what he did. He had two whole families, separate and apart, one in Williamsburg and the other in the Bronx. The two wives knew about each other. The wife in the Bronx was younger; she's close to seventy now. When he got sore at one wife he went to live with the other one. Meanwhile he ran his chicken business in New Jersey. By one wife he had four kids, and by the other six. They're all grown, but they never have met their half-brothers and sisters and don't want to. The whole bunch of them are listed in the telephone book."

"I can't believe it," said Wilhelm.

"He told me this himself. And do you know what else? While he had his eyesight he used to read a lot, but the only books he would read were by Theodore Roosevelt. He had a set in each of the places where he lived, and he brought his kids up on those books."

"Please," said Wilhelm, "don't feed me any more of this stuff, will you? Kindly do not—"

"In telling you this," said Tamkin with one of his hypnotic subtleties, "I do have a motive. I want you to see how some people free themselves from morbid guilt feelings and follow their instincts. Innately, the female knows how to cripple by sickening a man with guilt. It is a very special *de*struct, and she sends her curse to make a fellow impotent. As if she says, 'Unless I allow it, you will never more be a man.' But men like my old dad or Mr. Rappaport answer, 'Woman, what art thou to me?' You can't do that yet. You're a halfway case. You want to follow your instinct, but you're too worried still. For instance, about your kids—"

"Now look here," said Wilhelm, stamping his feet. "One thing! Don't bring up my boys. Just lay off."

"I was only going to say that they are better off than with conflicts in the home."

"I'm deprived of my children." Wilhelm bit his lip. It was too late to turn away. The anguish struck him. "I pay and pay. I never see them. They grow up without me. She makes them like herself. She'll bring them up to be my enemies. Please let's not talk about this."

But Tamkin said, "Why do you let her make you suffer so? It defeats the original object in leaving her. Don't play her game. Now, Wilhelm, I'm trying to do you some good. I want to tell you, don't marry suffering. Some people do. They get married to it, and sleep and eat together, just as husband and wife. If they go with joy they think it's adultery."

When Wilhelm heard this he had, in spite of himself, to admit that there was a great deal in Tamkin's words. Yes, thought Wilhelm, suffering is the only kind of life they are sure they can have, and if they quit suffering they're afraid they'll have nothing. He knows it. This time the faker knows what he's talking about.

Looking at Tamkin he believed he saw all this confessed from his usually barren face. Yes, yes, he too. One hundred falsehoods, but at last one truth. Howling like a wolf from the city window. No one can bear it any more. Everyone is so full of it that at last everybody must proclaim it. It! It!

Then suddenly Wilhelm rose and said, "That's enough of this. Tamkin, let's go back to the market."

"I haven't finished my melon."

"Never mind that. You've had enough to eat. I want to go back."

Dr. Tamkin slid the two checks across the table. "Who paid yesterday? It's your turn, I think."

It was not until they were leaving the cafeteria that Wilhelm remembered definitely that he had paid yesterday too. But it wasn't worth arguing about.

Tamkin kept repeating as they walked down the street that there were many who were dedicated to suffering. But he told Wilhelm, "I'm optimistic in your case, and I have seen a world of maladjustment. There's hope for you. You don't really want to destroy yourself. You're trying hard to keep your feelings open, Wilhelm. I can see it. Seven per cent of this country is committing suicide by alcohol. Another three, maybe, narcotics. Another sixty just fading away into dust by boredom. Twenty more who have sold their souls to the Devil. Then there's a small percentage of those who want to live. That's the only significant thing in the whole world of today. Those are the only two classes of people there are. Some want to live, but the great majority don't." This fantastic Tamkin began to surpass himself. "They don't. Or else, why these wars? I'll tell you more," he said. "The love of the dying amounts to one thing; they want you to die with them. It's because they love you. Make no mistake."

True, true! thought Wilhelm, profoundly moved by these revelations. How does he know these things? How can he be such a jerk, and even perhaps an operator, a swindler, and understand so well what gives? I believe what he says. It simplifies much—everything.

People are dropping like flies. I am trying to stay alive and work too hard at it. That's what's turning my brains. This working hard defeats its own end. At what point should I start over? Let me go back a ways and try once more.

Only a few hundred yards separated the cafeteria from the broker's, and within that short space Wilhelm turned again, in measurable degrees, from these wide considerations to the problems of the moment. The closer he approached to the market, the more Wilhelm had to think about money.

They passed the newsreel theater where the ragged shoeshine kids called after them. The same old bearded man with his bandaged beggar face and his tiny ragged feet and the old press clipping on his fiddle case to prove he had once been a concert violinist, pointed his bow at Wilhelm, saying, "You!" Wilhelm went by with worried eyes, bent on crossing Seventy-second Street. In full tumult the great afternoon current raced for Columbus Circle, where the mouth of midtown stood open and the skyscrapers gave back the yellow fire of the sun.

As they approached the polished stone front of the new office building, Dr. Tamkin said, "Well, isn't that old Rappaport by the door? I think he should carry a white cane, but he will never admit there's a single thing the matter with his eyes."

Mr. Rappaport did not stand well; his knees were sunk, while his pelvis only half filled his trousers. His suspenders held them, gaping.

He stopped Wilhelm with an extended hand, having somehow recognized him. In his deep voice he commanded him, "Take me to the cigar store."

"You want me—? Tamkin!" Wilhelm whispered, "You take him."

Tamkin shook his head. "He wants you. Don't refuse the old gentleman." Significantly he said in a lower voice. "This minute is another instance of the 'here-and-now.' You have to live in this very minute, and you don't want to. A man asks you for help. Don't think of the market. It won't run away. Show your respect to the old boy. Go ahead. That may be more valuable."

"Take me," said the old chicken merchant again.

Greatly annoyed, Wilhelm wrinkled his face at Tamkin. He took the old man's big but light elbow at the bone. "Well, let's step on it," he said. "Or wait—I want to have a look at the board first to see how we're doing."

But Tamkin had already started Mr. Rappaport forward. He was walking, and he scolded Wilhelm, saying, "Don't leave me standing in the middle of the sidewalk. I'm afraid to get knocked over."

"Let's get a move on. Come." Wilhelm urged him as Tamkin went into the broker's.

The traffic seemed to come down Broadway out of the sky, where the hot spokes of the sun rolled from the south. Hot, stony odors rose from the subway grating in the street.

"These teen-age hoodlums worry me. I'm ascared of these Puerto Rican kids, and these young characters who take dope," said Mr. Rappaport. "They go around all hopped up."

"Hoodlums?" said Wilhelm. "I went to the cemetery and my mother's stone bench was split. I could have broken somebody's neck for that. Which store do you go to?"

"Across Broadway. That La Magnita sign next door to the Automat."

"What's the matter with this store here on this side?"

"They don't carry my brand, that's what's the matter."

Wilhelm cursed, but checked the words.

"What are you talking?"

"Those damn taxis," said Wilhelm. "They want to run everybody down."

They entered the cool, odorous shop. Mr. Rappaport put away his large cigars with great care in various pockets while Wilhelm muttered, "Come on, you old creeper. What a poky old character! The whole world waits on him." Rappaport did not offer Wilhelm a cigar, but, holding one up, he asked, "What do you say at the size of these, huh? They're Churchill-type cigars."

He barely crawls along, thought Wilhelm. His pants are dropping off because he hasn't got enough flesh for them to stick to. He's almost blind, and covered with spots, but this old man still makes money in the market. Is loaded with dough, probably. And I bet he doesn't give his children any. Some of them must be in their fifties. This is what keeps middle-aged men as children. He's master over the dough. Think—just think! Who controls everything? Old men of this type. Without needs. They don't need therefore they have. I need, therefore I don't have. That would be too easy.

"I'm older even than Churchill," said Rappaport.

Now he wanted to talk! But if you asked him a question in the market, he couldn't be bothered to answer.

"I bet you are," said Wilhelm. "Come, let's get going."

"I was a fighter, too, like Churchill," said the old man. "When we licked Spain I went into the Navy. Yes, I was a gob that time. What did I have to lose? Nothing. After the battle of San Juan Hill, Teddy Roosevelt kicked me off the beach."

"Come, watch the curb," said Wilhelm.

"I was curious and wanted to see what went on. I didn't have no business there, but I took a boat and rowed myself to the beach. Two of our guys was dead, layin' under the American flag to keep the flies off. So I says to the guy on duty, there, who was the sentry, 'Let's have a look at these guys. I want to see what went on here,' and he says, 'Naw,' but I talked him into it. So he took off the flag and there were these two tall guys, both gentlemen, lying in their boots. They was very tall. The two of them had long mustaches. They were high-society boys. I think one of them was called Fish, from up the Hudson, a big-shot family. When I looked up, there was Teddy Roosevelt, with his hat off, and he was looking at these fellows, the only ones who got killed there. Then he says to me, 'What's the Navy want here? Have you got orders?' 'No, sir,' I says to him. 'Well, get the hell off the beach, then.' "

Old Rappaport was very proud of this memory. "Everything he said had such snap, such class. Man! I love that Teddy Roosevelt," he said, "I love him!"

Ah, what people are! He is almost not with us, and his life is nearly gone, but T. R. once yelled at him, so he loves him. I guess it is love, too. Wilhelm smiled. So maybe the rest of Tamkin's story was true, about the ten children and the wives and the telephone directory.

He said, "Come on, come on, Mr. Rappaport," and hurried the old man back by the large hollow elbow; he gripped it through the thin cotton cloth. Re-entering the brokerage office where under the lights the tumblers were speeding with the clack of drumsticks upon wooden blocks, more than ever resembling a Chinese theater, Wilhelm strained his eyes to see the board.

The lard figures were unfamiliar. That amount couldn't be lard! They must have put the figures in the wrong slot. He traced the line back to the margin. It was down to .19, and had dropped twenty points since noon. And what about the contract of rye? It had sunk back to its earlier position, and they had lost their chance to sell.

Old Mr. Rappaport said to Wilhelm, "Read me my wheat figure."

"Oh, leave me alone for a minute," he said, and positively hid his face from the old man behind one hand. He looked for Tamkin, Tamkin's bald head, or Tamkin with his gray straw and the cocoa-colored band. He couldn't see him. Where was he? The seats next to Rowland were taken by strangers. He thrust himself over the one on the aisle, Mr. Rappaport's former place, and pushed at the back of the chair until the new occupant, a red-head man with a thin, determined face, leaned forward to get out of his way but would not surrender the seat. "Where's Tamkin?" Wilhelm asked Rowland.

"Gee, I don't know. Is anything wrong?"

"You must have seen him. He came in a while back."

"No, but I didn't."

Wilhelm fumbled out a pencil from the top pocket of his coat and began to make calculations. His very fingers were numb, and in his agitation he was afraid he made mistakes with the decimal points and went over the subtraction and multiplication like a schoolboy at an exam. His heart, accustomed to many sorts of crisis, was now in a new panic. And, as he had dreaded, he was wiped out. It was unnecessary to ask the German manager. He could see for himself that the electronic bookkeeping device must have closed him out. The manager probably had known that Tamkin wasn't to be trusted, and on that first day he might have warned him. But you couldn't expect him to interfere.

"You get hit?" said Mr. Rowland.

And Wilhelm, quite coolly, said, "Oh, it could have been worse, I guess." He put the piece of paper into his pocket with its cigarette butts and packets of pills. The lie helped him out—although, for a moment, he was afraid he would cry. But he hardened himself. The hardening effort made a violent, vertical pain go through his chest, like that caused by a pocket of air under the collar bones. To the old chicken millionaire, who by this time had become acquainted with the drop in rye and lard, he also denied that anything serious had happened. "It's just one of those temporary slumps. Nothing to be scared about," he said, and remained in possession of himself. His need to cry, like someone in a crowd, pushed and jostled and abused him from behind, and Wilhelm did not dare turn. He said to himself, I will not cry in front of these people. I'll be damned if I'll break down in front of them like a kid, even though I never expect to see them again. No! No! And yet his unshed tears rose and rose and he looked like a man about to drown. But when they talked to him, he answered very distinctly. He tried to speak proudly.

". . . going away?" he heard Rowland ask.

"What?"

"I thought you might be going away too. Tamkin said he was going to Maine this summer for his vacation."

"Oh, going away?"

Wilhelm broke off and went to look for Tamkin in the men's toilet. Across the corridor was the room where the machinery of the board was housed. It hummed and whirred like mechanical birds, and the tubes glittered in the dark. A couple of businessmen with cigarettes in their fingers were having a conversation in the lavatory. At the top of the closet door sat a gray straw hat with a cocoa-colored band. "Tamkin," said Wilhelm. He tried to identify the feet below the door. "Are you in there, Doctor Tamkin?" he said with stifled anger. "Answer me. It's Wilhelm."

The hat was taken down, the latch lifted, and a stranger came out who looked at him with annoyance.

"You waiting?" said one of the businessmen. He was warning Wilhelm that he was out of turn.

"Me? Not me," said Wilhelm. "I'm looking for a fellow."

Bitterly angry, he said to himself that Tamkin would pay him the two hundred dollars at least, his share of the original deposit. "And before he takes the train to Maine, too. Before he spends a penny on vacation—that liar! We went into this as equal partners."

VII

I was the man beneath; Tamkin was on my back, and I thought I was on his. He made me carry him, too, besides Margaret. Like this they ride on me with hoofs and claws. Tear me to pieces, stamp on me and break my bones.

Once more the hoary old fiddler pointed his bow at Wilhelm as he hurried by. Wilhelm rejected his begging and denied the omen. He dodged heavily through traffic and with his quick, small steps ran up the lower stairway of the Gloriana Hotel with its dark-tinted mirrors, kind to people's defects. From the lobby he phoned Tamkin's room, and when no one answered he took the elevator up. A rouged woman in her fifties with a mink stole led three tiny dogs on a leash, high-strung creatures with prominent black eyes, like dwarf deer, and legs like twigs. This was the eccentric Estonian lady who had been moved with her pets to the twelfth floor.

She identified Wilhelm. "You are Doctor Adler's son," she said.

Formally, he nodded.

"I am a dear friend of your father."

He stood in the corner and would not meet her glance, and she thought he was snubbing her and made a mental note to speak of it to the doctor.

The linen-wagon stood at Tamkin's door, and the chambermaid's key with its big brass tongue was in the lock.

"Has Doctor Tamkin been here?" he asked her.

"No, I haven't seen him."

Wilhelm came in, however, to look around. He examined the photos on the desk, trying to connect the faces with the strange people in Tamkin's stories. Big, heavy volumes were stacked under the double-pronged TV aerial. *Science and Sanity*, he read, and there were several books of poetry. The *Wall Street Journal* hung in separate sheets from the bed-table under the weight of the silver water jug. A bathrobe with lightning streaks of red and white was laid across the foot of the bed with a pair of expensive batik pajamas. It was a box of a room, but from the windows you saw the river as far uptown as the bridge, as far downtown as Hoboken. What lay between was deep, azure, dirty, complex, crystal, rusty, with the red bones of new apartments rising on the bluffs of New Jersey, and huge liners in their berths, the tugs with matted beards of cordage. Even the brackish tidal river smell rose this high, like the smell of mop water. From every side he heard pianos, and the voices of men and women singing scales and opera, all mixed, and the sounds of pigeons on the ledges.

Again Wilhelm took the phone. "Can you locate Doctor Tamkin in the lobby for me?" he asked. And when the operator reported that she could not, Wilhelm gave the number of his father's room, but Dr. Adler was not in either. "Well, please give me the masseur. I say the massage room. Don't you understand me? The men's health club. Yes, Max Schilper's—how am I supposed to know the name of it?"

There a strange voice said, "Toktor Adler?" It was the old Czech prizefighter with the deformed nose and ears who was attendant down there and gave out soap, sheets, and sandals. He went away. A hollow endless silence followed. Wilhelm flickered the receiver with his nails, whistled into it, but could not summon either the attendant or the operator.

The maid saw him examining the bottles of pills on Tamkin's table and seemed suspicious of him. He was running low on Phenaphen pills and was looking for something else. But he swallowed one of his own tablets and went out and rang again for the elevator. He went down to the health club. Through the steamy windows, when he emerged, he saw the reflection of the swimming pool swirling green at the bottom of the lowest stairway. He went through the locker-room curtains. Two men wrapped in towels were playing Ping-pong. They were awkward and the ball bounded high. The Negro in the toilet was shining shoes. He did not know Dr. Adler by name, and Wilhelm descended to the massage room. On the tables naked men were lying. It was not a brightly lighted place, and it was very hot, and under the white faint moons of the ceiling shone pale skins. Calendar pictures of pretty girls dressed in tiny fringes were pinned on the wall. On the first table, eyes deeply shut in heavy silent luxury lay a man with a full square beard and short legs, stocky and black-haired. He might have been an orthodox Russian. Wrapped in a sheet, waiting, the man beside him was newly shaved and red from the steambath. He had a big happy face and was dreaming. And after him was an athlete, strikingly muscled, powerful and young, with a strong white curve to his genital and a half-angry smile on his mouth. Dr. Adler was on the fourth table, and Wilhelm stood over his father's pale, slight body. His ribs were narrow and small, his belly round, white, and high. It had its own being, like something separate. His thighs were weak, the muscles of his arms had fallen, his throat was creased.

The masseur in his undershirt bent and whispered in his ear, "It's your son," and Dr. Adler opened his eyes into Wilhelm's face. At once he saw the trouble in it, and by an instantaneous reflex he removed himself from the danger of contagion, and he said serenely, "Well, have you taken my advice, Wilky?"

"Oh, Dad," said Wilhelm.

"To take a swim and get a massage?"

"Did you get my note?" said Wilhelm.

"Yes, but I'm afraid you'll have to ask somebody else, because I can't. I had no idea you were so low on funds. How did you let it happen? Didn't you lay anything aside?"

"Oh, please, Dad," said Wilhelm, almost bringing his hands together in a clasp.

"I'm sorry," said the doctor. "I really am. But I have set up a rule. I've thought about it, I believe it is a good rule, and I don't want to change it. You haven't acted wisely. What's the matter?"

"Everything. Just everything. What isn't? I did have a little, but I haven't been very smart."

"You took some gamble? You lost it? Was it Tamkin? I told you, Wilky, not to build on that Tamkin. Did you? I suspect—"

"Yes, Dad, I'm afraid I trusted him."

Dr. Adler surrendered his arm to the masseur, who was using wintergreen oil.

"Trusted! And got taken?"

"I'm afraid I kind of—" Wilhelm glanced at the masseur but he was absorbed in his work. He probably did not listen to conversations. "I did. I might as well say it. I should have listened to you."

"Well, I won't remind you how often I warned you. It must be very painful.

"Yes, Father, it is."

"I don't know how many times you have to be burned in order to learn something. The same mistakes, over and over."

"I couldn't agree with you more," said Wilhelm with a face of despair. "You're so right, Father. It's the same mistakes, and I get burned again and again. I can't seem to—I'm stupid, Dad, I just can't breathe. My chest is all up—I feel choked. I just simply can't catch my breath."

He stared at his father's nakedness. Presently he became aware that Dr. Adler was making an effort to keep his temper. He was on the verge of an explosion. Wilhelm hung his face and said, "Nobody likes bad luck, eh Dad?"

"So! It's bad luck, now. A minute ago it was stupidity."

"It is stupidity—it's some of both. It's true that I can't learn. But I—"

"I don't want to listen to the details," said his father. "And I want you to understand that I'm too old to take on new burdens. I'm just too old to do it. And people who will just wait for help— must *wait* for help. They have got to stop waiting."

"It isn't all a question of money—there are other things a father can give to a son." He lifted up his gray eyes and his nostrils grew wide with a look of suffering appeal that stirred his father even more deeply against him.

He warningly said to him, "Look out, Wilky, you're tiring my patience very much."

"I try not to. But one word from you, just a word, would go a long way. I've never asked you for very much. But you are not a kind man, Father. You don't give the little bit I beg you for."

He recognized that his father was now furiously angry. Dr. Adler started to say something, and then raised himself and gathered the sheet over him as he did so. His mouth opened, wide, dark, twisted, and he said to Wilhelm, "You want to make yourself into my cross. But I am not going to pick up a cross. I'll see you dead, Wilky, by Christ, before I let you do that to me."

"Father, listen! Listen!"

"Go away from me now. It's torture for me to look at you, you slob!" cried Dr. Adler.

Wilhelm's blood rose up madly, in anger equal to his father's, but then it sank down and left him helplessly captive to misery. He said stiffly, and with a strange sort of formality, "Okay, Dad. That'll be enough. That's about all we should say." And he stalked out heavily by the door adjacent to the swimming pool and the steam room, and labored up two long flights from the basement. Once more he took the elevator to the lobby on the mezzanine.

He inquired at the desk for Dr. Tamkin.

The clerk said, "No, I haven't seen him. But I think there's something in the box for you."

"Me? Give it here," said Wilhelm and opened a telephone message from his wife. It read, "Please phone Mrs. Wilhelm on return. Urgent."

Whenever he received an urgent message from his wife he was always thrown into a great fear for the children. He ran to the phone booth, spilled out the change from his pockets onto the little curved steel shelf under the telephone, and dialed the Digby number.

"Yes?" said his wife. Scissors barked in the parlor.

"Margaret?"

"Yes, hello." They never exchanged any other greeting. She instantly knew his voice.

"The boys all right?"

"They're out on their bicycles. Why shouldn't they be all right? Scissors, quiet!"

"Your message scared me," he said. "I wish you wouldn't make 'urgent' so common."

"I had something to tell you."

Her familiar unbending voice awakened in him a kind of hungry longing, not for Margaret but for the peace he had once known.

"You sent me a postdated check," she said. "I can't allow that. It's already five days past the first. You dated your check for the twelfth."

"Well, I have no money. I haven't got it. You can't send me to prison for that. I'll be lucky if I can raise it by the twelfth."

She answered, "You better get it, Tommy."

"Yes? What for?" he said. "Tell me. For the sake of what? To tell lies about me to everyone? You—"

She cut him off. "You know what for. I've got the boys to bring up."

Wilhelm in the narrow booth broke into a heavy sweat. He dropped his head and shrugged while with his fingers he arranged nickels, dimes, and quarters in rows. "I'm doing my best," he said. "I've had some bad luck. As a matter of fact, it's been so bad that I don't know where I am. I couldn't tell you what day of the week this is. I can't think straight. I'd better not even try. This has been one of those days, Margaret. May I never live to go through another like it. I mean that with all my heart. So I'm not going to try to do any thinking today. Tomorrow I'm going to see some guys. One is a sales manager. The other is in television. But not to act," he hastily added. "On the business end."

"That's just some more of your talk, Tommy," she said. "You ought to patch things up with Rojax Corporation. They'd take you back. You've got to stop thinking like a youngster."

"What do you mean?"

"Well," she said, measured and unbending, remorselessly unbending, "you still think like a youngster. But you can't do that any more. Every other day you want to make a new start. But in eighteen years you'll be eligible for retirement. Nobody wants to hire a new man of your age."

"I know. But listen, you don't have to sound so hard. I can't get on my knees to them. And really you don't have to sound so hard. I haven't done you so much harm."

"Tommy, I have to chase you and ask you for money that you owe us, and I hate it."

She hated also to be told that her voice was hard.

"I'm making an effort to control myself," she told him.

He could picture her, her graying bangs cut with strict fixity above her pretty, decisive face. She prided herself on being fairminded. We could not bear, he thought, to know what we do. Even though blood is spilled. Even though the breath of life is taken from someone's nostrils. This is the way of the weak; quiet and fair. And then smash! They smash!

"Rojax take me back? I'd have to crawl back. They don't need me. After so many years I should have got stock in the firm. How can I support the three of you, and live myself, on half the territory? And why should I even try when you won't lift a finger to help? I sent you back to school, didn't I? At that time you said—"

His voice was rising. She did not like that and intercepted him. "You misunderstood me," she said.

"You must realize you're killing me. You can't be as blind as all that. Thou shalt not kill! Don't you remember that?"

She said, "You're just raving now. When you calm down it'll be different. I have great confidence in your earning ability."

"Margaret, you don't grasp the situation. You'll have to get a job."

"Absolutely not. I'm not going to have two young children running loose."

"They're not babies," Wilhelm said. "Tommy is fourteen. Paulie is going to be ten."

"Look," Margaret said in her deliberate manner. "We can't continue this conversation if you're going to yell so, Tommy. They're at a dangerous age. There are teen-aged gangs—the parents working, or the families broken up."

Once again she was reminding him that it was he who had left her. She had the bringing up of the children as her burden, while he must expect to pay the price of his freedom.

Freedom! he thought with consuming bitterness. Ashes in his mouth, not freedom. Give me my children. For they are mine too.

Can you be the woman I lived with? he started to say. Have you forgotten that we slept so long together? Must you now deal with me like this, and have no mercy?

He would be better off with Margaret again than he was today. This was what she wanted to make him feel, and she drove it home. "Are you in misery?" she was saying. "But you have deserved it." And he could not return to her any more than he could beg Rojax to take him back. If it cost him his life, he could not. Margaret had ruined him with Olive. She hit him and hit him, beat him, battered him, wanted to beat the very life out of him.

"Margaret, I want you please to reconsider about work. You have that degree now. Why did I pay your tuition?"

"Because it seemed practical. But it isn't. Growing boys need parental authority and a home."

He begged her, "Margaret, go easy on me. You ought to. I'm at the end of my rope and feel that I'm suffocating. You don't want to be responsible for a person's destruction. You've got to let up. I feel I'm about to burst." His face had expanded. He struck a blow upon the tin and wood and nails of the wall of the booth. "You've got to let me breathe. If I should keel over, what then? And it's something I can never understand about you. How you can treat someone like this whom you lived with so long. Who gave you the best of himself. Who tried. Who loved you." Merely to pronounce the word "love" made him tremble.

"Ah," she said with a sharp breath. "Now we're coming to it. How did you imagine it was going to be—big shot? Everything made smooth for you? I thought you were leading up to this."

She had not, perhaps, intended to reply as harshly as she did, but she brooded a great deal and now she could not forbear to punish him and make him feel pains like those she had to undergo.

He struck the wall again, this time with his knuckles, and he had scarcely enough air in his lungs to speak in a whisper, because his heart pushed upward with a frightful pressure. He got up and stamped his feet in the narrow enclosure.

"Haven't I always done my best?" he yelled, though his voice sounded weak and thin to his own ears. "Everything comes from me and nothing back again to me. There's no law that'll punish this, but you are committing a crime against me. Before God—and that's no joke. I mean that. Before God! Sooner or later the boys will know it."

In a firm tone, levelly, Margaret said to him, "I won't stand to be howled at. When you can speak normally and have something sensible to say I'll listen. But not to this." She hung up.

Wilhelm tried to tear the apparatus from the wall. He ground his teeth and seized the black box with insane digging fingers and made a stifled cry and pulled. Then he saw an elderly lady staring through the glass door, utterly appalled by him, and he ran from the booth, leaving a large amount of change on the shelf. He hurried down the stairs and into the street.

On Broadway it was still bright afternoon and the gassy air was almost motionless under the leaden spokes of sunlight, and sawdust footprints lay about the doorways of butcher shops and fruit stores. And the great, great crowd, the inexhaustible current of millions of every race and kind pouring out, pressing round, of every age, of every genius, possessors of every human secret, antique and future, in every face the refinement of one particular motive or essence—*I labor, I spend, I strive, I design, I love, I cling, I uphold, I give way, I envy, I long, I scorn, I die, I hide, I want.* Faster, much faster than any man could make the tally. The sidewalks were wider than any causeway; the street itself was immense, and it quaked and gleamed and it seemed to Wilhelm to throb at the last limit of endurance. And although the sunlight appeared like a broad tissue, its actual weight made him feel like a drunkard.

"I'll get a divorce if it's the last thing I do," he swore. "As for Dad— As for Dad— I'll have to sell the car for junk and pay the hotel. I'll have to go on my knees to Olive and say, 'Stand by me a while. Don't let her win. Olive!'" And he thought, I'll try to start again with Olive. In fact, I must. Olive loves me. Olive—

Beside a row of limousines near the curb he thought he saw Dr. Tamkin. Of course he had been mistaken before about the hat with the cocoa-colored band and didn't want to make the same mistake twice. But wasn't that Tamkin who was speaking so earnestly, with pointed shoulders, to someone under the canopy of the funeral parlor? For this was a huge funeral. He looked for the singular face under the dark gray, fashionable hatbrim. There were two open cars filled with flowers, and a policeman tried to keep a path open to pedestrians. Right at the canopy-pole, now wasn't that that damned Tamkin talking away with a solemn face, gesticulating with an open hand?

"Tamkin!" shouted Wilhelm, going forward. But he was pushed to the side by a policeman clutching his nightstick at both ends, like a rolling pin. Wilhelm was even farther from Tamkin now, and swore under his breath at the cop who continued to press him back, back, belly and ribs, saying, "Keep it moving there, please," his face red with impatient sweat, his brows like red fur. Wilhelm said to him haughtily, "You shouldn't push people like this."

The policeman, however, was not really to blame. He had been ordered to keep a way clear. Wilhelm was moved forward by the pressure of the crowd.

He cried, "Tamkin!"

But Tamkin was gone. Or rather, it was he himself who was carried from the street into the chapel. The pressure ended inside, where it was dark and cool. The flow of fan-driven air dried his face, which he wiped hard with his handkerchief to stop the slight salt itch. He gave a sigh when he heard the organ notes that stirred and breathed from the pipes and he saw people in the pews. Men in formal clothes and black homburgs strode softly back and forth on the cork floor, up and down the center aisle. The white of the stained glass was like mother-of-pearl, the blue of the Star of David like velvet ribbon.

Well, thought Wilhelm, if that was Tamkin outside I might as well wait for him here where it's cool. Funny, he never mentioned he had a funeral to go to today. But that's just like the guy.

But within a few minutes he had forgotten Tamkin. He stood along the wall with others and looked toward the coffin and the slow line that was moving past it, gazing at the face of the dead. Presently he too was in this line, and slowly, slowly, foot by foot, the beating of his heart anxious, thick, frightening, but somehow also rich, he neared the coffin and paused for his turn, and gazed down. He caught his breath when he looked at the corpse, and his face swelled, his eyes shone hugely with instant tears.

The dead man was gray-haired. He had two large waves of gray hair at the front. But he was not old. His face was long, and he had a bony nose, slightly, delicately twisted. His brows were raised as though he had sunk into the final thought. Now at last he was with it, after the end of all distractions, and when his flesh was no longer flesh. And by this meditative look Wilhelm was so struck that he could not go away. In spite of the tinge of horror, and then the splash of heartsickness that he felt, he could not go. He stepped out of line and remained beside the coffin; his eyes filled silently and through his still tears he studied the man as the line of visitors moved with veiled looks past the satin coffin toward the standing bank of lilies, lilacs, roses. With great stifling sorrow, almost admiration, Wilhelm nodded and nodded. On the surface, the dead man with his formal shirt and his tie and silk lapels and his powdered skin looked so proper; only a little beneath so—black, Wilhelm thought, so fallen in the eyes.

Standing a little apart, Wilhelm began to cry. He cried at first softly and from sentiment, but soon from deeper feeling. He sobbed loudly and his face grew distorted and hot, and the tears stung his skin. A man—another human creature, was what first went through his thoughts, but other and different things were torn from him. What'll I do? I'm stripped and kicked out. . . . Oh, Father, what do I ask of you? What'll I do about the kids—Tommy, Paul? My children. And Olive? My dear! Why, why, why—you must protect me against that devil who wants my life. If you want it, then kill me. Take, take it, take it from me.

Soon he was past words, past reason, coherence. He could not stop. The source of all tears had suddenly sprung open within him, black, deep, and hot, and they were pouring out and convulsed his body, bending his stubborn head, bowing his shoulders, twisting his face, crippling the very hands with which he held the handkerchief. His efforts to collect himself were useless. The great knot of ill and grief in his throat swelled upward and he gave in utterly and held his face and wept. He cried with all his heart.

He, alone of all the people in the chapel, was sobbing. No one knew who he was.

One woman said, "Is that perhaps the cousin from New Orleans they were expecting?"

"It must be somebody real close to carry on so."

"Oh my, oh my! To be mourned like that," said one man and looked at Wilhelm's heavy shaken shoulders, his clutched face and whitened fair hair, with wide, glinting, jealous eyes.

"The man's brother, maybe?"

"Oh, I doubt that very much," said another bystander. "They're not alike at all. Night and day."

The flowers and lights fused ecstatically in Wilhelm's blind, wet eyes; the heavy sea-like music came up to his ears. It poured into him where he had hidden himself in the center of a crowd by the great and happy oblivion of tears. He heard it and sank deeper than sorrow, through torn sobs and cries toward the consummation of his heart's ultimate need.

GABRIEL
GARCÍA MÁRQUEZ

No One Writes
to the Colonel

Translated by J. S. Bernstein

Introduction

As we make our way into this novella, we immediately become aware that we are approaching an unfamiliar, perhaps a strange world. We first meet a fragile old man called the "Colonel." He is impoverished, scraping the last spoonful of coffee from a can. Hardly the image of a high military officer. In the second paragraph, the Colonel is said to be "innocent"—again, somewhat odd to American ears, especially those of us who have been in the army. Where is this Colonel, in which country, and why so desperate and hungry?

We are not told, at least not yet. Perhaps the author, Gabriel García Márquez, simply takes for granted that his public in Latin America and elsewhere will quickly assume the story is set in his native Colombia. Perhaps he wants to leave the setting deliberately vague—as if to suggest any small, poor, wretched country in Latin America ruled by an oppressive dictatorship. And perhaps, when he was composing *No One Writes to the Colonel*, García Márquez already knew that much of the historical background would later be provided in his brilliant, highly successful novel *One Hundred Years of Solitude*, published in 1967. Like such novelists as Balzac and Faulkner, both of whom seem to have influenced him, García Márquez has created a "world of his own," one that keeps reappearing in somewhat different ways from book to book. But here we will treat

No One Writes to the Colonel as a self-sufficient work, complete in itself, without referring to García Márquez's other writings.

In the opening few pages we encounter a setting and a central character that we cannot quickly make out, yet we are also drawn into an atmosphere of muted suspense. Something is very wrong in this unnamed town; something that makes us a little nervous. The Colonel has been waiting for sixty years "since the end of the last civil war"—a piece of information crucial for everything to come in the story. And "October was one of the few things that arrived"—the sort of sardonic remark that punctuates the story repeatedly, building up a tone of extreme bitterness.

So let's assume that the first several pages of *No One Writes to the Colonel* are an opening scene that provides some preliminary information—answers to such questions as who? where? maybe even why? And let's also assume that this "opening scene" ends at the point on page 574 where the Colonel is seen making one of his anxious, fruitless visits to the post office. "No one writes to me," he says there, and that seems like a good place at which to conclude the story's "opening scene."

Now, let's go over these first few pages and see how tightly packed they are with clues and hints:

+ *The time of the story is October. It is the rainy reason, and it makes the Colonel, an old man, feel sick, as if "fungus and poisonous lilies were taking root in his gut."*

+ *Poverty-stricken, though for reasons not yet clear to us, the Colonel owns a rooster, a fighting cock. Half-playfully, half-desperately, he ties the rooster to the leg of the bed in which his wife sleeps. The rooster is valuable; the Colonel hopes to win some money betting on a cockfight a few months from now; and anyway, there is no place else to keep it. The rooster also brings out the Colonel's humor, at once dry and extravagant: "Stop looking at that animal," he tells some children, "roosters wear out if you look at them so much." And if the rooster were to "wear out," what hope would be left the Colonel?*

+ *The Colonel had a son, Augustín, born in 1922.*

+ *Little details, sprinkled through these opening pages, tell us something about the Colonel's past. At a raffle held for the Colonel's party, his wife won an umbrella. It's very old, for that raffle was held twenty-four years ago, in 1930. (We aren't told the name of the Colonel's party, but it's the Liberal Party. For over a century two parties in Colombia, the Liberal and the Conservative, by no means as clearly distinguishable as their names might suggest, have been fighting civil wars and engaging in electoral contests and deals.) The Colonel and his wife live in the past, with things from the past. And now they are so poor, the Colonel doesn't even have a mirror: he must shave by touch.*

✦ *Though they quarrel under the pressures of shared trouble, the Colonel and his wife still have strong feelings for one another. "His wife saw him at that moment, dressed as he was on their wedding day." She sees an old man, 75 years of age, but one who "did each thing as if it were a transcendent act." That's a striking description: it suggests perhaps a man who endows even the routine things of life with an aura of significance, a man who in good "Latin style" accords dignity to each moment, each gesture. Manners play an important part in the Colonel's life, as the outward expression of his dignity, a kind of defense against the chaos of circumstances.*

✦ *The Colonel is going to a funeral, "the first death from natural causes which we've had in many years." This is a country of violence. Perhaps the Colonel, in his ironic way, is exaggerating somewhat; perhaps it's not literally true that no one in the town has died of "natural causes" for "many years." We don't know. But the Colonel's remark is pointed enough to give us a clear indication of how he sees the state of things.*

✦ *At the funeral we meet Sabas, a man who will be important in the novella later on. Sabas is "the only leader of [the Colonel's] party who had escaped political persecution. . . ." We may guess, and soon confirm, that Sabas is morally the opposite of the Colonel. Sabas is a turncoat who has betrayed the cause—and the story itself, through its biases of language, persuades us that we should feel this cause to have been (at least in the past) a good one. We will never learn completely from this novella what that cause was, though it's not hard to surmise that it was some sort of liberal or populist movement.*

✦ *A bit later we learn something crucial: the country is under martial law and apparently has been so for a long time. In the arbitrary way of police states, the funeral procession is not allowed to pass in front of the police barracks. Because of a fear that some action might be taken by the mourners against the police? Because a dictatorship likes to demonstrate its power through arbitrary means? Because the police feel uneasy about a death not caused by them?*

✦ *Home from the funeral, the Colonel talks with his wife. More crucial information: their son was shot nine months ago "at the cockfights distributing clandestine literature." The cause for which the Colonel fought sixty years ago seems to have survived, and his son has become its martyr. "We are," says the Colonel's wife, "the orphans of our son"—a vivid, moving way to suggest how these people feel about their lives. Notice, however, that the wife does not berate the Colonel for their painful circumstances or the loss of their son. We don't know (and aren't going to find out) whether she agrees with the Colonel's politics; but it seems clear that she stands shoulder to shoulder with her husband, honoring his convictions and courage.*

✦ *Finally we learn that the Colonel has been waiting fifteen years for something to come in the mail: word of the pension to which he is entitled and which might keep him and his wife from starving. It does not come, of course. Each Friday he goes to the post office—nothing. "No one writes to me." No one writes because the Colonel is neglected, forgotten. And the tone of the story leads us to expect that it will remain so to the end.*

With the sentence, "No one writes to me," we reach a convenient breaking-point, the place at which we can say the introduction to the novella has concluded. We have by now *almost* all the information we need in order to grasp the essential theme of the novella; and everything that is still to come will serve mostly as detailed reinforcement, tragic accumulation. This is a sleepy backwater Central American town, with sun and rain both merciless. The Colonel, a man of pride, lives on memories of past glories and delusions of future relief. The author's style is terse, dry, understated, though every once in a while one of the characters will rise to dramatic eloquence, usually in the form of a sharp single sentence. And above all, it should be clear even after reading only a few pages, that García Márquez has planned his narrative with great care, planting cues that prepare us for later developments while writing with extreme economy and control.

Having lingered for a "close-up" of the first several pages, let's now move back for a "long shot" of the novella as a whole, seeing what we can make of its meaning, characters, and structure.

Gabriel García Márquez is one of the most distinguished Latin American writers. Like many other novelists from that part of the world, he hates the military oligarchies that usually dominate the Latin American countries—hates their oppression of the poor, their denial of liberties. García Márquez thinks of himself as an unorthodox leftist, one who believes that revolution is necessary for creating a better life in the "third world" countries. But he also knows that as a writer of fiction he cannot and should not be a mere propagandist; that a novelist has an obligation, first of all, to depict the human situation as he honestly sees it, even if that may not square with his political opinions; and that a work of literature cannot, or at least should not, be judged by whether it has the "right" or "wrong" politics. (For if it were, what need would there be for the work of literature to begin with?) And García Márquez seems also to understand that the changes he wants for his country aren't likely to come about very quickly.

In the central figure who towers over *No One Writes to the Colonel*, García Márquez has created a man who really belongs to an earlier era, that of populist nationalism, largely a nineteenth-century phenomenon. We are not told if some of the young people he meets in the tailor shop hold political opinions more "advanced" than those of the Colonel—and for the purposes of this novella, it barely matters. For in a country dominated by a bureaucratic-military tyranny, all its opponents have to huddle together for comfort and safety. What matters finally about the Colonel is not so much his opinions as his example—*the example of a man who will not yield*, who remains firms into old age, who will not allow even the death of his son to break his spirit. Nor is this Colonel romanticized. He has obvious flaws: he is vain and, sometimes, indecisive. Still, he is also a man to admire and emulate. Insofar as García Márquez is trying to "make a point" through this novella, it seems to be a celebration of integrity, the need for endurance, the readiness to pay a price for one's convictions.

All of this comes through in a series of little touches, some humorous, others sad. There is, for example, the biting conversation between the Colonel and his wife on p. 588, where he says "Nobody dies in three months," and when she asks in reply, "What do we eat in the meantime," he says, "I don't know. But if we were going to die of hunger, we would have died already." There is, again, a razor-sharp comment of the Colonel about his hat: "I don't wear one, so I won't have to take it off for anyone." A touch of bravado, perhaps, but a touch the Colonel has earned.

More important is the whole business with the rooster, which forms a strand of the narrative clearly meant to have symbolic overtones. The rooster represents the Colonel's last hope of escaping starvation; it is an emotionally-laden tie with the mourned son; it has become a kind of totem for the young people, both personal friends and political allies, who gather in the tailor shop. Toward the end of this novella, we come to realize that the rooster symbolizes the Colonel's last-ditch struggle for independence. Sell it to Sabas? That means physical survival for a while longer, a slow eking out of life by carefully-measured pesos; but it would also mean a kind of surrender. Close to the end of the story, the Colonel says to his wife, "The rooster is not for sale." It's as if he were also saying, *and neither am I for sale*. At this point García Márquez permits himself one of the few departures from his severe detachment: the Colonel's remark, he writes, was made with "a sort of bottomless sweetness."

Despite the small tensions, and the one major outburst, between the Colonel and his wife, we glimpse in their life together what a true marriage can be: an unbreakable bond for sharing both good and bad. The wife is religious, as the Colonel evidently is not; he teases her a little about this, but with a nice affection; and she supports him unquestioningly, though she also worries about their survival. They stand together, "orphans of their son."

At this point, it may be useful for us to consider the problem that García Márquez must have faced in *No One Writes to the Col onel.* What he has done is, essentially, to compose a *portrait* of a single character, shown in his strength and suffering. The point of this portrait is finally that nothing changes: the pension will never come, no one will write to the Colonel (don't we already know this after the first few pages?), and still he will hold fast. This is moving as an idea, moving also as a portrait—but the problem García Márquez had to face was, how to achieve some tension and drama in a story where "nothing happens," indeed, where the central fact is that nothing can happen to change the lot of the Colonel. I think García Márquez solves this problem brilliantly, through a number of devices:

✦ *By not filling in a good part of the historical background of the revolution and its aftermath, García Márquez forces the reader to grapple for bits of knowledge, to keep an eye open for clues to fill in the picture. Once our interest has been aroused, it's only natural that we should want to know more.*

✦ *In the conversations between the Colonel and his wife, at least part of what we have grown curious to find out is gradually revealed—not in an orderly, abstract exposition put together by the author, but through dialogues between two people sharing a common past, remembering bits of it now and then, hopping about in memory so as, in effect, to keep feeding the reader a little here, a little there. We are thus forced to engage in a process of step-by-step discovery.*

✦ *The character Sabas is especially important, underlining through contrast what the Colonel stands for. Sabas represents the all-too-common temptation to give up, to live comfortably, to care more about one's own digestion than the hunger of other human beings. Through a series of interactions with Sabas, the Colonel defines himself all the more vividly.*

✦ *There are a few incidents where drama is created through sudden pressures placed upon the Colonel. One of these occurs in a tense exchange on p. 597 between the Colonel and his wife:*

Her voice began to darken with rage. "I'm fed up with resignation and dignity."

The colonel didn't move a muscle.

"Twenty years of waiting for the little colored birds which they promised you after every election, and all we've got out of it is a dead son," she went on. "Nothing but a dead son." . . .

"We did our duty."

This outburst of the Colonel's wife, which does not, I think, signify a lack of underlying solidarity with him, is not to be judged harshly. It is entirely understandable, and in the context of the novella helps to create an additional degree of tension.

Another dramatic moment comes when the Colonel is trapped in a police raid with "the clandestine paper in his pocket." García Márquez's description of this moment is wonderful:

The colonel felt the dry snap, articulate and cold, of a rifle being cocked behind his back. He realized that he had been caught fatally in a police raid with the clandestine paper in his pocket. He turned halfway around without raising his hands. And then he saw, close up, for the first time in his life, the man who had shot his son. The man was directly in front of him, with his rifle barrel aimed at the colonel's belly. He was small, Indian-looking, with weather-beaten skin, and his breath smelled like a child's. The colonel gritted his teeth and gently pushed the rifle away with the tips of his fingers.

"Excuse me," he said.

Incidents such as these, dramatizing the undramatic experience of hopeless waiting, lead to the great climax of the story, on the very last page. The concluding expletive, in this context, has the power to shock not because it's a "dirty word" but because it finally reveals the strength, the purity, and the hard realism of the Colonel's mind. He does not delude himself. He knows that what awaits him is death, the death that comes so cheaply in his country, the death that is a great obsession of almost all Latin American writers. There is a fine sentence in an essay about García Márquez by the English literary critic V. S. Pritchett, which could stand as an epitaph for the Colonel: "Life is ephemeral but dignified by fatality."

No One Writes
to the Colonel

The colonel took the top off the coffee can and saw that there was only one little spoonful left. He removed the pot from the fire, poured half the water onto the earthen floor, and scraped the inside of the can with a knife until the last scrapings of the ground coffee, mixed with bits of rust, fell into the pot.

While he was waiting for it to boil, sitting next to the stone fireplace with an attitude of confident and innocent expectation, the colonel experienced the feeling that fungus and poisonous lilies were taking root in his gut. It was October. A difficult morning to get through, even for a man like himself, who had survived so many mornings like this one. For nearly sixty years—since the end of the last civil war—the colonel had done nothing else but wait. October was one of the few things which arrived.

His wife raised the mosquito netting when she saw him come into the bedroom with the coffee. The night before she had suffered an asthma attack, and now she was in a drowsy state. But she sat up to take the cup.

"And you?" she said.

"I've had mine," the colonel lied. "There was still a big spoonful left."

The bells began ringing at that moment. The colonel had forgotten the funeral. While his wife was drinking her coffee, he unhooked the hammock at one end, and rolled it up on the other, behind the door. The woman thought about the dead man.

"He was born in 1922," she said. "Exactly a month after our son. April 7th."

She continued sipping her coffee in the pauses of her gravelly breathing. She was scarcely more than a bit of white on an arched, rigid spine. Her disturbed breathing made her put her questions as assertions. When she finished her coffee, she was still thinking about the dead man.

"It must be horrible to be buried in October," she said. But her husband paid no attention. He opened the window. October had moved in on the patio. Contemplating the vegetation, which was bursting out in intense greens, and the tiny mounds the worms made in the mud, the colonel felt the sinister month again in his intestines.

"I'm wet through to the bones," he said.

"It's winter," the woman replied. "Since it began raining I've been telling you to sleep with your socks on."

"I've been sleeping with them for a week."

It rained gently but ceaselessly. The colonel would have preferred to wrap himself in a wool blanket and get back into the hammock. But the insistence of the cracked bells reminded him about the funeral. "It's October," he whispered, and walked toward the center of the room. Only then did he remember the rooster tied to the leg of the bed. It was a fighting cock.

After taking the cup into the kitchen, he wound the pendulum clock in its carved wooden case in the living room. Unlike the bedroom, which was too narrow for an asthmatic's breathing, the living room was large, with four sturdy rockers around a little table with a cover and a plaster cat. On the wall opposite the clock, there was a picture of a woman dressed in tulle, surrounded by cupids in a boat laden with roses.

It was seven-twenty when he finished winding the clock. Then he took the rooster into the kitchen, tied it to a leg of the stove, changed the water in the can, and put a handful of corn next to it. A group of children came in through a hole in the fence. They sat around the rooster, to watch it in silence.

"Stop looking at that animal," said the colonel. "Roosters wear out if you look at them so much."

The children didn't move. One of them began playing the chords of a popular song on his harmonica. "Don't play that today," the colonel told him. "There's been a death in town." The child put the instrument in his pants pocket, and the colonel went into the bedroom to dress for the funeral.

Because of his wife's asthma, his white suit was not pressed. So he had to wear the old black suit which since his marriage he used only on special occasions. It took some effort to find it in the bottom of the trunk, wrapped in newspapers and protected against moths with little balls of naphthalene. Stretched out in bed, the woman was still thinking about the dead man.

"He must have met Agustín already," she said. "Maybe he won't tell him about the situation we've been left in since his death."

"At this moment they're probably talking roosters," said the colonel.

He found an enormous old umbrella in the trunk. His wife had won it in a raffle held to collect funds for the colonel's party. That same night they had attended an outdoor show which was not interrupted despite the rain. The colonel, his wife, and their son, Agustín—who was then eight—watched the show until the end, seated under the umbrella. Now Agustín was dead, and the bright satin material had been eaten away by the moths.

"Look what's left of our circus clown's umbrella," said the colonel with one of his old phrases. Above his head a mysterious system of little metal rods opened. "The only thing it's good for now is to count the stars."

He smiled. But the woman didn't take the trouble to look at the umbrella. "Everything's that way," she whispered. "We're rotting alive. And she closed her eyes so she could concentrate on the dead man.

After shaving himself by touch—since he'd lacked a mirror for a long time—the colonel dressed silently. His trousers, almost as tight on his legs as long underwear, closed at the ankles with slip-knotted drawstrings, were held up at the waist by two straps of the same material which passed through two gilt buckles sewn on at kidney height. He didn't use a belt. His shirt, the color of old Manila paper, and as stiff, fastened with a copper stud which served at the same time to hold the detachable collar. But the detachable collar was torn, so the colonel gave up on the idea of a tie.

He did each thing as if it were a transcendent act. The bones in his hands were covered by taut, translucent skin, with light spots like the skin on his neck. Before he put on his patent-leather shoes, he scraped the dried mud from the stitching. His wife saw him at that moment, dressed as he was on their wedding day. Only then did she notice how much her husband had aged.

"You look as if you're dressed for some special event," she said.

"This burial is a special event," the colonel said. "It's the first death from natural causes which we've had in many years."

The weather cleared up after nine. The colonel was getting ready to go out when his wife seized him by the sleeve of his coat.

"Comb your hair," she said.

He tried to subdue his steel-colored, bristly hair with a bone comb. But it was a useless attempt.

"I must look like a parrot," he said.

The woman examined him. She thought he didn't. The colonel didn't look like a parrot. He was a dry man, with solid bones articulated as if with nuts and bolts. Because of the vitality in his eyes, it didn't seem as if he were preserved in formalin.

"You're fine that way," she admitted, and added, when her husband was leaving the room: "Ask the doctor if we poured boiling water on him in this house."

They lived at the edge of town, in a house with a palm-thatched roof and walls whose whitewash was flaking off. The humidity kept up but the rain had stopped. The colonel went down toward the plaza along an alley with houses crowded in on each other. As he came out into the main street, he shivered. As far as the eye could see, the town was carpeted with flowers. Seated in their doorways, the women in black were waiting for the funeral.

In the plaza it began to drizzle again. The proprietor of the pool hall saw the colonel from the door of his place and shouted to him with open arms:

"Colonel, wait, and I'll lend you an umbrella!"

The colonel replied without turning around.

"Thank you. I'm all right this way."

The funeral procession hadn't come out of church yet. The men—dressed in white with black ties—were talking in the low doorway under their umbrellas. One of them saw the colonel jumping between the puddles in the plaza.

"Get under here, friend!" he shouted.

He made room under the umbrella.

"Thanks, friend," said the colonel.

But he didn't accept the invitation. He entered the house directly to give his condolences to the mother of the dead man. The first thing he perceived was the odor of many different flowers. Then the heat rose. The colonel tried to make his way through the crowd which was jammed into the bedroom. But someone put a hand on his back, pushed him toward the back of the room through a gallery of perplexed faces to the spot where—deep and wide open—the nostrils of the dead man were found.

There was the dead man's mother, shooing the flies away from the coffin with a plaited palm fan. Other women, dressed in black, contemplated the body with the same expression with which one watches the current of a river. All at once a voice started up at the back of the room. The colonel put one woman aside, faced the profile of the dead man's mother, and put a hand on her shoulder.

"I'm so sorry," he said.

She didn't turn her head. She opened her mouth and let out a howl. The colonel started. He felt himself being pushed against the corpse by a shapeless crowd which broke out in a quavering outcry. He looked for a firm support for his hands but couldn't find the wall. There were other bodies in its place. Someone said in his ear, slowly, with a very gentle voice, "Careful, Colonel." He spun his head around and was face to face with the dead man. But he didn't recognize him because he was stiff and dynamic and seemed as disconcerted as he, wrapped in white cloths and with his trumpet in his hands. When the colonel raised his head over the shouts, in search of air, he saw the closed box bouncing toward the door down a slope of flowers which disintegrated against the walls. He perspired. His joints ached. A moment later he knew he was in the street because the drizzle hurt his eyelids, and someone seized him by the arm and said:

"Hurry up, friend, I was waiting for you."

It was Sabas, the godfather of his dead son, the only leader of his party who had escaped political persecution and had continued to live in town. "Thanks, friend," said the colonel, and walked in silence under the umbrella. The band struck up the funeral march. The colonel noticed the lack of a trumpet, and for the first time was certain that the dead man was dead.

"Poor man," he murmured.

Sabas cleared his throat. He held the umbrella in his left hand, the handle almost at the level of his head, since he was shorter than the colonel. They began to talk when the cortege left the plaza. Sabas turned toward the colonel then, his face disconsolate, and said:

"Friend, what's new with the rooster?"

"He's still there," the colonel replied.

At that moment a shout was heard:

"Where are they going with that dead man?"

The colonel raised his eyes. He saw the Mayor on the balcony of the barracks in an expansive pose. He was dressed in his flannel underwear; his unshaven cheek was swollen. The musicians stopped the march. A moment later the colonel recognized Father Angel's voice shouting at the Mayor. He made out their dialogue through the drumming of the rain on the umbrella.

"Well?" asked Sabas.

"Well nothing," the colonel replied. "The burial may not pass in front of the police barracks."

"I had forgotten," exclaimed Sabas. "I always forget that we are under martial law."

"But this isn't a rebellion," the colonel said. "It's a poor dead musician."

The cortege changed direction. In the poor neighborhoods the women watched it pass, biting their nails in silence. But then they came out into the middle of the street and sent up shouts of praise, gratitude, and farewell, as if they believed the dead man was listening to them inside the coffin. The colonel felt ill at the cemetery. When Sabas pushed him toward the wall to make way for the men who were carrying the dead man, he turned his smiling face toward him, but met a rigid countenance.

"What's the matter, friend?" Sabas asked.

The colonel sighed.

"It's October."

They returned by the same street. It had cleared. The sky was deep, intensely blue. It won't rain any more, thought the colonel, and he felt better, but he was still dejected. Sabas interrupted his thoughts.

"Have a doctor examine you."

"I'm not sick," the colonel said. "The trouble is that in October I feel as if I had animals in my gut."

Sabas went "Ah." He said goodbye at the door to his house, a new building, two stories high, with wrought-iron window gratings. The colonel headed for his home, anxious to take off his dress suit. He went out again a moment later to the store on the corner to buy a can of coffee and half a pound of corn for the rooster.

The colonel attended to the rooster in spite of the fact that on Thursday he would have preferred to stay in his hammock. It didn't clear for several days. During the course of the week, the flora in his belly blossomed. He spent several sleepless nights, tormented by the whistling of the asthmatic woman's lungs. But October granted a truce on Friday afternoon. Agustín's companions—workers from the tailor shop, as he had been, and cockfight fanatics—took advantage of the occasion to examine the rooster. He was in good shape.

The colonel returned to the bedroom when he was left alone in the house with his wife. She had recovered.

"What do they say?" she asked.

"Very enthusiastic," the colonel informed her. "Everyone is saving their money to bet on the rooster."

"I don't know what they see in such an ugly rooster," the woman said. "He looks like a freak to me; his head is too tiny for his feet."

"They say he's the best in the district," the colonel answered. "He's worth about fifty pesos."

He was sure that this argument justified his determination to keep the rooster, a legacy from their son who was shot down nine months before at the cockfights for distributing clandestine literature. "An expensive illusion," the woman said. "When the corn is gone we'll have to feed him on our own livers." The colonel took a good long time to think, while he was looking for his white ducks in the closet.

"It's just for a few months," he said. "We already know that there will be fights in January. Then we can sell him for more."

The pants needed pressing. The woman stretched them out over the stove with two irons heated over the coals.

"What's your hurry to go out?" she asked.

"The mail."

"I had forgotten that today is Friday," she commented, returning to the bedroom. The colonel was dressed but pantsless. She observed his shoes.

"Those shoes are ready to throw out," she said. "Keep wearing your patent-leather ones."

The colonel felt desolate.

"They look like the shoes of an orphan," he protested. "Every time I put them on I feel like a fugitive from an asylum."

"We are the orphans of our son," the woman said.

This time, too, she persuaded him. The colonel walked toward the harbor before the whistles of the launches blew. Patent-leather shoes, beltless white ducks, and the shirt without the detachable collar, closed at the neck with the copper stud. He observed the docking of the launches from the shop of Moses the Syrian. The travelers got off, stiff from eight hours of immobility. The same ones as always: traveling salesmen, and people from the town who had left the preceding week and were returning as usual.

The last one was the mail launch. The colonel saw it dock with an anguished uneasiness. On the roof, tied to the boat's smokestacks and protected by an oilcloth, he spied the mailbag. Fifteen years of waiting had sharpened his intuition. The rooster had sharpened his anxiety. From the moment the postmaster went on board the launch, untied the bag, and hoisted it up on his shoulder, the colonel kept him in sight.

He followed him through the street parallel to the harbor, a labyrinth of stores and booths with colored merchandise on display. Every time he did it, the colonel experienced an anxiety very different from, but just as oppressive as, fright. The doctor was waiting for the newspapers in the post office.

"My wife wants me to ask you if we threw boiling water on you at our house," the colonel said.

He was a young physician with his skull covered by sleek black hair. There was something unbelievable in the perfection of his dentition. He asked after the health of the asthmatic. The colonel supplied a detailed report without taking his eyes off the postmaster, who was distributing the letters into cubbyholes. His indolent way of moving exasperated the colonel.

The doctor received his mail with the packet of newspapers. He put the pamphlets of medical advertising to one side. Then he scanned his personal letters. Meanwhile the postmaster was handing out mail to those who were present. The colonel watched the compartment which corresponded to his letter in the alphabet. An airmail letter with blue borders increased his nervous tension.

The doctor broke the seal on the newspapers. He read the lead items while the colonel—his eyes fixed on the little box—waited for the postmaster to stop in front of it. But he didn't. The doctor interrupted his reading of the newspapers. He looked at the colonel. Then he looked at the postmaster seated in front of the telegraph key, and then at the colonel.

"We're leaving," he said.

The postmaster didn't raise his head.

"Nothing for the colonel," he said.

The colonel felt ashamed.

"I wasn't expecting anything," he lied. He turned to the doctor with an entirely childish look. "No one writes to me."

They went back in silence. The doctor was concentrating on the newspapers. The colonel with his habitual way of walking which resembled that of a man retracing his steps to look for a lost coin. It was a bright afternoon. The almond trees in the plaza were shedding their last rotted leaves. It had begun to grow dark when they arrived at the door of the doctor's office.

"What's in the news?" the colonel asked.

The doctor gave him a few newspapers.

"No one knows," he said. "It's hard to read between the lines which the censor lets them print."

The colonel read the main headlines. International news. At the top, across four columns, a report on the Suez Canal. The front page was almost completely covered by paid funeral announcements.

"There's no hope of elections," the colonel said.

"Don't be naïve, Colonel," said the doctor. "We're too old now to be waiting for the Messiah."

The colonel tried to give the newspapers back, but the doctor refused them.

"Take them home with you," he said. "You can read them tonight and return them tomorrow."

A little after seven the bells in the tower rang out the censor's movie classifications. Father Angel used this means to announce the moral classification of the film in accordance with the ratings he received every month by mail. The colonel's wife counted twelve bells.

"Unfit for everyone," she said. "It's been about a year now that the movies are bad for everyone."

She lowered the mosquito netting and murmured, "The world is corrupt." But the colonel made no comment. Before lying down, he tied the rooster to the leg of the bed. He locked the house and sprayed some insecticide in the bedroom. Then he put the lamp on the floor, hung his hammock up, and lay down to read the newspapers.

He read them in chronological order, from the first page to the last, including the advertisements. At eleven the trumpet blew curfew. The colonel finished his reading a half-hour later, opened the patio door on the impenetrable night, and urinated, besieged by mosquitoes, against the wall studs. His wife was awake when he returned to the bedroom.

"Nothing about the veterans?" she asked.

"Nothing," said the colonel. He put out the lamp before he got into the hammock. "In the beginning at least they published the list of the new pensioners. But it's been about five years since they've said anything."

It rained after midnight. The colonel managed to get to sleep but woke up a moment later, alarmed by his intestines. He discovered a leak in some part of the roof. Wrapped in a wool blanket up to his ears, he tried to find the leak in the darkness. A trickle of cold sweat slipped down his spine. He had a fever. He felt as if he were floating in concentric circles inside a tank of jelly. Someone spoke. The colonel answered from his revolutionist's cot.

"Who are you talking to?" asked his wife.

"The Englishman disguised as a tiger who appeared at Colonel Aureliano Buendía's camp," the colonel answered. He turned over in his hammock, burning with his fever. "It was the Duke of Marlborough."

The sky was clear at dawn. At the second call for Mass, he jumped from the hammock and installed himself in a confused reality which was agitated by the crowing of the rooster. His head was still spinning in concentric circles. He was nauseous. He went out into the patio and headed for the privy through the barely audible whispers and the dark odors of winter. The inside of the little zinc-roofed wooden compartment was rarefied by the ammonia smell from the privy. When the colonel raised the lid, a triangular cloud of flies rushed out of the pit.

It was a false alarm. Squatting on the platform of unsanded boards, he felt the uneasiness of an urge frustrated. The oppressiveness was substituted by a dull ache in his digestive tract. "There's no doubt," he murmured. "It's the same every October." And again he assumed his posture of confident and innocent expectation until the fungus in his innards was pacified. Then he returned to the bedroom for the rooster.

"Last night you were delirious from fever," his wife said.

She had begun to straighten up the room, having recovered from a week-long attack. The colonel made an effort to remember.

"It wasn't fever," he lied. "It was the dream about the spider webs again."

As always happened, the woman emerged from her attack full of nervous energy. In the course of the morning she turned the house upside down. She changed the position of everything, except the clock and the picture of the young girl. She was so thin and sinewy that when she walked about in her cloth slippers and her black dress all buttoned up she seemed as if she had the power of walking through the walls. But before twelve she had regained her bulk, her human weight. In bed she was an empty space. Now, moving among the flowerpots of ferns and begonias, her presence overflowed the house. "If Agustín's year were up, I would start singing," she said while she stirred the pot where all the things to eat that the tropical land is capable of producing, cut into pieces, were boiling.

"If you feel like singing, sing," said the colonel. "It's good for your spleen."

The doctor came after lunch. The colonel and his wife were drinking coffee in the kitchen when he pushed open the street door and shouted:

"Everybody dead?"

The colonel got up to welcome him.

"So it seems, Doctor," he said, going into the living room. "I've always said that your clock keeps time with the buzzards."

The woman went into the bedroom to get ready for the examination. The doctor stayed in the living room with the colonel. In spite of the heat, his immaculate linen suit gave off a smell of freshness. When the woman announced that she was ready, the doctor gave the colonel three sheets of paper in an envelope. He entered the bedroom, saying, "That's what the newspapers didn't print yesterday."

The colonel had assumed as much. It was a summary of the events in the country, mimeographed for clandestine circulation. Revelations about the state of armed resistance in the interior of the country. He felt defeated. Ten years of clandestine reports had not taught him that no news was more surprising than next month's news. He had finished reading when the doctor came back into the living room.

"This patient is healthier than I am," he said. "With asthma like that, I could live to be a hundred."

The colonel glowered at him. He gave him back the envelope without saying a word, but the doctor refused to take it.

"Pass it on," he said in a whisper.

The colonel put the envelope in his pants pocket. The woman came out of the bedroom saying, "One of these days I'll up and die, and carry you with me, off to hell, Doctor." The doctor responded silently with the stereotyped enamel of his teeth. He pulled a chair up to the little table and took several jars of free samples out of his bag. The woman went on into the kitchen.

"Wait and I'll warm up the coffee."

"No, thank you very much," said the doctor. He wrote the proper dosage on a prescription pad. "I absolutely refuse to give you the chance to poison me."

She laughed in the kitchen. When he finished writing, the doctor read the prescription aloud, because he knew that no one could decipher his handwriting. The colonel tried to concentrate. Returning from the kitchen, the woman discovered in his face the toll of the previous night.

"This morning he had a fever," she said, pointing at her husband. "He spent about two hours talking nonsense about the civil war."

The colonel started.

"It wasn't a fever," he insisted, regaining his composure. "Furthermore," he said, "the day I feel sick I'll throw myself into the garbage can on my own."

He went into the bedroom to find the newspapers.

"Thank you for the compliment," the doctor said.

They walked together toward the plaza. The air was dry. The tar on the streets had begun to melt from the heat. When the doctor said goodbye, the colonel asked him in a low voice, his teeth clenched:

"How much do we owe you, Doctor?"

"Nothing, for now," the doctor said, and he gave him a pat on the shoulder. "I'll send you a fat bill when the cock wins."

The colonel went to the tailor shop to take the clandestine letter to Agustín's companions. It was his only refuge ever since his copartisans had been killed or exiled from town and he had been converted into a man with no other occupation than waiting for the mail every Friday.

The afternoon heat stimulated the woman's energy. Seated among the begonias in the veranda next to a box of worn-out clothing, she was again working the eternal miracle of creating new apparel out of nothing. She made collars from sleeves, and cuffs from the backs and square patches, perfect ones, although with scraps of different colors. A cicada lodged its whistle in the patio. The sun faded. But she didn't see it go down over the begonias. She raised her head only at dusk when the colonel returned home. Then she clasped her neck with both hands, cracked her knuckles, and said:

"My head is as stiff as a board."

"It's always been that way," the colonel said, but then he saw his wife's body covered all over with scraps of color. "You look like a magpie."

"One has to be half a magpie to dress you," she said. She held out a shirt made of three different colors of material except for the collar and cuffs, which were the same color. "At the carnival all you have to do is take off your jacket."

The six-o'clock bells interrupted her. "The Angel of the Lord announced unto Mary," she prayed aloud, heading into the bedroom. The colonel talked to the children who had come to look at the rooster after school. Then he remembered that there was no corn for the next day, and entered the bedroom to ask his wife for money.

"I think there's only fifty cents," she said.

She kept the money under the mattress, knotted into the corner of a handkerchief. It was the proceeds of Agustín's sewing machine. For nine months, they had spent that money penny by penny, parceling it out between their needs and the rooster's. Now there were only two twenty-cent pieces and a ten-cent piece left.

"Buy a pound of corn," the woman said. "With the change, buy tomorrow's coffee and four ounces of cheese."

"And a golden elephant to hang in the doorway," the colonel went on. "The corn alone costs forty-two."

They thought a moment. "The rooster is an animal, and therefore he can wait," said the woman at first. But her husband's expression caused her to reflect. The colonel sat on the bed, his elbows on his knees, jingling the coins in his hands. "It's not for my sake," he said after a moment. "If it depended on me I'd make a rooster stew this very evening. A fifty-peso indigestion would be very good." He paused to squash a mosquito on his neck. Then his eyes followed his wife around the room.

"What bothers me is that those poor boys are saving up."

Then she began to think. She turned completely around with the insecticide bomb. The colonel found something unreal in her attitude, as if she were invoking the spirits of the house for a consultation. At last she put the bomb on the little mantel with the prints on it, and fixed her syrup-colored eyes on the syrup-colored eyes of the colonel.

"Buy the corn," she said. "God knows how we'll manage."

"This is the miracle of the multiplying loaves," the colonel repeated every time they sat down to the table during the following week. With her astonishing capacity for darning, sewing, and mending, she seemed to have discovered the key to sustaining the household economy with no money. October prolonged its truce. The humidity was replaced by sleepiness. Comforted by the copper sun, the woman devoted three afternoons to her complicated hairdo. "High Mass has begun," the colonel said one afternoon when she was getting the knots out of her long blue tresses with a comb which had some teeth missing. The second afternoon, seated in the patio with a white sheet in her lap, she used a finer comb to take out the lice which had proliferated during her attack. Lastly, she washed her hair with lavender water, waited for it to dry, and rolled it up on the nape of her neck in two turns held with a barrette. The colonel waited. At night, sleepless in his hammock, he worried for many hours over the rooster's fate. But on Wednesday they weighed him, and he was in good shape.

That same afternoon, when Agustín's companions left the house counting the imaginary proceeds from the rooster's victory, the colonel also felt in good shape. His wife cut his hair. "You've taken twenty years off me," he said, examining his head with his hands. His wife thought her husband was right.

"When I'm well, I can bring back the dead," she said.

But her conviction lasted for a very few hours. There was no longer anything in the house to sell, except the clock and the picture. Thursday night, at the limit of their resources, the woman showed her anxiety over the situation.

"Don't worry," the colonel consoled her. "The mail comes tomorrow."

The following day he waited for the launches in front of the doctor's office.

"The airplane is a marvelous thing," the colonel said, his eyes resting on the mailbag. "They say you can get to Europe in one night."

"That's right," the doctor said, fanning himself with an illustrated magazine. The colonel spied the postmaster among a group waiting for the docking to end so they could jump onto the launch. The postmaster jumped first. He received from the captain an envelope sealed with wax. Then he climbed up onto the roof. The mailbag was tied between two oil drums.

"But still it has its dangers," said the colonel. He lost the postmaster from sight, but saw him again among the colored bottles on the refreshment cart. "Humanity doesn't progress without paying a price."

"Even at this stage it's safer than a launch," the doctor said. "At twenty thousand feet you fly above the weather."

"Twenty thousand feet," the colonel repeated, perplexed, without being able to imagine what the figure meant.

The doctor became interested. He spread out the magazine with both hands until it was absolutely still.

"There's perfect stability," he said.

But the colonel was hanging on the actions of the postmaster. He saw him consume a frothy pink drink, holding the glass in his left hand. In his right he held the mailbag.

"Also, on the ocean there are ships at anchor in continual contact with night flights," the doctor went on. "With so many precautions it's safer than a launch."

The colonel looked at him.

"Naturally," he said. "It must be like a carpet."

The postmaster came straight toward them. The colonel stepped back, impelled by an irresistible anxiety, trying to read the name written on the sealed envelope. The postmaster opened the bag. He gave the doctor his packet of newspapers. Then he tore open the envelope with the personal correspondence, checked the correctness of the receipt, and read the addressee's names off the letters. The doctor opened the newspapers.

"Still the problem with Suez," he said, reading the main headlines. "The West is losing ground."

The colonel didn't read the headlines. He made an effort to control his stomach. "Ever since there's been censorship, the newspapers talk only about Europe," he said. "The best thing would be for the Europeans to come over here and for us to go to Europe. That way everybody would know what's happening in his own country."

"To the Europeans, South America is a man with a mustache, a guitar, and a gun," the doctor said, laughing over his newspaper. "They don't understand the problem."

The postmaster delivered his mail. He put the rest in the bag and closed it again. The doctor got ready to read two personal letters, but before tearing open the envelopes he looked at the colonel. Then he looked at the postmaster.

"Nothing for the colonel?"

The colonel was terrified. The postmaster tossed the bag onto his shoulder, got off the platform, and replied without turning his head:

"No one writes to the colonel."

Contrary to his habit, he didn't go directly home. He had a cup of coffee at the tailor's while Agustín's companions leafed through the newspapers. He felt cheated. He would have preferred to stay there until the next Friday to keep from having to face his wife that night with empty hands. But when the tailor shop closed, he had to face up to reality. His wife was waiting for him.

"Nothing?" she asked.

"Nothing," the colonel answered.

The following Friday he went down to the launches again. And, as on every Friday, he returned home without the longed-for letter. "We've waited long enough," his wife told him that night. "One must have the patience of an ox, as you do, to wait for a letter for fifteen years." The colonel got into his hammock to read the newspapers.

"We have to wait our turn," he said. "Our number is 1823."

"Since we've been waiting, that number has come up twice in the lottery," his wife replied.

The colonel read, as usual, from the first page to the last, including the advertisements. But this time he didn't concentrate. During his reading, he thought about his veteran's pension. Nineteen years before, when Congress passed the law, it took him eight years to prove his claim. Then it took him six more years to get himself included on the rolls. That was the last letter the colonel had received.

He finished after curfew sounded. When he went to turn off the lamp, he realized that his wife was awake.

"Do you still have that clipping?"

The woman thought.

"Yes. It must be with the other papers."

She got out of her mosquito netting and took a wooden chest out of the closet, with a packet of letters arranged by date and held together by a rubber band. She located the advertisement of a law firm which promised quick action on war pensions.

"We could have spent the money in the time I've wasted trying to convince you to change lawyers," the woman said, handing her husband the newspaper clipping. "We're not getting anything out of their putting us away on a shelf as they do with the Indians."

The colonel read the clipping dated two years before. He put it in the pocket of his jacket which was hanging behind the door.

"The problem is that to change lawyers you need money."

"Not at all," the woman said decisively. "You write them telling them to discount whatever they want from the pension itself when they collect it. It's the only way they'll take the case."

So Saturday afternoon the colonel went to see his lawyer. He found him stretched out lazily in a hammock. He was a monumental

Negro, with nothing but two canines in his upper jaw. The lawyer put his feet into a pair of wooden-soled slippers and opened the office window on a dusty pianola with papers stuffed into the compartments where the rolls used to go: clippings from the *Official Gazette*, pasted into old accounting ledgers, and a jumbled collection of accounting bulletins. The keyless pianola did double duty as a desk. The lawyer sat down in a swivel chair. The colonel expressed his uneasiness before revealing the purpose of his visit.

"I warned you that it would take more than a few days," said the lawyer when the colonel paused. He was sweltering in the heat. He adjusted the chair backward and fanned himself with an advertising brochure.

"My agents write to me frequently, saying not to get impatient."

"It's been that way for fifteen years," the colonel answered. "This is beginning to sound like the story about the capon."

The lawyer gave a very graphic description of the administrative ins and outs. The chair was too narrow for his sagging buttocks. "Fifteen years ago it was easier," he said. "Then there was the city's veterans' organization, with members of both parties." His lungs filled with stifling air and he pronounced the sentence as if he had just invented it:

"There's strength in numbers."

"There wasn't in this case," the colonel said, realizing his aloneness for the first time. "All my comrades died waiting for the mail."

The lawyer didn't change his expression.

"The law was passed too late," he said. "Not everybody was as lucky as you to be a colonel at the age of twenty. Furthermore, no special allocation was included, so the government has had to make adjustments in the budget."

Always the same story. Each time the colonel listened to him, he felt a mute resentment. "This is not charity," he said. "It's not a question of doing us a favor. We broke our backs to save the Republic." The lawyer threw up his hands.

"That's the way it is," he said. "Human ingratitude knows no limits."

The colonel also knew that story. He had begun hearing it the day after the Treaty of Neerlandia, when the government promised travel assistance and indemnities to two hundred revolutionary officers. Camped at the base of the gigantic silk-cotton tree at Neerlandia, a revolutionary battalion, made up in great measure of youths who had left school, waited for three months. Then they went back to their homes by their own means, and they kept on waiting there. Almost sixty years later, the colonel was still waiting.

Excited by these memories, he adopted a transcendental attitude. He rested his right hand on his thigh—mere bone sewed together with nerve tissue—and murmured:

"Well, I've decided to take action."

The lawyer waited.

"Such as?"

"To change lawyers."

A mother duck, followed by several little ducklings, entered the office. The lawyer sat up to chase them out. "As you wish, Colonel," he said, chasing the animals. "It will be just as you wish. If I could work miracles, I wouldn't be living in this barnyard." He put a wooden grille across the patio door and returned to his chair.

"My son worked all his life," said the colonel. "My house is mortgaged. That retirement law has been a lifetime pension for lawyers."

"Not for me," the lawyers protested. "Every last cent has gone for my expenses."

The colonel suffered at the thought that he had been unjust.

"That's what I meant," he corrected himself. He dried his forehead with the sleeve of his shirt. "This heat is enough to rust the screws in your head."

A moment later the lawyer was turning the office upside down looking for the power of attorney. The sun advanced toward the center of the tiny room, which was built of unsanded boards. After looking futilely everywhere, the lawyer got down on all fours, huffing and puffing, and picked up a roll of papers from under the pianola.

"Here it is."

He gave the colonel a sheet of paper with a seal on it. "I have to write my agents so they can cancel the copies," he concluded. The colonel shook the dust off the paper and put it in his shirt pocket.

"Tear it up yourself," the lawyer said.

"No," the colonel answered. "These are twenty years of memories." And he waited for the lawyer to keep on looking. But the lawyer didn't. He went to the hammock to wipe off his sweat. From there he looked at the colonel through the shimmering air.

"I need the documents also," the colonel said.

"Which ones?"

"The proof of claim."

The lawyer threw up his hands.

"Now, that would be impossible, Colonel."

The colonel became alarmed. As Treasurer of the revolution in the district of Macondo, he had undertaken a difficult six-day journey with the funds for the civil war in two trunks roped to the back of a mule. He arrived at the camp of Neerlandia dragging the mule, which was dead from hunger, half an hour before the treaty was signed. Colonel Aureliano Buendía—quartermaster general of the revolutionary forces on the Atlantic coast—held out the receipt for the funds, and included the two trunks in his inventory of the surrender.

"Those documents have an incalculable value," the colonel said. "There's a receipt from Colonel Aureliano Buendía, written in his own hand."

"I agree," said the lawyer. "But those documents have passed through thousands of offices, before they reached God knows which department in the War Ministry."

"No official could fail to notice documents like those," the colonel said.

"But the officials have changed many times in the last fifteen years," the lawyer pointed out. "Just think about it; there have been seven Presidents, and each President changed his Cabinet at least ten times, and each Minister changed his staff at least a hundred times."

"But nobody could take the documents home," said the colonel. "Each new official must have found them in the proper file."

The lawyer lost his patience.

"And moreover if those papers are removed from the Ministry now, they will have to wait for a new place on the rolls."

"It doesn't matter," the colonel said.

"It'll take centuries."

"It doesn't matter. If you wait for the big things, you can wait for the little ones."

He took a pad of lined paper, the pen, the inkwell, and a blotter to the little table in the living room, and left the bedroom door open in case he had to ask his wife anything. She was saying her beads.

"What's today's date?"

"October 27th."

He wrote with a studious neatness, the hand that held the pen resting on the blotter, his spine straight to ease his breathing, as he'd been taught in school. The heat became unbearable in the closed living room. A drop of perspiration fell on the letter. The colonel picked it up on the blotter. Then he tried to erase the letters which had smeared but he smudged them. He didn't lose his patience. He wrote an asterisk and noted in the margin, "acquired rights." Then he read the whole paragraph.

"When was I put on the rolls?"

The woman didn't interrupt her prayer to think.

"August 12, 1949."

A moment later it began to rain. The colonel filled a page with large doodlings which were a little childish, the same ones learned in public school at Manaure. Then he wrote on a second sheet down to the middle, and he signed it.

He read the letter to his wife. She approved each sentence with a nod. When he finished reading, the colonel sealed the envelope and turned off the lamp.

"You could ask someone to type it for you."

"No," the colonel answered. "I'm tired of going around asking favors."

For half an hour he heard the rain against the palm roof. The town sank into the deluge. After curfew sounded, a leak began somewhere in the house.

"This should have been done a long time ago," the woman said. "It's always better to handle things oneself."

"It's never too late," the colonel said, paying attention to the leak. "Maybe all this will be settled when the mortgage on the house falls due."

"In two years," the woman said.

He lit the lamp to locate the leak in the living room. He put the rooster's can underneath it and returned to the bedroom, pursued by the metallic noise of the water in the empty can.

"It's possible that to save the interest on the money they'll settle it before January," he said, and he convinced himself. "By then, Agustín's year will be up and we can go to the movies."

She laughed under her breath. "I don't even remember the cartoons any more," she said. The colonel tried to look at her through the mosquito netting.

"When did you go to the movies last?"

"In 1931," she said. "They were showing *The Dead Man's Will*."

"Was there a fight?"

"We never found out. The storm broke just when the ghost tried to rob the girl's necklace."

The sound of the rain put them to sleep. The colonel felt a slight queasiness in his intestines. But he wasn't afraid. He was about to survive another October. He wrapped himself in a wool blanket, and for a moment heard the gravelly breathing of his wife—far away—drifting on another dream. Then he spoke completely conscious.

The woman woke up.

"Who are you speaking to?"

"No one," the colonel said. "I was thinking that at the Macondo meeting we were right when we told Colonel Aureliano Buendía not to surrender. That's what started to ruin everything."

It rained the whole week. The second of November—against the colonel's wishes—the woman took flowers to Agustín's grave. She returned from the cemetery and had another attack. It was a hard week. Harder than the four weeks of October which the colonel hadn't thought he'd survive. The doctor came to see the sick woman, and came out of the room shouting, "With asthma like that, I'd be able to bury the whole town!" But he spoke to the colonel alone and prescribed a special diet.

The colonel also suffered a relapse. He strained for many hours in the privy, in an icy sweat, feeling as if he were rotting and that the flora in his vitals was falling to pieces. "It's winter," he repeated to himself patiently. "Everything will be different when it stops raining." And he really believed it, certain that he would be alive at the moment the letter arrived.

This time it was he who had to repair their household economy. He had to grit his teeth many times to ask for credit in the neighborhood stores. "It's just until next week," he would say, without being sure himself that it was true. "It's a little money which should have arrived last Friday." When her attack was over, the woman examined him in horror.

"You're nothing but skin and bones," she said.

"I'm taking care of myself so I can sell myself," the colonel said. "I've already been hired by a clarinet factory."

But in reality his hoping for the letter barely sustained him. Exhausted, his bones aching from sleeplessness, he couldn't attend to his needs and the rooster's at the same time. In the second half of November, he thought that the animal would die after two days without corn. Then he remembered a handful of beans which he had hung in the chimney in July. He opened the pods and put down a can of dry seeds for the rooster.

"Come here," she said.

"Just a minute," the colonel answered, watching the rooster's reaction. "Beggars can't be choosers."

He found his wife trying to sit up in bed. Her ravaged body gave off the aroma of medicinal herbs. She spoke her words, one by one, with calculated precision:

"Get rid of that rooster right now."

The colonel had foreseen that moment. He had been waiting for it ever since the afternoon when his son was shot down, and he had decided to keep the rooster. He had had time to think.

"It's not worth it now," he said. "The fight will be in two months and then we'll be able to sell him at a better price."

"It's not a question of money," the woman said. "When the boys come, you'll tell them to take it away and do whatever they feel like with it."

"It's for Agustín," the colonel said, advancing his prepared argument. "Remember his face when he came to tell us the rooster won."

The woman, in fact, did think of her son.

"Those accursed roosters were his downfall!" she shouted. "If he'd stayed home on January 3rd, his evil hour wouldn't have come." She held out a skinny forefinger toward the door and exclaimed:

"It seems as if I can see him when he left with the rooster under his arm. I warned him not to go looking for trouble at the cockfights, and he smiled and told me, 'Shut up; this afternoon we'll be rolling in money.' "

She fell back exhausted. The colonel pushed her gently toward the pillow. His eyes fell upon other eyes exactly like his own. "Try not to move," he said, feeling her whistling within his own lungs. The woman fell into a momentary torpor. She closed her eyes. When she opened them again, her breathing seemed more even.

"It's because of the situation we're in," she said. "It's a sin to take the food out of our mouths to give it to a rooster."

The colonel wiped her forehead with the sheet.

"Nobody dies in three months."

"And what do we eat in the meantime?" the woman asked.

"I don't know," the colonel said. "But if we were going to die of hunger, we would have died already."

The rooster was very much alive next to the empty can. When he saw the colonel, he emitted an almost human guttural monologue and tossed his head back. He gave him a smile of complicity:

"Life is tough, pal."

The colonel went into the street. He wandered about the town

during the siesta; without thinking about anything, without even trying to convince himself that his problem had no solution. He
walked through forgotten streets until he found he was exhausted.
Then he returned to the house. The woman heard him come in and
called him into the bedroom.

"What?"

She replied without looking at him.

"We can sell the clock."

The colonel had thought of that. "I'm sure Alvaro will give you
forty pesos right on the spot," said the woman. "Think how quickly
he bought the sewing machine."

She was referring to the tailor whom Agustín had worked for.

"I could speak to him in the morning," admitted the colonel.

"None of that 'speak to him in the morning,' " she insisted. "Take
the clock to him this minute. You put it on the counter and you tell
him, 'Alvaro, I've brought this clock for you to buy from me.' He'll
understand immediately."

The colonel felt ashamed.

"It's like walking around with the Holy Sepulcher," he protested.
"If they see me in the street with a showpiece like that, Rafael Es-
calona will put me into one of his songs."

But this time, too, his wife convinced him. She herself took down
the clock, wrapped it in newspaper, and put it into his arms. "Don't
come back here without the forty pesos," she said. The colonel went
off to the tailor's with the package under his arm. He found Agustín's
companions sitting in the doorway.

One of them offered him a seat. "Thanks," he said. "I can't
stay." Alvaro came out of the shop. A piece of wet duck hung on a
wire stretched between two hooks in the hall. He was a boy with a
hard, angular body and wild eyes. He also invited him to sit down.
The colonel felt comforted. He leaned the stool against the doorjamb
and sat down to wait until Alvaro was alone to propose his deal. Suddenly he realized that he was surrounded by expressionless faces.

"I'm not interrupting?" he said.

They said he wasn't. One of them leaned toward him. He said
in a barely audible voice:

"Agustín wrote."

The colonel observed the deserted street.

"What does he say?"

"The same as always."

They gave him the clandestine sheet of paper. The colonel put it in his pants pocket. Then he kept silent, drumming on the package, until he realized that someone had noticed it. He stopped in suspense.

"What have you got there, Colonel?"

The colonel avoided Hernán's penetrating green eyes.

"Nothing," he lied. "I'm taking my clock to the German to have him fix it for me."

"Don't be silly, Colonel," said Hernán, trying to take the package. "Wait and I'll look at it."

The colonel held back. He didn't say anything, but his eyelids turned purple. The others insisted.

"Let him, Colonel. He knows mechanical things."

"I just don't want to bother him."

"Bother, it's no bother," Hernán argued. He seized the clock. "The German will get ten pesos out of you and it'll be the same as it is now."

Hernán went into the tailor shop with the clock. Alvaro was sewing on a machine. At the back, beneath a guitar hanging on a nail, a girl was sewing buttons on. There was a sign tucked up over the guitar: "TALKING POLITICS FORBIDDEN." Outside, the colonel felt as if his body were superfluous. He rested his feet on the rail of the stool.

"Goddamn it, Colonel."

He was startled. "No need to swear," he said.

Alfonso adjusted his eyeglasses on his nose to examine the colonel's shoes.

"It's because of your shoes," he said. "You've got on some goddamn new shoes."

"But you can say that without swearing," the colonel said, and showed the soles of his patent-leather shoes. "These monstrosities are forty years old, and it's the first time they've ever heard anyone swear."

"All done," shouted Hernán, inside, just as the clock's bell rang. In the neighboring house, a woman pounded on the partition; she shouted:

"Let that guitar alone! Agustín's year isn't up yet."

Someone guffawed.

"It's a clock."

Hernán came out with the package.

"It wasn't anything," he said. "If you like I'll go home with you to level it."

The colonel refused his offer.

"How much do I owe you?"

"Don't worry about it, Colonel," replied Hernán, taking his place in the group. "In January, the rooster will pay for it."

The colonel now found the chance he was looking for.

"I'll make you a deal," he said.

"What?"

"I'll give you the rooster." He examined the circle of faces. "I'll give the rooster to all of you."

Hernán looked at him in confusion.

"I'm too old now for that," the colonel continued. He gave his voice a convincing severity. "It's too much responsibility for me. For days now I've had the impression that the animal is dying."

"Don't worry about it, Colonel," Alfonso said. "The trouble is that the rooster is molting now. He's got a fever in his quills."

"He'll be better next month," Hernán said.

"I don't want him anyway," the colonel said.

Hernán's pupils bore into his.

"Realize how things are, Colonel," he insisted. "The main thing is for you to be the one who puts Agustín's rooster into the ring."

The colonel thought about it. "I realize," he said. "That's why I've kept him until now." He clenched his teeth, and felt he could go on:

"The trouble is there are still two months."

Hernán was the one who understood.

"If it's only because of that, there's no problem," he said.

And he proposed his formula. The other accepted. At dusk, when he entered the house with the package under his arm, his wife was chagrined.

"Nothing?" she asked.

"Nothing," the colonel answered. "But now it doesn't matter. The boys will take over feeding the rooster."

"Wait and I'll lend you an umbrella, friend."

Sabas opened a cupboard in the office wall. He uncovered a jumbled interior: riding boots piled up, stirrups and reins, and an aluminum pail full of riding spurs. Hanging from the upper part, half a dozen umbrellas and a lady's parasol. The colonel was thinking of the debris from some catastrophe.

"Thanks, friend," the colonel said, leaning on the window. "I prefer to wait for it to clear." Sabas didn't close the cupboard. He settled down at the desk within range of the electric fan. Then he took a little hypodermic syringe wrapped in cotton out of the drawer. The colonel observed the grayish almond trees through the rain. It was an empty afternoon.

"The rain is different from this window," he said. "It's as if it were raining in another town."

"Rain is rain from whatever point," replied Sabas. He put the syringe on to boil on the glass desk top. "This town stinks."

The colonel shrugged his shoulders. He walked toward the middle of the office: a green-tiled room with furniture upholstered in brightly colored fabrics. At the back, piled up in disarray, were sacks of salt, honeycombs, and riding saddles. Sabas followed him with a completely vacant stare.

"If I were in your shoes I wouldn't think that way," said the colonel.

He sat down and crossed his legs, his calm gaze fixed on the man leaning over his desk. A small man, corpulent, but with flaccid flesh, he had the sadness of a toad in his eyes.

"Have the doctor look at you, friend," said Sabas. "You've been a little sad since the day of the funeral."

The colonel raised his head.

"I'm perfectly well," he said.

Sabas waited for the syringe to boil. "I wish I could say the same," he complained. "You're lucky because you've got a cast-iron stomach." He contemplated the hairy backs of his hands which were dotted with dark blotches. He wore a ring with a black stone next to his wedding band.

"That's right," the colonel admitted.

Sabas called his wife through the door between the office and the rest of the house. Then he began a painful explanation of his diet. He took a little bottle out of his shirt pocket and put a white pill the size of a pea on the desk.

"It's torture to go around with this everyplace," he said. "It's like carrying death in your pocket."

The colonel approached the desk. He examined the pill in the palm of his hand until Sabas invited him to taste it.

"It's to sweeten coffee," he explained. "It's sugar, but without sugar."

"Of course," the colonel said, his saliva impregnated with a sad sweetness. "It's something like a ringing but without bells."

Sabas put his elbows on the desk with his face in his hands after his wife gave him the injection. The colonel didn't know what to do with his body. The woman unplugged the electric fan, put it on top of the safe, and then went to the cupboard.

"Umbrellas have something to do with death," she said.

The colonel paid no attention to her. He had left his house at four to wait for the mail, but the rain made him take refuge in Sabas's office. It was still raining when the launches whistled.

"Everybody says death is a woman," the woman continued. She was fat, taller than her husband, and had a hairy mole on her upper lip. Her way of speaking reminded one of the hum of the electric fan. "But I don't think it's a woman," she said. She closed the cupboard and looked into the colonel's eyes again.

"I think it's an animal with claws."

"That's possible," the colonel admitted. "At times very strange things happen."

He thought of the postmaster jumping onto the launch in an oil-skin slicker. A month had passed since he had changed lawyers. He was entitled to expect a reply. Sabas's wife kept speaking about death until she noticed the colonel's absentminded expression.

"Friend," she said. "You must be worried."

The colonel sat up.

"That's right, friend," he lied. "I'm thinking that it's five already and the rooster hasn't had his injection."

She was confused.

"An injection for a rooster, as if he were a human being!" she shouted. "That's a sacrilege."

Sabas couldn't stand any more. He raised his flushed face.

"Close your mouth for a minute," he ordered his wife. And in fact she did raise her hands to her mouth. "You've been bothering my friend for half an hour with your foolishness."

"Not at all," the colonel protested.

The woman slammed the door. Sabas dried his neck with a hand-kerchief soaked in lavender. The colonel approached the window. It was raining steadily. A long-legged chicken was crossing the deserted plaza.

"Is it true the rooster's getting injections?"

"True," said the colonel. "His training begins next week."

"That's madness," said Sabas. "Those things are not for you."

"I agree," said the colonel. "But that's no reason to wring his neck."

"That's just idiotic stubbornness," said Sabas, turning toward the window. The colonel heard him sigh with the breath of a bellows. His friend's eyes made him feel pity.

"It's never too late for anything," the colonel said.

"Don't be unreasonable," insisted Sabas. "It's a two-edged deal. On one side you get rid of that headache, and on the other you can put nine hundred pesos in your pocket."

"Nine hundred pesos!" the colonel exclaimed.

"Nine hundred pesos."

The colonel visualized the figure.

"You think they'd give a fortune like that for the rooster?"

"I don't think," Sabas answered. "I'm absolutely sure."

It was the largest sum the colonel had had in his head since he had returned the revolution's funds. When he left Sabas's office, he felt a strong wrenching in his gut, but he was aware that this time it wasn't because of the weather. At the post office he headed straight for the postmaster:

"I'm expecting an urgent letter," he said. "It's air mail."

The postmaster looked in the cubbyholes. When he finished reading, he put the letters back in the proper box but he didn't say anything. He dusted off his hand and turned a meaningful look on the colonel.

"It was supposed to come today for sure," the colonel said.

The postmaster shrugged.

"The only thing that comes for sure is death, Colonel."

His wife received him with a dish of corn mush. He ate it in silence with long pauses for thought between each spoonful. Seated opposite him, the woman noticed that something had changed in his face.

"What's the matter?" she asked.

"I'm thinking about the employee that pension depends on," the colonel lied. "In fifty years, we'll be peacefully six feet under, while that poor man will be killing himself every Friday waiting for his retirement pension."

"That's a bad sign," the woman said. "It means that you're beginning to resign yourself already." She went on eating her mush. But a moment later she realized that her husband was still far away.

"Now, what you should do is enjoy the mush."

"It's very good," the colonel said. "Where did it come from?"

"From the rooster," the woman answered. "The boys brought him so much corn that he decided to share it with us. That's life."

"That's right." The colonel sighed. "Life is the best thing that's ever been invented."

He looked at the rooster tied to the leg of the stove and this time he seemed a different animal. The woman also looked at him.

"This afternoon I had to chase the children out with a stick," she said. "They brought an old hen to breed her with the rooster."

"It's not the first time," the colonel said. "That's the same thing they did in those towns with Colonel Aureliano Buendía. They brought him little girls to breed with."

She got a kick out of the joke. The rooster produced a guttural noise which sounded in the hall like quite human conversation. "Sometimes I think that animal is going to talk," the woman said. The colonel looked at him again.

"He's worth his weight in gold," he said. He made some calculations while he sipped a spoonful of mush. "He'll feed us for three years."

"You can't eat hope," the woman said.

"You can't eat it, but it sustains you," the colonel replied. "It's something like my friend Sabas's miraculous pills."

He slept poorly that night trying to erase the figures from his mind. The following day at lunch, the woman served two plates of mush, and ate hers with her head lowered, without saying a word. The colonel felt himself catching her dark mood.

"What's the matter?"

"Nothing," the woman said.

He had the impression that this time it had been her turn to lie. He tried to comfort her. But the woman persisted.

"It's nothing unusual," she said. "I was thinking that the man had been dead for two months, and I still haven't been to see the family."

So she went to see them that night. The colonel accompanied her to the dead man's house, and then headed for the movie theater, drawn by the music coming over the loudspeakers. Seated at the door of his office, Father Angel was watching the entrance to find out who was attending the show despite his twelve warnings. The flood of light, the strident music, and the shouts of the children erected a physical resistance in the area. One of the children threatened the colonel with a wooden rifle.

"What's new with the rooster, Colonel?" he said in an authoritative voice.

The colonel put his hands up.

"He's still around."

A four-color poster covered the entire front of the theater: *Midnight Virgin*. She was a woman in an evening gown, with one leg bared up to the thigh. The colonel continued wandering around the neighborhood until distant thunder and lightning began. Then he went back for his wife.

She wasn't at the dead man's house. Nor at home. The colonel reckoned that there was little time left before curfew, but the clock had stopped. He waited, feeling the storm advance on the town. He was getting ready to go out again when his wife arrived.

He took the rooster into the bedroom. She changed her clothes and went to take a drink of water in the living room just as the colonel finished winding the clock, and was waiting for curfew to blow in order to set it.

"Where were you?" the colonel asked.

"Roundabout," the woman answered. She put the glass on the washstand without looking at her husband and returned to the bedroom. "No one thought it was going to rain so soon." The colonel made no comment. When curfew blew, he set the clock at eleven, closed the case, and put the chair back in its place. He found his wife saying her rosary.

"You haven't answered my question," the colonel said.

"What?"

"Where were you?"

"I stayed around there talking," she said. "It had been so long since I'd been out of the house."

The colonel hung up his hammock. He locked the house and fumigated the room. Then he put the lamp on the floor and lay down.

"I understand," he said sadly. "The worst of a bad situation is that it makes us tell lies."

She let out a long sigh.

"I was with Father Angel," she said. "I went to ask him for a loan on our wedding rings."

"And what did he tell you?"

"That it's a sin to barter with sacred things."

She went on talking under her mosquito netting. "Two days ago I tried to sell the clock," she said. "No one is interested because they're selling modern clocks with luminous numbers on the installment plan. You can see the time in the dark." The colonel acknowledged that forty years of shared living, of shared hunger, of shared suffering, had not been enough for him to come to know his wife. He felt that something had also grown old in their love.

"They don't want the picture, either," she said. "Almost everybody has the same one. I even went to the Turk's."

The colonel felt bitter.

"So now everyone knows we're starving."

"I'm tired," the woman said. "Men don't understand problems of the household. Several times I've had to put stones on to boil so the neighbors wouldn't know that we often go for many days without putting on the pot."

The colonel felt offended.

"That's really a humiliation," he said.

The woman got out from the mosquito netting and went to the hammock. "I'm ready to give up affectation and pretense in this house," she said. Her voice began to darken with rage. "I'm fed up with resignation and dignity."

The colonel didn't move a muscle.

"Twenty years of waiting for the little colored birds which they promised you after every election, and all we've got out of it is a dead son," she went on. "Nothing but a dead son."

The colonel was used to that sort of recrimination.

"We did our duty."

"And they did theirs by making a thousand pesos a month in the Senate for twenty years," the woman answered. "There's my friend Sabas with a two-story house that isn't big enough to keep all his money in, a man who came to this town selling medicines with a snake curled around his neck."

"But he's dying of diabetes," the colonel said.

"And you're dying of hunger," the woman said. "You should realize that you can't eat dignity."

The lightning interrupted her. The thunder exploded in the street, entered the bedroom, and went rolling under the bed like a heap of stones. The woman jumped toward the mosquito netting for her rosary.

The colonel smiled.

"That's what happens to you for not holding your tongue," he said. "I've always said that God is on my side."

But in reality he felt embittered. A moment later he put out the light and sank into thought in a darkness rent by the lightning. He remembered Macondo. The colonel had waited ten years for the promises of Neerlandia to be fulfilled. In the drowsiness of the siesta he saw a yellow, dusty train pull in, with men and women and animals suffocating from the heat, piled up even on the roofs of the cars. It was the banana fever.

In twenty-four hours they had transformed the town. "I'm leaving," the colonel said then. "The odor of the banana is eating at my insides." And he left Macondo on the return train, Wednesday, June 27, 1906, at 2:18 P.M. It took him nearly half a century to realize that he hadn't had a moment's peace since the surrender of Neerlandia.

He opened his eyes.

"Then there's no need to think about it any more," he said.

"What?"

"The problem of the rooster," the colonel said. "Tomorrow I'll sell it to my freind Sabas for nine hundred pesos."

The howls of the castrated animals, fused with Sabas's shouting, came through the office window. If he doesn't come in ten minutes I'll leave, the colonel promised himself after two hours of waiting. But he waited twenty minutes more. He was getting set to leave when Sabas entered the office followed by a group of workers. He passed back and forth in front of the colonel without looking at him.

"Are you waiting for me, friend?"

"Yes, friend," the colonel said. "But if you're very busy, I can come back later."

Sabas didn't hear him from the other side of the door.

"I'll be right back," he said.

Noon was stifling. The office shone with the shimmering of the street. Dulled by the heat, the colonel involuntarily closed his eyes and at once began to dream of his wife. Sabas's wife came in on tiptoe.

"Don't wake up, friend," she said. "I'm going to draw the blinds because this office is an inferno."

The colonel followed her with a blank look. She spoke in the shadow when she closed the window.

"Do you dream often?"

"Sometimes," replied the colonel, ashamed of having fallen asleep. "Almost always I dream that I'm tangled up in spider webs."

"I have nightmares every night," the woman said. "Now I've got it in my head to find out who those unknown people are whom one meets in one's dreams."

She plugged in the fan. "Last week a woman appeared at the head of my bed," she said. "I managed to ask her who she was and she replied, 'I am the woman who died in this room twelve years ago.' "

"But the house was built barely two years ago," the colonel said.

"That's right," the woman said. "That means that even the dead make mistakes."

The hum of the fan solidified the shadow. The colonel felt impatient, tormented by sleepiness and by the rambling woman who went directly from dreams to the mystery of the reincarnation. He was waiting for a pause to say goodbye when Sabas entered the office with his foreman.

"I've warmed up your soup four times," the woman said.

"Warm it up ten times if you like," said Sabas. "But stop nagging me now."

He opened the safe and gave his foreman a roll of bills together with a list of instructions. The foreman opened the blinds to count the money. Sabas saw the colonel at the back of the office but didn't show any reaction. He kept talking with the foreman. The colonel straightened up at the point when the two men were getting ready to leave the office again. Sabas stopped before opening the door.

"What can I do for you, friend?"

The colonel saw that the foreman was looking at him.

"Nothing, friend," he said. "I just wanted to talk to you."

"Make it fast, whatever it is," said Sabas. "I don't have a minute to spare."

He hesitated with his hand resting on the doorknob. The colonel felt the five longest seconds of his life passing. He clenched his teeth.

"It's about the rooster," he murmured.

Then Sabas finished opening the door. "The question of the rooster," he repeated, smiling, and pushed the foreman toward the hall. "The sky is falling in and my friend is worrying about that rooster." And then, addressing the colonel:

"Very well, friend. I'll be right back."

The colonel stood motionless in the middle of the office until he could no longer hear the footsteps of the two men at the end of the hall. Then he went out to walk around the town which was paralyzed in its Sunday siesta. There was no one at the tailor's. The doctor's office was closed. No one was watching the goods set out at the Syrians' stalls. The river was a sheet of steel. A man at the waterfront was sleeping across four oil drums, his face protected from the sun by a hat. The colonel went home, certain that he was the only thing moving in town.

His wife was waiting for him with a complete lunch.

"I bought it on credit; promised to pay first thing tomorrow," she explained.

During lunch, the colonel told her the events of the last three hours. She listened to him impatiently.

"The trouble is you lack character," she said finally. "You present yourself as if you were begging alms when you ought to go there with your head high and take our friend aside and say, 'Friend, I've decided to sell you the rooster.' "

"Life is a breeze the way you tell it," the colonel said.

She assumed an energetic attitude. That morning she had put the house in order and was dressed very strangely, in her husband's old shoes, and oilcloth apron, and a rag tied around her head with two knots at the ears. "You haven't the slightest sense for business," she said. "When you go to sell something, you have to put on the same face as when you go to buy."

The colonel found something amusing in her figure.

"Stay just the way you are," he interrupted her, smiling. "You're identical to the little Quaker Oats man."

She took the rag off her head.

"I'm speaking seriously," she said. "I'm going to take the rooster to our friend right now, and I'll bet whatever you want that I come back inside of half an hour with the nine hundred pesos."

"You've got zeros on the brain," the colonel said. "You're already betting with the money from the rooster."

It took a lot of trouble for him to dissuade her. She had spent the morning mentally organizing the budget for the next three years without their Friday agony. She had made a list of the essentials they needed, without forgetting a pair of new shoes for the colonel. She set aside a place in the bedroom for the mirror. The momentary frustration of her plans left her with a confused sensation of shame and resentment.

She took a short siesta. When she got up, the colonel was sitting in the patio.

"Now what are you doing?" she asked.

"I'm thinking," the colonel said.

"Then the problem is solved. We will be able to count on that money fifty years from now."

But in reality the colonel had decided to sell the rooster that very afternoon. He thought of Sabas, alone in his office, preparing himself for his daily injection in front of the electric fan. He had his answer ready.

"Take the rooster," his wife advised him as he went out. "Seeing him in the flesh will work a miracle."

The colonel objected. She followed him to the front door with desperate anxiety.

"It doesn't matter if the whole army is in the office," she said. "You grab him by the arm and don't let him move until he gives you the nine hundred pesos."

"They'll think we're planning a hold-up."

She paid no attention.

"Remember that you are the owner of the rooster," she insisted. "Remember that you are the one who's going to do him the favor."

"All right."

Sabas was in the bedroom with the doctor. "Now's your chance, friend," his wife said to the colonel. "The doctor is getting him ready to travel to the ranch, and he's not coming back until Thursday." The colonel struggled with two opposing forces; in spite of his determination to sell the rooster, he wished he had arrived an hour later and missed Sabas.

"I can wait," he said.

But the woman insisted. She led him to the bedroom where her husband was seated on the throne-like bed, in his underwear, his colorless eyes fixed on the doctor. The colonel waited until the doctor had heated the glass tube with the patient's urine, sniffed the odor, and made an approving gesture at Sabas.

"We'll have to shoot him," the doctor said, turning to the colonel. "Diabetes is too slow for finishing off the wealthy."

"You've already done your best with your damned insulin injections," said Sabas, and he gave a jump on his flaccid buttocks. "But I'm a hard nut to crack." And then, to the colonel:

"Come in, friend. When I went out to look for you this afternoon, I couldn't even see your hat."

"I don't wear one, so I won't have to take it off for anyone."

Sabas began to get dressed. The doctor put a glass tube with a blood sample in his jacket pocket. Then he straightened out the things in his bag. The colonel thought he was getting ready to leave.

"If I were in your shoes, I'd send my friend a bill for a hundred thousand pesos, Doctor," the colonel said. "That way he wouldn't be so worried."

"I've already suggested that to him, but for a million," the doctor said. "Poverty is the best cure for diabetes."

"Thanks for the prescription," said Sabas, trying to stuff his voluminous belly into his riding breeches. "But I won't accept it, to save you from the catastrophe of becoming rich." The doctor saw his own teeth reflected in the little chromed lock of his bag. He looked at the clock without showing impatience. Sabas, putting on his boots, suddenly turned to the colonel:

"Well, friend, what's happening with the rooster?"

The colonel realized that the doctor was also waiting for his answer. He clenched his teeth.

"Nothing, friend," he murmured. "I've come to sell him to you."

Sabas finished putting on his boots.

"Fine, my friend," he said without emotion. "It's the most sensible thing that could have occurred to you."

"I'm too old now for these complications," the colonel said to justify himself before the doctor's impenetrable expression. "If I were twenty years younger it would be different."

"You'll always be twenty years younger," the doctor replied.

The colonel regained his breath. He waited for Sabas to say something more, but he didn't. Sabas put on a leather zippered jacket and got ready to leave the bedroom.

"If you like, we'll talk about it next week, friend," the colonel said.

"That's what I was going to say," said Sabas. "I have a customer who might give you four hundred pesos. But we have to wait till Thursday."

"How much?" the doctor asked.

"Four hundred pesos."

"I had heard someone say that he was worth a lot more," the doctor said.

"You were talking in terms of nine hundred pesos," the colonel said, backed by the doctor's perplexity. "He's the best rooster in the whole province."

Sabas answered the doctor.

"At some other time, anyone would have paid a thousand," he explained. "But now no one dares pit a good rooster. There's always the danger he'll come out of the pit shot to death." He turned to the colonel, feigning disappointment:

"That's what I wanted to tell you, friend."

The colonel nodded.

"Fine," he said.

He followed him down the hall. The doctor stayed in the living room, detained by Sabas's wife, who asked him for a remedy "for those things which come over one suddenly and which one doesn't know what they are." The colonel waited for him in the office. Sabas opened the safe, stuffed money into all his pockets, and held out four bills to the colonel.

"There's sixty pesos, friend," he said. "When the rooster is sold we'll settle up."

The colonel walked with the doctor past the stalls at the waterfront, which were beginning to revive in the cool of the afternoon. A barge loaded wtih sugar cane was moving down the thread of current. The colonel found the doctor strangely impervious.

"And you, how are you, Doctor?"

The doctor shrugged.

"As usual," he said. "I think I need a doctor."

"It's the winter," the colonel said. "It eats away my insides."

The doctor examined him with a look absolutely devoid of any professional interest. In succession he greeted the Syrians seated at the doors of their shops. At the door of the doctor's office, the colonel expressed his opinion of the sale of the rooster.

"I couldn't do anything else," he explained. "That animal feeds on human flesh."

"The only animal who feeds on human flesh is Sabas," the doctor said. "I'm sure he'd resell the rooster for the nine hundred pesos."

"You think so?"

"I'm sure of it," the doctor said. "It's as sweet a deal as his famous patriotic pact with the Mayor."

The colonel refused to believe it. "My friend made that pact to save his skin," he said. "That's how he could stay in town."

"And that's how he could buy the property of his fellow-partisans whom the Mayor kicked out at half the price," the doctor replied. He knocked on the door, since he didn't find his keys in his pockets. Then he faced the colonel's disbelief.

"Don't be so naïve," he said. "Sabas is much more interested in money than in his own skin."

The colonel's wife went shopping that night. He accompanied her to the Syrians' stalls, pondering the doctor's revelations.

"Find the boys immediately and tell them that the rooster is sold," she told him. "We mustn't leave them with any hopes."

"The rooster won't be sold until my friend Sabas comes back," the colonel answered.

He found Alvaro playing roulette in the pool hall. The place was sweltering on Sunday night. The heat seemed more intense because of the vibrations of the radio turned up full blast. The colonel amused himself with the brightly colored numbers painted on a large black oilcloth cover and lit by an oil lantern placed on a box in the center of the table. Alvaro insisted on losing on twenty-three. Following the game over his shoulder, the colonel observed that the eleven turned up four times in nine spins.

"Bet on eleven," he whispered into Alvaro's ear. "It's the one coming up most."

Alvaro examined the table. He didn't bet on the next spin. He took some money out of his pants pocket, and with it a sheet of paper. He gave the paper to the colonel under the table.

"It's from Agustín," he said.

The colonel put the clandestine note in his pocket. Alvaro bet heavily on the eleven.

"Start with just a little," the colonel said.

"It may be a good hunch," Alvaro replied. A group of neighboring players took their bets off the other numbers and bet on eleven after the enormous colored wheel had already begun to turn. The colonel felt oppressed. For the first time he felt the fascination, agitation, and bitterness of gambling.

The five won.

"I'm sorry," the colonel said, ashamed, and, with an irresistible feeling of guilt, followed the little wooden rake which pulled in Alvaro's money. "That's what I get for butting into what doesn't concern me."

Alvaro smiled without looking at him.

"Don't worry, Colonel. Trust to love."

The trumpets playing a mambo were suddenly interrupted. The gamblers scattered with their hands in the air. The colonel felt the dry snap, articulate and cold, of a rifle being cocked behind his back. He realized that he had been caught fatally in a police raid with the clandestine paper in his pocket. He turned halfway around without raising his hands. And then he saw, close up, for the first time in his life, the man who had shot his son. The man was directly in front of him, with his rifle barrel aimed at the colonel's belly. He was small, Indian-looking, with weather-beaten skin, and his breath smelled like a child's. The colonel gritted his teeth and gently pushed the rifle barrel away with the tips of his fingers.

"Excuse me," he said.

He confronted two round little bat eyes. In an instant, he felt himself being swallowed up by those eyes, crushed, digested, and expelled immediately.

"You may go, Colonel."

He didn't need to open the window to tell it was December. He knew it in his bones when he was cutting up the fruit for the rooster's breakfast in the kitchen. Then he opened the door and the sight of the patio confirmed his feeling. It was a marvelous patio, with the grass and the trees, and the cubicle with the privy floating in the clear air, one millimeter above the ground.

His wife stayed in bed until nine. When she appeared in the kitchen, the colonel had already straightened up the house and was talking to the children in a circle around the rooster. She had to make a detour to get to the stove.

"Get out of the way!" she shouted. She glowered in the animal's direction. "I don't know when I'll ever get rid of that evil-omened bird."

The colonel regarded his wife's mood over the rooster. Nothing about the rooster deserved resentment. He was ready for training. His neck and his feathered purple thighs, his saw-toothed crest: the animal had taken on a slender figure, a defenseless air.

"Lean out the window and forget the rooster," the colonel said when the children left. "On mornings like this, one feels like having a picture taken."

She leaned out the window but her face betrayed no emotion. "I would like to plant the roses," she said, returning to the stove. The colonel hung the mirror on the hook to shave.

"If you want to plant the roses, go ahead," he said.

He tried to make his movements match those in the mirror.

"The pigs eat them up," she said.

"All the better," the colonel said. "Pigs fattened on roses ought to taste very good."

He looked for his wife in the mirror and noticed that she still had the same expression. By the light of the fire her face seemed to be formed of the same material as the stove. Without noticing, his eyes fixed on her, the colonel continued shaving himself by touch as he had done for many years. The woman thought, in a long silence.

"But I don't want to plant them," she said.

"Fine," said the colonel. "Then don't plant them."

He felt well. December had shriveled the flora in his gut. He suffered a disappointment that morning trying to put on his new shoes. But after trying several times he realized that it was a wasted effort, and put on his patent-leather ones. His wife noticed the change.

"If you don't put on the new ones you'll never break them in," she said.

"They're shoes for a cripple," the colonel protested. "They ought to sell shoes that have already been worn for a month."

He went into the street stimulated by the presentiment that the letter would arrive that afternoon. Since it still was not time for the launches, he waited for Sabas in his office. But they informed him that he wouldn't be back until Monday. He didn't lose his patience despite not having foreseen this setback. "Sooner or later he has to come back," he told himself, and he headed for the harbor; it was a marvelous moment, a moment of still-unblemished clarity.

"The whole year ought to be December," he murmured, seated in the store of Moses the Syrian. "One feels as if he were made of glass."

Moses the Syrian had to make an effort to translate the idea into his almost forgotten Arabic. He was a placid Oriental, encased up to his ears in smooth, stretched skin, and he had the clumsy movements of a drowned man. In fact, he seemed as if he had just been rescued from the water.

"That's the way it was before," he said. "If it were the same now, I would be eight hundred and ninety-seven years old. And you?"

"Seventy-five," said the colonel, his eyes pursuing the postmaster. Only then did he discover the circus. He recognized the patched tent on the roof of the mail boat amid a pile of colored objects. For a second he lost the postmaster while he looked for the wild animals among the crates piled up on the other launches. He didn't find them.

"It's a circus," he said. "It's the first one that's come in ten years."

Moses the Syrian verified his report. He spoke to his wife in a pidgin of Arabic and Spanish. She replied from the back of the store. He made a comment to himself, and then translated his worry for the colonel.

"Hide your cat, Colonel. The boys will steal it to sell it to the circus."

The colonel was getting ready to follow the postmaster.

"It's not a wild-animal show," he said.

"It doesn't matter," the Syrian replied. "The tightrope walkers eat cats so they won't break their bones."

He followed the postmaster through the stalls at the waterfront to the plaza. There the loud clamor from the cockfight took him by surprise. A passer-by said something to him about his rooster. Only then did he remember that this was the day set for the trials.

He passed the post office. A moment later he had sunk into the turbulent atmosphere of the pit. He saw his rooster in the middle of the pit, alone, defenseless, his spurs wrapped in rags, with something like fear visible in the trembling of his feet. His adversary was a sad ashen rooster.

The colonel felt no emotion. There was a succession of identical attacks. A momentary engagement of feathers and feet and necks in the middle of an enthusiastic ovation. Knocked against the planks of the barrier, the adversary did a somersault and returned to the attack. His rooster didn't attack. He rebuffed every attack, and landed again in exactly the same spot. But now his feet weren't trembling.

Hernán jumped the barrier, picked him up with both hands, and showed him to the crowd in the stands. There was a frenetic explosion of applause and shouting. The colonel noticed the disproportion between the enthusiasm of the applause and the intensity of the fight. It seemed to him a farce to which—voluntarily and consciously—the roosters had also lent themselves.

Impelled by a slightly disdainful curiosity, he examined the circular pit. An excited crowd was hurtling down the stands toward the pit. The colonel observed the confusion of hot, anxious, terribly alive faces. They were new people. All the new people in town. He relived—with foreboding—an instant which had been erased on the edge of his memory. Then he leaped the barrier, made his way through the packed crowd in the pit, and confronted Hernán's calm eyes. They looked at each other without blinking.

"Good afternoon, Colonel."

The colonel took the rooster away from him. "Good afternoon," he muttered. And he said nothing more because the warm deep throbbing of the animal made him shudder. He thought that he had never had such an alive thing in his hands before.

"You weren't at home," Hernán said, confused.

A new ovation interrupted him. The colonel felt intimidated. He made his way again, without looking at anybody, stunned by the applause and the shouts, and went into the street with his rooster under his arm.

The whole town—the lower-class people—came out to watch him go by followed by the school children. A gigantic Negro standing on a table with a snake wrapped around his neck was selling medicine without a license at a corner of the plaza. A large group returning from the harbor had stopped to listen to his spiel. But when the colonel passed with the rooster, their attention shifted to him. The way home had never been so long.

He had no regrets. For a long time the town had lain in a sort of stupor, ravaged by ten years of history. That afternoon—another Friday without a letter—the people had awakened. The colonel remembered another era. He saw himself with his wife and his son watching under an umbrella a show which was not interrupted despite the rain. He remembered the party's leaders, scrupulously groomed, fanning themselves to the beat of the music in the patio of his house. He almost relived the painful resonance of the bass drum in his intestines.

He walked along the street parallel to the harbor and there, too, found the tumultuous Election Sunday crowd of long ago. They were watching the circus unloading. From inside a tent, a woman shouted something about the rooster. He continued home, self-absorbed, still hearing scattered voices, as if the remnants of the ovation in the pit were pursuing him.

At the door he addressed the children:

"Everyone go home," he said. "Anyone who comes in will leave with a hiding."

He barred the door and went straight into the kitchen. His wife came out of the bedroom choking.

"They took it by force," she said, sobbing. "I told them that the rooster would not leave this house while I was alive." The colonel tied the rooster to the leg of the stove. He changed the water in the can, pursued by his wife's frantic voice.

"They said they would take it over our dead bodies," she said. "They said the rooster didn't belong to us but to the whole town."

Only when he finished with the rooster did the colonel turn to the contorted face of his wife. He discovered, without surprise, that it produced neither remorse nor compassion in him.

"They did the right thing," he said quietly. And then, looking through his pockets, he added with a sort of bottomless sweetness:

"The rooster's not for sale."

She followed him to the bedroom. She felt him to be completely human, but untouchable, as if she were seeing him on a movie screen. The colonel took a roll of bills out of the closet, added what he had in his pockets to it, counted the total, and put it back in the closet.

"There are twenty-nine pesos to return to my friend Sabas," he said. "He'll get the rest when the pension arrives."

"And if it doesn't arrive?" the woman asked.

"It will."

"But if it doesn't?"

"Well, then, he won't get paid."

He found his new shoes under the bed. He went back to the closet for the box, cleaned the soles with a rag, and put the shoes in the box, just as his wife had brought them Sunday night. She didn't move.

"The shoes go back," the colonel said. "That's thirteen pesos more for my friend."

"They won't take them back," she said.

"They have to take them back," the colonel replied. "I've only put them on twice."

"The Turks don't understand such things," the woman said.

"They have to understand."

"And if they don't?"

"Well, then, they don't."

They went to bed without eating. The colonel waited for his wife to finish her rosary to turn out the lamp. But he couldn't sleep. He heard the bells for the movie classifications, and almost at once— three hours later—the curfew. The gravelly breathing of his wife became anguished with the chilly night air. The colonel still had his eyes open when she spoke to him in a calm, conciliatory voice:

"You're awake."

"Yes."

"Try to listen to reason," the woman said. "Talk to my friend Sabas tomorrow."

"He's not coming back until Monday."

"Better," said the woman. "That way you'll have three days to think about what you're going to say."

"There's nothing to think about," the colonel said.

A pleasant coolness had taken the place of the viscous air of October. The colonel recognized December again in the timetable of the plovers. When it struck two, he still hadn't been able to fall asleep. But he knew that his wife was also awake. He tried to change his position in the hammock.

"You can't sleep," the woman said.

"No."

She thought for a moment.

"We're in no condition to do that," she said. "Just think how much four hundred pesos in one lump sum is."

"It won't be long now till the pension comes," the colonel said.

"You've been saying the same thing for fifteen years."

"That's why," the colonel said. "It can't be much longer now."

She was silent. But when she spoke again, it didn't seem to the colonel as if any time had passed at all.

"I have the impression the money will never arrive," the woman said.

"It will."

"And if it doesn't?"

He couldn't find his voice to answer. At the first crowing of the rooster he was struck by reality, but he sank back again into a dense, safe, remorseless sleep. When he awoke, the sun was already high in the sky. His wife was sleeping. The colonel methodically repeated his morning activities, two hours behind schedule, and waited for his wife to eat breakfast.

She was uncommunicative when she awoke. They said good morning, and they sat down to eat in silence. The colonel sipped a cup of black coffee and had a piece of cheese and a sweet roll. He spent the whole morning in the tailor shop. At one o'clock he returned home and found his wife mending clothes among the begonias.

"It's lunchtime," he said.

"There is no lunch."

He shrugged. He tried to block up the holes in the patio wall to prevent the children from coming into the kitchen. When he came back into the hall, lunch was on the table.

During the course of lunch, the colonel realized that his wife was making an effort not to cry. This certainly alarmed him. He knew his wife's character, naturally hard, and hardened even more by forty years of bitterness. The death of her son had not wrung a single tear out of her.

He fixed a reproving look directly on her eyes. She bit her lips, dried her eyelids on her sleeve, and continued eating lunch.

"You have no consideration," she said.

The colonel didn't speak.

"You're wilful, stubborn, and inconsiderate," she repeated. She crossed her knife and fork on the plate, but immediately rectified their positions superstitiously. "An entire lifetime eating dirt just so that now it turns out that I deserve less consideration than a rooster."

"That's different," the colonel said.

"It's the same thing," the woman replied. "You ought to realize that I'm dying; this thing I have is not a sickness but a slow death."

The colonel didn't speak until he finished eating his lunch.

"If the doctor guarantees me that by selling the rooster you'll get rid of your asthma, I'll sell him immediately," he said. "But if not, not."

That afternoon he took the rooster to the pit. On his return he found his wife on the verge of an attack. She was walking up and down the hall, her hair down her back, her arms spread wide apart, trying to catch her breath above the whistling in her lungs. She was there until early evening. Then she went to bed without speaking to her husband.

She mouthed prayers until a little after curfew. Then the colonel got ready to put out the lamp. But she objected.

"I don't want to die in the dark," she said.

The colonel left the lamp on the floor. He began to feel exhausted. He wished he could forget everything, sleep forty-four days in one stretch, and wake up on January 20th at three in the afternoon, in the pit, and at the exact moment to let the rooster loose. But he felt himself threatened by the sleeplessness of his wife.

"It's the same story as always," he began a moment later. "We put up with hunger so others can eat. It's been the same story for forty years."

The colonel kept silent until his wife paused to ask him if he was awake. He answered that he was. The woman continued in a smooth, fluent, implacable tone.

"Everybody will win with the rooster except us. We're the only ones who don't have a cent to bet."

"The owner of the rooster is entitled to twenty per cent."

"You were also entitled to get a position when they made you break your back for them in the elections," the woman replied. "You were also entitled to a veteran's pension after risking your neck in the civil war. Now everyone has his future assured and you're dying of hunger, completely alone."

"I'm not alone," the colonel said.

He tried to explain, but sleep overtook him. She kept talking dully until she realized that her husband was sleeping. Then she got out of the mosquito net and walked up and down the living room in the darkness. There she continued talking. The colonel called her at dawn.

She appeared at the door, ghostlike, illuminated from below by the lamp which was almost out. She put it out before getting into the mosquito netting. But she kept talking.

"We're going to do one thing," the colonel interrupted her.

"The only thing we can do is sell the rooster," said the woman.

"We can also sell the clock."

"They won't buy it."

"Tomorrow I'll try to see if Alvaro will give me the forty pesos."

"He won't give them to you."

"Then we'll sell the picture."

When the woman spoke again, she was outside the mosquito net again. The colonel smelled her breath impregnated with medicinal herbs.

"They won't buy it," she said.

"We'll see," the colonel said gently, without a trace of change in his voice. "Now, go to sleep. If we can't sell anything tomorrow, we'll think of something else."

He tried to keep his eyes open but sleep broke his resolve. He fell to the bottom of a substance without time and without space, where the words of his wife had a different significance. But a moment later he felt himself being shaken by the shoulder.

"Answer me."

The colonel didn't know if he had heard those words before or after he had slept. Dawn was breaking. The window stood out in Sunday's green clarity. He thought he had a fever. His eyes burned and he had to make a great effort to clear his head.

"What will we do if we can't sell anything?" the woman repeated.

"By then it will be January 20th," the colonel said, completely awake. "They'll pay the twenty per cent that very afternoon."

"If the rooster wins," the woman said. "But if he loses. It hasn't occurred to you that the rooster might lose."

"He's one rooster that can't lose."

"But suppose he loses."

"There are still forty-four days left to begin to think about that," the colonel said.

The woman lost her patience.

"And meanwhile what do we eat?" she asked, and seized the colonel by the collar of his flannel night shirt. She shook him hard.

It had taken the colonel seventy-five years—the seventy-five years of his life, minute by minute—to reach this moment. He felt pure, explicit, invincible at the moment when he replied:

"Shit."

DORIS LESSING

The Temptation
of Jack Orkney

Introduction

My name is Jack Orkney. I'm the main character in Doris Lessing's novel, *The Temptation of Jack Orkney*. Most literary critics seem to think that characters in novels and stories have no existence before the opening page or beyond the last one. But I deny that. There obviously are great characters of literature —Don Quixote, Faust, Captain Ahab, Ivan Karamazov—who seem to "exist" outside the works in which they first appeared; they have become, you might say, shared possessions of the human imagination. And while I'm not claiming that Ms. Lessing has drawn me as vividly or profoundly as the characters I've just mentioned, still, here I am, a reasonably familiar type of twentieth century Englishman.

There's also a precedent for my "stepping out" of my own story, so to speak. Earlier in our century a brilliant Italian dramatist named Luigi Pirandello wrote a play called *Six Characters in Search of an Author*, in which the six characters step out of the play to speak as individuals in their own right or, if your prefer, as potentialities that Pirandello did not entirely fulfill. They comment on what Pirandello has done with them, and they complain too. That's what I propose to do here—comment and complain.

The novella in which I appear is entirely interwoven with contemporary history. It bears the stamp of a particular moment, and its characters speak in the tone and accents that were then dominant. This is not one of those works of fiction which one can call "timeless" or "eternal." Its action occurs in 1970 or 1971, slightly before India defeated Pakistan in a war that helped create the new nation of Bangladesh. Some of us in England were upset by the brutality with which Pakistan had treated its former province of Bangladesh, and were glad when Bangladesh became an independent country. I suppose that you chaps in America have only a vague idea of where Bangladesh is, and you may wonder why people like myself in England cared enough to undertake a twenty-four-hour fast. Well, that's the sort we were. We worried about the fate of the world, or at least persuaded ourselves that we were worried. Some of us were socialists, others pacifists, still others a bewildering range of free-lance radicals. If you like, you might call us idealists; if not, you might call us busy-bodies; and if you wanted really to be fair, you could say we were something of both. Evidently, that's the way Doris Lessing saw us— at least until a certain point in the story that I'll get to later. She herself, by the way, came out of a similar political milieu.

I had spent most of my life as a public man. Being a public man meant traveling around the world as a reporter and sometimes participant in civil wars and revolutions; it meant making speeches at innumerable meetings (half my life seems to have been spent at those meetings); it meant going to conferences, writing reports, turning out articles. Even now, when I've begun to change, I still think that this wasn't a bad life, and I think it also fair to say that I led this life out of genuine convictions. Still, *because every kind of life has within it the danger of becoming too self-satisfied and therefore blind to other possibilities,* I began to sink into the motions of routine. It was a satisfying routine, perhaps too satisfying, for as I now see it, I was gradually succumbing to the vanity of the more-or-less successful public man, succumbing even to that lust for power which is the great curse of public life. As I reached my early fifties, I began to get depressed, I felt that I was gasping for air, and without quite knowing why, I had increasing difficulty in falling asleep. You might call it a mid-life crisis, one that, in my case, combined public and private, ideological and intimate problems. Now this part of my experience Doris Lessing has captured very well: she really knows what it's like— perhaps because she herself has gone through it—to find all your long-held certainties crumbling in your hands.

Then came the news of my father dying. I hadn't been very close to him all those years—I hadn't been close to anyone, except maybe one or two of the women with whom I had love affairs. Still, it's now obvious to me that my father played more of a role in my inner life than I was ready to admit. So I went up to the town in which he lived, thinking that the unavoidable reunion with my family would work out pretty much according to my thoughtless expectations. I was wrong. I expected my brother and sister, good middle-class people, to be boring, trite, and utterly conventional. But they had changed over the years, and they were by no means the conventionally pious folk that I thought they would be, my sister, in fact, displaying an aliveness and sensitivity that surprised me. The point is that I had gotten to be as rigid and predictable in my personal responses as in my political responses. For I didn't recognize that even ordinary people, the kind who never get written up in newspapers or invited to conferences, can also grow and develop as human beings. After seeing my brother and sister again I felt a bit like a fool.

Then there was my niece Ann, who found a path to my father I no longer could take, perhaps didn't even want to take. It made me uneasy to hear her singing those hymns to the old man; well, all right, let me admit it: I felt a little jealous too. Now all this, if I say so myself, Doris Lessing handles beautifully. She has a way of getting under my skin, knowing intuitively how I thought and felt during that difficult time—which is no small achievement for a writer. In rather blunt but effective language she shows how people approach one another with hardened notions—fixed expectations of class, status, sex—and then become a bit rattled to discover that in actuality each human being is a little more individual, nuanced, unpredictable. Lessing doesn't strike me as the kind of writer whose strength is probing into the depths of a character's psyche, though who knows, maybe she got as deeply into my psyche as she needed to for the purposes of this novella. (Maybe I didn't even have any more depths for her to probe . . .) In fact, it was perhaps the crusted shallowness of my life that really interested her most. I think she also caught my sister Ellen and brother Cedric pretty well, and Ann too, that neat little body who seemed to feel she had Jesus in the palm of her hand. (For all I know, she did.)

Anyway, the story now enters its first crisis. My father's death caused a loosening up in me of feelings that had been suppressed for a long time. To know that there's no longer anyone in the family from the previous generation, to realize that you are now next in line at the door marked "exit," can be a strange, somewhat frightening experience.

All that remained of my dad was memory, guilt, and those dreams, really nightmares, that meshed memory and guilt. Here, for the first time, I have to "talk back" to Doris Lessing and wonder whether she got things exactly right. It must be very hard for a writer to describe dreams convincingly—at least as hard as it is for most of us to remember dreams—since by their very nature dreams are imprecise, chaotic, full of inner contradiction, and soon blurred. So I wonder whether the dreams Doris Lessing says I had don't come out a little too pat, overly simplified. But then, maybe a writer who describes dreams *has* to engage in some degree of simplification.

To keep returning to those nightmares of mine was probably essential for Ms. Lessing in order to make clear the central theme of the novella. For this was her way of trying to show what was *really* happening to me: a change of life that went deeper than mere opinions. The dreams represented, I guess, long-suppressed impulses and desires of my inner being; they reflected, in their grotesque way, the needs of my inner life; they spoke for the Jack Orkney who was more than that familiar public figure but was also a man of erupting desires, needs, frustrations. So Lessing took a risk in using those dreams repeatedly in the story, but a risk she probably could not avoid. Even if some of the dreams aren't individually so vivid or persuasive, it may not matter in considering the action as a whole, since they do succeed in suggesting the depth and intensity of my unheaval. Long-buried feelings started to pour out, with a strength that broke past any impulse I might have had to block them. And of course, as Lessing understood, it was my father's death that triggered the whole crisis. I think she manages nicely here the relation between private and public difficulties.

But now I'm going to be a little more critical of the author who created me. Once she gets to that twenty-four-hour fast and my complicated relations to the Old Guard (that loose gang of old friends who had been steady campaigners in left-wing causes), I think she loses her grip, maybe her cool also. By contrast, when she writes about my charming daughters and their friends, Lessing is quite wonderful. Her eye is keen and her heart is open. She shows nice touches of humor, capturing the charm of Carrie and Liz, their dewy innocence, their fondness for brightly-colored clothes, their openness to people, and, not least of all, their limited intellectual capacities. Because she writes about these young people without excessive involvement, she can be affectionate, humorous, and objective. But when she gets to my friends, to the Old Guard and especially Walter, she grows irritable, even at a few points malicious. She loses her calm, as if she were now intent upon settling some scores with remembered friends of *her* Old Guard. That's her business, but it mars my story. I think of a few examples:

✦ *Ms. Lessing seems really to have it in for poor old Walter, making him into some sort of inhuman monster all aglow with the lust for power. I don't doubt that if you were to meet Walter and study him carefully, you'd see things like that in him; but that's not all there is to Walter, or the Walters of this world. He is really more complicated than Ms. Lessing is willing to acknowledge. It's true that his character seems to have a tendency to keep away from intimate difficulties of human life, especially difficulties to which politics has no "answer"—and that this side of him is described well enough. But Walter also has a genuine interest in ideas, a strong concern with justice, a feeling for the public interest. I can't avoid the feeling that there's a touch of vindictiveness in Ms. Lessing's treatment of Walter, something that has more to do with personal memories than literary obligations.*

✦ *Ms. Lessing has her fun in writing about those conferences that left-wing intellectuals used to go in for. OK, it's fair game. But when she resorts to the pat sarcasm of capital letters—describing a conference on ecology as a Conference on Saving Earth from Man—she is making things just a little too easy for herself. There's a touch of spite in her treatment of the Old Guard and it undermines the reader's confidence, I suspect, in her work as a novelist.*

✦ *On a more personal level, Ms. Lessing makes a big to-do about my wish to sound off to the younger generation, telling them to avoid the mistakes of my generation, urging them not to get caught up in sectarian political divisions etc. Well, maybe. It's always a temptation for older people to distribute their wisdom freely to the young. But I don't think I was, or could have been, quite so naïve on this score as she would have me be: after all, I'd been around a long time and knew that divisions of opinion on the left were just as unavoidable as divisions of opinion*

> *everywhere else in modern society. Frankly, I find these*
> *pages a little boring.*

> ✦ *Finally, a difficult problem. I wonder whether Ms. Lessing*
> *doesn't make my changes of thought and feeling seem too*
> *rapid and abrupt. I recall them as slower, more uncertain,*
> *more agonized, which all such changes are likely to be.*
> *Now, a writer has to speed up the pace of narration, first*
> *to avoid boredom and second to move into more interest-*
> *ing and dramatic experiences. Nothing can be shown in*
> *fiction at the pace it has in actual life. Still, I wonder . . .*

Perhaps I'm being unfair. It must be very hard for a writer to describe mental and emotional confusion without making the description itself seem confused. It's not exactly true, however, that I "got religion," as both Ms. Lessing and some of my Old Guard friends seem to feel at various points. If you look at the story closely, you'll see that in her more careful moments Ms. Lessing makes it clear that what was really happening was that I was trying to open myself up to a wider range of experience than I had previously allowed myself to know. In the last page or two, where Ms. Lessing shows me sinking deeply and happily into the unfamiliar terrain of the self, she does me as much justice as any writer could do to a character.

For you Americans at this time, all this business about self-discovery has become something of a platitude, a cliché, and intelligent people among you have apparently come to be repelled by "me-ism" as a form of narcissistic indulgence. But for people like myself, who had surrendered themselves almost entirely to the demands of public life, the question, "Who am I?" was one we seldom asked or answered, and it therefore took on an intense importance and genuine freshness at the point in my life that's described in the last few pages of the novella. "The sleep [that] had become another country, lying just behind [the] daytime one," brought me a bracing, enriching aware-ness. As Ms. Lessing says, behind the face of the "skeptical" public world there "was another one," that of imagination and the inner life, to which I now gave myself with a luxurious new freedom. As for what I discovered in that inner life . . .

The Temptation
of Jack Orkney

His father was dying. It was a telegram, saying also: *you unob-tainable telephone.* He had been on the telephone since seven that morning. It was the housekeeper who had sent the telegram. Did Mrs. Markham not know that she could have asked the telephone authorities to interrupt his conversations for an urgent message? The irritation of the organiser who is manipulating intractable people and events now focussed on Mrs. Markham, but he tried to alleviate it by reminding himself that Mrs. Markham was housekeeper not only to his father but to a dozen other old people.

It had been a long time since he had actually organised some-thing political; others had been happy to organise *him*—his name, his presence, his approval. But an emotional telephone call from an old friend, Walter Kenting, before seven that morning, appealing that they "all" should make a demonstration of some sort about the refugees—the nine million refugees of Bangladesh, this time—and the information that he was the only person available to do the organis-ing, had returned him to a politically active past. Telephoning, he soon discovered that even the small demonstration they envisaged would be circumscribed, because people were saying they could see no point in a demonstration when television, the radio and every news-paper did little else but tell the world about these millions of suf-ferers. What was the point of a dozen or twenty people "sitting down" or "marching" or even being hungry for twenty-four hours in some prominent place? Surely the point of these actions in the past had been to draw public attention to a wrong?

Now the strength of his reaction to Mrs. Markham's inadequacy made him understand that his enthusiastic response to Walter so early that morning had been mostly because of weeks, months, of inactivity. He could not be so exaggerating details if he were not under-employed. He had been making occupation for himself, calling it stocktaking. He had been reading old diaries, articles of his own twenty or more years old, letters of people he had not seen, sometimes, for as long. Immersing himself in his own past had of course been uncomfortable; this is what it had been really like in Korea, Israel, Pretoria, during such-and-such an event: memory had falsified. One knew that it did, but he had believed himself exempt from this law. Every new day of this deliberate evocation of the past had made his own part in it seem less worthwhile, had diminished his purposes and strengths. It was not that he now lacked offers of work, but that he could not make himself respond with the enthusiastic willingness which he believed every job of work needed. Of his many possibilities the one that attracted him most was to teach journalism in a small college in Nigeria, but he could not make up his mind to accept: his wife didn't want to go. Did he want to leave her in England for two years? No; but at one time this certainly would not have been his reaction!

Nor did he want to write another adventure book; in such empty times in the past he had written, under *noms de plume*, novels whose attraction was the descriptions of the countries he had set them in. He had travelled a great deal in his life, often dangerously, in the course of this war or that, as a soldier and as a journalist.

He might also write a serious book of social or political analysis: he had several to his credit.

He could do television work, or return to active journalism.

The thing was that now the three children were through university he did not need to earn so much money.

"Leisure, leisure at last!" he had cried, as so many of his friends were doing, finding themselves similarly placed.

But half a morning's energetic organising was enough to tell him—exactly as his mother had been used to tell him when he was adolescent: "Your trouble is, you haven't got enough to do!"

He sent a telegram to Mrs. Markham: *Arriving train early evening.* Flying would save him an hour; proper feeling would no doubt choose the air, but he needed the train's pace to adjust him for what

was ahead. He rang Walter Kenting to say that with the organising
still undone, urgent family matters were claiming him. Walter was
silent at this, so he said: "Actually, my old man is going to die in
the next couple of days. It has been on the cards for some time."

"I am sorry," said Walter. "I'll try Bill or Mona. I've got to go
to Dublin in fifteen minutes. Are you going to be back by Saturday—
oh of course you don't know." Realising that he was sounding careless or callous, he said: "I do hope things will be all right." This was
worse and he gave up: "You think that a twenty-four-hour fast meets
the bill better than the other possibilities? Is that what most people
feel, do you think?"

"Yes. But I don't think they are as keen as usual."

"Well, of course not, there's too much of bloody everything,
that's why. You could be demonstrating twenty-four hours a day.
Anyway, I've got to get to my plane."

While Jack packed, which he knew so well how to do, in ten
minutes, he remembered that he had a family. Should everyone be
at the deathbed? Oh surely not! He looked for his wife; she was out.
Of course! The children off her hands, she too had made many exclamations about the attractions of leisure, but almost at once she
signed up for a Psychology Course as part of a plan to become a
Family Counsellor. She had left a note for him: "Darling, there's
some cold lamb and salad." He now left a note for her: "Old man
on his way out. See you whenever. Tell girls and Joseph. All my love.
Jack."

On that train he thought of what he was in for. A family reunion, no less. His brother wasn't so bad, but the last time he had
seen Ellen, she had called him a Boy Scout, and he had called her
a Daughter of the British Empire. Considering it a compliment, she
had been left with the advantage. A really dreadful woman, and as
for her husband—surely he wouldn't be there too? He would have to
be, as a man? Where would they all fit in? Certainly not in that tiny
flat. He should have put in his note to Rosemary that she should
telephone hotels in S———. Would the other grandchildren be there?
Well, Cedric and Ellen would be certain to do the right thing, whatever that was: as for himself, he could telephone home when he had
found what the protocol was. But good God, surely it was bad
enough that three of them, grownup and intelligent people—
grownup, anyway, were going to have to sit about waiting, in a deathbed scene, because of—superstition. Yes, that was what it was. Certainly no more than outdated social custom. And it all might go on

for days. But perhaps the old man would be pleased? At the approach of a phrase similar to those suitable for deaths and funerals, he felt irritation again: this would lead, unless he watched himself, to self-mockery, the spirit of farce. Farce was implicit, anyway, in a situation which had himself, Ellen and Cedric in one room.

Probably the old man wasn't even conscious. He should have telephoned Mrs. Markham before rushing off like—well, like a journalist, with two pairs of socks, a spare shirt, and a sweater. He should have bought a black tie? Would the old man have wished it? Jack noted the arrival of an indubitably "suitable" phrase, and feared worse for the immediate future.

The old man had not worn black or altered his cheerfulness when his wife died.

His wife, Jack's mother.

The depression that he had suspected was in wait for him now descended. He understood that he had been depressed for some time; this was like dark coming down into a fog. He had not admitted that he was depressed, but he ought to have known it by the fact that what he had woken up to each morning was not his own expectation of usefulness or accomplishment, but his wife's.

Now, if Rosemary died . . . but he would not think about that; it would be morbid.

When his mother died, his father had made the simplest of funerals for her—religious, of course. All the family, the grandchildren too, had stayed in the old house, together for the first time in years. The old man had behaved like a man who knew that his grief ought not to be inflicted on others. Jack had not been close to his mother; he had not liked her. He was close to no member of the family. He now knew that he loved his wife, but that had not been true until recently. There were his beautiful daughters. There was his son Joseph, who was a chip off the old block—so everyone insisted on saying, though it infuriated Joseph. But they could not meet without quarrelling. That was closeness of a kind?

He ought to have been more attentive, when the mother died, to the old man, who had probably been concealing a good deal behind his mild dignity. Of course! And, looking back ten years, Jack knew that he had known what his father was feeling, had been sympathetic, but had also been embarrassed and unable to give anything of himself—out of fear that more would be asked?—had pretended obtuseness.

The old house was Church property, divided into units for old people who had been good parishioners. None had been friends before going to live there, but now it seemed that they were all close friends, or at least kept each other company in a variety of ways under the eyes of Mrs. Markham, who also lived there, looked after the house, after them. She put flowers in the Church and mended surplices and garments of that sort—she was fifty, poor old thing. Jack now told himself that he was over fifty, although "the baby of the family," and that his sister, Ellen, with whom he was to spend an unknown number of days, was fifty-five, while his boring brother Cedric was older still.

This train was not full and moved pleasantly through England's green and pleasant land. There were two other people in the compartment. Secondclass. Jack traveled secondclass when he could: this was one of the ways he used to check up on himself that he was not getting soft with success—if you could call what he had success. His brother and sister did, but that was the way they looked at life.

One fellow passenger was a middleaged woman, and one a girl of about twenty-three or twenty-four who leaned an elbow on the window ledge and stared at Buckinghamshire, then Berkshire, then Wiltshire, all green and soft on this summery day. Her face was hidden behind glittering yellow hair. Jack classed her as a London secretary on her way home for a family visit, and as the kind of young person he would get on with—that is, like his daughters rather than his son.

He was finding the company of his girls all pleasure and healing. It seemed to him that everything he had looked for in women now flowed generously towards him from Carrie and Elizabeth. It was not that they always approved him, far from it; it was the quality of their beauty that caressed and dandled him. The silk of their hair flattered, their smiles, even when for somebody else, gave him answers to questions that he had been asking of women—so it seemed to him now—all his life.

Though of course he did not see much of them; while living in the same house, upstairs, they led their own lives.

The woman, whom he disliked because she was not young and beautiful—he was aware that he should be ashamed of his reaction, but put this shame onto an agenda for the future—got off the train, and now the girl at the window turned towards him and the rest of the journey was bound to be delightful. He had been right—of course, he was always right about people. She worked in an office in Great Portland Street, and she was going for a visit to her parents—no, she

628 / DORIS LESSING

"got on" with them all right, but she was always pleased to be back in her flat with her friends. She was not a stranger to Jack's world; that is, she was familiar with the names of people whose lives expressed concern for public affairs, public wrong and suffering, and she used the names of his friends with a proprietary air—she had, as it were, eaten them up to form herself, as he, Jack, had in his time swallowed Keir Hardie, Marx, Freud, Morris and the rest. She, those like her, now possessed "the Old Guard," their history, their opinions, their claims. To her, Walter Kenting, Bill, Mona, were like statues on plinths, each representing a degree of opinion. When the time came to give her his own name, he said it was Jack Sebastian, not Jack Orkney, for he knew he would join the pantheon of people who were her parents-in-opinion and, as he had understood, were to be criticised, like parents.

The last time he had been Jack Sebastian was to get him out of a tight spot in Ecuador, during a small revolution; he had escaped prison and possible death by this means.

If he told this girl about that, he knew that as he sat opposite her, she would gaze in judiciously measured admiration at a man retreating from her into history. He listened to her talk about herself, and knew that if things had been otherwise—he meant not his father's dying, but his recently good relations with his wife—he could easily have got off the train with the girl, and persuaded her to spend the rest of her holiday with him, having made excuses to her family. Or he could have met her in London. But all he wanted now was to hear her voice, and to let himself be stimulated by the light from her eyes and her hair.

She got off the train, with a small laughing look that made his heart beat, and she strode off across the platform with her banners of yellow hair streaming behind her, leaving him alone in the brown compartment full of brown air.

At the station he was looking for a taxi when he saw his brother Cedric. A brown suit that discreetly confined a small stomach came towards him. That suit could only clothe a member of the professional classes; it had to be taken into account before the face, which was, as it happened, a mild pale face that had a look on it of duty willingly performed.

Cedric said, in his way of dealing all at once with every possible contingency: "Mrs. Markham said it had to be this train. I came because Ellen has only just come herself; I arrived first."

He had a Rover, dark blue, not new. He and Jack, defined by

this car and particularly accurately in this country town, drove through soothingly ancient streets.

The brothers drove more or less in silence to the church precincts. As they passed in under a thirteenth-century stone archway, Cedric said: "Ellen booked a room for you. It is the Royal Arms, and she and I are there too. It is only five minutes from Father."

They walked in silence over grass to the back door of this solid brick house which the Church devoted to the old. Not as a charity of course. These were the old whose own saved money or whose children could pay for their rooms and for Mrs. Markham. The poor old were elsewhere.

Mrs. Markham came forward from her sittingroom and said: "How do you do, Mr. Orkney?" to Jack, smiling like a hostess at Cedric. "I am sure you would like some tea now," she directed. "I'll bring you some up." She was like the woman on the train. And like Ellen.

He followed his brother up old wooden stairs that gleamed, and smelled of lavender and wax polish. As always happened, the age of the town, and of the habits of the people who lived in it, the smell of tradition, enveloped Jack in well-being; he had to remind himself that he was here for an unpleasant occasion. At the top of the stairs various unmarked doors were the entrances to the lives of four old people. Cedric opened one without knocking, and Jack followed him into a room he had been in twice before on duty visits. It was a smallish but pleasant room with windows overlooking the lawns that surrounded the church.

Sister Ellen, in thick grey tweed, sat knitting. She said: "Oh Jack, there you are, we are all here at last."

Jack sat. Cedric sat. They had to arrange their feet so as not to entangle in the middle of the small floor. They all exchanged news. The main thing that had happened to the three of them was that the children had all grown up.

The grandchildren, eight of them, knew each other, and had complicated relationships: they were a family, unlike their parents.

Mrs. Markham brought tea, of the kind appropriate to this room, this town: scones, butter, jam, comb honey, fruit buns, cherry cake, fruit cake. Also cream. She left giving the three a glance that said: At last it is all as it should be.

Jack asked: "Have you seen him?"

"No," said Cedric, a fraction of a second before Ellen did. It was clear that here was competition for the perfect disposition of his death. Jack was remembering how these two had fought for domination over each other, and over, of course, himself.

"That is to say," said Ellen, "we have seen him, but he was not conscious."

"Another stroke?" asked Jack.

"He had another before Christmas," said Cedric, "but he didn't tell us, he didn't want to worry us."

"I heard about it through Jilly," said Ellen. Jilly was her daughter.

"And I through Ann," said Cedric. Ann was his.

Jack had now to remind himself that these names represented persons, not samples of pretty infancy.

"He is very close to Ann," said Cedric.

"He is fond of Jilly too," said Ellen.

"I suppose there is a nurse in there?" asked Jack. "Oh, of course, there must be."

"There is a day nurse and a night nurse, and they change places at dawn and dusk," said Ellen. "I must say I am glad of this tea. There was no restaurant on the train."

"I wonder if I could see him?" asked Jack, and then corrected it: "I shall go in to see him." He knew, as he spoke, that all the way on the train he had in fact been waiting for the moment when he could walk into the little bedroom, and his father would smile at him and say—he had not been able to imagine what, but it must be something that he had been waiting to hear from him, or from somebody, for years. This surely was the real purpose of coming here? That what he had in fact been expecting was something like a "deathbed scene," with vital advice and mutual comfort, embarrassed him, and he felt that he was stupid. Now he understood that embarrassment was the air of this room: the combat between elder brother and sister was nominal; they skirmished from habit to cover what they felt. Which was that they were in a position not allowed for by their habits of living. Jack had a vision of rapidly running trains—their lives; but they had had to stop the trains, had had to pull the emergency cords, and at great inconvenience to everyone, because of this ill-timed death. Death had to be ill-timed? It was its nature? Why was it felt to be? There was something ridiculous about this scene in which he was trapped: three middleaged children sitting about in one room, idle, thinking of their real lives which stagnated, while in another room an old man lay dying, attended by a strange woman.

"I'm going in," he said, and this time got up, instinctively careful of his head: he was tall in this lowceilinged room.

"Go in without knocking," said Ellen.

"Yes," Cedric confirmed.

Jack stooped under the doorframe. An inappropriate picture had come into his mind. It was of his sister, in a scarlet pinafore and bright blue checkered sleeves, tugging a wooden horse which was held by a pale plump boy. Jack had been scared that when Ellen got the horse a real fight would start. But Cedric held on, lips tight, being jerked by Ellen's tugs as a dog is tugged by the other dog who has fastened his teeth into the bit of meat or the stick. This scene had taken place in the old garden, for it had been enclosed by pink hydrangeas, while gravel had crunched underfoot. They must all have been very young, because Ellen had still been the classic golden-haired beauty; later she became large and ordinary.

What he was really seeing was his father sitting up against high pillows. A young woman in white sat with her hands folded watching the dying man. But he looked asleep. It was only when he saw the healthy young woman that Jack understood that his father had become a small old man: he had definitely shrunk. The room was dark, and it was not until Jack stood immediately above his father that he saw the mouth was open. But what was unexpected was that the eyelids had swelled and were blue, as if decomposition had set in there already. Those bruised lids affected Jack like something in bad taste, like a fart at a formal meal, or when making love of a romantic sort. He looked in appeal at the nurse who said in a normal voice which she did not lower at all: "He did stir a moment ago, but he didn't really come to himself."

Jack nodded, not wanting to break the hush of time that surrounded the bed, and bent lower, trying not to see the dying lids, but remembering what he could of his father's cool, shrewd, judging look. It seemed to him as if the bruised puffs of flesh were trembling, might lift. But his stare did not have the power to rouse his father, and soon Jack straightened himself—cautiously. Where did the Church put its tall old people, he wondered, and backed out of the room, keeping his eyes on the small old man in his striped pyjamas, which showed very clean under a dark grey cardigan that was fastened under the collar with a gold tiepin, giving him a formal, dressed-up look.

"How does he seem?" asked Ellen. She had resumed her knitting.

"Asleep."

"Unconscious," said Cedric.

Jack asserted himself—quite easily, he saw with relief. "He doesn't look unconscious to me. On the contrary, I thought he nearly woke up."

They knew the evening was wearing on: their watches told them so. It remained light; an interminable summer evening filled the sky above the church tower. A young woman came through the room, a coat over her white uniform, and in a moment the other nurse came past them, on her way out.

"I think we might as well have dinner," said Ellen, already folding her knitting.

"Should one of us stay perhaps?" corrected Cedric. He stayed, and Jack had hotel dinner and a bottle of wine with his sister; he didn't dislike being with her as much as he had expected. He was even remembering times when he had been fond of Ellen.

They returned to keep watch, while Cedric took his turn for dinner. At about eleven the doctor came in, disappeared for five minutes into the bedroom, and came out saying that he had given Mr. Orkney an injection. By the time they had thought to ask what the injection was, he had said that his advice was they should all get a good night's sleep, and had gone. Each hesitated before saying that they intended to take the doctor's advice: This situation, traditionally productive of guilt, was doing its work well.

Before they had reached the bottom of the stairs, the nurse came after them: "Mr. Orkney, Mr. Orkney . . ." Both men turned, but she said: "Jack? He was asking for Jack?"

Jack ran up the stairs, through one room, into the other. But it seemed as if the old man had not moved since he had last seen him. The nurse had drawn the curtains, shutting out the sky so full of light, of summer, and had arranged the lamp so that it made a bright space in the dark room. In this was a wooden chair with a green cushion on it, and on the cushion a magazine. The lit space was like the detail of a picture much magnified. The nurse said: "Really, with that injection, he ought not to wake now." She took her place again with the magazine on her lap, inside the circle of light.

Yet he had woken, he had asked for himself, Jack, and for nobody else. Jack was alert, vibrating with his nearness to what his father might say. But he stood helpless, trying to make out the bruises above the eyes, which the shadows were hiding. "I'll stay here the night," he declared, all energy, and strode out, only just remembering to lower his head in time, to tell his sister and his brother, who had come back up the stairs.

"The nurse thinks he is unlikely to wake, but I am sure it would be what he would wish if one of us were to stay."

That he had used another of the obligatory phrases struck Jack with more than amusement: now it was with relief as well. Now the fact that the prescribed phrases made their appearance one after the other was like a guarantee that he was behaving appropriately, that everything would go smoothly and without embarrassment, and that he could expect his father's eyes to appear from behind the corrupted lids—that he would speak the words Jack needed to hear. Cedric and Ellen quite understood, but demanded to be called at once if . . . They went off together across the bright grass towards the hotel.

Jack sat up all night; but there was no night, midsummer swallowed the dark; at midnight the church was still glimmering and people strolled, talking softly, over the lawns. He had skimmed through Trollope's *The Small House at Allington*, and had dipped into a book of his own called *With the Guerrillas of Guatemala*. The name on the spine was Jack Henge, and now he wondered if he had ever told his father that this was one of his *noms de plume*, and he thought that if so, it showed a touching interest on his father's part, but if not, that there must have been some special hidden sympathy shown in the choice or chance that led to its sitting here on the old man's shelves side by side with the complete works of Trollope and George Eliot and Walter Scott. But of course, it was unlikely now that he would ever know. . . . His father had not woken, had not stirred, all night. Once he had tiptoed in, and the nurse had lifted her head and smiled; clearly, though the old man had gone past the divisions of day and night, the living must still adhere to them, for the day nurse had spoken aloud, but now it was night, the nurse whispered: "The injection is working well. You try to rest, Mr. Orkney." Her solicitude for him, beaming out from the bright cave hollowed from the dark of the room, enclosed them together in the night's vigil, and when the day nurse came, and the night nurse went yawning, looking pale, and tucking dark strands of hair as if tidying up after a night's sleep, her smile at Jack was that of a comrade after a shared ordeal.

Almost at once the day nurse came back into the livingroom and said: "Is there someone called Ann?"

"Yes, a granddaughter; he was asking for her?"

"Yes. Now, he was awake for a moment."

Jack suppressed: "He didn't ask for me?"—and ran back into the bedroom, which was now filled with a stuffy light that presented the bruised lids to the nurse and to Jack.

"I'll tell my brother that Ann has been asked for."

Jack walked through fresh morning air that had already brought a few people onto the grass around the church, to the hotel, where he found Cedric and Ellen at breakfast.

He said that no, he had not been wanted, but that Ann was wanted now. Ellen and Cedric conferred and agreed that Ann "could reasonably be expected" never to forgive them if she was not called. Jack saw that these words soothed them both; they were comforting himself. He was now suddenly tired. He drank coffee, refused breakfast, and decided on an hour's sleep. Ellen went to telephone greetings and the news that nothing had changed to her family; Cedric to summon Ann, while Jack wondered if he should telephone Rosemary. But there was nothing to say. He fell on his bed and dreamed, woke, dreamed again, woke, forced himself back to sleep but was driven up out of it to stand in the middle of his hotel room, full of horror. His dreams had been landscapes of dark menacing shapes that were of man's making—metallic, like machines, steeped in a cold grey light, and scattered about on a plain where cold water lay spilled about, gleaming. This water reflected, he knew, death, or news, or information about death, but he stood too far away on the plain to see what pictures lay on its surfaces.

Now, Jack was one of those who did not dream. He prided himself on never dreaming. Of course he had read the "new" information that everyone dreamed every night, but he distrusted this information. For one thing, he shared in the general distrust of science, of its emphatic pronouncements; for another, travelling around the world as he had, he had long ago come to terms with the fact that certain cultures were close to aspects of life which he, Jack, had quite simply forbidden. He had locked a door on them. He knew that some people claimed to see ghosts, feared their dead ancestors, consulted witchdoctors, dreamed dreams. How could he not know? He had lived with them. But he, Jack, was of that part of mankind delivered from all that; he, Jack, did not consult the bones or allow himself to be afraid of the dark. Or dream. He did not dream.

He felt groggy, more than tired: the cold of the dream was undermining him, making him shiver. He got back into bed, for he had slept only an hour, and continued with the same dream. Now he and Walter Kenting were interlopers on that death-filled plain, and they were to be shot, one bullet each, on account of non-specified crimes. He woke again: it was ten minutes later. He decided to stay awake. He bathed, changed his shirt and his socks, washed the shirt and socks he had taken off, and hung them over the bath to drip. Restored by these small ritual acts which he had performed in so many hotel rooms and in so many countries, he ordered fresh coffee, drank it in the spirit of one drinking a tonic or prescribed medicine, and walked back across sunlit grass to the old people's house.

He entered on the scene he had left. Ellen and Cedric sat with their feet almost touching, one knitting and one reading the *Daily Telegraph*. Ellen said: "You haven't slept long." Cedric said: "He asked for you again."

"*What!*" While he had slept, his energies draining into that debilitating dream, he might have heard, at last, what his father wanted to say. "I think I'll sit with him a little."

"That might not be a bad idea," said his sister. Was she annoyed that she had not been "asked for"? If so, she showed no sign of it.

The little sitting room was full of light; sunshine lay on the old wood sills. But the bedroom was dark, warm and smelled of many drugs.

The nurse had the only chair—today just a piece of furniture among many. He made her keep it, and sat down slowly on the bed, as if this slow subsidence could make his weight less.

He kept his eyes on his father's face. Since yesterday the bruises had spread beyond the lids: the flesh all around the eyes and as far down as the cheekbones was stained.

"He has been restless," said the nurse, "but the doctor should be here soon." She spoke as if the doctor could answer any questions that could possibly ever be asked; and Jack, directed by her as he had been by his sister and his brother, now listened for the doctor's coming. The morning went past. His sister came to ask if he would go with her to luncheon. She was hungry, but Cedric was not. Jack said he would stay, and while she was gone the doctor came.

He sat on the bed—Jack had risen from it, retreating to the window. The doctor took the old man's wrist in his hand and seemed to commune with the darkened eyelids. "I rather think that perhaps . . ." He took out a plastic box from his case that held the ingredients of miracle-making: syringes, capsules, methylated spirits.

Jack asked: "What effect does that have?" He wanted to ask: Are you keeping him alive when he should be dead?

The doctor said: "Sedative and painkiller."

"A heart stimulant?"

Now the doctor said: "I have known your father for thirty years." He was saying: I have more right than you have to say what he would have wanted.

Jack had to agree; he had no idea if his father would want to be allowed to die, as nature directed, or whether he would like to be kept alive as long as possible.

The doctor administered an injection, as light and as swift as the strike of a snake, rubbed the puncture with one gentle finger, and said, "Your father looked after himself. He has plenty of life left in him yet."

He went out. Jack looked in protest at the nurse: what on earth had been meant? Was his father not dying? The nurse smiled, timidly, and from that smile Jack gathered that the words had been spoken for his father's sake, in case he was able to hear them, understand them, and be fortified by them.

He saw the nurse's face change; she bent over the old man, and Jack took a long step and was beside her. In the bruised flesh the eyes were open and stared straight up. This was not the human gaze he had been wanting to meet, but a dull glare from chinks in damaged flesh.

"Ann," said the old man. "Is Ann here?"

From the owner of those sullen eyes Jack might expect nothing; as an excuse to leave the room, he said to the nurse, "I'll tell Ann's father."

In the livingroom sunlight had left the sills. Cedric was not there. "It's Ann he wants," Jack said. "He has asked again."

"She is coming. She has to come from Edinburgh. She is with Maureen."

Ellen said this as if he was bound to know who Maureen was. She was probably one of Cedric's ghastly wife's ghastly relations. Thinking of the awfulness of Cedric's wife made him feel kindly towards Ellen. Ellen wasn't really so bad. There she sat, knitting, tired and sad but not showing it. When you came down to it she didn't look all that different from Rosemary—unbelievably also a middle-aged woman. But at this thought Jack's loyalty to the past rebelled. Rosemary, though a large, fresh-faced, greying woman, would never wear a suit which looked as if its edges might cut, or hair set in a helmet of ridges and frills. She wore soft pretty clothes, and her hair was combed straight and long, as she had always worn it: he had begged her to keep it like that. But if you came to think of it, probably the lives the two women led were similar. Probably they were all more alike than any one of them would care to admit. Including Cedric's awful wife.

He looked at Ellen's lids, lowered while she counted stitches. They were her father's eyes and lids. When she lay dying probably her lids would bruise and puff.

Cedric came in. He was very like the old man—more like him than any of them. He, Jack, was more like their mother, but when he was dying perhaps his own lids . . . Ellen looked up, smiled at Cedric, then at Jack. They were all smiling at each other. Ellen laid down her knitting, and lit herself a cigarette. The brothers could see that this was the point when she might cry. But Mrs. Markham came in, followed by a well-brushed man all white cuffs and collar and pink fresh skin.

"The Dean," she breathed, with the smile of a girl.

The Dean said: "No, don't get up. I dropped in. I am an old friend of your father's, you know. Many and many a game of chess have we played in this room . . ." and he had followed Mrs. Markham into the bedroom.

"He had Extreme Unction yesterday," said Ellen.

"Oh," said Jack. "I didn't realise that Extreme Unction was part of his . . ." He stopped, not wanting to hurt feelings. He believed both Ellen and Cedric to be religious.

"He got very High in the end," said Cedric.

Ellen giggled. Jack and Cedric looked enquiry. "It sounded funny," she said. "You know, the young ones talk about getting high."

Cedric's smile was wry: and Jack remembered there had been talk about his elder son, who had threatened to become addicted. What to? Jack could not remember; he would have to ask the girls.

"I suppose he wants a church service and to be buried?" asked Jack.

"Oh yes," said Cedric. "I have got his will."

"Of course, you would have."

"Well, we'll have to get through it all," said Ellen. It occurred to Jack that this was what she probably said, or thought, about her own life: Well, I've just got to get through it. The thought surprised him; Ellen was pleasantly surprising him. Now he heard her say: "Well, I suppose some people have to have religion."

And now Jack looked at her in disbelief.

"Yes," said Cedric, equally improbably, "it must be a comfort for them, one can see that." He laid small strong hands around his crossed knees and made the knuckles crack.

"Oh, Cedric," complained Ellen, as she had as a girl: this knuckle-cracking had been Cedric's way of expressing tension since he had been a small boy.

"Sorry," said Cedric. He went on, letting his hands fall to his sides, and swing there, in a conscious effort toward relaxing himself, "From time to time I take my pulse—as it were. Now that I am getting on for sixty one can expect the symptoms. Am I getting God? Am I still myself? Yes, no, doubtful? But so far, I can report an even keel, I am happy to say."

"Oh one can understand it," said Ellen. "God knows, one can understand it only too well. But I really would be ashamed . . ."

Both Ellen and Cedric were looking to him, to add his agreement of which they were sure, of course. But he could not speak. He had made precisely the same joke a month ago, in a group of "the Old Guard" about taking his pulse to find out if he had caught religion. And everyone had confessed to the same practice. To get God, after a lifetime of enlightened rationalism, would be the most shameful of capitulations.

Now his feelings were the same as those of members of a particularly exclusive Club on being forced to admit the lower classes; or the same as the Victorian Bishop who, travelling to some cannibal-land to baptise the converted, had been heard to say that he could wish that his Church admitted degrees of excellence in its material: he could not believe that his lifetime of impeccable service would weigh the same as those of these so recently benighted ones.

Besides, Jack was shocked: to hear these ideas from Ellen, looking as she did, leading the life she did—she had no right to them! She sounded vulgar.

She was saying: "Of course I do go to church sometimes to please Freddy." Her husband. "But he seems to be losing fervour rather than gaining it, I am glad to say."

"Yes," said Cedric. "I am afraid I have rather the same thing with Muriel. We have compromised on Christmas and Easter. She says it is bad for my image not to be a church-goer. Petersbank is a small place you know, and the good people do like their lawyers and doctors to be pillars of society. But I find that sort of trimming repulsive and I tell her so."

Again they waited for Jack; again he had to be silent. But surely by now they would take his opinions for granted? Why should they? If they could become atheist, then what might he not become? The next thing, they'll turn out to be socialists, he thought. Surely all this godlessness must be a new development? He could have sworn that Ellen had been devout and Cedric correct towards a Church which—as far as Jack had been concerned—had been irritation, humiliation, tedium, throughout his childhood. Even now he could not think of the meaningless services, the Sunday school, the fatuity of the parsons, the social conformity that was associated with the Church, without feeling as if he had escaped from a sticky trap.

Ellen was saying: "As for me, I am afraid I find it harder to believe as I get older. I mean, God, in this terrible world, with new horrors every minute. No, I am afraid it is all too much."

"I quite agree," said Cedric. "The devil's more like it."

"Yes," said Jack, able to speak at last. "Yes, that's about it, I'm afraid." It was the best he could do. The room was now full of good feeling, and they would have begun to talk about their childhood if the bedroom door had not opened, and the Dean come out. The smile he had shed on the nurse was still on his healthy lips, and he now let it benefit the three, while he raised his hand in what looked like a benediction. "No, don't get up!" He was almost at once out of the door, followed close by Mrs. Markham.

The look the three now shared repudiated the Dean and all his works. Ellen smiled at her brother exactly as—he realised in capitulation to a totally unforeseen situation—his own wife would have done. Cedric nodded private comment on the stupidities of mankind.

Soon Cedric went to the bedroom, to return with the report that the old man looked pretty deep in. Then Ellen went and came back saying that she didn't know how the nurse could bear it in that dark room. But as she sat down, she said: "In the old days, one of us would have been in there all the time?"

"Yes," said Cedric. "All of us."

"Not just a nurse," said Ellen. "Not a stranger."

Jack was thinking that if he had stuck it out, then he would have been there when his father called for him, but he said: "I'm glad it is a nurse. I don't think there is very much left of *him*."

Ann arrived. What Jack saw first was a decided, neat little face, and that she wore a green jacket and trousers that were not jeans but "good" as her Aunt Ellen used the word. Ellen always had "good" clothes that lasted a long time. Ann's style was not, for instance, like Jack's daughters', who wore rags and rubbish and cast-offs and who looked enchanting, like princesses in disguise. She kissed her father, because he was waiting for her to do this. She stood examining them with care. Her father could be seen in her during that leisurely, unembarrassed examination: it was both her right and her duty to do this. Now Jack saw that she was small, with a white skin that looked greenish where it was shaded, and hair as pale as her father's had been. Her eyes, like her father's, were green.

She said: "Is he still alive?"

The voice was her father's, and it took her aunt and her uncle back, back—she did not know the reason for their strained, reluctant smiles as they gazed at her.

They were suffering that diminution, that assault on individuality which is the worst of families: some invisible dealer had shuffled noses, hands, shoulders, hair and reassembled them to make—little Ann, for instance. The dealer made out of parts a unit that the owner would feed, maintain, wash, medicate for a lifetime, thinking of it as "mine," except at moments like these, when knowledge was forced home that everyone was put together out of stock.

"Well," said Ann, "you all look dismal enough. Why do you?"

She went into the bedroom, leaving the door open. Jack understood that Ann had principles about attitudes toward death: like his own daughters.

The three crowded into the room.

Ann sat on the bed, high up near the pillow, in a way that hid the old man's face from them. She was leaning forward, the nurse—whom Ann had ignored—ready to intervene.

"Grandad!" she said. "Grandad! It's me!"

Silence. Then it came home to them that the improbable had happened, that she had called up Lazarus. They heard the old man's voice, quite as they remembered it: "It's you, is it? It is little Ann?"

"Yes, Grandad, it's Ann."

They crowded forward, to see over her shoulder. They saw their father, smiling normally. He looked like a tired old man, that was all. His eyes, surrounded by the puffy bruises, had light in them.

"Who are these people?" he asked. "Who are all these tall people?"

The three retreated, leaving the door open.

Silence from the bedroom, then singing. Ann was singing in a small clear voice: All Things Bright and Beautiful.

Jack looked at Cedric, Ellen looked at Cedric. He deprecated: "Yes, I am afraid that she is. That's the bond, you see."

"Oh," said Ellen, "I see, that explains it."

The singing went on:

> *All things bright and beautiful,*
> *All creatures great and small,*
> *All things wise and wonderful,*
> *The Lord God made them all.*

The singing went on, verse after verse, like a lullaby.

"She came to stay with him," said Cedric. "At Easter, I think it was. She slept here, on the floor."

Jack said: "My girls are religious. But not my son of course."

They looked blankly sympathetic; it occurred to Jack that his son's fame was after all circumscribed to a pretty small circle.

"He takes after me," said Jack.

"Ah," said Cedric.

"A lot of them are religious," said Ellen, brisk.

"It's the *kind* of religion that sticks in one's craw," said Jack. "Simple faith and Celtic crosses."

"I agree," said Cedric. "Pretty low-level stuff."

"Does the level matter?" asked Ellen. "Surely *c'est le premier pas qui coûte?*"

At which Jack looked at his sister in a disbelief that was meant to be noticed. Cedric, however, did not seem surprised: of course, he saw Ellen more often. He said mildly: "I don't agree. One wouldn't mind if they went on to something a bit more elevated. It's this servants'-hall village-green mother's-meeting sort of thing. You spend a fortune trying to educate them decently and then it ends up in . . . My eldest was a Jesus freak for a few months, for example. After Winchester, Balliol, the lot."

"What is a Jesus freak?" enquired Ellen.

"What it sounds like."

Normally Jack would have cut out emotionally and mentally at the words "servants' hall," but he was still with them. He said: "What gets me is that they spout it all out, so pat and pretty, you know, and you get the feeling it might be anything, anything they had picked up or lay to hand—*pour épater le bourgeois,* you know." At this he had to think that the other two must be thinking, but were too polite to say, that his own socialism, a degree or two off full communism, when he was in his teens, had had no deeper cause. This unspoken comment brought the conversation to a stop.

The singing had stopped too. It was getting dark.

"Well," said Ellen, "I tell you what I am going to do, I am going to have a bath and then dinner and then a good night's sleep. I think Ann is meeting Father's requirements better than we could."

"Yes," said Cedric.

He went to the door, and communicated this news to his daughter, who said she would be fine, she would be super, she would stay with her grandad, and if she got tired she could sleep on the floor.

Over the dinner table at the hotel, it was a reunion of people who had not met for a long time. They drank some wine, and were sentimental.

But the little time of warmth died with the coffee, served in the hall, which let in draughts from the street every time somebody came in.

Jack said: "I'll turn in, I didn't sleep last night."

"Nor I."

"Nor I."

They nodded at each other; to kiss would have been exaggerated. Jack went upstairs, while Cedric and Ellen went to telephone their families.

In the bedroom he stood by the window and watched how the light filled the lime outside. Breaths of tree-air came to his face. He was full of variegated emotions, none, he was afraid, to do with his father: they were about his brother and his sister, his childhood, that past of his which everything that happened to him these days seemed to evoke, seemed to present to him, sharp, clear, and for the most part painful; he did not feel he could sleep, he was over-stimulated. He would lie on his bed for a rest. Waking much later, to a silence that said the night had deepened all around him, with the heaviness of everybody's sleeping, he started up into a welter of feeling that he could not face, and so burrowed back into sleep again, there to be met by—but it was hard to say what.

Terror was not the word. Nor fear. Yet there were no other words that he knew for the state he found himself in. It was more like a state of acute attention, as if his whole being—memory, body, present and past chemistries—had been assaulted by a warning, so that he had to attend to it. He was standing, as it were, at the alert, listening to something which said: Time is passing, be quick, listen, attend.

It was the knowledge of passing time that was associated with the terror, so that he found himself standing upright in the dark room crying out: "Oh, no, no, no, I understand, I am sorry, I . . ." He was whimpering like a puppy. The dark was solid around him, and he didn't know where he was. He believed himself to be in a grave, and he rushed to the window, throwing it open as if he were heaving a weight off himself. The window was hard to open. At last he forced it, leaning out to let the tree-air come to his face, but it was not air that came in, but a stench, and this smell was confirmation of a failure which had taken place long ago, in some choice of his, that he had now forgotten. The feeling of urgency woke him: he was lying on his bed. Now he really did shoot into the centre of the room, while the smell that had been the air of the dream was fading around him. He was terrified. But that was not the word. . . . He feared that the terror would fade, he would forget what he had dreamed; the knowledge that there was something that had to be done, done soon, would fade, and he would forget even that he had dreamed.

What *had* he dreamed? Something of immense importance.

But as he stood there, with the feeling of urgency draining away and his daytime self coming back, even while he knew, as powerfully as he had ever known anything, that the dream was the most important statement ever made to him, the other half of him was asserting old patterns of thought, which said that to dream was neurotic and to think of death morbid.

He turned on the light, out of habit, a child chasing away night-fears, and then at once switched it off again, since the light was doing its job too well: the dream was dwindling into a small feeling that remarked in a tiny nagging voice that he should be attending to something. And Jack was chasing after the dream: No, no, don't go. . . .

But the feeling of the dream had gone, and he was standing near the window, telling himself—but it was an intellectual statement now, without force—that he had had a warning. A warning? Was it that? By whom? To whom? He must do something . . . but what? *He had been terrified of dying*: he had been forced to be afraid of that. For the first time in his life he had been made to feel the fear of death. He knew that this is what he would feel when he was in his father's position, lying propped on pillows, with people around him waiting for him to die. (If the state of the world would allow his death such a degree of civilisation!)

All his life he had said lightly: Oh, death, I'm not afraid of death; it will be like a candle going out, that's all. On these occasions when, just like his brother Cedric, he checked up on himself for internal weakness, he had said to himself: I shall die, just like a cat or a dog, and too bad, when I die, that's that. He had known the fear of fear of course: he had been a soldier in two wars. He had known what it was to rehearse in his mind all the possible deaths that were available to him, removing pain and horror by making them familiar, and choosing suitable ways of responding—words, postures, silences, stoicisms—that would be a credit to him, to humanity. He knew very well the thought that to be hit over the head like an ox, stunned before the throat was cut, was the highest that he could hope for: annihilation was what he had elected.

But his dream had been horror of annihilation, the threat of nothingness. . . . It already seemed far away. He stretched his arms up behind his head, feeling the strength of his body. *His* body, that was made of fragments of his mother and his father, and of their mothers and their fathers, and shared with little Ann, with his daughters, and of course with his son—exactly like him, his copy. Yes, his, his body, strong, and pulsing with energy—he pushed away the warning from the dream, and switched on the light again, feeling that *that* was over. It was one in the morning, hardly the hour, in an English country hotel, to ask for tea, for coffee. He knew he would not dare to lie again on that bed, so he went down to let himself out. He was going to his father.

Ann was wrapped in blankets, lying on the floor of the living-room. He knelt by her and gazed at the young face, the perfect eyelids that sealed her eyes shut like a baby's, incisive but delicate, shining, whole.

He sat on his father's bed where Ann had sat, and saw that the old man was slipping away. Jack could not have said why he knew, but he did know the death would be this day: it occurred to him that if he had not had that dream, he would not have known; he would not have been equipped to know, without the dream.

He walked the rest of the night away, standing to watch the bulk of the old church dwindling down under a sky lightening with dawn. When the birds began, he returned to the hotel, bathed, and with confidence woke his sister and brother, saying that yes, they could have breakfast but should not take too much time over it.

At eight-thirty they arrived to find Ann again crouched up on the bed near the old man, crooning to him bits of hymn, old tunes, nursery rhymes. He died without opening his eyes again.

Cedric said he would deal with all the arrangements, and that he would notify them of the funeral, which would probably be on Monday. The three children of the old man separated in good feeling and with kisses, saying that they really ought to see more of each other.

And Jack said to Ann that she must come and visit. She said yes, it would be super, she could see Elizabeth and Carrie again, how about next weekend? There was to be a Pray-in for Bangladesh.

Jack returned to his home, or rather, to his wife. She was out. He suppressed grievance that there was no note from her; after all, he had not telephoned. She was at another class, he supposed.

He went to see if anybody was in the girls' flat. Carrie and Elizabeth had made rooms for themselves on the top floor, and paid rent for them. They both had good jobs. There was an attic room used occasionally by Joseph.

Hearing sounds, he knocked, with a sense of intruding, and was bidden to come in by Carrie, who seemed in conflict at the sight of him. This was because she, like the others, had been waiting for his coming, waiting for the news of the death. She had prepared the appropriate responses, but had just finished cooking a meal, and was putting dishes on the table. A young man whose face he did not know was coming towards the table, ready to eat.

Carrie was flushed, her long dark hair fell about, and she was wearing something like a white sack, bordered with deep white lace.

"My father died," he said.

"Oh poor you," said Carrie.

"I don't know," said Jack.

"This is Bob," said Carrie. "My father. Dad, would you like to eat with us? It is a business lunch, actually."

"No, no," said Jack. "I'll see you later." She called after him: "Dad, Dad, I'm sorry about Grandad."

"Oh, he was due to go," Jack called back.

He cut himself bread and cheese, and rang Walter's office. Walter was back from Dublin, but had to fly to Glasgow that afternoon: he was to appear on television in a debate on the Common Market. He would be back by midday Saturday: the Twenty-four-Hour Fast would start at two o'clock Saturday. Thirty people were expected to take part. It was a good thing Jack was back: he could take over again.

But what was there to be done?

Nothing much, really; he should keep a tag on the names; some might decide to drop out again. Considering the scale of the horror at that moment taking place in India, the mass misery, it would be a surprisingly small turn-out—he was sorry, he had to leave, a car was waiting.

It is normal to feel, on returning to the place one lives in, after having been away, that one has not left at all: this is not what Jack was feeling now. Whether it was because he was so tired, or because he was more upset by his father's death than he knew, he felt at a distance from his commonplace self, and particularly at a distance from the Jack Orkney who knew so well how to organise a sit-down, or a march, or how to produce such occasions properly for the Press or television.

Walter's contrasting the numbers of the people involved in the Bangladesh tragedy with the numbers who were prepared not to eat, publicity, for twenty-four hours in London, had struck him as bathos, as absurdity, but he knew that normally that was how he would be reacting himself.

Now he tried to restore himself by summoning well-tried thoughts. Every time the radio or television was turned on, every time you saw a newspaper, the figure *nine million* was used, with the information that these refugees had no future, or none of the normal kind. (India's short, sharp, efficient war that reprieved these same nine million was of course months in the future.) But there was nothing to be done; this catastrophe had the same feeling as the last, which had been Nigeria: a large number of people would die of starvation or would be murdered, but there was no power strong enough to stop this.

It was this feeling of helplessness that seemed to be the new factor; each time there was something of this kind, the numbers of people grew larger, and the general helplessness augmented. Yet all that had happened was that great catastrophes were being brought to general attention more forcefully than in the past. Not long ago, as recently as thirty years, it had been a commonplace for small paragraphs in newspapers to say that six, seven, eight million people had died, were dying of starvation, in China; communism had put an end to famine, or to the world's hearing about it. A very short time ago, a decade, several million might die in a bad season in India; the green revolution had (possibly temporarily) checked that. In Russia millions had died in the course of some great scheme or other: the collectivisation of the peasants, for instance.

The most shocking thing that had happened to his generation was the event summed up by the phrase "six million Jews." Although so many millions of people had been killed or had died in that war, and in a thousand awful ways, it was that one thing, the *six million*, which seemed worst. Because, of course, as everyone knew, it had been willed and deliberate murder. . . . Was it really any more deliberate than the *nine million* of Stalin's forcible collectivisation? And how about that *nine*, or *ninety million*, the figure for the deaths of black men in Africa caused by white men in the course of bringing civilisation to that continent? (This figure, whatever it was, never could accumulate about it the quality of senseless horror that had the figure for the death camps and gas chambers under Hitler. Why not?) During the next twelve months, between *twelve* and *twenty-four* million would die of starvation in the world (the figure depended on the source of calculation). The twelve months after, this figure would double—by the end of a decade, the numbers of people expected to die annually of hunger was beyond calculation. . . . These figures, and many more, clicked through his well-stocked journalist's head, and against them he heard Walter's voice, rather tetchy, critical, saying that there would only be thirty people for the Twenty-four-Hour Fast.

Yes, of course it was ridiculous to think on these lines and particularly when you were tired; he had been thrown off balance worse than he knew. He would sleep for a little—no, no, better not, he would rather not; he would not go to his bed unless Rosemary could be with him. Well, there were things that he ought to be doing, he was sure: for one thing, he had not read the newspapers for three days, nor listened to the news. He regarded it as his responsibility to read all the newspapers every day as if knowing what was bad could prevent worse. He did not want to read the papers; he wanted to sit down and wait quietly for his wife. This made him guilty, and he was associating his reluctance to plunge into the misery and threat of the newspapers with the brutalising of everybody, everyone's acceptance of horror as normal—well, it was, when had storms of blood and destructions *not* swept continuously over the globe?

His will was being attacked: he had no will. This was why he needed to see Rosemary. This thought, he knew, had put a small whimsical grimace onto his face; the grimace was for the benefit of an observer. The observer was himself; it was there for the sake of his pride—a very odd thing had happened between him and his wife. For a long time, in fact for most of the marriage, they would have said that they were unhappily married. It had been a war marriage of course, like those of most of their contemporaries. It had begun in passion, separation, dislocation. They had felt, on beginning to live together for the first time, when they had been married for nearly six years, that their good times had been stolen from them. Then three children: they had turned Rosemary into an obsessed complaining woman; so he had seen her, and so she now saw herself during that period. He was most often out of England, and had many affairs, some of them serious. He knew she had been in love with someone else; she, like himself, had refused to consider a divorce because of the effect on the children. There was of course nothing remarkable in this history; but some of the men he knew had divorced, leaving first wives to bring up children. He knew that many of his friends' wives, like Rosemary, had been obsessed with grievance at their lot, yet had been dutiful mothers.

Various unhappy balances had been achieved by himself and Rosemary, always regarded as secondbest. Best was in fantasy, or what other people had. Then the children grew up, and were no longer there to be cooked for, worried about, shopped for, nursed—suddenly these two people who had been married thirty years discovered they were enjoying each other. They could not use the words "a second honeymoon" because they had never had a first. Jack remembered that at the other end of what now seemed like a long tunnel of responsibility, worry, guilt—relieved by frequent exile, whose enjoyability caused more guilt—had been a young woman with whom he had been more in love than with anybody since. He relaxed into the pleasures of his home, pleasure with Rosemary, who, appreciated at last, took on energy and poise, lost her listlessness, her reproach, her patience under neglect.

It had been the completeness of her revival that was the only thing disturbing about their being in love again: Jack lived marvelling that so little a thing as his own attention should be enough to nourish this creature, to burnish her with joy. He could not help being guilty anew that so little an effort towards self-discipline would have produced the kindness which could have made this woman's life happy, instead of a martyrdom. Yet he knew he had not been capable of even so small an effort: he had found her intolerable, and the marriage a burden, and that was the truth. But the thought he could not come to terms with was this: what sort of a creature was she, to be fed and made happy by the love of a creature like himself?

And Rosemary was not the only woman he observed enjoying a new lease on life. At parties of "the Old Guard" it was enough simply to look around at the wives of the same age as his own wife, the women recently released from nursery and kitchen, to see many in the same condition, without having to ask if a second honeymoon was in progress—and here was another source of unease. He was not able to ask, to discuss frankly, or even to raise the matter at all, and yet these were friends, he had been with them, worked with them, faced a hundred emergencies with them—but they did not have with each other the friendship of the kind that would enable them to talk about their relationships with each other, with their wives, their wives with them. Yet this was friendship, or at least it was as close to friendship as he was likely to get. Intimacy he had known, but with women with whom he was having affairs. Intimacy, frankness, trust, had, as it were, been carried inside him, to be bestowed on loved women, and withdrawn when that love had ended because he was married. So it was not that he had not known perfect intimacy; it was that he had known it with several people, one after another. What was left now of these relationships was a simplicity of under- standing when he met these women again—those that he did meet, for after all, many of these affairs had taken place in other countries. But even now he had to admit that this state had never been achieved with his wife, as good as their relation now was; for what he could not share with her was a feeling he could not control that he had to value her less for being so satisfied—more, fulfilled—with so little. Himself.

Yet, for all these reservations, the last two years had been better than anything he had expected with a woman, except in the expecta- tions of his dreams about marriage so long ago. They went for holi- days together, for weekends to old friends, to the theatre, for special meals at restaurants, and for long walks. They made little treats for each other, gave each other presents, had developed the private lan- guage of lovers. And all the time her gaiety and energy grew, while she could not prevent herself watching him—not knowing that she did it, and this humbled him and made him wretched—for the re- turn of the old tyrant, the boor. Always he was aware that their hap- piness lacked a foundation.

But what foundation ought there to be?

Now he wanted to tell his wife the dream he had had about death. This is why he had been longing to see her. But he had not allowed himself to understand the truth, which was that he couldn't tell her. She dreaded change in him; she would feel the dream as a threat. And it was. For another thing, this new easy affection they had would not admit the words he would have to use. What words? None he knew could convey the quality of the dream. The habits of their life together made it inevitable that if he said: Rosemary, I had a terrible dream; well, no, that was not it, its terribleness is not the point, wait, I must tell you—she would reply: Oh, Jack, you must have eaten something. Are you well?—And she would run off to get him a glass of medicine of some sort. Her smile at him, while she handed it to him, would say that she knew, they both knew, that he didn't really need it, but she enjoyed looking after him when at last he was enjoying being looked after.

Tea time came. Jack watched the young man from upstairs walk away under the summer's load of leaf. The telephone rang twice, both times for Rosemary. He took messages. He saw Elizabeth come up the path to the side door, nearly called to her, but decided not. He sat on into the summer afternoon, feeling that it was appropriate to be melancholy: it was what was expected of him. But that was not it! It was as if he had no substance at all, there was nothing to him, no purpose, no worth. . . . Something was draining quietly away from him, had been for a long time.

Elizabeth came running in, saying: "Oh, Father, I am so sorry, you must be feeling low." Caroline came after her. Carrie was now dressed in a purple shawl over tight red cotton trousers. Elizabeth, still in what she had worn to work, had on a dark green trouser suit, but her own personality had been asserted since she came home: she had tied her hair back with an exotic-looking piece of red material, and it was making a froth of gold curls around her face. His cold heart began to stir and to warm, and they sat themselves down opposite ready to share his grief.

Rosemary now came in, a large, tall woman, smiling and shedding energy everywhere.

"Oh, darling," said she, "you didn't telephone. I am so sorry. You have had tea, I hope?"

"He's dead," said Elizabeth to her mother.

"He died this morning," said Jack, not believing that it had been that morning.

Rosemary slowed her movements about the room, and when she turned to him, her face, like the faces of her daughters, was not smiling.

"When is the funeral?"

"I don't know yet."

"I'll come with you," said Elizabeth.

"I won't," said Carrie. "I don't like funerals. Not our kind of funeral."

"And I won't either, if you don't mind," said Rosemary. "That is, not unless you want me there." A glass and decanter had appeared beside him, and Rosemary was causing whisky to descend into the glass in a gold stream.

The whisky was not the point, the women's serious faces not the point, the funeral and who was at it, not the point.

"There is no need for any of you to come," he said. And added, as he had been afraid he might: "It wouldn't be expected of you."

All three showed relief, even Elizabeth.

Rosemary hated funerals: they were morbid. Carrie, being sort of Buddhist, believed, apparently, in putting corpses out for the vultures. Elizabeth's Christianity, like Ann's, was without benefit of church services.

"Oh no, I want to come with you," said Elizabeth.

"Well, we'll see."

He told them about the death—a mild and well-ordered affair. He said that Ellen and Cedric had been there, and watched for his wife's humorous glance so that he could return it: she wanted to convey sympathy for having to be with his family even for two days. Then he began speaking about the Twenty-four-Hour Fast. He did not ask if they would join him, but he was hoping they would.

Now, while Rosemary had early on been inculcated with his left-wing opinions, during all the years of their unhappiness his activities had been seen by her as being in some subtle way directed against her, or, at any rate, as depriving her of something. But recently she had several times gone with him to a meeting or a demonstration. Looking guilty, she said that she couldn't join the Fast, because she had a lecture on Saturday night on Stress in the Family. She made it sound funny, in her way of appearing like an intelligent child submitting to official pedantry; but there was no doubt she would be at the lecture. Carrie said nothing: she thought any kind of politics silly. Elizabeth said she would have joined the Fast, but she had a demonstration of her own on Saturday.

Jack now remembered Ann's programme, said that Ann was coming down at the weekend for a Pray-in. It turned out that this was the same as Elizabeth's. Both girls were pleased that Ann was coming, and starting talking about her and her relations with her parents. These were not very good: Ann found them materialistic, conventional, bourgeois. Jack was not able to be much amused; he found himself in sympathy with Cedric, possibly even with his sister-in-law. Probably Elizabeth and Carrie said to their friends that their parents were materialistic and bourgeois. He knew that his son Joseph did.

The girls had been going out for the evening, but because of the death, and wanting to cheer their father up, they stayed in to supper. Rosemary's new practice, now that the decades of compulsive cooking, buying, fussing, were done with, was to keep food to its simplest. She offered them soup, toast, and fruit. The girls protested: the parents could see that this was because they needed to do something to show their sympathy. Rosemary and Jack sat hand in hand on the sofa, while the girls made a long and delicious meal for them all.

They went to bed early: it was still not quite dark outside. But he needed to make love with his wife, feeling that here at least the cold which threatened him would be held at bay.

But the shell of himself loved, the shell of himself held Rosemary while she fell asleep and turned away from him. He was awake, listening to the tides of blood moving in his body.

He crept downstairs again. He read the newspapers—making himself do so, like a penance for callousness. He listened to the radio, avoiding news bulletins. He did not go to bed again until it was fully light, and was woken an hour later by Cedric: practical reasons had set the funeral for tomorrow, Saturday, at Eleven.

Friday he spent in the activities that the journalist was so good at. Saturday was not a good day for train and air services: to reach S—— in time for the funeral, and to be back by two, would need luck and ingenuity. He checked the weather forecast: rain and mist were expected. Having made the arrangements, he rang Mona, since Walter was still in Glasgow. Mona was not only a wife of an "Old Guard," but one in her own right. It had been agreed that he, Jack, would be on the steps of the church at ten, to welcome the fasters as they arrived, and to see that the posters proclaiming the event were in place. He now asked Mona to do all this, explaining why.

"Oh dear," she said, "I am so sorry about your father. Yes, luckily I can do it. Who is coming?—wait, I'll get a pencil."

He gave her the names over the telephone, while she wrote them down.

They were the names of people with whom he had been associated in a dozen different ways, ever since the war ended; it seemed now as if the war had been an instrument to shake out patterns of people who would work and act together—or against each other—for the rest of their lives. They had not known about this process while it was happening, but that was when "the Old Guard" had been formed. The phrase was a joke of course, and for family use: he certainly would never use it to Walter, Bill, Mona and the rest—they would be hurt by it. Carrie had said one day, reporting a telephone call, "I didn't get his name, but it sounded like one of the Old Guard."

These names appeared constantly together on dozens, hundreds, of letterheads, appeals, protests, petitions; if you saw one name, you could assume the others. Yet their backgrounds had been very different, of all classes, countries, even races. Some had been communists, some had fought communism. They were Labour and Liberal, vegetarian and pacifist, feeders of orphaned children, builders of villages in Africa and India, rescuers of refugees and survivors of natural and man-made calamities. They were journalists and editors, actors and writers, film makers and trade unionists. They wrote books on subjects like Unemployment in the Highlands and The Future of Technology. They sat on councils and committees and the boards of semicharitable organisations; they were Town Councillors, members of Parliament; creators of documentary film programmes. They had taken the same stands on Korea and Kenya, on Cyprus and Suez, on Hungary and the Congo, on Nigeria, the Deep South and Brazil, on South Africa and Rhodesia and Ireland and Vietnam and . . . and now they were sharing opinions and emotions on the nine million refugees from Bangladesh.

Once, when they had come together to express a view, it had been a minority view, and to get what they believed publicised had sometimes been difficult or impossible. Now something had happened which not all of them had understood: when they expressed themselves about this or that, it was happening more and more often that their views were identical with conventional views put forward freely by majorities everywhere. Once they had been armed with aggressive optimistic views about society, about how to change it; now they were on the defensive. Once they had forecast utopias; now they forecast calamity, failed to prevent calamity, and then worked to minimize calamity.

This view of the Old Guard had been presented to Jack by his son, the chip off the old block.

When Jack had finished the list of names, Mona said "Surely we can do better than that?" and he said, apologetically (why, when it was not his fault?): "I think a lot of people are feeling that the media are doing it for us."

Then he decided to ring his son, who had not yet heard about his grandfather. To reach Joseph was not easy, since he worked for a variety of "underground" organisations, slept in many places, might even be out of the country.

At last Jack rang Elizabeth, who was already at her place of work, heard where Joseph was likely to be, and finally reached his son. On hearing that his grandfather was dead, Joseph said: "Oh that's bad, I am sorry." On being asked if he and his friends "with nothing better to do" would like to join the Twenty-four-Hour Fast, he said: "But haven't you been reading the newspapers?" Jack did not want to say that he had not read them enough to know what his son's programme was likely to be, but it turned out that "all of us" were organising a Protest March for that Sunday.

In his son's briskness, modified because of the death, Jack heard his own youth speaking, and a sense of justice made him sound apologetic towards his son. He felt, too, the start of exhaustion. This was because his effort to be fair made it necessary to resurrect his own youth as he talked to Joseph, and it took the energy that in fantasy he would be using to bring Joseph around to see his point of view. He had recently been indulging fantasies of confronting Joseph with: Look, I have something of great importance to say, can you let me have an hour or two? He was on the point of saying this now, but Joseph said: "I have to rush off, I'm sorry, see you, give my love to everyone."

He knew exactly what he wanted to say, not only to his son—to his own youthful self—but to the entire generation, or rather, to that part of it which was political, the political youth. What he felt was, he knew, paradoxical: it was because his son was so much like him that he felt he had no son, no heir. What he wanted was for his son to carry on from himself, from where he, Jack, stood now: to be his continuation.

It was not that his youthful self had been, was, conceited, crude, inexperienced, intolerant: he knew very well that his own middleaged capacities of tact and the rest were not much more than the oil these same qualities—not much changed—used to get their own way; he wasn't one to admire middleaged blandness, expertise.

What he could not endure was that his son, all of them, would have to make the identical journey he and his contemporaries had made, to learn lessons exactly as if they had never been learned before.

Here, at precisely this point, was the famous "generation gap"; here it had always been. It was not that the young were unlike their parents, that they blazed new trails, thought new thoughts, displayed new forms of courage. On the contrary, they behaved exactly like their parents, could not listen to this simple message: that it had all been done before.

It was this that was so depressing, and which caused the dryness of only just achieved tolerance on the part of the middleaged towards "the youth"—who, as they themselves had done, behaved as if youth and the freedom they had to "experiment" was the only good they had, or could expect in their lives.

But this time the "gap" was much worse because a new kind of despair had entered into the consciousness of mankind: things were too desperate, the future of humanity depended on humanity being able to achieve new forms of intelligence, of being able to learn from experience. That humanity was unable to learn from experience was written there for everyone to see, since the new generation of the intelligent and consciously active youth behaved identically with every generation before them.

The endless cycle, of young people able to come to maturity only in making themselves into a caste which had to despise and dismiss their parents, insisting pointlessly on making their own discoveries— it was, quite simply, uneconomic. The world could not afford it.

Every middleaged person (exactly as his or her parents had done) swallowed the disappointment of looking at all the intelligence and bravery of his or her children being absorbed in—repetition, which would end, inevitably in them turning into the Old Guard. Would, that is, if Calamity did not strike first. Which everybody knew now it was going to.

Watching his son and his friends was like watching laboratory animals unable to behave in any way other than that to which they had been trained—as he had done, as the Old Guard had done. . . . At this point in the fantasy, his son having accepted or at least listened to all this, Jack went on to what was really his main point. What was worst of all was that "the youth" had not learned, were repeating, the old story of socialist recrimination and division. Looking back over his time—and after all recently he had had plenty of time to do just this, and was not that important, that a man had reached quiet water after such a buffeting and a racing and could think and reflect?—he could see one main message. This was that the reason for the failure of socialism to achieve what it could was obvious: that some process, some mechanism was at work which made it inevitable that every political movement had to splinter and divide, then divide again and again, into smaller groups, sects, parties, each one dominated, at least temporarily, by some strong figure, some hero, or father, or guru figure, each abusing and insulting the others. If there had been a united socialist movement, not only in his time—which he saw as that since the Second World War—but in the time before that, and the epoch before that, and before that, there would have been a socialist Britain long ago.

But as night followed day, the same automatic process went on . . . but if it *was* automatic, he imagined his son saying, then why talk to me like this?—Ah, Jack would reply, but you have to be better, don't you see? You have to, otherwise it's all at an end, it's finished, can't you see that? Can't you see that this process where one generation springs, virginal and guiltless—or so it sees itself—out of its debased predecessors, with everything new to learn, makes it inevitable that there must soon be division, and self-righteousness and vituperation? Can't you see that that has happened to your lot? There are a dozen small newspapers, a dozen because of their differences. But suppose there had been one or two? There are a dozen little groups, each jealously defending their differences of dogma on policy, sex, history. Suppose there had been just one?

But of course there could not be only one; history showed there could not—history showed this, clearly, to those who were prepared to study history. But the young did not study history, because history began with them. Exactly as history had begun with Jack and his friends.

But the world could no longer afford this. . . . The fantasy did not culminate in satisfactory emotion, in an embrace, for instance, between father and son; it ended in a muddle of dull thoughts. Because the fantasy had become increasingly painful, Jack had recently developed it in a way which was less personal—less challenging, less real? He had been thinking that he could discuss all these thoughts with the Old Guard and afterwards there could perhaps be a conference? Yes, there might be a confrontation, or something of that kind, between the Old Guard and the New Young. Things could be said publicly which never seemed to get themselves said privately? It could all be thrashed out and then . . . Meanwhile there was the funeral to get through.

That night, Friday, the one before the funeral, no sooner had he gone to sleep than he dreamed. It was not the same dream, that of the night in the hotel room, but it came as it were out of the same area. A corridor, long, dark, narrow, led to the place of the first dream, but at its entrance stood a female figure which at first he be-

lieved was his mother as a young woman. He believed this because
of what he felt, which was an angry shame and inadequacy: these
emotions were associated for him with some childhood experience
which he supposed he must have suppressed; sometimes he thought
he was on the point of remembering it. The figure wore a straight
white dress with loose lacy sleeves. It had been his mother's dress,
but both Elizabeth and Carrie had worn it "for fun." This monitor
was at the same time his mother and his daughters, and she was di-
recting him forward into the darkness of the tunnel.

His wife was switching on lights and looking at him with concern. He soothed her back to sleep and, for the second night running, left his bed soon after he had got into it to read the night away
and to listen to radio stations from all over the world.

Next morning he travelled to the airport in light fog, to find the
flight delayed. He had left himself half an hour's free play, and in
half an hour the flight was called and he was airborne, floating west
inside grey cloud that was his inner state. He who had flown unmoved through the skies of most countries of the world, and in every
kind of weather, was feeling claustrophobic, and had to suppress
wanting to batter his way out of the plane and run away across the
mists and fogs of this upper country. He made himself think of
something else: returned to the fantasy about the Conference. He
imagined the scene, the hall packed to the doors, the platform
manned by the well known among the various generations of socialists. He saw himself there, with Walter on one side, and his son on
the other. He imagined how he or Walter would speak, explaining
to the young that the survival of the world depended on them, that
they had the chance to break this cycle of having to repeat and repeat experience: they could be the first generation to consciously take
a decision to look at history, to absorb it, and in one bound to tran-
scend it. It would be like a willed mutation.

He imagined the enthusiasm of the Conference—a sober and intelligent enthusiasm, of course. He imagined the ending of the Conference when . . . and here his experience took hold of him, and
told him what would happen. In the first place, only some of the
various socialist groups would be at the Conference. Rare people indeed would be prepared to give up the hegemony of their little
groups to something designed to end little groups. The Conference
would throw up some strong personalities, who would energize and
lead; but very soon these would disagree and become enemies and
form rival movements. In no time at all, this movement to end

schism would have added to it. As always happened. So, if this was what Jack knew was bound to happen, why did he . . . They were descending through heavy cloud. There was heavy rain in S——. The taxi crawled through slow traffic. By now he knew he would not be in time to reach the cemetery. If he had really wanted to make sure of being at the funeral, he would have come down last night. Why hadn't he? He might as well go back now for all the good he was doing; but he went on. At the cemetery the funeral was over. Two young men were shovelling earth into the hole at the bottom of which lay his father: like the men in the street who continually dug up and rebury drains and pipes and wires. He took the same taxi back to the house in the church precincts where he found Mrs. Markham tidying the rooms ready to hold the last years of another man or woman, and his brother Cedric sorting out the old man's papers. Cedric was crisp: he quite understood the delay; he too would have been late for the funeral if he had not taken the precaution of booking rooms in the Royal Arms. But both he and Ellen had been there, with his wife and Ellen's husband. Also Ann. It would have been nice if Jack had been there, but it didn't matter.

It was now a warm day, all fog forgotten. Jack found a suitable flight back to London. High in sunlight, he wondered if his father had felt as if he had no heir? He had been a lawyer: Cedric had succeeded him. In his youth he had defended labour agitators, conscientious objectors, taken on that kind of case: from religious conviction, not from social feeling. Well, did it make any difference why a thing was done if it was done? This thought, seditious of everything Jack believed, lodged in his head—and did not show signs of leaving. It occurred to Jack that perhaps the old man had seen himself as his heir, and not Cedric, who had always been so cautious and respectable? Well, he would not now know what his father had thought; he had missed his chance to find out.

Perhaps he could talk to Ann and find out what the old man had been thinking? The feebleness of this deepened the inadequacy which was undermining him—an inadequacy which seemed to come from the dream of the female in a white dress? Why had that dream fitted his two lovely daughters into that stern unforgiving figure? He dozed, but kept waking himself for fear of dreaming. That he was now in brilliant sunshine over a floor of shining white cloud so soon after the flight through fog dislocated his sense of time, of continuity even more: it was four days ago that he had had that telegram from Mrs. Markham?

They ran into fog again above Heathrow, and had to crawl around in the air for half an hour before they could land. It was now four, and the Twenty-four-Hour Fast had begun at two. He decided he would not join them, but he would drop in and explain why not.

He took the underground to Trafalgar Square.

Twenty people, all well known to him and to the public, were grouped on the steps and porch of St. Martin's. Some sat on cushions, some on stools. A large professionally made banner said: THIS IS A TWENTY-FOUR-HOUR FAST FOR THE STARVING MILLIONS IN BANGLA-DESH. Each faster had flasks of water, blankets and coats for the night ahead. Meanwhile it was a warm misty afternoon. Walter had a thick black sweater tied around his neck by the sleeves. Walter was the centre of the thing; the others related to him. Jack stood on the other side of the road thinking that his idea of talking with these his old friends about a joint conference with "the youth" was absurd, impractical; now that he was again in the atmosphere of ordinary partisan politics, he could see that it was.

He was longing to join them, but this was because he wanted to be enclosed in a group of like-minded people, to be supported by them, to be safe and shielded from doubts and fears. And dreams.

By Walter was his wife, Norah, a small pretty woman whom he had always thought of as Walter's doormat. He had done, that is, until he had understood how afraid Rosemary had been of himself. Norah had once said to him after a meeting: "If Walter had been an ordinary man, I might have resented giving up my career, but when you are married to someone like Walter, then of course you are glad to submerge yourself. I feel as if this has been my contribution to the Movement." Norah had been a journalist.

Walter's face, usually a fist of intention and power, was beaming, expansive: they all looked as if they were at a picnic, Jack thought. Smug, too. That he should think this astounded him, for he knew that he loved and admired them. Yet now, looking at Walter's handsome face, so well known to everyone from newspaper and television, it had over it a mask of vanity. This was so extraordinary a metamorphosis of Jack's view of his friend that he felt as if an alien was inhabiting him: a film had come over his eyes, distorting the faces of everyone he looked at. He was looking at masks of vanity, complacency, stupidity or, in the case of Walter's Norah, a foolish admiration. Then Jack's sense of what was happening changed; it was not that he was looking through distorting film, but that a film had been stripped off what he looked at. He was staring at faces that horrified him because of their naked self-centredness: he searched faces that must be like his own, for something he could admire, or need. And hastily he wiped his hand down over his own face, for he knew that on it was fastened a mask of vanity; he could feel it there. Under it, under an integument that was growing inwards into his flesh, he could feel something small, formless, blind—something pitiful and unborn.

Now, disgusted with his treachery, but still unable to take his hand down from his face, unable to prevent himself from trying to tug off that mask fastened there, he walked over to his friends who, seeing him come, smiled and looked about them for a place where he could sit. He said: "I can't join you, I am afraid. Transport trouble," he added ridiculously, as first surprise, then incomprehension showed on their faces. Now he saw that Walter had already registered: *His father!* and saw that this born commander was framing the words he would use as soon as Jack turned his back: "His father has died, he has just come from the funeral." But this was no reason why he shouldn't be with them: he agreed, absolutely. Now he moved away, but glanced back with a wave and a smile; they were all gazing after the small drama embodied in: His father has just died. They looked as if they were hungry for the sensation of it—he was disliking himself for criticising people whom he knew to be decent and courageous, who, ever since he had known them, had taken risks, given up opportunities, devoted themselves to what they believed to be right. To what *he* believed was right. . . . He was also a bit frightened. Thoughts that he would never have believed he was capable of accommodating were taking root in him; he felt as if armies of others waited to invade.

He decided to walk down to the river, perhaps even to take a trip to Greenwich, if he could get on to a boat at all on a warm Saturday afternoon. He saw coming towards him a little procession under banners of: JESUS IS YOUR SAVIOUR and JESUS LIVES! All the faces under the banners were young; these young people were in no way distinguished by their clothes from the young ones he had watched marching, with whom he had marched, for the last fifteen years or more. Their clothes were gay and imaginative, their hair long, their faces all promise. He was smiling at Ann, who carried a square of cardboard that said: JESUS CARES ABOUT BANGLADESH. A voice said, "Hello, Dad!" and he saw his Elizabeth, her golden hair in heavy pigtails over either shoulder. Hands, Ann's and Elizabeth's, pulled him in beside them. In this way one of the most prominent members of the Old Guard found himself marching under a poster which said: CHRIST CAME TO FEED THE HUNGRY. REMEMBER BANGLADESH! Ann's little face beamed with happiness and the results of the exercise. "It was a nice funeral," she said. "I was telling Liz about it. It had a good feeling. Grandad liked it, I am sure."

To this Jack found himself unable to reply, but he smiled and, with a couple of hundred Jesus-lovers, negotiated the Square, aided by some indulgent policemen. In a few moments he would pass his friends on the steps of the church.

"I shouldn't be here," he said. "False pretences."

"Oh why?" enquired his daughter, really disappointed in him. "I don't see that at all!"

Ann's look was affectionate and forgiving.

Around him they were singing Onward, Christian Soldiers. They sang and marched or, rather, shuffled and ambled, and he modified his pace to theirs, and allowed his depression to think for him that whether the banners were secular and atheist on principle, or under the aegis of Jesus, twenty-four million people would die in the world this year of starvation, and that he would not give a new penny for the chances of anybody in this Square living another ten years without encountering disaster.

He was now aware that Mona was staring at him: in her decisive face, in her unequivocal eyes, was not a trace of what he usually saw there—the reminder of their brief but pleasurable affair. She turned to tug at Walter's sleeve, in a way that betrayed panic—more than ordinary shock, anyway. Now they all turned to look at him; they were all blank, they could not take it in. He had a need to wave his arms and shout: Nonsense, can't you see that I am with my daughter and my niece? He felt he should apologise. He could not stand being condemned by them, his side, his family, but even as he nodded and smiled embarrassed greeting, he saw that Walter, whose mouth at first had really dropped open, had seen Elizabeth, whom of course he had known all her life. All was explainable! For the second time in half an hour Jack watched Walter framing words with which to exculpate him: Jack was with his daughter, that was it! After all, Jack was not the only one among them whose offspring had caught God in various extraordinary forms!

Jack entered the Square with the children, was informed that they would come to visit him later, and he left them singing energetic hymns by a fountain.

He took busses home. He was looking forward to letting the false positions of the day dissolve themselves into unimportance while he laughed over them with his wife; but now he remembered that she would not be there, nor expect him to be.

There was a note, not to him but to Carrie, saying: "Please feed the cat, shall be very late, might stay at Judy Miller's, please lock all doors much love."

It was seven: it seemed like midafternoon. He drew the curtains to make a night, and sat in it with a glass of whiskey. Later Ann came in to tell him about the funeral, about Jesus. He moved his position in his chair so that he could look at her shining eyelids. Carrie came in, and he looked at her, but her eyes were a woman's. He knew about her love life, because she talked freely to her parents about it, but if she had never said a word he would have known from her knowledgeable breasts, from the way the flesh was moulded to her eyeballs by kisses. She breathed tenderness, and care for him; he was happy she was there, but it was Ann he wanted to look at.

They discussed their respective faiths. Ann did not need to join a church because she had a direct relationship with Jesus, who loved her as she loved Him. Carrie defined her religion as "sort of Eastern, she supposed." No, she didn't think it was Buddhist so much as Hindu. She believed in reincarnation but could not see the point of cow-worship, though anything that made people be nice to animals was worth it, she thought. Had Ann read the Upanishads? That was what she believed in. She was taking it for granted that her father had not, and would not. She would like to be a vegetarian, but after all she shared a kitchen with Elizabeth, who would object. . . . Here Elizabeth came in, having bathed and put on an ancient peacock-blue lace dinner dress that had holes in the sleeves; Jack remembered Rosemary in it, twenty years before. Elizabeth was indignant, and said she would not at all mind Carrie turning vegetarian, she was ready to be one herself. But what would they feed the cat on? Were human beings going to kill all the cats and dogs in the world because they weren't vegetarian? Carrie got angry at this, and said: There you are; I told you, I knew you didn't want to be vegetarian! Ann restored good feeling by laughing at them both.

They went on discussing the exact nuances of their beliefs, I believe that, no, I don't agree with that, no I think it is more that . . . surely not, oh no, how can you believe that? An hour or so went by. Jack lifted the drawn curtain: there was a heavy golden light everywhere, thunder in the evening sky, the tree had damp yellow aureoles.

He dropped the curtain, and they were in a small low lamplight, and the three girls were discussing Women's Liberation. Jack hated women talking about this, not because he disagreed with any of it, but because he had never been able to cope with it; it was all too much for him. He felt increasingly that he had reason to feel guilty about practically every relationship he ever had with a woman except for two or three special love affairs, which were outside ordinary categorisation, but did not know how to change himself—if, indeed, he wanted to. These three young women had different, but precisely defined, opinions about the roles of women, with Carrie representing an extreme of femininity, and Ann, surprisingly, militant. Elizabeth talked about the lot of working women and had no time for what she called "futile psychologising." This phrase made them quarrel, and for the first time Jack saw Ann strident. The quarrel went on, and then they saw that Jack was silent, and they remembered that his father was just dead, and they cooked for him, handing him many dishes, each as if it were a poultice for some wound he had suffered. Then, with an effort towards being reasonable, they went on discussing their ideological positions about Women's Liberation. Jack was again in the condition he had been in in the Square, when he had looked across traffic at his old friends. All he had been able to see there was a variety of discreditable emotions; all he could see in these charming faces was self-importance. What mattered to them was the moment when they said: I think so-and-so; no, I don't think that. He knew that what they believed was not as important to them as that they had come to an opinion and the reasons why they had reached that opinion. They possessed their beliefs or opinions; they owned them.

Now they were back to religion again: the other two attacked Ann for being Christian when Christianity's history in relation to women was so retrogressive. To which Ann said to Carrie: "You can talk, how about women in India?"

"Yes," said Carrie, "but then I don't believe in women being the same as men."

This started the quarrel again, and their voices rose.

He had to stop himself saying that they sounded like a Conference of World Churches debating doctrinal differences, because he knew that if it came to dogmas, and disagreements about historical personalities, then his faith, socialism, beat them all. He looked at, listened to, his daughters, his brother's daughter, and knew that in two, three, ten years (if they were all allowed to live so long) they would be laying claim, with exactly the same possessiveness, to other creeds, faiths, attitudes.

Again he felt like a threatened building, the demolition teams at work on its base. He was seeing, like a nightmare, the world like a little ball covered over with minuscule creatures all vociferously and viciously arguing and killing each other over beliefs which they had come to hold by accident of environment, of geography.

He told the girls he had not been sleeping well, must go to bed: he could no longer stand listening while they staked precise claims in fields of doctrine. They went off, kissing him fondly: he knew from the warmth of the kisses that they had talked about his reactions to Grandad's death; everything was bound to be much worse for him of course because he was an atheist and did not believe in survival after death.

They each had a different version of their futures. Ann for instance believed that she would sit up after her death, exactly as she was now, but better, and would recognise her friends and family, and Jesus would be there too.

Jack was thinking that his own attitude to life after death had been collected quite casually: when he was young and forming (or acquiring) his opinions, the people and writers he admired wore atheism like a robe of honour. Not to believe in an after-life was like a certificate of bravery and, above all, clarity of thinking. If he had been young now, he might have collected, according to the chances of his experience, and just as lightly, any one of a variety of opinions. Reincarnation? Why not? After all, as Carrie said, it was an optimistic and forward-looking creed. But when he was young he couldn't have taken to a belief in reincarnation, if for no other reason than that he never met anyone who had it. He had known that a few cranks believed in it, and people in India, but that was about it.

Now he made a ritual of going to bed. The sky was still full of light, so he made the room black. He drank hot milk. He wooed sleep, which he had never done in his life, and soon lay awake, hands behind his head. But he could not spend a third night reading and listening to the radio. Then lights crashed on and his wife was in the room. She was apologetic, and quite understood that he hadn't felt like joining the Fast. Her mind, he could see, was on her lecture and the friends she had met afterwards. He watched her dimming her vitality, damping her good mood, because she was afraid of it disturbing him. She lay in bed smiling, bright-eyed. She asked about the funeral, was sorry he had not reached it. Poor Jack! Smiling, she offered her arms, and grateful, he went into them. He would have gone on making love all night, but she went to sleep. In the close protective dark he lay beside his wife and in imagination saw the sky fill with dawn.

He fell asleep; he fell into a dream. In the dream he was thinking of what he had kept out of his consciousness all day, for to think of it was morbid. His father lay in a tight box under feet of wet soil. He, Jack, lay with him. He stifled and panicked, and the weight on him was as if he had been buried alive, in wet cement. He woke, and finding that although a cool damp light lay everywhere, and birds were at work on the lawn, it was only half past four; he went downstairs, turned on the radio, and made pictures in his head of the towns the stations were in, and lists of the people he had known in these towns, and then divided these into friends and enemies, and then, by a different classification, into the dead and the living, and so he returned in memory to the wars he had fought in or had reported, and relived, in a half-sleep, crisis-points, moments of danger, when he might have been killed, that now made him sweat and tremble but which he had simply lived through. When it seemed to him as if hours of a new day had already passed, he went back upstairs and got into bed beside his wife.

But at breakfast she betrayed that she had known he had not been beside her: she started to talk about the job in Nigeria. He knew that she did not want to go away for two years, leaving all her new interests, new friends, new freedom. There she would be back inside duties she had escaped from. There would be much social life. Yet it sounded as if she was trying to bring herself to believe she wanted to go if he did: she was worried about him.

He said, instead of replying about Nigeria, that he would like to go to church, just to see what it was like these days. She took in a puzzled but patient breath, let it sigh out of her, and looked at him with loving and respectful eyes—just like, he thought, the way Norah looked at Walter. She said: "Oh, I can understand why. You mean, you missed the funeral service?"

Perhaps it was because he had missed the funeral service. He put on a suit and she a dress, and they went to church together, for the first time, except for weddings. Carrie and Elizabeth went with them, Carrie because God was everywhere, Elizabeth because He was particularly in churches. Ann would not come; she had Jesus by the hand as she sat on the floor reading the Sunday newspapers.

He sat through the service in a rage, perhaps it was a retrospective rage; certainly this was what he had felt throughout years of compulsory attendance at Evensong and Matins, and Services Early and Late, at his public school. He did not mind that it was mumbo jumbo: it was bound to be! What he minded was that people voluntarily submitted themselves to the ministry of men palpably no better than themselves, men whose characters were written on their faces. This was perhaps what had first directed him towards socialism? He had not been able to stand that people submitted to being lied to, cheated, dominated by their equals? He was again afflicted by yesterday's disability: a film had rolled away from what he looked at. That man, wearing black with white lace and embroidery, and dangling strips of this and that colour—the sort of attractive nonsense that Carrie and Liz might wear—that man intoning and dancing and posturing through the service, had a face like Walter's. They were both public men, performers. Their features were permanently twisted by vanity and self-importance. Jack kept passing his hand across his own face, feeling the ugliness of the love of power on it. And Rosemary put her arm in his, asking if he felt well, if he had toothache? He replied with violence that he must have been mad to want to come; he apologized for inflicting it on her.

"Oh it doesn't matter for once," she said, with mildness, but glanced over her shoulder to see if Carrie and Elizabeth had heard: it was extraordinary how they all kowtowed to their children, as if they feared to offend them.

After the midday meal he felt as if he could sleep at last, and did so.

The dream pulled him down into itself as he rolled onto his bed in the sultry yellow afternoon light—and passed out. This time, as he sank down beside his father, who was very cold—he could feel the cold coming out and claiming him—the weight pressed them both down, right through the earth that was below the tight box. His father disappeared and he, Jack, quite alone, was rocking on a light blue sea. This too dissolved into air, but not before he had been pierced through and through with an extraordinary pain that was also a sweetness. He had not known anything like this before; in the dream he was saying to himself: That's a new thing, this sweetness. It was quickly gone, but astonishing, so that he woke up, pleased to wake up, as if out of a nightmare, yet what he had been happy to wake from was that high, piercing sweetness. Unhealthy, he judged it. It was not yet tea time; he had slept an hour and not been refreshed. He went down to be told as a joke by his wife that a journalist had rung that morning to find out his views on the Twenty-four-Hour Fast; did his not having been there mean that he was against it? Ann had answered, and had said that Mr. Orkney was at church. The journalist had seemed surprised, Ann said. She had had to repeat it more than once. Had she meant that Jack Orkney was at a wedding? At a christening? No, no, at church, a Sunday morning service.

Jack knew the journalist; they had been in several foreign fields together. Jack was now seriously worried, as a man is when faced with the loss of reputation. He said to himself: I was not worried what people thought of me when I was young. He was answered: You mean, you were not worried by what people said who were not *your side*. He said: Well, but now it is a personal thing, criticism of me is a criticism of my side; surely it is right to worry about letting my own side down?

There was no answer to this, except a knowledge he was dishonest.

Rosemary suggested a long walk. He could see she had been thinking how to make him whole again—how to protect her own happiness, he could not prevent himself thinking. He was more than ready to walk as many miles away as they could before dark; when they had first met, before they married, one of their things had been to walk miles, sometimes for days on end. Now they walked until it was dark, at eleven o'clock; they worked out it was over fifteen miles, and were pleased that this was still so easy for them, at their age, and in the middle of their undemanding life. But the night now confronted Jack, a narrow tunnel at the end of which waited a white-robed figure, pointing him to annihilation. That night he did not sleep. The windows were open, the curtains drawn back, the room full of light from the sky. He pretended to sleep, so as to protect his wife from anxiety, but she lay alert beside him, also pretending sleep.

Next morning it was a week since Mrs. Markham's wire, and he became concerned for his health. He knew that not to sleep for night after night, as he was doing, was simply not possible. During the following days he went further into this heightened, over-sensitised state, like a country of which he had heard rumours, but had not believed in. On its edges his wife and daughters smiled and were worried about him. He slept little, and when he did he was monitored by the female figure in white, now a composite of his mother, his wife and his daughters, but quite impersonal; she used their features but was an imposter. This figure had become like an angel on a wedding cake, or on a tomb, full of false sentiment; its appearance was accompanied, like a strain of particularly nauseating and banal music, by the sweetly piercing emotion, only it was much worse now; it was the essence of banality, of mawkishness, like being rolled in powdered sugar and swallowed into an insipid smile. The horror of this clinging sickliness was worse even than the nightmare—he could no longer remember the quality of that, only that it had occurred—of the night in the hotel. His bed, the bedroom, soon the entire house, was tainted by this emotion, which was more a sensation, even like nausea, as if he could never rid himself of the taste of a concentration of saccharin which he had accidentally swallowed. He was all day in a state of astonishment, and self-distrust; he made excuses not to go to bed.

Walter came to see him. Unannounced. As soon as Jack saw him getting out of his car, he remembered something which told him why Walter had come. About four years before, Mona had reviewed a religious book, the memoirs of some sort of mystic, in a way which surprised them all. They would have expected a certain tone—light, carefully non-solemn, for it did not do to give importance to something which did not deserve it—not mocking, of course, which would have had the same result, but the tone you use to indicate to children that while you may be talking about, let's say, ghosts, or telling a story about a witch, the subject is not one to be taken seriously. But Mona had not used this subtly denigrating tone. Various of the Old Guard had commented on this. Then she had reviewed a book of religious poetry, which of course could not be dismissed in the light disinfecting tone, since poetry was obviously in a different category—but the point was that none of them would have reviewed it at all. For one thing no editor would think of asking them to. It was all very upsetting. There had been a party at Bill's house and Mona was not there. She had been discussed: she was at the age when women "get" religion. Jack, fond of Mona, offered to go and see her. His visit was to find out, as he put it to himself, if she was "still with us." He had found her amiable, and her usual self, helping to organise a conference for the coming week. He had probed—oh tactfully, of course. He mentioned an article in one of the Sundays about a certain well-known religious figure, and said he found the man a nauseating self-seeker. Mona had said that she was inclined to agree.

He had said casually, "Of course I am only too ready to forgive somebody who can't face old age and all that without being cushioned by God." Mona had remarked that for her part she could not believe in personal survival after death. Well, of course not, but for years that she could not would have been taken for granted. He remembered feeling protective affection for her, as if he were helping to save her from a danger. Seeing Walter at a meeting to do with the Crisis in Our Communications a week later, he had said that he had made a point of visiting Mona and that she had seemed quite sound to him.

He knew now what to expect from Walter.

Walter was looking furtive. Of course Jack knew that this furtiveness was not anything he would have noticed normally: this state he was in exaggerated every emotion on other people's faces into caricatures. But Walter was playing a double part, almost that of a spy (as he had with Mona, of course, now he came to think of it), and Furtiveness was written large on him.

Walter mentioned the Fast—a success—and then made a clumsy sort of transition which Jack missed, and was talking about Lourdes. Jack wondered why Lourdes? And then he laughed: it was a short laugh, of astonishment, and Walter did not notice it. Or rather, had not expected a laugh in this place, found it discordant, and therefore discounted it, as if it had not happened. Walter was trying to find out if Jack's religious conversion—the rumour had spread that he went to church on Sundays—included a belief in miracles, such as took place, they said, at Lourdes. Jack said he had been to Lourdes once for the *Daily* . . . over some so-called miracles some years ago. Walter nodded, as if to say: That's right. He was already feeling relieved, because Jack had used the right tone. But he was still showing the anxiety of a priest who knew his beliefs to be the correct ones and was afraid of a lamb straying from the flock. He mentioned that Mona was suspected of having become a Roman Catholic. "Good God, no," said Jack, "she can't have." He sounded shocked. This was because his reaction was that she had been deceiving him, had lied. He sat silent, trying to remember the exact tones of her voice, how she had looked. If she was a Catholic, could she have said she did not believe in a personal survival? But he knew nothing at all of what Catholics thought, except that they did not believe in birth control, but did believe in the Pope.

Remembering that Walter was still there, and silent, he looked up to see him smiling wtih relief. The smile seemed to him extraordinary in its vulgarity, yet he knew that what he was seeing was the pleasure of a good comrade: Walter was happy that nothing was going to spoil their long friendship. The spontaneity of his reply over Mona had reassured him; now, mission accomplished, Walter was already thinking about the various obligations he had to get back to. But he stayed a little, to discuss some committee on pollution he was helping to set up.

He talked: Jack listened, wondering if this was the right time to raise the question of "the young." Walter's two sons were both classic revolutionaries and they despised their father for his success, his position in the socialist world, for "his compromises with the ruling class." Jack was thinking that of all the people in the world it was Walter, so like himself in experience, position and—he was afraid—character, with whom he should be able to talk about his preoccupation. But he was beginning to realise that there was a difference, and it was obviously an important one, between them. Jack was more on the outskirts of politics. He was more of a freelance, but Walter was always in the thick of every political struggle, always involved with the actual details of organisation. He never did anything else. And this was why he was so far from Jack's present vision of things, which saw them all—the people like them—continually planning and arranging and organising towards great goals, but fated to see these plans fail, or becoming so diluted by pressures of necessity that the results resembled nothing of what had been envisaged at the start. Sitting there, looking at his old friend's forceful and energetic face, it was in a double vision. On the one hand he thought that this was the one man he knew whom he would trust to see them all through any public or private tight spot; but at the same time he wanted to howl out, in a protest of agonised laughter, that if the skies fell (as they might very well do), if the seas rolled in, if all the water became undrinkable and the air poisoned and the food so short everyone was scratching for it in the dust like animals, Walter, Bill, Mona, himself, and all those like them, would be organising Committees, Conferences, Sit-downs, Fasts, Marches, Protests and Petitions, and writing to the authorities about the undemocratic behavior of the police.

Walter was talking about some negotiation with the Conservatives. Normally, Jack would be listening to an admirably concise and intelligent account of human beings in conflict. Now Jack could see only that on his friend's face was a look which said: *I am Power.*

Jack suddenly got up, with a gesture of repulsion. Walter rose automatically, still talking, not noticing Jack's condition. Jack reminded himself that in criticising Walter he had forgotten that he must be careful about himself: he had again, and suddenly, become conscious of the expressions that were fitting themselves down over his face, reflecting from Walter's, horrifying him in their complacency or their cruelty. And his limbs, his body, kept falling into postures of self-esteem and self-approval.

Walter was moving to the door, still talking. Jack, trying to keep his face blank, to prevent his limbs from expressing emotions which seemed to him appropriate for a monster, moved cautiously after him. Walter stood in the door—talking. Jack wanted him to go. It tired him, this self-observation he could not stop: there was his image at the door, oblivious to anything in the world but his own analysis of events. Yet at last, as Walter said goodbye and he saw Jack again—which he had not done for some minutes, being too self-absorbed—a worried look came into his face, and because of this look Jack knew that what Walter saw was a man standing in a rigid unnatural position who had his hands at his lower cheeks, fretfully fingering the jawbone, as if it were out of place.

Walter said, in a simple and awkward voice: "It's a bit of a shock when your old man goes. I know when mine died it took me quite a time to get back to normal."

He left, like a health visitor, and Jack thought that Walter had had to get back to normal when his father died. He was thinking, too, that the cure for his condition was activity. Walter was more sensible than himself: he filled every moment of his time.

He decided to go to the family doctor for sleeping pills. This was a house that self-consciously did not go in for pills of any kind. Or did not now: Rosemary, during what she now called "my silly time"—which after all had gone on for some years—had taken sleeping pills a lot. But that, even while she did it, had seemed to her a betrayal of her real nature. The girls went in for health in various ways—diets, yoga, homemade bread. His son was too strong—of course!—to need medicine. He smoked pot, Jack believed, and on principle—well, so would Jack have done at his age; the law on marijuana was absurd.

He told the doctor he was not sleeping well. The doctor asked for how long. He had to think. Well, for about a month, perhaps six weeks.

The doctor said: "That's not going to kill you, Jack!"

"All right, but before I get into the habit of not sleeping I'd like something—and *not* a placebo, please." The glance the doctor gave him at this told him that he had in fact been deciding to prescribe a placebo, but there had been something in Jack's voice to make him change his mind.

"Is there anything else worrying you?"

"Nothing. Or everything."

"I see," said the doctor, and prescribed sleeping pills and anti-depressants.

Jack had the prescriptions made up, then changed his mind; if he started taking these pills, it would be some sort of capitulation. To what, he did not know. Besides, he was thinking: Perhaps they might make it worse? "It" was not only the sweet mawkishness which threatened him at every turn, in a jingle of a tune for an advertisement on television, a shaft of light from behind a cloud at sunrise, a kitten playing in the next garden, but the feeling, getting worse, that he was transparent, an automaton of unlikable and predictable reactions. He was like a spy in his own home, noticing the slightest reactions of thought or emotion in his wife and daughters, seeing them as robots. If they knew how he was seeing them, how loathsome they were in their predictability, their banality, they would turn and kill him. And quite rightly. For he was not human. He was outside humanity. He even found himself walking abruptly out of rooms where he was sitting with Rosemary, or one or other of the girls; he could not stand his own horror and pity because of them, himself, everybody.

Yet they were treating him with perfect kindness. He knew that this was what it really was: even if he had to see it all as falsity, mere habits of kindness, sympathy, consideration, tact, which none of them really felt, wanting him to get back to normal, so that life could go on without stress. His wife particularly longed for this. While he took care that he did not betray the horror he was immersed in, she knew well enough their time was over—the gaiety and charm of it, the irresponsibility. Probably for good. Being what she was, thoughtful, considerate (taught by society to show thoughtfulness and sympathy when she wasn't really feeling it, he could not stop himself thinking), she was trying to decide what to do for the best. Sometimes she even asked if he didn't think he should write another book—even if he would like to make a trip abroad without her; she talked about Nigeria. Each time Nigeria was mentioned his response to it was strong: it was the idea of forgetting himself entirely in an active and tightly planned life.

But he did not want to commit himself. He felt he would be losing an opportunity—but of what? And besides, how could he? He believed he was seriously ill, in some inconceivable, unprecedented way; how could he take a job when his energies had to go into presenting a bland and harmless surface to those around him, into preventing his hand rising furtively up to his face, to see if the masks of greed or power were fastened there, into watching the postures his body assumed, which must betray his vices to anyone looking his way—or would betray them, if everybody wasn't blind and deaf, absorbed in their kindness, their awful, automatic, meaningless "sympathy."

One night his son arrived upstairs. Joseph used sometimes to come, unannounced, and went up through the girls' room to the attic to sleep. He took food from his sisters' kitchen. Sometimes he brought friends.

About a year ago there had been a row over the friends. Feeling one evening as if the top part of his house had been invaded by a stealthy army, Jack had gone up and found a dozen or so young men, and a couple of girls, all lying about on sleeping bags and blankets under the rafters. They had moved in. A girl was cooking sausages in a frying pan that was on a camping stove; about a foot away was a drum that had written on it: PARAFFIN. INFLAMMABLE. The flame from the stove was turned too high, and showed around the edges of the frying pan. Jack jumped forward, turned it down, removed the pan, and stood up, facing them, the pan in his hand. His usual responses to his son—apology, or the exhaustion due to the effort to be fair, had been cut, and he asked: "What's the matter with you lot? What's wrong? You aren't stupid!"

Coming up the stairs he had been preparing a "humorous" remark—which he was afraid would sound pompous, to the effect: "How about introducing me to my guests?" Now he stared at them, and the young faces stared back. There was a half-scared smile on the face of the girl who had been cooking, but no one said anything. "I think you had better get out," said Jack at last, and went downstairs. Soon after he had watched the whole lot cross the garden like a tribe on the move, with their stove, their cartons, their paper-carriers, their guitars, their sleeping bags.

Now he came to think of it, this incident had been the beginning of his inadmissible depression. He had spent days, weeks, months, thinking about it. He felt there was a contempt there, in the carelessness, that went beyond anything he knew how to cope with; he did not understand it, them—his son. Who, meanwhile, had resumed his habits, and continued to drop in for a night or two when he had nowhere better to sleep. So it was not, Jack reasoned, that Joseph despised a roof over his head, as such? They had all been so stoned they had not known what they were doing? No, it hadn't seemed like it. They had not bothered to look at the drum, had not known it was full? But that was scarcely an excuse—no, it was all too much, not understandable. . . . He had not talked to his son since, only seen him go past.

The telephone rang from upstairs: Carrie said that Joseph would be down to see him in a few moments, if Jack "had nothing better to do."

Instantly Jack was on the defensive: he knew that Joseph criticised him for having been away so much when the three children were growing up. This message was a reference to that—*again*? If it was simply careless, what had come into his head, then that made it even worse, in a way. . . . Joseph came running lightly down the stairs and into the livingroom. A muscular young man, he wore skin-tight blue jeans, a light blue sweatshirt, and a small red scarf at his throat tied like a pirate's. The clothes were old, but as much care had gone into their choosing, preparation and presentation as a model getting ready for a photograph. . . . While Jack knew he had already begun the process of comparison that always left him exhausted, he could not stop, and he was wondering: Was it that we were as obsessed with what we wore but I've forgotten it? No, it's not that: our convention was that it was bourgeois to spend time and money on clothes, that was it, but their convention is different; that's all it is and it is not important.

Joseph had a strong blue gaze, and a strong straight mouth. The mouth was hidden under a wiry golden beard. A mane of wiry yellow hair fell to his shoulders. Jack thought that the beard and the long hair were there because they were fashionable, and would be dropped the moment they were not. . . . *Well, why not? He wished very much he could have swaggered about in beard and mane—that was the truth.*

This aggressively vivid young man sat on a chair opposite Jack, put his palms down on his thighs with his fingers pointing towards each other, and the elbows out. In this considering, alert position he looked at his father.

Jack, a faded, larger, softer version of what he was seeing, waited.

Joseph said: "I hear you have got religion."

"The opium," said Jack, in a formal considering way, "of the people: Yes. If that's what it is, I have got it."

Jack felt particularly transparent, because of his son's forceful presence. He knew that his posture, the smile on his face, were expressing apology. He already knew the meeting was doomed to end unpleasantly. Yet he was looking for the words to appeal to his son, to begin the "real" talk that they should be having. Joseph said: "Well, that's your business." He sounded impatient; having raised the subject, or at least used it as an opener, now he was saying that his father's processes were of no interest or importance.

"You've been following the Robinson affair?"

Jack could not remember for a moment which affair that was, but did not like to say no.

"We have to pay the defence lawyer. And there's the bail. We need at least three thousand pounds."

Jack did not say anything. It was not from policy, but inadequacy, yet he saw his son beginning to make the irritable movements of power, of confidence, checked and thwarted. It crossed his mind that of course his son saw him as powerful and confident, and this it was that accounted for the aggression, the hostility, the callousness. Into Jack's mind now came sets of words framed rhetorically; since this was not how he was feeling, he was surprised. "Why does it have to be like this, that more hate is used on people of the same side, thus preventing us ever from uniting in a common front, preventing us from bringing down the enemy?" These were words from the imaginary conversation with Joseph that he so often indulged in: only now did it strike him that he never had fantasies of a personal relationship—of their going for a holiday together, for instance, or just spending and evening, or walking for an hour or so. "Can't you see?"—the inner rhetoric-maker was continuing, "that the vigour of your criticism, your iconoclasm, your need to condemn the past without learning from it, will take you relentlessly to stand exactly where your despised elders stand now?"

It suddenly occurred to Jack, and for the first time, that he had repudiated his past. This so frightened him, leaving him, as it must, by himself out in the air somewhere, without comrades and allies—

without a family—that he almost forgot Joseph's presence. He was thinking: For weeks now, ever since the old man's death—before, even?—I've been thinking as if I have abandoned socialism.

Joseph was saying: "I don't have to tell you what the conditions are like in that prison, how they are being treated."

Jack saw that the "I don't have to tell you" was in fact an admission that in spite of everything he said, Joseph saw him as an ally. "You've come to me for money?" he asked, as if there could be another reason.

"Yeah. Yeah. That's about it, I suppose."

"Why do you have to be American?" Jack asked in sudden real irritation. "You're not American. Why do you all have to?"

Joseph said, with a conscious smile: "It's a mannerism, that's all." Then he looked stern again, in command.

Jack said: "I'm one of the old rich lefties you were publicly despising not long ago. You didn't want to have anything to do with us, you said."

Joseph frowned and made irritable movements which said that he felt that the sort of polemic which abused people not standing exactly where he stood was rather like breathing, a tradition, and he genuinely felt his father was being unreasonable in taking such remarks personally. Then he said, as if nothing better could be expected: "Then I take it it is no?"

"No," said Jack, "I am sorry."

Joseph got up; but he looked hesitant, and even now could sit down—if Jack said the right things. If he could push aside the rhetorical sentences that kept coming to his tongue: how should they not?—he had spent many hours of fantasy ensuring that they would!

Jack suddenly heard himself saying, in a low, shaking, emotional voice: "I am so sick of it all. It all just goes on and on. Over and over again."

"Well," said Joseph, "they say it is what always happens, so I suppose that ought to make us feel better." His smile was his own, not forced, or arranged.

Jack saw that Joseph had taken what he had said as an appeal for understanding between them personally: he had believed that his father was saying he was sick of their bad relations.

Had that been what he was saying? He had imagined he was talking about the political cycle. Jack now understood that if in fact he made enough effort, Joseph would respond, and then . . . He heard himself saying: "Like bloody automatons. Over and over again. Can't you see that it is going to take something like twenty years for you lot to become old rich lefties?"

"Or would if we aren't all dead first," said Joseph, ending the thing as Jack would, and with a calm, almost jolly smile. He left, saying: "The Robinson brothers are likely to get fifteen years if we don't do something."

Jack, as if a button had been pushed, was filled with guilt about the Robinson brothers and almost got up to write a cheque there and then. But he did not: it had been an entirely automatic reaction.

He spent a few days apparently in the state he had been in for weeks; but he knew himself to have reached the end of some long inner process that had proved too much for him. This interview with his son had been its end, as, very likely, the scene in the attic had been its beginning? Who knew? Who could know! Not Jack. He was worn out, as at the end of a long vigil. He found himself one morning standing in the middle of his livingroom saying over and over again: "I can't stand any more of this. I can't. I won't."

He found the pills and took them with the same miserable determination that he would have had to use to kill something that had to be killed. Almost at once he began to sleep, and the tension eased. He no longer felt as if he was carrying around, embodied in himself, a question as urgent as a wound that needed dressing, but that he had no idea what the language was in which he might find an answer. He ceased to experience the cloying sweetness that caused a mental nausea a hundred times worse than the physical. In a few days he had already stopped seeing his wife and daughters as great dolls who supplied warmth, charm, sympathy, when the buttons of duty or habit were pressed. Above all, he did not have to be on guard against his own abhorrence: his fingers did not explore masks on his face, nor was he always conscious of the statements made by his body and his limbs.

He was thinking that he was probably already known throughout the Left as a renegade; yet, examining the furniture in his mind, he found it not much changed.

It occurred to him, and he went on to consider it in a brisk judicious way, that it was an extraordinary thing that whereas he could have sat for an examination at a moment's notice on the history, the ideas, and the contemporary situation of socialism, communism and associated movements, with confidence that he would know the answers even to questions on the details of some unimportant sect in some remote country, he was so ignorant of religious history and thought that he could not have answered any questions at all. His condition in relation to religious questions was like that of a person hearing of socialism for the first time and saying: "Oh yes, I've often thought it wasn't fair that some people should have more than others. You agree, do you?"

He decided to go to the British Museum Reading Room. He had written many of his books there. His wife was delighted, knowing that this meant he was over the crisis.

He sent in his card for books on the history of the religions, on comparative religion, and on the relation of religion to anthropology.

For the first few days it seemed that he was still under the spell of his recent experience: he could not keep his attention from wandering from the page, and the men and women all around him bending over books seemed to him insane; this habit of solving all questions by imbibing information through the eyes off the printed page was a form of self-hypnotism. He was seeing them and himself as a species that could not function unless it took in information in this way.

But this soon passed and he was able to apply himself.

As he read, he conscientiously examined what he thought: was this changing at all? No, his distaste for the whole business could be summed up by an old idea of his, which was that if he had been bred, let us say, in Pakistan, that would have been enough for him to kill other people in the name of Mohammed, and if he had been born in India, to kill Moslems without a qualm. That had he been born in Italy, he would have been one brand of Christian, and if he had stuck with his family's faith, he would be bound to suspect Roman Catholicism. But above all what he felt was that this was an outdated situation. What was he doing sitting here surrounded by histories and concordances and expositions and exegetics? He would be better occupied doing almost anything else—a hundred years ago, yes, well, that had been different. The struggle for a Victorian inside the Church had meant something; for a man or a woman then to say: "If I had been born an Arab I would be praying five times a day looking at Mecca, but had I been a Tibetan I would have believed in the Dalai Lama"—that kind of statement had needed courage then, and the effort to make it had been worthwhile.

There were, of course, the mystics. But the word was associated for him with the tainted sweetness that had so recently afflicted him, with self-indulgence, and posturing, and exaggerated behaviour. He read, however, Simone Weil and Teilhard de Chardin; these were the names he knew.

He sat, carefully checking his responses: he was more in sympathy with Simone Weil, because of her relations with the poor, less than Teilhard de Chardin, who seemed to him not very different from any sort of intellectual: he could have been a useful sort of politician, for instance? It occurred to him that he was in the process of choosing a degree or class of belief, like a pipe from a display of pipes, or a jacket in a shop, that would be on easy terms with the ideas he was already committed to and, above all, would not disturb his associates. He could imagine himself saying to Walter: "Well, yes, it is true that I am religious in a way—I can see the point of Simone Weil, she took poverty into account. She was a socialist of a kind, really."

He bought more books by both Simone Weil and Teilhard de Chardin, and took them home, but did not read them; he had lost interest, and besides an old mechanism had come into force. He realised that sitting in the Reading Room he had been thinking of writing a book describing, but entirely as a tourist, the varieties of religious behaviour he had actually witnessed: a festival in Ceylon involving sacred elephants, for instance. The shape of this book was easy to find: he would describe what he had seen. The tone of it, the style—well, there might be a difficulty. There should not of course be the slightest tone of contempt; a light affectionate amusement would be appropriate. He found himself thinking that when the Old Guard read it they would be relieved as to the health of his state of mind.

Abandoning the Reading Room, he found that Carrie was becoming seriously interested in a young man met through her brother. He was one of the best of the new young revolutionaries, brave, forthright, everything a young revolutionary should be. Carrie was in the process of marrying her father? A difficulty was that this young man and Joseph had recently quarrelled. They had disagreed so violently over some policy that Joseph had left his particular group, and had formed another. Rosemary thought the real reason for the quarrel was that Joseph resented his sister loving his friend but did not realise it. Jack took his wife to task over this, saying that to discredit socialist action because it had, or might have, psychological springs was one of the oldest of reaction's tricks. But, said Rosemary, every action had a psychological base, didn't it, so why shouldn't one describe what it was? Jack surprised himself by his vehemence in this discussion—it was, in fact, a quarrel. For he believed with Rosemary, that probably Joseph was reacting emotionally: he had always been jealous of his sisters. Whatever the truth of it was, Carrie was certainly forgetting her "Eastern thing." She was already talking about it as of a youthful and outgrown phase. Rosemary, in telling Jack this, kept glancing apologetically at him; the last thing she wanted to do, she said, was to disparage any experience which he might be going through himself. Or had gone through.

Had gone through.

There was a Conference on the theme of Saving Earth from Man, and he had been afraid he wasn't going to be asked. He was, and Mona rang up to say she would like to go with him. She made some remarks that could be openings to his joining her in a position that combined belief in God with progressive action; he could see that she was willing to lay before him this position, which she had verbalised in detail. He closed that door, hoping it did not sound like a snub. He was again thinking of something called "religion" as an area coloured pink or green on a map and in terms of belief in an afterlife like a sweetened dummy for adults. In addition to this, he had two sets of ideas, or feelings, in his mind: one, those he had always held, or held since his early maturity; the other, not so much a set of ideas as a feeling of unease, disquiet, guilt, which amounted to a recognition that he had missed an opportunity of some sort, but that the failure had taken place long before his recent experience. Which he now summarised to himself in Walter's words as: It's a shock when your old man dies. His life had been set in one current, long ago; a fresh current, or at least, a different one, had run into it from another source; but, unlike the springs and rivers of myth and fairy tale, it had been muddled and unclear.

He could see that his old friends were particularly delighted to see him at the Conference, ready to take an active part. He was on the platform, and he spoke several times, rather well. By the time the Conference was over, there was no doubt he was again confirmed as one of the Old Guard, trusted and reliable.

Because of the attention the Conference got, he was offered a good job on television, and he nearly took it. But what he needed was to get out of England for a bit. Again Rosemary mentioned Nigeria. Her case was a good one. He would enjoy it, it was work he would do well, he would be contributing valuably. She would enjoy it too, she added loyally. As of course she would, in many ways. After all, it was for only two years, and when she came back it would be easy for her to pick up what she had dropped. And Family Counsellors would still be needed after all! Something that had seemed difficult now seemed easy, not much more than a long trip to Europe. They were making it easy, of course, because of that refusal to look at the consequences of a thing that comes from wanting to leave options open. Spending two years in Africa would change them both, and they did not want to admit that they had become reluctant to change.

On the night after he had formally agreed to go to Nigeria he had the dream again, the worst. If worst was the word?—in this region of himself different laws applied. He was dropping into nothingness, the void; he was fighting his way to a window and there he battered on panes to let in air, and as he hit with his fists and shouted for help the air around him thinned and became exhausted—and he ceased to exist.

He had forgotten how terrible—or how powerful—that dream had been.

He paced his house, wearing the night away. It was too late: he was going to Nigeria because he had not known what else it was he could do.

During that night he could feel his face falling into the lines and folds of his father's face—at the time, that is, when his father had been an elderly, rather than an old man. His father's old man's face had been open and sweet, but before achieving that goodness—like the inn at the end of a road which you have no alternative but to use?—he had had the face of a Roman, heavy-lidded, sceptical, obdurate, facing into the dark: the man whose pride and strength has to come from a conscious ability to suffer, in silence, the journey into negation.

During the days that followed, when the household was all plans and packing and arranging and people running in and out, Jack was thinking that there was only one difference between himself now and himself as he had been before "the bit of a shock." He had once been a man whose sleep had been—nothing, non-existent, he had slept like a small child. Now, in spite of everything, although he knew that fear could lie in wait there, his sleep had become another country, lying just behind his daytime one. Into that country he went nightly, with an alert, even if ironical interest—the irony was due to his habits of obedience to his past—for a gift had been made to him. Behind the face of the sceptical world was another, which no conscious decision of his could stop him exploring.

Notes on the Authors

FYODOR DOSTOEVSKY   1821–1881

Fyodor Mikhailovich Dostoevsky was born in Moscow of prosperous parents. He attended military engineering school in St. Petersburg and in 1842 became a lieutenant in the army. But, his interests having changed, he left his military life in 1844 for a literary career. Dostoevsky's father, a notoriously cruel man, was murdered by his serfs in 1839; Dostoevsky himself felt intense sympathy for the sufferings of the peasants. This sympathy led him into political activity, and in 1849 he was arrested and sentenced to death by the czarist government for belonging to a revolutionary activist group. The sentence, however, had really been a theatrical gesture by the czar to terrorize sympathizers, and Dostoevsky was told, only at the very moment it was supposed to have been carried out, that it had been commuted. He was then sent to a penal colony in Omsk, in Siberia, where he worked at hard labor from 1850 to 1854. His sufferings in prison were the basis for his book *The House of the Dead*, memoirs which began to appear in a periodical in 1861.

The terms of his sentence required Dostoevsky to remain in Siberia as a soldier after his release from prison, and it was not until 1859 that he returned to St. Petersburg to resume his writing. During the next fifteen years he published a remarkable series of novels including *Crime and Punishment* (1866), *The Idiot* (1868–69), *The Possessed* (1871), and *The Brothers Karamazov* (1880). He was also active as a journalist. But during these same years, he suffered from a variety of personal afflictions: frequent financial trouble, a mania for gambling, bouts of epilepsy, the death of his wife and brother. His political opinions changed from radical to reactionary, but he remained intensely open to the ordeals of other men and his work is infused with a mystique of suffering and redemption.

The standard biography is Avrahm Yarmolinsky's *Dostoevsky: A Life* (2nd ed., 1957). Another valuable work is David Magarshack's *Dostoevsky* (1963). André Gide's *Dostoevsky* (1949) provides interesting evidence of the impact of one great writer upon another. In René Wellek (editor), *Dostoevsky: A Collection of Critical Essays* (1962) the student will find a useful sampling of critical opinion. A major multi-volume biography by Joseph Frank is now in progress; the first volume, *Dostoevsky: Seeds of Revolt* appeared in 1976.

LEO TOLSTOY   1828–1910

Count Leo Nikolayevich Tolstoy was born to a wealthy, aristocratic family in central Russia. He entered the Kazan university in 1844 but studied little and, after having spent most of his time socializing, he left in 1847. Tolstoy returned to his estate, where his social conscience was stirred by the wretched living conditions of the serfs. But he failed in his attempts to help them and to improve the farming of his land. Restless, Tolstoy followed the example of an older brother and became a soldier in 1851. At the same time, he began his literary career. *Childhood*, his first completed work, was published in 1852. After being posted with the Danubian army, Tolstoy was sent to the Crimea in 1854 and there wrote the *Sevastopol* stories (1855), a strong attack on romantic glorifications of military life. Tired of war, Tolstoy resigned from the army in 1857. He then traveled west; in Paris he witnessed an execution, an experience that would prove crucial to his later thinking. This event and the ensuing death of his brother Nicholas in 1860 marked his turn to a kind of primitive Christianity and a preoccupation with the theme of death. From this point on, while also running the affairs of his estate, Tolstoy was to establish an almost universal reputation as the greatest writer of prose fiction. His major novels include *War and Peace* (1865–69), *Anna Karenina* (1875–77), and *The Kreutzer Sonata* (1889).

In his later years Tolstoy became an anarchic pacifist, rejecting not only war and military conscription but all forms of service to the state. The czarist government was fearful of persecuting a world-famous writer, but it vigorously persecuted his followers. Tolstoy was excommunicated in 1901 for his biting attacks on the Russian Orthodox Church. Renouncing the comforts of aristocratic life, he discarded his title, undertook acts of contrition and humility, and sought an ascetic existence.

Periodically he left his wife and home; it was during one such flight that he died.

The critical literature on Tolstoy is enormous. Perhaps the best standard biography is Ernest J. Simmons' *Leo Tolstoy* (2 vols., 1946): *Years of Development, 1828–79* and *Years of Maturity, 1880–1910*. A recent excellent volume of criticism is John Bayley's *Tolstoy and the Novel* (1967). An especially useful essay on Tolstoy appears in Philip Rahv's *Image and Idea* (rev. ed., 1957).

E. M. FORSTER   1879–1971

E. M. Forster is generally considered one of the best English novelists of the twentieth century. Born into a family with equally strong ties to English commercial and intellectual life, he spent his youth at a "public school" (the equivalent of an American private school) and then at Cambridge University; he was extremely unhappy in the first, mostly happy in the second. Shortly after the turn of the century Forster came into contact with the Bloomsbury group, a circle of cosmopolitan intellectuals that included such famous figures as the novelist Virginia Woolf and the economist J. M. Keynes; but Forster was essentially a solitary, a retiring bachelor who lived privately, for many of his later years in Cambridge, apart from public affairs and devoting most of his time to writing and reading.

His novels dealing with English life investigate, in a cool, slightly acerb style, the problems of cultivated middle-class people. Among the best of these are *Where Angels Fear to Tread* (1905), *The Longest Journey* (1907), and *Howard's End* (1910), the last a powerful study of conflict between refined and philistine ways of life. In 1924 Forster published his masterpiece, *A Passage to India*. He also wrote essays, stories, and other works.

The single most trenchant critical work on Forster is Lionel Trilling's *E. M. Forster* (1943). Wilfred Stone's *The Cave and the Mountain: A Study of E. M. Forster* (1966) is sympathetic, thorough, and informative. A vivid biography by P. N. Furbank, *E. M. Forster: A Life*, came out in 1978.

JOSEPH CONRAD   1857–1924

Joseph Conrad was born in the Ukraine of Polish parents, aristocratic patriots who gave their lives to the cause of freeing Poland from the domination of czarist Russia. As a child Joseph shared with them a period of exile in Russia. Most of his youth was spent in Cracow, Poland, where he learned French and developed a taste for novels, even as he kept witnessing the intrigues and desperation of the Polish nationalists. Originally his name was Teodor Józef Konrad Korzeniowski; he changed it to Joseph Conrad upon becoming a British citizen.

While still in his teens he journeyed to Marseille and became a seaman, and, teaching himself English, he enlisted in 1878 in the British merchant marine, where he served until 1894, having risen to a high rank of command. Two of the areas he traveled—the Orient and the Congo —were to become major locales in his fiction, as was the sea itself. Conrad did not begin to write until he was thirty-two. After publication of his first novel, *Almayer's Folly* (1894), he left the sea, married, and settled down to write. Although his work quickly won the admiration of critics, he was at first rewarded only by small sales and troublesome debts; moreover, he suffered from poor health. But he persevered, and in the end won financial success as well as literary acclaim. Conrad is best known as an adventure novelist, but in all his books he deals with the problems of human isolation, panic, and fear. Among his best-known works are *Lord Jim* (1900), *Nostromo* (1904), *Under Western Eyes* (1911), and *Victory* (1915).

The best general critical study of Conrad is Albert J. Guerard's *Conrad the Novelist* (1958). Jocelyn Baines has written a valuable biography, *Joseph Conrad* (rev. ed., 1959). An essay on Conrad's political fiction appears in Irving Howe's *Politics and the Novel* (1957). Various critical opinions can be found in Marvin Mudrick (editor), *Conrad: A Collection of Critical Essays* (1966). Frederick Karl's *Joseph Conrad: The Three Lives* (1979) is a thorough biography.

THOMAS MANN   1875–1955

Born of a distinguished German family in Lübeck, Thomas Mann became one of the great literary artists of the twentieth century. Although a mediocre student who disliked the discipline of school, Mann composed poems and plays while still a youth. At the university in Munich, Mann pursued the intellectual life, reading Schopenhauer and Nietzsche. As a young man he wrote his family novel *Buddenbrooks* (1900) and *Tristan* (1903) and joined the staff of a satirical review, *Simplicissimus*. He traveled widely in Europe and tried to represent in his writings the spirit of European humanism, as distinct from German nationalism. His major novel, *The Magic Mountain* (1924), deals with the problematical nature of life and death.

When the Nazis came to power, Mann left Germany in 1933 as a voluntary exile, and in 1934 he made his first visit to America, accompanied by his family. Denounced by the Nazi government, he replied by attacking the rulers of Germany as enemies of Christianity, occidental morality, and civilization itself. As a result, Mann was deprived of German citizenship and his name was removed from the University of Bonn's roll of honorary doctors. As if in compensation, Harvard bestowed an honorary degree upon him in 1935 and Czechoslovakia gave him the rights of citizenship. From 1938 to 1941 Mann was at Princeton and in 1941 he moved to California. He became a U.S. citizen in 1944.

By far the best book on Mann in English is Erich Heller's *The Ironic German: A Study of Thomas Mann* (1958). Also useful for its criticism is Henry Hatfield's *Thomas Mann* (rev. ed., 1962).

FRANZ KAFKA   1883–1924

One of the major writers of the first part of this century, Franz Fafka was born to a well-to-do middle-class Jewish family in Prague. He studied law at the German university in Prague and received his law degree in 1906. Afterward he obtained a position with the workmen's accident-insurance office of the Austrian civil service at the urging of his strong-willed father, whom he idolized. But his real devotion was to literature, and he wrote for some years though publishing little. *The Metamorphosis* appeared in 1916, and work on *The Trial* was begun that same year. During this period of literary productivity, Kafka's personal life was stormy. In 1917, his five-year engagement to Fraulein F. B. was broken, and the respiratory disease he was suffering from was diagnosed as tuberculosis. Still he continued to try to earn his living by writing. He spent the last year of his life in hospitals and died of consumption in one outside Vienna.

Little of Kafka's work was published during his lifetime, and none of his three novels had been completed. That his work is so widely known and admired is due largely to the efforts of his friend Max Brod. Instead of acceding to Kafka's command that his unpublished manuscripts be burned after his death, Brod edited them and had them published. *The Trial* appeared in 1925, *The Castle* in 1926, and *Amerika* in 1927. In these novels, as well as in Kafka's other writings, the theme is the frustration, bewilderment, and loneliness of modern man, who struggles against incomprehensible forces.

The standard biography is by Max Brod, *Franz Kafka: A Biography* (2nd ed., 1963). A valuable group of essays has been brought together by Ronald Gray in *Kafka: A Collection of Critical Essays* (1963). A stimulating critical study is Martin Greenberg, *The Terror of Art*, 1968.

FLANNERY O'CONNOR   1925–1964

Outwardly, Flannery O'Connor's life was uneventful. She was born in Savannah in 1925; she lived most of her life in a small town called Milledgeville, Georgia; she suffered for some years from an incurable tuberculous skin disease called lupus, which often prevented her from working; she indulged her hobby, which, readers of *The Displaced Person* will be interested to know, was the raising of peacocks; she took occasional trips, once to a creative writing session at the University of Iowa, another time to Lourdes, a third time to New York; and she died in 1964 at the age of 39, generally recognized as one of the best writers of American fiction of her time.

Her imaginative life, however, was very rich. In the short time granted her, she wrote a great deal. Her first novel, *Wise Blood*, appeared in 1952 and her second and better novel, *The Violent Bear It Away*, in 1960. Collections of her stories were published in 1955 (*A Good Man Is Hard to Find*) and in 1965 (*Everything That Rises Must Converge*). Her *Complete Stories* appeared in 1971 and won the National Book Award in 1972. Almost all of her fiction is set in Georgia or in a cut of Tennessee bordering on northern Georgia. Occasionally she gave literary interviews or brief literary lectures at colleges, but she kept away from the usual kinds of publicity, for she understood that the main task of a writer is to write.

A good critical study is Josephine Hendin's *The World of Flannery O'Connor* (1970).

SAUL BELLOW   b. 1915

The son of Russian Jewish immigrants, Saul Bellow was born in Lachine, Quebec, but spent most of his childhood in Chicago. He attended the University of Chicago, received his bachelor's degree from Northwestern University in 1937, and went to graduate school at the University of Wisconsin. He worked for a short time on the WPA Writer's Project and served in the merchant marine during World War II. At present a member of the Committee on Social Thought at the University of Chicago, Bellow has taught at New York University, Bard College, Princeton University, and the University of Minnesota.

After completing his first two novels—*Dangling Man* (1944) and *The Victim* (1947)—Bellow was awarded a Guggenheim Fellowship and spent a year in Paris, where he began *The Adventures of Augie March* (1953), his best-known novel and the winner of the National

Book Award for fiction. His later novels include *Seize the Day* (1956), *Henderson the Rain King* (1959), and *Herzog* (1964). Bellow has also written a play, *The Last Analysis*, which received a production in New York City.

Criticism of Bellow's work has appeared in many magazines. A useful collection of critical essays, edited by Irving Malin, is *Saul Bellow and the Critics* (1967).

GABRIEL GARCÍA MÁRQUEZ   b. 1928

There has been during the last few decades a major flowering of the novel in Latin America, and one of the most brilliant among the new writers is Gabriel García Márquez. Born in a small town in Colombia, he has lived most of his life in Mexico and Europe. After attending the University of Bogotá he worked for a time on a Colombian newspaper as reporter and film critic. He now resides in Spain.

García Márquez has published two collections of short fiction, *No One Writes to the Colonel* (1968) and *Leaf Storm* (1972). His masterpiece, *One Hundred Years of Solitude* (1970), is a splendid novel depicting the fortunes of a family in a Colombian town and, in its larger ramifications, constitutes a powerful indictment of political tyranny in Latin America. So far, almost all of García Márquez's work presents a complex and interrelated portrait of an imagined world, with incidents in the stories being referred to in his novels and vice versa. (In this respect, it resembles the work of William Faulkner.) Though a man of the left, García Márquez does not propagandize in his novels; they are marked by a mixture of realism, fantasy, and outlandish humor. Without question he is one of the half dozen leading novelists in the world today.

There is, as yet, very little solid criticism in English of García Márquez's work, but you will find a fascinating interview with him in Rita Guibert's book, *Seven Voices*, 1973.

DORIS LESSING   b. 1919

Perhaps one of the most influential novelists writing in English today, Doris Lessing has been extremely prolific both as the author of novels and of short stories. She has more than twenty books to her credit, the best-known and probably the most interesting of which is *The Golden Notebook* (1962), a complex narrative set in post-World War II England with special emphasis upon a group of women intellectuals.

Lessing was born in Persia of British parents, but at the age of five was taken by them to Southern Rhodesia. Some of her strongest works of fiction are in a collection of short stories and novellas entitled *African Stories* (1975), many of which depict the tensions between blacks and whites in southern Africa. In her younger years Lessing entered the world of left-wing politics shown in *The Temptation of Jack Orkney*, but at some point in the late 1950's she broke from this milieu. In her more recent works she has concentrated on interior psychological life and the kinds of experiences that can sometimes be described as "mystical." All of her novels and stories are marked by a great intensity of feeling, and for many younger people in England and America she seems to have become a sort of culture heroine who articulates their sense of contemporary life. Her most ambitious recent work consists of a multi-volume series of related novels entitled *Children of Violence*.

A mixed bag of critical essays is *Doris Lessing: Critical Studies*, edited by Annis Pratt and L. S. Dembo (1974). Paul Schleuter's *The Novels of Doris Lessing*, 1973, provides some useful information and analysis. See also the essay on Lessing in Irving Howe, *Celebrations and Attacks*, 1979.